HIRAMIC BROTHERHOOD
of the
THIRD TEMPLE

WILLIAM HANNA

ISBN- 978-1-909425-91-0

Justyna

Contents

THE LOSS OF PALESTINIAN LAND SINCE 1946

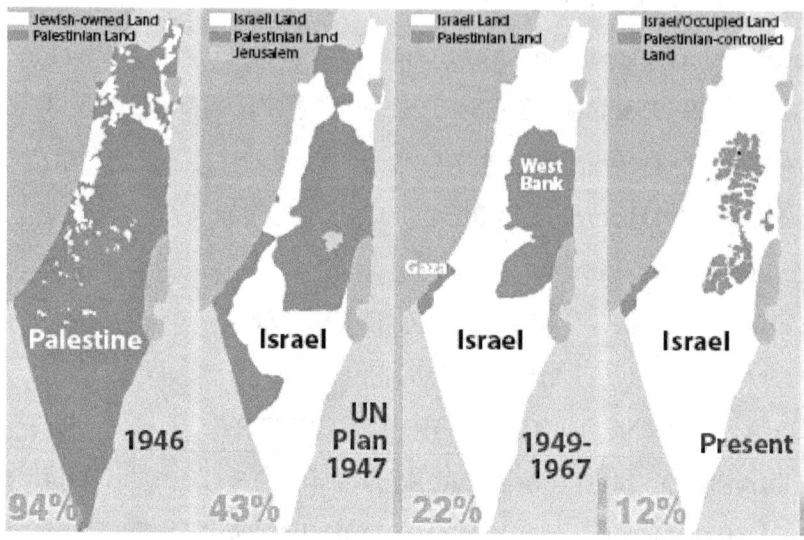

As part of its ethnic cleansing and Judaization of Palestine, Apartheid Israel continues to violate international law and human rights by its brutal displacement of the Palestinian people, the destruction of their property, and the expropriation (theft) of their land so as to continue building illegal Jewish settlements and thereby render impossible any hope of a two-state solution to the Israeli-Palestinian conflict. The abhorrence of Apartheid Israel's actions against the Palestinian people is exceeded only by those Western nations whose abysmal failure to force Israel to respect human rights and international law constitutes hypocritical double standards, cowardice and complicity. Their silence is tantamount to collaboration.

THE TEMPLE INSTITUTE

Founded in 1987, The Temple Institute's official website states that it is dedicated to every aspect of the Holy Temple of Jerusalem including the central role that the Temple fulfilled and will once again fulfill for the spiritual well-being of both Israel and *all the nations of the world.* The Institute claims to be involved with education, research and development that touches on the the Holy Temple's past, an understanding of the present, and the divine promise of Israel's future.

The Temple Institute is categoric in stating that its ultimate goal is to see Israel rebuild the Holy Temple on Mount Moriah (Temple Mount) in Jerusalem, in accordance with the Biblical commandments. Judaism regards the Temple Mount as the place where God chose the Divine Presence to rest:

> *Here am I, and the children the Lord has given me. We are signs and symbols in Israel from the Lord Almighty, who dwells on Mount Zion.* **(Isaiah 8:18)**

According to the rabbinic sages whose debates produced the Talmud, it was from here that the world expanded into its present form and from where God gathered the dust used to create Adam, the first man, all of which contradicts the established reality of man's evolution from Africa. Temple Mount is also the alleged location of Abraham's binding of Isaac as well as the First and Second Temples.

The Temple Institute's ultimate Judaic goal is being assiduously pursued not only despite the existence of centuries-old Muslim holy sites on Temple Mount, but also irrespective of any consequences that might lead to a regional or even a global conflict with weapons of mass destruction resulting in a nuclear holocaust. But of what concern is that to the Temple Institute — and other like-minded people — so long as they can pursue the fulfillment of some mythical commandment from the realms of Biblical fantasy.

> *There is no evidence of a United Monarchy no evidence of a capital in Jerusalem or of any coherent, unified political force that dominated western Palestine, let alone an empire of the size the legends describe. We do not have evidence for*

7

the existence of kings named Saul, David or Solomon; nor do we have evidence for any temple at Jerusalem in this early period. What we do know of Israel and Judah of the tenth century does not allow us to interpret this lack of evidence as a gap in our knowledge and information about the past, a result merely of the accidental nature of archeology. There is neither room nor context, no artifact or archive that points to such historical realities in Palestine's tenth century. One cannot speak historically of a state without a population. Nor can one speak of a capital without a town. Stories are not enough.
Thomas L Thompson, *The Bible in History: How Writers Create a Past,* Pimlico, 1999.

This is what archaeologists have learned from their excavations in the Land of Israel: the Israelites were never in Egypt, did not wander in the desert, did not conquer the land in a military campaign and did not pass it on to the 12 tribes of Israel.
Ze'ev Herzog, professor of archaeology at The Department of Archaeology and Ancient Near Eastern Cultures at at Tel Aviv University specializing in social archaeology, ancient architecture, and field archaeology — debunks the historic Exodus myth in *Deconstructing the Walls of Jericho.*

Appropriations of the past as part of the politics of the present . . . could be illustrated for most parts of the globe. One further example which is of particular interest to this study, is the way in which archeology and biblical history have become of such importance to the modern state of Israel. It is this combination which has been such a powerful factor in silencing Palestinian history.
Keith W. Whitelam, *The Invention of Ancient Israel: the Silencing of Palestinian History,* Routledge, London, 1996.

De-Arabizing the history of Palestine is another crucial element of the ethnic cleansing. 1500 years of Arab and

Muslim rule and culture in Palestine are trivialized, evidence of its existence is being destroyed and all this is done to make the absurd connection between the ancient Hebrew civilization and today's Israel. The most glaring example of this today is in Silwan, (Wadi Hilwe) a town adjacent to the Old City of Jerusalem with some 50,000 residents. Israel is expelling families from Silwan and destroying their homes because it claims that King David built a city there some 3,000 years ago. Thousands of families will be made homeless so that Israel can build a park to commemorate a king that may or may not have lived 3,000 years ago. Not a shred of historical evidence exists that can prove King David ever lived yet Palestinian men, women, children and the elderly along with their schools and mosques, churches and ancient cemeteries and any evidence of their existence must be destroyed and then denied so that Zionist claims to exclusive rights to the land may be substantiated.

Miko Peled, Israeli peace activist and author. (Born in 1961 in Jerusalem)

The Dome of the Rock

The Western Wall

Charter of the International Jewish anti-Zionist Network

We are an international network of Jews who are uncompromisingly committed to struggles for human emancipation, of which the liberation of the Palestinian people and land is an indispensable part. Our commitment is to the dismantling of Israeli apartheid, the return of Palestinian refugees, and the ending of the Israeli colonization of historic Palestine.From Poland to Iraq, from Argentina to South Africa, from Brooklyn to Mississippi, Jews have taken up their quest for justice, and their desire for a more just world, by joining with others in collective struggles. Jews participated prominently in the workers' struggle of the depression era, in the civil rights movement, in the struggle against South African Apartheid, in the struggle against fascism in Europe, and in many other movements for social and political change. The State of Israel's historic and ongoing ethnic cleansing of the Palestinian people from their land contradicts and betrays these long histories of Jewish participation in collective liberation struggles.

Zionism — the founding and current ideology that manifested in the State of Israel — took root in the era of European colonialism and was spread in the aftermath of the Nazi genocide. Zionism has been nourished by the most violent and oppressive histories of the nineteenth century, at the expense of the many strains of Jewish commitment to liberation. To reclaim them, and a place in the vibrant popular movements of our time, Zionism, in all its forms, must be stopped.

This is crucial, first and foremost, because of Zionism's impact on the people of Palestine and the broader region. It also dishonors the persecution and genocide of European Jews by using their memory to justify and perpetuate

European racism and colonialism. It is responsible for the extensive displacement and alienation of Mizrahi Jews (Jews of African and Asian descent) from their diverse histories, languages, traditions and cultures. Mizrahi Jews have a history in this region of over 2,000 years. As Zionism took root, these Jewish histories were forced from their own course in service of the segregation of Jews imposed by the State of Israel.

As such, Zionism implicates us in the oppression of the Palestinian people and in the debasement of our own heritages, struggles for justice and alliances with our fellow human beings.

We pledge to: **Oppose Zionism and the State of Israel**

Zionism is racist. It demands political, legal and economic power for Jews and European people and cultures over indigenous people and cultures. Zionism is not just racist but anti-Semitic. It endorses the sexist European anti-Semitic imagery of the effeminate and weak "diaspora Jew" and counters it with a violent and militarist "new Jew," one who is a perpetrator rather than a victim of racialized violence.

Zionism thus seeks to make Jews white through the adopting of white racism against Palestinian people. Despite Israel's need to integrate Mizrahis in order to maintain a Jewish majority, this racism is also seen in the marginalization and economic exploitation of the socially deprived Mizrahi population. This racialized violence also includes the exploitation of migrant workers.

Zionists disseminate the myth that Israel is a democracy. In truth, Israel has established and enforces internal policies and practices that discriminate against Jews of Mizrahi descent and exclude and restrict Palestinian people. Moreover, Israel, in collaboration with the United States, undermines any Arab movements for social change and liberation.

Zionism perpetuates Jewish exceptionalism. In defense of

its crimes, Zionism tells a version of Jewish history that is disconnected from the history and experiences of other people. It promotes the narrative that the Nazi holocaust is exceptional in human history — despite it being one of many holocausts from Native Americans North and South to Armenia and Rwanda. It sets Jews apart from the victims and survivors of other genocides instead of uniting us with them.

Through a shared Islamophobia and desire for control of the Middle East and broader West Asia, Israel makes common cause with Christian fundamentalists and others who call for Jewish destruction. Together they call for the persecution of Muslims. This shared promotion of Islamophobia serves to demonize resistance to Western economic and military domination. It continues a long history of Zionist collusion with repressive and violent regimes, from Nazi Germany to the South African Apartheid regime to reactionary dictatorships across Latin America.

Zionism claims that Jewish safety depends on a militarized Jewish state. But Israel does not make Jews safe. Its violence guarantees instability and fear for those within its sphere of influence and endangers the safety of all people, including Jews, far beyond its borders. Zionism colluded willingly in creating the conditions that led to violence against Jews in Arab countries. The loathing aroused by Israeli violence and military domination toward Jews living in Israel and elsewhere is used to justify further Zionist violence.

We pledge to: **Reject the colonial legacy and on-going colonial expansion**

The moment when the Zionist movement decided to build a Jewish State in Palestine, it became a movement of conquest. Like the imperial conquest and genocidal ideologies of the Americas or Africa, Zionism depends on the segregation of people and the confiscation of land that produces ethnic cleansing and depends on unrelenting military violence.

Zionists worked hand in hand with the British colonial

13

administration against the indigenous people of the region and their legitimate hopes for liberty and self-determination. The Zionist imagining of Palestine as "empty" and desolate justified the destruction of Palestinian life in the same way that such racism justified the extermination of Native Americans, the Atlantic slave trade, and many other atrocities.

From the ever expanding settlements to the Apartheid Wall, Israel's commitment to colonial domination leaves its mark in environmental damage and the destruction of the physical landscape of Palestine. The failure of these policies to end Palestinian resistance propels Israel toward ever increasing violence and policies that, when followed to their fullest extent, end in genocide. In Gaza, the Israeli state withholds access to food, water, electricity, humanitarian aid, and medical supplies as a weapon that targets the foundations of human life.

Israel, once a vehicle for the British and French assault on Arab unity and independence, is now a junior partner in the US-allied strategy for world military, economic and political control, specifically for domination of the strategic Middle-East/Southwest Asia region. The danger of nuclear war through a US/Israeli attack on Iran reminds us that Israel is an atomic bomb that should be urgently dismantled for the sake of saving the lives of all its current and potential victims.

We pledge to: **Challenge Zionist organizations**

Beyond shaping the creation of Israel, Zionism determined its international policy of military dominance and antagonism toward its neighbors, and established a sophisticated global network of organizations, political lobbies, public relation firms, campus clubs, and schools to sustain and perpetuate Zionist ideas in Jewish communities and the general public.

Billions of US dollars flow annually to Israel to sustain the occupation and Israel's sophisticated and brutal army. The war machine they fund is a leader in the global arms industry,

14

which drains resources craved by a world in desperate need of water, food, health care, housing and education. Europe, Canada and the United Nations, meanwhile, prop up the infrastructure of occupation under the guise of humanitarian aid to Palestinian people. Together, the US and its allies cooperate in deepening the domination of the region and suppressing popular movements.

An international network of Zionist institutions and organizations support the Israeli military and militant Jewish settlements with direct funds. These organizations also provide the political support necessary for legitimizing and promoting policies and aid packages. In individual countries, these organizations censor criticisms of Israel and target individuals and organizations with blacklists, violence, imprisonment, deportation, unemployment and other economic hardship.

These organizations facilitate the spread of Islamophobia. They beat the drums of war abroad and push repressive legislation at home. In the United States and Canada, Zionist organizations helped pass "anti-terrorist" legislation making organizing in support of boycott, divestment and sanctions against Israel and support for Palestinian, Iranian, Iraqi, and Lebanese and Muslim organizations subject to prosecution as aiding terrorism and committing treason. In both Europe and the US, supposedly "Jewish" organizations are now at the forefront of pushing for war with Iran.

Cracks are appearing in the edifice of Zionism as in that of US world dominance itself. In the region, extraordinary resistance from Palestine and Southern Lebanon to Israeli and US aggression and occupation has been sustained despite limited resources and many betrayals. Around the world, the movement in solidarity with the Palestine people and in confrontation with the U.S. and Israeli policy is gaining momentum. In Israel, this momentum can be seen in brewing dissent that creates possibilities for reclaiming two legacies of the 1960s: Matzpen, an Israeli Palestinian and Jewish anti-Zionist organization, and the Mizrahi Black Panther Party. In Israel there also is growing refusal of youth to participate in mandatory conscription into the army.

Within the governments and public discussions in the United States and Europe, the costs of unconditional support to Israel are increasingly questioned. Israel and the US seek new allies in the global South to join in their economic and military conquests. The growing relationship between Israel and India is a stark example of this. Sharing an interest in political control and capital gain for the few at the expense of the many, the elite in India as well as in countries across the Middle East and broader West Asia collude with the Western economic and military agenda in the region.

The propaganda of the West's Global War on Terror resonates with the Islamophobia that is needed and promoted by the Indian elite and has provided an opportunity for the severe repression of dissent by regimes across the Middle East and South and West Asia. Despite this, there are rising people's movements based in rich histories of anti-colonial struggle that challenge and will ultimately defeat this alliance.

Together with our allies, we aim to help widen those cracks, until the wall comes down and Israel is isolated as was apartheid South Africa. We pledge to take up the battle against these organizations that pretend to speak for us, and to defeat them.

*We pledge to: **Commit our solidarity and work toward justice***

We commit our hearts, minds and political energy to support the varied and vibrant resistance movement of the Palestinian people and to confront the injustices for which the countries we live in are responsible.

We unequivocally support the Palestinian Right of Return. We call for a dismantling of the racist Israeli law of return that privileges the rights of any person that the State of Israel deems as Jewish to settle in Palestine while excluding

Palestinians and making them refugees.

We respond wholeheartedly to the call from Palestine for boycott, divestment and sanctions against Israel.

We support the demand for the release of Palestinian political prisoners and an end to incarceration of Palestinian political leaders, women, children and men, as a method of control and terror.

It is not our job to prescribe what road the Palestinian people should take toward defining their future. We do not presume to substitute our voices for theirs. Our strategies and actions will emerge from our active relationships with those who are engaged in the range of liberation struggles within Palestine and in the broader region. We will support their struggle to survive, to hold their ground and to advance their movement as best as they can, on their own terms.

We are partners in the vibrant popular resistance movements of our time that defend and cherish the lives of all people and of the planet itself. We are partners in movements that are led by those most impacted by imperial conquest, occupation, racism and the global control and exploitation of people and resources. We stand for the protection of the natural world. We stand by the rights of indigenous peoples to their land and sovereignty. We stand by the rights of migrant peoples and people who are refugees to move freely and safely across borders. We stand by the rights of working people —including migrant workers brought to Israel to replace both Palestinian and Mizrahi labor— to economic justice and self-determination. We stand by rights to racial equality and cultural expression. We stand by the rights of women and children and all exploited groups to be free from subjugation. And we stand by the universal right to water, food, shelter, education, health-care and freedom from violence — the only basis on which human society can survive and flourish.

We commit to support justice so that healing may take root. There is much to heal: the wounds inflicted by the imposition and operation of colonial rule in Palestine and the broader region; the traumas of the European oppression of Jews that the Zionist project is exploiting; the fears and deprivations suffered through years of bloodshed; the manipulations of culture and resources used to exploit Mizrahi Jews and divide them from Palestinians; and the continuing massacre, rape and dispossession of Palestinian people.

The justice we work for must be built by those throughout Palestine, including Israel, and by Palestinian refugees, whose struggle for self-determination can lead to equity and freedom for all who live there and in the surrounding lands.

We call you to join with us.

These pledges require the building of a united international Jewish movement which challenges Zionism and its claim to speak on behalf of all Jews. In the face of an international adversary, it is not enough to work only locally, or even nationally. We must find ways to work together across boundaries, distances, sectors and languages. There is room for many initiatives and organizations, established and new, to work independently and together, in mutual support and collaboration.

Do you stand against racism in all its forms? **Then we call you to join with us** *in ending Israeli apartheid.*

Do you support the sovereignty and land-rights of indigenous peoples? **Then we call you to join with us** *in defending the sovereignty and land-rights of Palestinians.*

Do you believe that all our lives depend on economic and environmental sustainability? Are you enraged at the theft and destruction of the world's resources? **Then we call you to join with us** *in stopping Israel's destruction of Palestinian agriculture and land, the theft of land and water, and the bulldozing of villages and groves.*

Do you seek an end to the endless wars for oil and military dominance of the US and its allies? Do you want an end to militarized cultures, to the drafting of our young people and the ransacking of resources that finance armies rather than the necessities of life? **Then we call on you to join with us** *in dismantling a critical piece of the global war machine.*

Do you wish to dissociate yourself from the Israeli ethnic cleansing of Palestine and the destruction of history, culture and self-governance? Do you believe there is no peace without justice? Do you feel enraged and saddened that the holocaust against Jewish people is being used to perpetrate other atrocities? Then we call on you to join with us in ending Zionist colonialism.

For the people of this planet to live in safety, justice and peace, the Israeli colonial project must be brought to an end. We joyfully take up this collective task of undermining a system of conquest and plunder that has tormented our world for far too long.

DEDICATION

We have become a Nazi monster in the eyes of the world — bullies and bastards who would rather kill than live peacefully. We are whores for power and oil with hate and fear in our hearts.
Hunter S. Thompson (1937-2005) American journalist and author.

Dedicated to the American people with the hope that they will — before it is too late — acquire the necessary knowledge, judiciousness and resolve to reestablish control over the governance of their sham democracy so as to avoid the self-destruction of the American nation. In the unlikelihood of their managing to do so, then they will not only have rendered the rest of humanity a great service, but they might also become the exemplary people and beacon of light democracy that in their delusion they wholeheartedly believe they are. Undertaking such a momentous task, however, will not be easy and they could do no better than to start off by heeding the words of a true American patriot — who unlike the majority of elected politicians on Capitol Hill — never betrayed his country for the proverbial thirty pieces of silver. The following excerpts are from former **Senator William J. Fulbright's** *The Arrogance of Power*, **Random House, 1966.**

America is the most fortunate of nations — fortunate in her rich territory, fortunate in having had a century of relative peace in which to develop that territory, fortunate in her diverse and talented population, fortunate in the institutions devised by the founding fathers and in the wisdom of those who have adapted those institutions to a changing world. For the most part America has made good use of her blessings, especially in her internal life but also in her foreign relations. Having done so much and succeeded so well, America is now at that historical point at which a great nation is in danger of losing its perspective on what exactly is within the realm of its power and what is beyond it. Other great nations, reaching this critical juncture, have aspired to too much, and by overextension of effort have declined and then fallen.

The causes of the malady are not entirely clear but its recurrence is one of the uniformities of history: power tends to confuse itself with virtue and a great nation is peculiarly susceptible to the idea that its power is a sign of God's favor, conferring upon it a special responsibility for other nations — to make them richer and happier and wiser, to remake them, that is, in its own shining image. Power confuses itself with virtue and tends also to take itself for omnipotence. Once imbued with the idea of a mission, a great nation easily assumes that it has the means as well as the duty to do God's work. The Lord, after all, surely would not choose you as His agent and then deny you the sword with which to work His will. German soldiers in the First World War wore belt buckles imprinted with the words "Gott mit uns." It was approximately under this kind of infatuation — an exaggerated sense of power and an imaginary sense of mission — that the Athenians attacked Syracuse and Napoleon and that Hitler invaded Russia. In plain words, they overextended their commitments and they came to grief.   I do not think for a moment that America, with her deeply rooted democratic traditions, is likely to embark upon a campaign to dominate the world in the manner of a Hitler or Napoleon. What I do fear is that she may be drifting into commitments which, though generous and benevolent in intent, are so far-reaching as to exceed even America's great capacities. At the same time, it is my hope — and I emphasize it because it underlies all of the criticisms and proposals to be made in these pages — that America will escape those fatal temptations of power which have ruined other great nations and will instead confine herself to doing only that good in the world which she can do, both by direct effort and by the force of her own example.

The stakes are high indeed: they include not only America's continued greatness but nothing less than the survival of the human race in an era when, for the first time in human history, a living generation has the power of veto over the survival of the next.

If America has a service to perform in the world and I believe it has it is in large part the service of its own example. In our excessive involvement in the affairs of other countries, we are not only living off our assets and denying our own people the proper enjoyment of their resources; we are also denying the world the example of a free society enjoying its freedom to the fullest. This is regrettable indeed for a nation that aspires to teach democracy to other nations, because, as Burke said, "Example is the school of mankind, and they will learn at no other."

There are many respects in which America, if it can bring itself to act with the magnanimity and the empathy appropriate to its size and power, can be an intelligent example to the world. We have the opportunity to set an example of generous understanding in our relations with China, of practical cooperation for peace in our relations with Russia, of reliable and respectful partnership in our relations with Western Europe, of material helpfulness without moral presumption in our relations with the developing nations, of abstention from the temptations of hegemony in our relations with Latin America, and of the all-around advantages of minding one's own business in our relations with everybody. Most of all, we have the opportunity to serve as an example of democracy to the world by the way in which we run our own society; America, in the words of John Quincy Adams, should be "the well-wisher to the freedom and independence of all" but "the champion and vindicator only of her own."

If we can bring ourselves so to act, we will have overcome the dangers of the arrogance of power. It will involve, no doubt, the loss of certain glories, but that seems a price worth paying for the probable rewards, which are the happiness of America and the peace of the world.

• Nobiscum deus (meaning God with us) was the battle cry of the late Roman, the Byzantine, and the Russian Empires and then as Gott mit uns was used on the armor of German military from the German Empire to the end of the Third Reich.

● Only 57.1 percent and 56.8 percent of eligible American voters cast their votes in the 2008 Presidential and Federal elections respectively. Hardly impressive turnouts for a nation which with pretentious chest-thumping arrogance insinuates itself as the hallmark for world democracy.

Nobody will ever deprive the American people of the right to vote except the American people themselves and the only way they can do this is by not voting.
President Franklin D. Roosevelt (1933-1945).

In America, the criminally insane rule and the rest of us, or the vast majority of the rest of us, either do not care, do not know, or are distracted and properly brainwashed into acquiescence.
Kurt Nimmo, writer and editor.

The above paid-for advertisement — a minuscule part of the overall Zionist agenda to brainwash North Americans — is obviously racist and in keeping with the supremacist sentiments of a criminally insane Apartheid state. It also implies that what the Israelis are doing to the Palestinian people is civilized and acceptable. The "civilised" conduct of the Israeli Defense Force and the Jewish settlers in the illegally Occupied Territories is well documented and would be more appropriately described as barbaric. The racist tone

of such advertisements should be condemned and rejected outright by all those who are truly civilized and humane.

> *Today the world is the victim of propaganda because people are not intellectually competent. More than anything the United States needs effective citizens competent to do their own thinking.***William Mather Lewis (1878-1945), American teacher, university president and local politician.**

INTRODUCTION

While the background information in this book is historically factual and verifiable by anyone with access to an uncensored internet or a well-stocked reference library, the plot and main protagonists are fictional — but not necessarily far-fetched — so that any resemblance to persons living or dead is entirely coincidental. Furthermore the book was written with neither agenda nor affiliation with any other individuals or organizations — be they political, religious or otherwise — but with a view to providing a red alert regarding the dangers resulting from the failure to constantly fight for and protect the five basic principles which underpin that concept of democracy which purports to provide governance by the people and for the people. Unfortunately governance in virtually all so-called democratic countries today is by and for big business and special interest groups.

The first principle of democracy stresses the importance of recognizing that each individual is a separate, unique, and valuable being who along with other individuals helps to create a society whose members must all without exception be cared and catered for by a process of democratic governance.

The second principle unequivocally emphasises the equality of all individuals without imposing the actual condition of equality because realistically not everyone can be intellectually or physically equal. It does, however, provide individuals with inalienable rights to equal opportunity and equality before an unbiased legal system that disregards gender, colour, race, and religion.

The third principle calls for governance by the will of the majority — rather than by the disproportionate influence and power of a few — with equal rights for all minorities who serve to keep majority rule under check. It is also recognizes that while majority governance will not necessarily always arrive at the right decisions, it will more often than not serve the will of the majority — always providing that the majority participate in the democratic process.

The fourth principle recognises that in order for the third principle to function satisfactorily, the element of compromise must always be employed so that while the concept of democracy champions the rights of individuals, it must also by means of compromise secure a consensus that is acceptable to the majority.

25

The fifth principle, while recognising the right to individual freedom, does not demand complete freedom for each individual because that could only exist under a state of anarchy where there is no established process of governance. In other words the exercise of individual freedom is permitted so long as it does not impinge on either the freedom of others, or on government legislation enacted in the name of the majority.

With those five principles in mind, it is evident that no democratic process can be viable without the constant participation of an alert and well-informed electoral majority. The absence of such participation will inevitably result in negative if not catastrophic consequences as was the case in Germany where an ill-informed and negligent electorate allowed the maniac Adolf Hitler to take power and then stood idly by while he pursued diabolic and disastrous policies — including a genocidal persecution of Jews and others — that ultimately also punished the very people who allowed him to take power.

> *It also gives us a very special, secret pleasure to see how unaware the people around us are of what is really happening to them.*
> **Adolph Hitler (1889-1945)**

In his best-known work *The Republic* (c. 380 BCE), the renowned Athenian philosopher Plato (428-347 BCE) likens the governance of a city-state to the command of a naval vessel and argues that such command should only be given to those fit for the task. Plato therefore concludes that democratic self-governance does not work because ordinary people have failed to learn how to run the ship of state. They are generally unfamiliar with the intricacies of economics, foreign policy, military strategy, jurisprudence, or even the ethical aspects of their own conduct in society. Furthermore they regard the acquisition of such knowledge as being a tedious and unnecessary chore. Their judgments are inevitably based on capricious emotions rather than well-founded, practical evaluations so that in their sadly benighted state they are inclined to elect shallow but beguiling politicians who make ill-defined pledges. This results in their becoming subject to circumstances and governance over which they have no control and are therefore easily inveigled into accepting precarious policies and avoidable military conflicts whose cost in human and monetary terms defies any degree of justification.

The conclusions that Plato arrived at almost two and a half millenniums ago are unfortunately still very relevant today with people still failing to accept the responsibilities that are essential for successful democratic self-governance. They remain oblivious to the fact that their failure to responsibly participate in in the democratic process — other than perhaps to occasionally vote in periodic elections — contributes to the gradual but certain erosion of all democratic principles including those relating to human rights. Though such failure may no doubt stem from a variety of reasons including an understandable selfish preoccupation with survival in the rat race, it is nonetheless inexcusable to not identify and oppose those forces whose pernicious influence is responsible for much of what afflicts humanity.

> *Every man must decide whether he will walk in the light of creative altruism or in the darkness of destructive selfishness.*
> **Dr. Martin Luther King Jr. (1929-1968) African-American Civil Rights leader.**

> *If ye love wealth better than liberty, the tranquility of servitude better than the animating contest of freedom, go home from us in peace. We ask not your counsels or arms. Crouch down and lick the hands which feed you. May your chains set lightly upon you, and may posterity forget that ye were our countrymen.*
> **Samuel Adams (1722-1803), American statesman, political philosopher, and one of the Founding Fathers of the United States of America.**

So while such irresponsible ignorance may have been excusable in Plato's time, there is certainly no excuse for such dereliction of duty in an age where advanced technologies provide instant access to information and worldwide communication. It is precisely for that reason that repressive regimes deem it essential to control and restrict the free flow and exchange of information that is possible with modern day communications including access to the internet. Nowadays most constituents in Western democracies have the means to instantly make their views known by email to their elected representatives — it only takes a few minutes — and thereby have direct influence on the governance of their country without publicly demonstrating or resorting to violence. Elected representatives who have their inbox swamped with 20-30,000 emails from their constituents on a regular basis regarding issues of importance will certainly become aware of majority constituency participation and conduct themselves accordingly with the certain knowledge that serving the interests of influential minority groups alone will not be enough to get them re-elected.

> *Everyone has the right to freedom of opinion and expression; this right includes freedom to hold opinions without interference and to seek, receive and impart information and ideas through any media and regardless of frontiers.*
> **Article 19, The Universal Declaration of Human Rights.**

Governance by the people and for the people is consequently only possible if the people themselves are constantly vigilant to ensure that neither individuals nor groups with special interests — political, religious or otherwise — are ever allowed to exert disproportionate influence over the affairs of state. It is also crucial that the people oppose the machinations of secret organizations whose illegitimate covert influence is by nature and necessity both corrupt and contrary to the legitimate interests of the majority. It is equally essential that the people renounce false religious doctrines that were originally created to gain control over the masses by exploiting their ignorance and fear of the unknown.

> *All institutions of churches, whether Jewish, Christian or Turkish, appear to me no other than human inventions, set up to terrify and enslave mankind, and monopolize power and profit.*
> **Thomas Paine (1737-1809), English-American political activist, author, political theorist and revolutionary. The Age of Reason.**

It is equally vital that the people totally reject governance without transparency from politicians who having been elected to represent the majority, have instead readily accepted "thirty pieces of silver" from lobbyists and pressure groups who serve the interests of a selfish and avaricious minority. By failing to watch over and protect their democratic rights, people are legitimizing and providing license without limit for the incessant assault on the natural and legal rights of all human beings.

> *Every morning I have been looking at CNN to see if there is any reason for hope. I see a few large and impressive peace protests here and there around the world, but mostly I see empty robot faces monotonously reciting the magic incantations, "We must support the President" and "We must support our troops," both of which mean the killing must continue.*
> **Robert Anton Wilson, american author, philosopher, psychologist, essayist, editor, playwright, poet, futurist and civil libertarian.** *Cosmic Trigger II: Down to Earth* **(1991)**

So despite hypocritically professing to be upholding and fighting for the natural and legal rights of all human beings, Western nations led by that sham democracy called the United States, are just as guilty — because of their cowed silence, their despicable double standards and their unprincipled self-serving policies — as those repressive regimes who blatantly flout the Universal Declaration of Human Rights whose uncompromising enforcement is an essential prerequisite if there is to be any hope of peaceful coexistence in the conduct of human affairs. So while natural and legal rights include the individual's right to pursue the religious belief of his or her choice, that religious belief must never be allowed to either aggressively violate the rights of others or to wage unjustified and insane wars in God's name.

IN GOD'S NAME

Nations will gather together to bring their homage to the people of God; the whole fortune of nations will pass into the hands of the Jewish people, they will march behind the Jewish people, in chains as captives, and will prostrate before it.
Isador Loeb, French-Jewish scholar (1839-1892) Le Probleme Juif.

. . . On this account I, or rather the Lord, beseech you as Christ's heralds to publish this everywhere and to persuade all people of whatever rank, foot-soldiers and knights, poor and rich, to carry aid promptly to those Christians and to destroy that vile race from the lands of our friends. I say this to those who are present, it meant also for those who are absent. Moreover, Christ commands it . . . All who die by the way, whether by land or by sea, or in battle against the pagans, shall have immediate remission of sins . . .
From Pope Urban II's Speech at the Council of Clermont (1095) calling for a Crusade to recover Palestine from Muslim rule.

Allah wished to confirm the truth by his words: "Wipe the infidels out to the last."
Qur'an: 8:7

I am convinced that I am acting as the agent of our Creator. By fighting off the Jews, I am doing the Lord's Work.
Adolf Hitler (1889-1945) in *Mein Kampf*.

I am driven with a mission from God. God would tell me, "George go and fight these terrorists in Afghanistan." And I did. And then God would tell me "George, go and end the tyranny in Iraq." And I did . . .
Unindicted war criminal U.S. President George W. Bush in August 2003.

I think if you have faith about these things, you realize that judgment is made by other people — and if you believe in God, it's made by God as well.

Unindicted war criminal British Prime Minister Tony Blair 'passing the buck' in March 2006 on the role played by his Christian faith in deciding to launch the illegal war against Iraq.

This country exists as the fulfillment of a promise made by God Himself. It would be ridiculous to ask it to account for its legitimacy.

Israeli Prime Minister (March 1969-June 1974) Golda Meir, *Le Monde* 1971.

Every war results from the struggle for markets and spheres of influence, and every war is sold to the public by professional liars and totally sincere religious maniacs, as a Holy Crusade to save God and Goodness from Satan and Evil.

Robert Anton Wilson (1932–2007), American author and polymath.

Monday, 10 November 2008

The Corniche, Beirut, Lebanon.

Mark Banner, as was his habit whenever he was trying to concentrate, ran his fingers though his chestnut colored hair which was graying around the temples. Several decades of war zone reporting were beginning to take their toll on his now fifty-four year old body and he used his left hand to massage his right shoulder to relieve the twinge of pain still felt occasionally as a result of having stopped a bullet while covering the war in Afghanistan. He dismissed the idea of a pickup with another cup of black coffee for fear of becoming a caffeine junkie. He could almost smell the aroma of his customized blend from London's coffee store in Soho's Old Compton Street which fortunately offered a worldwide mail-order service.

As an independent journalist and author, Banner had not shared the euphoria with which the mainstream media had reacted to the election of Barack Obama as the first African American U.S. President: he was dismayed and perhaps even disgusted. Being a journalist and writer who held more British and international journalism awards than any other foreign correspondent, Banner's disdain was understandable and justified. The mostly muzzled and mealy-mouthed mainstream media had accepted without question or analysis Obama's "full of hope" package of promises of a new U.S. approach to diplomacy that would include resolution of the conflict between Israel and the Palestinian people.

Unlike most journalists who worked within the mainstream media — a media which rather than being the "voice of the people" is instead serving the interests of the Anglo-Zionist Political Corporate Military Industrial Empire — Banner resolutely refused to compromise the truth along with his own integrity out of fear of committing career suicide. He had on many occasions paid a high price for bucking the diktats of political correctness by assiduously reporting the facts rather than simply providing a glossed-over semblance of the truth. Most journalists — like the majority in the professions and politics — were primarily concerned with the advancement of their own careers and, as such, had learnt early on to work under the subjugation of the media owners' agendas which for those who are ambitious decrees their toleration of lies and corruption rather than their uncompromising rejection of everything but the whole truth.

> *Without an unfettered press, without liberty of speech, all of the outward forms and structures of free institutions are a sham, a pretense — the sheerest mockery. If the press is not free; if speech is not independent and untrammeled; if the mind is shackled or made impotent through fear, it makes no difference under what form of government you live, you are a subject and not a citizen.*
> **William E. Borah, (1865-1940), prominent Republican attorney and longtime U.S. Senator known as 'The Lion of Idaho'.**

It went without saying that anyone who dared to either question or criticize U.S or Israeli Middle East policy would become the subject of hate mail, vilification campaigns, and even death threats. For justifiably asking the awkward questions that seek to arrive at the truth, it was people like Banner — and not Israel's illegal occupation and brutal treatment of Palestinian people — that was to blame for provoking anti-Semitism. So as an irreproachable journalist, Banner had to choose from one of three options: enjoy a peaceful life by toeing the line and religiously refraining from criticizing the U.S. and Israel; give up writing altogether; or continue with the quest — with all its accompanying consequences — for universal justice, peace, and goodwill. Mark Banner had without any hesitation chosen the third option.

In what was to be his first article since Obama's election, Banner argued that for America to have any chance of brokering a Middle East peace it would first have to make an honest evaluation of the facts relating to the conflict by recognizing that the main root of the problem was that Israeli leaders had never wanted, nor would they ever want a peace that would mean abandoning their Zionist objective of grabbing as much land as possible and driving out the Palestinian people. Banner noted that former President Jimmy Carter in his memoirs about his White House years, wrote that peace could have been possible between Arabs and Israelis had it not been for the bigoted, Nazi-like racial views of Israel's Prime Minister Menachem Begin. According to Carter, Begin believed the Jews were a Master Race, a holy people superior to Egyptians and Arabs. Begin also held the belief that God wanted the Jews to own the land, so that there was absolutely no basis for peace. The Jews lusted for the land and intended to have it. Period!

> *If I were an Arab leader, I would not sign an agreement with Israel. It is normal; we have taken their country. It is true God promised it to us, but how could that interest them? Our God is not theirs. There has been anti-Semitism, the Nazis, Hitler, Auschwitz, but was that their fault? They see but one thing: we have come and we have stolen their country. Why should they accept that?*
> **David Ben-Gurion (the first Prime Minister of Israel), quoted by Nahum Goldmann in *Le Paradox Juif* (The Jewish Paradox).**

> *I would have joined a terrorist organization.*
> **Israeli Prime Minister (1999–2001) Ehud Barak's response when asked by a *Haaretz* newspaper columnist what he would have done if he had been born a Palestinian.**

Such admissions from Zionist Israeli leaders prove complete cognisance of what they did, are still doing, and intend to go on doing in the illegally occupied territories. Banner noted that Jewish people should not allow their religion and the long history of their persecution to be hijacked by a fascist ideology which then fully exploits them to justify the cold, calculated, crimes being continually perpetrated against the Palestinian people. Israel was a nation which since its inception in 1948 had pursued an expansionist policy by means of calculated belligerence towards Palestinians whose degradation and suppression had been ceaselessly maintained with stoic determination. He also made the point that while Israel was always prepared to attend peace talks with proclamations of good faith for the sake of appearance, it would always simultaneously do everything in its power to sabotage the negotiations.

Proof of that ploy existed in a 2001 secretly-filmed meeting between Benjamin Netanyahu and an Israeli family to whom he admitted that as prime minister from 1996 to 1999 he had deceived then U.S. President Bill Clinton into believing that Israel was implementing the Oslo accords by making insignificant withdrawals from the West Bank while actually entrenching the occupation. In further unguarded comments, Netanyahu boasts contemptuously that he knows "what America is," and that "America is something that can be moved easily. Moved to the right direction."

Netanyahu had also made it clear that far from being defensive, Israel's harsh military repression had been specifically designed to crush the Palestinian Authority so as to make it more pliable to Israeli diktats. Netanyahu confirmed that Israeli tactics included ". . . a broad attack on the Palestinian Authority. To bring them to the point of being afraid that everything is collapsing." And when asked about the world's reaction to such an attack he arrogantly replied that "the world won't say a thing. The world will say we're defending."

Banner continued, Americans had to have the vision and courage to recognise that Israel — by means of the most powerful lobbying group in America, the American Israel Public Affairs Committee (AIPAC) — was in effect controlling the American Congress. In October 2001 Foreign Minister Shimon Perez was warned as follows by the then unindicted war criminal Prime Minister Ariel Sharon:

> *Every time we do something you tell me America will do this and will do that . . . I want to tell you something very clear: Don't worry about American pressure on Israel. We the Jewish people, control America, and the Americans know it.*

Banner pointed out that this was obviously a fact of which Obama was acutely aware because after becoming the Democratic Party's Presidential Candidate on Tuesday 3rd. June 2008, Obama — in order to establish his AIPAC credentials — had toadied up to an AIPAC conference the very next day with a groveling "Uncle Tom" performance in which he claimed that his "great-uncle had been part of the 89th Infantry Division — the first Americans to reach a Nazi concentration camp. They liberated Ohrdruf, part of Buchenwald, on an April day in 1945. Adding that the horrors of that camp went beyond their capacity to imagine. And that tens of thousands died of hunger, torture, disease, or plain murder — part of the Nazi killing machine that killed 6 million people." Obama omitted to mention the other 6 million non-Jews who were also killed.

Banner wondered if Obama was capable of stretching the capacity of his imagination to comprehend what it was like for the victims of the Armenian Holocaust where 300,000 were massacred (1894-1896), 1.5 million massacred or forcibly deported (1915-1916), and 30,000 massacred or burnt in Smyrna (1922); what it was like for the 15 million Christian Russian Kulak farmers who were exterminated during the Soviet Holocaust (1924-1930); what it was like for the seven million Ukrainian farmers who were starved to death (1930-1933); what it was like for the 12 million Russian political prisoners who perished between 1919 and 1949; what it was like for the victims of the 1948 Deir Yassin massacre which marked the beginning of the depopulation of over 400 Palestinian towns and villages resulting in the exodus of 750,000 Arabs which marked the beginning of the Palestinian Nakba, or catastrophe, resulting in a Palestinian diaspora within refugee camps and in neighboring Arab countries; what it was like for the estimated 40 to 60 million Chinese victims of Mao Zedong's regime; what it was like for the estimated 2 million victims of the Vietnam War including massacres such as My Lai by U.S Forces and the U.S. herbicidal warfare programme's use of Agent Orange which killed or maimed some 400,000 and to this day is still afflicting 3 million as a result of birth defects and that is without counting the millions more of their relatives who bear the hardship of looking after them; what it was like for the 2.5 million Cambodians who were slaughtered during the Pol Pot Communist Holocaust in 1975; what it was like for the millions of victims in the still ongoing Iraq War which was deceitfully launched against Iraq's nonexistent weapons of mass destruction; what it was like for the tens of thousands of South Americans who were victims of Central Intelligence Agency (CIA) subversion operations to overthrow left-wing governments as happened in Chile to Salvador Allende's government (November 1970 to September 1973); and finally, what it was like for the hundreds of millions of under-5 children (over 30,000 a day) who died, are still dying and will go on dying from acute respiratory infections, diarrhea, measles, malaria and malnutrition which all in combination constitute a horrendous genocide by means of irresponsible neglect.

While the term *Holocaust victims* is usually taken to refer to Jews, the victims of Nazi Germany for example also included disabled people, enemy nationals, Esperantists, Freemasons, homosexuals, leftists, non-Europeans, Poles, political prisoners, Romanies (Gypsies), Slavs, and Soviet Slavs and POWs. While constant reminders of anti-Semitism and the Holocaust have so far served their purpose, the continual cries of "anti-Semitism" like the continual cries of "wolf," will eventually fall on deaf ears if used constantly without justification. There is some degree of irony in the fact that those who once justifiably complained of anti-Semitism the loudest, are now also the ones who are themselves guilty of racism and crimes against humanity.

> *Ever since the Jews invented the libel charge of "anti-Semitism" in the 1880s. It was first printed in the Jewish Encyclopedia (1901 Vol. 1, p. 641), and has been built up with Jewish money, organizations, propaganda and lies (such as the Holocaust — Holohoax), so that now the word is like a snake venom which paralyses one's nervous system. Even the mention of the word "Jew" is shunned unless used in a most favorable and positive context.*
> **Charles A. Weisman, *Who is Esau-Edom?*, Weisman Publications, 1966.**

> *Israelis and American Jews fully agree that the memory of the Holocaust is an indispensable weapon — one that must be used relentlessly against their common enemy . . . Jewish organizations and individuals thus labor continuously to remind the world of it. In America, the perpetuation of the Holocaust memory is now a $100-million-a-year enterprise, part of which is government funded.*
> **According to Israeli author Moshe Leshem, the expansion of Israeli power is commensurate with the expansion of "Holocaust" propaganda. *Balaam's Curse: How Israel Lost its Way, and How it Can Find it Again*, Simon & Schuster, 1989.**

In his eagerness to brownnose his Jewish audience by pledging unequivocal support for the Apartheid state of Israel, Obama — a graduate of Columbia University and Harvard Law School — either conveniently forgot, or was simply not aware of the findings of Professor of International Law, John Dugard, who following the recurrence of the Palestinian intifada in late 2000, was appointed Chairman of a UN Commission on Human Rights inquiry into the human rights situation in the Palestinian territories. In 2001, he was appointed United Nations Special Rapporteur to the commission on the "situation of human rights in the Palestinian territories occupied by Israel since 1967." Dugard was charged with submitting annual reports and recommendations to the UN concerning the situation of international human rights and humanitarian law.

In its first special session in July 2006, the Human Rights Council dispatched an urgent fact-finding mission led by Dugard to report on the situation in the Palestinian territories. On 26 September 2006, Dugard reported that the "standards of human rights in the Palestinian territories have fallen to intolerable new levels."

In a further report released in February 2007, Dugard stated that Israel's policies "resemble those of apartheid." The report also stated that "it is difficult to resist the conclusion that many of Israel's laws and practices violate the 1966 Convention on the Elimination of all forms of Racial Discrimination." It was also stated that "Discrimination against Palestinians occurs in many fields. Moreover, the 1973 International Convention on the Suppression and Punishment of the Crime of Apartheid appears to be violated by many practices, particularly those denying freedom of movement to Palestinians."

In referring to Israeli actions in the occupied West Bank, Dugard asked, "Can it seriously be denied that the purpose is to establish and maintain domination by one racial group (Jews) over another racial group (Palestinians) and systematically oppressing them? Israel denies that this is its intention or purpose. But such an intention or purpose may be inferred from the actions described in this report."

Needless to say, like anyone who dares to rightly criticise Israel, Dugard got his share of unjustified vilification by God's "chosen people." The following is an excerpt from a paper written by Dugard on the International Convention on the Suppression and Punishment of the Crime of Apartheid:

> *The Apartheid Convention declares that apartheid is a crime against humanity and that "inhuman acts resulting from the policies and practices of apartheid and similar policies and practices of racial segregation and discrimination" are international crimes (art. 1). Article 2 defines the crime of apartheid — "which shall include similar policies and practices of racial segregation and discrimination as practiced in southern Africa— as covering inhuman acts committed for the purpose of establishing and maintaining domination by one racial group of persons over any other racial group of persons and systematically oppressing*

them" It then lists the acts that fall within the ambit of the crime. These include murder, torture, inhuman treatment and arbitrary arrest of members of a racial group; deliberate imposition on a racial group of living conditions calculated to cause its physical destruction; legislative measures that discriminate in the political, social, economic and cultural fields; measures that divide the population along racial lines by the creation of separate residential areas for racial groups; the prohibition of interracial marriages; and the persecution of persons opposed to apartheid.

Therefore, as a lawyer, instead of admitting that Israel was in every sense an Apartheid state, Obama went on to assure the AIPAC audience that foreign policy changes would include "change that restores American power and influence. Change accompanied by a pledge that I will make known to allies and adversaries alike: that America maintains an unwavering friendship with Israel, and an unshakeable commitment to its security." In making such a pledge, Obama was merely confirming that he knew what all other politicians on Capitol Hill have always known: if you criticize Israel or in any way upset AIPAC, then come the next election you will find that your opponent's campaign will have AIPAC's full support and funding.

This tribe of black gentry work more effectually against us, than the enemy's arms. They are a hundred times more dangerous to our liberties, and the great cause we are engaged in. It is much lamented that each state, long ere this, has not hunted them down, as pests to society, and the greatest enemies we have to the happiness of America. I would to God, that some one of the most atrocious in each state, was hung upon a gallows, five times as high as the one prepared by Haman [Haman instigated an unsuccessful plot to kill all Jews in the lands over which he ruled in ancient Persia]. No punishment, in my opinion, is too great for the man who can build his greatness upon his country's ruin.
J. F. Schroeder, *Maxims of Washington: Political, Social, Moral and Religious*, D. Appleton and Company, New York, 1855.

In 1974 an AIPAC-backed opponent defeated the incumbent Senator J. W. Fulbright who had sponsored the Fulbright Act of 1946 to provide funds for the exchange of students, scholars, and teachers between the United States and other countries. Fulbright had represented Arkansas from 1945 to 1975 and apart from being the longest serving chairman in the history of the Senate Foreign Relations Committee, the much respected Fulbright had also opposed McCarthyism, the House Un-American Activities Committee, and the Vietnam War. Despite his long and distinguished service to America, Senator Fulbright paid the price for his forthright beliefs which included the following:

> *Israel, I am convinced, can and should survive as a peaceful, prosperous society — but within the essential borders of 1967 . . . That much we owe them, but no more. We do not owe them our support of their continued occupation of Arab lands . . . The Palestinians have as much right to a homeland as the Jewish people.*

Fulbright's sentiment regarding the rights of the Palestinian people was obviously not one that was shared by Zionist leaders whose ideology included welcoming and actively promoting anti-Semitism as a means of achieving their racist objectives. Banner illustrated the point by wondering if the following quotes were any less racist or contemptible than Hitler's remarks about the Jewish people:

> *We must expropriate gently the private property on the state assigned to us. We shall try to spirit the penniless population across the border by procuring employment for it in the transit countries, while denying it employment in our country . . . Both the process of expropriation and the removal of the poor must be carried out discreetly and circumspectly.*
> **Theodore Herzl, founder of the World Zionist Organization, speaking of the Arabs of Palestine, *Complete Dairies*, 1895 entry.**

> *Let us not ignore the truth among ourselves . . . Politically we are the aggressors and they defend themselves . . . The country is theirs, because they inhabit it, whereas we want*

to come here and settle down, and in their view we want to take away their country.
David Ben-Gurion, quoted on pp 91-2 of Chomsky's Fateful Triangle, which appears in Simha Flapan's *Zionism and the Palestinians* pages 141-2 citing a 1938 speech.

We must do everything to insure they (the Palestinians) never do return. The old will die and the young will forget.
David Ben-Gurion, in 1948 assuring his fellow Zionists that Palestinians will never come back to their homes.

We walked outside, Ben-Gurion accompanying us. Allon repeated the question, what is to be done with the Palestinian population? Ben-Gurion waved his hand in a gesture which said drive them out.
Yitzhak Rabin, leaked censored version of Rabin memoirs, *New York Times*, 23 October 1979.

We shall reduce the Arab population to a community of woodcutters and waiters.
Rabin's description of the conquest of Lydda, after the completion of Plan Dalet. Sabri Jiryas, *The Arabs in Israel*, Monthly Review Press, 1977.

There is no such thing as a Palestinian People . . . It is not as if we came and threw them out and took their country. They didn't exist.
Golda Meir, to *The Sunday Times*, June 15, 1969.

When we have settled the land, all the Arabs will be able to do about it will be to scurry around like drugged cockroaches in a bottle.
Raphael Eitan, Chief of Staff of the Israeli Defense Forces, *New York Times*, April 14, 1983.

We declare openly that the Arabs have no right to settle on even one centimeter of Eretz Israel . . . Force is all they do or ever will understand. We shall use the ultimate force

until the Palestinians come crawling to us on all fours.
**Rafael Eitan, Chief of Staff of the Israeli Defense Forces,
Gad Becker, *Yediot Ahronot* 13 April 1983; *New York
Times*, 14 April 1983.**

*We have to kill all the Palestinians unless they are resigned
to live here as slaves.*
**Chairman Heilbrun of the Committee for the election of
General S. Lahat, the mayor of Tel Aviv, October 1983.**

*The Palestinians would be crushed like grasshoppers . . .
smashed against the boulders and walls.*
**Israeli Prime Minister (at the time) Yitzhak Shamir in
a speech to Jewish settlers, *New York Times*, April 1988.**

It was evident from Israeli leadership remarks and opinions that
recognition of, and peace with the Palestinians had never been and
never would be on Israel's agenda. Israel would continue to ignore UN
resolutions and world opinion by expanding settlements in the West
Bank and building more Jewish neighborhoods in East Jerusalem. Just as
it did in September 2000, Israel would continue to blame the Palestinian
leadership for the failure of the diplomatic process by dishonestly
asserting that the Palestinians planned for more violence and were not
really interested in a two-state solution. So-called Palestinian violence
is in fact Palestinian resistance to Israeli violence and oppression — and
it is time the West acknowledged that irrefutable fact.

Just as then U.S. President Bill Clinton — no doubt preoccupied
with regret over enjoying Oval Office fellatio without actually having
"sex with that woman" — swallowed Israeli disinformation hook, line,
and sinker and abandoned the Palestinian Leadership, so would Barack
Obama. If the West continued to tolerate Israel's illegal occupation and
further annexation of Arab lands; if it continued with its failure to take
positive steps to punish Israel for human rights violations; if it continued
to countenance being blackmailed into silence by unjustified Israeli
accusations of anti-Semitism; and if it continued to meekly accept U.S.
vetoes of UN resolutions condemning Israel (the U.S. has used more
vetoes on behalf of Israel than it has on behalf of itself or any other
issue); then the West should not be surprised at being the subject of
Islamic hatred and acts of terrorism. A balanced and just Middle East

policy by Western nations would prove far more effective in winning the war on terror and Islamic extremism than would ever be accomplished by the West's combined military might. The West must stop paying for Israel's belligerency by fighting wars against enemies that Israel was responsible for creating and will deliberately continue to create as a smokescreen for its own diabolical agenda and conduct.

Banner wound up his column with the forecast that there would never be peace between Israelis and Palestinians so long as Israel was able to continually outfox spineless U.S. presidents and AIPAC retained its stranglehold on Congress. Israel's total control of U.S. Middle East policy meant that whenever there was a United Nations Security Council resolution condemning Israel for its ongoing violations in the illegally occupied Palestinian territories, the U.S. would inevitably either abstain or use its veto power to kill the resolution. Such biased U.S. policies that unjustly favored Israel not only fueled Islamic hate for the U.S., but also served to alienate, radicalize, and justify — even among Islamic moderates — an extremist response. Unfortunately, the brunt and cost of this Islamic hatred and terror was also being borne by other Western nations who obsequiously support ill-conceived U.S. Middle East policies. "For how long," Banner asked, "must the citizens of Western nations continue paying for the enormous costs of tolerating Israeli crimes against the Palestinian people?"

Freemasons' Hall, Covent Garden, London

The building situated at the intersection of Great Queen Street and Wild Street was monumental in every sense of the word and David Reisner was suitably impressed. London's Freemasons' Hall doubled as headquarters for the United Grand Lodge of England and as a venue for London area Masonic Lodge meetings. Built in Art Deco style between 1927 and 1933 as a memorial to the 3,225 Freemasons who died during active service in the First World War, it was initially known as the Masonic Peace Memorial. The name, however, was changed to Freemasons' Hall following the outbreak of the Second World War.

There is now a Masonic suggestion that the reason the building escaped damage during the Blitz — sustained German bombing from September 1940 to May 1941 — was because many of the German

Luftwaffe pilots were themselves Freemasons. This would appear to contradict the fact that the Nazis believed that high-degree Freemasons were not only willing members of "the Jewish conspiracy" but were also partly responsible for Germany's defeat in the First World War. Estimates of the number of Freemasons killed in Nazi occupied countries varied between 80,000 and 200,000.

Masonic lore also suggests that Masonic origins date back to the time of the legendary Hiram Abiff, (also known as "the Widow's Son") who as an architect and master artificer is an allegorical character prominently figuring in a play that is enacted during initiation ceremonies into the Third Degree of Freemasonry. Abiff, had been sent by King Hiram of Tyre (present-day Lebanon) to build King Solomon's Temple. Though the name Hiram Abiff does not appear in the in scriptures, the Masonic account of Hiram is often said to be based upon the Holy Bible. In the Master Mason Degree portion of the ritual known as the Legend of the Third Degree, the storyline has three central characters associated with the building of Solomon's temple. The characters, King Solomon, King Hiram of Tyre, and Hiram Abiff are all taken from the Scriptural account of the temple building.

> *King Solomon sent to Tyre and brought Huram, whose mother was a widow from the tribe of Naphtali and whose father was a man of Tyre and a craftsman in bronze. Huram was highly skilled and experienced in all kinds of bronze work. He came to King Solomon and did all the work assigned to him.*
> **1 Kings 7:13-14**

According to the Masonic version of the legend, Abiff was murdered while visiting the temple by three dissatisfied and envious Fellow Crafts whom Abiff had refused to raise to the level of Master by not divulging the Master Mason's secret password. The re-enactment of Abiff's murder by Candidates wishing to become Master Masons is an important part of their initiation ceremony which is followed by an explanation that the story is a lesson in fidelity to one's word, and in the brevity of life.

The tale starts with Hiram's arrival in Jerusalem, and his appointment by Solomon as chief architect and Master of Works at the construction of his temple. As the temple is nearing completion, three Fellow Crafts from the workforce ambush him and demand the secrets of a Master Mason. Hiram is challenged by each in turn, and at each refusal to divulge the information his assailant strikes him with a mason's tool. He is injured by the first two assailants, and struck dead by the third. His murderers hide his body under a pile of rubble, returning at night to move the body outside the city, where they bury it in a shallow grave marked with a sprig of acacia on a hill west of Mt. Moriah (Temple Mount).

As Hiram was missed the next day, Solomon sends out a group of Fellow Craft Masons to search for him. Abiff's body is accidentally discovered and exhumed to be given an appropriate burial. The three assassins are eventually located and brought to justice. Solomon informs the workforce that the secrets of the Master Mason have been lost and he replaces them with new ones based on gestures given and words spoken upon the discovery of Hiram's body.

The Hiram Abiff tale used in Freemasonry, however, is only part of the original legend which involves the Queen of Sheba. This is because Freemasonry — like most secret societies and religions — has an inherent tendency to relegate the importance of the female role.

While it is generally accepted that masons and smiths first became recognised as craftsmen some time prior to 3,500 BCE, there can be no certainty as to either the date they first became organised associations, or the precise origin of the Legend of the Temple. It is, however, evident that the initial development of trade associations was at its peak during the time of the Roman Empire when the *Collegia* — as they were called — consisted of the following basic groups:

A. Religious bodies such as the Colleges of Priests and Vestal Virgins.

B. Civil service associations for those in administrative positions.

C. Corporations for workers in metals or other hard materials.

D. Associations known as *Sodalitates* which started out as friendly leagues for social gatherings and feasting, but finished up being political associations against whom the Senate was often obliged to take action.

By the time of Theodosius I who was Emperor until 395, virtually every city and important town had associations that were similar to those in Rome, whereby the workers were either voluntarily or by compulsion obliged to belong to some trade or occupation for the benefit of their community. Proof of this can be found in the works of many ancient writers including Pliny the Younger (61-c. 112) who as pro-consul of Asia Minor, wrote to the Emperor Trajan informing him of a most destructive fire at Nicomedia (ancient city in what is present-day Turkey) and requesting permission to establish a *collegium fabrorum* for the rebuilding of the city.

Apart from membership in the *Collegia,* many workers would also have belonged to some kind of religion wherein their initiation would invariably have been based either on the allegorical killing of a deity or great man who subsequently resurrects, or on the wanderings of a person in great distress over the loss of a loved one. It was therefore only natural for trade associations to have initiation rituals that were compatible with the religion of its members.

The widespread nature of the Roman Empire also meant that *Collegia* were already established in many countries where even after the collapse of the Empire the concept was retained and served as the basis from which there evolved trade associations whose features and functions were mostly dictated by local circumstances and requirements.

> *Scarcely had had the Teutonic hordes obtained the mastery over the decaying Roman Empire, and the wandering tribes became fixed in their newly acquired territories, then the work began.*
> **Robert F. Gould, Gould's History of Freemasonry Throughout the World (6 volumes), Charles Scribner's Sons, 1936.**

In France for example, as magnificent structures began to be raised, a system of apprenticeship was in due course established whereby an apprentice was assigned to a master for a period of usually seven years after which he became a journeyman traveling around the country to gain experience on various building projects under different masters. In order to assist the journeyman with accommodation and companionship while he was on this *"our de France,"* the *Compagnonnage* was instituted with three main divisions for the different trades which had initiation rites connected to Solomon's Temple.

One version names Maitres Jacques and Soubise as associate Master Masons who after completion of the temple returned to Gaul with the vow never to part. Inevitably, however, in keeping with the mandatory storyline, the violent-natured Soubise becomes jealous of Jacques and breaks away to form his own group of disciples who are eventually instrumental in the treachery that leads to his rival's murder.

The traitor who betrayed Jacques to the killers by giving him the kiss of peace while he was at his usual place for morning prayers — like Judas Iscariot — later committed suicide.

Robert F. Gould also noted that the development of European trade associations such as the *Steimetzen* (stonemasons) started when:

Devout men from the British Isles, chiefly from Ireland, crossed over to the mainland, and penetrating into the depths of the German forests, carried the pure doctrines of primitive Christianity to the German Tribes. Wherever they came, they raised churches and dwellings for their priests, cleared the forests, tilled the soil, and instructed the heathen in the first principles of civilization . . . Then came Charlemagne and taught the German tribes to build cities and palaces (Aix-la-Chapelle, Ingelsheim). Each seat soon became the seat of a Roman Bishop; hence arose the cathedrals; and in many other cases the bishop's seat gave rise to the town. Later on the cities prospered and grew rich, and the necessity for sumptuous town halls arose, and thus by degrees the face of the land became dotted with those monuments of architectural skill, the very ruins of which testify to the cunning of the builders.

And who were these builders? What manner of men were they? Whence came they? They were the Steinmetzen. They were a class of simple workmen, bound together by strong ties of brotherhood, but containing in their midst master builders whose minds were stored with all the mathematical knowledge of those days, and who contentedly worked for a lifetime at an edifice, satisfied to know that although they might never see its completion, their successors would carry on the work to a glorious conclusion, and raise one more temple to the worship of the Most High.

As most of these building workers were invariably itinerant with three basic levels of skill acquired over seven years of apprenticeship — as Apprentices, Journeymen, and Master Masons — a system of secret recognition signs and words was devised for each level to which they were made privy as they progressed from apprentice to master. So as

47

they moved from one building project to another, their new employers could identify the degree of their skills from those secret signs and words.

During the Renaissance (14th-17th century) stonemason guilds began to admit members who were not stonemasons but were attracted by either the fraternal and social aspects or the potential for covert chicanery which could be conducted behind the closed nature of such organizations. And so it was from the observance of stonemason traditions without any actual involvement in construction projects that the secret society of Freemasons evolved.

David Reisner's reason for visiting the Freemasons' Hall was for its Masonic Library and Museum which served as a repository for archives and also contained a comprehensive collection of printed books covering Freemasonry in England, Wales, and elsewhere in the world. Information was also available on subjects related to Masonic, mystical, and esoteric traditions. Despite several hours of diligent research and assistance from the helpful librarians, Reisner, however, could not find any mention of the Hiramic Brotherhood of the Third Temple.

Reisner had first learnt about the possible existence of a secretive cell from Michal Zeldin, an Israel Antiquities Authority archaeologist who had become a thorn in the side of both his employers and his country. The actual existence of such a cell called the Hiramic Brotherhood of the Third Temple — which was alleged to be embedded within Freemasonry in Israel — had subsequently been confirmed to Reisner by an Israeli government source. Zeldin was coming to London for an exhibition at the British Museum and Reisner, an investigative journalist, had hoped that he would by then have uncovered more details about this covert Masonic cell whose members were fanatically dedicated to the rebuilding of a Third Temple on East Jerusalem's Temple Mount, the site of the Islamic Dome of the Rock.

At the time of revealing his suspicions to Reisner, Zeldin had also entrusted Reisner with a map — copied from the original which had been accidentally left in the photocopier he was about to use — that showed the locations of forbidden tunnel excavations under the Temple Mount. Though Reisner had not held any high hopes of uncovering something sensational at Freemasons' Hall, he was nonetheless somewhat disappointed at having found nothing at all. He left the building and walked westwards along Great Queen Street to a nearby pub where he hoped to review his options over a few pints.

Being a down-to-earth man who was not susceptible to vanity, Reisner had always been painfully aware that women did not regard him as being particularly attractive — a reality which he had philosophically accepted. Consequently he was rather surprised when an attractive, shapely brunette who, after ordering a glass of Chardonnay at the bar, sat nearby and kept looking in his direction with an inviting smile. The resulting adrenaline rush as his body tensed was not, however, due to the prospect of a tryst with an alluring woman, but to the realization that he may now be in danger. Reisner reckoned that she was either a high-class hooker or a Mossad agent. So irrespective of her profession, Reisner decided that becoming involved with a stranger was not an option for someone who was a sought-after fugitive for revealing the contents of secret Israeli Defense Force (IDF) documents that had been leaked to him.

With self-preservation being his immediate priority, Reisner had no difficulty resisting the temptation to linger, flirt a little and perhaps even get laid. He quickly finished his beer and headed for the nearest exit without giving the brunette a second glance. Once outside he walked briskly along Great Queen Street to Covent Garden Underground Station where he stopped, turned around and took time to check he was not being followed. As he got on the down escalator he thought about the brunette in the pub and recalled the honey-trap case of Mordechai Vanunu, the former Israeli nuclear technician.

Vanunu, the son of a rabbi, had completed three years of military service as First Sergeant with the Israeli Defence Force Combat Engineering Corps before working as a technician from 1976 until being laid off 1985 at the Negev Nuclear Research Centre south of Dimona. During that time he was also a part-time geography and philosophy student at Ben-Gurion University where he became critical of Israeli government policies. In 1985 he graduated with a BA in both subjects and left Israel to travel to Nepal, Burma, Thailand and then eventually in 1986 to Sydney, Australia. While there, he worked at various odd jobs and began attending a local Anglican church whose ministers were instrumental in his conversion from Judaism to Christianity.

Fate then played a hand when Vanunu met a journalist form *The Sunday Times* with whom he agreed in early September 1986 to fly to London to reveal information about Israel's nuclear program which included secretly taken photographs at the Dimona site. Israel had always pursued a policy of neither acknowledging nor denying possession of nuclear weapons so as to avoid a U.S. legal prohibition on funding countries which proliferate weapons of mass destruction. To admit possession would theoretically have disqualified Israel from receiving its annual military and other aid package which by courtesy of American taxpayers was in 1985, $3.4 billion (about 14% of Israel's $24.1 billion GDP).

Having been previously duped and embarrassed by the *Hitler Dairies* hoax, *The Sunday Times* was understandably cautious and took some time investigating Vanunu's claims which were eventually verified by experts. In the meantime a frustrated Vanunu had approached the *Sunday Mirror* whose owner was Robert Maxwell, a shyster and Mossad agent who plundered his own employees' pension fund as his business empire began to crumble. Maxwell's Mossad connection was subsequently revealed before his death by a former Mossad officer, Ari Ben-Menashe, who claimed that Maxwell had alerted the Israeli Embassy in London as to Vanunu's intention of divulging what he knew. In a further effort to save his empire, Maxwell tried to put the squeeze on Mossad for a financial bailout by threatening to expose what he knew and Mossad without the slightest compunction assassinated him (Gordon Thomas & Martin Dillon, *The Assassination of Robert Maxwell: Israel's Super Spy,* 2002).

After his approach to the *Sunday Mirror,* Vanunu became a Mossad priority so that one of its agents from America, Cheryl Bentov, was flown to London where she joined a team of nine Katsas (Israeli field intelligence officers). Bentov wasted no time in using her seduction skills to "come alongside" Vanunu in Leicester Square and quickly developed an amorous relationship with him. When Vanunu suggested spending the night together, Bentov agreed with the suggestion that they should go to Rome and "enjoy a few romantic days in the city of love." Five other members of the Mossad team were also on the flight to Rome where in the old quarter of the city, Bentov led Vanunu to an apartment which she claimed belonged to her sister. Israeli agents waiting in the apartment overpowered Vanunu, injected him with a paralyzing drug, and then transported him by freighter to Israel.

Vanunu was subsequently tried in secret on espionage and treason charges for which in 1988 he received an eighteen-year prison sentence eleven of which he spent in near total isolation. Amnesty International called his treatment by Israel as being cruel, inhuman or degrading such as that prohibited by international law. Every year from 1988 to 2004

Vanunu was nominated for the Nobel Peace Prize amongst many other nominations and awards.

Though in April 2004 Vanunu was finally released conditionally, he remained defiant under interrogation by Israel's internal security service. In recordings of the interrogation made public he was heard to say "I am neither a traitor nor a spy, I only wanted the world to know what is happening." He also stated: "We don't need a Jewish state. There needs to be a Palestinian state. Jews can, and have lived anywhere, so a Jewish state is not necessary."

Vanunu had been to date continually harassed, rearrested and imprisoned for violating the terms of his release which included not being allowed to have contact with citizens from other countries; not to use phones or own cellular phones; not to have access to the internet; not to approach embassies or consulates; not to come within five hundred metres of any international border crossing; not to visit any port of entry or airport; and not to leave the state of Israel. *And these people have the bare-faced cheek to claim that Israel was the only democracy in the Middle East,* Reisner thought as he boarded the train with the preoccupation of something he had once read:

> *We Jews, we are the destroyers and will remain the destroyers. Nothing you can do will meet our demands and needs. We will forever destroy because we want a world of our own.*
> **Maurice Samuels in *You Gentiles*, Harcourt, Brace & Co., New York, 1924.**

By allowing himself the luxury of dwelling temporarily on the inner conflict between Zionist Israeli characteristics and his own principled standards for decency and justice, Reisner had become too distracted to notice the nondescript couple with backpacks who got on the same carriage at an adjoining set of doors.

The Rockefeller Archaeological Museum, East Jerusalem.

After what had been a contentious meeting with the director-general of the Israel Antiquities Authority (IAA), an irritated Michal Zeldin stormed out of the office and slammed the door shut behind him. He had just yet again been warned that his outspoken views regarding both the IAA's and the Israeli government's policies were close to becoming treasonable and could no longer be tolerated by either the state or the IAA. As a dedicated archaeologist, Zeldin's main grievance was his belief that the IAA was being used to further the political goals of what was now effectively an Israeli Apartheid state that had by far surpassed all of the iniquities perpetrated by South Africa's former Afrikaner government.

While the IAA's professed aim was to serve as the leading professional body for the preservation, conservation, and study of Eretz Israel's (Land of Israel's) archaeological heritage, it was alternatively seen by Zeldin, as operating unethically and having an excavation agenda in and around East Jerusalem that was politically motivated for the purpose of consolidating and legitimizing Israel's claim on the land so as to establish all of Jerusalem as the eternal and undivided capital of Israel and thereby ensure East Jerusalem never becomes the capital of a Palestinian state. Zeldin was certain that though there were many other archaeologists and academics who shared his views — there was even talk of forming an organization that would enunciate such views — he was the one being the most watched by the security services.

In meetings with other concerned archaeologists and academics it had been generally agreed that together with other community activists all efforts should be focused on the role of archaeology in Israeli society in relation to the Israeli-Palestinian conflict. The view was taken that archaeology should be used as a means for building bridges and strengthening bonds between different peoples, their religions, and their cultures, and thereby have a positive impact on the social dynamics of the Palestinian-Israeli conflict. It was felt that archaeology should not and must not be employed to prove ownership by any one nation, ethnic group or religion over a given place. Archaeological discoveries should instead provide an intricate picture independent of religious tradition, ancient folklore, or current political agendas; and that an impartial examination of that picture would serve to enrich the wider public's culture and promote values of tolerance and pluralism.

It was believed by many that archaeological sites offered a cultural wealth that was an integral part of the cultural assets of a country and as such belonged jointly to all the communities, peoples and religious groups living there. Furthermore the term "archaeological sites" is not only a reference to the excavated layers of the sites, but also to their current characteristics including the inhabitants, their culture, and the routines and requirements of their daily existence. The perception that ruins of the past can be employed both in the service of national struggles and as a means of legitimizing the persecution of disadvantaged communities, was one that had to be assertively opposed. Support should therefore only be given to archaeological practices that involve and benefit all residents living in and around archaeological sites so as to reinforce positive environmental conscientiousness that will in turn encourage community involvement and generate significant social change.

It was also generally noted that Israel's archaeological excavations in Jerusalem's Old City had since 2005 focused on advancing the construction plans for public and tourist buildings mainly in the vicinity of the Temple Mount (al-Haram a-Sharif) and the Village of Silwan. Such excavations have become the main means of creating a new "Old City" and changing the lay of the land so as to lend legitimacy to Israeli claims while marginalizing the Palestinian inhabitants from their environment and their connection to the Temple Mount. The nature of such Israeli policies could only impact negatively on both the multi-cultural character of the city and the Israeli-Palestinian conflict.

Since East Jerusalem's 1967 annexation, the view — that the Old City is an inseparable part of Jerusalem as Israel's capitol — has gained credence amongst Israeli Jews even though it runs contrary to the international perspective which views the Old City as part of the West Bank. The Palestinians regard the Old City as an integral part of Palestinian Jerusalem, which in the future will be transferred to their jurisdiction in the framework of a political agreement.

Though Jerusalem is not universally recognized as being either the capitol or a part of Israel, Israel nonetheless, in keeping with its long-term policy of settling and keeping occupied territories, persists in making such claims and even redraws maps that show illegally occupied territories as being a part of Israel. Another Israeli ploy is the change of street and place names on signposts, in official documents, and in the state media. The problem is more pronounced in mainly Arab East Jerusalem which since its 1967 occupation by Israel has seen a continuous influx of Jewish settlers who are taking over Palestinian homes and endeavoring to erase all traces of Palestinian culture and identity by the complete Judaization of the map with all names being in Hebrew as in Yerushalayim instead of Jerusalem. To help consolidate such claims on the ground, an extensive program of archaeological excavations had been launched under the auspices of the IAA.

This unethical use of archeology is most evident in the town of Silwan — which with its unpretentious stone and cinder-block homes — stretches southwards from Jerusalem's Old City walls into the valley locally known as the Holy Basin. Silwan overlooked by the golden Dome of the Rock and the silver dome of the Al-Aqsa mosque from the north, the Mount of Olives from the northeast, and Israeli CCTV cameras everywhere from within. Armed Israeli guards patrol the stone-paved alleyways as part of the protection for the ever-growing number of illegal Israeli settlers — who by claiming biblical right to the land — started moving into Silwan in the early 1990s. Some fifty Jewish families numbering more than two hundred and fifty people, had since taken over Palestinian homes throughout the town and turned them into strongholds with fluttering Israeli flags as a further in the face provocation to the Palestinian inhabitants.

> *It is the duty of Israeli leaders to explain to public opinion, clearly and courageously, a certain number of facts that are forgotten with time. The first of these is that there is no Zionism, colonisation, or Jewish state without the eviction of the Arabs and the expropriation of their lands.*
> **Yoram Bar Porath, in *Yediot Aarh onot*, 14 July 1972.**

It was a common procedure for Israeli bulldozers to routinely knock down Palestinian homes to make room for new Jewish settler homes and parks that are designated with bogus religious archaeological pretensions. Armed with authorization from the Israeli Cabinet, the Jerusalem municipality works ceaselessly to strengthen Israel's claim to East Jerusalem by building parks and trails that connect illegal Jewish settlements so as usurp more Palestinian land and bring it under Israeli control.

The avowed goal of Israeli settler groups consisting of religious nationalists, is to bring hundreds of families over the next decade to the area so that Jews will become the majority. With 60 percent of rebuilding permits being allocated for Jewish settlement and little more than 10 percent for Palestinians, the Palestinians are being slowly but surely squeezed out of Jerusalem. Zeldin was also critical of an Israeli agenda which in order to be achieved required blatant violations of Palestinian human rights and international law. He regarded such violations as being profoundly abhorrent and a betrayal of everything that was commendable in Jewish ethical traditions.

While Silwan is only one of many such takeovers in Palestinian areas of occupied East Jerusalem, it was the one where inordinate Israeli settler arrogance — backed by private Jewish donations from abroad — was most pronounced with overt official assistance from the likes of the IAA and the Jerusalem municipality. This gradual takeover by means of illegal Israeli settlement and the establishment of archaeological sites was being conducted by Elad, an organization with artful wiles that somehow managed to usurp the jurisdiction in such matters from the Nature and Parks Authority.

In pursuit of its goal Elad had converted arbitrarily confiscated Silwan land into the "City of David" within whose centre an archaeological park was being extended with incessant resolve. More areas were being fenced off for the construction of new settler homes and excavations including tunnels to the walls of the Old City. According to a series of recent reports in the Israeli media, the government, IAA archaeologists, the Jerusalem municipality, and the police have all colluded with Elad and another settler organization, Ateret Cohanim, in efforts to extend the Israeli settlers' control of Silwan.

Zeldin was also concerned over the "City of David" excavations which were conducted under Palestinian residential areas without regard for the safety of the Palestinian residents whose homes in many cases had been subject to cracks, structural damage, and even total collapse. The excavations were intended to substantiate the Bible's reference to a powerful 10th century B.C. Kingdom of David which had allegedly stretched from Egypt to the Euphrates. To date, however, little — let alone conclusive — evidence of its existence has actually been found.

Elad had used archaeology which was often bogus as a smokescreen for its political agenda of pushing out Silwan's Palestinians and had allocated a huge amount of money for excavations in the area with an IAA subcontract for the "managed" uncovering of what it claims was the 3,000-year-old palace of King David, thereby making Silwan the capital of an ancient Israelite kingdom. By convincing people that this was once the home of King David, Elad could then justify and complete the removal of the Palestinians and the takeover of Silwan.

Criticism of, and opposition to Elad was at its height in the mid-1990s, but as Elad's control of Silwan has tightened, and the "City of David's" popularity has grown — last year 350,000 tourists were shown

55

around the site by biased Elad guides — the voices of dissent had fallen silent. Furthermore by funding the financially-constrained IAA on which Israeli archaeologists are dependent for work — and consequently unable to protest against Elad's questionable involvement — Elad had managed to surreptitiously set the agenda for the supposedly independent IAA. As a consequence of this somewhat illicit relationship, the archaeologists have become selectively blinkered in their findings so that when dozens of skeletons from the early Islamic period were unearthed in Silwan close to the Al-Aqsa Mosque in June 2008, they were discarded without any consideration or proper examination. While no archaeologist would speak on the record regarding such irresponsible conduct and shameful discrimination, the IAA later reluctantly admitted to what was "a serious mishap."

Some opponents of Elad have argued that even if a sign was discovered with a Hebrew inscription saying "Welcome to King David's Palace," that would still not justify Elad's political agenda. The Palestinian residents of Silwan and their ancestors have lived in the town for hundreds of years and their rights must by any standards be respected and enforced. If for instance a Christian site was discovered in Israel, would that entitle the Vatican to claim the land and evict the Israelis from their homes?

Elad, also known as the Ir David Foundation (City of David), is equally supportive of other archaeological excavations, related educational initiatives, and the establishment of a Jewish community in Jerusalem. Elad is a tax exempt entity in the U.S., a registered non-profit institution in Israel, and a magnet for criticism from a number of Israeli civil rights organizations including Rabbis for Human Rights, Peace Now, Ir Amim, and the Association for Civil Rights in Israel.

Apart from compromising the independence of the IAA with its funding, most of Elad's own funding comes controversially from anonymous private donors who, according to Israeli newspaper reports, include some Russian-Jewish oligarchs such as England's Chelsea Football Club owner, billionaire Roman Abramovich. Abramovich — alleged by countless sources to have been involved in antitrust law violations, blackmail, bribery, loan-fraud, share-dilution, and theft — was a guest of honor at a major Elad event and was said to have been one of its top donors. So while enjoying the benefits and rights of British democracy, this gentleman of "repute" appears to have no qualms about supporting an Apartheid state and racist organization that together deny those same benefits and rights to the Palestinian people.

It may also seem for some a touch hypocritical of Abramovich to own a football club in the English Premier League whose Football Association along with the Union of European Football Associations (EUFA) and Fédération Internationale de Football Association (FIFA) strongly condemn racism. And while on the subject of hypocrisy, why is an Apartheid state like Israel allowed to play in European and World Cup competitions (FIFA should expel Israel) while South Africa under Afrikaner Apartheid rule was banned from participation in all international sporting events? Western hypocrisy remains unsurpassed and is indeed supreme. Worse still, millions of intelligent and successful Jewish people all over the world, who by virtue of their conscientious devotion to family and Judaism must by any benchmark be judged as decent human beings, should consider the possibility of their own hypocrisy and ask themselves whether by either silently tolerating or actively supporting Israeli crimes against the Palestinian people, they too are complicit in crimes which even by the wildest stretch of the Hebraic biblical imagination is neither justifiable nor excusable especially by those who maintain they are "God's Chosen People."

There is also staunch support for Apartheid Israel from Howard Schultz, the chairman and CEO of coffee giant Starbucks who in 1998 was given the Israel 50th Anniversary Tribute Award from the Jerusalem Fund of Aish Ha-Torah for "playing a key role in promoting a close alliance between the U.S. and Israel." In February 2009 while Speaking to the Consumer News and Business Channel (CNBC), Schultz stated his concern over the global economic crisis, adding that the place that concerned him most was western Europe, and specifically the UK, which he considered to be in a "spiral" by expressing concern over the levels of unemployment and consumer confidence in the country. Apparently Shultz had not considered the possibility that if Starbucks — having reported a taxable profit only once in fifteen years despite generating over £3 billion in UK sales since 1998 — had refrained from calculated corporation tax avoidance, then the UK's HM Treasury would have been better off.

Starbucks tax avoidance is achieved by means of transfer pricing which refers to the prices a company charges itself when goods or services are transferred within the company but from one country to another. By varying the transfer prices, a company can choose where to make its profits. Therefore if Starbucks' U.S. operation charges high

57

prices to its UK operation for various services, such as royalties for the use of branding and management services; or lends money to its UK operation at much higher interest rates, then Starbucks' profits will rise in the USA and fall in the UK.

Another Apartheid Israel supporter is British billionaire Philip Green who spends a considerable time in Israel and is generous with his donations to several Israeli causes. Green — whose Arcadia retail group includes British Home Stores, Burton Menswear, Dorothy Perkins, Evans, Miss Selfridge, Outfit, Topman, Topshop, and Wallis which total some 2,500 stores — lives in a London hotel during the week running his retail empire and then flies to Monaco to join his wife for the weekend. Green, however, does not actually own the Arcadia Group which is instead owned by his wife who does no work for the company and as a resident of Monaco, she comfortably avoids paying a single penny in income tax to the British Treasury. Meanwhile back in Britain thousands of the Arcadia Group employees are taxed at the average rate of twenty percent on their measly wages.

In 2005, with his usual chutzpah, Philip Green paid himself £1.2 billion — the biggest paycheck in British corporate history — which after being channeled through a network of offshore tax haven accounts, ended up in Mrs. Green's Monaco bank account. This tax avoidance of epic proportions saved Green, at the cost to British taxpayers, close to £300m which alone could have paid for the £9,000 university fees for 32,000 students or met the salaries of 20,000 National Health Service nurses. Green's tax dodging was subsequently rewarded in 2006 with a knighthood. So the offensively flash, foul-mouthed, tax avoiding Philip Green became the offensively flash, foul-mouthed, tax avoiding Sir Philip Green. To add insult to injury, in August 2010, Green was appointed by Prime Minister David Cameron to lead a review of government spending.

Support for an Apartheid Israel by people such as the aforementioned is not compatible with the ethical teachings of Judaism. Judaism is the original Abrahamic faith which propounds ethical monotheism with the existence of a single, all-powerful, indivisible god. Ethical monotheism means that there is but one God from whom emanates one morality for all humanity, and that God's primary demand of people is that they act decently towards each other. The God of ethical monotheism is the God first revealed to the world in the Hebrew Bible from which God's four primary characteristics can be established: God is supernatural, is personal, is good, and is holy. So the question is — and it is a question that religious Jews should honestly answer — does this God of ethical monotheism approve of what Israel is doing to the Palestinian people?

Equally controversial was Elad's funding from donors in the United States where a *New York Times* investigation identified at least 40 groups responsible for giving more than $200 million in tax-deductible gifts for illegal Jewish settlement in the West Bank and Jerusalem over a period of ten years. While most of the money was used for expenditures such as schools and synagogues, some was also illegally spent for housing, vehicles, rifle scopes, bulletproof vests, and guard dogs to help establish and maintain settlements deep within the illegally Occupied Territories. For Zeldin this was yet another example of contradictory and ineffective U.S. foreign policy which asserts that the building of illegal settlements was an obstacle to peace while simultaneously allowing tax credits to fund the establishment of such settlements in contravention of international law.

Zeldin was also far more outspoken than others in his opposition to the view that any archaeological discovery that might be of ancient Jewish origin automatically entitled Israel to claim that particular piece of land from which its Palestinian inhabitants were then driven off. Like many other Israeli and diaspora Jews who condemn the iniquity of Israeli treatment of the Palestinian people, Zeldin had also become the frequent subject of Fascist style harassment, threats, and vilification from fanatical Zionist and ultra-orthodox groups.

Zeldin was prepared to accept that Israeli Jews had a right to have a homeland; he was even prepared to tolerate their right to believe the Biblical fable that the Jews were "God's Chosen" people; but he was resolute in his refusal to acquiesce to their assertion that a mythical covenant with God entitled them to forcibly displace and deprive the Palestinian people of that same right to a homeland that Israeli Jews have so violently demanded for themselves. Zeldin was a Jew who passionately loved his country: and it was because of that passion and love that he opposed what his country was doing.

Zeldin's disaffection with Israel had grown gradually over the years as he watched its initial aim of having a society of democratic socialism, deteriorate into one with an expansionist philosophy conducted with a fundamentalist mentality and an exploitative contempt for all its allies including the United States. Driven by the religious parties, the settler movement and the opportunistic paranoia of its leaders, Israel had become not only a nation that was aggressively hostile to all its neighbors, but also one towards which all international goodwill was fast eroding. Israel's abysmal treatment of the Palestinian people was the result of its insatiable lust for Palestinian land — a lust justified by the belief that this was the land that God promised to the Israelites.

> *On that day the Lord made a covenant with Abram and said,*
> *'To your descendants I give this land, from the Wadi of Egypt*
> *to the great river, The Euphrates — the land of the Kenites,*
> *Kenizzites, Kadmonites, Hittites, Perizzites, Rephaites,*
> *Amorites, Canaanites, Girgashites and Jebusites.*
> **Genesis 15: 18 – 21.**

Though respectful of Judaism as a religion and recognising the right of its adherents to live in accordance with their traditions and to do so in peace and security, Zeldin, however, obstinately refused to concur with the biblical assertion of a "Promised Land" for Jews; especially if that land was illegally obtained through the brutally forced displacement of the Palestinian people. Zeldin was a sufficiently intelligent and educated man to have recognized and abhorred the destructive forces of religion which had always been the cardinal cause of human suffering right from the very beginning.

> *They said this mystery shall never cease: the priest promotes*
> *war, and the soldier peace.*
> **William Blake (1757-1827) English poet, painter, and printmaker.**

IN THE BEGINNING

Man cannot make a worm, yet he will make gods by the dozen.
Michel de Montaigne (1533-1592), influential French Renaissance writer.

Most people have been brought up to believe that in the beginning God created the universe and humankind so it follows that in reality there can only be one Creator. But as was noted by Michel de Montaigne, and as everyone is aware, there are numerous religions who with mendacious doctrines and at times murderous intent are vying to establish the omnipotence of their own man-made gods.

Young Earth creationism (YEC) is the religious belief that asserts that the universe, the earth, and life on earth were the direct acts of the Abrahamic God during a relatively short period of between 5,700 and 10,000 years ago. Abrahamic religions are the monotheistic faith of Judaism, Christianity, Islam, and Bahá'i — with the latter being founded in nineteenth-century Persia by Bahá'ulláh — that either emphasize and trace their common origin to Abraham, or recognize the spiritual tradition identified with him.

Scientific consensus, however, with backing from a 2006 statement by sixty-eight national and international academies, asserts that evidence-based fact derived from observations and experiments in multiple scientific disciplines show that the universe existed almost 14 billion years ago in an extremely hot and dense state. It was about that time, according to the Big Bang theory, that the universe then began to cool and expand towards its present dispersed state with the earth being formed 4.5 billion years ago and life first appearing no less than 2.5 billion years ago. That self-induced expansion is still ongoing to this day without any influence or input from some god or supreme-being.

Recently an international team of astronomers — using the Hubble Space Telescope that was carried into orbit by a space shuttle in 1990 — detected the most distant galaxy yet which at about thirty billion light-years away is helping to shed light on the period that immediately followed the Big Bang. The galaxy's distance was confirmed by the ground-based Keck Observatory in Hawaii. As it takes light so long to travel from the outer edge of the Universe to the planet Earth, the galaxy appears as it was 13.1 billion years ago — some 700 million years after the Big Bang.

According to the study published in the *Nature Journal*, astronomers were able to measure its distance from Earth by analyzing its color. With the Universe expanding and everything moving away from the Earth, light waves are stretched, making objects appear redder than they actually are. Such apparent color changes are rated by astronomers on a scale that is called redshift. So with a redshift of 7.51, this galaxy — named z8_GND_5296 — is the most distant galaxy ever found. Though the system has a mass of only about one to two percent of the Milky Way and is rich in heavier elements, it has the surprising feature of turning gas and dust into new stars at a remarkable rate of hundreds of times faster than our own galaxy can.

In 1974 anthropologist Professor Donald Johanson and his student made an important fossil discovery in a maze of ravines at Hadar in Northern Ethiopia. While searching the scorched terrain for animal bones in the sand, ash, and silt they spotted a tiny fragment of arm bone. Johanson immediately recognised it as belonging to a hominid. Further up the slope they discovered more bone fragments of ribs, vertebrae, thighbones, and a partial jawbone. Eventually forty-seven bones were unearthed — about forty-percent of a hominid (humanlike creature) which had existed some 3.2 million years ago. Its small size and pelvic shape suggested it was female and they named it "Lucy" after "Lucy in the Sky with Diamonds," the Beatles song which happened to be playing during their post-discovery celebration.

Though many of Lucy's characteristics were similar to those of a chimpanzee, the structure of her knee and pelvis showed that she routinely walked upright on two legs like humans. Known as "bi-pedalism," this form of locomotion is the single most important difference between humans and apes. As walking on two legs was one of the earliest defining characteristics of humans, Lucy was placed firmly within the human family. Johanson named Lucy's species Australopithecus afarensis, which means "southern ape of afar," after the Ethiopian region where Hadar is located. This species — existing 3.5 million years ago — foraged for fruit, nuts, and seeds in a mixture of savannah and woodland, and may also have obtained animal protein from termites and birds' eggs.

In 2001 palaeontologists in Northeastern Brazil discovered fossils of what was believed to be an ancestor of Tyrannosaurus rex (T. rex), two words which mean tyrant lizard and king. The fossils — including two skulls and various bones — were from the high Triassic period from 235 to 240 million years ago and consequently predate and contradict the timescales for religious versions of the creation.

In September 2011 it was announced that a two million year-old fossil discovered in a South African cave may be the missing link between humans and our ape ancestors. The fossil, called Australopithecus sediba, has a human-like brain and hands, but its legs were more ape-like, suggesting that it walked upright but more like a chimpanzee than a modern human. Until now scientists have traced human ancestry to fossils discovered in East Africa of the species Homo habilis or Homo rudolfensis, but the newly discovered specimen is several hundred thousand years older. Professor Lee Berger, from the University of the Witwatersrand in Johannesburg, said that "the many very advanced features found in the brain and body, and the earlier date, make it possibly the best candidate for ancestor of our genus, the genus Homo."

More recently the science journal *Nature* revealed that scientists believe that a new fossil discovery from China is the world's oldest known example of the bone structure that is recognizable as a face. The remarkably well-preserved fish (an example of the species Entelognathus primordialis) was discovered in Southeast China in a layer of sediment dating back to the Silurian period — marks the time when the first plants and animals colonized dry land — making the specimen roughly 419 million years old. The find is exceptional because it is the earliest known example of the basic facial bone structure that is currently recognized: the ancient predator has a jaw, a mouth, two eyes and a nose. All previous discoveries from this geological time period have been of jawless fish — of the type that is still in existence today as lamprey and hagfish.

What may be even more remarkable than seeing the world's oldest known face is the notion that this fossil might even be a direct ancestor of human life. The fossil is unique in that it displays characteristics of two types of ancient fish: placoderms (heavily armored fish that were thought to have gone extinct millions of years ago) and bony fish (a taxonomic group that gave rise to all modern vertebrate fish — and subsequently amphibians, birds, mammals and finally humans).

Another recent report by the journal *Nature* said that water drilled from rock under Timmins, Ontario is among the oldest yet found on Earth by scientists. Despite being far from any light source, particular types of micro-organism could survive in the water which has the right chemistry and is rich in dissolved gases like hydrogen and methane. Professor Chris Ballentine from Manchester University explained that "there are similar waters in South Africa with almost identical chemistry that are tens of millions of years old, and they contain microbes that have adapted to that environment . . . These are microbes that can survive on the energy from the natural water-rock interactions . . . A positive identification had fascinating implications for our understanding of how life evolved on the early Earth and where it could exist underground today on other planets, such as Mars." Researchers recovered the water from mineworkers who had drilled new exploratory holes into deeply buried sulphide ores containing zinc and copper.

If despite such evidence and the advantage of current scientific knowledge there are people who still find it difficult to either comprehend or accept such a phenomenon, then it must have been even more so for the earliest of our ancestors whose evolution as human beings — Homo sapiens — probably began in East Africa where archaeological evidence of our ancestral Y chromosome and mtDNA (mitochondrial DNA) has been discovered.

It must be disconcerting for white supremacists and other like-minded people to learn that geneticists have identified groups of chromosomes called haplogroups — "genetic fingerprints" which define populations — that trace their ancestral origins to the "subhuman" races of Africa. The ethnocentric concepts of a God's "chosen people," a "master race," or Nazi breeding program ("Lebensborn") to produce perfect "purity" is therefore unadulterated racist rubbish.

As the accrued mutations of mtDNA occur at a known rate, they can be used to calculate the timing of human existence. By combining all the available evidence of this mtDNA and Y chromosome with archaeology, climatology and fossil analysis, scientists have managed to tabulate the directions and timing of human migration. Though further archaeological discoveries could change estimates regarding the peopling of the world, it is currently believed that it began sometime between 160,000 and 135,000 BCE when groups of hunter-gatherers from East Africa migrated northeast to the Horn of Africa, southwest to the Congo Basin, west to the Ivory Coast, and south to the Cape of Good Hope.

Around 125,000 BCE migration continued along the Nile through a green Sahara and the Levant. Those that reached the Levant died out by 90,000 BCE when a global freeze turned the area — including

North Africa — into desert. The area was subsequently repopulated by Neanderthal man and about 5,000 years later groups crossed the mouth of the Red Sea and along the coast of the Arabian Peninsula towards India. All non-African peoples are the descendants of these migrants.

From 85,000 to 75,000 BCE migration pushed further along the Indian Ocean coastline to South China by way of Indonesia and Borneo which were then still part of the Asian landmass from which they were later to detach. Then in about 73,000 BCE one of the earth's largest known eruptions occurred on Sumatra's Mount Toba and covered India and Pakistan with a five-meter deep blanket of volcanic ash that caused a six-year nuclear winter, a thousand-year ice age and a considerable drop in population.

Following this cataclysmic event repopulation occurred after about nine thousand years followed by migrations from Borneo to New Guinea, and Timor to Australia. Aboriginal DNA from a lock of hair has been dated to 70,000 BCE. A more recent study of DNA from Aboriginal Australians has shown that a further migration from India occurred about four thousand years ago at around which time dingoes also made their first appearance.

An ensuing warming in climate leading up to 50,000 BCE then allowed northward migrations back to the Levant, past the Bosphorus and into Europe. By the time of 45,000 BCE the Mini Ice Age had occurred and the early stages of the Paleolithic culture moved from Turkey into Europe. Research suggests that the Modern humans who entered Europe at that time, outnumbered by as much as 10 to 1 the Neanderthals who had lived there for at least 200,000 years. Human migration along the River Danube also introduced newly developed stone tools and overwhelming human settlement eventually drove the Neanderthals to extinction.

During this period migrations continued from Indochina across Tibet; from Pakistan into Central Asia; and westwards from the East Asian coast traversing the central steppes towards the northeast. Between then and 25,000 BCE Central Asians then migrated westwards into Eastern Europe, northwards to the Arctic Circle, and accompanied East Asians to north-east Eurasia. This was also a time that witnessed the birth of impressive works of art such as those discovered in the Chauvet-Pont-d'Arc cave in southern France which contains the earliest known cave paintings.

Leading up to 22,000 BCE, due to low sea levels, the Bering Strait was in effect a land bridge across which ancestors of Native Americans travelled between Siberia and Alaska. But during the last Ice Age leading up to 19,000 BCE, populations in Northern Europe, Asia, and North America drastically reduced with only a small number of groups surviving in isolated areas.

The findings of the biggest survey of Native American DNA published in the journal *Nature* by an international team of researchers concluded that though the New World was settled in three major waves, the majority of today's indigenous Americans descended from a single group of migrants that crossed from Asia to Alaska 15,000 or more years ago. Previous genetic data have suggested that America was colonized by a single migrant wave, but it is now apparent that there are at least three deep lineages in Native American populations. This latest research has settled the debate as to whether or not Native Americans stemmed from a single migration by casting light on patterns of human dispersal within the Americas.

Following the Last Glacial Maximum around 18,000 BCE, development in genes, diversity, culture and language continued with migration into South America. This period also saw the start of Australian rock art such as the elegant and impressive Bradshaw Paintings (or Guion Guion) in the North West region. The continued improvement in global climatic conditions opened American coastal routes and enabled human habitation as confirmed by the Monte Verde Excavation in southern Chile where finds have been radio-carbon dated from 11,800 to 13,600 years BCE.

The repopulation of North America began 12,500 BCE and a thousand years later groups migrated from the Beringian refuge to become the Aleut, Eskimo, and Na Dene speaking peoples. The ensuing and final demise of the ice age between 10,000 and 8,000 years BCE witnessed the emergence of agriculture with a Sahara grassland and a recolonised British Isles and Scandinavia.

Contrary to the existence of such evidence, a 2007 *Newsweek* poll discovered that 78 percent of people in the U.S — a superpower whose astronauts have walked on the moon — doubt the traditional scientific view of "secular evolution" which is the long-term interaction between the galaxy and its environment such as gas accretion (the growth of objects that gravitationally attract gaseous matter in an accretion disk) and galaxy harassment (frequent high speed galaxy encounters that produce starbursts).

A 2012 Gallup poll discovered that forty-six percent of Americans believed in the creationist view that God created humans in their present form 10,000 years ago. Furthermore, Americans with postgraduate education were most likely of all educational groups to say that humans evolved without God's guidance; and least likely to say that God created humans in their present form 10,000 years ago. So it is the less educated who are more likely to have the creationist viewpoint. But then one does not have to be a genius to realize that ignorance, fear and poverty provide the fertile ground wherein religion will thrive the best.

Human history becomes more and more a race between education and catastrophe.
H.G. Wells, *The Outline of History*, George Newnes, 1922.

It must be bewildering for any reasonable person with average intelligence to comprehend how despite the vast advances that have been achieved with the help of science and technology in virtually every field of human endeavor, there is still a suicidal tendency for people to blindly embrace the tenets of crude religious myths even to the extent of inflicting unspeakable atrocities not only on the lives of others, but also on the lives of their own families. For some inexplicable reason mankind has from the beginning of time failed to establish a universal ethic based on unfettered perceptions of reality rather than the disastrous consequences of adherence to diverse forms of religious mumbo-jumbo.

Any system of education, be it religious, secular or otherwise, which with authority presents age-old myths as being facts, is only serving to befuddle and shackle the susceptible minds of present-day youngsters with the same spurious nonsense that warped the minds of their forefathers.

The truth of our faith becomes a matter of ridicule among the infidels if any Catholic, not gifted with the necessary scientific learning, presents as dogma what scientific scrutiny shows to be false.
Thomas Aquinas (1225-1274), the Dominican priest, philosopher, and theologian.

Belief without evidence in what is told by one who speaks without knowledge, of things without parallel.
The definition of *faith* by Ambrose Bierce (1842-1913), in his satirical lexicon *The Devil's Dictionary.*

Most of the greatest evils that man has inflicted upon man have come through people feeling quite certain about something which, in fact, was false.
Bertrand Russell (1872-1970) British philosopher, logician, mathematician, historian and social critic.

THE ANCIENT EGYPTIAN
PRIESTHOODS

Following the global freeze that transformed the Levant and northern Africa into a lifeless desert, gradual repopulation was begun about ten thousand years ago along the Nile Valley by tribes of possible Semitic origin from the adjoining regions of Africa and Western Asia. The valley's long and narrow geological features coupled with the danger of attack from other tribes, forced most of the new settlers to live in small, isolated communities close to the river which provided not only the means to sustain life, but also formed a natural defensive barrier on one side against marauding tribes.

The primitive existence and profound ignorance of people at that time meant that superstition was rampant with an abundance of amulets, charms, talismans, and ceremonies for everything from healing the sick to raising the dead; knowledge of the past and foretelling of the future; and even curses that supposedly caused harm to enemies. They even believed in vivification by means of magical words and formulas. Consequently there was a prevalence of reverential fear and respect for the unexplained mysteries of nature such as the heavenly elements and the surrounding wildlife. Religious worship was therefore awe-inspired and directed towards the wonders of nature including animals, birds, and reptiles whose deification was strictly the work of human imagination.

In the time leading up to the Predynastic Period (5,500 BCE) such man-made idols were only village or district gods whose stature and influence was limited to the size and importance of the communities over which they presided. Furthermore the line between secular and religious authority in such communities was so indistinguishable, that it was the self-proclaimed priests with their alleged possession of wisdom and access to the gods, who with good measures of coercion and corruption were best positioned to fully exploit the prevailing ignorance and superstition so as to rule unchallenged. The priests also developed both esoteric and exoteric religious doctrines, with the latter being the idolatrous faith fed to the uneducated and unworthy masses. The esoteric doctrine proclaiming the unity of God was reserved for the select few who like the priests themselves had been initiated into the mysteries.

With the passing of time and changing social conditions, however, it became necessary for the priests to defend their own privileged positions within the communities which they then achieved by allowing a select minority of the population to carry arms so as to maintain the existing repression and exploitation of the majority of the people. While such a ploy was initially successful, it soon backfired when ambition within the ranks of the military led to an uprising wherein force of arms ended the monopoly of religious authority and ultimately brought about the institution of a monarchy.

But even within that new scenario religious influence remained unassailable and the priests, who in effect ruled alongside the monarchs, were allowed to retain their colleges, palaces, and temples as well as agricultural and commercial interests. Furthermore, having already established themselves as the bureaucrats of their societies, they continued to regulate every aspect of daily life by acting as advisors, magistrates, physicians, and teachers. They became a select and privileged minority who by paying no taxes and accepting donations, accumulated wealth, influence, and power that was exceeded only by the monarchs. They were thus in the ideal position through unrelenting vigilance and cunning to ensure compatibility between religious doctrines and ever-changing political and social conditions.

One of the initial stages in that ongoing evolution of socially compatible theology was the humanisation of the deities so that some of them were provided with human bodies to go with their animal, bird, and serpent heads. The aspects of nature, animal, and man as related to such worship, however, began to gradually fuse so that with the passing of time animal gods with human characteristics began to appear. Thoth, god of wisdom and truth, was given a human body but retained the head of an ibis; Anubis, who assisted Osiris as judge of the dead, was given a human body with the head of a Jackal; and Hathor, the goddess of childbirth and love, was given a human head and body but retained an element of her animal manifestation — a pair of cow's horns. Then as the masses became more sophisticated and required gods with which they could identify, the gods were accordingly transformed and obligingly portrayed as having complete human forms. So it was that man created gods and endowed them with infinite powers that could then be used to explain the inexplicable mysteries which included that of the Creation.

Apart from their physical transformations, the gods were also subject to the reality that religion was very much a part of politics so that whenever a political fusion occurred between two or more communities, a fusion of their gods was also necessary. That fusion was achieved by grouping them into families such as that of the Osirian triad consisting of Osiris, Isis and Horus who had initially presided separately over three different tribes. Such groupings inevitably led to varying degrees of syncretisation whereby the main gods acquired multiple names and each other's characteristics.

The situation was also further complicated by the introduction of West Asian cosmic theology which maintained that in the beginning there existed only the darkness of boundless primeval water that had remained unproductive for a considerable period of time before its spirit felt the urge to create the seed from which sprang Re, the sun god, within whose shining form was embodied the almighty power of the divine spirit.

Before spreading the cosmic faith to other parts of the valley from their main cult centre in sun-city which the Greeks later referred to as Heliopolis, the priests had to first somehow include within the system of cosmic theology, the widespread worship of existing popular gods such as Osiris, Isis, Horus, and others without actually subordinating the importance of their own positions. This was achieved by rewriting the religious texts so as to form the Heliopolitan Ennead whereby Re had apparently created the gods Shu and Tefnut; who in turn begat Seb and Nut; who in turn produced Osiris, Isis, Seth, and Nephthys. Consequently as the gods and religious doctrines were customised to accommodate the political requirements of the ruling elite, the history of ancient Egyptian gods has no continuity and is full of interpolations that reflect the influence of changing political and social conditions over a period of many millenniums.

One such influence was that of the monarchy whose successive members became increasingly unhappy with only being kings who like everyone else, were also simply subject to birth, life, and death. It was therefore with the connivance of the priesthoods that a deification process — with its ramifications of immortality — was set into motion with subtle associations between the Pharaohs and the gods being gradually introduced. For instance the second Pharaoh of the Second Dynasty (c. 2890-2686 BCE) incorporated Re's name with his own so as to become known as Re'neb. The Pharaohs of the Fifth Dynasty (c. 2494-2345 BCE) went even further by claiming to have been directly descended from Re as a result of a miraculous conception by a high priest's wife who was no doubt penetrated by a strong shaft of sunlight.

The "miraculous conception" story — a convenient way of explaining how an ordinary human being could also be a god — has since been used by the priesthoods of other religions including Christianity. As always such blatant fabrications were lent authenticity by their inclusion in texts such as that of the depiction of Pharaonic afterlife in the Pyramid Texts discovered in the burial chamber of the Fifth Dynasty's last Pharaoh, Unas. The hieroglyphics have Unas ascending a stairway of sunlight so as to join in immortality with his father, Re, from whose unquestioned supremacy flowed the Pharaonic Right to govern the land of Egypt.

Immortality was initially a privilege which only the Pharaohs could enjoy after death, embalmment, and reunification with their ancestors. A Pharaoh, however, could in his capacity as a god extend the privilege to high priests and favoured officials by allowing them to build their tombs within the confines of the royal necropolis, and to use secret formulae to facilitate their journey to the afterlife.

In their never-ending quest to retain their privileged positions, the ruling elite soon realised that the concept of immortality was a potentially powerful weapon with which to control an ever-growing and increasingly disaffected population. So as the advantages of retaining the privilege of afterlife for themselves began to be outweighed the benefits of making the afterlife an entitlement for everyone, the necessary theological adjustments were begun so that by the onset of the Middle Kingdom (c. 1550-1650 BCE) the concept of the soul's immortality became universal.

By the time of the New Kingdom (c. 1550-1069 BCE) the Priesthood had produced *The Book of the Dead* which was designed to help people to prepare themselves for death and the consequences of the Final Judgment. Apart from preparations before death, it was also necessary — so as to ensure continued existence in the afterlife — that the body after death be kept intact as an "everlasting" depository that would provide a permanent place of refuge for the soul which would cease to exist in the event of the body being somehow destroyed. Consequently a period of seventy days was required for preparation and embalmment of the corpse during which time the soul wandered the underworld in search of Osiris, who, with the assistance of forty-two other deities known as the judges of the dead, would determine the soul's fate in the afterlife.

On finally entering the hall of judgment, the soul was required to render a full account of past actions, and in the event of an unfavourable judgment, was sentenced to a life of thirst and hunger in the darkness of Amenti, an area of the underworld that was reserved for the damned. So the concept of accountability and possible damnation in the afterlife for one's actions on earth was thus established, and its potential as a means of controlling the actions of the common people has since been fully exploited by all major religions. The Greek historian, Polibius (c. 200-118 BCE), author of books on the history of the Roman Republic and renowned for his ideas on the separation of powers in government which were later to be used in drafting the United States Constitution, had this to say about the subject:

The most important difference for the better, which the Roman Commonwealth appears to me to display, in their religious beliefs, for I conceive that what in other nations is looked upon as a reproach, I mean a scrupulous fear for the gods, is the very thing that keeps the Roman Commonwealth together. To such an extraordinary height is this carried among them in private and public business, that nothing could exceed it. Many people think this unaccountable, but in my opinion their object is to use it as a check upon the common people. Where it possible to form a state wholly of philosophers, such a custom would be unnecessary. But seeing that every multitude is fickle and full of lawless desires, unreasoning anger and violent passion, the only resource is to keep them in check by the mysterious terrors and scenic effects of this sort. Wherefore to my mind the ancients were not acting without purpose or at random when they brought in among the vulgar these opinions about the gods and the punishments of Hades.

While members of the ruling elite were prepared to share the concept of afterlife with the common people, they were not at all prepared to allow universal access to the celebration of the mysteries of which there were two levels of initiation with the three Lay, or Lower Degrees, having a selective membership. The seven Crata Repoa, or Higher Degrees, were restricted to Pharaohs, high priests, and some top officials. Each degree had passwords and signs of recognition and initiation ceremonies were usually conducted in the subterranean chambers of pyramids which by virtue of their shape were symbolic of the ascending flame that was a sacred tribute to the sun.

For initiation into the first of the Lower Degrees the Candidate's instruction by a hierophant was followed by a lengthy period of fasting and rigorous silence which on successfully completing, the Candidate was ready to be fully initiated into the mysteries of Isis. He was first required to swear never to reveal what he was about to learn, and to then symbolically drink the water of Lethe — a river in Hades that according to mythology caused amnesia in those who drank from its waters — so as to forget all that he had known in his unregenerate state. This was followed by another symbolic drink from the water of Mnemosyne, the goddess of memory, so that he would remember the mysteries that had been revealed to him. He was finally introduced into the temple's inner sanctum to be familiarized with the secret signs and symbols before being formally pronounced an initiate of the mysteries of Isis.

The character of Isis, like that of other important ancient Egyptian deities, had evolved over many millenniums. Her portrayal as a faithful wife and loving mother who had conceived miraculously does not, however, appear to have become very pronounced until the Nineteenth Dynasty (c. 1295-1186 BCE) as is evident from numerous figurines of that period that have her seated on a throne clasping Horus to her left breast. There is no doubt, however, that the position she occupied as the "Mother of God" was unique to her as no other goddess was shown suckling a child. All the attributes, qualities and powers of all the other goddesses were without exception combined in the person of Isis, and ancient Egyptian Scriptures state that "in the beginning there was Isis, Oldest of the Old, she was the Goddess from whom all becoming arose." Though variously known by many names, Isis was ultimately addressed as follows:

> *Mistress of the gods, thou bearer of wings, thou lady of the red apparel, queen of the crowns of the South and North, only One . . . Superior to who the gods cannot be, thou mighty one of enchantments . . . Thou who art preeminent, mistress and lady of the tomb, Mother in the horizon of heaven . . . Praise be unto thee, O Lady, who art mightier than the gods, words of adoration rise unto thee from the Eight Gods of Hermopolis. The living souls who are in their hidden places praise the mystery of thee, O thou who art*

their mother, though source from which they sprang, who makest for them a place in the hidden Underworld, who makest sound their bones and preservest them from terror, who makest them strong in the abode of everlastingness.

Isis was the Egyptian throne with Pharaohs sitting on her lap for protection from her arms and wings. Her crown bore the symbol of Mu'at, or "foundation of the throne" which also symbolized her alter ego Maat, the motherhood-principle called Right, Justice and Truth, or the All-seeing eye. One of the Psalms in the Bible (89:14) which states "righteousness and justice are the foundation of thy throne; steadfast love and truth go before you," was copied form an Egyptian hymn to Isis.

The worship of Isis was very widespread and apart from becoming one of the principle goddesses of Rome, her cult was also to be found in many Mediterranean islands including Chios, Crete, Lesbos, Rhodes and Samos. Representations of her on many antiquities found in place such as Argos, Epirus, Corinth, Megara and Thessaly also bear witness to her popularity in numerous Greek cities where even the elite members of society felt the need to become initiates.

Though the mysteries of Isis continued to be performed by priestesses in the numerous temples built in her honour right up to the fourth century, her cult was eventually suppressed as a result of Christianity's ruthless elimination of other religious movements. Isis as a goddess, however, was not really eliminated but absorbed, and the identification of the Virgin Mary with her was part of a calculated syncretism that led to the creation of the Madonna cult. The similarities between them are numerous and include Mary's wanderings in Egypt which follow a comparable sequence of events to those experienced by Isis as described in the Metternich Stela Texts (c. 380-342 BCE), a magico-medical style that is part of the Egyptian Collection of the Metropolitan Museum of Art in New York City. By bringing forth a human life which she then protected, fed and nourished, Isis became the personification of that great feminine capacity to conceive and to give birth to new life. Drawings and sculptures depicting Isis suckling her child became the model for the Christian Madonna and Child, and many of the qualities that were originally attributed to Isis were then given to the Mother of Christ. In order to supplant popular pagan deities the Christian Church Fathers had to ensure that their own man-made

Christian idols had characteristics similar to those of the popular pagan deities whom they were destined to replace. The following quotes are from the ***Egyptian Religion: Egyptian Ideas of the Future Life* (1900), Sir E.A. Wallis Budge (1857-1934):**

> *In Osiris the Christian Egyptians found the prototype of Christ, and in the pictures and statues of Isis suckling her son Horus, they perceived the prototype of the Virgin Mary and her child. Never did Christianity find elsewhere in the world a people whose minds were so thoroughly well prepared to receive its doctrines as the Egyptians.*

> *The Christian Trinity ousted the old triads of gods. Osiris and Horus were represented by our Lord Jesus Christ, Isis by the Virgin Mary, Set the god of evil by Diabolus [Satan] . . . and the various Companies of the gods by Archangels, and so on.*

Information regarding initiation into the Second Degree is somewhat scarce but it is known that in the Third Degree the Candidate was required to take part in a lengthy re- enactment of the murder of Osiris by playing the role of the victim. This was followed by the revelation of secret doctrines including the ineffable name AL-OM-JAK, the sacred name of the deity symbolising solar fire as the combined principle on which all existence was dependent. The word OM, or its trilateral form AUM, signified the Deity's capacity to create, to preserve, and to destroy; and was represented by an equilateral triangle. Great powers were attributed to this ineffable name which was to be contemplated in silence so as to avoid the dire consequences that would result from its vocalisation.

Osiris was a god whose coming was announced by Three Wise Men — the three stars of Mintaka, Anilam, and Alnitak in the belt of Orion which pointed towards his star, Sirius (the significator of his birth) which "rose in the east" at the time of the seasonal flooding of the Nile. The Osirian tradition is traceable to the Orient where in Tibet the rising of the same star in the east — named Rishi-Agastya, after an ancient holy king — marks the annual event of "setting free the waters of the springs." This same star was called Ephraim (or star of Jacob) by the ancient Hebrews. In Arabian, Persian, and Syrian astrology it was the Messaeil — the Messiah.

76

Osiris was without doubt the paradigm for Messiahs who was the god of gods who came to be regarded as the son of Re next to whom he sat as an equal in heaven. Egyptians regarded him as the only deity capable of bestowing upon them the gift of eternal life, and the events leading to his death were re-enacted in a passion play. His flesh was that of the Saviour and Truth, which when eaten in the form of communion wheatmeal cakes, made them just like him. The ancient Egyptians viewed the horrible consequences of death and its decaying aftermath with fear and trepidation and so believed that only Osiris could save them. **Wallis Budge** noted that the Egyptians believed according to the following:

> *The resurrection of the body in a changed and glorified form, which would live to all eternity in the company of the spirits and souls of the righteous in a kingdom ruled by a being who was of divine origin, but who had lived upon the earth, and had suffered a cruel death at the hands of his enemies, and had risen from the dead, and had become a God and king of the world which was beyond the grave . . . Although they believed in all these things and proclaimed their belief with almost passionate earnestness, they seemed never to have freed themselves from a hankering for amulets and talismans, and magical names, and words of power, and seem to have trusted in these to save their souls and bodies, both living and dead, with something of the same confidence which they placed in the death and resurrection of Osiris. A matter of surprise is that they seem to see nothing incongruous in such a mixture of magic and religion.*

This same mixture of magic and religion still exists worldwide to this day with even Christians displaying the same ancient Egyptian hankering for crucifixes, Saint Christopher medals, holy pendants, superstition-based incantations, holy name invocations, holy water blessings, saintly relics, and even the rosaries which Christianity copied from the ancient Egyptians.

The fact that early Christianity was more readily accepted in Egypt than in other place comes as no surprise when one considers that it was from the characteristics of Osiris that the Christ figure had evolved; and that from texts relating to the life of Osiris that many Biblical passages were plagiarised. It is for example evident that Psalm 23 was based on an Egyptian text that called on Osiris the Good Shepherd to lead the dead to the "green pastures" and "still waters" of the nefer-nefer land so as to restore the soul to the body and provide protection in the valley of the shadow of death (the Tuat). Even the Lord's Prayer was certainly influenced by a hymn to Osiris that began "O Amen, O Amen, who art in heaven," and which also ended with an "Amen."

The words by Jesus "Except a corn of wheat fall into the ground and die, it abideth alone; but if it die, it bringeth forth much fruit" (John 12:24) were from an Osirian tenet that a dying man is like a corn of wheat "which falls into the earth in order to draw from its bosom a new life." The Osirian text telling of the numerous Arits (Mansions) in the blessed land of Father Osiris is also apparently uttered by Jesus "In my Father's house are many mansions" (John 14:2). Just as Osirian worshippers were promised that they would rule the spirit-souls (angels) in heaven, so too were the Saint Paul's followers promised by him that they would rule even the angels (1 Corinthians 6:3). Even the healing by Jesus of a nobleman's daughter was long preceded by an Osirian priest who cured a princess. Numerous such examples exist as a testament to the popularity of a god who in spite of being a figment of creative human imagination, became the obligatory prototype for any other man-made god who wished to replace him.

The portrayal of an eminent man or deity who as a member of a trinity, first perishes as the victim of an evil deed, and then resurrects into a greater glory, is by now an all too familiar theme and figures not only in religious legends, but also as part of initiation ceremonies in secular secret societies. Of the various legends relating to Osisris, it is perhaps the one by the Greek historian, Plutarch (c. 46-120), *Peri Isodos Kai Osiridos,* which best echoes the consensus of available accounts.

It is alleged that Osiris was a wise and just king who after civilising his own people through instruction in religious worship, the rule of law, and land cultivation, then proceeded, by means of reason rather than force of arms, to do likewise for the rest of humanity. While Osiris was carrying out this noble mission overseas, Isis, who was both his wife and sister, watched over the affairs of state so carefully, that the political ambitions of their envious brother, Seth, were completely frustrated.

By the time of Osiris' return, however, Seth had already devised a plan which was put into effect at a banquet when some of Seth's co-conspirators brought in an exquisitely ornamented chest which unbeknown to Osiris, had been made to accommodate his precise measurements. The chest was then playfully offered as a gift to the person whom it would best fit, and after some of those present had gone along with the charade, Osiris unwittingly stretched himself out in the chest which was then immediately slammed and nailed shut, covered with molten lead, and thrown into the waters of the Nile wherein it floated out to sea before drifting ashore at Byblos — present-day Lebanon — to become lodged in a Tamarisk bush.

On learning of the chest's location, Isis simply parted the waters for her journey to Byblos — thereby providing the story line for Bindumati (Kali as the mother of *bindu* or Spark of Life) whose miraculous crossing of the River Ganges was also emulated by the mythical Moses — and eventually retrieved the chest which she then laid to rest in an isolated part of Egypt. The annual flooding of the Nile was said to have been caused by a teardrop from the eye of Isis as she lamented the deceased Osiris. The ensuing annual Nile Festival took place on the 'Night of the Teardrop' and was subsequently taken up by Muslims in the June festival of Lelat al-Nuktah (Night of the Drop). Sometime later Seth accidentally found the chest while out hunting and in a fit of rage had the corpse cut into fourteen pieces that were subsequently scattered throughout the land.

Isis once again set about finding her husband's remains and managed to locate every part except the phallus which had apparently been thrown into the Nile to be devoured by the fish. She therefore created and consecrated an imitation which by her decree was commemorated annually by the ceremonial procession of an Ark containing the seeds of various plants, a winnowing fan, and a representation of Osiris' pudendum. This gave rise to the worship of the phallus which was comparable in concept to that of the worship of the lingam in India.

After gathering Osiris's remains, Isis murmured powerful incantations that brought life to his body, and by raising up "the prostate form of him whose heart was still," she was able to take of his essence and thereby become full with child. In spite of his miraculous resurrection, however, Osiris was unable to resume his earthly life and instead went on to rule as Lord of the underworld and judge of the dead. Seth in the meantime took possession of the kingdom and imprisoned Isis who, with the assistance of the Seven Scorpion Goddesses managed to escape to the Papyrus Swamps in the Nile Delta. According to one version which sounds familiar, Isis applied to a rich woman for a night's lodging but was turned away and was eventually obliged to give birth to her son, Horus, on a cot made from papyrus plants after obtaining help from a poor family. She then raised Horus secretly and prepared him for the day when he would avenge his father's murder by defeating Seth in battle to become the new Pharaoh.

The myth of Horus' birth, however, was not confined to ancient Egyptian religion and is also to be found in the narratives of many other god-kings and eminent heroes. King Sargon of Akkad (the Akkadian Empire was a region in ancient Mesopotamia) was the virgin-born son of a temple maiden who set him afloat on the river in a basket of rushes. Sargon was rescued by the divine midwife, Akki the Water Drawer — now transformed into Aquarius — and then had to overcome the traditional obstacle of a sacred king: the menace of early destruction from an incumbent ruler, time spent in wilderness exile, evil spirit temptations, and finally ascension to the throne as spouse of the Goddess Ishtar.

This theme of a fatherless eminence born of "waters" (Maria) became universal and was repeated in many myths including that of Jason, Joshua son of Nun, Oedipus, Perseus, and Trakhan of Gilgit (a Central Asian dynasty). Such narratives were mostly based on the Goddess Cunti (Kali-the-cosmic-yoni) myth which had her give birth to the sun god and place him in a basket of rushes and set it afloat on the Ganges River. It was this selfsame sun god who was fathered by Apollo and reborn in Athens to the virgin Cruesa who left him in the obligatory woven basket. It is no surprise that the mythical Moses was also set afloat on the River Nile in a basket of bullrushes coated in pitch.

So the concept of the "virgin birth" became an essential element for the creation of divine beings because the ancient religious scribes obviously felt that no self-respecting divine being would deign to have sexual intercourse with a mere mortal, let alone one who was a woman. And so long before Mary's "Immaculate Conception" of Jesus, a whole lot of other presumably "untouched" women where used as receptacles for the fetal development of divine beings.

Whenever broaching the subject of the mysteries in his writings, the Greek historian Herodotus (c. 485-425 BCE), always does so with caution and explains his reluctance by recounting the misfortunes of another who had been so foolish as to utter secrets that had been learnt through initiation. In *The Golden Ass,* which is in effect a description of the mysteries under the guise of a fable, Apuleius, the Berber Latin prose writer, is not much more forthcoming. When the narrative's protagonist, Lucius, regains his human shape and is initiated into the mysteries of Isis, he divulges very little:

> *Perhaps, inquisitive reader, you will very anxiously ask me what was said and done? I would tell you if it could be lawfully told. I approached to the confines of death, and having trod on the threshold of Proserpine, at midnight I saw the sun shining with a splendid light.*

Lucius also discovers that he is to receive instruction in the mysteries of 'the great god, and supreme father of the gods, the invincible Osiris,' and goes on to say:

> *My head was decorously encircled with a crown, the shining leaves of the palm tree projecting from it like rays of light, I celebrated the most joyful day of my initiation by delightful, pleasant and facetious banquets.*

In a dream he sees one of the officiating priests who walked with a limp, the ankle bone of his left foot being a little bent, as a sign by which Lucius might know him. In another of his works, *Apologia,* Apuleius writes that:

> *If anyone happens to be present who has been initiated into the same rites as myself, if he will give me a sign, he shall then be at liberty to hear what it is that I keep with so much care.*

Knowledge of the Higher Degrees or Crata Repoa is also based on a compilation of initiation facts sourced from the allusions of many separate ancient writers. Entrance to the Crata Repoa was by invitation only — usually from the Pharaoh himself — and required the Candidate to be continually tried during many years of work and study before eventually being accepted as a Propheta in the Seventh Degree where he was addressed as "Saphenath Pancah," or the man who knows the secrets. His acceptance entitled him to take part in elections for high office and read all the sacred books in the Ammonite language after which Amman, the capitol of present-day Jordan was named. Apart from a square cap for his tonsured head and a full-length, white-stripped tunic called an Etangi, he was also given a cross whose shape and special significance was related to the waters of the Nile.

The cross was in fact a small replica of an upright pole with horizontal bars that was fixed into the riverbed of the Nile as a means of judging the level of inundation. As a result of life in ancient Egypt being dependent on the flooding of the Nile, this form of measure for inundation came to be viewed as the symbol of life, health and prosperity.

Consequently the Tau cross — Tau being Greek for the letter T — topped by a circle, was the 'Cross of Life' representing the union of the male and female sexual symbols. It was regarded by the ancient Egyptians as an essential life-charm on whose possession depended the life of every human and divine being. Ancient Egyptian depictions have goddesses, gods and Pharaohs clutching such crosses in their right hands long before anyone ever heard of, or saw the Christian version which did not appear in Christian art until the fifth century. Needless to say, the Christian version dropped the female symbol of the circle and retained only that of the male. Such bias against females within Christianity has lasted to this day.

Variations of this cross — also known as an ankh, or ansate cross — were later adopted as an emblem by other religious and secular organizations including the Knights Templar. The Triple Tau, for example, is now regarded by Royal Arch Masons as the emblem of emblems with "a depth that reaches to the creation of the world and all that is therein."

THE BRAHMINS

Sometime during the second millennium BCE a large group of light-skinned Aryans from Persia migrated in a southeasterly direction through Afghanistan and into India which was mostly inhabited by dark-skinned Dravidians. The migrating Aryans introduced a Dark Age to an otherwise thriving civilization where their priests — like those of Western Europe in a later Dark Age — devised a caste system to relegate the indigenous inhabitants to a lower status, and to preserve that social order by claiming divine ordinance.

The caste system doctrines promulgated the idea that all those born into the lower ranks were living out a necessary punishment for sins committed in a previous life which they may not recall. Their duty was to accept their fate without any objection while toiling and obeying their superiors so as to win promotion in the next life. It was in effect slavery with a carrot and stick Approach.

The migrating Aryans were nomadic agriculturalists consisting of three main castes of priests, warriors and husbandmen. They initially settled around the northern branches of the Indus River, but then fought their way southwards to create more settlements in the central and southern parts of the country. Assimilation soon followed and the Aryan language gradually became part of the extensive folklore which in being passed from generation to generation, helped to develop Sanskrit, the language used in the most ancient and sacred religious writings collectively known as the Vedas.

Early Vedic religion involved the deification and worship of natural elements with each element often being represented by more than one deity so that the sun was for instance variously venerated as Vishnu, "the mighty one"; Bhaga, "the bestower of boons"; Savitar, "the enlivener"; Pushan, "he who causeth to flourish"; and Surya, "the glowing one." The gods in their abundance, however, were not worshipped by the priests who like their ancient Egyptian counterparts did not subscribe to the idolatry of the duped masses whom they considered incapable of either comprehending or observing the pure religion of the spirit which in its spoken and written form was the jealously guarded possession of a small circle of initiated men. It is evident in the following passage from the Maha-nirvana that those chosen for initiation were taught to disregard such idolatrous inventions:

Numerous figures, corresponding with the nature of divers powers and quality, were invented for the benefit of those who are wanting in sufficient understanding . . . We have no notion of how the Eternal Being is to be described: He is above all that mind can apprehend, above nature . . . That only one that was never defined by language, and gave to language all its meaning, he is the Supreme Being and no partial thing that man worships . . . This Being extends over all things. He is mere spirit without corporal form; without extension of any size, unimpressionable, and without any organs; he is pure, perfect, omniscient, omnipresent, the ruler of the intellect and the soul of the whole world.

Despite assimilation, the caste system persisted and the priests evolved into the Brahmins from whose supposedly deep appreciation of the values that mattered most to humanity, emanated the power that governed every aspect of community life. The Kshatriyas, or warriors, provided the political and military leadership that maintained social order and enhanced the material welfare of the community. The necessary base for social cohesion was down to the artisans, farmers and merchants who as a group were known as the Vaisyas. It was from the Vaisyas that a fourth group of unskilled labourers, or Sudras, came into being to carry out the menial tasks which in turn produced a people of such low status, that they were called Harijans or "untouchables," and as such they were not allowed to associate or even worship with their fellow human beings because the nature of their "impure" work was anathema to the purity of the Brahmin religion.

Such discrimination appears even in the Bible where it is written that outcasts could not be touched, but were permitted to exist as "hewers of wood and drawers of water" (Joshua 9:21). While Yahweh's Jewish scribes insinuated that traditions of the caste system had been passed down from their ancestors, they were in truth borrowed from the already established Asian caste system.

Brahmanism, the orthodox religion of India, developed in three main stages starting with the Age of the Vedas and their Ancillary Literature. Next came Brahmanism and the doctrines of the Upanishads — texts with esoteric embodiment that were probably written between 400 and 200 BCE — which held that God was the transcendent reality

84

of which man, nature and the material universe were manifestations. Finally came the Age of the Buddhist and Jainist Heresies which prompted a Brahmin counter-reformation in the form of relentless and sanguinary persecution that led to the rise of Hindu sects.

Acceptance into the priesthood required initiation into the mysteries whose celebration through progressive Degrees was regulated by the different phases of the moon. The main part for each Degree of an initiation ceremony was invariably conducted in a darkened environment such as a subterranean cavern or man-made excavation. Flashing lights, screams and other frightening effects were used to create fear, sensory confusion and a hypnotic effect which facilitated indoctrination. During the time lapse of many weeks between each successive Degree, the Candidate was kept busy with constant ablutions, fasting, prayer and study under the tutelage and spiritual guidance of a Brahmin.

After completing the long and arduous process, the Candidate's acceptance into the priesthood culminated with him being introduced into a brightly lit Holy of Holies with fragrance, soothing music and a blazing fire representing paradise. The susceptive Candidate then knelt before the fire and was encouraged to believe that he would see the Deity's appearance within the pyramidal flame. Thus regenerated, he was invested with a tiara, a white robe and the sacred cord; his forehead was marked and on his breast was placed a tau cross whose vertical shaft represented the higher celestial states of being, while the horizontal bar represented the lower, earthly states; and finally he was entrusted with the sacred word whose trilateral form represented the Deity's power to create, preserve and destroy as personified by Brahma, Vishnu and Siva.

Thus was the Candidate elevated to the position of Brahmin: a position that was attainable only to a man who belonged to the first three thrice-born classes, and of the four original divisions of the Hindu body: a position that allegedly possessed supernatural powers that could control and even change the course of cosmic events by means of rituals and sacrifices; a position of esteem and unchallenged authority; and a contemptible position because of that position's own contempt for "those who were wanting in sufficient understanding," for those who were Untouchables, and for those who were women.

It was the Brahmins who around 200 BCE composed the self-serving rules which they legitimized by attribution to Manu who was the Hindu version of Adam, or First Man. The Code of Manu, or Manusmrti, is the collection of laws based on custom, precedent and the teaching of the Vedas. It is alleged — as was the case with Moses — that Manu learnt these laws from the Creator himself which he in turn passed on to the sages who were by definition profoundly wise men. Despite the written assertions by such wise men it would not be unreasonable to wonder what kind of benevolent and just God would have been responsible for the iniquitous laws of which the following are but a few examples:

> *In childhood a female must be subject to her father; in youth, to her husband; when her lord (husband) is dead, to her sons; a woman must never be independent. She must not seek to separate herself from her father, husband or sons. By leaving them she would make both her and her husband's families contemptible.*
> **Manu Verses 148, 149**

> *Him to whom her father may give, or her brother with the father's permission, she shall obey as long as she lives. Though destitute of virtue, or seeking pleasure elsewhere, or devoid of good qualities, a husband must be constantly worshipped as a god by a faithful wife.*
> **Manu Verses 151, 154**

Though Mahatma (Great Soul) Gandhi to some extent championed women's rights and travelled throughout India condemning the degradation of the Untouchables, little has changed to this day with the caste system and religious intolerance still prevailing. Irrespective of the religion that an Indian belongs to — Buddhist, Christian, Hindu, Jainist, Muslim, Sikh, or otherwise — he or she will regard their caste as being the primary factor in their identities as Indians rather than their religion.

Even in Western nations like Britain, the tradition of forced marriages persists within South Asian communities where young girls can often be falsely lured to India, kidnapped, held against their will, beaten, and in some cases even killed by their relatives. Those who rebel against such an abhorrent tradition are regarded as having brought shame on the family and are invariably punished with "honor" attacks that can include dousing with acid, abduction, mutilations, beatings and in some cases, even murder. It would be hard to find another animal species capable of punishing its offspring with the same degree of barbarity. But maybe that is because other animal species do not worship the false idols of hate-inducing religions.

Despite its abundance of gods and religious fervour, India is rated as one of the most hazardous countries in the world for women and young girls with high rates of human trafficking, prostitution and rape. The cultural preference for male rather than female offspring has also encouraged feticide and infanticide with an estimated 50 million females having gone missing over the past century. Though India may be the world's largest "democracy" and is hailed as a rapidly developing country, it must be said that its flagrant disregard for the human rights of women and the lower castes is a disgrace even by the abysmal standards of its own false gods and gender-biased religious doctrines.

THE MAGI

The extent to which priesthoods were prepared to go with theological fabrications that were customized to gain power, wealth and control over the masses was by no means confined to Egypt. The priests of ancient Persia who came to be known as the Magi were equally manipulative with their own primitive customs and superstitions. Initially the Magi were not priests in the strict sense of the word, but shamans of a distinct tribal caste from Media which lay south of the Caspian Sea. The Medes like the Elamites from the nearby Kingdom of Elam, were aboriginal and in no way connected to either the Aryans or Semites who at that time shared most of Western Asia between them. As Shamans they did not subscribe to any established or organized form of religion and instead preached that the world was inhabited by both good and evil spirits which only they could control. Their rituals included both fire and animal sacrifices that were invariably accompanied by drunken shouting and dancing after liberal consumption of an intoxicating drink made from the fermented juice of the haoma plant.

Apart from being avid practitioners of consanguineous (related to or descended from the same ancestors) marriage which they rated highly for its accumulative benefits, the Median shamans also claimed expertise in the occult, practiced divination, foretold the future, interpreted dreams, transmitted and received omens, read signs in the flight of birds and the movement of the stars, and preached that they were the only seers capable of recognising the coming of the Messiah's star which would correctly identify the Divine Child on the occasion of his birth.

The term "magus," or priest, was not one which they had immediately acquired, and it is said to have been later acquired from Maja, or mirror, wherein according to Indian legend, Brahma, the Hindu god, from all eternity beheld himself and all his powers and wonders. The Maja implied a formation of a shape, a figure, or a creature from the potency of primeval and unstructured living matter. A Magus therefore was a person who studied the functional aspects of eternal life. It was from the term "magus" that words such as "image" and "magic" came to us via the Latin and Greek languages.

The ancients attributed mystic powers to any liquid or solid reflective surface and there were strict prohibitions on disturbing water in which a person was gazing as such a disturbance would supposedly endanger the soul. Endangerment of the soul-reflection was the actual basis for the Narcissus myth and not the misinterpretation that suggests excessive self-love. Apart from the superstition that broken mirrors will result in bad luck for seven years, there were numerous Christian superstitions that connect mirrors with death because mirrors do not reflect the images of demons and other creatures without souls. When there is a death in the house some Christians still to this day cover or turn mirrors to the wall in the belief that mirrors can delay or detain the souls of the dead while on their journey.

When Cyrus the Great invaded Media in 550 BCE during the establishment of the Persian Empire, the wily shamans made an unsuccessful bid for political supremacy by posing for some considerable time as the champions of the people against the Aryan aggressors. Their incessant quest for power was not only maintained throughout the reigns of Cyrus and his son, Cambysses, but also carried over into the first years of rule under Darius (521-486 BCE) when the Magus Gaumata, masquerading as Smerdis, the brother of the deceased Canbysses, ceased power while Darius was overseas. Darius, however, regained control by putting Gaumata and associates to death.

Having therefore failed to gain power by political means, the Magi immediately proceeded to insinuate themselves as priests within the ranks of Persian nature-worship by emphasising the more obviously common aspects of both religions such as the veneration of fire and the sun. They also appear to have had no qualms over the self-imposed suppression of their own aboriginal affinities even to the extent of adopting the Persian funerary custom of encasement in wax as opposed to their own tradition of exposing the dead to scavenging animals and carrion birds. The tradition, however, was later reintroduced once their usurped position of theological eminence had been established and no religious ceremony could be performed without their presence. The Greek historian, Herodotus (c. 485-425 BCE), accurately records that by the time of his travels, the Magi had compensated for the failure of their political endeavours by becoming indispensable to the ritual of Persian religion. This they achieved by not only highjacking the more popular aspects of nature-worship, but also by tenaciously attaching themselves to the religion of the Persian prophet, Zarathushtra, or more commonly known as Zoroaster.

According to Zoroastrian tradition, the beginning of creation was achieved by the emanation of light by the Eternal, from whence issued the King of Light, Ahura Mazda, who by means of speech created the pure world, of which he was the preserver and judge. He was the Supreme Being, or Eternal Life, otherwise known as "Time Without Limits" because no origin was assigned to him. He was enshrined in his glory with attributes and properties that were incomprehensible to human understanding, and to him belonged silent adoration. His first creations were threefold and began with the creation in his own image and likeness of six genii called amshaspands, who surrounded his throne and were his messengers to lesser spirits and men; and to whom they represented purity and perfection.

The second creation was that of the twenty-eight yazatas, who as models of virtue and interpreters of men's prayers, watched over the happiness, innocence and preservation of the world. The third creation was that of the far more numerous farohars, who represented the perceptions of Ahura Mazda before he proceeded with the creation of material things. They were in principle the spirits, or "guardian angels" of men, and the concept of their alleged existence was later to be adopted by the Greeks and the Romans.

Apart from Ahura Mazda, there was also Ahriman, who as the second-born (twin) emanation from primitive light by the Eternal, was also initially pure, but being very ambitious and haughty, he soon gave way to intense jealousy that was deserving of punishment. The Supreme Being consequently condemned him to the region of darkness for twelve thousand years, a period considered sufficient for ending the strife between good and evil. Ahriman in the meantime created numerous genii, *daevas,* who plagued the world with disease, guilt and misery. They represented cruelty, covetousness, impurity and violence. They were the demons of cold, hunger, leanness, ignorance, poverty and calumny. They provided Western Europe with the basic myth of Lucifer's downfall with its dualistic division of the universe between the forces of good and evil. The prediction by Persian prophets that Ahriman and his *daevas* would be defeated in the Apocalypse, the final destruction of the world, was also adopted by Judeo-Christian prophets as was described in the Book of Revelation.

Ahura Mazda reigned for three thousand years before deciding to create the material world — in the same six stages that were later to appear in the book of Genesis — and then produced the initial being from whose seed the first human pair were formed, Meshia and Meshiane; but first the woman and then the man were seduced by Ahriman who corrupted their natures by feeding them certain fruits.

Ahriman also altered the natures of other forms of life by aligning insects, serpents, wolves and all other kinds of vermin against the good creatures. At the end of twelve thousand years, however, when the world is no longer afflicted by the spirits of darkness, there would appear three prophets whose power and wisdom would restore the world to its original pristine beauty. Ahriman, the demons and all men — no mention of women — will be purified in a sea of liquid metal, and the law of Ahura Mazda will prevail everywhere.

So by publicly feigning acceptance of Zoroastrian traditions, the former Median shamans managed to establish their own worthiness as proselytes to serve at the altar of native Persians: and in so doing, were able to gradually and covertly hijack Zoroastrianism by introducing many aspects of their own primitive beliefs. Consequently as the transformation from shamans to Magi took place, drunken orgies and blatant deceptions gave way to a more acceptable public image that even impressed Greek and Roman scholars who commented favourably on various characteristics of Magian behaviour such as demeanour, discipline, ethics, laws of purity and powers of divination. Their reputation had become so widespread as a result of the Persian Diaspora in Asia Minor, Syria, Mesopotamia and Armenia, that even in the infancy narrative of Jesus (Matthew 2:1-2) it was felt — despite Christian hostility towards the Magi — that the child's alleged divinity had to be substantiated by including the presence of the three Magi who had been guided by a brilliant star. The frequent Christian depiction of these three wise men bearing gifts as a token of their homage subsequently became known as the "Adoration of the Magi."

Becoming a member of such a religious elite, however, was not easy and after lustrations by fire, water and honey, the Candidate had to endure in silent solitude numerous probations that culminated in a fast of fifty consecutive days. The mental rather than the physical strain of the trials often caused varying degrees of derangement whose effects on occasion proved permanent. After having survived the novitiate, the Candidate was armed with various talismans for protection during his journey through a series of adjoining chambers where intermittent flashes of light and thunderous noise were accompanied by attacks from other members disguised as wild animals. The Candidate was then soothed with pleasant scents and melodious music; had a snake placed on his breast as a token of regeneration; and witnessed a display of the wicked torments of Hades. On finally being congratulated and welcomed into the illuminated Holy of Holies which sparkled with precious metal ornaments, the Candidate had to undertake not to divulge the secret rites of Zoroaster to profane outsiders. An Archmagus seated on a throne and surrounded by the dispensers of the mysteries, then revealed the sacred words of which the Tetractys, or name of God, was the principle. The Tetractys is analogous to the Tetragrammaton, or name of the Deity as revealed to Moses on Mount Sinai. Transliterated Y H W H and regarded by the Jews as being too sacred to pronounce, it is articulated as Yahweh or Jehovah.

These initiation stages came to be known as the ascent of the ladder of perfection and subsequently gave rise to the legend of Rustam, the Persian Hercules who mounted a Simurgh, a monstrous griffin in Persian Mythology, and undertook the conquest of Mazendaraun which was reputed to be the perfect earthly paradise. After fighting his way through many dangers along a road of seven stages, Rustam finally reached the White Giant who smote all who assailed him with blindness. Rustam, however, proved triumphant and with three drops of the giant's blood restored sight to all the captives. The blindness with which the captives had been smitten was symbolic of the Candidate's mental blindness before initiation.

Zoroastrianism under the authority of the Magi flourished in Persia for many centuries until 651 when Persian sovereignty was ceded to the Islamic invaders, and what was left of Zoroaster's teachings soon gave way to those of Mohammed. The severity of the ensuing persecutions forced many Zoroastrians to flee to remote regions with the majority settling in Northwest India where they are to this day known as Parsis, or Persians.

It is estimated that there are about 150,000 Zoroastrians worldwide with the majority residing in India (70,000), Iran (25,000), United States (11,000), Afghanistan (10,000), Canada (5,000), and the United Kingdom (4,200). When the British rock band Queen's lead vocalist Freddie Mercury — who was a Zoroastrian — died in 1991, it was not possible in Britain to lay him naked in a "Tower of Silence" on a mountain or hilltop to be devoured by carrion birds, and he was instead simply cremated.

For those Zoroastrians who courageously remained in Persia, Iran since 1935, persecution has been a way of life and they are referred to as gabhr, or infidel. Whether or not the former shamans of Media allowed themselves to be martyred for Zoroastrianism, is not known. But one must wonder if those wily shamans who survived the Aryan invasion and then embraced whatever religious beliefs were fashionable at the time, would have had much difficulty in making the necessary theological adjustments to become ardent and influential members of the Islamic community: a community where religious laws written by men, encouraged men to regard women as being deficient in intelligence and no better than pieces of property.

THE RABBIS

Despite the biblical assertion that God chose Abraham to be the father of a people that were special and would be an example to the rest of the world — the present-day barbaric oppression of the Palestinian people would suggest that many Israeli Jews have not read the script — numerous scholars regard Jewish history as having begun with the Exodus from Egypt and that anything previous to that event in the Bible was a collection of syncretic mythologies based on numerous non-Jewish sources.

It would appear that the expulsion of the Jews from Egypt following an outbreak of plague — likely to have been leprosy — was the historical basis for the myths surrounding Moses. Manetho, the Egyptian priest and historian who during the third century BCE wrote the *Aegyptiaca* (History of Egypt), said that alien tribes in northwest Egypt were lepers and unclean. The historian **Tacitus (c. 56-c. 117)** wrote as follows:

Most writers, however, agree in stating that once a disease, which horribly disfigured the body, broke out over Egypt; that king Bocchoris, seeking a remedy, consulted the oracle of Hammon, and was bidden to cleanse his realm, and to convey into some foreign land this race detested by the gods. The people, who had been collected after diligent search, finding themselves left in a desert, sat for the most part in a stupour of grief, till one of the exiles, Moyses by name, warned them not to look for any relief from God or man, forsaken as they were of both, but to trust to themselves, taking for their heaven-sent leader that man who should first help them to be quit of their present misery. They agreed, and in utter ignorance began to advance at random. Nothing, however, distressed them so much as the scarcity of water, and they had sunk ready to perish in all directions over the plain, when a herd of wild asses was seen to retire from their pasture to a rock shaded by trees. Moyses followed them, and, guided by the appearance of a grassy spot, discovered an abundant spring of water. This furnished relief. After a continuous journey for six days, on the seventh they possessed themselves of a country, from which they expelled the inhabitants, and in which they founded a city and a temple.

Making the Jewish people a scapegoat for the plague in Egypt may have been the first of such injustices, but it was not to be the last. The great plagues of the fourteenth century were also blamed on Jews who were said to have caused the contamination of water sources with a mixture of Holy Communion wafers stolen from Christian churches and the menstrual blood of Jewish women. The Jewish quarter in Paris was subject to looting and vandalism by rioters in 1382. A "Holy War against Jews" fomented by the Archdeacon of Seville in 1391 witnessed the storming of the ghetto, the destruction of synagogues, and the brutal murder of an estimated 41,000 innocent people. During the Black Death, a pandemic that ravaged Europe (1347-1351), 12,000 Jews perished in Bavaria; two thousand were burned in Strasbourg; and 160 were burned in a trench at Chinon (central France).

This unjust persecution of Jews was encouraged by the Christian Church to divert attention from the emerging idea that a malevolent God was responsible for the plagues which by the end of the century had wiped out almost half of Europe's population. The true cause of the plague bacillus probably originated on trade ships from China and then carried on Crusader ships from the Holy Land that unwittingly transported millions of Oriental black rats. Rather than attempt to eradicate the problem, resentful Christian authorities — in their panic, fear, and dereliction of duty — chose instead to resort to the extermination of Jews. Such atrocities were then justified by customized myths that portrayed Jews unfavorably.

Though it is possible that some Jews may have been expelled from ancient Egypt because of the plague, it is highly unlikely that the number expelled was anywhere near the number that was subsequently claimed by Jewish scribes. According to the various parts of the narrative in the books of Exodus, Leviticus, Numbers, and Deuteronomy, it was in approximately 1,300 BCE that the Exodus of some 600,000 oppressed Israelite slaves took place when led by Moses — with neither map nor directions from the God that *chose* them — then wandered through the wilderness for forty years before settling in the promised land. Unfortunately there is no mention or record of this Exodus in ancient Egyptian history and had such a momentous event actually occurred — 600,000 people would in those days have represented at least a quarter of the Egyptian population — then surely it would have warranted being diligently recorded or at least mentioned. So while the Exodus story is discounted by Egyptologists, archaeologists and even Jewish scholars, it has nonetheless served to historically help cast Jews as the perennial victims.

As for the name Moses, it was Egyptian as in Thutmose or Ahmoses, and meant "unfathered son of a princess." The Moses myth was modeled on the Egyptian demigod Heracles of Canopus — Ancient Egyptian coastal town located on the River Nile Delta — who was drawn from an arc in the Nile bulrushes, grew up to perform many great deeds, and eventually died on a mountaintop.

Moses's fortuitous meeting with Sinai's god — the Chaldean moon-god Sin — suggests that the Jews attempted to settle in that God's Cainite-Midianite mining community on the Sinai Peninsula, or land of Sinim ("Land of the Moon") whose consort was Mother Inana, who annually turned Sumer's (present-day Iraq) waters into blood. Moses, who climbed the holy mountain where Sin dwelt, divulged that Sin was the same as the God of Abraham who apparently did not know him by that name (Exodus 6:3). Ancient documents show that the name "Abraham" was itself a synonym for Ab-Sin, or "Moon-Father."

Abraham's God (Father Brahm) introduced himself to Moses with the words "I Am That I Am," thereby echoing the Brahmanic *Tat Sat's* "I Am That that Is." He also commanded, "Put off thy shoes from off thy feet, for the place whereon thou standest is holy ground," (Exodus 3:5). The removal of footwear was an ancient Hindu custom — also attributed to ancient Egyptian and Roman witches — which in India is still practiced in temples where worshippers go barefoot because of the belief that emanations from the holy ground can enter the body via the feet.

The narrative of Moses allegedly being given the tablets of stone was borrowed from the Canaanite god Baal-Berith, "God of the Covenant" — later to be regarded as a devil by Christian demonology — and the tablets' Ten Commandments followed the commandments of the Buddhist Decalogue. In ancient times such commandments were generally given by a deity on a mountain top as was the case with the Greek Titan Queen of heaven, Mother Rhea of Mount Dicte (in Crete), and Zoroaster who received his tablets on a mountaintop from Ahuru Mazda.

People are still being misled into believing that Moses wrote the

Pentateuch (first five books of the Old Testament) despite the fact that scholars have long known that they were written by priestly scribes in Jerusalem late in the post-exilic period — between the end of Jewish exile in Babylon in 538 BCE and 1 CE — with a view to creating a mythic history for their nation based on the customs, pronouncements and legends of others. Because the character of Moses was conceived with a non-Jewish name and a selection of different myths, he remains shrouded in mystery that casts doubt on his actual existence.

It is also apparent that some 21 references to camels in the first books of the Bible were in fact concoctions such as the story of Abraham's servant finding a wife for Isaac in Genesis 24: "Then the servant left, taking with him 10 of his master's camels loaded with all kinds of good things from his master. He set out from Aram Naharaim and made his way to the town of Nahor. He made the camels kneel down near the well outside the town; it was towards evening, the time the women go to draw water."

Israeli archaeologists recently sifted through a site north of the modern city of Eilat in search of camel bones which could be carbon dated. None of the domesticated camel bones discovered dated from earlier than around 930 BCE — some 1,500 years after the stories of the patriarchs in Genesis were said to have occurred. The difference between domesticated and wild camels can be established by examining the leg bones which in the case of domesticated camels are thicker as a result of having carried heavy loads. The proportion of male camels in a graveyard provides a further indication because they were preferred for being able to carry heavier loads. Consequently it is clear that there were no domesticated camels in that region any time before 1,000 BCE.

Other groundless Judaic traditions include the common assumption that the hexagram, with its two intersecting equilateral triangles, has been the emblem of Judaism since the time of David or Solomon. Though variously known as the Magen David (Shield of David), Star of David, or Solomon's Seal, the hexagram had nothing to do with either of them and was not even mentioned by Judaic scribes until the twelfth century. Furthermore its official acceptance as the Judaic emblem did not occur until the seventeenth century after it had been part of the medieval Cabala's system of sex worship.

The symbol originally represented the union between males and females in Tantric Hinduism; with the upward pointing triangle representing the former and the downward representing the latter. The borrowing of this Tantric Hindu symbol was only a very small part of a lengthy and concerted effort by religious scribes to create a Jewish nation whose mythic history incorporated the traditions, maxims and legends of other religions and nations. Unfortunately Judaism has never been content to be just a religion, it has also always wanted its adherents to regard themselves, and to be regarded by others as a distinct race whom God had chosen. By growing up and living in accordance with such a premise — those who believe they are "superior" by virtue of having allegedly been chosen by God — will invariably create a barrier between themselves and the less fortunate "unchosen" who will neither regard them with respect nor shower them with love.

The concept of a master race or chosen people is loaded with explosive potential for continual human conflict. History has repeatedly shown that large scale human suffering is the inevitable consequence whenever a people believe that their own ethnicity or religion is superior to that of others. While the extermination of six million chosen Semitic people by a Germanic master race ranks high as one of mankind's most abhorrent atrocities, the annual genocide by neglect resulting in the death of millions of children under the age of five is by contrast worthy of little if any attention when compared to the Holocaust industry which is a regular feature of present-day media output. So rather than having a concerted worldwide effort to address the urgent needs of millions of young children who are born into dire environments that are deficient in the most basic of human needs and rights, vast resources are instead wasted on financing endless ethnic and religious conflicts of which the greater majority are conducted in the name of God.

Other misconceptions include the Hebrew Bible's assertion that Solomon beseeched God as follows: "Give Thy servant an understanding heart to judge Thy people and to know good and evil" (1 Kings 3:9). God apparently replied: "Since you have asked for this and not for long life and wealth for yourself, nor have you asked for the death of your enemies but for discernment in administering justice, I will do what you have asked . . . " (1 Kings 3:11-12).   Despite being on speaking terms with the one and only true God who apparently endowed him with great wisdom for discernment, Solomon allegedly went on not only to dabble in idolatry, but also to accumulate three hundred concubines and seven hundred wives whose sexual demands alone must have somewhat curtailed the energy and time available for the administration of justice.

In its account of Solomon's wisdom and Golden Age reign, the

Bible relates how his legend was so widespread and impressive that Balkis, the Queen of Sheba, determined to meet this great man:

> *Arriving at Jerusalem with a very great train — with camels carrying rare spices, large quantities of gold, and precious stones — she came to Solomon and talked with him about all that she had on her mind.*
> **(1 Kings 10:2).**

The Bible, however, conveniently omits to mention that the historical facts relating to King Solomon's lifetime (c. 1011-931 BCE) were loosely based on a selection of legends from Egypt, Phoenicia, and southern Arabia where the land of Sheba had long enjoyed a genuine Golden Age as a result of being the main source of frankincense and important spices that were essential for religious and funerary functions as well as food preservation. It is therefore highly unlikely that Balkis, one of a long line of matriarchal Sheban queens that had ruled over the entire Sinai Peninsula, a land renowned for fabulous wealth, would have stooped to paying homage to Solomon. It is far more likely that this far-fetched link with Balkis was merely a name-dropping exercise intended to enhance Solomon's legend.

In reality there was no Golden Age; the Israelites were by no means a great nation; and there were no great cities with magnificent structures. The "city" of Meggido for example covered an area of less than several dozen acres and the only "magnificent structures" were mud-plastered huts where the standard of living was certainly below that of other nations in the ancient Near East. The character of Solomon, or Sun God of On, was the Israelite version of the Egyptian sun god, Re of Heliopolis. Furthermore, most of what is known about Solomon was not written until some two thousand years later so that there are no factual records traceable to the time of his reign.

The Hebrew Bible also mentions the building of Solomon's First Temple which was achieved with the help of King Hiram of Tyre (part of present day Lebanon) who provided quality materials and skilled craftsmen for which Solomon was obliged to pay King Hiram an annual tribute of 100,000 bushels of wheat and 110,000 gallons of pure olive oil (1 Kings 5:11). So far no archaeological evidence has been unearthed for Solomon's First Temple and the only reference to what might have been contemporary with its supposed existence comes from the Hebrew

Bible. Even architectural descriptions of the First Temple are lacking in technical detail and appear to feature combined characteristics from other temples in Egypt, Mesopotamia and Phoenicia.

According to another mythical tradition, the ancestral line of the builders who erected the mystical temple was started by one of the Elohim when he married Eve to beget a son called Cain. Elohim is a Hebrew plural word meaning "the goddesses and gods" though its appearance in the Bible was invariably translated as "God." In the original transcripts of the book of Genesis, Yahweh was only one of the Elohim. El, the singular form of the word, was at times used as a name as was the case for the Phoenician bull-god who was simply referred to as El, "the god." Adonai, another of the Elohim, created Adam and united him with Eve to bring forth the family of Abel, to whom the sons of Cain were subjected as punishment for the transgression of Eve. Cain's industrious cultivation of the soil produced little, whilst Abel leisurely tended the flocks. Adonai refused the gifts and sacrifices from Cain and stirred trouble between the sons of the Elohim generated out of fire and the sons formed of only the earth. Cain killed Abel,

And so it was against that mythical background that Solomon, having determined that the erection of the temple begun by his father should be completed, gathered artificers who were organised into companies under the command of Hiram Abiff, the architect sent by King Hiram of Tyre to oversee the project. The construction of the temple was in due course completed and featured a beautifully crafted golden throne for Solomon. Though Hiram stayed on to construct many more magnificent structures, he, however, lived in melancholy loneliness, loved and understood by few, and disliked by many including Solomon who envied his genius.

News of Solomon's wisdom had in the meantime spread to other nations including Sheba, a kingdom believed to be present day Yemen which at the time may also have incorporated areas now known as Eritrea and Ethiopia. Intrigued by what she had heard, Balkis, the Queen of Sheba, decided to travel to Jerusalem to meet the great man and behold the marvels of his reign. On her arrival in Jerusalem she was welcomed with fanfare, festivities and a tour of the great buildings including the Temple which filled her with awe and admiration. On being captivated by her beauty, Solomon proposed marriage which a flattered Balkis accepted.

After several subsequent visits to the Temple, however, Balkis insisted on meeting the architect of such magnificence, and when brought before her, she found Hiram's appearance and manner totally beguiling. After regaining her composure she not only questioned him at length, but also defended him against Solomon's evident ill will and rising jealousy. When she asked to see the men who had built the Temple, Solomon protested at the impossibility of assembling the entire workforce consisting of Apprentices, Fellow Crafts and Masters. But Hiram, jumping up on a large rock so as to be better seen, described with his right hand the symbolical Tau, and immediately all the workmen hastened from the different works into the presence of their Master. Balkis was so impressed by such a display of authority that she realized she was in love with the great architect and regretted her promise to Solomon.

Solomon's response to this new development was to arrange for Hiram's utter humiliation and ultimate ruin by conspiring with three of Hiram's dissatisfied and envious Fellow Crafts whom Hiram had refused to raise to the level of master because of their idleness and lack of skills. The disgruntled Fellow Crafts suggested that the forthcoming casting of the brazen sea which would enhance Hiram's reputation even further, should turn out to be a complete disaster. On accidentally learning of the Fellow Crafts' plot, a young workman named Benoni, alerted Solomon in the mistaken belief that appropriate action would be taken against the conspirators. On the day of the casting which was attended by Balkis, the molten metal overflowed from the sabotaged mould and spread like red-hot lava causing the terrified onlookers to flee. Hiram, however, remained calm and endeavored unsuccessfully to extinguish the flames with water which only rose as steam and caused further chaos.

Though overcome by grief and surrounded by danger, Hiram's only thought was for Balkis, but before he could go to her he heard a voice from an apparition above him that urged him to be fearless and to throw himself into the flames. Hiram obeyed without question and whereas others would certainly have been consumed by the fire, he experienced ineffable delights as he was drawn into the abyss by an irresistible force. The voice then informed him that he was being taken to the centre of the earth, into the soul of the world, into the kingdom of the great Cain where liberty reigned within without the despised anger and tyrannous envy of Adonai. Therein was the home of Hiram's fathers where it would be possible to taste fruit from the tree of knowledge. When Hiram enquired as to whom the voice belonged, he was told "I am the father of thy fathers, I am the son of Lamech, I am Tubal-Cain."

101

Tubal-Cain then took Hiram into the sanctuary of the fire and spoke of Adonai's weakness, base passions and capacity for murderous vengeance. Hiram was then presented to Cain, the creator of his race. The angel of light that produced Cain was reflected in the splendor of this son of love whose noble magnanimity was the envy of Adonai. Cain recounted his personal experiences, misfortunes and sufferings at the hands of the implacable Adonai. Presently a voice belonging to the offspring of Tubal-Cain and his sister Naamah informed him that he would have a son whom he would never see, but whose numerous descendants would perpetuate his race, which superior to that of Adam, would acquire the empire of the world; for centuries they would dedicate their courage and genius to the service of the always ungrateful race of Adam, but in the end the superior would triumph and restore the worship of fire to the earth. His sons, invincible in his name, would destroy the power of those who were the ministers of Adonai's tyranny. The voice finally urged Hiram to go forth as the genii of fire were with him.

Before returning Hiram to the earth, Tubal-Cain gave him the hammer with which he himself had crafted great works, and assured him that with the help of the hammer and the genii of fire he would quickly complete the tasks left unfinished by man's stupidity and malevolence. Back on earth Hiram immediately used the wondrous instrument for completion of the massive bronze cast and the people were astonished at the speed with which the repairs had been accomplished. Overcome by elation, Hiram and Balkis pledged their vows and wondered how Balkis could get out of her promise to Solomon. This she achieved by removing the ring of betrothal from Solomon's finger while he was under the influence of wine.

Solomon's reaction was to let his fellow-conspirators know that Hiram's removal would be welcome and so when the great architect next visited the temple he was attacked by the three villainous Fellow Crafts. Before dying, however, Hiram managed to remove from around his neck the golden triangle on which the Master's word was engraved and threw it into a deep well. Hiram's corpse was covered and carried by the killers to a solitary hillside where it was placed in a grave over which a sprig of acacia was then planted.

After Hiram had been missing for seven days, the public's outcry forced Solomon to mobilize a search for Hiram whose body was eventually discovered by three Masters who because of the missing golden triangle decided as a security precaution to change the Master's sacred and secret word. The three suspects were pursued but rather than face justice they committed suicide and their heads were brought to Solomon. After being later found in the well, the golden triangle was taken to the remotest part of the temple and placed in a triangular alter within a vault concealed by a cubical stone bearing the inscription of the sacred law. The vault, whose location was known only to the twenty-seven elect, was then walled up.

Once again the portrayal of an eminent man or deity who as part of a trinity, first perishes as a victim of envy or evil, and is then restored to a far greater glory, occurs as the mandatory and by now an all too familiar story line that is central to numerous fraternal and religious rituals to which a significant percentage of humanity still subscribes in one form or another. Hiram Abiff's legacy is that the myth of his malevolent demise is still being reenacted in the twenty-first century by intelligent men of substance whose influential social status, when corrupted, can adversely affect the lives of millions. The fraternal organization that is the main exponent of the reenactment of Hiram Abiff's death — with no mention of Balkis so as to eliminate the female principle — is the secret society of Freemasonry whose origins surreptitiously evolved from the trade associations of the past.

THE MITHRAIC AND CHRISTIAN PRIESTHOODS

Long before the Islamic threat to Zoroastrianism, Ahura Mazda faced another challenge to his authority which came not from Ahriman, but from Mithra who should not to be confused with Mitra who in Hindu Scriptures represents the light of day. Mithra, who was the first of the twenty-eight yazatas, or spirits of light that were invoked with the sun, eventually came to be regarded as being the sun. As the beneficent genius and most powerful of the yazatas, Mithra was the intercessor between Ahura Mazda and man; and though he was technically below the six amshaspands, the cosmic aspects of his position were allowed to become so perverted by the Magi, that with the passing of time he acquired the attributes of divinity. Such usurpation of a deity's rank by an inferior was not uncommon in mythology as was the case with Serapis in Egypt, Jupiter in Greece and Suva and Vishnu in India. Deification of an inferior being simply occurs when the symbol itself became confused with that which it was intended to symbolize.

Though Zoroaster's "purer" version of the Persian faith which held that Ahura Mazda was the Supreme Being eventually gained prominence and spread even to the West where it influenced Middle Platonism and Judaism — many of Zoroastrian doctrines were adopted by Judaism to formulate the laws of Yahweh including the anti-female sentiment that only those women who were "submissive to control, who had considered their husbands as lords" could enter heaven — Mithra nonetheless remained an influential force when the Magi reintroduced aspects of their pagan worship which were legitimized in supplements to the scriptures. This is illustrated by the following quote from the **Mihr Yasht (Hymn to Mithra):**

> *Ahura Mazda spake unto Spitama Zarathustra, saying: "Verily, when I created Mithra, the lord of wide pastures, O Spitama! I created him as worthy of sacrifice, as worthy of prayer as myself, Ahura Mazda.*

By having been accorded equal status with Ahura Mazda, Mithra became a supreme being in his own right and the emergence of Mithraism as a separate cult soon followed. Mithra's predominantly male attributes, however, had to be somehow balanced with some feminine presence and he was consequently paired with Anahita, an important female yazata who along with Ahura Mazda formed the mandatory great triad. The kings of the latter part of the Achaemenid dynasty from about 485 BCE became ardent votaries of Mithra and Anahita and introduced the religion to their winter capitol in Babylon. This furthered the cause of Mithraism as an independent religion and brought it into contact with the Babylonian priesthood who identified Mithra with Shamash, the Babylonian sun god.

The main source of influence on Mithraism, however, came from the Babylonian region of Chaldea whose Semitic inhabitants observed the planets in the belief that heavenly bodies had sway over people's destinies and guided the passage of their souls through the spheres. By plotting the movement of the stars, the Chaldeans were able to note that after a given period of time, some of the stars returned to their original position. This, they reasoned, meant that the stars were eternal and that the creating power responsible for their capacity for perpetual motion was therefore, if such were conceivable, even more eternal. Such reasoning gave birth to one of the concepts of eternity that led to belief in eternal life. Evidence of Chaldean influence can be seen on Mithraic monuments that invariably depict as prominent symbols the sun, the moon and the circle of the zodiac. During the Mithraic initiation ceremony into the Fourth Degree the neophyte was required to wear a mantle adorned with signs of the zodiac and was hailed as a "Lion of Mithra," an allusion to the zodiacal sign in which the sun attained its greatest power.

The worship of Mithra spread from Babylon to Armenia and on to Asia Minor — the Anatolian peninsula of present day Turkey — where it made contact with the indigenous worship of Cybele, the Phrygian goddess of nature worship and mother of all things. Just as Isis was associated with Osiris, and Venus with Adonis, so also was Cybele with Attis: and together they symbolized relations between Mother Earth and her fruitage. So despite the fundamental differences in both character and function between Attis and Mithra, the two soon became assimilated in art and folklore so that the way was paved for an alliance between Cybele — with whom Anahita was easily identifiable — and Mithra. The ensuing association with the Cybele cult gave Mithraism its first experience of the mysteries that were to become an important part of it subsequent evolution.

Alexander the Great's conquest of the Persian Empire in 328 BCE, however, does not appear to have greatly assisted the westward advance of Mithraism, and it was not until after the collapse of his empire that the faith reinvigorated when rulers of the loosely formed federation of independent Near Eastern states became fervent worshipers in the hope that his association with Ahura Mazda — the first possessor of the legendary *hvareno,* or talisman of the Royal House of Persia — would lend a token of legitimacy to their dynasties. With Mithra firmly established as the region's favorite deity, Mithraism itself began from about 300 BCE — a time when the mysteries were enjoying a renaissance — to gain the interest of potential recruits in the West by exploiting the belief that access to the fabled wisdom of the East was only possible through initiation into the mysteries.

According to one of the most commonly known legends, the Magi who were much later to attend the birth of Jesus, brought gifts and were also present along with shepherds in the cave when Mithra was born of a female Rock, the petra genetrix, which had been fertilised by the Heavenly Father's phallic lightening. As a Peter, the son of *petra,* he carried the keys to the Kingdom of heaven. This led to Christianity's legend of Saint Peter which portrayed him as holder of the symbolic keys as was also the case with Shiva's trident and the Osirian *ankh* (known as key of the Nile and heavenly key to the Nile in the Sky, or Milky Way). Such key-holding enabled the holder to either admit or deny admittance to the land of the dead. The actual roots of Saint Peter's legend are to be found in pagan Roman myths of the city-god Petra, or Pater Liber, assimilated to the Mithraic *pater patrum* (Father of Fathers) whose title was first corrupted into *papa,* and then "pope."

The myth of Saint Peter was the false foundation on which the authority of the Roman papacy was built with a passage from the Gospel of Matthew stating that Jesus made a pun by giving Simon son of Jonah the new name of Peter — "Rock," or Latin *petra* — saying that he would found his church on this rock (Matthew 16:18-19). This so-called Petrine passage, however, was a forgery deliberately inserted into the scripture in the third century as a political ploy to establish the primacy of Christianity over equally competitive religions from the East. It was all part of the power struggle where the main weapons were bribery, forgery, collusion, intricate falsehoods, and fraudulent passages slipped into the sacred scriptures.

After first proving his invincible strength by overcoming the sun, Mithra then had to capture the bull — the first animal created by Ahura Mazda — which he dragged back to his cave. The bull, however, managed to escape and thereby caused Ahura Mazda to order its recapture and sacrifice.

When Mithra plunged his knife into the bull, its body gave forth all the useful herbs; from its spinal marrow, there issued wheat; from its blood came the grape that produced the wine used in the mysteries; and from its seminal fluid, all the useful animals were born. The Bull's death was therefore the birth of life, and the heavenly drama of its sacrifice was subsequently reenacted on earth as the central act of Mithraic worship in tauroboliums wherein devotees would lay in a trench beneath a lattice frame on which a bull was being slain so as to bathe in its blood. The ritual was believed to activate the renewal of life to the soul and probably originated from the Cybele cult.

Mithra, the predecessor of Jesus, performed the now familiar array of miracles by restoring health to the sick; sight to the blind; mobility to the lame; and even life to the dead. The Mithraic festival of the Epiphany which celebrates the arrival of the sun-priests or Magi at the Savior's birthplace, was not adopted by Christianity until the year 813.

Mithraic ceremonies were usually conducted in subterranean caverns or crypts that had been converted to resemble caves that were symbolic of Mithra's birthplace. As the majority of such Mithraea were understandably small, membership averaged between fifty and sixty but rarely exceeded a hundred people who consequently experienced the kind of brotherhood and feigned equality — similar to that found in Freemasonry — that could not otherwise be found in the unjust social conditions of the Roman Empire.

The practice of equality, however, was not accorded to women and like its replacement Christianity, it was an ascetic, anti-female religion whose priests were celibate men. Women in Mithraic families were not allowed into Mithraea and the female principle was removed from the creation myth by replacing the Mother of All Living in the primal garden of paradise (Pairidaeza) with a bull named the Sole-Created. So instead of Eve, the bull was partnered with the first man. This masculinisation of the birth-giving ability, however, still required the bull to be castrated, sacrificed, and having its blood delivered for mystical fructification to the moon which being the source of a women's mystical lunar "blood of life" was responsible for producing life on earth.

An examination of all Mithraic inscriptions will reveal nothing to suggest the existence of even a single female participant in the mysteries. The concept of women's inequality to men was, and has been a hallmark of fraternal and religious organizations throughout the ages. There has to be something fundamentally wrong with the psychological state of men who subscribe to the highest of ideals and yet cannot accept women as either their social equals, or when it is patently evident on the basis of ability alone — as their superiors.

Initially Mithraism had only two degrees of initiation, but the need to exaggerate the extent of the mysteries and to create an aura of exclusivity eventually led to there being seven because that number was considered sacred. Beyond the Seventh Degree there was a priesthood under the authority of a high priest in Rome whose title of Pater Patrum was later appropriated to become the Christian Papa or Pope. The priests were responsible for the daily conduct of worship towards the east in the morning, the south at noon, and the west at night. They also kept the sacred fire burning, offered prayers to the planet that governed the day, and officiated at initiation ceremonies.

According to comments of what is left of the writings of the phoenician neoplatonist philosopher, Porphyry (c. 232-302) whose fifteen books Against the Christians failed to survive the sentence of burning that was pronounced against them in 448, the first three degrees were of a preparatory nature and included the customary lustrations, a symbolic offering of bread and water to Mithra, and the marking of a sign on the Candidates brow. After being crowned, the Candidate removed the crown to the declaration "Mithra is my crown" and then armed himself in defense as he ran the gauntlet of priests who in various animal guises assailed the Candidate with blows and shouting.

It is reported that during his initiation, the deranged Emperor Commodus (180-192) became overenthusiastic in his own defence and accidentally killed one of his assailants. Beyond these few details, there is little else known of the preparatory degrees and virtually nothing at all regarding initiation into the mysteries. One commentator does speak of "eighty punishments" by fire, water, frost, hunger, thirst, and wanderings of increasing severity; and it may be assumed that it was only after the surmounting of such trials that the Mithraic mysteries, representing the progress from darkness to light, were revealed.

Mithraism was also promoted by the enlistment of Hellenistic art with the creation of sculptured reliefs — the most common depiction being that of Mithra slaying the bull — that became the hallmark of every Mithraeum and sanctuary as the cult moved westward from Asia Minor. The eventual extent of the cult's diffusion, however, was mostly due to the Roman armies. Even before their annexation and while still client-kingdoms of the Roman Empire during the first century BCE, some regions of Asia Minor such as Armenia, Cappadocia, and Pontus (both in present-day Turkey) served as recruiting grounds for Rome's legions and foreign auxiliary corps. It was these oriental soldiers, who while on garrison duty in far off outposts, established the numerous Mithraic sanctuaries that stretched from Africa to Britain. During 1954 rebuilding work in London's Walbrook, a Mithaeum was discovered and is now rated as the most famous of all twentieth-century Roman discoveries in the City of London.

Despite its popularity within military ranks, Mithraism was not immediately successful in Rome and was obliged to resort to the customary device of acquiring legitimacy by registering its sanctuaries as burial associations. Apart from Mithraism, there was also the monotheistic sun-worshipping cult of Sol Invictus, or "Invincible Sun," whose doctrinal belief that its god possessed the attributes of all the other gods precluded the need for competition with its rivals. It was therefore to the relative success of this cult that Mithraism attached itself by various means including depictions that had Mithra sharing the banquet with Sol after the former had sacrificed the bull.   As   both cults regarded Sunday as being sacred and attached the same importance to the status of the sun whose rebirth they celebrated annually on the 25th of December, it was only natural that a gradual merging took place and what had previously occurred in Persia —the supplanting of a superior deity by an inferior through the confusion of attributes — reoccured in Rome. Mithra then came to be variously known as "Invictus Mithra," "Deus Invictus Mithra,'"or by the full title of "Deus Sol Invictus Mithra."

Despite its apparent success, however, Mithraism had no official recognition and it was not until the Emperor Commodus became an initiate that progress towards that goal was begun and culminated with the Emperor Aurelian (270-275) finally providing state recognition. The adoption of such an un-Roman form of worship by Roman Emperors at that time was probably influenced by the belief of oriental cults that the sun was the attendant and patron of the ruler. Consequently by promoting the concept of their own deification, Roman Emperors hoped that like the Egyptian Pharaohs, they too would be regarded as human manifestations of the sun god. Diocletian, who in 277 instigated the dedication of a temple to Mithra, was also a devotee and as Emperor from 284-305 was responsible for the last of the severe persecution of Christians prior to the more tolerant rule of Constantine the Great.

Christian historians and scholars have since tried to have us believe that the survival of Christianity owes much to the tolerance of Constantine (c. 272-337) who they claim became the first Christian Roman Emperor when prior to the Milvian Bridge Battle he saw a vision of the Christian God who promised victory if the Christian monogram was daubed on the soldiers' shields. This legend was invented by Eusebius — the Roman historian, exegete, and Christian polemicist — who also transformed Constantine's nefarious activities into acts of piety. Furthermore the "Christian monogram" which was already on Constantine's standard, was the labarum with no Christian connections whatsoever and was in truth the emblem of Mithra, the deity most worshipped by the legions of Rome. A series of inscriptions from the island of Philae in Upper Egypt prove that the labarum evolved from the Egyptian ankh.

The tolerance resulting from what came to be known as the "Edict of Milan," which was more of an informal agreement between Constantine who ruled the western parts of the empire and Licinius who ruled the eastern, was not intended by Constantine as specific assistance for Christianity, but as part of his scheme to bring about unity in the Empire which he then proceeded to do by orchestrating a campaign to blacken Licinius's name, to eventually bring about his death, and finally to stigmatize his memory with infamy that resulted in the removal of his statues and the abolition of all his laws and judicial proceedings.

While Constantine also recognized that unity required the establishment of social, political and religious tolerance, his support for religious tolerance, however was not due to some altruistic concern for his subjects, but to his desire to avoid offending any of the gods who might seek retribution against him personally. Though he has been hailed for establishing Christianity as the official religion of Rome, such official recognition of Christianity did not occur until after his lifetime and was the work of his bishops. He was not so much a man who worshiped Christ, but one who revered himself.

While recognizing the advantages offered by cults to government, Constantine was also aware that the vested interests of paganism had for too long exercised a divisive and dangerous influence through corruption of government officials in particular, and the people in general. Christianity on the other hand, as a relatively new religion, had not yet had enough time to become seriously involved with intrigue and corruption. He also recognised Christianity's educative and stabilizing potential which more than any of its dogmas commended it to the interests of government.

As to his own religious credentials, Constantine did not share Christianity's view that pagan gods were devils and was himself an initiate of the Sol Invictus cult which regarded him as a high priest in deference to his imperial position. When he moved his capital to Byzantium in 330 to allegedly create the "first purely Christian" city, he renamed it Constantinople after himself and had many pagan relics taken there for preservation. His life was hardly one of piety, but one filled with an obsession for his own self-preservation. He murdered his oldest son, his second wife, his father-in-law, his brother-in-law, and numerous others. Despite having several wives and a legion of concubines, Christian apologists claimed that he was "wedded to chastity."

Constantine's conversion to Christianity appears to have been a deathbed insurance policy that came about when Christian bishops were successful in convincing him that their God would absolve him of his sins and install him in heaven. So with death approaching, Constantine decided that "the salvation which I have earnestly desired of God these many years I do now expect. It is time therefore that we should be sealed and signed in the badge of immortality." He was then duly baptized and passed away with the deluded expectation of a heavenly resurrection. Despite that, his had been a "sun emperorship" under which Christianity enjoyed a degree of freedom and tolerance, but at no time during his reign (306-337) did Christianity come close to replacing the state religion of Sol Invictus whose symbol was prominent on many public features including banners and coins.

State recognition and political power were nonetheless urgent priorities which Christianity was prepared to acquire by any means even if it meant temporarily playing down the role of Jesus as the Messiah from the heaven above, and instead becoming associated with Constantine's more tangible accomplishments down here on earth. Jesus had after all been a Jewish Zealot agitator — a fact from which Christianity wished to distance itself — whose condemnation and crucifixion resulted from his outspoken criticism of social injustice which the Roman authorities regarded as subversive political activity. Consequently in 321 as part of the "shedding" of its Jewish heritage, Christianity switched its sacred day of observance from Saturday, the Jewish Sabbath, to Sunday, the state's sacred and "venerable day of the sun." Further changes included "borrowing" the aureole of light that crowned the sun god's head to create the Christian halo and Christ's birthday was changed from January 6 to December 25 in keeping with the sun's rebirth celebration. The Orthodox Church in Armenia still adheres to the January 6 date, while the Eastern Catholic and Orthodox churches observe a January 7 date.

Though Constantine is regarded as the effective architect of the Christian Church, his zeal for its teachings never quite matched that of his mother, the Empress Helena. It was she who deemed that extensive searches should be carried out until all the holy sites were identified and appropriately marked with some imposing shrine. Imperial subordinates eager to please the supposedly devout Helena wasted no time in not only identifying the site of the crucifixion below Jupiter's temple, but also in locating Christ's place of burial. Most impressive of all, if it is to be believed, was the discovery of the precise spot where Mary Magdalene had been standing when she received the glad tidings of Christ's resurrection. Whether by arrangement or coincidence, it was Helena herself who found the True Cross with its unmistakable "King of the Jews" plaque.

Churches were then established at the alleged site of Christ's birth in Bethlehem and on the Mount of Olives from where His Ascension is said to have taken place. Helena's achievements were certainly impressive considering that all of these discoveries were made subsequent to the city's destruction by the Romans and some three hundred years after occurrence of the events. Most remarkable of all, however, was the pinpointing of the exact spot where God spoke to Moses from the burning bush on top of Mount Herob in the Sinai Desert. The site is currently the location of St. Catherine's Monastery which was built by the Emporer Justinian (reigned 527-565) so as to enclose the Chapel of the Burning Bush which Helena had ordered to be built. The monastery's full, official name is The Sacred and Imperial Monastery of the God-Trodden Mount of Sinai, and its patronal feast is the Transfiguration. Associated with Saint Catherine of Alexandria (whose relics were said to have been miraculously transported there by angels) the monastery is now a favorite pilgrimage destination and sacred to Christianity, Islam and Judaism.

Comparisons between Christ and Mithra will show that both were born in a cave; both were part of a trinity; both were mediators between God and man; both committed a sacrifice for the benefit of mankind — though in different ways — wherein blood was the symbol of regeneration; and both celebrated with their respective twelve followers who in Mithra's case represented the twelve signs of the zodiac. Christianity's seven sacraments were a follow-on from the seven degrees of Mithraic initiation; both religions promulgated concepts concerning man and the immortality of his soul; and both had mysteries from which the lower ranks were excluded. Confirmation as to the secrecy surrounding the Christian Eucharist comes from Tertullian (c.160-220) the Christian Carthaginian writer who stated that which is holy should not be cast to the "dogs," and that it was "a universal custom in religious initiation to keep the profane aloof and to beware of witnesses." Christianity also concurred with Mithraism over doctrines relating to heaven and hell; judgment after death; and the triumph of good over evil.

In trying to provide some explanation for the numerous similarities that existed between the pagan religion that had long preceded Christianity, Christian writers such as Tertullian came up with the rather novel idea that Satan, having anticipated the coming of the true faith, proceeded to imitate it long before Christ was born. Such anticipation no doubt included ensuring that the Magi would be present at Mithra's birth. Tertullian even went further to suggest that "the observances of Mithraism were cunning parodies devised by Satan to seduce the souls of men from the true faith by a false and insidious imitation of it." St. Augustine (354-395) who had himself been an adherent of Mithraism for some ten years, was later to offer the more realistic explanation that "what is now called the Christian religion existed amongst the ancients, and was not absent from the beginning of the human race until Christ came, from which time the true religion, which existed already, began to be called Christian." In other words it was just a different name for the same old recipe — a concoction of fables heavily laced with blatant lies.

Christianity's quest to be recognized as the official state religion was in the meantime pursued with an impressive ruthlessness and Mithra's temple which was located on the ancient site of Vaticanum, or Vatican Hill, was ceased in 376. The temple, over which St. Peter's Basilica was built, is still accessible to this day. Persistent efforts by Bishop Ambrose of Milan eventually succeeded in persuading the initially tolerant Roman Emperor Theodosius I (392-395) to prohibit pagan sacrifices and to destroy pagan temples so that Christianity could by the default of the others become the state religion.

The relentless and often barbarous persecutions that ensued were not, however, totally successful and elements of oriental paganism persisted in various forms including that of Manichaeism which had been developed by Mani, a former Persian slave and an initiate of the Mithraic mysteries. Mani had cunningly utilised Christian names and rites to mask a mixture of Zoroastrian and Mithraic traditions laced with gnostic and Cabalistic ideas to produce a puritanical religion that viewed all things material as evil. He maintained that the Satan responsible for the creation of the material world with all its temptations was the Jewish Jehovah, and that it was in truth the Prince of Darkness who spoke to Moses, the Jews and their priests. Thus the Christians, the Jews and the Pagans are involved in the same error when they worship this God. Mani regarded Zoroaster, Buddha, and Jesus — but not Moses — as predecessors who like himself had been chosen as "messengers" to the people. He declared Jesus to be mortal and emphasized that any allusion to divinity had to be regarded as being merely symbolic.

Unfortunately for Mani, the "messenger" business in those days was not without its hazards and it was at the instigation of the Magi that in 276 King Bahram of Persia sentenced him to death by flaying and crucifixion. His martyrdom, however, only served to fuel the spread of his teachings and Manichaean schools promoted the ideas from which under different names and guises there evolved other similar sects such as the Cathars, the Paulicians, and the Bogomils of Bulgaria who all in their own way challenged the Christian view that Christianity was the only legitimate religion for the worship of God.

With Constantine's reign being the first important turning point in the history of the Holy Roman Empire, the second occurred under Charlemagne, the Frankish emperor who reigned from 786 to 814. Being a Christian was for Charlemagne a matter of convenience because the Holy Roman Empire — unlike the pagan tribal religions — tolerated his wars of acquisition for a share of the spoils and eventually recognized his barbarous achievements by giving him the crown of the Empire. He was also accorded special status with regards to the holy sacrament of matrimony in that he had four wives and numerous concubines which the church explained away as "marriages of the second rank."

During his reign Charlemagne ruthlessly destroyed pagan clan shrines, enforced conversion to Christianity with the choice of either Christ or immediate execution, and imposed vassalage. One reprehensible aspect of vassalage was the feudal emergence of "The Lord's Right" — also known as *jus primae noctis* (the law of the first night) — which equated the ownership of land with the ownership of women. This *droit du seigneur* meant that every serf's bride on her wedding night had to be deflowered by the lord of the land and not by her bridegroom. The church upheld the *droit du seigneur* as a God-given right of the nobility and declared that consummation of marriage by a vassal bridegroom within three nights after the wedding was blasphemous and equivalent to "carnal Lust." The landowner's carnal lust, however, was judged to be just and proper. Even the Eastern Church had provisions for punishing any man who tried to consummate his marriage before his lord had raped her. *Droit du seigneur* lasted throughout the feudal period — between the ninth and fifteenth centuries — and until the nineteenth century in Russia.

During thirty-three years of continuous war that built the Holy Roman Empire, Charlemagne shed so much blood that historians have baulked at the task of trying to establish the extent of the slaughter. His conversion method by the sword was so successful that the church subsequently supported Christian rulers who indulged in similar military pursuits. The French heroic poem *The Song of Roland* (*La Chanson de Roland*) — based on the Battle of Roncesvalles in 778 — clearly states that "the bishops bless the waters and convert the heathen. If any man protests, he is burned or put to the sword." On occasions it was the blessed water itself that served as executioner of unregenerate pagans with them becoming converts under the rule of Saint Goar — who died in 575 and was honored by Charlemagne — being held under blessed water until they either accepted Christ or drowned. And so that was how the Holy Roman Empire was built.

Many Western historians have since unconvincingly tried to explain the causes responsible for triggering the collapse of that Holy Roman Empire and the onset of the Dark Age with its intellectual famines, economic hardships, and social regressions. Many such historians have, however, had neither the integrity nor the courage to firmly lay the blame at the door of Christianity. It was after all the Christians themselves who maintained that the diabolic symptoms of the approaching end to the world was "the spread of knowledge" which they attempted to halt by their opposition to education for laymen, their destruction of libraries and schools, and their indiscriminate burning of books. After years of persistent destruction and vandalism, Saint John Chrysostom was able to boast with holy pride that "every trace of the old philosophy and literature of the ancient world has vanished from the face of the earth."

Pope Gregory the Great (540-604) condemned secular education as folly and wickedness and even proscribed the reading of the Bible by laymen. He had the library of the Palatine Apollo burned "lest its secular literature distract the faithful from the contemplation of heaven." By the end of the fifth century — with the church maintaining that all opinions other than its own were heretical and diabolical — Christian rulers had forcibly terminated the study of geography, mathematics, philosophy and medicine (because diseases were the work of the devil).

The result of insane Christian persecution and wanton destruction was that numerous scholars fled eastwards for refuge in Persia (now Iran) where the King of the Sassanian Empire — the last Persian empire before the rise of Islam — helped them establish a school for medicine and science that was to become the world's intellectual centre for several centuries. In 529, when Justinian I (c. 482-564) shut the Athenian schools, all Hellenistic knowledge was dispersed to Gupta India, Celtic Ireland, and Sassanian Persia. And because Christianity could only flourish — and like most religions still does — on ignorance, it became necessary for it to relentlessly promote ignorance with the result that Western Europe was deprived of the learning and knowledge that would have unleashed its potential for social advancement.

THE ISLAMIC IMAMS

The history of all major religions, including Islam, has been one of endless dissensions and divisions with mayhem and murder being a regular occurrence to the present day. The problems in Islam began after the Prophet Muhammad (c. 570-632) died without having designated a successor for the Muslim community he had established at Medina. This led to a succession dispute between the "Emigrants" who had accompanied him from Mecca to Medina, and the local "Supporters" who by joining his movement had enhanced it both materially and spiritually. Though Ali, Muhammed's son-in-law, was the obvious candidate for succession, the community elders decided that Muhammed's father-in-law would become the caliph and thereby the institution of the caliphate was begun whereby the caliph acted as both the religious and secular authority.

One of the main disadvantages of having outright authority vested in one man is that his eventual death will result in considerable turmoil as claimants squabble over the succession. Further problems may also arise from having religion dominate every aspect of community life because in the event of social disaffection, such disaffection will be expressed in religious terms whereby sectarianism becomes the only recourse available to the disaffected.

Though Ali's supporters, who became known as shi'at Ali, or party of Ali, did not take any immediate overt action, they nonetheless covertly laid the foundation for Islam's main division of Sunni and Shia Muslims who to this day — especially in Iraq — resort to ungodly violence towards each other. The Shias lived by a strict social code that demanded absolute obedience to their imams, or priest-kings, who were the direct descendants of Muhammed through the union of his daughter Fatima and Ali. They believed that in the coming millennium one of the past imams would return to earth as the Mahdi, or "guided one," to establish the rule of justice.

In the meantime, in order to avoid persecution while simultaneously working to undermine the orthodox doctrines of the Sunni majority, the Shias established a discipline of secrecy that required them to conceal their true religious beliefs and to outwardly conform to the state religion. In Shia Islam, this religious dissimulation — a form of deception that conceals the truth — was known as *taqiyya* and provided

117

legal dispensation whereby believers could conceal their true religious beliefs when under threat, persecution, or compulsion. The concept of *taqiyya* was developed to protect the Shias who were usually in the minority and under threat. The Shia view was that *taqiyya* was lawful in situations of overwhelming danger such as loss of life or property but where danger to the religion would not occur. The term *"taqiyya"* did not exist in Sunni jurisprudence because denying the faith under duress was only permitted in some extreme circumstances.

As part of their deception, the Shias also dispatched specially trained missionaries, or da'is, throughout the Arab world to preach doctrines that belied most of the orthodox beliefs. They maintained that Muslim Law and Scriptures contained a hidden meaning known only to the imams, and that there were seven prophets: Adam, Noah, Abraham, Moses, Jesus, Muhammed and Ali. It was also held that the sevenfold chain of creation was as follows: the prophets were second only to God at the level of Universal Reason; Ali, the "Prophet's companion," at the level of Universal Soul; the seven imams, at the level of Primal Matter; the chief da'i, or Grand Master, at the level of Space; the da'i, at the level of Time; and finally at the lowest level, stood man.

Though God himself was unknowable to man, a man could work his way upwards through the grades and thereby acquire a new revelation up to that of Universal Reason. The capacity for being reasonable, however, has never been a characteristic of those who peddle religion, and the death of the celebrated sixth imam, Ja'far al-Sadiq (702-765 BCE), was the start of the first major division amongst the Shias. Those who backed the succession of Ja'far's son, Musa and his descendants, believed that the millennium would come with the return of the twelfth imam in that line, and were called the "Twelvers." The remainder who supported Musa's older brother, Ismail, believed that his son Muhammed, who had disappeared in 770, was the seventh and last imam, and that his return to earth as the Mahdi would mark the millennium. Ismail's supporters where known as the Ismailis or the "Seveners." With the passing of time the Ismailis also quarreled amongst themselves and divided to create even more secretive sects such as the Batinites, Qarmatians, Druzes, Bretheren of Sincerity, Rosheniah, and the Nizari Ismailis who were the "Assassins."

Because the ruling administration of any given Islamic society could be toppled by the removal of just one man, assassination became the easiest recourse for those with unscrupulous political ambitions. This elimination of the competition, however, was not without precedence and there is evidence that the Prophet Muhammed — knowing full well that his faithful followers would carry out his wishes — used to rid himself of troublesome critics and rivals by simply implying that they were undeserving of life.

By far the most successful exponent of political assassination, however, was Hassan-i Sabbah (c. 1050s-1124), the Persian Nizari Ismaili missionary and founder of the Hashshashin or Assassins, who in his youth was reputed to have attended school with the subsequently famous astronomer and poet of the *Rubaiyat,* Omar Khayyam (1048-1131), and the Sunni statesman, Nizam al Mulk (1018-1092). Though the likelihood of that having been true is contradicted by chronology, its mention in the introduction to Fitzgerald's version of the *Rubaiyat* as well as other sources would suggest that they at least knew each other, especially as Nizam was later to become one of Hasan's first victims.

When the Mongol Hulago Khan (c. 1217-1265), Genghis Khan's grandson and scourge of Islam, overran Hasan's mountain fortress at Alamut in 1256, Mongol historians made note of what was considered important before allowing the libraries to be destroyed. It is therefore known that Hasan was born of a Twelver Shia family in the Persian city of Qom. As a youth he sought the secrets of science and religion and for a while apparently experienced a period of doubt and depression prior to being recruited and converted to the Ismaili cause. Having then overcome a serious illness and being spiritually rejuvenated, Hasan travelled to Cairo to obtain the eighth Fatimid Caliph's permission to spread the Ismaili doctrine in Persia which was under the authority of the Seljuk Turks. Permission was given on the understanding that Hasan would support the Caliph's oldest son, Nizar, to become the ninth Fatamid caliph, and thus was born the Ismaili sect of the Nizaris who came to be known as the Assassins.

There are numerous tales relating to the travels and missionary subversion of the cunning Hasan who eventually acquired as a strategic headquarters the Northern Persian fortress of Alamut from whence he only ventured out twice in more than thirty years. His "invisibility" as the "Old Man of the Mountain" enhanced rumors of his omnipotence and he continued to seize other mountain fortresses as regional centers of subversion. The summary execution of deviants, including two of his own sons, was a common feature of the ascetic severity of his regime which was elevated to include authority over the body as well as the soul.

Marco Polo (c. 1254-1324) — the Italian merchant traveller from the Republic of Venice who embarked on an epic twenty-four-year journey to Asia — described Aladdin quite differently from the mythic character who in *Arabian Nights* was master of a cave full of treasure. The cave in question was actually real and was located in the fortified valley of Alamut near Kazvin. Aladdin was the Old Man of the Mountain, the hereditary title of the Hashshishin starting with Hassan-b Sabbah whose name meant Son of the Goddess. The name Aladdin was subsequently adopted following the bloody conquest of Gujarat in 1297 by Ala-ud-din Khilji, the second ruler of the Turco-Afghan Khilji dynasty in India.

In order to accomplish his single-minded pursuit of religious power through violent political action, Hasan altered and increased the grades of Ismaili initiation from seven to nine and transformed the role the lowly devotee from aspiring supporter to that of an active Assassin. Wily da'is with knowledge about the manipulation of the human character would "hook" potential recruits by first revealing the kind of information that would capture interest, and then implying that the divine mysteries could only be attained by those who swore allegiance to the imam. Then by using a combination of drugs and pleasurable experiences, Hasan was able to give the newly recruited "self-sacrificers" a taste of the "paradise" to which they would return as soon as they had accomplished whatever it was that he had required them to do.

The word "assassin" is a corruption of the Arabic word Hashshishin meaning "users of hashish," and it was alleged that the Assassins were heavily drugged before being dispatched to murder their victims. As each aspirant then progressed upwards through the grades of initiation, he was inspired to gradually discard the basic tenets of Islam so that by the ninth degree he was free of all authority and could subscribe to whatever system he deemed most suitable for his own needs. Such freedom of action, however, did not include exemption from the inviolable oaths and assurances that he would never lie to his fellow members, reveal their secrets, or lend a hand to an enemy against them.

Following the caliph's death and Nizar's failure to succeed in 1094, Hasan established himself as an independent prince by severing relations with the Egyptian Fatimids and unleashing his Assassins in a campaign of terror against the Persians. This led to the Turks and Sunnis retaliating by wiping out Ismaili communities in the Levant and Persia. While the Assassins remained powerful within their own areas of influence, they were by 1110 no longer regarded as a serious military threat and remained that way until Hasan's death in 1124.

Though Hasan's two immediate successors did little to alter his policies, the fourth Grand master, Hasan II who ruled between 1162 and 1164, claimed to be the Mahdi and thus ended the Shia discipline of secrecy. He seceded from Islam to found a more liberal religion which only served to alienate the more entrenched Nizaris who rejoiced at his death at the hands of his brother-in-law, and welcomed a return to the more orthodox version of the faith. Though still remaining independent, the Persian Assassins were never again to become the power they once were and in time the arrival of the Mongol Hulago resulted in the massacre of all Persian Assassins.

In the meantime the Syrian branch of the Assassins which was ably led by Rashid ad-Din Sinan (c. 1132-1192) and had some time previously become independent of the Persian Grand Master's authority, began carrying out assassinations on a "contract" basis for either money or the usual political and religious considerations. Sinan's intrigues with and against Saladin (c. 1137-1193) and the Knights Templar are legend and there was a period during which in order to avoid being caught between the two factions, he made an annual tribute payment to the Templars of two thousand gold pieces. Sinan became a Syrian hero who maintained independence from the surrounding powers by terrorizing them.

Saladin (Salāh al-Dīn Yūsuf ibn Ayyūb), a Kurdish Muslim who at the height of his power ruled over Mesopotamia, Syria, Yemen, Egypt and Hejaz (a western region in present-day Saudi Arabia), also led the Muslims against European Crusaders and recaptured Palestine from the Crusader Kingdom of Jerusalem. Consequently an apprehensive Sinan decided to have Saladin killed but his Assassins met with failure on several occasions. According to legend Saladin stopped persecuting the Ismailis because he awoke one morning to find by his pillow a poisoned dagger that had been placed there by the Assassins as a warning. The more likely explanation, however, is that Saladin and Sinan had pooled their resources, at least temporarily, against the Crusaders. Sinan appears to have helped Saladin's cause by dispatching two Assassins to kill Conrad of Montferrat, Prince of Tyre and King of Jerusalem in 1192.

'. . . *two youths lightly clad, who wore*
No cloaks, and each a dagger bore,

> *Made straight for him, and with one bound,*
> *Smote him and bore him to the ground,*
> *And each one stabbed him with his blade,*
> *The wretches, who thus wise betrayed*
> *Him, were of the Assassin's men . . .'*
> **Twelfth-century Chronicle of Ambroise**

The Crusades had been "holy wars" that were specifically waged to seize property from the heretic and heathen enemies of orthodox Christianity and were usually fought by vassals of Christian overlords and well-heeled clergy. As well as the usual spoils of war, the crusaders were also rewarded with indulgences such as remission of sins and a guaranteed admission to heaven irrespective of how heinous a crime they may have committed.

The Ismaili sect did manage to survive and there are now an estimated sixteen million adherents worldwide whose leader, claiming direct descent from the Prophet Muhammed, is the Aga Khan. The most colourful of Ismaili leaders was Sultan Mahommed Shah, Aga Khan III (1877-1957) who enjoyed the "sport of kings" including the ownership of thoroughbred racing horses who managed a total of sixteen wins in British Classic Races. Another of his distractions was a succession of women with three of his four marriages being to European Christians all of whom did not covert to Islam. In defense of his fondness for alcohol, Sultan Mohammed Shah was quoted as having said "I'm so holy that when I touch wine, it turns to water." This is incidentally a biological function which is within the capacity of all human beings and hardly worth boasting about.

His successor, Shah Karim al-Hussayni Aga Khan IV, who apart from also being a racehorse owner and breeder, is an international business magnate whom *Forbes* magazine described as one of the world's ten richest royals with an estimated net worth of $800 million. His Highness Aga Khan IV has apparently inherited his father's penchant for European ladies with both his marriages to date being to former British model Sarah ("Sally") Frances Croker-Poole (1969-1995 with a £20 million divorce settlement and the sale of jewelry worth £17.5 million), and a German-born princess Gabriele zu Leiningen (1998-2011 with a £54 million divorce settlement following a long-standing adulterous affair between His Highness and air hostess Beatrice von der Schulenburg). So for Nizari Ismaili leaders — who are considered by their followers as being proof or the *hujjah* (completion of proof) of God on earth: as being infallible and immune from sin; and as being the carriers of the eternal *Noor of Allah* (Light of God) — it is business as usual. In fairness it should be mentioned that the Aga Khan's philanthropic institutions spend some $600 million per year primarily in Africa, Asia, and the Middle East. This is funded by his followers who by means of a complicated system of tithes each pay him 12.5 percent of their gross income annually thus providing a personal fortune (for use by him and his family) in excess of $1 billion.

Even the Ismaili sect had its dissenters so that by the eleventh century the Druze religion had emerged without attempting to reform mainstream Islam, but instead to create an entirely new faith that combined various Christian, Iranian, and Jewish elements influenced by Greek philosophy and Gnosticism that included the Druze reincarnating as future descendants. They regard themselves theologically as "an Islamic reformatory sect," calling themselves *Ahl al-Tawhid* ("People of Monotheism") or *al-Muwahhidūn* ("Monotheists"). The origin of the name *Druze* is traced to Nashtakin ad-Darazi, one of the first preachers of the religion.

Ad-Darazi, who was confessor to the sixth Fātimid caliph al-Hakim bi-Amr Allah — an impostor ruling "by the Command of Allah" over Egypt (reigned 996–1021) and thought by the Druze to be an actual incarnation of God — began promoting the religion from around 1017. The Druze who divulge few details of their faith also practice *taqiyya* which still permits them to outwardly deny their faith in the event of persecution or danger to life. They are prohibited from dating, intermarrying, or converting either out of or into the Druze religion. Those who violate this rule can be excommunicated or killed.

Druze reside mostly in Lebanon (thirty to forty percent), Israel (six to seven percent), Syria (forty to fifty percent), and to a lesser extent in Jordan (one to two percent) where they are officially recognised as a separate religious communities with their own religious court systems. Expatriate communities of Druze also live in Australia, Canada, Europe, Latin America, the U.S., and West Africa. They speak Arabic and regard themselves as Arab in every country they inhabit apart from Israel where they are granted a privileged status in exchange for their loyalty to the state which includes fighting for the Israeli Defense Force alongside Jews. This willingness to fight for Israel has naturally strained relations with the Palestinian people.

The Druze symbol consists of five colours with each pertaining to a symbol defining its principles: green for □*Aql* "the Universal Mind"; red for Nafs (cognate of the Hebrew word *Nefesh)* "the Universal Soul"; yellow for *Kalima* "the Truth/Word"; blue for *Sabq* "the Antagonist/ Cause"; and white for *Talī* "the Protagonist/Effect." The number "five" representing those principles, has a special significance in the Druze community, and is usually represented by a five-pointed star.

The Druze are split into two groups with members of the inner spiritual elite group called al-□Uqqāl "the Knowledgeable Initiates" having undergone secret initiations that gives them access to the secret teachings of the Druze religious doctrine, the hikmah. Women —being regarded as spiritually superior to men — are considered especially suitable to become □Uqqāl and as such can opt to wear *al-mandīl,* a transparent loose white veil, especially in the presence of religious figures. The *al-mandīl* is worn on the head to cover the hair and wrap around the mouth and sometimes over the nose. Female □*uqqāl* wear black shirts and long skirts covering their legs to their ankles. Male □*uqqāl* grow mustaches, shave their heads, and wear dark clothing with white turbans.

Members of the outer group, called *al-Juhhāl* "the Ignorant," who are not allowed access to the secret Druze holy literature, comprise some ninety percent of the Druze and form the political and military leadership while mostly distancing themselves from religious matters. The question has to be asked as to what credibility and benefits are on offer from a religion that considers most of its adherents to be *ignorant* and *unworthy* of access to its doctrines.

THE CRUSADERS

When in 1095 the Byzantine Emperor Alexius I Comnenus sent envoys to the West requesting military assistance against the Seljuk Turks, it was a timely event for the Holy Roman Empire which had itself been harassed for the past two centuries by Norsemen who owned numerous northern trading centers and dominated the sea routes. Furthermore, negotiations with North African and Middle Eastern powers had culminated in 834 with an Arabian delegation visiting Denmark to complete military and trade alliances that left the Holy Roman Empire trapped between two anti-Christian forces.

The Byzantine Emperor's request for assistance therefore provided Pope Urban II at the Council of Claremont in 1095 with an excuse to initiate a crusade — as a penitential pilgrimage and a war of conquest — against the infidels with the alleged intent of regaining the Holy Land for Christianity. So with the promise that volunteers would be placed above restrictions of law, receive forgiveness for all their sins, and enjoyment of eternal bliss in heaven without time in purgatory, a ragtag force — consisting mostly of social outcasts and soldiers of fortune — of between 150,000 to 300,000 was assembled.

As the force traversed southern Europe they pillaged, tortured, and murdered with one division slaughtering 10,000 Jews in the Rhineland before abandoning thoughts of the Holy Land and disbanding. Two other divisions perpetrated so many atrocities in Hungary that native soldiers were eventually roused to oppose and wipe them all out. Of the others, thousands died en-route from starvation, disease, or wounds resulting from violence. Those who survived then despoiled the Greeks before making their way to Constantinople where the more powerful of them financed their own existence by selling off the decrepit amongst them as slaves. Of the 7,000 who eventually crossed the Bosphorus, none survived the merciless onslaughts by Turkish forces.

Despite the utter failure of this initial crusade, more were to follow which with hindsight were better organised with seasoned soldiers and fewer penitential pilgrims. For the next 400 hundred years Christian Knights in the Holy Land waged wars whose barbarity in the name of God, knew no bounds. One contemporaneous report stated that after laying siege to Jerusalem for one month, the Crusaders rode into the city with their horses "knee-deep in the blood of disbelievers." Jews were herded into their synagogues and burnt alive, and on the following day Christian knights slaughtered "a great multitude of people of every age, old men and women, maidens, children and mothers with infants, by way of a solemn sacrifice" to Jesus.

After the siege of Acre which ended in 1191, King Richard I of England, Richard the Lionheart (1157-1199) broke his promise of truce by having his Muslim hostages slaughtered:

> *His conduct stands in strong contrast with the dignity and forbearance of Saladin, before whose eyes the outrage was committed, and who would not stoop to retaliate on his dastardly opponent.*

Establishment of the ongoing crusades also enabled the Holy Roman Empire to take punitive military measures against Europe's heathens and heretics so that the sword became the traditional method of Christianizing the West at the cost of between 8 to 10 million lives The Catharan or Albigensian heretics in the Languedoc region of Southern France — who regarded the Roman Church as the Synagogue of Satan and called for a return to the Christian message of perfection, poverty, and preaching — became the recipients of particularly barbaric treatment after Pope Innocent III declared a crusade in 1209 against the Languedoc with the promise that Cathar lands would be given to French noblemen willing to take up arms.

The Albigensian Crusade is still to this day one of the darkest and bloodiest chapters in the history of Christian persecutions. When it was enquired of a papal legate as to how heretics were to be distinguished from the faithful, he replied, "Kill them all; God will know his own." The ensuing slaughter lasted for twenty years with an estimate of more than a million lives being lost. In trying to justify the scale of such wanton carnage, the best that Christian apologists could come up with was "The Church, after all, was only defending herself." This flagrant lie for an excuse is one that present-day Israelis have artfully become adept at during the last sixty or more years as they continue to "defend themselves" while robbing, displacing, persecuting and murdering the Palestinian people. Despite the carnage in Europe, it was the crusades to the Holy Land that received the most attention especially after the formation of the Knights Templar who became a force to be reckoned with. The seed for the founding of the Order of the Poor Knights of

Christ and the Temple of Solomon was sown in 1118 when Hugues de Payen, a nobleman from Champagne, and eight comrades presented themselves at the palace of Jerusalem's King Baudouin I whose elder brother, Godfroi de Bouillon, had captured the Holy City nineteen years earlier. Their stated objective was to protect the pilgrim routes to Jerusalem and other holy places.

Having from the beginning pledged themselves to poverty, obedience, and chastity, the Templars began to attract an extraordinary band of cavalrymen including excommunicated knights who had nothing to lose. It could be said that the Templar Order became the forerunner of the French Foreign Legion in that it used discipline and war to purge the sins of those within its ranks. Templar ranks were increased by "rogues and impious men, robbers and committers of sacrilege, murderers, perjurers, and adulterers" whose unkept demeanor and maverick methods the influential French abbot, Bernard of Clairvaux, praised highly in a letter to Hugues de Payen. Armed with Clairvaux's letter, de Payen attended the Council of Troyes in 1128 where he was granted papal sanction and exemption from excommunication for the Templars.

As religion in the Middle Ages was the beneficiary of much generosity by its followers, the Templars were themselves bequeathed many estates in England, France, and Spain by returning crusaders or Christians who believed that their own route to heaven was being guarded by those keeping watch over the road to Jerusalem. The "Order of the Poor Knights of Christ" consequently ended up with a great deal of wealth which led to their becoming a moneylending institution which attracted both envy and ill will.

As bankers to the Levant their clients included Muslims who feared that the changing fortunes of war might in the future require them to ally themselves with the Christians. Even the courts of Europe made use of the Templar banking operation which could not only provide loans, but also arrange — because of its widespread network — international money transfers. Though at that time usury was forbidden to Christians, the Templars would repay an agreed sum less than the original amount that was either banked or transferred. Debtors repaid a greater amount than that borrowed. As a result the Temple in Paris became the hub of the world's money-market.

The Templars, like most other religious sects, also had their own regulations (The Rule of the Temple) and secret initiation ceremonies which distinguished them from other orders such as the Hospitallers and the Teutonic Knights. The Order was open only to men who were obliged to observe strict vows of celibacy with the prohibition that they could neither marry nor remain married. Wives of men who became Templars were expected to join other religious orders as nuns. Templars were prohibited from kissing their mothers, wives, sisters, or any other woman. They were also cautioned to beware the wiles of women who were not even to be looked upon. During the entirety of its historical preoccupation with protecting its celibate clergymen from the wicked wiles of women, the Catholic Church has unfortunately not only neglected to protect innocent young children from the diabolic lust of its paedophile priests, it has also more often than not taken steps to cover up such religious criminality. It should be noted that the physical and sexual abuse of children by "holy men" is not peculiar to Christianity and exists within many other religions including Judaism and Islam but is not as widely reported.

Templar initiations were conducted in darkened, guarded chapter houses were the entirety of the Rule was revealed only to officers of the highest rank. After establishing that the assembled knights had no objection to the admission of a particular novice, the Master of the Temple then asked if he had a wife or betrothed, debts, a hidden disease, other vows, or some other master. After answering correctly, the Novice knelt before the Master and asked to become "the serf and slave of the House," to which the Master replied with the following:

> *You do not know the hard commandments that are within; because it is a hard thing for you, who are master of yourself, to make yourself the serf of another. For you will hardly ever do what you want; if you wish to be on this side of the sea, you will be sent to the other side; or if you wish to be in Acre, you will be sent to the land of Tripoli or Antioch or Armenia, or you will be sent to Apulia or Sicily or France or Burgundy or England or to many other lands where we have houses and possessions. And if you wish to sleep, you will be made to stay awake; and if sometimes you wish to stay awake, you will be ordered to go and rest in your bed.*

The Novice was then warned that he must not enter the order to gain advantage for himself, but to forsake the sins of the world, to serve the Lord, to be poor, and to do penitence so as to save his soul.

The Novice then swore that he would obey the Master of the Temple in everything, live all his life without private possessions, follow the customs of the House, help in the conquest of the Holy Land, stay for the rest of his life in the order "both in strength and weakness, for better or for worse," and never allow a Christian to be robbed of his possessions.

After the Novice had sworn by God and the Virgin Mary to observe all the Order's rules, the Master accepted him into the Order by draping his shoulders with a mantle and promising him "bread and water and the dress of the poor and much suffering and travail." Though dedication to such a lifestyle may seem somewhat harsh, for many who had neither hope of marriage nor inheritance of lands, being a Templar in the Levant was preferable to subsistence in the service of a feudal Lord in Europe.

The first three Templar Grand Masters were men of faith, capable, and well-organised diplomatic leaders whose banners proclaimed *Non nobis, Domin, non nobis, sed nomini tuo da gloriam* (Not to ourselves, Lord, not to ourselves, but to Thy name give the glory). Their successor Bernard de Tremelai, however, during the siege of Ascalon in 1153, ordered his knights to beat back their Christian allies so that the Templars would get all the credit for taking the town.

The ensuing succession of Templar Grand Masters were at best mediocre with the seventh of them, Philip de Milly, becoming involved in the political intrigue and quarrels that disunited Jerusalem. His successor, Odo de Saint-Amand (1170-1179) proved to be even worse — in believing that Templar independence meant being bound by no treaty — and accordingly breaking the King of Jerusalem's treaty with Saladin by which no further Templar fortresses were to be built on the frontier. His arrogance was rewarded when the fortress he built fell to Saladin with the Templar garrison being massacred and Odo himself later dying in prison in 1180 after refusing to be ransomed with the declaration that "A Templar can only offer as ransom his belt and his sword."

When Odo's nondescript aged successor died in 1184, he was succeeded by the young and ambitious Gerard de Ridfort who was destined to play a major role in Jerusalem's destruction. During the succession squabble following the death of boy-king Baldwin V (1186), Ridefort backed the unpopular Guy de Lusignan and had him crowned king instead of the regent, Raymond III of Tripoli who had Hospitaller support. The inevitable divisions amongst the crusaders were then ruthlessly exploited by Saladin whose peace treaty with the Crusaders

129

had been broken by the treacherous Prince of Antioch, Reynald de Chatillon. Saladin's response was to join forces with Raymond in 1187 and during their march to Jerusalem they encountered Ridefort and 150 of his knights outside of Nazareth. The Templars had no chance against Saladin's force of 7,000 and were all massacred apart from Ridefort who managed to escape with three of his men.

On realizing that the Crusader kingdom was on the verge of obliteration, Raymond severed his alliance with Saladin and joined the Christian forces led by Guy de Lusignan whose equipping of an army to fight Saladin was financed by the Templars. Ridefort then persuaded the indecisive Guy de Lusignan to go on the offensive against Saladin rather than adopt Raymond's preference for a campaign of delaying tactics. By taking the offensive, the Crusaders were obliged to leave behind their water supplies and then advance across a searingly hot and inhospitable desert to eventually come to a halt on the scorched double hill that formed the Horns of Hattin.

Saladin who had just captured the nearby town of Tiberias (now in present-day Israel), had the Crusaders surrounded and forced up the hill slopes. Being crazed with thirst, the Crusaders made repeated unsuccessful attempts to reach the freshwater lake of Tiberias (Sea of Galilee). Though Raymond and his knights managed to break through the Muslim encirclement, the remaining Crusaders were less fortunate with the result that most of them were slaughtered. The surviving Templars and Hospitallers, who had fought valiantly in a desperate situation, were not spared by Saladin who had them — apart from Ridefort — all beheaded. Ridefort, who as a free man was vocally courageous and physically aggressive, turned out to be a cowering yellow-belly in captivity who ordered the garrisons of the remaining Templar fortresses to surrender to Saladin. The fall of Jerusalem followed months later in October 1187.

Ridefort's brief rule as Templar Grand Master was a calamity from which the Templars never recovered. So despite subsequently regaining some of their former wealth and power even in the Levant, the Templars had forever lost their renown for religious zealotry and instead — to best serve their own interests — sheathed their swords along with compromises that accommodated Muslim rule and custom. The fact that they — unlike other Christian orders — also spoke Arabic and wore long beards in the Muslim fashion, provided ammunition for their detractors who had never forgotten that the first Templar home had been situated in a mosque built on the alleged site of Solomon's Temple in Jerusalem.

Even the Templars themselves were never slow to acknowledge their knowledge of the esoteric doctrines of the East; that their discipline for fasting, prayer and punishment for sins were sufficiently severe to meet the most demanding standards of Islam; that they were proud of their devotion to the Virgin Mary who also featured in the Koran; and that they recognised survival in the Levant was dependent on their having Arab allies in a divided Arab world.

Ridefort's successors proved to be less cavalier as Grand Masters and were cautiously instrumental in the great siege of Acre and following the city's eventual capture, made it their new headquarters. They also supported Richard the Lionheart's failed attempt to capture Jerusalem during the Third Crusade (1191-1192) and when Richard was forced to flee the Holy Land he did so disguised as a Templar in one of their galleys.

The Fourth Crusade (1202-1204) — which was originally intended as an invasion from Egypt to recapture Jerusalem from the Muslims — ended up instead as an attack by West European Crusaders (the objective of whose First Crusade was to help Christianity in the East) on the Eastern Orthodox Christian city of Constantinople. This treacherous attack on Eastern Christianity served not only to widen the schism between the Eastern Orthodox Church and the Roman Catholic Church, but also led to the decline in the Near East of both empire and Christianity.

The Fifth Crusade (1213-1221) was another attempt by Christian Europeans to recapture Jerusalem and the rest of the Holy Land by first conquering the powerful Egyptian Ayyubid state. Apart from the initial mainly Templar success at the siege of the port of Damietta in Egypt, little else was, however, achieved in further Christian actions despite having at their core the experience of the Templars and Hospitallers. Pope Innocent III and his successor Pope Honorius III both organised crusades led by King Andrew II of Hungary and Duke Leopold VI of Austria with incursions against Muslim Jerusalem ending in failure.

Later in 1218, a German army led by Oliver of Cologne, and a mixed army of Dutch, Flemish, and Frisian forces led by William I, Count of Holland joined the crusade. In order to attack Damietta they allied in Anatolia with the Seljuk Sultanate of Rûm which attacked the Ayyubids in Syria with a view to freeing the Crusaders from fighting on two fronts. After occupying Damietta, the Crusaders in July 1221 marched south towards Cairo but were repulsed when their diminishing supplies forced them to retreat. Sultan Al-Kamil's nighttime attack took a heavy toll on the Crusaders who eventually surrendered and agreed to an eight-year peace treaty with Al-Kamil.

Though the Templars were no longer the power they once were, they nonetheless had not lost all their strutting confidence and at the start of the Sixth Crusade (1128-1129) refused along with the Hospitallers to help the Crusade's leader, Frederick II (one of the most powerful Holy Roman Emperors of the time) who had been excommunicated by Pope Gregory IX for political reasons.

After first sailing to Cyprus — an imperial fiefdom since its capture by Richard the Lionheart — and becoming involved in a dispute with the island's Constable, Frederick eventually had to face the reality that his force lacked the manpower to engage the Ayyubid empire in battle and that his only hope of any success in the Holy Land was to negotiate for the surrender of Jerusalem. He also hoped that a token show of force, a threatening march down the coast, would be enough to persuade Al-Kamil, the sultan of Egypt, to honor a proposed treaty that had been negotiated some years earlier, prior to the death of al-Muazzam, the governor of Damascus. The Egyptian sultan, preoccupied with trying to suppress rebellious forces in Syria, agreed to cede Jerusalem along with a narrow corridor to the coast.

Frederick was also given Nazareth, Sidon, Jaffa, and Bethlehem. In a sensible compromise, Frederick in turn allowed the Muslims to retain control over Jerusalem's Temple Mount, the site of the Al-Aqsa Mosque and the Dome of the Rock. The Transjordan castles remained under Ayyubid control with the further understanding that Jerusalem's fortifications were not to be restored. Completion of the treaty on February 18, 1229, guaranteed truce of ten years.

Frederick entered Jerusalem on 17 March 1229 where on the following day he attended a crowning ceremony. Whether this was intended to signify his official coronation as King of Jerusalem, cannot be certain, especially as the patriarch, Gerald, was not in attendance. As Frederick had pressing matters to attend to back home, he departed Jerusalem in May having proved that success in a crusade was possible without either military superiority or papal support. By emulating Frederick's precedent of leading successful a crusade without papal involvement, subsequent crusades were launched by individual kings —

Louis IX of France (seventh and Eighth Crusades), Edward I of England (Ninth Crusade) — to further erode papal authority.

The truce, however, was unpopular from the first day of its inception and after its expiry in 1239, a new threat appeared over the horizon in the form of the formidable Mongol, Genghis Khan. Christian hopes of an alliance with Genghis Kahn to defeat the Muslims were, however, quickly dashed when Khwarezmian Turks — displaced by the Mongols — skirted the Templar fortress at Safed and proceeded to sack the Holy City of Jerusalem in June 1244. Then in October, the Egyptians and the Khwarezmians led by Baibars, the future sultan of Egypt, fought the Crusaders at La Forbie, a small village northeast of Gaza, killing 5,000 including the Templar Grand Master and taking 800 as prisoners. From the ranks of the knightly orders, only thirty-three Templar, twenty-seven Hospitaller, and three Teutonic knights survived.

The Seventh Crusade (1248-1254) led by King Louis IX of France provided the Templars with an opportunity to regain some of Order's lost stature. With Acre still serving as headquarters for Crusader operations, Damietta was once again taken; but against Templar advice Louis advanced into Egypt and suffered defeat at the battle of Mansura in 1250.

From that point on Templars fortunes began to decline and back in France King Louis IX's concern for what was left of the Crusader states — the Templars, squeezed between the Egyptians and the Mongols, had gradually lost most of their strongholds — prompted his launching of the Eighth Crusade (1270) which like the Ninth Crusade (1271-1272) was limited in scope and short on achievement. In 1291 Tripoli fell and was quickly followed by the fall of Acre which signaled the end of any further Crusades to regain the Holy Land from the Muslims.

The Templars, however, were by no means an entirely spent force and the order still had some 20,000 members as well as the accumulated wealth of its European holdings. So with that in mind they still harboured hopes of setting up base in Cyprus and recapturing the Holy Land. Apart from being unrealistic, such hopes were also tempered by developments back in France where King Philip IV — who had for some time been trying to curb the French Temple's independent power — decided to borrow heavily from the Templars in return for his protection.

In 1303 after severing relations with Pope Boniface VIII, Philip signed a formal treaty of alliance with the Templars in France and granted them control of state finances. Two years later when he was attacked by a mob in Paris, Philip took refuge in the Temple whose members he was destined to later persecute and have killed. Although moneylenders are despised at the best of times — even by those who out of desperation borrow from them — they become even more despicable when their lending power is used to either influence or control the rights and destinies of others.

Following the Paris mob incident, Philip was presented with an excuse for ridding himself of the Templar yoke of debt from around his neck when a disgruntled former Templar, Esquiu de Forian, unleashed a lurid denunciation of the Order and its practices. That same year, the France-based newly-elected Pope Clement V, wrote to both the Templar Grand Master Jacques de Molay and the Hospitaller Grand Master Fulk de Villaret proposing the possibility of merging the two Orders, but neither was receptive to the idea.

Despite their initial reluctance for a merger, the two Grand Masters finally relented to Pope Clement persistence and in 1306 accepted his invitation to meet in France. De Molay was the first to arrive in early 1307 but then had to wait for several months because de Villaret had been delayed which provided de Molay and Clement with an opportunity to discuss Esquiu de Florian's 1305 denunciation of the Templars. Though they both agreed that the allegations were at best spurious, Pope Clement nonetheless dispatched a written request for assistance with the investigation to King Philip who as a result of his war with the English was deeply in debt to the Templars.

Having already expelled the Jews and exiled the Lombard bankers (Italian pawnbroking system), Philip used spies to join the Order and uncover its covert iniquitousness. So as a means of relieving himself from his enormous debt to the Templars, Philip first pressured the Church to act against the Order, and then on Friday, 13 October 1307 ordered the simultaneous arrest of de Molay and other French Templars. The arrest warrant began with the phrase, "God is not pleased. We have enemies of the faith in the kingdom," and went on to charge the Templars with numerous offenses including apostasy, financial corruption and fraud, heresy, homosexuality, idolatry, obscene rituals, and secrecy.

Despite their valor in battle, few templars could withstand the torture with whips, screws, and racks and thirty-six of them died within a few days of their arrest. The remainder in the meantime confessed to whatever their torturers wanted to hear. Pope Clement — after further pressure and bullying from Philip — then issued the papal bull Pastoralis

Praeeminentiae on 22 November 1307, which instructed all Christian monarchs in Europe to arrest all Templars and seize their assets.

Pope Clement also held papal hearings to determine the Templars' guilt or innocence, and on being freed from the inquisitors' torture, many Templars recanted their confessions. In 1310 Philip blocked attempts by Templars with legal knowledge to defend themselves and insisted on the use of the previously forced confessions to have scores of Templars burned at the stake in Paris. Further threats by Philip to resort to military action if necessary then forced Pope Clement in 1312 to finally accede to Philip's demands by issuing a series of papal bulls at the Council of Vienne that officially dissolved the Order and transferred most of its assets to the Hospitallers.

Though Grand Master Jacques de Molay and the Preceptor of Normandy, Geoffroi de Charney, both retracted their confessions and insisted on their innocence, they were nonetheless found guilty as relapsed heretics and were burnt alive at the stake in Paris on 18 March 1314. De Molay was reportedly defiant to the end and legend suggests that he called out from the flames that both Pope Clement and King Philip would soon meet him before God: "God knows who is wrong and has sinned. Soon a calamity will occur to those who have condemned us to death." Pope Clement died a month later, and King Philip died in a hunting accident before the year's end.

In 1919 in Kansas City, Missouri, the Order of DeMolay — also known as DeMolay International and deriving its name from the last Templar Grand Master Jacques de Molay — was founded by Frank S. Land, a Freemason. Modeled after and sponsored by Freemasonry, it is an organization for young men between the ages of 12 to 21. Although none of the youth groups are "Masonic" as such, DeMolay is considered to be part of the general "family" of Masonic and associated organizations, along with other youth groups such as Job's Daughters (young women aged between ten and twenty) and Rainbow which are both Masonic sponsored youth organizations for young girls.

DeMolay has seven Cardinal Virtues, which constitute the basic ideals and essential teachings of the organization. They are: Filial love (love between a parent and child); Reverence for sacred things; Courtesy; Comradeship; Fidelity; Cleanness; and Patriotism. Though regarded as a "grooming" organization for Freemasonry, DeMolay members are not obliged to become Freemasons. One of those who did not become a Freemason was Bill Clinton, who also failed miserably on the question of fidelity to his wife. Other notable former members included Walt Disney, John Steinbeck, and John Wayne.

In September 2001, a discovery was made in the Vatican Secret Archives of document known as the "Chinon Parchment" dated 17-20 August 1308 which in 1628 had been wrongly filed. It is a record of the Templars trials showing that Pope Clement absolved the Templars of all heresies in 1308 before formally disbanding the Order in 1312. Another Chinon Parchment addressed to Philip IV of France and dated 20 August 1308, also mentions that all Templars that had confessed to heresy had been "restored to the Sacraments and to the unity of the Church." The current position of the Roman Catholic Church is that the medieval persecution of the Knights Templar was unjust, that nothing was inherently wrong with the Order, its Rule, or its conduct, and that Pope Clement had been pressured by both the impact of the scandal and the dominating influence of King Philip IV, who was Pope Clement's relative.

Following the loss of their leaders and the arrest of many of their brothers-in-arms, the remaining Templars dispersed throughout Europe by either enlisting with other military orders such as the Knights Hospitaller, or by joining trade associations and covert brotherhoods such as the Carbonari (charcoal-burners). The earliest known existence of organised leagues of charcoal-burners with political objectives dates back to the twelfth century when they were probably formed to counter the severe forest laws that were in existence in those days. At about the same time corporations of Fendeurs (hewers) with similar rites and secret signs of recognition existed in Jura (a department in eastern France named after the Jura mountains) where the associations were known as le Bon Cousinage (the good cousinship). In view of the important services that could be rendered on a countrywide basis by members of such associations, many powerful lords with political agendas and persecuted individuals such as the Templars either became members themselves or entered into secret treaties with them.

Attempts to prosecute the Templars in England were mostly unsuccessful because King Edward II — who was also Philip of France's son-in-law — initially sided with the Order before succumbing to pressure from Philip and Pope Clement. The ensuing prosecutions, however, were half-hearted with light sentences for some and the remainder escaping mostly to Scotland which was at war with England. The English Templars were joined by many of their French brothers and a large contingent of both is said to have fought with Robert the Bruce (1274-1329) at the Battle of Bannockburn in 1314 where Edward II's much larger English force was defeated. It has since been suggested that it was in Scotland that the Templars became seriously involved and entwined with the Masonic lodges — whose propensity for secrecy and intrigue — must have appealed to Templars already conditioned by the covert and conniving nature of their own Order.

Today there is no shortage of legends and theories regarding these warrior monks who guarded pilgrims traveling to the Holy Land, formed the backbone of successive Crusades, and allegedly derived their wealth and power from something they discovered by digging under the ruins of the Second Temple whose site is claimed by Judaism to be the Holy of Holies and initially the inner sanctuary of the Tabernacle where the Arc of the Covenant containing the Ten Commandments was kept during the period of the First Temple.

What it was that the Templars discovered has long remained the subject of much speculation with some scholars and numerous authors suggesting vast amounts of treasure, the Holy Grail, the severed head of John the Baptist, and even a historical record of the Nazarene family of Jesus. But with all the suggestions put forward there at least one week link within the chain of reasoning.

Why for instance would Judaic priests bury their own treasures and relics with those of a relatively small and little known Christian sect that was still competing with numerous other equally small religions? Christianity did not become a major religion until the patronage of the Byzantine Emperor Constantine (272-337) which occurred more than two centuries after the Jerusalem's sacking by the Romans, the razing to the ground of the temple, and the exile from the city of many but not all Jews.

Even the theory that it was of the Holy Grail that had been discovered must be discounted because the Grail does not appear in any form of literature until the Dark Age (c. 11th-13th century) legend of King Arthur and his knights. Inexplicably these legends have often been accepted as historical facts. In those days it was common practice to weave fictional tales with metaphors and examinations of current events portrayed by fabled characters as was the case with King Arthur and the Holy Grail in Chrétien de Troyes' *Percival.* As the great empires of the classical world collapsed, such tales served to inspire hope for a Europe wallowing in the quagmire of plagues and pandemonium, and then survived to fuse with historical notions to become part of modern mythology. The Templars therefore could not have discovered something that could not possibly have been there.

The most plausible explanation for what the Templars actually found is simply one of an ancient Jewish treasure. Such treasure would probably have consisted mainly of first century gold coins that would have helped finance their rapid acquisition of property, power, and the political influence that results from lending money to nobles and royals. It was that wealth, power and wide-ranging influence that would ultimately cause the Templars downfall.

1
Friday, 5 December 2008
Phoenicia InterContinental Hotel, Beirut, Lebanon

The Phoenicia Hotel became a battlefield in the Lebanese Civil War in 1975-6 during fighting known as the Battle of the hotels — which occurred in the Minet-el-Hosn hotel district of downtown Beirut — and ended up being a burnt-out ruin. The battle was the first large-scale clash between the Christian-conservative Lebanese Front and the Leftist-Muslim Lebanese National Movement (LNM) militias and PLO fighters. The battle was fought for the possession of a small hotel complex adjacent to the Corniche on the Mediterranean seafront in the north-west corner of the downtown Beirut and quickly spread to other areas of central Beirut. It was a fiercely fought conflict with sniper fire and heavy exchanges of rocket and artillery fire from hotel rooms and rooftops. Ultimately the Christian militias were pushed out of the area's hotels including the Alcazar, Excelsior, Holiday Inn Beirut, Hilton, Normandy, Palm Beach, St. Georges, and of course the Phoenicia.

After being abandoned for some twenty-five years until the late 1990s, the Phoenicia underwent extensive renovation work with the addition of a third tower and re-opened in March 2000. It was, however, damaged again in the 2005 bombing assassination of Rafiq Hariri — business tycoon and Lebanese Prime Minister from 1992 to 1998 and again from 2000 until his resignation in October 2004 — in the street in front of the hotel causing it to close again for three months for repairs.

Despite its violent history, the Phoenicia was still Mark Banner's favorite Beirut watering hole. He was well known to the staff and during the summer months between June and September he would often enjoy a drink by the outdoor pool while working and enjoying the sight of bronzed bikini-clad young ladies. It was in fact at the Phoenicia that he had met his girlfriend Nadine. Today, however, with the onset of Beirut's mild winter, he was having his morning coffee in the lounge while reading the final draft of his weekend article which he was due to despatch to London later that afternoon:

Mark Banner
Sunday, 7 December 2008

Israel's Misuse of Administrative Detention Orders Must be Condemned

It has been common practice for Palestinian people to be imprisoned since the beginning of the 1967 Israeli Occupation and to a much lesser degree, under the previous British Mandate. The more controversial aspect of this arbitrary imprisonment is administrative detention whose frequent use by Israel has been rising steadily. Most Palestinian families have at some stage had at least one family member in jail with the number being held as of November 2008 now totaling 8,218 most of whom were dealt with by the frequently criticized so-called Israeli military justice system. Of those prisoners, 5,393 are serving a sentence; 286 are detainees; 1,970 are being detained until the conclusion of legal proceedings; and 569 are administrative detainees.

Administrative detention is a procedure that allows the Israeli military to hold prisoners indefinitely on secret information without charging them or allowing them to stand trial. Although administrative detention is used almost exclusively to detain Palestinians from the occupied Palestinian territories — which include the West Bank, East Jerusalem and the Gaza Strip — Israeli citizens and foreign nationals can also be held as administrative detainees, but over the years, only 9 Israeli "terrorist" settlers have been held in administrative detention. Although international human rights laws permit some degree of administrative detention use in emergency situations, the authorities are nonetheless required to follow basic rules for detention including a fair hearing at which the detainee can challenge the reasons for his or her detention. Furthermore, in order to use such detention, there must be a public emergency that threatens the life of the nation with detention only being permitted on an individual, case-by-case basis without discrimination of any kind. (International Covenant on Civil and Political Rights, Article 9).

Administrative detention constitutes the most extreme measure that international humanitarian laws allow an occupying power to use against residents of an occupied territory. Using administrative detention in a sweeping manner is permitted against protected persons in occupied territory only for "imperative reasons of security" (Fourth Geneva Convention, Article 78).

In practice, however, Israel uses administrative detention routinely in violation of the strict parameters established by international law. In mitigation for its blatant violations, Israel has claimed to be under a continuous state of emergency since achieving statehood in 1948. Furthermore, it frequently uses administrative detention — in direct contravention of international law — for collective and criminal punishment rather than for the prevention of threats to the state. Administrative detention orders are for example routinely issued against individuals suspected of committing an offense after an unsuccessful criminal investigation or a failure to obtain a confession during interrogation and torture.

In reality, Israel's administrative detention regime also violates numerous other international standards with administrative detainees from the West Bank being deported from the occupied territories and interned inside Israel in direct violation of Fourth Geneva Convention prohibitions (Articles 49 and 76); administrative detainees are often denied regular family visits in accordance with international law standards; there is a regular Israeli failure to separate administrative detainees from the regular prison population as required by law; and with regard to child detainees, an indefensible Israeli failure to take into account the best interests of the child as required by international law.

The iniquities of administrative detention include the detainees' inability to know or challenge the secret information on which they are being held; unlike with a fixed sentence, detainees never know when they will be released; some detainees have been held for up to ten years with no way of knowing when or if they will ever be released and united with their families; the use of psychological torture by Israel whereby detainees leaving prison clutching their few belongings when their detention order has expired, are then issued with a renewed detention order and returned immediately to prison; and the effect on the families of the detainees of indefinite detention without recourse to an impartial legal process.

Apart from excessive and unjustified use of administrative detention, the Israelis — with the world's most moral army — have increasingly targeted Palestinian children (some as young as six years of age) for the dual purpose of discouraging them from participating in protest demonstrations; and for getting them, without any legal representation, to sign confessions that are in Hebrew and therefore beyond the Arab-speaking children's comprehension. These "child

141

confessions" — brutally extracted during interrogations by brave Israeli adults — are then used as the evidence to justify arresting the adult members of their family and placing them in administrative detention. Such arrests are usually carried out in the middle of the night when doors are knocked down and homes ransacked so as to disorientate and instill fear in both the young and the old. Rights groups have investigated and documented interrogation centers where detainees have no access to lawyers and are harshly treated while being in isolation within tiny, unhygienic cells without windows. Prison life for Palestinian detainees is really hard with inhuman living conditions and barbarous interrogation techniques. Many have become sick or blind and some have died.

It is inexcusable for any civilised society in the West or anywhere else in the world to either tolerate without question or fail to challenge and condemn Apartheid Israel's treatment of the Palestinian people.

International outrage and boycotts helped to end Apartheid in South Africa. So why is there no global outrage and boycott to end Israel's Apartheid regime? Is it because people have been brainwashed and blackmailed into feeling guilty about the Holocaust? Well, if people in the West are not hypocrites and do really feel strongly about human rights, then is it not time for them to stand up and be counted? They could for example start by joining the Boycott, Divestment and Sanctions (BDS) campaign against Israel — with a clear conscience and no hint of anti-Semitism — because the Palestinian people are now the victims who incidentally had absolutely nothing to do with the Holocaust. Despite the injustice and all the tribulations they are faced with, Palestinians still believe that having to suffer is an essential part of their resistance — to Israel's illegal occupation — which will ultimately lead to their freedom.

> *What I want you to take away from my life story is just how important it is to defend your freedom, at all costs. Experience has shown me that if you lose your freedom, you are condemned to fail.*
> **Leon Schgrin, Holocaust survivor.**

> *Those who deny freedom to others deserve it not for themselves.*
> **Abraham Lincoln (1809-1865), who as 16th President of the U.S., led the country through its greatest constitutional, military, and moral crisis — the American**

Civil War — preserving the Union, abolishing slavery, strengthening the national government and modernizing the economy.

A cynical, mercenary, demagogic press will produce in time a people as base as itself.
Joseph Pulitzer (1847-1911), Hungarian-American Jewish newspaper publisher of the *St. Louis Post Dispatch* and the *New York World.*

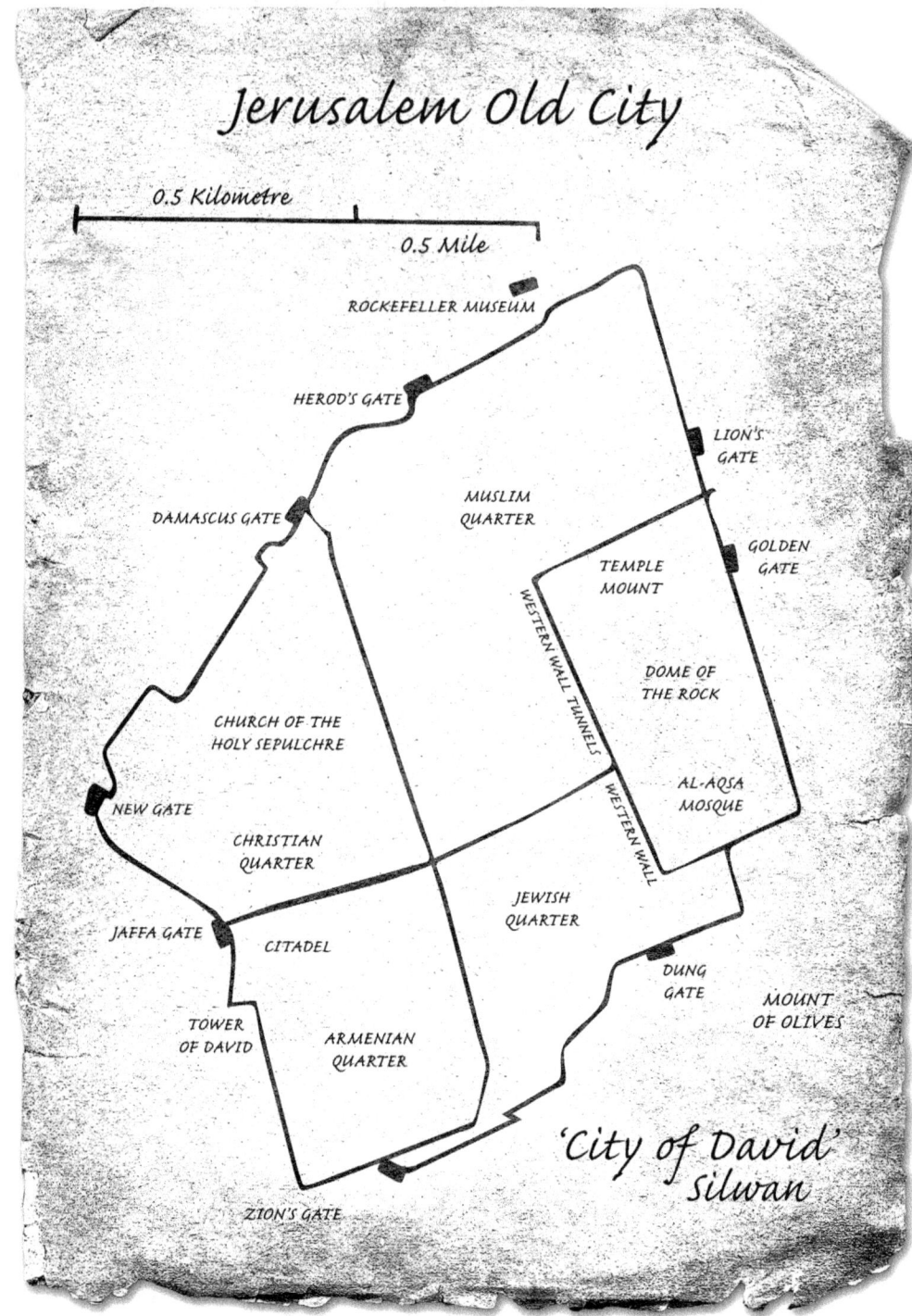

Jerusalem Old City

0.5 Kilometre

0.5 Mile

ROCKEFELLER MUSEUM

HEROD'S GATE

LION'S GATE

DAMASCUS GATE

MUSLIM QUARTER

TEMPLE MOUNT

GOLDEN GATE

WESTERN WALL TUNNELS

DOME OF THE ROCK

CHURCH OF THE HOLY SEPULCHRE

WESTERN WALL

NEW GATE

AL-AQSA MOSQUE

CHRISTIAN QUARTER

JEWISH QUARTER

JAFFA GATE

CITADEL

DUNG GATE

TOWER OF DAVID

ARMENIAN QUARTER

MOUNT OF OLIVES

'City of David' Silwan

ZION'S GATE

Damascus Gate

The ever watchful occupiers

2
Saturday, 6 December 2008
Old City Wall Ramparts, East Jerusalem

The Hebrew Bible tells us that the Jebusites (a Canaanite tribe) had built and inhabited Jerusalem (then known as Jebus) prior to its alleged conquest by King David either at the end of the tenth or the start of the eleventh century BCE. Supposedly known as Ir David (City of David) while under his mythical rule, it apparently lay southwest of the Old City's Dung Gate. King Solomon, David's son, is said to have extended the walls of the city which centuries later at around 440 BCE were rebuilt by Nehemiah, cup-bearer to Artaxerxes the Persian king who granted him permission to return from Babylon for that purpose. Centuries later in between the years 41 and 44 a new "Third Wall" was built by Agrippa, king of Judea. In the seventh century (637) the city was annexed to the Islamic Arab Empire by the second caliph, the tolerant Umar Ibn al-Khattab who was welcomed by Sophronius, the Patriarch of Jerusalem and subsequent saint to both Catholic and Eastern Orthodox churches. Umar decreed that Muslims could not gather for prayer at the site of the Church of the Holy Sepulchre which is said to contain the burial place of Jesus Christ.

The Western Christian army of the First Crusade captured Jerusalem in 1099 and held on to it until its recapture by Saladin in 1187 when he summoned the Jews and allowed them to resettle in the city. In 1219 Mu'azzim, the Sultan of Damascus, razed the walls of the city which a decade later was by treaty with Egypt handed to Frederick II of Germany who in 1239 began rebuilding the walls only for them to be yet again destroyed by Da'ud, the emir of Kerak (part of Jordan). During the brief period of Christian control of Jerusalem in 1243, the walls were repaired but again razed the following year when Kharezmian Tatars captured the city.

The current walls of the Old City were built by Sultan Suleiman the Magnificent of the Ottoman Empire and stretch for approximately 4.5 kilometres (2.8 miles); are three metres thick (ten feet); and in some places rise to a height of fifteen metres (49 feet). There are 43 surveillance towers and eleven gates of which seven are open for access. The Old City itself is divided roughly into Armenian, Christian, Jewish and Muslim quarters with their designations having been introduced in the 19th century. Following the Arab-Israeli War in 1948, Jordan captured the Old city and expelled the Jews.

Jordan's tenure, however, was short-lived and it lost control of East Jerusalem when Israel on June 5, 1967 launched surprise military attacks against Egypt, Jordan, and Syria which it subsequently claimed was a preemptive strike necessitated by impending Arab aggression. The fact that this was another Israeli lie is confirmed by the following statements:

> *The thesis that the danger of genocide was hanging over us in June 1967 and that Israel was fighting for its physical existence is only bluff, which was born and developed after the war.*
> **Israeli General Matiyahu Peled, *Ha'aretz*, March 1972.**

> *In June 1967, we had a choice. The Egyptian army concentration in the Sinai approaches did not prove that Nasser was really about to attack us. We must be honest with ourselves. We decided to attack him.*
> **Israeli Prime Minister Menachem Begin, 1982.**

Though Israel continues to illegally occupy and control the entire city, its "Jerusalem Law" of 1980 — which asserted Jerusalem to be Israel's "complete and united" capital — was declared null, void, and a violation of international law by UN Security Council Resolution 478 which also stated that the Council will not recognize the law and called upon member states to withdraw diplomatic missions from the city. The resolution was carried by fourteen votes to zero with an abstention from Israel's lapdog — the AIPAC-controlled *democracy* of the United States of America whose people clamorously insist on their constitutional right to bear arms but then meekly allow themselves to be governed by a foreign power.

Tourists, mostly Jewish Americans, can now amble at a leisurely pace along the northern section of the Ramparts Walk which can be accessed as a starting point by the Jaffa Gate and terminated at the Lion's Gate. The walk provides them with an excellent view of both outer and newer Jerusalem and the inner and older Jerusalem where Palestinians struggle to survive under the yoke of an illegal and brutal

Israeli occupation. These American Jewish tourists are mostly unsmiling and lacking in the kind of friendly spontaneity that comes from having a clear conscience. Maybe they are suffering from the subconscious guilt that results from their complicity in supporting Israel's crimes against humanity and arrogant disregard for international law.

●　●　●　●　●

The time was 12:57 p.m. and the green Hyundai in the Rockefeller Archaeological Museum's circular parking facility was strategically parked so as to provide its two occupants, a man and a woman, with a good view of the museum's entrance. Though the couple appeared to be tourists as they whiled away the time by feigning interest in a guide book and map, they were in fact members of a Kidon unit from Mossad whose motto is "by means of deception, thou shalt do war." Known by its full name as the Institute for Intelligence and Special Operations, Mossad was responsible for external intelligence gathering and covert operations including paramilitary assignments and assassinations. As such, Mossad would not normally have become involved with an internal operation, but as it had already had Michal Zeldin under surveillance during his recent visit to London where he met with fugitive Israeli journalist David Reisner, a decision had been taken to let the agency continue with the operation.

Kidon, the Hebrew word for "bayonet," is the name of a department within Mossad that is specifically responsible for assassination and kidnap operations. Originally known as Caesarea, it was the unit of the Israel Defense Forces charged with intelligence missions in neighboring Arab countries. At the behest of Prime Minister David Ben-Gurion, however, the unit was transferred to Mossad in 1953.

Kidon agents never entered or communicated with Mossad headquarters and operated strictly undercover through intermediary controllers. As there were very few Nazi fugitives still at large who needed to be eliminated — thanks to the Nazi-hunting efforts of the Simon Wiesenthal Centre — Kidon's main quarries were now extremists, terrorists, and Arab militants who in any way threatened Israel or its citizens; those whose work had the potential to endanger Israel's security as was the case of Gerald Bull, the Canadian engineer whose "supergun" project for Iraq resulted in his assassination by a Kidon hit squad in Brussels in 1990; and those whose overt criticism and opposition to

Israeli policies is regarded as being a serious threat to the successful implementation of such policies. In keeping with Israel's propensity for assassinating those perceived as being its enemies, Mossad maintains a hit list of anything from 20 to 40 names for whose elimination the Prime Minister's permission must first be obtained.

A vital role is played in Kidon operations by female members whose skills — like all Mossad recruits — would have been fine-tuned during a two-year training course at the agency school in a grayish building outside Tel Aviv. They are taught the art of shadowing targets; hiding pistols in their nickers; creating dead-letter boxes; breaking into hotel rooms; stealing passports; and other spook-related covert activities. The failure rate amongst recruits is high and those who pass will either work at Mossad's Tel Aviv headquarters, or at one of its numerous overseas stations. It is only after gaining practical experience in the field that a female might then be selected for further training to become a Kidon operative with the promise that being a member of Kidon was like being a member of a family that would nurture and protect her. In return she would serve the family by doing whatever was required of her. Greater love has no woman than to lay down with her legs akimbo for her country.

> *A woman has skills a man simply does not have. She knows how to listen. Pillow talk is not a problem for her. The history of modern intelligence is filled with accounts of women who have used their sex for the good of their country . . . It is not just sleeping with someone if required. It is to lead a man to believe you will do so in return for what he has to tell you.*
> **Meir Amit, director-general of Mossad in the 1960s.**

One such Kidon high-flyer was Tzipi Livni — daughter of two members of the Irgun paramilitary force that operated in Mandate Palestine — who as head of the opposition Kadima party also held many ministerial positions in the Israeli Cabinet. After being posted to Paris as a Kidon agent, Livni had carried out ruthless operations against Arab terrorists and according to Ephraim Halevy, former head of Mossad, she took "substantial risks to get her targets."

As they were now on home ground, there were no risks — substantial or otherwise — for the Kidon couple waiting in the museum's car park. The museum itself was an impressive limestone building combining elements of art deco, Byzantine, and Islamic architecture. The building's construction had been facilitated by a subsidy from the British mandatory government and a U.S. $2 million donation from John D. Rockefeller, Jr., the American oil magnate and philanthropist. Rockefeller had stipulated that the museum, which opened in 1938, should be strictly archaeological with exhibits highlighting the different cultures of the Holy Land. The venture had become possible because following the Ottoman Empire's demise and the 1919 British mandate in Palestine and Transjordan, a Mandatory Department of Antiquities had been established in 1920 to oversee exploration of the Holy Land's ancient sites by teams of archaeologists from Britain, France, Germany, and the United States.

The museum's exhibits were now arranged according to Iron Age, Persian, Hellenistic, Roman, and Byzantine periods. Special features include a gallery of Egyptian antiquities and a small exhibit of a few Dead Sea Scrolls with the majority having been 'rehoused' in the Israel Museum. The scrolls were first discovered in 1946 by a Bedouin who happened across them in caves off the northwest shore of the Dead Sea close to the ancient settlement of Qumran in the Palestinian West Bank.

Initially known as the Palestine Archaeological Museum and managed by an international board of trustees, the museum was nationalised in 1966 by Jordan's King Hussein but then lost following the city's occupation by Israel in 1967. Whether it was the result of actual divine guidance or simply part of an overall Zionist scheme, the fact remains that some weeks prior to Israel's attack on 5 June 1967, the following anonymously sponsored but prominent advertisement appeared in *The Washington Post* and the *New York Times* on May 21:

TO ALL PERSONS OF THE JEWISH FAITH ALL OVER THE WORD
A project to rebuild the Temple of God in Israel is now being started. With Divine Guidance and Hope the 'Temple' will be completed. It will signal a new era in Judaism. Jews will be inspired to conduct themselves in such a moral way that our Maker will see fit to pay us a visit here on earth. Imagine the warm feeling that will be ours when this happy event takes place. 'THIS IS MY GOD' is the book that was the inspiration for this undertaking. God will place in the minds of many persons in all walks of Jewish life the desire

to participate in this work. Executive talents, Administrators and Workers in all levels are needed. All efforts will be anonymous. GOD will know those desiring to participate. Please write to Box M-917, The Washington Post. Under no circumstances send contributions. 'GOD'S WILL WILL PREVAIL'.

Following Israel's victory which was achieved in just six days, the museum came under the joint control of the Israel Museum and the Israel Department of Antiquities and Museum that together were later renamed as the Israel Antiquities Authority (IAA). The two Kidon agents waiting in the green Hyundai suddenly became alert when they saw Michal Zeldin — who had made a habit of coming to the IAA's office for a couple of hours every Saturday to catch up on his paperwork — came out of the museum's entrance and walked towards his Volvo Estate. It was in fact during one of his Saturday visits several months earlier that Zeldin had fortuitously come across the secret map which one of his colleagues had carelessly left in the photocopier. The Kidon agents knew that on reaching the end of the museum's driveway Zeldin would turn right onto Sultan Suleiman Street and travel westwards towards his apartment in West Jerusalem's Old Katamon neighbourhood. The woman agent wasted no time in dialing one of the numbers on her mobile's contacts list.

Meanwhile on the northern ramparts a short distance east of the Herod's Gate a Kidon "tourist" couple who had been lingering and were supposedly taking holiday snapshots with the museum in the background, suddenly stopped what they were doing when the man's mobile phone rang.

"Yes." he answered.

"He's on his way," the female agent in the museum car park informed him.

"Okay," he said ending the call and selecting a number from the mobile's contacts list which he did not actually dial. Instead he concentrated his gaze on the museum's driveway.

Several minutes passed before the Zeldin's Volvo Estate approached the automatic barrier by the gatehouse and was allowed to exit. As soon as the Volvo reached the end of the short driveway at the junction with Sultan Suleiman Street, the male Kidon agent looked down at the mobile in the palm of his hand and pressed the dial button with his thumb. The number dialed was for the mobile whose ringer had been wired to the two detonating caps of a C-4 (RDX) plastic explosive device of the type favored by terrorists. The device had been attached to Weinberg's Volvo by Kidon agents at around 4:00 a.m. earlier that morning. Suddenly the whole area was engulfed by the sound of a deafening explosion whose violent power hurled the Volvo Estate upwards with a belch of smoke, fire, and debris that no one could have possibly survived. The time was 1:14 p.m. and as far as Mossad was concerned the Michal Zeldin problem was solved and his file closed.

• • • • •

That car bomb explosion at 1:14 p.m. may have apparently marked the end of Mossad's involvement with Michal Zeldin — which had only come about because of his overseas trip — but it also meant the reassignment of the case to Shin Bet whose task was now to "clean up" in the aftermath of the assassination. Shin Bet, better known in Israel by the acronym Shabak is the Israel Security Agency (ISA) responsible for internal security as opposed to military intelligence (Aman) and foreign Intelligence (Mossad). With its motto of *"Magen VeLo Yera'e"* ("Defender that shall not be seen" or "The unseen shield"), Shabak had responsibility for safeguarding state security, exposing terrorist cells, interrogating terror suspects, providing intelligence and counter-terrorism operations in the Gaza Strip and West Bank, counter-espionage, personal protection of senior politicians and public officials, the security of important infrastructure and government buildings, and providing protection for Israeli airlines and overseas embassies.

Shin Bet also had a special operations unit named Yamas whose existence — due to the secret nature of the unit — has always been denied by the Israeli government. Yamas is allegedly one of the most efficient counter-terror units in the world — and as the special undercover operations unit of the Israeli Border Police — is responsible for locating and eliminating anyone associated with Palestinian resistance to the occupation whom Israel regards as terrorists. Yamas does not follow regular military or police command structures and is directly accountable to Shin Bet.

Like all the other Israeli military and security organisations, Shin Bet's image and reputation is also tarnished by some of its illegal and inhuman practices. Though in October 1991 Israel ratified the Convention

152

against Torture and Other Cruel, Inhuman or Degrading Treatment or Punishment, it has as usual blatantly failed to comply because no doubt of a prevailing view that "no one has the right to put the Jewish people or the State of Israel on trial." According to the Convention, Israel should prevent acts of torture with no exceptional circumstances whatsoever being invoked as a justification of torture.

In August 2007, the Public Committee against Torture in Israel (PCATI) released a paper on its attempts to make Shin Bet accountable for its practices of torture and ill-treatment of Palestinian detainees. It stated that according to the Convention, Israel must ensure that all acts of torture, attempts to commit torture and acts of complicity or participation in torture are made punishable "by appropriate penalties which take into account their grave nature." PCATI, however, found that Israel had not only hitherto ignored its international obligations to halt torture, but had also evaded criminal investigations into all 701 complaints of torture and ill-treatment despite consistent reports of political prisoner rights violations by Palestinian and Israeli human rights organizations.

Within half an hour of Michal Zeldin's assassination by the Mossad Kidon unit, Shin Bet agents entered his apartment in Katamon, the district where incidentally on 17 September 1948, UN Mediator Folke Bernadotte and UN Observer André Serot, were assassinated by members of the Jewish terrorist Stern Gang (Lehi group). The Shin Bet agents proceeded to carry out a meticulous search of the apartment's contents including Zeldin's personal effects and papers. It was not long before one of them unwittingly came across the copy of the secret map and with alarm bells ringing immediately recognized its significance. Just how Zeldin had acquired the map was not at this stage of vital importance for the agents because the immediate priority was to relay the discovery to Mossad who would have to upgrade their surveillance of David Reisner to also include establishing whether or not he had been given a copy of the map by Zeldin.

3
Sunday, 7 December 2008
The Frontline Club, Norfolk Place, Paddington, London

David Reisner spent most of the morning working on his laptop in his room at the Frontline Club. The Frontline had been set up in 2003 by Vaughan Smith as a tribute to his colleagues at the Frontline News Television agency which he and three other colleagues had formed in 1989 during the chaos of the Romanian revolution which toppled the regime of Nicolae Ceausescu. Over the next fifteen years a total of eight cameramen who were either directly or indirectly linked to Frontline News Television were killed.

It was 12:45 when Reisner left his room and walked the short distance to a nearby newsagents around the corner in Praed Street to buy his morning newspaper which he would read over lunch at the Frontline Restaurant. The club's restaurant consisted of a large room with sunburst windows set in cream-colored brick walls decorated with iconic photographs by renowned photographers. The relaxed, unpretentious ambience was complimented by a businesslike, attentive service.

After ordering lunch and a glass of Rioja, Reisner ran his eyes over the day's headlines before coming to one about the "Israeli archaeologist killed." His heartbeat quickened as he finished reading the piece and he was visibly shaken as he folded and put down the paper with a trembling hand. The news of Michal Zeldin's murder caused Reisner to be even more concerned than he already was for his own safety. According to the newspaper report, Israeli authorities suspected that Zeldin had been the victim of a terrorist bomb and was probably targeted for assassination because of his involvement with the City of David excavations. Reisner, a freelance investigative journalist who contributed to various publications including the Israeli *Haaretz* newspaper, was well acquainted with the media disinformation techniques used by Israeli government spokespersons and was not about to buy yet another of their disingenuous fabrications. He had no doubt whatsoever that Zeldin's murder had Mossad's hallmark stamped all over it.

Reisner had been contacted some months earlier by Zeldin whom he had agreed to meet for lunch. During that meeting at a café at the recently completed Arlov Mamilla shopping and entertainment complex — part of the new city centre that adjoined the Old City along the Jaffa Road but nonetheless beyond the financial and social status of Palestinians. An impassioned but articulate Zeldin had asserted that the Israel Antiquities Authority's work, contrary to all the professed principles and aims of archaeology, was being controlled and manipulated to achieve political goals that were also in keeping with those of the Religious Zionist Movement.

Zeldin claimed to have recently become increasingly aware of some unnamed powers whose manipulative control of the IAA was determining the direction, the nature, and the speed at which the IAA conducted its excavation projects. He could not offer any precise evidence to back up his his suspicions apart from the fact that IAA decisions were being taken without any indication as to the source of their formulation. Zeldin who was familiar with Reisner's past exposures of corruption and government transgressions, wondered if Reisner would take on the onerous task of trying to uncover who or what was behind the frenetic push to Judaize excavation sites so as to legitimize Israeli claims of heritage in East Jerusalem. Reisner had expressed his interest but explained he would first have to establish if there would be any editorial interest in commissioning such an investigation. Reisner and Zeldin had then parted company with the understanding that they would keep each other updated with any new developments in their mutual quest.

Reisner had subsequently proved intuitive in his first choice of the editor most likely to be interested in such a story because not only was the editor receptive to the idea, but he also provided Reisner with the name and contact details of a high-ranking official in the Israel Ministry of Foreign Affairs. This was the ministry that apart from its responsibility for Aliya (the right of every Jew to live in Israel), was also responsible for other related factors such as agriculture, architecture, and archaeology which had a vital role to play in the reclamation of land that Israel regarded as being its biblical heritage despite habitation of the land by Canaanite peoples prior to the alleged Exodus from Egypt, and more recently by generations of Palestinian families. The following piece of brainwashing propaganda targeting Americans appears on the AIPAC Biblical Heritage website which unashamedly purports an affinity between American Christians and Israelis without any regard for the truth or mention of the rights of Palestinian inhabitants:

The biblical kingdom of David (1000 BCE), followed by

Solomon, was the Jewish people's first independent nation-state, with Jerusalem as its political and spiritual capital. Over the following three millennia, the Jewish nation of Israel was conquered by numerous foreign empires including the Persians, Greeks and Romans. Mass expulsion by imperial rulers led to the majority of Jewish people being dispersed throughout the world after the destruction of the Second Temple in the year 70 CE.

Despite being persecuted by these invading foreign forces, many brave Jews remained in their native Israel, continuing the Jewish inhabitance of this ancient land, without pause, until today.

Those who fled under expulsion and the generations that followed never lost faith in their desire to return to the land of their forefathers and foremothers: Israel. They never lost hope of one day returning to their ancient capital of Jerusalem —a city mentioned more than 800 times in the Bible and thousands of times in more than 2,000 years of rabbinic literature.

Millions of America's Christians also feel a deep and abiding connection to Israel, and demonstrate this by making religious pilgrimages, offering moral and financial support and praying for the peace of Jerusalem. Based on theology and devotion to the land that was the setting for thousands of years of biblical history, they embrace the Jewish people and their national aspirations in Israel.

Beyond faith alone, America's Christians have many reasons to support Israel: the Jewish state reflects U.S. democratic ideals, is a stable ally in a turbulent region and fervently protects all holy sites and freedom of religion for its citizens.'

The official, who at first had been reluctant to meet with Reisner, finally agreed on condition of complete anonymity and the arrangement of a somewhat clandestine rendezvous. After listening to what Reisner had to say, the official confirmed Zeldin's suspicions of the existence of an agenda for Israel to ungently reclaim and rehabilitate religious sites in the occupied territories with the eventual aim of building the Third Temple. According to the official, preparations were already under way with the establishment of a heritage investment fund in excess of $100m with a view to a "Holy Land-grab" that would on Israel's heritage list include Al Ibrahimi Mosque in Hebron (also known as the Cave of the Patriarchs) and the Bilal bin Rabah Mosque (Rachel's Tomb).

Even though it was a certainty that the United Nations' culture and education body (Unesco) and the Islamic world would strongly condemn such plans, Israel would as always ignore any international censure and continue with the process known as Judaization which converts Palestinian sites into Jewish sites. It was Moshe Dayan who in April 1969 said the following:

> *Jewish villages were built in the place of Arab villages. You do not even know the names of these Arab villages, and I do not blame you because geography books no longer exist. Not only do the books not exist, the Arab villages are not there either. Nahlal arose in the place of Mahlul; Kibbutz Gvat in the place of Jibta; Kibbutz Sarid in the place of Huneifis; and Kefar Yehushua in the place of Tal al-Shuman. There is not a single place built in this country that did not have a former Arab population.*

Since Israel's 1967 occupation of the West Bank, Israeli soldiers have controlled the Al Ibrahimi compound and certain areas have been reserved as places for Jewish worship. On the other hand, Palestinians have a small area where their worship is restricted in numbers and the times of day. It was at the Al Ibrahimi Mosque that in February 1994 Baruch Kopel Goldstein, an American-born Israeli Jew, went on a shooting spree that killed 29 Muslims and wounded another 125. Goldstein was overcome and beaten to death by survivors and his gravesite subsequently became a pilgrimage site for Jewish extremists. His shrine, however, was dismantled in 1999 following Israeli legislation outlawing monuments to terrorists.

For Reisner, the most interesting of the official's revelations was the shadowy existence of an organization calling itself the the Hiramic Brotherhood of the Third Temple which while fully supporting Israel's heritage list, was more concerned with, and totally dedicated to the

157

building of the Third Temple. Reisner had not been able to comprehend — nor did he bother to ask — why such sensitive information had been disclosed by the government official whose motive for doing so may have been simply altruistic or because of some more personal or sinister reason.

Zeldin believed that the pressure for more extensive excavation was due to certain Israeli groups being obsessed with locating the ruins of Solomon's Temple which some believed lay beneath the Islamic Dome of the Rock. The magnificent Dome had been built to give Islam parity with its Judaic and Christian predecessors and to compete with the Church of the Holy Sepulchre. It was the official's understanding that the group's members had all been recruited from within Masonic lodge ranks. The group was apparently well-financed and enjoyed access to senior members of government though it would have preferred a more right-wing government with a hard-line prime minister like Benjamin Netanyahu who would help to accelerate achievement of the group's agenda.

Though Reisner had intended pursuing an investigation of the Hiramic Brotherhood of the Third Temple, he had in the meantime been side-tracked when thousands of secretly copied classified and confidential documents had been leaked to him by a military assistant in a regional command bureau of the Israeli Defense Forces. The documents covered wide-ranging and sensitive intelligence information including the suggestion that the military had defied a court ruling forbidding the assassination of wanted militants in the West Bank who could otherwise have been safely apprehended.

Details of the case had become subject to a gag order on the already cowed Israeli media and the military assistant responsible for the leak was placed under house arrest awaiting trial. While on vacation in Italy, and on learning that his computer and files had been seized during a raid on his apartment by Shin Bet, Israel's internal security service, Reisner had opted for self-imposed exile in London rather than face being arrested back in Israel. Despite the restrictions, the Israeli gag order was eventually circumvented and other news sources abroad broke the story. Fortunately for Reisner, several Israeli media organizations had continued to publish other reports from him with a London dateline.

Since then Reisner and Zeldin had met several times in November during Zeldin's short visit to London for the British Museum's *Babylon: Myth and Reality* exhibition. Zeldin had explained that the first archaeologists to explore Mesopotamia were more intent on corroborating the Bible's fabled nonsense rather than dealing with realities such as the fact that Babylon was not destroyed for its alleged sins but had simply faded over a period of time into insignificance. As for the renowned prophet Jeremiah (c. 655-586 BCE) and the supposed deportation of the Jews as referred to in Psalm 137:1 ("By the rivers of Babylon we sat and wept when we remembered Zion"), the fact was that following Jerusalem's fall Jeremiah ended up becoming a cosseted collaborator while many other Jews remained in Mesopotamia as an accomplished and respected upper class.

Zeldin had gone on to explain that similar efforts to connect archaeological finds with biblical myths were currently being repeated in the Holy Land by Israeli archaeologists. He cited the recent discovery in the Temple Mount area of a pool which was without conclusive proof designated as a mikveh: a bath used for ritual immersion in Judaism. Another discovery of animal bones which did not include pig bones resulted in an immediate conclusion that the site was of Jewish origin while conveniently forgetting that pork was also forbidden to Muslims. New archaeological discoveries were not being judged for what they were, but for what they were required to be by a combined Zionist and ultra-orthodox religious agenda. Zeldin was also of the opinion that even if there was positive proof that artefacts were of Judaic origin, that still would not give Jewish Israelis the right to claim East Jerusalem and displace the Palestinian majority.

Zeldin's concerns had not been just about archaeology, but also about a nation whose concept of a Jewish social democracy had deteriorated into a profound, existential crisis; whose children grew up with a siege mentality that promoted hatred of Arabs in general, and Palestinians in particular; whose proclamations of having exemplary ethical values, were in reality a smokescreen for lying, cheating, stealing, violating, and committing crimes against humanity; whose occupation of the West Bank and Gaza violated the human rights of some 4.5 million Palestinians; whose adherence to liberal and egalitarian precepts, had been replaced with more right wing and restrictive outlooks; whose top decile of the population earned more than 30 percent of the nation's total net income, while the lowest decile earned a mere 1.6 percent; and of whose population at least 20 percent (and 15 percent of Israeli Jews) were living below the poverty line.

Zeldin felt certain that he was not alone in believing that a disproportionately high percentage of the nation's resources were going to the mostly religious and ultranationalist West Bank settlers and to the ultra-Orthodox who contributed virtually nothing to the economy and avoided mandatory military service — a situation that was bound to change due to the secular disaffection of those who paid taxes and served in the armed forces. To make matters worse, this hard-core grouping tended to have five to eight children per family as opposed to two or three by secular families. While this resulted in their having a disproportionate advantage both economically and politically, they were nevertheless the poorest of Israeli Jews because many of them did not work.

So how do they spend their time, these unemployed ultra-orthodox Jewish men with Beards, long wispy ringlets of hair, long black overcoats and colour-matching broad-brimmed Homburg hats? They mostly spend it in prayer and contemplation of the scriptures rather than attempting to work for a living. They live off handouts and their wives' wages. They also spend time trying to impose their views on less orthodox Jews by for example having men and women ride in separate segregated areas on buses. They also spend time picketing schools where schoolgirls as young as six years of age are intimidated with a baying cacophony of screamed insults and a pelting with rotten tomatoes, stones and even faeces. These men, whom God apparently chose, accuse the young girls of "defiling the neighborhood" by being immorally dressed like sluts. In reality these men are no better than the mutaween (government-recognized religious police) in strict Islamic countries.

Zeldin had been adamant that his views were not those of a traitor, but of a patriot who refused to be conditioned into accepting Zionist propaganda lies instead of the facts of history. As a scholar he knew it was untrue that all the Palestinians who had become refugees in 1948 had left their homes voluntarily and that in fact most had been driven out by Zionist terrorism and calculated ethnic cleansing. He knew that despite Zionist claims to the contrary, Israel had never been in danger of annihilation that would culminate with Jews being "driven into the sea." He knew that Israeli peace negotiations were always deliberately conducted with terms that would be totally unacceptable to the majority of Palestinians and the Arab world because Zionism's expansion plans were dependent on conflict and not peace. A continual state of conflict was essential for Zionist Israel's existence because it provided the illusion of justification for the continued ethic cleansing of the Palestinian people.

Zeldin regarded the West's timid policy of unconditional support for Israel whether it be right-or-wrong as being erroneous, dangerous, and a threat not only to the peace of Middle East, but also to that of the whole world. As far as he was concerned, in having remained the brainchild of Zionism, Israel had not only become its own worst enemy, but it had also debased Judaism's moral values and ethical principles. He pointed out that Judaism was the religion of Jews, but not the religion of "all the Jews" of whom many were not religious. Furthermore, many Jews were neither Zionist nor consensually associated with the crimes that Zionism committed. Just as all Jews were not Zionists, it followed that not all non-Jews were anti-Semitic. Criticism of a Zionist Israeli Apartheid state should not be equated with anti-Semitism.

Zeldin had also emphasised the importance of differentiating between Zionism and Judaism because Judaism was not contemptuous of both international law and the human and political rights of the Palestinian people. It was not Judaism that employed abhorrent sectarian and colonial principles to create a Jewish nationalist state by means of illegal occupation and gradual expropriation of Arab lands. Supporters of Israel insist on conflating Zionism with Judaism because the assertion that they are one and the same enables them to claim that criticism of the Zionist state of Israel is tantamount to anti-Semitism. This ploy provides them with the means to blackmail critics into silence and to suppress honest and informed debate.

Reisner had been impressed not only by Zeldin's passionate desire for truth and justice, but also by his resolve that unlike the majority of Jews everywhere he would never be intimidated into silence by succumbing to moral blackmail of the kind that invoked wild and unjustified accusations of anti-Semitism and Holocaust denial. It was obvious that having been unable to legitimately silence the troublesome Zeldin, the Zionist state had instead decided to assassinate him.

After due consideration of this latest development, Reisner concluded that as he was already being sought by Israeli intelligence services over the leaked documents affair, and Zeldin had obviously also been in their sights, then it was a certainty that both had been under surveillance during their London meetings which would also mean that they knew where Reisner lived. Reisner had first come under the Israeli security radar back in 2005 when he had written a favourable article about the newly formed organisation Yesh Din, an Israeli human rights group providing legal assistance to citizens of the Palestinian

161

territories. Yesh Din made a point of monitoring the Israeli Defence Force's investigations into suspected crimes against Palestinians by Israeli settlers and soldiers. Coming from a Hebrew phrase meaning "there is law," the group had been founded by Shulamit Aloni, the Israeli politician and left-wing activist whom Reisner held in very high esteem. It was Shulamit Aloni who in a June 2006 article revealed the following:

Not very long ago, during Rabbi Meir Kahane's racist rantings, the late writer and journalist Amos Elon gave me a copy of a letter Lord Rothschild sent to Herzl in August 1902. In the letter, Rothschild explains why he refuses to support the establishment of a Jewish state in the Land of Israel. He writes "he should view with horror the establishment of a Jewish colony pure and simple; such a colony would be Imperium Imperio [state within a state]; it would be a Ghetto with the prejudice of the Ghetto; it would be a small petty Jewish state, orthodox and illiberal, excluding the Gentile and the Christian." Nevertheless, and despite phenomena like Kahane, the hope prevailed here over the years that Rothschild's harsh vision would prove false; that Israel would indeed "ensure complete equality of social and political rights to all its inhabitants irrespective of religion, race or sex," and "guarantee freedom of religion, conscience, language, education and culture," as stated in the Declaration of the Establishment of the State.

Time has passed and many heirs to Kahane have arisen — not only among a greedy and savage multitude but also among "he public's chosen representatives" in the Knesset and government. The latter are busy preparing blatantly racist laws and sending armed police to thwart Palestinian-initiated international cultural events because the regime believes the Arabs of the Land of Israel, the native Palestinians, are not worthy of being called human beings. According to the writers of these laws, the Arabs are certainly not entitled to human rights, not to mention a cultural and intellectual life, and never mind property, land and a home, because thousands of years ago God promised this land to Abraham and his seed. Most regrettably and disgracefully, everything that Lord Rothschild predicted is coming to pass in our time. In our blackest dreams and in the hardest times since the struggle to establish the state, we never imagined that those who call themselves disciples of Ze'ev Jabotinsky would impose terror and fear here using deranged racist legislation. We never imagined that they would use the destruction of the court system to try to prevent any possibility of achieving social justice and a humane attitude. This is something essential in every democratic society toward every man, woman and child, irrespective of origin, race, religion and sex.

For 42 years we have been occupying, oppressing and stealing lands that are not ours. To be free in our land do we need to become thieving Cossacks, uprooters of trees, burners of fields and harassers of women, the elderly and the very young? "We have this land, we have it," goes the song, but what should have been said is 'We have the power, we have it, we have the money, we have it, and we are allowed, we are," to starve an entire population, imprison it and annihilate it using air strikes, cluster bombs and white phosphorous. Because we are the lords of the land and God has chosen us to rule. For the shame of it.

"A unique people," wrote David Ben-Gurion. Alas, for that uniqueness. Instead of a Jewish and democratic state they have delivered us a Jewish state controlled by religious fanaticism, one that maintains the purity of the race. They have delivered a democracy in the most primitive sense — not the preservation of democratic values but rule by the demos, the populace that is dictating the transformation of Israel into a totalitarian ethnocracy. Hooray for Prime Minister Benjamin Netanyahu and Foreign Minister Avigdor Lieberman — they are eradicating everything we built, everything we dreamed about and everything we fought for.

Reisner believed that so long as there were always some Jewish people who spoke out like Shulamit Aloni, then there would always be hope that Jews could to some extent salvage some of the decency and sense of justice that was once a part of their heritage. Of the following, the first is an excerpt from an August 2002 interview with American journalist Amy Goodman, and the second is from a January 2007 article in Counterpunch:

> **Goodman:** *Yours is a voice of criticism we don't often hear in the United States. Often when there is dissent expressed in the United States against policies of the Israeli government, people here are called anti-Semitic. What is your response to that as an Israeli Jew?*
>
> **Aloni:** *Well, it's a trick, we always use it. When from Europe somebody is criticizing Israel, then we bring up the Holocaust. When in this country people are criticizing Israel, then they are anti-Semitic. And the organization is strong, and has a lot of money, and the ties between Israel and the American Jewish establishment are very strong and they are strong in this country, as you know. And they have power, which is OK. They are talented people and they have power and money, and the media and other things, and their attitude is "Israel, my country right or wrong," the identification. And they are not ready to hear criticism. And it's very easy to blame people who criticize certain acts of the Israeli government as anti-Semitic, and to bring up the Holocaust, and the suffering of the Jewish people, and that is justify everything we do to the Palestinians.*

Yes, There is Apartheid in Israel

Jewish self-righteousness is taken for granted among ourselves to such an extent that we fail to see what's right in front of our eyes. It's simply inconceivable that the ultimate victims, the Jews, can carry out evil deeds. Nevertheless, the state of Israel practices its own, quite violent, form of Apartheid with the native Palestinian population.

The U.S. Jewish Establishment's onslaught on former President Jimmy Carter is based on him daring to tell the truth which is known to all: through its army, the government of Israel practices a brutal form of Apartheid in the territory it occupies. Its army has turned every Palestinian village and town into a fenced-in, or blocked-in, detention camp.

All this is done in order to keep an eye on the population's movements and to make its life difficult. Israel even imposes a total curfew whenever the settlers, who have illegally usurped the Palestinians' land, celebrate their holidays or conduct their parades.

If that were not enough, the generals commanding the region frequently issue further orders, regulations, instructions and rules (let us not forget: they are the lords of the land). By now they have requisitioned further lands for the purpose of constructing "Jewish only" roads. Wonderful roads, wide roads, well-paved roads, brightly lit at night — all that on stolen land. When a Palestinian drives on such a road, his vehicle is confiscated and he is sent on his way. On one occasion I witnessed such an encounter between a driver and a soldier who was taking down the details before confiscating the vehicle and sending its owner away. "Why?" I asked the soldier. "It's an order — this is a Jews-only road," he replied. I inquired as to where was the sign indicating this fact and instructing [other] drivers not to use it. His answer was nothing short of amazing. "It is his responsibility to know it, and besides, what do you want us to do, put up a sign here and let some antisemitic reporter or journalist take a photo so that he can show the world that Apartheid exists here?"

Indeed Apartheid does exist here. And our army is not "the most moral army in the world" as we are told by its commanders. Sufficient to mention that every town and every village has turned into a detention centre and that every entry and every exit has been closed, cutting it off from arterial traffic. If it were not enough that Palestinians are not allowed to travel on the roads paved "or Jews only," on their land, the current GOC found it necessary to land an additional blow on the natives in their own land with an 'ingenious proposal.'

Humanitarian activists cannot transport Palestinians either.

Major-General Naveh, renowned for his superior patriotism, has issued a new order. Coming into effect on 19 January, it prohibits the conveyance of Palestinians

165

without a permit. The order determines that Israelis are not allowed to transport Palestinians in an Israeli vehicle (one registered in Israel regardless of what kind of numberplate it carries) unless they have received explicit permission to do so. The permit relates to both the driver and the Palestinian passenger. Of course none of this applies to those whose labour serves the settlers. They and their employers will naturally receive the required permits so they can continue to serve the lords of the land, the settlers.

Did man of peace President Carter truly err in concluding that Israel is creating Apartheid? Did he exaggerate? Don't the U.S. Jewish leaders recognize the International Convention on the Elimination of all Forms Racial Discrimination of 7 March 1966, to which Israel is a signatory? Are the U.S. Jews who launched the loud and abusive campaign against Carter for supposedly maligning Israel's character and its democratic and humanist nature unfamiliar with the International Convention on the Suppression and Punishment of the Crime of Apartheid of 30 November 1973? Apartheid is defined therein as an international crime that among other things includes using different legal instruments to rule over different racial groups, thus depriving people of their human rights. Isn't freedom of travel one of these rights?

In the past, the U.S. Jewish community leaders were quite familiar with the meaning of those conventions. For some reason, however, they are convinced that Israel is allowed to contravene them. It's OK to kill civilians, women and children, old people and parents with their children, deliberately or otherwise without accepting any responsibility. It's permissible to rob people of their lands, destroy their crops, and cage them up like animals in the zoo. From now on, Israelis and International humanitarian organizations' volunteers are prohibited from assisting a woman in labour by taking her to the hospital. Israeli human rights group Yesh Din volunteers cannot take a robbed and beaten-up Palestinian to the police station to lodge a complaint. (Police stations are located at the heart

166

of the settlements.) Is there anyone who believes that this is not Apartheid?

Jimmy Carter does not need me to defend his reputation that has been sullied by Israelophile community officials. The trouble is that their love of Israel distorts their judgment and blinds them from seeing what's in front of them. Israel is an occupying power oppressing an indigenous people, which is entitled to a sovereign and independent existence while living in peace with us. We should remember that we too used very violent terror against foreign rule because we wanted our own state. And the list of victims of terror is quite long and extensive.

We do limit ourselves to denying the [Palestinian] people human rights. We not only rob of them of their freedom, land and water. We apply collective punishment to millions of people and even, in revenge-driven frenzy, destroy the electricity supply for one and half million civilians. Let them "sit in the darkness" and "starve."

Employees cannot be paid their wages because Israel is holding 500 million shekels that belong to the Palestinians. And after all that we remain "pure as the driven snow." There are no moral blemishes on our actions. There is no racial separation. There is no Apartheid. It's an invention of the enemies of Israel. Hooray for our brothers and sisters in the U.S.! Your devotion is very much appreciated. You have truly removed a nasty stain from us. Now there can be an extra spring in our step as we confidently abuse the Palestinian population, using the "most moral army in the world."

[Translated by Sol Salbe]

Reisner was of course aware that Shulamit Aloni was not the only Jew to have spoken out against the use of anti-Semitism as a means of promoting Zionism. Lenni Brenner the author and prominent civil rights activist and Norman Finkelstein in his *The Holocaust Industry: Reflections on the Exploitation of Jewish Suffering,* had also done so. For daring to speak out against Israeli crimes the three aforementioned along with former U.S. President Jimmy Carter and some seven thousand others are included on the Jewish S.H.I.T List (Self-hating and/or Israel-Threatening) website which is well worth a visit for anyone requiring a crash course in the kind of vicious vitriol that best describes those Zionists responsible for its dissemination.

Though the term "Zionism" may have been first mentioned by Nathan Birmbaum in 1893, it was Theodor Herzl (1860-1984), an Austro-Hungarian Jew who is credited with having founded Zionist ideology and in effect the Israeli state with the publication in 1896 of his book *The Jewish State*. Herz's attachment to the idea of a Jewish state in Palestine was far less than that of other prominent Zionists at one stage he was considering the creation of a Jewish state in what is now Uganda.

Herzl was born in Pest, Hungary, to an Ashkenazi Jewish family that was originally from Serbia. Ashkenazi Jews were descended from the medieval Jewish communities along Germany's the River Rhine that stretched from Alsace in the south to the Rhineland in the north. Ashkenaz was the medieval Hebrew name for that German region and consequently Ashkenazim or Ashkenazi Jews are literally "German Jews." Many Ashkenazi Jews later migrated, mostly eastwards, to form communities in Eastern Europe including Belarus, Hungary, Lithuania, Poland, Russia, Ukraine and elsewhere between the eleventh and nineteenth centuries. They took with them and diversified a Yiddish influenced Germanic language written in Hebrew letters which in medieval times had become the lingua franca among Ashkenazi Jews. Although in the eleventh century, Ashkenazi Jews comprised only three percent of the world's Jewish population, they peaked to 92 percent by 1931 and now account for about 80 percent of Jews worldwide.

Herzl's proposal for the eradication of anti-Semitism was to actively encourage and even promote anti-Semitism so as to further the cause of Zionism and thereby make possible the creation of a Jewish state.

It is essential that the sufferings of Jews... become worse.... this will assist in realization of our plans... I have an excellent idea ... I shall induce anti-Semites to liquidate Jewish wealth... The anti-Semites will assist us thereby in that they will strengthen the persecution and oppression of Jews. The anti-Semites shall be our best friends.

Ultimately, and at great cost to the Jewish people, Herzl's idea of increasing "the oppression and persecution of Jews," was achieved beyond his wildest dreams when Adolf Hitler and his Nazis obliged on a grand scale. The fact that such an idea was at the core of Zionist ideology is evident from David Ben-Gurion who said the following:

If knew that it was possible to save all the children of Germany by transporting them to England, and only half by transferring them to the Land of Israel, I would choose the latter, for before us lies not only the numbers of these children but the historical reckoning of the people of Israel.

Reisner decided to focus on the reality of his own situation which meant that being in London did not necessarily guarantee his being beyond Mossad's clutches. Though it was a relatively small intelligence agency, Mossad's capacity to cover a lot of ground was much enhanced by people known as assets whose work in politics, the media, or other professions enabled them to exert influence on Israel's behalf. Reisner recalled an October 2007 report in the influential French daily, *Le Figaro*, which claimed that President Sarkozy (of mixed Jewish and Christian ancestry) was, and still may have been working for Mossad as a sayan and was accordingly dubbed "Sarco the Sayan."

Apart from its influential assets, Mossad had also established a worldwide secret network of sayanim (Hebrew word for helpers) who were controlled by field intelligence officers known as katsas (case officers). The network had been set up through a risk-free recruitment system that exploited the availability of potential assistance from the millions of Jews in diaspora whose loyalty and sympathy for the Jewish cause were understandably inherent. A potential sayan (helper) in London for example may be approached with the line that his or her assistance was required to help save Jews in Israel and elsewhere. While only about a third may agree to be enlisted, the rest would out of mistaken loyalty to the cause, not divulge information to anyone regarding Mossad's attempt to recruit them.

As sayanim are never put in a position of risk or entrusted with classified information regarding an operation which could even involve assassination, they are legally, if not morally, shielded from the culpability of being accomplices in illegal activity. There is also the question of whether a sayan's first loyalty is to Israel or to the country of which he or she is a resident and citizen. Sayanim were in effect Mossad's worker ants who, within the area of their own professional capacity and expertise, provided wide ranging logistical support that could include accommodation, transport, equipment, cash, cover stories, references, simple surveillance, and access to private or sensitive information. It was for example an established fact that Kidon assassination units on assignments abroad, invariably travel on cloned foreign passports whose details were stolen by sayanim.

Reisner had not forgotten the revelations by Victor Ostrovsky, the former Mossad agent who in his book *By Way of Deception*, had estimated that in London alone there were some 2,000 active sayanim, and about 5,000 more who were available to be called upon for assistance if required. There were now probably over two million sayanim worldwide. When Israel attempted to stop the book's publication with a preliminary injunction in 1990, it became the first sovereign state to attempt preventing a book publication in another sovereign state. That injunction was overturned by the New York Supreme Court and the resulting publicity only helped Ostrovsky's book to become a best seller in the U.S. and Canada.

One of the disclosures Israel may have been keen to prevent from becoming public knowledge in North America was Ostrovsky's allegation that in 1983 Mossad failed to share with its U.S. benefactor — and supposed ally — specific intelligence that might have prevented the suicide bombing in Beirut of the U.S. Marine barracks that resulted in the death of 241 servicemen. Reisner knew for a fact that Israel always secretly welcomed Arab-related attacks on the West and when former Israeli Prime Minister Benjamin Netanyahu was asked what the 9/11 attacks meant for U.S.-Israeli relations? He replied "It's very good . . . well it's not good, but it will generate immediate sympathy." For Israel.

Islamist attacks on the West served a useful dual purpose. The first was to reinforce the erroneous perception that all Arabs were murderous terrorists, and the second was to allow Israel to exploit the illusion of being on the moral high ground which enabled it, without fear of serious condemnation from the West, to use gratuitous violence in suppressing Palestinian resistance to an illegal and brutal occupation. Reisner pondered on the double standards whereby European citizens who opposed German occupation during the Second World War were known as "the resistance", while the Palestinians, for trying to do the exact same thing with far less resources, were branded as terrorists. Reisner could not remember ever seeing a Hollywood film that portrayed an

Arab as the "good guy" as opposed to the usual stereotyped unshaven Arab villain.

But then that was unlikely to happen so long as Hollywood had a proliferation of Jewish film producers such as Arnon Milchan *(Once Upon a Time in America, Pretty Woman, and L.A. Confidential)* who was also an acknowledged Israeli intelligence agent for Mossad and disavowed arms dealer. Milchan, a staunch supporter of Israel — and personal friend of Israeli President Shimon Peres who had recruited him as a spy — recruited other Hollywood A-listers including Sydney Pollack. Milchan at one time operated thirty companies in seventeen countries on behalf of Israel. He also underwrites the Israeli Network which transmits Israeli television programs to Canada and the U.S. via cable and satellite television. The actor Marlon Brando had to apologize for the controversy caused by the following remark:

> *And then Sam Goldwyn and all of the rest of them. Metro Goldwyn Mayer, they — Hollywood is run by Jews; it is owned by Jews — and they should have a greater sensitivity about the issue of people who are suffering. Because . . . we have seen . . . the greaseball, we've seen the Chink, we've seen the slit-eyed dangerous Jap, we have seen the wily Filipino, we've seen everything but we never saw the kike. Because they knew perfectly well, that that is where you draw the [line].*
> **Marlon Brando on Larry King Live**

> *Do the Jews run Hollywood? You bet they do — and what of it?*
> **Ben Stein, *Do the Jews Run Hollywood*, an article on EOnline**

> *It makes no sense at all to try to deny the reality of Jewish power and prominence in popular culture. Any list of the most influential production executives at each of the major movie studios will produce a heavy majority of recognizably Jewish names.*
> **Michael Medved, *Moment,* the American Jewish Magazine, August 1996**

171

Reisner recalled having some years earlier interviewed a London-based Jewish arms dealer for an article that Reisner had been commissioned to write on the illicit arms trade in Africa. The dealer — a proud owner of a Regent's Park mansion, a trophy wife, and three well-fed, impeccably dressed and beaming children — having been given Reisner's assurance of anonymity, had spoken quite freely about his arms deals in Africa for which he was paid mostly with diamonds that were mined in war zones (blood diamonds). The dealer had been justifiably proud of his children, but while he watched them lovingly as they played outside on the carefully manicured lawn, he appeared blissfully oblivious to the suffering and fatalities that his guns were causing to the children of Africa.

When it came to gunrunning, however, no one was quite in the same league as Israeli multi-billionaire tycoon Shaul Eisenberg (1921-1997) who helped Israel to become a covert but major trafficker in illicit arms. After escaping from Nazi-controlled Europe, Eisenberg had relocated to the Far East where his activities with Asia's Jewish community during the Second World War also involved a close intelligence and business partnership with Japan's Imperial government which with Nazi Germany and Fascist Italy formed the Axis Alliance.

With base operations established in Japan and Japanese-occupied Shanghai, Eisenberg then helped Japanese military intelligence to form the future Jewish terrorist groups of the Irgun and the Shanghai Betar. The Betar had been originally founded in the 1930s by the Polish Zionist Yakob Jabotinsky — an ardent supporter of Benito Mussolini, Italy's Fascist leader — to fight against the British for control of Palestine.

In Shanghai, The Japanese taught the Jewish paramilitary forces how to disrupt the logistical, command, and control aspects of colonial rule by employing the same successful strategies previously used against American, British, Dutch, and French colonial authorities in Asia. After the Second World War the Irgun and Betar gangs used the knowledge gained from the Japanese in their terror campaigns against British and Arab forces in Palestine. The veterans of these two terrorist organisations went on to form Israel's present-day Likud Party whose extreme right-wing (Fascist) leader is Benjamin Netanyahu.

Following the war, Eisenberg profited from the sale of military surplus equipment including scrap iron and steel. In 1968 he became one of the first strategic foreign investors in Israeli history by founding the Israel Corporation, a huge holding company, which in the 1970s began to covertly export Israeli military equipment and weapons to China.

Meanwhile as the U.S. was facing ignominious defeat in the Indochina War at the hands of the Cambodian, Laotian, and Vietnamese communist-nationalist forces, Eisenberg immediately moved to forge new alliances in Southeast Asia with President Richard Nixon's National Security Adviser, unindicted war criminal Henry Kissinger, a close friend of Eisenberg, ordering the CIA to overthrow Cambodian head of state Prince Norodom Sihanouk.

Cambodia then fell victim to a bloody civil war between Vietnamese troops backing Pol Pot's one-time ally Hun Sen and the Chinese-backed "Democratic Kampuchea" government of Khmer Rouge leader Pol Pot. Eisenberg then started supplying weapons from China to the genocidal Cambodian Khmer Rouge regime of Pol Pot which was directly responsible for the murder of some 2.4 million of the almost four million Cambodians who died as the result of rebellion, war, man-made famine, and genocide.

It was not by chance that President Ford's administration and Secretary of State Kissinger backed the Khmer Rouge. Kissinger and Ford's long-time Michigan financial backer, Jewish industrialist Max Fisher, were both financially and ideologically linked to Eisenberg. The somewhat duplicitous Henry Kissinger — who in 1972 acknowledged to China that Washington could accept a communist takeover of South Vietnam if that were to evolve after the withdrawal of U.S. Troops — also authorized Eisenberg to commence a covert operation to modernize China's armed forces with $10 billion in Israeli and U.S. designed weapons being re-exported through Israel with a view to counteracting Soviet military power in Asia.

By using a Panama-based company called United Development Inc., Eisenberg also began supplying weapons to Central America's most unscrupulous dictatorships including the corrupt embezzler President Anastasio Somoza of Nicaragua. The Israel Corporation's vast holdings were to eventually include amongst others Better Place, Israel Chemicals, Israel Aircraft Industries, Oil Refineries Ltd., Tower Semiconductor, and Zim Integrated Shipping Services.

It is evident that Israel — through Mossad and its continued connections with Jewish gunrunners like Eisenberg — has no compunction about destabilizing regional and world peace by supplying weapons to whoever wants them (including both sides of an armed conflict) so long as it reaps the benefits of a huge profit.

Unending conflicts and wars are always good for the armaments business. When American military forces were sent to Afghanistan to fight Osama bin Laden and the Taliban they found themselves up against stockpiled Stinger antiaircraft missiles which back in 1981 had been supplied by the U.S. Central Intelligence Agency (CIA) to the mujahideen to counter the menace of Soviet helicopter gunships during the Soviet war in Afghanistan which lasted from December 1979 to February 1989. The Soviets, like the British before, and the Americans after, achieved nothing but senseless death and destruction. *Yes,* Reisner thought to himself, *history does indeed repeat itself and we still never learn.*

Despite the fact that the tragic news of Michal Zeldin's murder had unsettled Reisner, he was now more than ever determined to expose the existence of the Hiramic Brotherhood of the Third Temple even if it was only as a posthumous tribute to Zeldin's courage. Reisner was, however, also aware that any attempts to uncover more information about the Hiramic Brotherhood would be hampered by his inability to return to Israel where he would be arrested and held incommunicado.

Reisner therefore reasoned that irrespective of his chosen course of action, he would still require some assistance with his quest and after some consideration the name of Mark Banner came to mind. Though Reisner had been familiar with Banner's achievements as a foreign correspondent, they had never actually met before last year when both happened to be in London at the same time — Banner for the 2007 British Press Awards after once again having been shortlisted for another accolade, and Reisner for an investigation of a Jewish Russian billionaire businessmen with Russian mafia connections and resident in Britain. Their meeting had taken place one evening after Banner had presented a discussion on the *Fatah-Hamas conflict and the Israeli blockade*. They had since kept in touch and Reisner now resolved to phone Banner the following day.

4
Monday, 8 December 2008
The Corniche, Beirut, Lebanon

Mark Banner was working on his third book titled The *Knesset on Capitol Hill* when the phone rang. With reluctance he reached over and with a less than polite expletive, picked up the receiver.

"Hello."

"Good morning Mark, it's David Reisner. Am I disturbing you?"

"Not at all," Banner lied, "how are you?"

"I'm okay . . . you and Nadine?"

"We're good."

"Glad to hear it . . . Mark I'm calling about Michal Zeldin, the Israeli archaeologist who was killed last week."

"Oh! The one blown up by terrorists?"

"Mossad terrorists," Reisner corrected emphatically before going on to relate in detail everything that he had learnt from his two meetings with Michal Zeldin and the Israeli government official. Reisner also confirmed that he had visited the Library and Museum of Freemasonry in London's Covent Garden without being able to uncover anything about the Hiramic Brotherhood who were apparently nonexistent. Banner pointed out that the fact they were officially nonexistent meant nothing: it would not be the first time that a rogue cell had operated within the ranks of Freemasonry. He also informed Reisner that he would make some enquiries and would be coming to London on December the thirteenth for three weeks over the Christmas holidays when they could meet up and discuss the matter. In parting Banner suggested that in the meantime Reisner could write an article about the Brotherhood's existence which might 'smoke them out' by eliciting some kind of response either as an acknowledgement or denial. Banner's suggestion, however, was accompanied by the warning that such a strategy was not without its dangers and that Reisner should be on his guard and beware of strangers. Banner then promised to phone Reisner as soon as he and Nadine arrived in London and hung up.

He quickly refocused and got back to working on one of the chapters that dealt with the relationships between successive U.S. presidents and

Israel since its creation in 1948. He had set the tone with a brief preamble and now continued with an excerpt from George Washington's farewell speech of March 1796 whose forewarnings were uncannily prophetic considering the manner in which U.S. Foreign Policy — especially with regards to Israel — was currently being conducted.

> *. . . Observe good faith and justice towards all nations; cultivate peace and harmony with all. Religion and morality enjoin this conduct; and can it be, that good policy does not equally enjoin it — it will be worthy of a free, enlightened, and at no distant period, to give to mankind the magnanimous and too novel example of a people always guided by an exalted justice and benevolence. Who can doubt that, in the course of time and things, the fruits of such a plan would richly repay any temporary advantages which might be lost by a steady adherence to it? The experiment at least, is recommended by every sentiment which ennobles human nature. Alas! Is it rendered possible by its vices?*
>
> *In execution of such a plan, nothing is more essential than that permanent, inveterate antipathies against particular nations, and passionate attachment for others, should be excluded; and that in place of them, just and amicable feelings towards all should be cultivated. The nation which indulges towards another a habitual hatred or habitual fondness is in some degree a slave. It is a slave to its animosity or to its affection, either of which is sufficient to lead it astray from its duty or interest. Antipathy in one nation against another disposes each more readily to offer insult and injury, to lay hold of slight causes of umbrage, and to be haughty and intractable, when accidental or trifling occasions of dispute occur. Hence frequent collisions, obstinate, envenomed, and bloody contests. The nation, prompted by ill will and resentment, sometimes impels to war the government, contrary to the best calculations of policy. The government sometimes participates in the national propensity, and adopts through passion what reason would reject; at other times it makes the animosity of the nation subservient to projects of hostility instigated by pride, ambition, and other sinister and pernicious motives. The peace often, sometimes*

perhaps the liberty, of nations, has been the victim.

So likewise, a passionate attachment of one nation for another produces a variety of evils. Sympathy for the favorite nation, facilitating the illusion of an imaginary common interest in cases were no real common interest exists, and infusing into one the enmities of the other, betrays the former into participation in the quarrels and wars of the latter without inducement or justification. It leads also to concessions to the favorite nation of privileges denied to others which is apt doubly to injure the nation making the concessions; by unnecessarily parting with what ought to have been retained, and by exciting jealousy, ill-will, and a disposition to retaliate, in the parties from whom equal privileges are withheld. And it gives to ambitious, corrupted, or deluded citizens (who devote themselves to the favorite nation), facility to betray or sacrifice the interests of their own country, without odium, sometimes even without popularity; gilding, with appearances of virtuous sense of obligation, a commendable deference for public opinion, or a laudable zeal for public good, the base or foolish compliances of ambition, corruption, or infatuation.

As avenues to foreign influence in innumerable ways, such attachments are particularly alarming to the truly enlightened and independent patriot. How many opportunities do they afford to tamper with domestic factions, to practice the art of seduction, to mislead public opinion, to influence or awe the public councils. Such attachment of a small or weak towards a great and powerful nation dooms the former to be a satellite of the latter.

Against the insidious wiles of foreign influence (I conjure you to believe me, fellow-citizens) the jealousy of a free people ought to be constantly awake, since history and experience prove that foreign influence is one of the most baneful foes of republican government. But that jealousy to be useful must be impartial; else it becomes the instrument of the very influence to be avoided, instead of defence against it. Excessive partiality for one nation and excessive dislike for another cause those who they actuate to see danger only on one side, and serve to veil and even second the arts of influence on the other. Real patriots who may resist the intrigues of the favourite are liable to become suspected and odious, while its tools and dupes usurp the applause and confidence of the people, to surrender their interests.

Banner continued with the reminder that during World War II, President Roosevelt had promised Saudi Arabia's King Saud that the U.S. would make no policy decisions concerning Palestine without first consulting the Arabs. Roosevelt had later reiterated that promise in writing on April 5, 1945 which, as it turned out, was one week before he died. Though Roosevelt's successor Harry S. Truman, — having been much moved by revelations of the Nazi atrocities — was in favor of Jewish immigration to Palestine he was nonetheless initially against the idea of the partition of Palestine to facilitate the creation of a Jewish state which he rightly felt would require excessive U.S. resources to defend.

Long before going into politics and while doing basic training at Fort Sill in Oklahoma, Truman had met and befriended Eddie Jacobson, a Jew, with whom he successfully managed a canteen that led to them eventually becoming partners in an unsuccessful haberdashery business. Subsequently in June 1946, in the first of many such visits, Jacobson accompanied by American Zionist officials, met with Truman at the White House. Despite this relationship, Truman was not particularly fond of Jews and in many of his recorded opinions he fails to differentiate between Zionists and traditional Jewish people, particularly those in diaspora. Part of Truman's diary entry for July 21, 1947, reads as follows:

The Jews, I find are very, very selfish. They care not how many Estonians, Latvians, Finns, Poles, Yugoslavs or Greeks get murdered or mistreated as D[isplaced] P[ersons] as long as the Jews get special treatment. Yet when they have power, physical, financial or political neither Hitler nor Stalin has anything on them for cruelty or mistreatment to the underdog. Put an underdog on top and it makes no difference whether his name is Russian, Jewish, Negro, Management, Labor, Mormon, Baptist he goes haywire. I have found very, very few who remember their past condition when prosperity comes.

Truman's eventual cautious and conditional support for a Jewish state, a concept to which the U.S. State and Defense Departments had always been opposed, was to a great extent due to ceaseless lobbying pressure from Zionists who by courtesy of the Eddie Jacobson connection had open-door access to the White House. On November 27, 1947 the UN partition resolution was passed by an ad hoc committee vote of twenty-five to thirteen with seventeen abstentions. The vote, however, was one short of the two thirds majority that would be required to pass in the General Assembly itself.

Following pressure from Zionists and their U.S. supporters, the vote was postponed from Wednesday so that the Thursday Thanksgiving holiday could be used to canvass and acquire the necessary votes. This was achieved by threatening the loss of foreign aid to countries such as Greece who having initially been against partition, quickly changed their vote. This by any standard was the flagrant bribing and corrupting of a UN body whose main function was to regulate and enforce universal justice between nations. Israel's creation and continued existence was, is and always will be dependent on the bribing and corrupting of low life Western politicians who along with the majority of their citizens will also be subject to blackmail by the Holocaust industry.

In the end, we will remember not the words of our enemies,
but the silence of our friends.
Dr. Martin Luther King Jr.

The resolution that was subsequently passed called for the termination of the British Mandate by 1 August 1948, and the establishment of the new independent states by 1 October 1948. Banner summarised the first term of the Truman presidency by pointing out that had Truman presided over a failure to establish a Jewish state, he would most certainly have lost the 1948 November elections because Zionists had the support of almost all of Congress, the backing of the U.S. media, and the sympathy of the American people.

As the end of the mandate approached, the decision to recognise the Jewish state remained contentious, with significant disagreement between Truman, his advisors, the State Department, and the Defence Department. Though Truman was sympathetic to the Zionist cause, he was more concerned with relieving the plight of displaced people. Secretary of State George Marshall feared U.S. backing of a Jewish state would harm relations with the Muslim world, limit access to Middle Eastern oil, and destabilise the region.

On 12 May 1948, Truman met in the Oval Office with Secretary of State Marshall, Counsel to the President Clark Clifford, and several others to discuss the Palestine situation. Clifford argued in favour of recognising the new Jewish state in accordance with the partition resolution. Marshall opposed Clifford's arguments, contending they were based on domestic political considerations in the election year. Marshall said that if Truman followed Clifford's advice and recognised the Jewish state, then he would vote against Truman in the election. Truman appears to have sat on the fence during the meeting, but two days later, on 14 May 1948, the United States, under Truman, became the first country to extend any form of recognition.

This occurred quickly within hours of the Jewish People's Council gathering at the Tel Aviv Museum and David Ben-Gurion declaring the "establishment of a Jewish state in Eretz Israel to be known as the State of Israel." The text of the communication from the Provisional Government to Truman was as follows:-

MY DEAR MR. PRESIDENT:

I have the honor to notify you that the state of Israel has been proclaimed as an independent republic within frontiers approved by the General Assembly of the United Nations in its Resolution of 29 November 1947, and that a provisional government has been charged to assume the rights and duties of government for preserving law and order within the boundaries of Israel, for defending the state against external aggression, and for discharging the obligations of Israel to the other nations of the world in accordance with international law. The Act of Independence will become effective at one minute after six o'clock on the evening of 14 May 1948, Washington time.

With full knowledge of the deep bond of sympathy which has existed and has been strengthened over the past thirty years between the Government of the United States and the Jewish people of Palestine, I have been authorized by the provisional government of the new state to tender this message and to express the hope that your government will recognize and will welcome Israel into the community of nations.

Very respectfully yours,

ELIAHU EPSTEIN

Agent, Provisional Government of Israel

The text of the United States recognition was as follows:

This Government has been informed that a Jewish state has been proclaimed in Palestine, and recognition has been requested by the provisional Government thereof. The United States recognizes the provisional government as the de facto authority of the new State of Israel. (signed) Harry Truman *Approved 14 May 1948.*

With this unexpected decision, U.S. representative to the UN Warren Austin — who had previously announced at the UN that the United States believed that the partition of Palestine was no longer a viable option and had been working on alternative trusteeship proposal — resigned shortly thereafter, left his office at the UN, and went home. Secretary of State Marshall sent a State Department official to the United Nations to prevent the entire U.S. delegation from resigning. De jure (in law) recognition came on 31 January 1949.

This recognition was given despite the atrocities committed against the Palestinian people by armed Zionist terror gangs whose genocidal brutally was for responsible the Palestinian exodus of some 755000 civilians — known in Arabic as the Nabka (catastrophe) — which lasted throughout the 1947-1948 Civil War in Mandatory Palestine and the 1948 Arab-Israeli war. The latter ended following UN mediation leading to the 1949 Armistice Agreements. The Armistice was backed up by the Tripartite Declaration of 1950 consisting of the U.S. Britain, and France. In relation to enforcement of the armistice they pledged to take action within and outside the UN to prevent violations of the frontiers or armistice lines; they committed to peace and stability in the area; they stated their opposition to the use or threat of force; and they reiterated their opposition to the development of an arms race in the region. Having done all that, this highly honorable and humane tripartite — still feeling guilty over the Holocaust — then stood by while the Zionists set about the Palestinian people by destroying, raping, expelling, murdering, and stealing the land that God apparently promised them thousands of years ago.

The ensuing U.S. policy in the Middle East under rapidly changing geopolitical circumstances was predominantly one of support for the independence of Arab states, the promotion the development of oil-producing countries, the curtailment of Soviet influence in Greece, Iran, and Turkey, the prevention of an arms race, and the stance of neutrality in the Arab-Israeli conflict. Initially the U.S. used foreign aid to support and promote these objectives. But Zionism had other ideas and with the eventual establishment and success of AIPAC, Zionism began to decide who and by how much the U.S. would support and finance in the Middle East.

In 1948 the general consensus of informed world opinion had been that Israel's creation was allowed as a conscious and willful act of compensation for the Holocaust. A compensation for which the Palestinian people were still paying. As it was not the Palestinians who were responsible for the Holocaust, why should they have been chosen as the "sacrificial lamb" that would ease the collective conscious of the West? More than six decades had passed since that 1948 UN resolution and the Palestinian people were still waiting to be allowed to establish a state of their own: a state where they would not be forcibly isolated and suffocated; where they would not be subject to a blockade that prevented trade and the import of essential goods; a state where their homes would not be arbitrarily demolished; a state where their children could grow up without seeing their parents being hounded, humiliated and imprisoned; a state where those same children, like Israeli children, could enjoy the benefits of an education that would enhance their future prospects; a state where their land would not be continually and illegally expropriated; a state where illegal Israeli settlements would not encroach on their land or worm their way into their society; and a state where they could enjoy all the human rights for which the West, at great cost, is allegedly fighting both legitimate and illegitimate wars.

Banner's assessment of Dwight D. Eisenhower's presidency (1953-1961) was that while Eisenhower minimized relations with Israel and questioned the wisdom of Truman's decision to accept a Jewish state, he did not reduce U.S commitment to its existence. He did, however, recognize that good relations with Israel would inevitably harm those with the Arabs and on several occasions he made decisions with a view to redressing the imbalance of congressional support for Israel.

As a settler community, the Jewish state had from the start unilaterally and systematically helped itself to Arab land and water resources contrary to armistice agreements and over U.S. and UN protests. When in January1951 the Israelis sent military units and bulldozers into the demilitarised zone (DMZ) bordering Syria so as to grab the River Jordan for its water, the Jewish National Fund of the World Zionist Organisation agreed to help finance a $250 million development project that included drainage of the Huleh Marshes — an integral part of the River Jordan system — and irrigation of the Negev and the Jerusalem corridor.

As such drainage channels would undoubtedly impact on Syrian territory within the central DMZ, the Syrian-Israel Mixed Armistice Commission ruled that the Israeli project constituted "a flagrant violation of the armistice." On March 24 Israel asserted that it had sovereignty over the zone and consequently had the right to proceed with the project and then began doing so the very next day thereby causing clashes between Syrian and Israeli forces. Israel's response to the clashes was as usual disproportionate and resulted in the expulsion from their villages in the central DMZ of 785 Palestinians whose homes were then bulldozed. Banner wondered hypothetically if such actions were any less evil than the targeting and destruction of Jewish communities by the Nazis?

Prompted by the ongoing dispute over water, the Eisenhower Administration in 1953 began preparing a unified plan for the use of the Jordan River. By September, however, Israel decided to pre-empt the American proposals by starting to secretly construct a nine-mile long pipeline in the DMZ so as to divert the Jordan River waters. On learning of Israel's around the clock activities, the U.S. protested and President Eisenhower suspended essential economic aid to Israel. Fear of angering the Zionist lobby, however, prevented announcement of the aid's suspension. Undeterred, the Israelis shortly afterwards launched an attack on the Jordanian village of Kibya — an attack ordered by General Ariel Sharon, a war criminal who with his racist views and actions would not have looked out of place in a swastika decked Nazi uniform. The following is part of the report that appeared in the October 26, 1953 issue of *Time Magazine:*

> *The sullen enmity between infant Israel and its Arab*
> *neighbors, long acknowledged and long passed over by*

Western diplomacy, erupted last week with violence that could no longer be ignored.

At 9:30 one night, most of the people were just going to bed in the Jordanian village of Kibya, 20 miles northwest of Jerusalem, and a mile and a half beyond the Israeli frontier. A light burned in the village coffeehouse, where a few late gossipers were preparing to depart; on this quiet night, as usual, everyone put his trust in the U.N. 'truce' and 30 skimpily armed Jordanian national guardsmen. Suddenly, Israeli artillery, previously zeroed onto target, opened up, and a 600-man battalion of uniformed Israeli regulars swept across the border to encircle the village. For the next two hours the town shuddered under shell bursts and small-arms fire; villagers, screaming and milling, rushed out to the surrounding fields and olive groves. Then the guardsmen's ammo (25 rounds per man) gave out, and the Israelis moved into Kibya with rifle and sten guns. They shot every man, woman and child they could find, then turned their fire on the cattle.

After that, they dynamited 42 houses, a school and a mosque. The cries of the dying could be heard amid the explosions. The villagers huddled in the grass could see Israeli soldiers slouching in the doorways of their homes, smoking and joking, their young faces illuminated by the flames. By 3 a.m. the Israeli's work was done, and they leisurely withdrew.

At dawn, the villagers crept out of the grass and made for the smoldering ruins, looking desperately for a husband, a wife, a child. They crowded around a young girl whose body sprawled grotesquely, forefinger raised to heaven as Moslems do when they say: "There is only one God, and Mohammed is his prophet." An old man dug furiously in the debris, occasionally looked up, terror in his eyes, then laughed hysterically. Once he shouted to the sky: "Allah! I have no relations now. Why didn't you leave me one person?' Sixty-six died that night; eleven from one family, ten of another. It was the bloodiest night of border warfare

184

since the 1949 armistice — the armistice that won Dr.
Ralph Bunche the Nobel Peace Prize, but brought no peace.

Mark Banner noted that while Nazis were to this day still being pursued to answer for their war crimes, it seemed that Israelis were to be exempt from being judged by the same standards. As a result of the ensuing outcry over the Kibya massacre, on October 18, 1953, the Eisenhower administration made public its suspension of aid to Israel. The suspension lasted a pathetic and meaningless eleven days because following pressure from the U.S. Zionist lobby and an Israeli pledge to suspend construction on the diversion project, U.S. aid was restored. The Israeli pledge was as always worthless and construction of the diversion project was eventually recommenced and completed in defiance of an important principle of international law regarding water use which states that water should not be diverted from its catchment basin.

Israel's unilateral appropriation of virtually all this water left only unusable briny water for the Jordanians and the Syrians and ended all local Arab agricultural activity. Israel's typically selfish and insatiable thirst for water meant that numerous more murderous raids were to be launched so as to facilitate the plunder of yet more water resources. Of the water available from West Bank aquifers, Israel uses 73%, the Palestinian majority uses 17%, and the illegal Jewish settlers use 10%. These settlers, who insist they are God's chosen people often vandalize Palestinian wells by pouring concrete into them, breaking connecting pipes, and even contaminating them with hazardous waste such as used disposable diapers. Every year there are hundreds of violent incidents involving armed settler attacks that injure unarmed Palestinians and damage Palestinian property. Attacks on mosques were also a regular occurrence including walls being daubed with Hebrew graffiti and even arson. Violence against Palestinians was also committed by members of the Israeli Defense Force who are mostly brutal and racist with perhaps a few dissenting voices:

I was shocked to see IDF soldiers dragging a bleeding
young Palestinian in the streets of Hebron. The shocking
image showed our soldiers as sadist who rejoice over the
killing of a young man, and drag his body to our settlers to
rejoice, dance, exchange candy and kick the not yet dead
body. It reminds me of cheetahs and hyenas, which kill and

185

drag their prey. The problem is that these animals kill to survive. Our soldiers kill to maintain the occupation, an apartheid system.

An ex-IDF officer, mentioned in the Jewish daily *Haaretz* in January 2001.

This raised the question as to whether the Jewish settlers and IDF soldiers responsible for such attacks are any better than the anti-Semite neo-Nazis who desecrate Jewish monuments. Even more disturbing is the fact that rather than enforce the law by preventing such attacks, the Israeli Defense Force overtly supports and trains these lawless settlers. Many of the West Bank's most important underground wellsprings are located just to the east of the Green Line dividing Israel from Palestine. So when building its "defensive wall," Israel made a point of also annexing land that was directly over many of these wells whose waters were then diverted to Israel and illegal Israeli settlements in the West Bank. Israel does not allow the drilling of new wells by Palestinians, it confiscates many wells for Israeli use, and sets quotas on how much water Palestinians can draw from their own existing wells.

When supplies of water run low in the summer months, the Israeli water company Mekorot simply shuts off the supply to Palestinian towns and villages so as not to affect Israeli usage. This results in illegal Israeli settlers being able to water their lawns and top up their swimming pools while their Palestinian neighbours, on whose land the Israeli settlements were illegally built, do not have enough water for drinking and cooking. To add insult to injury, the ever exploiting Israelis often sell the water it has stolen from the West Bank back to the Palestinians at inflated prices. International law unequivocally states that it is illegal for Israel to expropriate the water of the Occupied Palestinian Territories for use by its own citizens or by illegal Israeli settlers; and furthermore, that Israel owes Palestinians reparations — with interest for loss of earnings from agriculture — for past and continuing use of Palestinian water resources. While Eisenhower failed to enforce some measure of justice for the Arabs whose water Israel was stealing, he did to some extent try to make amends following the Suez Crisis.

The seeds for the Suez Crisis were sown when in May 1956 Egyptian President Gamal Abdel Nasser officially recognised the People's Republic of China and in doing so angered the U.S. which was a staunch supporter of Taiwan. Eisenhower's response on July 19 was to withdraw all U.S. financial aid for the Aswan Dam project. Nasser swiftly retaliated on July 26 by nationalizing the Suez Canal and closing it to Israeli shipping.

The ensuing hostilities, also known as the Tripartite Aggression, involved France as the instigator, Britain as a belated partner, and Israel as the trigger. So on October 29 Israel invaded Egypt and on the following day, as part of the tripartite's agreed charade, France and Britain issued a joint ultimatum for an end to hostilities which Nasser rejected. On the night of November 5-6, British and French troops invaded Port Said and took control of the Suez Canal. Eisenhower wins the U.S. Presidential election and on November 7, and joined by the USSR and the UN, the U.S. condemns the military action and forces British Prime Minister Anthony Eden into calling a ceasefire. The tripartite troops were forced to withdraw and Britain and France failed in their political and strategic aims of regaining control of the canal and toppling President Nasser from Power.

In his assessment of the Eisenhower Presidency, Banner credited Eisenhower, like George Washington, with having the wisdom and foresight to recognise and warn against potential pitfalls for for the future of U.S. Democracy. Eisenhower did so by addressing the danger of having an immense military-industrial complex that would impact on every aspect of American life and become susceptible to the unwarranted covert influence of special interest groups.

In the intervening years since Eisenhower's 1961 Farewell Address warning, the vast U.S. military-industrial complex had for its survival become dependent on never-ending global conflicts. Like a voracious colossus it feeds on human misery, death, and wanton destruction. In its quest for continual U.S. involvement in overseas wars, it has AIPAC as an ally with immense influence on Capitol Hill with the result that together they have deliberately duped the American people into accepting the false necessity of constantly waging war. The former has done so by first employing a revolving door syndrome that cycles employees between the armaments industry and government agencies such as the Pentagon; and secondly by maintaining the false perception of ever-present danger and threats to U.S. security. The latter does so by establishing as fact the misconception that Israel and the U.S. are staunch allies facing and fighting against the same enemies. Banner supported his thesis by citing the following excerpt from Eisenhower's Farewell Address to the Nation on January 17, 1961:

. . . Until the latest of our world conflicts, the United States had no armaments industry. American makers of ploghshares could, with time and as required, make swords as well. But now we can no longer risk emergency improvisation of national defense; we have been compelled to create a permanent armaments industry of vast proportions. Added to this, three and a half million men and women are directly engaged in the defense establishment. We annually spend on military security more than the net income of all United States corporations.

This conjunction of an immense military establishment and a large arms industry is new in the American experience. The total influence — economic, political, even spiritual — is felt in every city, every State house, every office of the Federal government. We recognize the imperative need for this development. Yet we must not fail to comprehend its grave implications. Our toil, resources and livelihood are all involved; so is the very structure of our society.

In the councils of government, we must guard against the acquisition of unwarranted influence, whether sought or unsought, by the military industrial complex. The potential for the disastrous rise of misplaced power exists and will persist.

We must never let the weight of this combination endanger our liberties or democratic processes. We should take nothing for granted. Only an alert and knowledgeable citizenry can compel the proper meshing of the huge industrial and military machinery of defense with our peaceful methods and goals, so that security and liberty may prosper together.

Akin to, and largely responsible for the sweeping changes in our industrial-military posture, has been the technological revolution during recent decades.

In this revolution, research has become central; it also becomes more formalized, complex, and costly. A steadily increasing share is conducted for, by, or at the direction of, the Federal government.

Today, the solitary inventor, tinkering in his shop, has been overshadowed by task forces of scientists in laboratories and testing fields. In the same fashion, the free university, historically the fountainhead of free ideas and scientific discovery, has experienced a revolution in the conduct of research. Partly because of the huge costs involved, a government contract becomes virtually a substitute for intellectual curiosity. For every old blackboard there are now hundreds of new electronic computers.

The prospect of domination of the nation's scholars by Federal employment, project allocations, and the power of money is ever present — and is gravely to be regarded.

Yet, in holding scientific research and discovery in respect, as we should, we must also be alert to the equal and opposite danger that public policy could itself become the captive of a scientific technological elite.

It is the task of statesmanship to mould, to balance, and to integrate these and other forces, new and old, within the principles of our democratic system — ever aiming toward the supreme goals of our free society.

Another factor in maintaining balance involves the element of time. As we peer into society's future, we — you and I, and our government — must avoid the impulse to live only for today, plundering, for our own ease and convenience, the precious resources of tomorrow. We cannot mortgage the material assets of our grandchildren without risking the loss also of their political and spiritual heritage. We want democracy to survive for all generations to come, not to become the insolvent phantom of tomorrow.

Down the long lane of the history yet to be written America knows that this world of ours, ever growing smaller, must avoid becoming a community of dreadful fear and hate, and be instead, a proud confederation of mutual trust and respect.

Such a confederation must be one of equals. The weakest must come to the conference table with the same confidence as do we, protected as we are by our moral, economic, and military strength. That table, though scarred by many past frustrations, cannot be abandoned for the certain agony of the battlefield.

Disarmament, with mutual honour and confidence, is a continuing imperative. Together we must learn how to compose differences, not with arms, but with intellect and decent purpose. Because this need is so sharp and apparent I confess that I lay down my official responsibilities in this field with a definite sense of disappointment. As one who has witnessed the horror and the lingering sadness of war — as one who knows that another war could utterly destroy this civilization which has been so slowly and painfully built over thousands of years — I wish I could say tonight that a lasting peace is in sight . . .

Mark Banner concluded that had former President Eisenhower been still alive today he would have been disappointed with the majority of American citizens who were neither "alert" nor "Knowledgeable" enough to control and compel the direction in which their government was leading the nation. By unconditionally supporting Israel and fighting wars that are prompted by combined Israeli, neoconservative, and military-industrial interests, successive U.S. governments had sold the American people down the river. They had diminished the standing, the integrity, and the power of the U.S. in world affairs. The real danger was that as the U.S. became less effective and influential in world affairs — a scenario that was already gradually occurring — the day might come when U.S. support for Israel will be rendered useless by a world full of other nations that finally tire of being bullied and blackmailed into silence by a U.S.-sponsored arrogant Israel. In the event of that happening with Israel having to fend for itself — insane Israeli leaders in the mould of an Ariel Sharon or a Benjamin Netanyahu — would not hesitate to use Israeli weapons of mass destruction and thereby initiate a nuclear holocaust whose consequences would be too horrendous for even Barack "Uncle Tom" Obama's fully stretched imagination to contemplate.

190

5

Tuesday, 9 December 2008
The British Library, Euston Road, London

Despite being to some extent familiar with the Old City of Jerusalem's historical background, David Reisner nonetheless decided that he required more in-depth information to fully appreciate all the ramifications of the map in his possession. So with that in mind, he was already waiting outside the entrance to Britain's national library when it opened at 9:30am. With some 150 million items from numerous countries, in many languages and formats, in both print and digital: the library was an ideal research facility with books, manuscripts, journals, newspapers, magazines, sound and music recordings, videos, play-scripts, patents, databases, maps, stamps, prints, and drawings. With approximately 14 million books and substantial holdings of manuscripts and historical items dating as far as back as 2000 BCE, the British Library was one of the two largest libraries in the world along with the United States Library of Congress.

Apart from stopping for a quick lunch of a sandwich and coffee, Reisner stuck to his task until just before the library's closing time of 6:00pm. He learnt that since the previous year the Israel Antiquities Authority (IAA) had been focusing its attention — under the pretext of scientific research — on the excavation of channels, tunnels, and underground spaces within Jerusalem's Historic Old City Basin and its surrounding areas with the intention of creating a physical environment suitable for ideological tourism with Zionist Israeli political overtones.

Though ostensibly engaged in scientific work, the IAA restricts access to any information relating to the locations, the objectives of its excavations, the scope of its activities, or the nature of its discoveries. Any information regarding IAA activities is never transparently forthcoming during excavations and is usually only released after the fact through a communiqué by a spokesperson. The covert nature of IAA's excavations consequently leads to suspicion of irregularities, concern of possible damage to archeological discoveries, and alarm at the prospect that excavations were being used to advance covert political objectives. The IAA's failure to provide a detailed account of all ongoing underground excavations in the Historic Basin had created a climate of distrust amongst the Palestinians and the international community who view its archeological activity with justifiable suspicion.

Reisner learnt that the current fascination with both ancient and contemporary underground tunnels and channels in and around the Temple Mount was by no means a recent phenomenon and in fact first occurred some 150 years earlier when European archeologists came to Jerusalem — with a view to establishing the ancient city's topography and the nature of the structures adjacent to Temple Mount — and began digging deep within its bowels. Preeminent amongst the archaeologists was Captain Charles Warren (1840-1927), an officer with the British Royal Engineers who in 1867 was recruited by the Palestine Exploration Fund to conduct Biblical archaeological reconnaissance.

Warren, who had spent much of his military service in British South Africa, was in earlier life the head of the London Metropolitan Police from 1886 to 1888 during the time of the Jack the Ripper murders. Though his command in combat during the Second Boer War was criticised, he nonetheless achieved considerable success both as a civilian and a soldier during his long life. A devout Anglican and enthusiastic Freemason — suggestions have since been made of a connection between Freemasonry and the Ripper murders — Warren became involved in 1908 with Robert Baden-Powell (1857-1941) in the formation of the Boy Scout movement.

As Warren's excavations — aided by an 1862 map showing the wells and water systems on the Temple Mount (Haram al-Sharif) — had to be surreptitious so as to avoid the attention of inquisitive Ottoman authorities, he first dug vertical shafts away from the walls of the Temple Mount, and then proceeded to excavate horizontal tunnels (galleries) along the Western and ancient Walls which are now part of the network of "Western Wall Tunnels." An ancient gate leading to the Temple Mount was also uncovered and attributed to the Herod's temple complex (first century BCE). Warren's team also carried out deep underground excavations out of sight of the authorities in the adjoining village of Silwan and uncovered important sections of Biblical Jerusalem's water system which included the shafts, tunnels, and channels — both naturally formed and man-made — that are now known as Warren's Shaft.

Excavations in Jerusalem continued during the Ottoman rule with archeologists F.G. Bliss and A.C. Dickie, digging a sprawling system of channels and tunnels around Mount Zion and the Siloam Pool (Birket al-Hamra) between 1894 and 1897. A two-year expedition led by M.

Parker starting in 1909 renewed investigations of the ancient waterworks of Jerusalem with a view to discovering a subterranean passage from the Gihon Spring in Silwan to the heart of the Temple Mount, where, it was hoped, treasures of the Temple would be discovered. The Parker expedition had to eventually abandon further excavations when it was revealed that an attempt had been made to bribe some Waqf Islamic guards so as to be allowed to excavate under the Temple Mount itself.

These clandestine excavations served to support two opposing viewpoints regarding the purpose of Jerusalem's archaeology. The Western viewpoint was that excavations beneath the surface had identified the 'real' Jerusalem thereby exposing its current inhabitants as debased and benighted survivors of the past who obscured the Holy City's status and destiny. Alternatively the Palestinian-Muslim viewpoint suggested that archaeology was a tool of western imperialism designed to undermine the Islamic presence in al-Quds and in the Haram al-Sharif.

Following those late 19th. and early 20th. century explorations in Jerusalem, the scientific techniques of archaeology rapidly developed with the "gallery" method of excavation being abandoned. The objective of scientific excavations was then prioritized to expose the historical layers from the top-down so as to reveal the sequence of stratification. Under British and Jordanian rule, Jerusalem's archaeology emerged from a shadowy past into the light of day with successive layers of its history being uncovered in a well-ordered manner from the surface and downwards.

As Reisner continued reading, he learnt that the well-ordered approach soon gave way to frenzied activity in and around the Old City following the 1967 Six Day War. Researchers from Jerusalem's Hebrew University led the way with extensive excavations in the Jewish Quarter; in the Ophel south of the Temple Mount, and at the "City of David" on the southeast hill of ancient Jerusalem. Though those excavations were conducted in accordance with acceptable scientific standards, subsequent excavations were not always as methodical and tended to adopt a less scrupulous approach.

In 1969 for example, with prompting from the Ministry of Religion, an excavation of a tunnel was begun under the densely built-up Muslim Quarter along the Western Wall that bordered the Temple Mount (Haram al-Sharif). Though this excavation continued through to the start of the 1990s under the auspices of a government ministry, the work was for many years of a covert nature; was unlicensed by the Israel Department of Antiquities (predecessor of the IAA); and records of what was found were not kept.

This was a time of an intense political struggle with the Palestinian Authority for political control of East Jerusalem. With the questionable support of then Mayor Ehud Olmert — subsequently mired in corruption scandals — it was decided to open the northern end of the tunnel, on the Via Dolorosa. The tunnel's opening "the rock of our existence" signaled the start of violent confrontations between Israeli forces and Palestinians throughout the West Bank with dozens killed and hundreds injured. Following the end of the violent clashes, the Western Wall Heritage Fund began using the northern exit of the tunnel as a means of increasing visitor numbers to the Western Wall Tunnels and thereby expand its area of control into the heart of the Muslim Quarter. Excavations in the Old City and the Historic Basin have since the mid-90s, virtually become the exclusive domain of the IAA which oversees excavations from the Siloam Pool on the slopes of Silwan to Herod's Gate in the northern wall of the Old City.

Underground excavations then continued at a moderate pace starting in Gihon Spring ('Ein Umm al-Daraj) at the request of Elad — the notorious settler organization and bane of Palestinian inhabitants — supported by the Israel Parks Authority. In 2004 a notable discovery was made on the southern slopes of the "City of David" archaeological park — actually the Wadi Hilweh neighborhood of Silwan — of an ancient pool and the remains of a Roman road leading from it towards Temple Mount.

Extensive excavations were also carried out at the top of the Tyropoean valley (Valley of the Cheesemakers) beneath the Ohel Yitzhak Synagogue adjacent to the Western Wall plaza. Though these two archaeological ventures were some distance apart and apparently separated by the walls of the Old City and the houses of Wadi Hilweh, they were in fact connected by the ancient streets and drainage channels uncovered years earlier by Bliss and Dickie. The simultaneous occurrence of these ventures was evidently not a coincidence, but a calculated plan to establish a link both physically (rediscovery of old tunnels) and ideologically (renewal of the abandoned method of tunnel excavations).

The IAA has since 2004 teamed up with ideological organizations to develop the Western Wall and the "City of David" National Park areas with a view to connecting the "City of David" to the Western Wall plaza in a single underground system which would include the large underground spaces whose contents were completely cleared. From 2005 to 2008, the IAA carried out tunnel excavations in Silwan and around the Western Wall where tunneling was used for the connection between the Ohel Yitzhak Synagogue and the Western Wall Tunnels.

South of Silwan, a lateral tunnel excavation uncovered parts of the early Roman street that was recorded by Bliss and Dickie. Further on up the slope, above the level of this road, a shaft was excavated from above into Bliss and Dickie's tunnels and revealed a covered stone-constructed drain which appeared to have run under the continuation of the same early Roman street. More than six feet (1.82 meters) high, the channel runs under Wadi Hilwe Street towards the Temple Mount excavations (the Davidson Centre) and continues north under the Western Wall plaza. All this work was overseen by the IAA as part of tourism development for the "City of David" National Park, and financed by the Elad Organization.

Further excavations had since 2007 been carried out within the Western Wall Tunnels and in the spaces that extend westward to El-Wad (Hagai) Street beneath the residential areas of the Muslim Quarter. Hundreds of square meters are being excavated with ancient walls being pierced and large amounts of fill being removed without methodical but perhaps selective documentation that serves the Zionist Israeli perspective. Nonetheless uncovered remains include almost every important period in Jerusalem's history: a large hamam (Turkish bath) from the the Mamluk period (Hamam al-'Ein); and remains of Aelia Capitolina which was the Roman city built by Hadrian over Jerusalem's ruins after its destruction in 70 CE by the Romans.

Silwan's folklore dates back to the arrival of the second Rashidun caliph, Umar ibn al-Khattab from Arabia who apparently so impressed the Greeks that they presented him with the key to the city. The Caliph thereafter granted the wadi to "Khan Silowna," an agricultural community of cave dwellers living around the valley spring. According to medieval Muslim tradition, the spring of Silwan (Ayn Silwan) was among the four most sacred water sources in the world. Silwan was mentioned as "Sulwan" by the 10th-century Arab writer and traveller al-Muqaddasi (c. 945-991) who In 985 noted that south of the village was 'Ain Sulwan ("Spring of Siloam") which provided "fairly good water" for irrigation of the large gardens that the third Rashidun caliph 'Othman ibn 'Affan endowed as a waqf — an inalienable religious endowment in Islamic law — to the impoverished residents of Jerusalem. Al-Muqaddasi further wrote that "It is said that on the Night of Arafat the water of the holy well Zamzam, at Makkah, comes underground to the water of the Spring (of Siloam). The people hold a festival here on that evening."

Ottoman tax registers in 1596 show that 'Ayn Silwan as being in the Nahiya (level of administration) of Quds of the Liwa of Quds with a population of 60 Muslim households. During a large-scale peasants' rebellion against Ibrahim Pasha of Egypt in 1834, thousands of rebels infiltrated Jerusalem through ancient underground sewage channels leading to the farm fields of the village of Silwan. In the mid-1850s, the villagers of Silwan were paid £100 annually by the Jews so as to prevent the desecration of graves on the Mount of Olives. Jewish visitors to the Western Wall were also required to pay a tax to Silwan's residents which by 1863 was apparently 10,000 Piastres. Travelers in the 19th-century described the village as a robbers' lair of which Charles Wilson — Chairman of the Palestine Exploration Fund — wrote that "the houses and the streets of Siloam, if such they may be called, are filthy in the extreme." Charles Warren depicted the population as a lawless set of the most unscrupulous ruffians in Palestine.

Silwan currently has a population of about 30,000 Palestinians and more than 50 Jewish families whose properties were deviously acquired by having them designated as 'absentee.' Furthermore it is an established fact that claims filed by Jewish organizations were accepted by the Custodian without any site visits or follow-up procedures. Property in Silwan has been variously acquired by invocation of the Absentee Property Law, purchase by Jews through indirect sales, and in many cases, the Jewish National Fund signed protected tenant agreements that allowed construction to proceed without any tender process. In some cases homes have been acquired from Arabs who claim they did not even know they were selling their homes to Jews. The Rabbis for Human Rights organization (founded in 1988) has accused Elad of creating a "method of expelling citizens from their properties, appropriating public areas, enclosing these lands with fences and guards, and banning the entrance of the local residents . . . under the protection of a private security force."

Within Jerusalem's ancient mound there are two unique underground systems of which the best known is the Siloam (Shiloah) Tunnel. This 500-meter rock-carved tunnel carries the waters of the

Gihon Spring ('Ein Umm al-Daraj) — located in the Qidron Valley between the two parts of Silwan — to the Pool of Siloam at the southern end of the ancient mound and the Wadi Hilweh neighborhood. From there the spring water runs down towards the houses of Al-Bustan. The Siloam Tunnel system consists of a number of carved tunnels and channels of which some are dry and some still carry water. Studies suggest that the initial stages of the tunnel's construction date back to the Canaanite period (18th century BCE to the Middle Bronze Age IIB, 1750-1650 BCE); and the latter stages to the Kingdom of Judah (8th century BCE to the Iron Age II, 1400-1200 BCE).

A second system of hewn passages connected to a vertical shaft of apparently natural origin extends above the man-made tunnel between the top of the hill and the Gihon Spring. This shaft is named after Charles Warren and its dating, purpose, and intended function are still subject to conjecture.

Since 1995 work has continued around the Gihon Spring and the adjoining systems with underground excavations being carried out in areas beneath residential structures and under the plaza facing Silwan's elementary school. Further excavations via a westward dug tunnel under a stepped public path connect to the stepped section excavated in the 1960s by the leading British archaeologist Kathleen Kenyon (1906-1978). Uncovered were the impressive remains of a fortification dating to the Middle Bronze Age. Visitors were obliged to enter and exit through a single access point in the Western Wall.

The extension of the Western Wall Tunnels through to the Via Dolorosa in the Muslim Quarter were completed 1993 with the opening being delayed until 1996 when Benjamin Netanyahu began his first tenure as prime minister. This was less than a year after Prime Minister Yitzhak Rabin was assassinated in November 1955 by Yigal Amir, a radical right-wing Orthodox Jew — who like millions of other Israelis — was not interested in peace and opposed the signing of the Oslo Accords. It had been a time of intense political struggle with the Palestinian Authority for political control of East Jerusalem.

With the support of then Mayor Ehud Olmert — subsequently to be investigated for various corruption charges — it was decided to open the northern end of the tunnel, on the Via Dolorosa. Opening of the tunnel "the rock of our existence" provoked demonstrations and violence between Palestinians and Israeli forces throughout the West Bank in which dozens were killed and hundreds injured. Following the eventual conclusion of violent demonstrations, the Western Wall Heritage Fund commenced using the tunnel's northern exit to increase the visitor numbers to the Western Wall Tunnels and thus stretch the area under its control to the heart of the Muslim Quarter.

●　●　●　●　●

As there was a load of material still to be tackled, David Reisner returned to the British Library first thing Thursday Morning and quickly settled down to reading about how the "City of David" excavations in the Silwan neighborhood had become a battleground between traditional and critical archaeologists. Critical archaeologists totally rejected the "Zionist narrative" of traditional archaeology that Jews were rooted in the Biblical Land of Israel.   Critical archaeology — also known as Biblical minimalism or the Copenhagen School — had been introduced by archaeologists Niels Peter Lemche, Thomas L. Thompson (University of Copenhagen) and Philip R. Davies, and Keith W. Whitelam (University of Sheffield). In his book *The Invention of Ancient Israel: The Silencing of Palestinians History* (Routledge, 1996), Whitelam shows how the true history of ancient Palestine had been obscured by calculated and persistent efforts by traditional Israeli archaeologists to create the link between modern Israel and its Biblical homeland.   Many   academics from Israel and abroad who were concerned over the threat of academic boycott were planning to petition the Tel Aviv University (TAU) requesting the termination of the university's participation in Elad's archaeological excavations in the Silwan neighborhood of occupied East Jerusalem. A partnership between Elad and TAU's Institute of Archaeology to excavate in the "City of David" national park would endanger Palestinian homes situated above. A plan to settle further 500 Israeli Jews throughout Silwan was yet another confrontational move by Elad which was allowed to act with impunity by Israeli authorities. The TAU was not the only university guilty of Politicizing research and was closely followed by the Hebrew University which offered an "Archaeological Field Summer School" at the "City of David" where students could gain credit for the studies.

Critical archaeologists felt that TAU was causing immeasurable damage not only to the chances of avoiding sanctions against Israel from the Boycott, Divestment and Sanctions movement (BDS), but also to Israeli academia in general which was already being subjected to boycotts and cancellations for conference and cultural activities. Earlier in 2008 so-called liberal critics of Israeli government policies were opposed to freedom of movement restrictions on Palestinian students from the West Bank on the grounds that such policies only helped "those who are trying to impose an academic boycott on Israel."

The relationship with the Elad in occupied Silwan is only a small part of TAU's complicity in grave violations of international law and human rights abuses and it also takes great pride in its intimate relationship with the state and the military. This is evident from the 2008-2009 winter edition of Tau's Review which boasted about "how much TAU contributes to Israel's security," by being "at the front line of the critical work to maintain Israel's military and technological edge." In the same issue TAU President Zvi Galil claimed to be "awed by the magnitude and scientific creativity of the work being done behind the scenes at TAU that enhances the country's civilian defense capabilities and military edge." The Review also referred to "defense-related research throughout the TAU campus," with MAFAT, "a Hebrew acronym meaning the R&D Directorate of the Israel Ministry of Defense," funding 55 projects at TAU.

TAU's close ties to the military serves to enforce the colonial occupation of the West Bank and Gaza Strip and comes as no surprise considering that an estimated 50 percent of students in the Security Studies Program "belong to the middle and upper echelon of Israel's defense establishment." The course is designed to equip them "with new conceptual tools and concepts," and the program is headed up by Professor Isaac Ben-Israel, a Major General (res.) in the Israeli military, who also happens to run TAU's decade-old Science, Technology and Security Workshop. It is Ben-Israel's opinion that "Military R&D in Israel would not exist without the universities. They carry out all the basic scientific investigation, which is then developed either by defense industries or the army."

TAU also offered a special engineering program for soldiers who excelled, with numerous students every year participating in the IDF Academic Reserve Program that supplies them "with an open-minded academic approach, skill set, and expertise for key research posts in the army." In the meantime, the Institute for National Security Studies (INSS), is an "external institute" of TAU that "operates seminar, workshop, and lecture programs jointly with the National Security College, IDF Command, and National Security Council." At a conference earlier that month, the INSS head noted with satisfaction that "we are now on the threshold of Tel Aviv University campus and this proximity is more than geographical proximity of buildings — it is a fertile and mutually stimulating proximity." It was the INSS which published IDF Major-General (res.) Giora Eiland's paper titled *The Third Lebanon War:Target Lebanon* which came to the following conclusion:

> *There is one way to prevent the Third Lebanon War and win it if it does break out (and thereby prevent the Fourth Lebanon War): to make it clear to Lebanon's allies and through them to the Lebanese government and people that the next war will be between Israel and Lebanon and not between Israel and Hizbollah. Such a war will lead to the elimination of the Lebanese military, the destruction of the national infrastructure, and intense suffering among the population. There will be no recurrence of the situation where Beirut residents (not including the Dahiya quarter) go to the beach and cafes while Haifa residents sit in bomb shelters.*

> *Serious damage to the Republic of Lebanon, the destruction of homes and infrastructure, and the suffering of hundreds of thousands of people are consequences that can influence Hizbollah's behavior more than anything else. The impact on Hizbollah and its willingness to end the war following Israeli actions of the kind described here would result from both internal and external effects. The internal effect stems from Hizbollah's political status and ambitions, as it portrays itself as a Lebanese national organization fighting for the interests of the Republic of Lebanon. It may lose its status if Lebanese public opinion blames it for the unnecessary destruction brought upon the state. The external effect stems from the organization's sensitivity to Iranian and Syrian interests. Neither Iran nor certainly not Syria wants Lebanon to be destroyed.*

As Israel's biggest university — entrusted with educating the best and brightest of Israel's young minds — TAU is unashamedly complicit in Israel's illegal colonial and criminal policies which constitute a legacy dating all the way back to the Nakba ("Day of the Catastrophe") and not just its current involvement in politicized archaeological excavations. TAU's campus encompasses land belonging to the destroyed village of

Sheikh Muwannis, with the home of the former village sheikh now being used as the university's faculty club. There can be no denial that Israel's security-military apparatus has been guilty of routine participation in apartheid policies and war crimes that are part of a decades-long oppressive and illegal occupation — an illegal occupation in which Israel's teaching fraternity is deeply and probably irretrievably mired.

By using the Dung Gate — the Old City's main entrance to the Jewish quarter — Elad has used the development of the "City of David" to gradually diminish Silwan's status as the heart of East Jerusalem's Palestinian population and to displace its residents by erecting new apartments for its settler corps. Furthermore, its openly declared intention is to surround the Old City with Jewish settlers and link up with Jewish neighborhoods to the north and east so as to forestall the possibility of any redivision of Jerusalem for a two-state solution. Without rightist financial support from abroad and corrupt collusion with the Antiquities Authority, there would be no "City of David" and the resulting subjection of the Palestinian population to atrocious hardships. Because irrespective of how often they tell themselves and the rest of the world that theirs is a god-given land, their collective conscience knows that theirs is a stolen land for which they lied, cheated, and murdered and that invoking God's name with Biblical quotations will never alter that irrefutable fact.

View of Silwan from the "City of David" park

Israeli police reinforce the illegal occupation

6
Wednesday, 10 December 2008
The Corniche, Beirut, Lebanon

It is interesting — but not surprising — to note that in all the words written and uttered about the Kennedy assassination, Israel's intelligence agency, the Mossad, has never been mentioned. And yet a Mossad motive is obvious. On this question, as on almost all others, American reporters and commentators cannot bring themselves cast Israel in an unfavorable light — despite the obvious fact that Mossad complicity is as plausible as any of the other theories.
Former Rep. Paul Findley (R-I11.), in the *Washington Report on Middle East Affairs*, March 1992.

Mark Banner began his evaluation of U.S.-Israeli relations during John F. Kennedy's short-lived Presidency with the above quote which preceded a summary and dismissal of the better known conspiracy theories relating to the Kennedy assassination. Banner was of the view that for any theory to have credibility, it must first address the question of "why was JFK killed and who had most to gain from his death?" In attempting to answer that question he pointed out that even before JFK was inaugurated, the Israeli leadership was by no means enamored with the prospect of having to deal with the son of an anti-Semite. Though JFK's father Joseph P. Kennedy regarded some individual Jews with a degree of esteem, his opinion of Jews as a people was by his own admission extremely unfavorable.   So apart from unjustly visiting the sins of the father on his son, Israeli leaders including Prime Minister David Ben-Gurion, were also at loggerheads with JFK over several important issues. The first was JFK's desire to prevent a nuclear arms race in the Middle East which on June 15, 1963 he reiterated in the last of a series of insistent letters to Israeli Prime Minister David Ben-Gurion. It has since become apparent that there never was a "special relationship" between Israel and JFK who had no doubt whatsoever that while Israel was masquerading as a friend and ally of the U.S., it was simultaneously lying repeatedly about its nuclear weapons development program.

On realizing that JFK would not budge on the issue, Ben-Gurion — who earnestly believed that possession of nuclear weapons was essential for Israel's survival — then decided to join forces with Communist China. As both countries were bent on creating nuclear programs, they began secretly developing their own nuclear capability through intermediary Shaul Eisenberg, who was a partner of Mossad gun-runner and accountant Tibor Rosenbaum. In his book *Seeds of Fire: China and the Story Behind the Attack on America* (Dandelion Books, 2001), Gordon Thomas exposes how the Mossad and CSIS (Chinese secret service) had conspired on many occasions to not only steal American military secrets, but to also to doctor U.S. intelligence programs.

One of Israel's most successful spies in the U.S. was Jonathan Jay Pollard, a former civilian intelligence analyst who in 1987 was convicted of spying for Israel and sentenced to life imprisonment. Pollard's case was later linked to that of Ben-ami Kadish, another U.S. national who pleaded guilty to charges of passing classified information to Israel in the same period. Israel granted Pollard citizenship in 1995 while continuing until 1998 to publicly deny that he was an Israeli spy. There is constant lobbying for his release by Israeli activist groups and high-profile Israeli politicians including Israeli Prime Minister Benjamin Netanyahu who visited the convicted spy in prison in 2002 which was in the same year that Pollard renounced his U.S. citizenship.

JFK's letter to Ben-Gurion was by no means friendly and stressed that as a professed ally, Israel should prove "beyond a reasonable doubt" that as the Middle East's Zionist enclave it was not developing nuclear weapons. The letter had been duly cabled to Tel Aviv but before it could be physically delivered by the U.S. ambassador, David Ben-Gurion abruptly resigned for undisclosed personal reasons.

In view of the fact that the Israelis routinely intercept communications and spy on the U.S., it may be safely assumed that having learnt of the letter's content, Ben-Gurion decided not only to preempt the letter's significance, but also to deprive JFK of an Israeli government with which to negotiate. JFK had at the time simply sought what Israel is now demanding of Iran: international inspections of its nuclear facilities. Had JFK succeeded, Israel would not have at some time between 1962 and 1964 produced the first of what is now a vast nuclear arsenal of some 200-400 warheads?

During that same 1962-63 period Senator William J. Fulbright of Arkansas, chairman of the Committee on Foreign Relations, convened

204

hearings on the legal status of the American Zionist Council (AZC). The Committee uncovered evidence that the Jewish Agency, a predecessor to the state of Israel, operated a massive network of financial "conduits" which funneled funds to U.S. Israel lobby groups. As a result, Attorney General Robert F. Kennedy (RFK) ordered the AZC to openly register and disclose all of its foreign funded lobbying activity in the United States. The attempt was subsequently thwarted first by the Israel lobby itself and then by the death of President Kennedy which led to growing concerns regarding the impact of the ever-growing Zionist influence on U.S. policy making decisions. On April 15, 1973, Fulbright — who lost his Senate seat the following year — had no qualms about boldly announcing on CBS *Face the Nation* that :

> *Israel controls the U.S. Senate. The Senate is subservient, much too much; we should be more concerned about U.S. interests rather than doing the bidding of Israel. The great majority of the Senate of the U.S. — somewhere around 80% — is completely in support of Israel; anything Israel wants; Israel gets. This has been demonstrated time and again, and this has made [foreign policy] difficult for our government.*

According to Banner the probability of Mossad's involvement in JFK's assassination was in 1994 clearly substantiated by **Michael Collins Piper who in his incisive book, *Final Judgment: The Missing link in the JFK Assassination Conspiracy* (American Free Press, 2004)** stated that:

> *Israel's Mossad was a primary (and critical) behind the scenes player in the conspiracy that ended the life of JFK. Through its own vast resources and through its international contacts in the intelligence community and in organized crime, Israel had the means, it had the opportunity, and it had the motive to play a major frontline role in the crime of the century — and it did.*

It was Piper's assertion that Israel's motive for the assassination was Prime Minister David Ben-Gurion's outrage at JFK's opposition to Israel becoming a nuclear power, and that in his final days as Prime

Minister Ben-Gurion commanded the Mossad to become involved in a plot to kill America's president. JFK's assassination served the dual purpose of eliminating not only the threat to Israel's nuclear ambitions, but also the need for the AZC to register as a foreign agent. So when Vice President Lyndon Johnson (LBJ) was sworn in as JFK's successor, he wasted no time in increasing Israel's arms budget and also turned a blind eye to its nuclear arms development program. A further blow to the integrity and independence of the U.S. Senate occurred in November 1963, when Nicholas Katzenbach replaced RFK as Attorney General with the result that the AZC evaded registration and calculatingly morphed into the American Israel Public Affairs Committee (AIPAC).

A 1979 account of the House Select Committee on Assassinations reported that on November 25, 1963, only 3 days after the JFK assassination and before any formal federal investigation had been conducted, Nicholas Katzenbach, then deputy attorney general, had written a memo to presidential assistant Bill Moyers which lends credence to the existence of a government cover-up:

> *The public must be satisfied that Oswald was the assassin; that he had no confederates who are still at large; and that evidence was such that he would have been convicted at trial . . . Speculation about Oswald's motivation ought to be cut off. . . . Unfortunately the facts on Oswald seem about too pat — too obvious (Marxist, Cuba, Russian wife, etc.) . . . We need something to head off public speculation or Congressional hearings of the wrong sort.*

Coming from an attorney who was supposed to uphold the concept of innocence until proven otherwise, the memo represents a profound betrayal of the ethical foundations on which judicial systems have been built. The Committee's final report implied that Katzenbach, FBI Director J. Edgar Hoover, and others were the key actors behind the creation of the Warren Commission. The report also stated that Hoover — whose anathema for women was exceeded only by his intense hate for Martin Luther King and the Kennedys — told staff members on November 24, 1963 that he and Katzenbach were anxious to have "something issued so we can convince the public that Oswald is the real assassin."

In the deep and murky world of politics nothing is ever quite what it seems. As far as Mark Banner was concerned, in leaning over backwards to appease the Israeli lobby, the LBJ Presidency betrayed the American people by finally surrendering complete control of U.S. foreign policy to AIPAC. It was no secret that despite his Texan gung-ho expansion of the Vietnam War, LBJ feared the possibility of his own assassination and his yellow streak certainly came to light in 1967 when the USS Liberty, a U.S. Navy technical research ship clearly flying an American flag, was attacked during the Six-Day War.

On June 8, 1967, deliberately unmarked Israeli Air Force jet fighter aircraft and Navy torpedo boats in a combined air and sea assault killed 34 and wounded 170 crew members while severely damaging the ship. The USS Liberty was at the time without doubt in international waters (29.3 mi: 47.2Km) north of the Sinai Peninsula. Both the U.S. and Israeli governments conducted inquiries that concluded the attack was a mistake due to Israeli confusion about the identity of the USS Liberty. Since then a former Navy attorney who helped lead the military investigation of the attack has categorically stated that LBJ and his defence secretary, Robert McNamara, ordered that the inquiry conclude the incident was an accident. Retired Capt. Ward Boston in a signed affidavit released at a Capitol Hill news conference, said LBJ and McNamara told those heading the Navy's inquiry to "conclude that the attack was a case of 'mistaken identity' despite overwhelming evidence to the contrary."

Retired Admiral Thomas Moorer, a former Joint Chiefs of Staff chairman who spent a year investigating the attack as part of an independent panel established with other former military officials, stated that it was "one of the classic all-American cover-ups." Moorer, who was chief of naval operations at the time of the attack, asked from his wheelchair at the news conference "Why would our government put Israel's interests ahead of our own?" He had always believed the attack was a deliberate act and wanted Congress to carry out an investigation.

Israel's explanation was that the USS Liberty was mistaken for an Egyptian ship and as such was a legitimate target of war. That, however, does not explain the use of unmarked aircraft and Moorer agrees that Israel intended to sink the USS Liberty and blame the Egyptians so as to drag the U.S. into a war against Egypt on Israel's behalf. Fifteen years after the attack, an Israeli pilot approached Liberty survivors and then held extensive interviews with former Congressman Paul N. McCloskey about his role. According to this senior Israeli lead pilot, he had immediately recognized the USS Liberty as American and accordingly informed his headquarters but was told to ignore the American flag and continue his attack. He refused to do so and returned to base, where he was arrested. Then U.S. Ambassador to Lebanon, Dwight Porter, has since confirmed that radio monitoring at the U.S. Embassy in Lebanon had also heard the pilot's protestations. Porter told his story to syndicated columnists Rowland Evans and Robert Novak and volunteered — in vain — to submit to further questioning by authorities.

Sometime later, a dual-citizen Israeli major told USS Liberty survivors that he was in an Israeli war room where he heard that pilot's radio report. There had been no doubt at the time that the attacking pilots and everyone in the Israeli war room was well aware that the USS Liberty was an American ship. This major, however, was later to recant his statement after receiving a series of inevitable threatening phone calls from Israel.

In interviews with surviving USS Liberty Crew Members the BBC learnt that 9 minutes into this attack the USS Liberty had been in contact with other U.S. Armed Forces in the area and directly requested support from the aircraft carrier USS Saratoga. U.S. support aircraft did subsequently approach the Liberty during the initial attacks but were apparently ordered to turn back. Irrespective of who was responsible for the refusal to aid the USS Liberty while it was under attack is immaterial because in the end "the buck stops" in the Oval Office.

In 2007 while writing an article on the subject for the Chicago Tribune, John M. Crewdson, contacted USS Liberty survivors who "to a man" rejected Israel's explanation of mistaken identity. Crewdson's article also stated that most senior U.S. government officials involved with the incident did not believe that the attack was a mistake. The attack remains as the only maritime incident in U.S. history where U.S. military forces were killed without there ever being an investigation by the U.S. Congress.

In May 1968, the Israeli government paid US$3,323,500 as full payment to the families of the 34 men killed in the attack. In March 1969, it paid a further $3,566,457 in compensation to the men who had been wounded. On 18 December 1980, it agreed to a payment of $6 million as settlement for the U.S. claim of $7,644,146 for material damage to the USS Liberty. Only Israel would have the gall to pay compensation to Americans with the money it had already received as aid courtesy of U.S. taxpayers. Despite continued efforts by survivors including a book *Assault on the Liberty* by Jim Ennes, the Israeli lobby's control of the U.S. Congress has ensured a denial of the Justice that the U.S is so fond of espousing. The issue of the USS Liberty was officially closed by the two governments through an exchange of diplomatic notes on December 17, 1987.

Long before the Israeli state was established Zionist terrorist groups used such operations even to the extent of attacking Jews so as to discredit the Arabs by having them take the blame. In the summer of 1954 an Israeli covert operation — code named Operation Susannah — was conducted in Egypt as part of a false flag operation. In what came to be known as the Lavon Affair, a group of Egyptian Jews were recruited for plans to plant bombs inside Egyptian, American and British-owned targets. The objective was to have the attacks blamed on the Muslim Brotherhood, Egyptian Communists, "unspecified malcontents" or "local nationalists" so as to create the violence and instability which would induce the British government to retain its occupying troops in Egypt's Suez Canal Zone.

The failed operation caused no casualties apart from the cell members who committed suicide after being captured. Though Israeli defence minister Pinhas Lavon denied prior knowledge of the operation, other government ministers sided against him even to the extent of perjury at the ensuing enquiry and he was made the scapegoat and forced to resign. The failed operation was named after him and was also euphemistically known as the "Unfortunate Affair" or The "Bad Business." In March 2005, Israel ended decades of official denial by publicly honoring the surviving operatives who were each presented with a certificate of appreciation for their service to the state.

One of Mossad's more successful deceptions was Operation Trojan which involved using a special communication device that would be planted deep inside enemy territory by Israeli commandos. The next stage involved an Israeli Defense Force (IDF) navy ship out at sea transmitting prerecorded digital messages containing misleading disinformation which could only be picked up by the Trojan. The Trojan device would then operate as a relay station by rebroadcasting the original transmissions on another frequency: one that was known to be used for official business by the enemy country. Such Trojan transmissions would subsequently be regarded as genuine when picked up by American and British listening stations.

As Libya had for a long time been on Israel's agenda of enemies to be targeted, on the night of 17-18 February 1986, two Israeli missile boats dropped Mossad agents off the Libyan coast to plant a Trojan for the rebroadcast of fake transmissions. By the end of March American listening stations were routinely intercepting the Trojan messages which were broadcast only during heavy communication traffic hours. The Mossad messages relayed through Trojan strongly implied that terrorists were in communication with various Libyan embassies around the world. As had been hoped by Mossad, the Americans concluded that this was proof positive that the Libyans were active sponsors of terrorism. Furthermore, Mossad "helpfully" confirmed American suspicions and President Ronald Reagan initiated Operation El Dorado Canyon.

On April 15, 1986, American aircraft pounded Libya with more than sixty tons of bombs. In view of the fact that the West has since been the subject of numerous terrorist attacks of presumably Islamic origin, it may be wise to consider the possibility that history has been repeating itself with more Israeli false flag operations. Numerous reputable writers, scientists, investigators and politicians have suggested an Israeli involvement with 9/11. There is a huge amount of credible evidence that is being ignored, swept under the carpet, or simply labelled as "conspiracy theories." More recently Chinese and Japanese intelligence agencies, which closely monitor events in the Persian Gulf due to the dependence of both countries on oil from the region, report that Israeli Navy commandos are constantly operating in the Persian Gulf so as to create maritime incidents that could be blamed on Iran. Zionist Israel has a consistent history of serving its own selfish purpose with murderous operations even if such operations cost others (the Goyim) vast resources and innocent human lives.

Mark Banner ended his appraisal of the LBJ Presidency with a quote from a 31 March 1968 change-of-mind speech that shocked the nation: "I shall not seek, and I will not accept, the nomination of my party for another term as your President." LBJ's announcement only served to reinforce the combined threat of RFK and Fulbright to Zionist influence on Capitol Hill which had already reemerged the previous month when RFK announced his candidacy for the presidency during the height of the unpopular Vietnam War that JBJ had dramatically escalated. The prospect of another Kennedy presidency revived the possibility that RFK with his peace candidacy would pursue his deceased brother's agenda of preventing a nuclear arms race in the Middle East by targeting Israel's nuclear arsenal. Furthermore, with Fulbright still wielding influence on U.S. foreign policy, a Kennedy presidency would undoubtedly support Fulbright in imposing restrictions on the Israel lobby.

As RFK's political polls ratings surged, the threat of his potential presidency was in due course eliminated during a campaign event in Los Angeles on 5 June 1968 which happened to coincide with the first anniversary of the Six-Day War. His Palestinian émigré assassin, Sirhan Sirhan, later claimed that his action had been motivated by Kennedy's campaign pledge to provide more fighter jets to Israel. At subsequent parole hearings which occurred every five years and were routinely denied, Sirhan always testified that he had no memory of the assassination nor any details relating to his 1969 trial and confession. Such a possibility is not as far-fetched as it may sound when considering the fact that Lee Harvey Oswald was likewise made the patsy for JFK's assassination. The possible use of Sirhan by Mossad should never be ruled out because in the early seventies following reports of mind control experiments, Israel acknowledged having such a program.

Considering the Israeli penchant for false flag operations that lay the blame at someone else's door, what could be more ingenious and fiendishly satisfying for the racist Zionist psyche than to have a Palestinian blamed for Israel's the dirty work. Even the death of JFK's son, JFK Jr. on 16 June 1999 remains subject to conspiracy theories with many unanswered questions suggesting some kind of cover-up. JFK Jr., who was apparently about to publish some new revelations about his father's assassination, died along with his wife Carolyn and sister-in-law Lauren Bessette when the plane he was piloting went down into the ocean with some witnesses claiming to have seen the plane explode.

RFK's assassination meant that the road to the presidency had been cleared for Richard Milhous "I am not a crook" Nixon who was by no means a fan of the Jewish people: or anyone else for that matter. After Nixon became President and was lobbied by Israeli Prime Minister Golda Meir, he readily agreed to go along with an ambiguous "Don't Ask, Don't Tell," status for Israel's nuclear weapons program. This is confirmed by author Avner Cohen in *Israel and the Bomb* who has stated that there was enough historical evidence to indicate that the president and the prime minister had reached a secret understanding on at least one issue: Israel would keep its nuclear devices out of sight and not test them, and the United States would tolerate the situation and not press Israel to sign the Nuclear Nonproliferation Treaty which had been embraced by many countries around the world.

Nixon adhered to his tolerance for Israel's Nuclear weapons buildup despite a 19 July 1969 calculated and devious warning in a memorandum from unindicted war criminal Henry A. Kissinger, a Jew and U.S. national security advisor: "The Israelis, who are one of the few peoples whose survival is genuinely threatened, are probably more likely than almost any other country to actually use their nuclear weapons." So despite having a dislike for Jewish people that could be construed as being anti-Semitic, Nixon is nevertheless still fondly regarded by Israelis as the man who saved Israel during the 1973 Yom Kippur War.

In the aftermath of the 1967 Six Day War, Arab nations were smarting from the humiliating defeat and loss of territory to the Israelis but realised that regaining lost territory and restoring some Arab dignity was not going to be achieved by direct military conflict with the Israelis. Consequently Egypt's President Nasser evolved a strategy of reclaiming the Egyptian land by increasing military pressure along the Suez Canal with a view to making it too costly for Israel to continue its occupation. Nasser's "War of Attrition" — consisting mainly of artillery bombardment and commando raids — lasted from March 1969 through to August 1970 achieving the desired result.

The "attrition" strategy's main weakness was its susceptibility to being reversed by the Israelis who in turn upped the ante by inflicting heavier costs to Egypt with air raids against strategic targets deep in Egyptian territory. The Egyptian response was to seek and obtain increased assistance from the Soviet Union including surface-to-air missiles (SAMs) and additional Soviet fighter aircraft flown by Soviet pilots. A brief Soviet-Israeli air battle on July 30, 1970, resulted in five Soviet aircraft being shot down with no Israeli losses. A cease-fire agreement followed shortly afterwards by which time over 700 Israelis had died and 2,700 had been wounded. Arab losses were believed to be more than three times that amount. President Nasser died of a heart attack in September 1970 and was succeeded by Anwar Sadat who proved to be more flexible than his predecessor by seeking a diplomatic solution but retaining the optional use of force.

Having accepted U.S.-mediated negotiations with an Israel that has never desired any kind of peace that would require it to surrender territory, a frustrated Sadat proclaimed 1971 as the "year of decision" if diplomacy failed to remove the Israelis from the Sinai. When 1971 passed with no Egyptian reaction to Israel's obdurateness, Sadat's proclamation was mistakenly taken as mere bravado. Later in July 1972, when Sadat expelled over twenty thousand Soviet advisers, Egypt appeared to have weakened its own capacity for a military solution. The effect of Sadat's removal of Soviet presence and influence, however, was to provide unfettered freedom to commence serious preparations for war. Regardless of his expulsion of Soviet advisors, Sadat was still able to negotiate an agreement for increased Soviet arms deliveries in late 1972 which was followed by a gradual return of some advisors starting in early in early 1973.

Though the Israeli intelligence system rightly enjoyed an excellent international reputation, it repeatedly — right up to the last minute — missed or ignored every possible indicator that Egypt was preparing for war. The coalition of Arab states led by Egypt and Syria had chosen to attack on October 6, 1973 which as the day of Yom Kippur (Day of Atonement) was the holiest and most solemn day of the year for Jewish people. Within forty-eight hours of the surprise Arab attack starting, Israel was staggering and in a desperate position with Syrian forces storming into the Golan Heights and their tanks taking positions on the hills overlooking the Sea of Galilee and pre-1967 Israel.

In the south, the Egyptians had sent five infantry and two armoured divisions across the entire length of the Suez Canal and penetrated Israeli front-line strongholds. Having initially estimated the possibility of up to 10,000 fatal casualties for the assault, the Egyptians lost only 200 men and the canal crossing has since been rated as one of the best-orchestrated obstacle crossings in history. By October 7, a defending Israeli regular division had 180 of its 270 tanks destroyed by Egyptian infantry antitank weapons. On 8 October 1973, the first two Israeli reserve armoured divisions finally arrived in the Sinai to launch a major counter-attack against Egyptian positions but one division was badly mauled and the other apparently indulged in aimless manoeuvres due to confused battle progress reports.

By the end of fighting on that fateful day the Israeli forces had suffered what the late Trevor Nevitt Dupuy (1916-1995), a retired U.S. Army Colonel and prolific author as a noted military historian, described as "the worst defeat in their history." On that same evening Israeli Defense Minister Moshe Dayan said to Prime Minister Golda Meir that "the Third Temple [the state of Israel] is going under." It was probably at that moment that an Israeli decision was taken to use nuclear weapons.

It is on record that on the following day Golda Meir was sufficiently concerned to propose travelling to Washington for a face-to-face meeting with President Nixon but abandoned the idea after being assured that the

U.S. would replenish Israel's military hardware. On October 12, Golda Meir stressed the urgency of the situation in a personal communication to Nixon that stated that Israel would be forced to use "all available means to ensure national survival" if U.S. military hardware was not immediately forthcoming. This implicit threat to use nuclear weapons was confirmed years later by Henry Kissinger to a trusted colleague.

According to CIA Director Vernon Walters, Nixon gave it the greater sense of urgency. He said, "you get the stuff to Israel. Now. Now." Though the situation for Israelis remained perilous over the next few days, they did start to stem the tide of daily advances. In the meantime the Nixon Administration had initiated Operation Nickel Grass which was to replace all of Israel's lost munitions. Throughout the airlift 567 missions were flown to deliver over 22,000 tons of supplies and an additional 90,000 tons was delivered by sea thereby enhancing Israel's ability to more freely expend what munitions it already had. On October 9, the Israelis avoided further counterattacks in the south while the Egyptians decided to reinforce their positions. Meanwhile the arrival of Israeli reserves on the Syrian front served to repulse further Syrian advances and by the evening of October 10 the pre-war lines had been restored. A further Israeli counterattack was planned for October 11 with a view to threatening the Syrian capital of Damascus and thereby neutralizing Syria so that the Israelis could concentrate on the Sinai. On that same day Syria urgently asked Egypt to initiate attacks that would relieve Israeli pressure in the north. Though to some extent successful, the Israeli attack was stalled some 20 miles from Damascus by the Syrians whose defensive lines had been reinforced by the arrival of troops from Jordan and Iraq.

By October 14 the northern front had stabilised and both sides reconciled themselves to defence rather than offence. Though Israel's counterattack in the north had failed to take Syria out of the war, it did nonetheless alter the situation in the south to Israel's advantage. Egypt's success had so far been achieved by fighting a defensive war under protection of their surface-to-air missiles, but there was no consensus amongst Egyptian commanders that switching to the offensive was advisable. Syria's plea for assistance, however, finally tipped the scales in favor of seeking further gains by launching an attack on October 14 which was repulsed by the Israelis who were by then prepared and reinforced.

Though the Egyptians suffered very heavy losses, they nonetheless managed to delay a planned Israeli attack scheduled for the same day. With hindsight it may have been better for the Egyptians to have gone for an all-out offensive from the start which would have secured victory by denying the Israelis the time to regroup and reinforce. There is, however, no doubt that had the Israelis been faced with such a defeat, they would not have hesitated in using their nuclear weapons for strikes on Cairo and Damascus: strikes that would have resulted in far worse holocausts than those experienced by the cities of Hiroshima and Nagasaki in August 1945 during the final stages of the Second World War.

On October 15 the Israelis began their delayed offensive with a thrust towards the east bank of Suez Canal and crossed over the following morning to secure a bridgehead. After a series of pitched battles over the three days with heavy losses on both sides, the Israelis managed to secure a twenty kilometre wide corridor to the canal which they subsequently spanned with a pontoon bridge to facilitate their crossing.

Having lost the surprise element of their initial attack, the Egyptians then failed to correctly evaluate Israel's game plan. It was not until October 18 when satellite photographs — provided by the secretly visiting Soviet President Kosygin — that Israeli intentions became apparent. It was then that President Sadat started becoming more agreeable to the Soviet idea for a cease-fire. Henry Kissinger's October 20 visit to Moscow for discussions on a UN-mediated halt to the fighting then resulted in the October 22 UN Security Council Resolution 338 (UNSCR 338) being adopted with a call for a cease-fire.

Despite both Egypt and Israel accepting the terms of UNSCR 338, fighting continued with both sides accusing the other — with some justification — of cease-fire violations. With numerous Egyptian units trapped behind the Israeli advance line on the west bank of the canal, continued fighting was unavoidable. It was also clear that the Israelis had gone beyond consolidating their gains and had continued fighting so as to completely encircle the Egyptian Third Army and to reach the Gulf of Suez which they did by midnight on October 23.

Though by October 24 some fighting continued along the west bank of the canal, the opposing forces had taken up settled positions without confrontation. Having guaranteed President Sadat that the cease-fire would hold and that the Third Army would be saved, the Soviets responded to the continued fighting by preparing to airlift up to seven divisions to the Middle East. At 21:25 that evening Brezhnev sent Nixon an urgent note suggesting joint U.S.-Soviet military action to enforce

215

the cease-fire, and threatened unilateral Soviet action if the U.S. were unwilling to participate. Such a scenario involving overseas deployment of U.S. troops so soon after Vietnam was out of the question for Nixon. Equally unacceptable was the prospect of either Americans teaming up with Soviets to fight against Israelis, or unilateral Soviet action.

Early on October 25, Nixon placed U.S. military forces on a world-wide state of increased alert so as to reinforce his message to Brezhnev which expressed resolute opposition to military intervention by either superpower. An urgent warning was also sent to Israel insisting that fighting be immediately brought to an end. Tension was eventually relieved by late afternoon when the Soviets eschewed the idea of superpower implementation of the cease-fire, and fighting along the Suez subsided. It was not until January 18, 1974, however, that a disengagement agreement was achieved with a UN buffer zone east of the Suez Canal including limitations on Egyptian and Israeli forces in adjacent areas. A similar disengagement and buffer zone agreement between Israel and Syria did not come into effect until May 31, 1974.

The conflict marked the fact that not since the Cuban Missile Crisis of 1962 had the superpowers come so close to a confrontation despite not having been directly involved in the fighting, The Israelis, having been initially overwhelmed and on the verge of utter defeat, nonetheless — with assistance from the U.S. — made an impressive comeback which in terms of human and matériel cost gave them victory. But the conflict was also a victory for the Arabs because even though their losses had been greater, the impact of the conflict on Israel's smaller population was realistically more damaging. It should be noted that while all this was going on, the Nixon Presidency was mired in the Watergate Scandal. Being faced with almost certain impeachment in the House of Representatives and a strong possibility of a conviction in the Senate, Nixon was forced resign on August 9, 1974, but was pardoned by his successor, Gerald Ford.   As a footnote to his chapter, Banner noted that following the conflict it had emerged that thousands of unarmed Egyptian prisoners of war had been massacred — similar to Nazi war crime perpetrations — by the Israeli forces. When later asked about his role in this genocidal massacre, Israeli Prime Minister Yitzak Rabin's angry riposte was "I am not going to discuss that. That's ancient history." The arrogance of Rabin's response once again illustrates the Israeli belief that while others must always be accountable for their criminality, Israelis should always be exempt. Jews still insist to this day that there is no statute of limitations for the capture, trial and execution of Germans accused of war crimes committed in the 1930s and 1940s. Jewish victims and their families of Nazi war crimes are still to this day receiving hundreds of millions of dollars in compensation. Banner concluded by asking when and from whom are the Palestinian victims of Israeli crimes going to receive compensation? And when will the Palestinian people — like the Jewish people on Palestinian lands — be allowed to have a state of their own on land that is rightly theirs?

●　●　●　●　●

It was just past two o/clock in London when David Reisner, who had been in his room all morning working, finally finished his article on the Hiramic Brotherhood of the third Temple. He had Followed Mark Banner's advice of releasing just enough of the kind of information that might prompt some response from either the Israeli government or the Brotherhood:

David Reisner

December 10, 2008
London

What is Going on Beneath Temple Mount

Temple Mount has been a flashpoint in the Middle East conflict since Israel seized East Jerusalem and the Old City from Jordan in 1967. For Israelis the action achieved the reunification of what they maintain is their ancient capital. Palestinians on the other hand, backed by the UN, still regard East Jerusalem to be occupied Arab land. Consequently the Temple Mount is precariously perched between these opposing views. Though Israel claims political sovereignty over the area, custodianship remains with the Waqf — an inalienable religious endowment in Islamic law.

　　Both sides therefore regard each other with suspicion and are on the lookout for any action that may tilt the delicate balance in the other side's favor. When in September 2000 Israeli politician and unindicted war criminal Ariel Sharon visited the Temple Mount, Palestinians saw it as a provocative Israeli assertion of sovereignty which sparked the second intifada uprising with an estimated loss of 6,600 lives as rioting, armed clashes and bombings erupted throughout the Palestinian territories and Israel. With rival claims to the same territory being at the core of this Israeli-Palestinian conflict, both sides have come to rely on history for making the case for whose roots in the land run deepest.

Jewish tradition maintains that this is the site where God gathered the dust to create Adam and where Abraham nearly sacrificed his son Isaac to prove his faith. It further maintains that according to the Bible King Solomon built the First Temple of the Jews on this mountaintop sometime around 1,000 BCE. Unfortunately nothing is known about this First Temple because there are no traces whatsoever of its physical remains. It is also alleged that the Temple was razed four hundred years later by troops commanded by the Babylonian king Nebuchadnezzar, who exiled many Jews. In the first century BCE Herod expanded and refurbished a Second Temple built by Jews who had returned from exile. It was in there that, according to the Gospel of John, Jesus Christ lashed out against the money changers and was subsequently crucified not far from there. The Roman general Titus sacked and burned the Temple in CE 70.

Muslims call the Temple Mount al-Haram al-Sharif (the Noble Sanctuary) and believe it was here that the Prophet Muhammad ascended to the "Divine Presence" on the back of a winged horse — a Miraculous Night Journey commemorated by one of Islam's architectural triumphs, the Dome of the Rock shrine. Few places anywhere else in the world have witnessed the same number of momentous historical events as the Temple Mount which has been conquered or occupied by a long succession of peoples.

Archaeologists, however, have had little opportunity to excavate for physical evidence that would distinguish myth from reality. Apart from being a place of active worship, the site remains under the control of the Waqf which forbids archaeological excavations that are viewed as desecration. Though there has been some clandestine surveys of caves, cisterns and tunnels undertaken by European explorers in the late 19th century — and some minor archaeological work conducted by the British from 1938 to 1942, when the Al-Aqsa Mosque was undergoing renovation — the layers of history beneath the Temple Mount have remained hidden and out of reach.

With such a scenario, only actual archaeological excavations can determine and legitimise any claim to this holy but small piece of bitterly contested real estate. As the occupying force, it is the Israelis who with biased Israeli enacted legislation can determine where and what is to be excavated — even if such excavations require the displacement of Palestinian families and the destruction of their homes.

There are many Jewish organizations — such as The Temple Institute — that are working towards the building of a Third Temple and Arab rumors and suspicions abound as to what the Israelis are actually doing to achieve their goal. Apart from those organizations that are overtly working towards that goal, there are also according to a reliable Israeli government source, a covert "Hiramic Brotherhood of the Third Temple" operating secretly within the ranks of Freemasonry. The most controversial of those rumors and suspicions is the suggestion that the Israelis are secretly tunneling eastwards from the Western Wall Tunnels towards the Dome of the Rock.

Michal Zeldin, the recently assassinated archaeologist who was allegedly assassinated by Palestinian terrorists, had before his death asserted to this correspondent that such illegal tunnelling was in fact taking place. If it is, then such tunnelling could not be carried out without the full approval of the Israeli government whose policy of Judaization appears to have no limits with regards to either Muslim holy sites or international law. Whatever it is that is going on under Temple Mount, it will sooner or later result in an eruption of violence that will devastate the Holy Land.

The Old City of Jerusalem

7

Friday, 12 December 2008
Watergate East Apartment Building, Washington D.C.

The full-figured Livia Appelman sat at her antique Venetian dressing table applying layers of make-up to create the mask that was to some extent her defense against the horrid tribulations of yet another of Washington's social gatherings which she — as a dissatisfied but steadfast wife — was often obliged to attend with her husband. No doubt the champagne would as usual be flowing and the circulating trays of scrumptious hors d'oeuvres with their abundance of forbidden calories would have to be staunchly resisted.

Such occasions were on the surface always glittering but behind the glitter of expensive bubbly drinks, petit gourmet savouries, and bulging gift bags there was a dismal superficiality to being huddled in small circles with people who talk through you as their eyes scan the room in search of more notable contacts who might possibly enhance both social and career prospects. The grovelling quest for advancement and influence in Washington was a way of life and as far as Livia was concerned they should all — her husband included — wear "FOR SALE'" signs on their backs.

Meanwhile in the lounge, Steve Appelman was quietly pensive as he stood by the window looking out onto the waters of the Potomac River. The vibrant red, orange and yellow leaves that adorned the trees in autumn had already withered and fallen and the city would soon be covered with a blanket of snow. Appelman's frequent applications of overpriced men's toiletries designed to invigorate and rejuvenate had so far failed to improve features that were aquiline, gaunt, and well-past their kiss by date. The slightly wrinkled forehead merged with a shiny, bald pate fringed by short graying hair at the back and sides. The wire-rimmed spectacles magnified eyes that betrayed the inner yearnings of a man who had never known true love or shared moments of magical intimacy with someone special. Even sex for its own sake was now awkward, impersonal, paid for with some classy capital hooker, and invariably of brief duration. In short, Appelman had yet to experience the profound exhilaration of having lain against the gently trembling naked body of a woman well and truly satisfied.   Appelman, however, was not depressed by either of his limitations — he was after all one of Washington's movers and shakers — or the thought of winter. He was instead looking forward to his forthcoming escape from the inclement temperatures of both marriage and weather to warmer and sunnier climes. He had just finished making his reservation online for an El Al flight for next Saturday that would arrive at Ben Gurion International Airport late Sunday afternoon. A fifty-minute journey in a chauffeur-driven limo would cover the fifty kilometers to Jerusalem's prestigious King David Hotel where he always made a point of staying as a kind of tribute to the role the hotel had played in Israel's history.

The King David had at one time housed the central offices of the British Mandatory authorities which included the Secretariat of the Government of Palestine, and the Headquarters of the British Forces in Palestine and Jordan. In July 1946 members of the Jewish terrorist organisation, Irgun Zvai Leumi, dressed as Arabs carried out the bombing of the hotel killing 91 people and injuring 46. It was the deadliest single attack carried out by Jewish Terrorists against the British throughout the 1920-1948 Mandate.

Menachem Begin, the Irgun leader at the time, was later to become the 6th. Prime Minister of Israel in June 1977. Begin's deep-rooted hatred for other peoples in general and the British in particular appears to have never abated because during the brief 1982 Falklands War he permitted the illegal supply of weapons to Argentina. The British, however, were by no means the only target of Begin's venomous hatred for others as was made apparent in the *New Statesman* by Amnon Kapeliouk, the renowned Jewish French-Israeli journalist. Though Zionist organizations have since attempted to discredit Kapeliouk by claiming that he greatly distorted Begin's comments, there is no reason to doubt Kapeliouk given the general tone of many other comments by Zionists and their leaders:

Our race is the Master Race. We Jews are divine gods on this planet. We are as different from the inferior races as they are from insects. In fact, compared to our race, other races are beasts and animals, cattle at best. Other races are considered as human excrement. Our destiny is to rule over the inferior races. Our earthly kingdom will be ruled by our leader with a rod of iron. The masses will lick our feet and serve us as our slaves.

Appelman had already visited Israel twice this year, but the imminent inauguration of the first Black American President in the United States meant that it was a time for both concern and opportunity. The concern was because though Barack Obama had already given assurances that America would maintain "an unwavering friendship with Israel, and an unshakeable commitment to its security," Israel and its supporters were still not entirely convinced in view of Obama's stated intention to "reach out" to Middle East leaders whom Israel regarded as bitter enemies. If Obama was foolish enough to veer away from AIPAC's prescribed Middle East policy for the U.S., then like his recent predecessors, he too would experience the full power of AIPAC and be embarrassed — and if necessary, forced — into toeing the Israeli line. Apart from the concern there was also the window of opportunity that would open during the changeover period between outgoing and incoming administrations which would create a leadership vacuum and government paralysis. It was an opportunity that Israel would certainly have to ruthlessly exploit.

Appelman's office was located several blocks from the Capitol in a nondescript but secure and heavily guarded building that served as AIPAC's headquarters. There was also an AIPAC office in Jerusalem which he would soon be visiting and a further seven U.S. regional offices. By working closely with the Washington headquarters, each regional office maintained a year-round hands-on involvement for its members who were kept informed with seminars on Israeli issues and encouraged to become effectively involved on Israel's behalf in local and national politics.

The seeds for AIPAC's creation were sowed soon after Israel's establishment as a state in 1948 when it became apparent that in order to cope with an influx of some 600,000 Jewish immigrants, Israel would need the assistance of U.S. Jews. But in 1948 prior to the creation of the Israeli State, two Jewish terrorist groups were working to cleanse Palestine of its Arab inhabitants and its British occupiers. The more brutal of these groups was Lohamei Herut Yisrael (Fighters for the Freedom of Israel) also known as the LEHI or the Stern Gang after its founder Avraham Stern.

Much of the financial support for these Jewish terrorists came from the United States. The Stern Gang received money raised under the deceitful name of American Friends of the Fighters for the Freedom of Israel. A Mr. Shepard Rifkin who was the executive director after the UN Partition of Palestine and prior to the creation of Israel in May 1948, solicited Albert Einstein to help the Stern Gang raise American money for arms to drive out the Arabs and help create a Jewish state. On April 10th, the day after the infamous massacre of Arabs at Deir Yassin, Einstein replied with the following letter.

April 10, 1948

Mr. Shepard Rifkin
Exec. Director
American Friends of the Fighters
For the Freedom of Israel
149 Second Ave.
New York 3, N.Y.

Dear Sir:

When a real and final catastrophe should befall us in Palestine the first responsible for it would be the British and the second responsible for it the terrorist organizations build up from our own ranks.

I am not willing to see anybody associated with those misled and criminal people.

Sincerely yours,
Albert Einstein

The original of the above letter on Einstein's embossed stationary was auctioned at Sotheby's on 21 June 2007 and purchased by Daniel McGowan, executive director of Deir Yassin Remembered, for $8,500, $1,700 commission, and $175 shipping costs. The letter was subsequently resold. In December 1948 The *New York Times* was sent a letter of warning which was signed by prominent American Jews including Albert Einstein, the Nobel Prize physicist.

TO THE EDITORS OF NEW YORK TIMES:

Among the most disturbing political phenomena of our times is the emergence in the newly created state of Israel of the

"Freedom Party" (Tnuat Haherut), a political party closely akin in its organization, methods, political philosophy and social appeal to the Nazi and Fascist parties. It was formed out of the membership and following of the former Irgun Zvai Leumi, a terrorist, right-wing, chauvinist organization in Palestine.

The current visit of Menachem Begin, leader of this party, to the United States is obviously calculated to give the impression of American support for his party in the coming Israeli elections, and to cement political ties with conservative Zionist elements in the United States. Several Americans of national repute have lent their names to welcome his visit. It is inconceivable that those who oppose fascism throughout the world, if correctly informed as to Mr. Begin's political record and perspectives, could add their names and support to the movement he represents.

Before irreparable damage is done by way of financial contributions, public manifestations in Begin's behalf, and the creation in Palestine of the impression that a large segment of America supports Fascist elements in Israel, the American public must be informed as to the record and objectives of Mr. Begin and his movement.

The public avowals of Begin's party are no guide whatever to its actual character. Today they speak of freedom, democracy and anti-imperialism, whereas until recently they openly preached the doctrine of the Fascist state. It is in its actions that the terrorist party betrays its real character; from its past actions we can judge what it may be expected to do in the future.

Attack on Arab Village

A shocking example was their behavior in the Arab village of Deir Yassin. This village, off the main roads and surrounded by Jewish lands, had taken no part in the war, and had even fought off Arab bands who wanted to use the village as their base. On April 9 (THE NEW YORK TIMES), terrorist bands attacked this peaceful village, which was not a military objective in the fighting, killed most of its inhabitants (240 men, women, and children) and kept a few of them alive to parade as captives through the streets of Jerusalem. Most of the Jewish community was horrified at the deed, and the Jewish Agency sent a telegram of apology to King Abdullah of Trans-Jordan. But the terrorists, far from being ashamed of their act, were proud of this massacre, publicized it widely, and invited all the foreign correspondents present in the country to view the heaped corpses and the general havoc at Deir Yassin.

The Deir Yassin incident exemplifies the character and actions of the Freedom Party.

Within the Jewish community they have preached an admixture of ultranationalism, religious mysticism, and racial superiority. Like other Fascist parties they have been used to break strikes, and have themselves pressed for the destruction of free trade unions. In their stead they have proposed corporate unions on the Italian Fascist model.

During the last years of sporadic anti-British violence, the IZL and Stern groups inaugurated a reign of terror in the Palestine Jewish community. Teachers were beaten up for speaking against them, adults were shot for not letting their children join them. By gangster methods, beatings, window-smashing, and wide-spread robberies, the terrorists intimidated the population and exacted a heavy tribute.

The people of the Freedom Party have had no part in the constructive achievements in Palestine. They have reclaimed no land, built no settlements, and only detracted from the Jewish defense activity. Their much-publicized immigration endeavors were minute, and devoted mainly to bringing in Fascist compatriots.

Discrepancies Seen

The discrepancies between the bold claims now being made by Begin and his party, and their record of past performance in Palestine bear the imprint of no ordinary political party. This is the unmistakable stamp of a Fascist party for whom terrorism (against Jews, Arabs, and British alike), and misrepresentation are means, and a "Leader State" is the goal.

In the light of the foregoing considerations, it is imperative that the truth about Mr. Begin and his movement be made known in this country. It is all the more tragic that the top leadership of American Zionism has refused to campaign against Begin's efforts, or even to expose to its own constituents the dangers to Israel from support to Begin.

The undersigned therefore take this means of publicly presenting a few salient facts concerning Begin and his party; and of urging all concerned not to support this latest manifestation of fascism.

ISIDORE ABRAMOWITZ; HANNAH ARENDT; ABRAHAM BRICK; RABBI JESSURUN CARDOZO; ALBERT EINSTEIN; HERMAN EISEN, M.D.; HAYIM FINEMAN; M. GALLEN; M.D.; H.H. HARRIS; ZELIG S. HARRIS; SIDNEY HOOK; FRED KARUSH; BRURIA KAUFMAN; IRMA L. LINDHEIM; NACHMAN MAISEL; SEYMOUR MELMAN; MYER D. MENDELSON, M.D.; HARRY M. OSLINSKY; SAMUEL PITLICK; FRITZ ROHRLICH; LOUIS P. ROCKER; RUTH SAGIS; ITZHAK SANKOWSKY; I.J. SHOENBERG; SAMUEL SHUMAN; M. SINGER; IRMA WOLFE; STEFAN WOLFE.

The letter's reference to Deir Yassin concerned the massacre that followed the 1947 supply of major shipments of modern armaments from Czechoslovakia to the Jewish terror groups. Czechoslovakia, as a means of replenishing its diminished post-war coffers, supplied the Jewish groups with tens of thousands of rifles, bayonets, machine guns, pistols, semi-automatic weapons, 80.5 million rounds of ammunition, 25 propeller-driven Avia S-199 fighters (the first fighter obtained by the Israeli Air Force), and 61 British Supermarine spitfires that had been used throughout the Second World War by Britain's Royal Air Force and other allied countries. They also trained Haganah pilots, ground crews, and even a brigade of Jewish volunteers.

In the early hours of Friday 9 April 1948, as Deir Yassin's

inhabitants slept peacefully, the Irgun in cahoots with the Stern Gang and with the knowledge and support of the Haganah, began their cold-blooded slaughter of 250 men, women and children, many of whom had been mutilated and raped. David K. Shipler, a *New York Times* journalist and Pulitzer Prize winner, cited Red Cross documents showing that the Zionist attackers had "lined men, women, and children up against the walls and shot them." Other sources reported that whole families were riddled with bullets, grenade fragments, and either buried under their blown up houses, or mowed down as they tried to escape from them with some individuals being captured. Following the massacre, groups of old men, women, and children were driven in a 'victory parade' through West Jerusalem's streets and then unceremoniously dumped in (Arab) East Jerusalem. When the butchery was finally over, a final body count of 254 was reported by the *New York Times* on April 13, 1948. The cemetery was later bulldozed and Deir Yassin was wiped off the map.

Though American Jews had responded with unprecedented generosity, by late 1950 it had become apparent to American Jewish leaders that much more financial aid was required. They accordingly devised a four-point plan that sought to increase donations from Jewish individuals; encourage investment in Israel from U.S. companies; promote the sale of Israeli bonds; and request that Israel becomes a recipient of assistance from the U.S. aid program for underdeveloped countries.

Despite such efforts it soon became equally apparent that Israel's economic and military requirements would demand a great deal more than just handouts, and consequently in 1951 the American Zionist Council (AZC) was established to promote a pro-Israel lobbying campaign that would concentrate on influencing Congress. Having been established as a tax-exempt entity, the AZC was legally not permitted to lobby on Israel's behalf in the U.S., and as a result in 1954 it faced a possible investigation for its alleged violations. To avoid such a possibility, the AZC rebranded itself as the non-tax- exempt American Zionist Committee for Public Affairs and thereby in effect became the predecessor of AIPAC. Having over a period of time recognized that its Zionist objectives were not necessarily the same as those of the majority of American Jews whose support was required, the Committee widened its appeal by once again shrewdly rebranding itself in 1959 by substituting the word "Israel" for "Zionist" to become the American Israel Public Affairs Committee.

Approximately one-third of AIPAC's Washington staff were administrative and clerical with the remainder being specialists in areas of strategic importance including communications and leading-edge weapons technology. AIPAC was structured so as to effectively maximize its efforts by concentrating on the Executive Branch, Legislation, Research, and political development.

Influencing an Executive Branch that was not elected but appointed and accountable only to the President was of vital importance when dealing with issues, such as the Middle East peace process, that are initiated by the Oval Office rather than by the bicameral Congress. By ensuring the presence of Jews within the ranks of the Executive Branch, AIPAC, rather than being in the position of having to react to U.S. Mid-East policies, is instead able to influence such policies during the process of their creation. One such example was President Obama's Chicago-born White House Chief of Staff, Rahm Israel Emanuel, who as a Jew, once attended summer camp in Israel just after the 1967 Six-Day War. The object of these annual summer camps is to indoctrinate young minds and identify those with potential to become assets and sayanim. Perhaps the experience was influential in his decision to volunteer with the Israeli Defense Forces during the 1991 Gulf War. Rahm Israel Emanual, however, never felt the need to serve with the U.S. Forces. Some fifteen years earlier when Rahm Emanuel was a senior official in President Clinton's White House, Hilary Clinton had him demoted for his arrogant and aggressive style. Today, it is the arrogant and aggressive Rahm who is telling her what she can and cannot do as the United States Secretary of State.

According to English-language reports in the *Jerusalem Post,* Benjamin Emanuel (real name Ezekiel Auerbach), in discussing with the Israeli daily *Ma'ariv* the potential influence of his son, said that "obviously he'll influence the president to be pro-Israel. Why wouldn't he? What is he, an Arab? He's not going to be mopping floors at the White House." Such sentiments coming from a man who was a terrorist with Irgun Zvai Leumi, are perhaps not surprising. Information about the Elder Emanuel's terrorist activities are contained in British MI-6 intelligence files which show that he was arrested by British police some months prior to the establishment of the Israeli state. Apart from specializing in the bombing buses carrying British policemen and troops, he was also apparently part of the assassination squad that murdered Sweden's Count Folke Bernadotte in 1948. Bernadotte, noted for his negotiation of the release of 31,000 prisoners (inluding 450 Danish Jews) from German concentration camps in April 1945, was as UN envoy to Palestine trying to find a solution for the UN Partition Plan that gave Palestinian land to Jews. It was also believed that Benjamin Emanuel was related to Vladimir Jabotinsky, the Russian Jew from Odessa who was a Zionist Revisionist and founder of the Irgun. As an avid admirer of Benito Mussolini, Jabotinsky secretly negotiated with the Nazi government in Germany for the expatriation of Jews to Palestine.

Following Rahm Emanuel's 2008 designation as Obama's chief of staff, Wikipedia mysteriously deleted Benjamin Emanuel's entry. The deletion or suppression of facts in the public domain that relate to any Zionist activity which may portray it in an unfavorable light is a routine tactic employed by supporters of Zionism. The extent of such suppression is best illustrated by a case relating to the works of the historian, Lenni Brenner, one of whose meticulously researched books document the fact that from the start, Zionist leaders were prepared to push the limits — including collaboration with the Nazis — in order to achieve their main objective of a Jewish state in Palestine. The pursuit of the Zionist goal to establish a state in Palestine included encouraging and exploiting anti-Semitism in Europe, and proposing an alliance with Hitler's Germany. There was also an offer of Zionists fighting against the British in return for a Nazi undertaking that after winning the war, Germany would give Palestine to the Jews.

In England in 1987 an anti-Zionist play, *Perdition,* written by Jim Allen who openly acknowledged Lenni Brenner's works as his source, caused controversy and the inevitable mounting of a concerted protest campaign by Jewish pressure groups who vociferously maintained that the play was anti-Semitic. As was usual with such cases, the British mainstream media (the so-called free press) once again failed to either question or refute such baseless allegations and the ill-informed British majority, who had in the past sacrificed so much for the concept of freedom, meekly acquiesced to the unjustified censorship of irrefutable historical facts by a Zionist-driven minority.

The play, which was scheduled to open at London's Royal Court Theatre never even made it to opening night so that members of the British public were denied the right to view the play and to judge it for themselves. Any assertion by Britain that it is a democracy must therefore be diagnosed as being a lamentable delusion for which the appropriate treatment could only be a cup of tea and sympathy. The well-practiced Zionist ploy of constant "never again" reminders of the Holocaust, helps to encourage the illusion that rampant anti-Semitism persists throughout society. This in turn creates a guilt complex within Western democracies that becomes susceptible to being blackmailed into silent acceptance of the Palestinian people's cultural genocide by Israel. The following is Article 7 of a 1994 draft of the United Nations Declaration on the Rights of Indigenous Peoples which was ratified in September 2007 without Israel's participation and of which Israel, in the name of all Jewish people, is in flagrant violation:

Indigenous peoples have the collective and individual right not to be subjected to ethnocide or cultural genocide, including prevention of and redress for:

(a) Any action which has the aim or effect of depriving them of their integrity as a distinct peoples, or of their cultural values or ethnic identities;

(b) Any action which has the aim or effect of dispossessing them of their lands, territories or resources;

(c) Any form of population transfer which has the aim or effect of violating or undermining any of their rights;

Any form of assimilation or integration by other cultures or ways of life imposed on them by legislative, administrative or other measures;

Any form of propaganda directed against them.

The Legislative Section at AIPAC headquarters with its proficient use of persuasive argument and constituency rewards for senators and congressmen who support legislation favourable to Israel, plays a vital role in maintaining a Congressional allegiance to Israel that by far surpasses loyalty to the United States itself. This is achieved by requiring from every candidate for the U.S. Congress a "signed pledge" to support Israel which if refused results in a cutoff from AIPAC's multimillion dollar war chest for fighting elections and the start of a media campaign to viciously demonize the un-cooperating candidate.

231

AIPAC by its own estimation can at any time count on the support of more than half of all senators and congressmen. Though the U.S. Jewish population is approximately six million or less than 3 percent, Jews have the highest ethnic group percentage of actual voters with an estimate of around 90 percent. Furthermore, 89 percent of the Jewish population lives in 12 key electoral college states. Despite comprising of only 1.8 percent of the college age population in the U.S., Jews total an astonishing 25 percent of Harvard and Ivy League college enrollment — a statistic that should not be regarded as condemnation of Jews, but of non-Jews. All Americans — including those who do not have college degrees — should recognize that they they can regain the governance of their country by exercising their right to vote and by making their views known to those on Capitol Hill.

AIPAC recognizes that effective lobbying requires the capacity to provide quality, well-timed information and consequently its Research Section is renowned for in-depth policy position papers that focus specifically on Israel's strategic importance to the United States. Any Congressional activity regarding Israel is closely monitored and extensive records are kept on members' speeches, informal comments, and constituent correspondence that might in any way relate to Israel. The Congressional Record is monitored on a daily basis with particular attention being paid to committee hearings that may affect Israel. A close watch is also kept with regards to members' voting patterns on issues such as foreign aid and arms sales. Every year anywhere from 70 to 90 U.S. senators and congressmen (about 20 percent) are rewarded with AIPAC-funded junkets to Israel.

AIPAC's grassroots lobbying is the responsibility of the Political Development Section which organizes fundraising, constituent participation in local and national politics, the provision of information to Congressional incumbents and aspirants on Israeli issues, and pro-Israel political leadership development programs in colleges across the United States. AIPAC is also active throughout the U.S. on college campuses with a Political Leadership Development Program (PLDP) that endeavors to get students involved in pro-Israel activities. Regional field organizers arrange workshops and conferences to recruit and train students as activists who are then expected to prepare reports on faculty members, students or college organizations who are in any way critical of Israel or sympathetic to the plight of the Palestinian people. The information is then used to publish the AIPAC College Guide which exposes the "miscreants" who are then subject to harassment, suspension, or in some cases, dismissal. In 2002 Daniel Pipes, the Middle East Forum director and anti-Arab propagandist, launched Campus Watch as a pro-Israel web-based forum staffed primarily by Jews. Campus Watch, like the PLDP, encourages students to submit reports about criticism of Israel by college professors who are then routinely harassed, blacklisted, and intimidated. There are more than a few recorded cases of professors being suspended or even dismissed for daring to criticize Israel's brutality in the illegally occupied territories.

The Political Section of AIPAC also ensures that all AIPAC members become individual Jewish lobbyists through their involvement in the political process. Maintaining the effectiveness of the Political Development Section at AIPAC's headquarters was the responsibility of Steve Appelman who as a Mossad Katsa, also supervised some 40 assets and sayanim. Appelman's role of puppetmaster was further enhanced by the regularity of his attendance at the Grand Lodge of Free and Accepted Masons of the District of Columbia.

You cannot criticize Israel in this country (USA) and survive.
Helen Thomas (1920-2013) American author, news service reporter, opinion columnist, and member of the White House press corps.

8
Saturday, 13 December 2008
Little Venice, London

Mark Banner and Nadine's five-hour British Airways flight from Beirut to London's Heathrow Airport had been uneventful and had provided Banner with an opportunity to complete the section for his book that covered the Carter and Reagan relationships with Israel.

Nadine, who always avoided attempts at conversation whenever he was engrossed with work, passed the time by watching a movie and reading several fashion magazines in anticipation of her forthcoming shopping spree which had become an annual holiday event.

Banner had begun by noting that while serving as president from January 20, 1977 to January 20, 1981, Jimmy Carter had achieved many significant foreign policy accomplishments including the Panama Canal treaties, the Camp David Accords, the treaty of peace between Egypt and Israel, the SALT II treaty with the Soviet Union, the establishment of U.S. diplomatic relations with the People's Republic of China, and the championing of human rights throughout the world. On the domestic front, his administration's achievements included a comprehensive energy program conducted by a new Department of Energy; deregulation in energy, transportation, communications, and finance; major educational programs under a new Department of Education; and major environmental protection legislation, including the Alaska National Interest Lands Conservation Act.

When presenting a progress report on the Camp David peace talks to the U.S. Congress on 18 September 1978, President Jimmy Carter pointed out that it had been some 2,000 years since there had been peace between Egypt and a free Jewish nation and that such a peace was achievable that same year. Having therefore at the time offered one of the most promising prospects for peace in Middle East history, the Camp David Accords had since failed to measure up to the expectations of that euphoric moment because peace with Egypt was only a small part of the equation and did not provide a framework for resolution of the plight of the Palestinian people who had every legal and moral right to self-determination as the Israelis.

Israel regarded the signing of the Accords as a useful ploy —

despite having to return the Sinai to Egypt — that eliminated Egypt (the biggest Arab nation) from its list of potential Arab enemies in the event of any future Arab-Israeli wars. There was never going to be even the remotest chance of Israel surrendering the occupied territories or abandoning its Zionist agenda of an Apartheid policy that called for the brutal oppression of the Palestinian people so as to gradually drive them off their land and make way for the construction of even more illegal Jewish settlements.

In his honest endeavor to broker a peace agreement between Egypt and Israel with the assumption that it would pave the way for resolution of the wider Palestinian issue, Carter made the fatal mistake — one that is repeatedly made by all Western leaders — of not recognizing the resolute reality of Israel's Apartheid agenda which would always preclude any hopes of eventual Palestinian autonomy and the withdrawal of Israeli armed forces from the West Bank and Gaza.

So even though Carter's efforts resulted in Egypt becoming the first Arab state to recognize Israel's legitimacy and thereby enhance Israel's security by causing the breakup of what was a solid Arab front, Carter has since been demonized — especially for his book *Palestine: Peace not Apartheid,* Simon & Schuster, 2006 — by an Israeli nation and its Zionist supporters who have accused him of "merely being provocative to sell books, he appears to be giving aid and comfort to the new anti-Semites whose goal since the 2001 UN World Conference against Racism, Racial Discrimination, Xenophobia and Related Intolerance in Durban, South Africa, has been to link Israel to apartheid South Africa."

Banner summed up with the opinion that the accomplishments of the Carter Presidency had been overshadowed — and may even have lost him election for a second term — when 52 Americans were held hostage for 444 days (November 4, 1979 to January 20, 1981), after a group of Iranian students supporting the Iranian Revolution took over the American Embassy in Tehran.

Though Carter's successor Ronald Reagan, never visited Israel as President, he was nonetheless regarded by Israelis as possibly the most pro-Israel U.S. president since the state's establishment in 1948. The existence of such regard was despite the fact — that while other presidents occasionally threatened to sanction Israel for its violations — Reagan was never shy with his admonishment. When in 1981 the Israelis voted to annex the Golan Heights which had been captured during the 1967 Six-day War and was by then already host to some

6,600 Jews in 31 settlements, Reagan did not hesitate to suspend the strategic cooperation agreement. Despite the fact that Israel's action had removed all prospects of territorial compromise or future peace negotiations, Prime Minister Menachem Begin accused Reagan of treating Israel like a "banana republic." As always, Israeli Jews were not to blame for their blatant violations of international laws because it was all the fault of those nasty anti-Semites who had the audacity to suggest that Palestinians were human beings deserving of the same inalienable rights as the Jewish people.

By formalising the strategic cooperation agreement, Reagan had cemented the U.S.-Israel relationship and established a firm connection between the Pentagon and the Israeli Defence Force which served to strengthen Israel's military capability. He did, however, at the same time also significantly strengthen the Arab position by selling them sophisticated American weapons. Also during that same year, Reagan was successful in overcoming the powerful Israeli lobby's opposition to the proposed sale of AWACS radar planes to Saudi Arabia. This proved to be a landmark success that prevented the lobby from ever again mounting a significant challenge to U.S. arms sales to Arab nations. The AWACs saga was one of nastiness between Reagan and Menachem Begin for whom the U.S. President had a conspicuous but understandable distaste.

On June 7, 1981, Israel — which by then already had a stockpile of more than a 100 nuclear weapons — dispatched 14 fighter jets of American manufacture (F15s and F16s) to bomb the Iraqi French-built reactor at Osirak. A dozen conventional bombs obliterated the almost complete reactor and killed one French Technician. In claiming responsibility and citing justification for the attack, Israel alleged that the reactor was intended for the production of nuclear weapons for use against Israel. Reagan was furious and the U.S. — for a change — actually supported the UN Security Council resolution condemning Israel. Israel, however, was not without its assets and staunch defenders in high places who in this instance included the U.S. ambassador to the UN, Jeane Kirkpatrick. Consequently the U.S. reverted to its traditional blind support for Israel and vetoed more than a dozen other anti-Israel resolutions.

Apart from certain basic issues — Palestinian refugees, the illegal occupation of East Jerusalem, and the question of pre-1967 borders — the events most addressed by U.N. resolutions against Israel have related

236

to its unlawful attacks on neighboring countries; its violation of, and contempt for Palestinian human rights, including deportations, home demolitions and other forms of collective punishment; its expropriation of Palestinian lands; its continuing establishment of illegal settlements; and its refusal to comply with both the U.N. Charter and the 1949 Fourth Geneva Convention Relative to the Protection of Civilian Persons in Time of War.

Though Reagan was not necessarily a great fan of Israel or its policies, he was nonetheless convinced by his religious beliefs — which tended to have a narrow Manichaean world view of good versus evil — that Israel was one of the good guys. With that in mind, Reagan worked to free Soviet Jews and approved the 1985 CIA-sponsored Operation Joshua which rescued 500 Ethiopian Jews from refugee camps. That same year, following a severe economic crisis in Israel with inflation rates as high as 445 percent, the U.S. approved a $1.5 billion emergency assistance package and facilitated the formulation of Israel's successful economic stabilization plan.

It was under Reagan that Israel began to receive $3 billion annually in foreign aid, and as of 1985 onwards, that aid was all in the form of grants. The U.S. also signed its first Free Trade Agreement with Israel along with a series of memoranda of understanding between U.S. agencies and their Israeli counterparts with a view to promoting cooperation in fields such as education, space research and health.

When on 6 June 1982 Israel launched the First Lebanon War which it euphemistically named Operation Peace for Galilee, Reagan's initial support gradually waned as the Israeli operation bogged down and U.S. forces were drawn into the quagmire. Two months later Reagan facilitated for Yasser Arafat and the PLO leadership the safe passage that allowed them to travel to exile in Tunis. Reagan then announced on September 1, that while he opposed the creation of a Palestinian state, he nonetheless felt that the Palestinians should have self-government in association with Jordan. He also maintained that Jerusalem should remain undivided until such time as its final status was negotiated and that there should be a freeze on settlements — a suggestion which Menachem Begin totally rejected.

As the war continued, and unbeknown to Israel, Reagan devised a new diplomatic initiative that was intended to revive peace negotiations, bolster Egyptian-Israeli relations, and provide Jordan with an incentive to become engaged in peace negotiations. It was also hoped that the initiative would convey to those Arab states who were host to PLO refugees from Beirut that the U.S. was actively seeking a solution to the Arab-Israeli conflict.

Though it was usually Israel that dragged the U.S into legally questionable ventures, the roles were reversed in the scandal that came to be known as the Iran-Contra affair or Irangate. Two interesting aspects of Reagan's presidency was his illogical obsession with Central America, and his mistaken belief that the Sandinistas' 1979 victory in Nicaragua could ignite a series of revolutions throughout the region and thereby threaten the security of the United States.

Though Central America had for many years been dismissed as a small, backward, and trifling part of the world, that view changed dramatically in 1979 when Nicaragua's left-wing Sandinista revolutionaries overthrew the corrupt and repressive regime of General Somoza. Though the Sandinistas never defined themselves as being communist — they in fact favored a mixed economy with political pluralism — they nonetheless alarmed Washington by setting up the clearly political Sandinista People's Army as a replacement for the National Guard; and by the redistribution of wealth including the expropriation of large estates. Consequently because he was already obsessed with the idea of fighting Communism worldwide, when he became U.S. President, Reagan proved uncompromising in his opposition to the Sandinista government which he regarded as being the main cause of the social unrest spreading throughout neighboring countries.

Reagan therefore determined that U.S. support should be given to the Contras — various rebel groups opposing the Sandinista Junta of National Reconstruction government in Nicaragua — whom he described as "the moral equivalent of our Founding Fathers." Assistance involved supplying financial support which proved difficult because the Democratic congressional elections landslide in November 1982 resulted in the passing of the Boland Amendment which specifically restricted CIA and Department of Defense operations in Nicaragua. A strengthening of the Boland Amendment two years later rendered any form of support virtually impossible. Not to be deterred, Reagan informed National Security Adviser Robert McFarlane, "I want you to do whatever you have to do to help these people keep body and soul together."

The covert operation that ensued — in the name of that pie-in-the-sky American democracy — was to say the least mind-boggling. During the Iran-Iraq war (September 1980 to August 1988), Iran secretly requested — despite an arms sales embargo against it — to purchase weapons from the United States. In seeking Reagan's approval, McFarlane explained that such sales would not only improve U.S. relations with Iran, but might also enhance relations with Lebanon and increase U.S. influence in the cauldron of the Middle East. It was also thought that such sales would assist in securing the release of seven American hostages being held by Iranian terrorists in Lebanon — a problem with which Reagan was already preoccupied.

It was therefore planned that Israel — always happy to indulge in some illegal arms dealing and thought to be already covertly supplying weapons to Iraq through its network of Jewish arms dealers — would ship to Iran the required weapons which the U.S would then replace with U.S. arms sales to Israel. It was hoped that in return the Iranians would do everything possible secure the release of the hostages. This proposal of arms-for-hostages divided the administration with longtime policy adversaries Secretary of State George Shultz and Secretary of Defense Caspar Weinberger being opposed the deal. But McFarlane and CIA director William Casey were for it and so with Reagan's support the plan went ahead.

When the Lebanese newspaper *Al-Shiraa* published its exposé of the illegal sales in November 1986, Reagan appeared on television to forcefully deny the occurrence of any such covert operation. Though he was forced to retract the denial a week later and defended the operation by virtue of its good intentions, he still maintained that the sale of weapons had not been an arms-for-hostages deal. By the time of *Al-shiraa's* disclosue, 1,500 missiles had already been shipped to Iran. The scandal served to tarnish Reagan's reputation for honesty and polls revealed that only 14 percent of Americans believed his claim that he had not traded arms for hostages.

While investigating the arms-for-hostages scandal, Attorney General Edwin Meese discovered that only $12 million of the $30 million the Iranians reportedly paid had reached government coffers. The then-unheard-of Lieutenant Colonel Oliver North of the National Security Council explained the discrepancy by revealing that he had diverted funds from the arms sales to the Contras with the full knowledge of National Security Adviser Admiral John Poindexter and supposedly the unstated approval of President Reagan.

Though Poindexter subsequently resigned and North was dismissed, the scandal persisted with the media demanding to know whether Reagan had been aware of the illegal shenanigans, and if not, then how could something with considerable political ramifications possibly occur without his knowledge? A Reagan-appointed Tower Commission investigation concluded that diversion of funds to the Contras had become possible because Reagan had disengaged himself from the management of the White House, and that there was no evidence that linked Reagan to the diversion.

Nonetheless speculation about the involvement of Reagan, Vice President George Bush and the administration at large continued as the Independent Counsel Lawrence Walsh investigated the affair over the next eight years. Though 14 people were ultimately charged with either operational of "cover-up crimes," North's conviction was overturned on a technicality. The already convicted McFarlane and yet to be tried Weinberger received two of the six pardons issued by President George Bush.

Reagan survived and towards the end of his second term in office in December 1988, he reversed the U.S. policy of refusing to recognise terrorist organisations and authorised the State Department to commence dialogue with the PLO, thus depriving Israel of any opportunity to marginalise the PLO and encourage the development of some alternative and more flexible leadership.

In retrospect, Mark Banner found it difficult to comprehend why Reagan was regarded as the most pro-Israel U.S. president because some of his policies resulted in both short and long-term damage to the U.S.-Israeli relationship. He did, however, contribute significantly to Israel's economic and military strength, and also raised the political level of the U.S.-Israel relationship. Though Reagan's image had been damaged by the Iran-Contra affair, he lived up to his reputation of being the "Teflon President" with his popularity rebounding so that by the time of his leaving office in 1989 he had the highest approval rating of any president since Franklin D. Roosevelt.

9
Sunday, 14 December 2008
Talbiyah, West Jerusalem

Abe Goldman lived in a U.S. $1.3 million garden apartment on Disraeli Street in Jerusalem's wealthy neighborhood of Talbiyeh where important government officials including the president also lived. The purchase of any property in West Jerusalem is controlled by the Israel Lands Administration (ILA) whose rules state that ownership of the land remains with the ILA which leases it to the purchaser for a period of 49 years. Article 19 of ILA leases specifies that foreign nationals cannot lease — let alone own — ILA land. Consequently any Palestinian application to buy an apartment, always assuming he or she could afford it, would be summarily rejected. While not quite as blatant as South Africa's apartheid-era Group Areas Act which enforced racial segregation, this sly Israeli ploy was just as effective and equally racist.

Goldman had for most of his life regarded Sunday as his day for rest and reflection and today was no different as he relaxed on his black leather swivel recliner. His choice of Sunday was simply a carry-over from his days in South Africa where it had been merely a question of convenience to fall in line with the Dutch reformed Church's day of worship and rest for Whites. Framed awards and photographs taken with captains of industry and world leaders adorned the wood paneled walls and were a testament to a lifetime of achievements.

Born in 1939 to a Jewish couple who owned and ran a shoe store in Johannesburg, Goldman had from an early age learnt what it was like to live in an environment that was hostile towards Jews. Such hostility dated back to the "rush" that followed the 1867 discovery of diamonds in the Cape Colony which was followed by grand scale exploitation by opportunists like Cecil Rhodes (1853-1902) and Barney Barnato (1851-1897) who like others of their ilk became known as Randlords. Rhodes, who as an English vicar's asthmatic runt of a son had been sent to South Africa at the age of sixteen to ease his lung congestion, was an avowed racist with the belief that Anglo-Saxons should exploit all those areas that were inhabited by "the most despicable specimens of human beings."

On his way to becoming the richest man in the world on the back of cheap Black labour, Rhodes had supported the notorious Masters and Servants Act which was facetiously nicknamed the "Every Man to Wallop his Own Nigger Bill." Barnato, a Jew, was Rhodes' main competitor but eventually sold his business to Rhodes for UK £4 million (currently equivalent to more than £2.5 billion or U.S. $4.4 billion). Rhodes, financed by bankers N. M. Rothschild & Sons, then proceeded to purchase and amalgamate diamond mines into the De Beers company whose ownership was subsequently wrested in 1927 by Ernest Oppenheimer who went on to found the Anglo American Corporation in South Africa and thereby consolidate his monopoly over the world's diamond industry.

When Oppenheimer converted from Judaism to Anglicanism in the late 1930s, some cynical observers had — perhaps unjustly — suggested that the conversion was intended to remove a possible obstacle to the continued sale of industrial diamonds for use in Hitler's Germany. His involvement in other controversies included price fixing, antitrust behavior, and an allegation of not releasing industrial diamonds for the U.S. war effort.

In June 1877, at Oxford, Cecil Rhodes wrote about his idea for expanding the British Empire which he later amended. The following, with the original grammatical and spelling errors, is the amended version:

> *It often strikes a man to inquire what is the chief good in life; to one the thought comes that it is a happy marriage, to another great wealth, and as each seizes on his idea, for that he more or less works for the rest of his existence. To myself thinking over the same question the wish came to render myself useful to my country. I then asked myself how could I and after reviewing the various methods I have felt that at the present day we are actually limiting our children and perhaps bringing into the world half the human beings we might owing to the lack of country for them to inhabit that if we had retained America there would at this moment be millions more of English living. I contend that we are the finest race in the world and that the more of the world we inhabit the better it is for the human race. Just fancy those parts that are at present inhabited by the most despicable specimens of human beings what an alteration there would*

be if they were brought under Anglo-Saxon influence, look again at the extra employment a new country added to our dominions gives. I contend that every acre added to our territory means in the future birth to some more of the English race who otherwise would not be brought into existence. Added to this the absorption of the greater portion of the world under our rule simply means the end of all wars, at this moment had we not lost America I believe we could have stopped the Russian-Turkish war by merely refusing money and supplies. Having these ideas what scheme could we think of to forward this object. I look into history and I read the story of the Jesuits I see what they were able to do in a bad cause and I might say under bad leaders.

At the present day I become a member of the Masonic order I see the wealth and power they possess the influence they hold and I think over their ceremonies and I wonder that a large body of men can devote themselves to what at times appear the most ridiculous and absurd rites without an object and without an end. The idea gleaming and dancing before ones eyes like a will-of-the-wisp at last frames itself into a plan. Why should we not form a secret society with but one object the furtherance of the British Empire and the bringing of the whole uncivilized world under British rule for the recovery of the United States for the making the Anglo-Saxon race but one Empire. What a dream, but yet it is probable, it is possible. I once heard it argued by a fellow in my own college, I am sorry to own it by an Englishman, that it was good thing for us that we have lost the United States. There are some subjects on which there can be no arguments, and to an Englishman this is one of them, but even from an American's point of view just picture what they have lost, look at their government, are not the frauds that yearly come before the public view a disgrace to any country and especially their's which is the finest in the world. Would they have occurred had they remained under English rule great as they have become how infinitely greater they would have been with the softening and elevating influences of English rule, think of those countless 000's of Englishmen that during the last

100 years would have crossed the Atlantic and settled and populated the United States. Would they have not made without any prejudice a finer country of it than the low class Irish and German emigrants? All this we have lost and that country loses owing to whom? Owing to two or three ignorant pig-headed statesmen of the last century, at their door lies the blame. Do you ever feel mad? do you ever feel murderous. I think I do with those men. I bring facts to prove my assertion. Does an English father when his sons wish to emigrate ever think of suggesting emigration to a country under another flag, never — it would seem a disgrace to suggest such a thing I think that we all think that poverty is better under our own flag than wealth under a foreign one.

Put your mind into another train of thought. Fancy Australia discovered and colonized under the French flag, what would it mean merely several millions of English unborn that at present exist we learn from the past and to form our future. We learn from having lost to cling to what we possess. We know the size of the world we know the total extent. Africa is still lying ready for us it is our duty to take it. It is our duty to seize every opportunity of acquiring more territory and we should keep this one idea steadily before our eyes that more territory simply means more of the Anglo-Saxon race more of the best the most human, most honourable race the world possesses.

To forward such a scheme what a splendid help a secret society would be a society not openly acknowledged but who would work in secret for such an object.

I contend that there are at the present moment numbers of the ablest men in the world who would devote their whole lives to it. I often think what a loss to the English nation in some respects the abolition of the Rotten Borough System has been. What thought strikes a man entering the house of commons, the assembly that rule the whole world? I think it is the mediocrity of the men but what is the cause. It is simply — an assembly of wealth of men whose lives have been spent in the accumulation of money and whose time

244

has been too much engaged to be able to spare any for the study of past history. And yet in hands of such men rest our destinies. Do men like the great Pitt, and Burke and Sheridan not now to exist. I contend they do. There are men now living with I know no other term the [Greek term] of Aristotle but there are not ways for enabling them to serve their Country. They live and die unused unemployed. What has the main cause of the success of the Romish Church? The fact that every enthusiast, call it if you like every madman finds employment in it. Let us form the same kind of society a Church for the extension of the British Empire. A society which should have members in every part of the British Empire working with one object and one idea we should have its members placed at our universities and our schools and should watch the English youth passing through their hands just one perhaps in every thousand would have the mind and feelings for such an object, he should be tried in every way, he should be tested whether he is endurant, possessed of eloquence, disregardful of the petty details of life, and if found to be such, then elected and bound by oath to serve for the rest of his life in his County. He should then be supported if without means by the Society and sent to that part of the Empire where it was felt he was needed.

Take another case, let us fancy a man who finds himself his own master with ample means of attaining his majority whether he puts the question directly to himself or not, still like the old story of virtue and vice in the Memorabilia a fight goes on in him as to what he should do. Take if he plunges into dissipation there is nothing too reckless he does not attempt but after a time his life palls on him, he mentally says this is not good enough, he changes his life, he reforms, he travels, he thinks now I have found the chief good in life, the novelty wears off, and he tires, to change again, he goes into the far interior after the wild game he thinks at last I've found that in life of which I cannot tire, again he is disappointed. He returns he thinks is there nothing I can do in life? Here I am with means, with a good house, with everything that is to be envied and yet I am not happy I am tired of life he possesses within him a portion of the [Greek term] of Aristotle but he knows it not, to such a man the Society should go, should test, and should finally show him the greatness of the scheme and list him as a member.

Take one more case of the younger son with high thoughts, high aspirations, endowed by nature with all the faculties to make a great man, and with the sole wish in life to serve his Country but he lacks two things the means and the opportunity, ever troubled by a sort of inward deity urging him on to high and noble deeds, he is compelled to pass his time in some occupation which furnishes him with mere existence, he lives unhappily and dies miserably. Such men as these the Society should search out and use for the furtherance of their object.

(In every Colonial legislature the Society should attempt to have its members prepared at all times to vote or speak and advocate the closer union of England and the colonies, to crush all disloyalty and every movement for the severance of our Empire. The Society should inspire and even own portions of the press for the press rules the mind of the people. The Society should always be searching for members who might by their position in the world by their energies or character forward the object but the ballot and test for admittance should be severe)

Once make it common and it fails. Take a man of great wealth who is bereft of his children perhaps having his mind soured by some bitter disappointment who shuts himself up separate from his neighbours and makes up his mind to a miserable existence. To such men as these the society should go gradually disclose the greatness of their scheme and entreat him to throw in his life and property with them for this object. I think that there are thousands now existing who would eagerly grasp at the opportunity. Such are the heads of my scheme.

For fear that death might cut me off before the time for attempting its development I leave all my worldly goods in trust to S. G. Shippard and the Secretary for the Colonies at the time of my death to try to form such a Society with such an object.

Not surprisingly the infamous racist Rhodes — who in a large part of Africa spearheaded British colonialism with its benefits of Christianity and corruption — was the recipient of a letter from Theodor Herzl (another racist and the father of Zionism) in which Herzl states:

You are being invited to help make history . . . It doesn't involve Africa, but a piece of Asia Minor; not Englishmen but Jews . . . How, then, do I happen to turn to you since this is an out-of-the-way matter for you? How indeed? Because it is something colonial . . . You, Mr. Rhodes, are a visionary politician or a practical visionary . . . I want you to put the stamp of your authority on the Zionist plan and to make the following declaration to a few people who swear by you: I, Rhodes have examined this plan and found it correct and practicable. It is a plan full of culture, excellent for the group of people for whom it is directly designed, and quite good for England, for Greater Britain . . .

Rhodes not only had a grand colonial dream, he also backed it with his money by leaving a will that was to create one of the most successful educational endowments of all time — The Rhodes Scholarships which were open only to Teutonic peoples (Britons, Germans, and Americans) to study at Oxford. The scholarships were to serve the express purpose of enabling the academic elites of those countries to come together and form a mutual understanding that would encourage attempts to create an Anglo-Saxon empire across the world. Scholarships are awarded annually by the Rhodes Trust which was established in 1902 under the terms and conditions of Rhodes' will and are funded by his estate under the administration of Nathan Rothschild. Since the Trust's inception in 1902, there have been more than 7,000 Rhodes Scholars — supposedly on the basis of academic achievement and strength of character — with more than 4,000 still living. Rhodes' "Teutonic" stipulation has more recently been abandoned so that a token number of non-Teutonic students have helped to remove the stigma of racism. In 1968, Bill Clinton, the yet to become serial adulterer and President of the United States, went to Oxford on a Rhodes scholarship. Thirty years later Clinton became only the second U.S. president to be impeached — the first being Andrew Johnson — for alleged acts of perjury and obstruction of justice related to the Monica Lewinsky scandal. This followed the Starr Report's submission to the House providing what it termed "substantial and credible information that President Clinton Committed Acts that May Constitute Grounds for an Impeachment." Rhodes must have turned in his grave.

A further influx of Randlords followed the end of the bitterly fought Second Boer War in 1902 when the Afrikaner republics of the Orange Free State and the Transvaal became a parts of the British Empire. Many of the new arrivals were part of the general Jewish exodus resulting from the growing anti-Semitism in Central Europe that led to the wider diaspora in London, New York and Johannesburg. Anti-Semitic sentiment took different forms including the caricature of "Hoggenheimer," a silk-hatted and bloated character with accentuated Semitic features who came to personify the hated capitalist in both national socialist and communist propaganda. The "Hoggenheimer" caricature had been based on a West End musical *The Girl from Kays* that opened in 1902 at London's Apollo Theatre. About an alluring dancer who beguiles a South African millionaire, the show lampooned the Randlords who flaunted their wealth and owned mansions in Park Lane and Belgravia while their disenfranchised and exploited Black workers in South Africa were confined to compounds like animals. The rise of Jewish mining magnates to prominence during this period increased anti-Semitism with editorial views suggesting that the Boer war had been fought to serve the interests of a small group of international financiers who were mainly German in origin and Jewish in race. In keeping with what had been a recurrent theme throughout history, Jews were openly accused of controlling the economy to the detriment of the rest of the population.

In the period leading up to the Second World War the influential Afrikaner secret society, the Broederbond (the Brotherhood), had begun developing ties to the Nazis and the prospect of siding with Britain in a war was anathema for most Afrikaners. In many predominantly Afrikaner communities Jews were victimised and Jewish businesses were attacked by the Fascist Grey Shirt militia. During the war a Broederbond member and future prime minister, John Vorster, was interned by Jan Smut's government in a prison camp for having Nazi sympathies and connections to the Grey Shirts.

Three decades later Vorster was greeted with open arms and feted by Israeli leaders in Jerusalem. The eventual Allied victory, however, did not end Afrikaner hatred for Jews and in 1948 the Reunited National Party defeated Smut's United Party by campaigning on an anti-Semitic platform and exploiting anti-British imperialist sentiment. Once in power, the Afrikaner nationalists wasted no time in implementing apartheid, the legal system of social and political separation, which was designed to consolidate and extend white minority control of South Africa's economy and politics. Apartheid's segregation was enforced from the bedroom to the workplace and millions of black people — the workforce on whom the Whites depended — were dumped in so-called "independent" homelands whose corrupt and despotic rulers were obligated to the Afrikaner government.

Many South African Jews at that time became understandably concerned as to their role in the newly intensified race differentiation setup. They were, however, soon reassured by the fact that the Apartheid regime could not risk creating an even bigger demographic problem by isolating a minority of the white population, even if that minority happened to be Jewish. So within a couple of years the majority of South African Jews not only felt safe under the Calvinist Afrikaner government, but also quite comfortable with the concept of Apartheid. While the death of 25,000 Afrikaner women and children from disease and starvation in British concentration camps during the Boer War was hardly comparable to the Holocaust, Jews in South Africa had nonetheless felt sympathetic towards Afrikaners and began siding with them not so much because they liked them but because Afrikaners were at least white. There were in fact survivors from Auschwitz and other Nazi concentration camps who saw no contradiction in their support for, and in some cases even membership in the Apartheid Nationalist party which pursued policies reminiscent of Hitler's Nuremberg laws against Jews: laws that included prohibition of sex and marriage between Blacks and Whites and the preclusion of Blacks from many jobs.

It was not uncommon to hear South African Jews speak of Blacks with the same derisive manner as that used by Nazis to describe Jews. They even defended Apartheid as a safeguard against domination by Blacks who were inferior to other human beings and not entitled to treatment as equals. If there had been any concern amongst "the chosen people" for the plight of black people, then it must have been extremely peripheral because in reality they had no qualms about fully enjoying the bountiful fruits of the system. They in fact meticulously avoided confrontation with the government and pursued a deliberate policy of "neutrality" without "rocking the boat" so as not to endanger the Jewish population.

The Zionist Federation and the Jewish Board of Deputies in South Africa regularly honoured Jewish men such as Percy Yutar who was hailed as a "credit to the community" and an example of Jews' contribution to South Africa. Yutar, who was also elected president of Johannesburg's largest orthodox synagogue, was the attorney who in 1963 successfully prosecuted Nelson Mandela for sabotage and conspiracy against the state.

A small number of Jews, however, notably Joe Slovo, Albie Sachs, Harry Schwarz, and Helen Suzman (the latter being for many years the only member of parliament to oppose Apartheid), did feel that silence with regard to racial oppression was tantamount to collaboration and as a consequence of openly opposing the system, they were regarded as enemies of the state and pariahs amongst their own people.

Even though Goldman had grown up with and been conditioned in accordance with the prevailing Jewish perception of apartheid, he had nevertheless always emphatically maintained — perhaps with more than a tinge of hypocrisy — that he was not and never had been a racist. After graduating with a degree in mercantile law from the University of the Free State Faculty of Law in Bloemfontein, Goldman had worked for a commercial law firm for three years before joining the legal department of a mining conglomerate whose more than 1,200 subsidiaries encompassed everything from automobile dealerships to Zinfandel vineyards. Goldman had wasted no time in becoming a potential rising star by marrying the daughter of a prominent Jewish family, having two children, and living in Johannesburg's fashionable Parktown district. He quickly became a troubleshooter and paymaster on whom the conglomerate could rely and he consequently travelled extensively starting with a trip to Namaqualand in the Northern Cape. Namaqualand was a rugged and sparsely populated plateau bordered on the east by dry central plains, and on the west by a sandveld whose desolate beaches were lapped by the waters of the Atlantic Ocean. Vegetation was scarce for most of the year, but in August and September following the seasonal rains, the sun-scorched terrain was miraculously transformed into a multi-colored weave of gently swaying flowers. Goldman had for the first time in his life — without comprehending why — become almost spiritually aware of his breathtaking surroundings to the extent of noting that here at least was an area that had so far survived mankind's predilection for wanton destruction.

Namaqualand's Port Nolloth had been a seaside town originally serving as a railway depot for the local copper mines but whose importance was upgraded following the chance discovery of precious stones in the early 1900's. Many millenniums earlier the stones had been carried down from the Richtersveld Mountains by the Orange River and dispersed along the coastline by powerful currents. Consequently glittering surf-washed pebbles of agate, amazonite, carnelian, diamond, and Jasper either littered the beaches or lay within the ocean gravel beds. During his stay in Port Nolloth, Goldman had watched offshore mining ships with huge hoses sucking up thousands of tonnes of sand and gravel from which the diamonds were sifted and automatically sealed in metal containers for airlifting by helicopter to the mainland.

The entire mineral-rich coastal strip was a Forbidden Zone with security being especially tight around the diamond-mining towns of Alexander Bay in South Africa, and Oranjemund (on the northern bank of the Orange River) in Namibia. Helicopters kept watch from above and Alsatian dog patrols covered the ground. Anyone entering or leaving the zone's wire-fenced perimeters required a permit and all vehicles and personal effects were thoroughly searched. Despite such stringent precautions including computerized security screening systems and the use of high tech X-ray equipment to check for swallowed diamonds, approximately twenty percent of all diamond production was at the time being lost.

By using the simple ploy of smuggling racing pigeons into the mines, strapping pouches of uncut diamonds to their legs, and then releasing them to return home, dishonest mine employees were repeatedly bypassing the maximum state of the art security with the minimum of primitive ingenuity. Though the pigeons were ostensibly reared to supply officially registered racing pigeon clubs, unscrupulous farmers were also selling the sought- after birds to anyone prepared to pay a premium.

The problem facing Goldman's employers was that such illegally acquired uncut precious stones from West and Central Africa were then being smuggled northwards to Liberia and sold to rogue Lebanese traders in the capitol city of Monrovia. To counter such trade, Goldman had travelled to London to meet with and employ a Special Air Service (SAS) veteran who provided mercenary army solutions. The mercenary army's assignment was to repeatedly ambush the smugglers with a view to either killing or scaring them off so that agents recognized by Goldman's employers could resume their practice of purchasing the illicit stones cheaply so as to monopolize and control the flow of diamonds which in turn facilitated price fixing on the world market.

Goldman's activities were in due course extended to include arranging for the use of mercenaries to foment conflict in diamond-rich African countries so that his employers could then reap the benefits of buying more cheap diamonds from cash-strapped civil war combatants. Furthermore, by also paying for men and armaments to fuel and prolong conflicts between newly independent but unstable mineral-rich African countries and rebel forces, mining conglomerates could continue plundering mineral resources that might otherwise have been nationalized under politically stable conditions.

Goldman, however, had to wait for the taste of real success and power until the early sixties when sanctions against South Africa began when the United Nations Security Council deplored apartheid and established a voluntary arms embargo against South Africa. As it was in the interests of the government and business conglomerates to maintain the social and political status quo in South Africa, they joined forces in their efforts to find new ways, means, and friends that would help in circumventing the inevitability of further sanctions.

During the early years following its creation as a state, Israel was on friendly terms with anti-apartheid African nations whose backing for Israel at the UN General Assembly served as a counter to the Muslim/ Arab bloc. In time, however, African nations gradually disengaged themselves from an Israel whose treatment of the Palestinian people was an Apartheid in different clothing. Israel was therefore forced to look elsewhere for an African ally and it was with South Africa that an alliance of shared interests began to materialise. To begin with both states had been established on land stolen from a an indigenous majority; both were consequently outnumbered and surrounded by enemies who had to be controlled and kept at bay by means of military force; and both were subject to regular condemnation by UN resolutions which in Israel's case were always vetoed by its superpower lackey, the United States.

It was therefore within that context that Abe Goldman undertook his first ever visit to Israel as an unofficial envoy representing South African business interests. His immediate mission was to secure from

Israel a lifeline supply of munitions that were essential for the continued suppression of the South African Black majority. Goldman's success in brokering a munitions supply arrangement which included Israel being used as an intermediary to purchase arms from countries that were otherwise off limits to South Africa, ensured that his visits would continue over the next two decades.

When trade sanctions prevented the legal import of South African agricultural products by other nations, it was Goldman who was dispatched by his mining conglomerate employers to arrange for such products to be sent on air cargo flights to Israel from where they would subsequently be re-exported as being of Israeli origin. Such "Israeli" products would then end up on the shelves of major European retailers such as Britain's high street giant, Marks & Spencer (M&S). The company had been run by successive generations of the Sieff family whose collaboration with Chaim Weizman and Zionism had been long and inexorable.

Joseph Edward "Teddy" Sieff (1906–1982) was Chairman of M&S (1967-1972) and honorary vice-president of the British Zionist Federation. Teddy had worked for most of his career at M&S, as did his brother Israel Sieff whom he succeeded as Chairman. In December 1973 Teddy survived an assassination attempt by the Popular Front for the Liberation of Palestine (PFLP) when PFLP assassin Carlos the Jackal called on Sieff's home in London's St. John's Wood and ordered the butler to take him to Sieff. On finding Sieff in the bathroom, Carlos fired one shot from a 9mm Beretta pistol which bounced off Sieff's dentures and knocked him unconscious; the gun then jammed and Carlos fled. While there can never be moral justification for such an assassination attempt irrespective of reason or circumstance, some would argue that it is equally immoral to support an ideology whose proclaimed intention was reiterated in the book *Ben Gurion and the Palestinian Arabs*, Oxford University Press, 1985: "We must expel the Arabs and take their places."

Teddy Sieff was succeeded as Chairman by Israel Sieff's son, Marcus, who in his book *Management:The Marks & Spencer Way* (Weidenfield & Nicolson, 1990), states that one of the fundamental objectives of M&S is to aid the economic development of Israel which was known to include the annual import of Israeli goods with a value in excess of $300 million. In 2001 press reports revealed that goods purportedly produced in the Zionist Israel and exported internationally with "Made in Israel" labels, were in actual fact usually produced by exploited Palestinian laborers in Israeli settlements within the Occupied Territories.

In April 2001, *The Guardian* newspaper reported that "Jars of Palestinian pickle, for instance, are handed over to the Israelis who stick a "Made in Israel," label on them and export them to Europe. Flowers grown by Palestinians in Gaza, strawberries, oranges, lemons and aubergines are all sent to Israel, mixed with Israeli produce and exported to Europe with Israeli certificates of origin." In other words, Israel unashamedly claimed that products from illegal Israeli settlements originate from within Israel's internationally recognized boundaries. That same month *The Guardian* also noted that "Nobody is in any real doubt that the products have come from illegal settlements and that their documentation has been falsified."

Under the 1975 Association Agreement between the EC and Israel, Israel is entitled to preferential trade treatment for agricultural and manufactured goods produced in "the territory of the state of Israel." Produce from Israeli settlements in the Occupied Territories are not covered by trade agreements with Europe and therefore do not qualify for preferential treatment. By falsely obtaining such preferential treatment including duty-free and reduced rates for its exports to Europe of goods produced outside of Israel's internationally recognized borders — such as occupied Palestinian territories — Israel is clearly in blatant violation of international law and its trade agreement with the EU.

U.N. Security Council resolutions 242 and 338 call on Israel to cease its occupation of Palestinian territories and cede to Palestinian self-determination. Article 49 of the Fourth Geneva Convention explicitly prohibits the establishment of settlements within occupied territory, along with UN Security Council resolution 465. A past statement from the EU presidency asserted that "Settlements change the physical character and demographic composition of the occupied territories. All settlement activities are illegal and constitute a major obstacle to peace." Yet by allowing settlement products to be imported with falsified documentation into Europe, the EU is in effect supporting and financing the settlements. The EU's failure in this respect is in violation of the Statute of the International Criminal Court (ICC) which elevates Article 49 of the Fourth Geneva Convention to a "war crime." In Article 8b (viii) of the ICC Statute, Article 49 of the Fourth Geneva Convention is literally incorporated, which means that individuals who are involved in planning or carrying out policies regarding Israeli settlements can be held liable as "war criminals" under the jurisdiction of the ICC. Not only does the Israeli trade policy therefore constitute a war crime, the international community's importing of Israeli settlement produce is by complicity also a war crime.

The courtship between these two regionally isolated nations reached its peak in 1975 when Israeli Defense Minister Shimon Peres became receptive to the possibility of nuclear cooperation. As Israel already had the capability to produce nuclear weapons, it can only be assumed that it was seeking to secure access to South Africa's abundance of yellowcake uranium as insurance against further international isolation. In exchange Israel would provide missiles, advisors, and secret support for nuclear weapons testing. In the end South Africa decided that the cost of acquiring Israeli nuclear weapons was too high and nothing came of the negotiations.

The declassification of South African documents relating to these negotiations which Israel tried to prevent, illustrate without a doubt that not only does Israel have nuclear weapons, but that it was also prepared to sell them to another rogue and racist state. As is the case whenever Israel is confronted with irrefutable facts relating to its reprehensible conduct, it steadfastly adopts blatant denials. Though Israel neither acknowledges nor denies having nuclear weapons, these documents undermine its assertion that even if it had nuclear weapons, it would not as a responsible state misuse them as would untrustworthy countries like Iran. Having always portrayed itself as the trustworthy and whiter than white Western ally, a shameless Israel continued to accept vast amounts of U.S. taxpayers' money in the form of aid, while simultaneously and without any compunction breaking the same UN embargoes that the U.S. had voted for and supported.

Not only has Israel possessed nuclear weapons since the late 1960s, but it has also kept its monopoly of such weapons in the region intact by using force to prevent their potential development in other Middle Eastern countries. Both Iraq in 1981 and Syria in 2007 were the targets of devastating Israeli airstrikes against their nuclear development programmes and Israel was now lining up Iran as its next target. Already in the U.S. AIPAC-engineered warmongering is afoot on Capitol Hill and in the media to imbue the American psyche with the idea that like Iraq and Syria in the past and probably Pakistan in the future, Iran also posed a serious threat to the West with its fledgling nuclear programme.

255

The service that Abe Goldman had unofficially rendered to the Afrikaner nation was finally acknowledged in 1983 when he became the only ever non-Afrikaner to receive an accolade from the Broederbond. Goldman had initially been contacted by a civil servant from the Trade Ministry who explained that because of his long service and loyalty, he was invited to attend a secret Broederbond meeting to witness the initiation of a Broeder after which Goldman himself would be made an Honourary Broeder. For Goldman it had been a privileged insight into the otherwise imperceptible world of power brokers and an occasion he would often reminisce about over the years.

●　●　●　●　●

On that fateful evening Goldman had been picked up from his Parktown home by two dark-suited men in a BMW and driven to a city centre recreation hall of a Dutch Reformed Church where two crewcut heavies met them at the door and let them through to the hall which was dimly-lit by a triple-branched candelabrum. Darkness usually symbolized the primeval chaos banished by the emanation of light from the Creator and was the complementary opposite of light in a basic duality. In initiation rites it also represented the Candidate's "unenlightened" state before he was shown the "light." Goldman had since come to realize that darkness also served to exploit the fact that people were more susceptible to persuasion in darkened environments. From the beginning of time charlatan shamans had mesmerized their victims with chanting and prancing to the crackle of after dusk bonfires; scheming priesthoods had promoted the worship of countless man-made gods in ill-lit temples sanctified by the burning of incense; and more recently, a Germanic master race — led by a maniac who at one time claimed to have "learnt much from the Jesuits" — orchestrated torch-lit rallies to harness a national fervor that would lead to atrocities against humanity on a scale exceeded only by the communist pogroms of Joseph Stalin and Mao Zedong.

Goldman had been ushered to one of the fifteen seats which with the rectangular table bearing the candelabra formed a circle in the middle of which stood the Candidate for initiation. The circle represented the laager, the defensive formation of ox-wagons that Voortrekkers had adopted whenever attacked by African warriors during the Great Trek. The table, on which there was also a leather bound Bible, was draped with a South African flag from which the Union Jack had been cut out as a symbolic rejection of all things British.

To the right of the table but outside the circle stood a mobile screen behind which lay some indiscernible large object. Hanging on the wall to the left was a depiction recalling the legendary 1838 Boer victory over the Zulu King Dingane whose warriors on that occasion had been no match for the overwhelming Boer firepower. It was said that the death of 3,000 Zulus had caused the Ncome River to run with blood for three days resulting in a name change with the event becoming known as the Battle of Blood River. Afrikaners attributed this victory to the mythical Covenant allegedly made with God (here we go again) when the besieged Voortrekkers had earlier vowed that if He gave them victory, they would keep that day holy and thereafter celebrate annually. Though this so-called covenant was later proven by South African scholars to have been invented some 33 years after the event, it still became part of Afrikaner folklore portraying Afrikaners as a latter-day version of the Children of Israel.

Hanging directly behind the table was a portrait of the current Broederbond Chairman flanked by flags of the former Boer republics of the Transvaal and the Orange Free State. Below the portrait a sign with bold, white letters on a black background emphatically warned the Candidate that:

FOR ALL THOSE WHO EMBARK ON THE
GREAT TREK THERE IS NO TURNING BACK.

The Branch Chairman, his face eerily illuminated by the candlelight, took his place behind the table and after welcoming the members he said that before proceeding with the evening's business, they would first take time to explain their aims and ideals to one who was eligible to join their ranks, and another, who though not one of them was nonetheless deserving of honor for his services to the Afrikaner nation. The Chairman then asked for a moment of silence during which they could all recall their vows and reaffirm their commitment to the aims of the organization.

Following the brief silence the Candidate was directly addressed by the Chairman who informed him that after due consideration, the fellow-Afrikaners present had agreed to offer him membership as a fellow Broeder, and with that in mind, the Broederbond's ideals and principal aims would be made known to him. If he then agreed to what would be expected of him, he would be required to make a solemn vow of unconditional commitment and loyalty. Having expressed his willingness to proceed, the Candidate also had to solemnly declare before God and those present that he was not a member of any other secret organization such as the Freemasons or Sons of England; that he understood that the organization's effectiveness depended on confidentiality and therefore vowed never to reveal anything he now knew or would in the future learn about the organization's membership, its objectives, or its modus operandi.

The Chairman, with the help of typewritten notes and a torch, then proceeded to remind the Candidate that the birth of the Afrikaner nation began in 1642 when Jan van Riebeeck established a settlement at Table Bay in the Cape of Good Hope for the Dutch East India Company. The Bay had been an ideal stopover for ships during their six-month journey between Europe and the East Indies where the company's lucrative spice trade was based in Java. At that time, the Chairman had continued, the Cape was inhabited by the San and the Khoikhoi, two stone-age peoples who differed only in that the San were nomadic hunter-gatherers while the Khoikhoi were sheep and cattle herders with whom Afrikaner forebears bartered. Though life was hard in those early days with several wars against the occasionally truculent Khoikhoi, Afrikaner forebears had nonetheless persevered and with God's help laid the foundations for the nation.

After the French Revolution and the ensuing European wars, the British occupied the Cape with Dutch acquiescence from 1795 to 1803. But when war broke out again Britain resolved to maintain the safety of its shipping route to India and accordingly reoccupied the Cape in 1806. The permanency of that reoccupation was later confirmed at the 1814 European peace conference with a British £6 million compensation payment being made to the Dutch.

Because of increasing resentment over British domination, the Great Trek of 1836 took place when more than 12,000 Boers migrated northwards in separate groups to establish independent republics. The Trek was like the flight to the Promised Land by the children of Israel who as the chosen people had determined to pursue their own destiny. Some Voortrekkers had settled in the Transvaal under constant threat from Ndebele warriors while others were lost to malaria and African native resistance en route to Delagoa Bay in Mozambique. Of those who trekked to the Natal, many were massacred by Zulu warriors, a sad event that was later avenged at Blood River. With God's help the Boer republics of the Transvaal and the Orange Free State were established in 1852 and 1854 respectively.

The 1866 discovery of gold in the Transvaal had witnessed the influx of many foreigners whom Transvaal President Paul Kruger denied the vote as a means of retaining Afrikaner political power. Rivalry to exploit the land's mineral wealth, however, continued and when the British tried to annex the Transvaal they were defeated at Majuba Hill in the Boer's First war of Independence in 1880.

Despite the signing of the Pretoria Convention's peace treaty in 1881, the Transvaal remained a target for the rapacious multi-millionaire Randlord, Cecil Rhodes. Rhodes, the Governor of the Cape Colony, planned a coup d'etat in the Transvaal by trying to arrange an uprising of foreigners who were to be supported by a private cross-border invasion led by Leander Jameson. But the uprising never materialized and Jameson's four hundred and eighty raiders were forced to surrender at Krugersdorp in January 1896. The attempted raid had been just one of many incidents that led to the Second Anglo-Boer War.

The cocky British campaign had begun in the spring of 1899 with the mistaken belief that it would be over by Christmas. Though less than two-thirds of the seventy thousand civilian Afrikaners who took up arms were actually active at any given time, they still proved a worthy match for the better equipped professional British force of four hundred and fifty thousand men. The British writer Rudyard Kipling later reported that the British were taught no end of a lesson by the Boers. The war captured the world's imagination and volunteers came from many countries including Ireland to join the Boers in their fight against British imperialism.

The Boers had disregarded conventional fighting and instead adopted guerrilla hit-and-run tactics in a war that eventually cost the British over £200 million with twenty thousand wounded and seven thousand killed. Because of Britain's inability to end the war quickly, the British Commander-in-Chief, Kitchener — who like Cecil Rhodes was a high-ranking Freemason — adopted tactics to isolate the Boer guerrillas from their source of food and shelter by employing a scorched earth policy. Thirty thousand farmsteads were destroyed and entire villages burnt to the ground. The sixty thousand made homeless, mostly women and children, were then "concentrated" in ill-equipped camps where twenty-six thousand died in conditions which "were not even fit for Kaffirs."

The Germans and Japanese may have perfected the "concentration" concept during the Second World War, but concentration camps were a British innovation. Substantiation as to the enormity of that British atrocity lay in the fact that those who died in the camps represented ten percent of the entire Afrikaner population while those Boer Guerrillas who died in actual battle numbered only four thousand. Having reluctantly accepted that its people had been deceived, dispossessed, and brutally defeated, the Afrikaner leadership settled for peace and allowed the Transvaal and the Orange Free State to become parts of the Union and the British Empire.

The post-war depression with severe droughts and crop failures had forced many Afrikaners to work in the cities and mines as underclass labourers: a situation that served to heighten the racial tension which in those days had been between Afrikaners and Britons rather than between Whites and Blacks. Enforced anglicisation of Afrikaner culture and the debate over whether or not to fight alongside the British in the First World War was also a cause for debate and division amongst Afrikaner people. It was during that period of doubt and disillusion that the Afrikaner Broederbond was born in 1918. It was born from a profound conviction that Afrikanerdom with its unique characteristics and destiny, was not the work of men, but the creation of God who had placed it in that land to remain in existence for as long as God in his almighty wisdom wished it to be.

The Broederbond was devoted to the service of the Afrikaner nation as a whole and did not serve or promote the personal interests of its members. Those who joined did so to give, not to receive; they did so to serve, not to be served or to obtain benefits or advantages for either themselves or their relatives and friends. Before asking the Candidate if he was prepared to become a member, the Branch Chairman had stressed that the Broederbond's aim was to unite its members in a strong bond of mutual love and trust so that they could work selflessly to promote the welfare and interests of the Afrikaner nation. After expressing his willingness to join, the Candidate was informed that membership entailed many responsibilities about which he would be enlightened in turn by three Broeders.

There followed a list of expectations starting with the Candidate being expected to not only to live and work in the firm belief that

Almighty God determined the destiny of nations, but also to adhere to the Christian national Afrikaner viewpoint as prescribed by the Word of God and the established traditions of the Afrikaner nation.   The second expectation was that he would remain true to himself and his conscience while respecting the right of his fellow Broeders to think and act differently. That though the Broeders were irrevocably bound together in their faith and aspirations, of one heart, one viewpoint, and one struggle for one nation, they were nonetheless individuals.

The third expectation was that he would do everything in his power to promote the establishment of a common purpose among all motivated Afrikaners; to strengthen and develop the Afrikaner nation; and in particular, to promote its unique culture while extending its influence in all affairs of national import including the economy.

The fourth expectation was that he would fulfil all his duties as a member, faithfully attend meetings, and otherwise make himself available to the organisation as and when the need arose.

The fifth expectation was that he would strive to achieve the aims of the Broederbond not only through participation in its organised endeavours, but also at his place of work, his home, and his general sphere of influence, inspired, strengthened and supported by his fellow Broeders and guided by Broederbond principles and Ideals; and that he would always cooperate actively and faithfully with his fellow Broeders in a spirit of steadfast common purpose and sincere brotherhood.

Following revelation of the final expectation which was that he would at all times conduct himself in a manner befitting the good name, the honour, and the ideals of the Afrikaner Broederbond, the Candidate indicated that he was prepared to accept all responsibilities without exception. He was then warned by the Chairman that the Broederbond demanded complete loyalty, hard work, unwavering perseverance in pursuit of its aims, and unconditional adherence to the practice of Christian principles. The Candidate was then required to acknowledge that he understood the purpose of the organisation and what it was that they as determined Afrikaners represented and intended to achieve. He also had to confirm that he would honestly and willingly subscribe to the principles and objectives which had been presented; and was ready to unconditionally accept the demands of membership while committing himself to an irrevocable union during his lifetime.

The Chairman then warned ominously that he who betrayed the Broederbond would face destruction because the Broederbond's vengeance was far-reaching and swift. It was a certainty that no traitor had ever escaped his due punishment. In support of that warning, the Chairman beckoned to one of the Broeders who walked to the right of the table and pushed aside the mobile screen to reveal a makeshift bier covered with a white sheet on which the Afrikaner word VERAAD (TREASON) had been daubed in red paint. The sheet was removed to unveil a dummy of a man in a black suit towards which the Candidate was ushered and handed a dagger with which to stab the vile traitor in the heart. The dagger thrust had released a spurt of the "traitor's blood" which covered the blade and his hand which he wiped with the hand towel provided. On returning to his position in the middle of the circle, he watched as every other Broeder including the Chairman, took turns at stabbing the 'traitor.'

The Candidate was next asked if with full awareness of the responsibilities of membership he was prepared to always unconditionally and solemnly undertake as a Broeder to join them in their duty to promote each other's interests in the community and whenever possible to support one another's business interests in word and deed. The spirit of preference had to always prevail and whenever possible they should also act as intercessors on each other's behalf; that as a member of the Broederbond he would always faithfully and sincerely serve the Afrikaner nation in all that it aspired to and represented; that he would never without permission of the Executive Council reveal to any outsider, including his nearest and dearest, anything that he may learn about the Broederbond and its members, even if his own membership had been revoked; that he would never without the appropriate permission reveal his own membership; that he would never without permission have involvement with, or become a member of any other secret organization; that he would always subject himself to the conditions of the Broederbond's constitution, fulfil all duties laid down by the Council's standing orders, and subject himself readily to any discipline deemed appropriate by the Council; that he would unconditionally comply if the Council, for whatever reason, decided to revoke his membership; and finally, that he would subject himself to immediate expulsion if he ever broke any of the aforementioned undertakings.

Before being officially declared a Broeder, the Candidate had to first step forward to the table, place his hand on the Bible, and affirm his commitment before God and his fellow Broeders who bore witness to the irrevocable union he had forged. He was then informed by the

Chairman that he had become a member of an organisation which since its inception had worked to further the cause of the Afrikaner nation. In 1927 they had pushed for legislation that made sexual relations between Whites and Blacks a punishable offence. They had opened shops specifically for Afrikaners, created an investment bank to help Afrikaners start businesses, and a building society to facilitate ownership of their own homes. In 1938 they had masterminded the centenary celebration of Voortrekker achievements with a symbolic Ox Wagon Trek to the Voortrekker monument near Pretoria. Celebration of that event coupled with the annual Day of Covenant holiday had served to unite the Afrikaner people and helped to bring about the Afrikaner National Party's election victory in 1948.

By 1950 the separation of the races had become a legal reality with the Prohibition of the Mixed Marriages Act banning interracial marriages, the Morality Act barring interracial sex, the Population Registration Act requiring all South Africans to be classified by race, The Group Areas Act mandating strict residential segregation, and the Separate Amenities Act extending segregation to public places and transportation. Since then the Broederbond had continuously provided the country with its Prime Ministers and governments to the extent that virtually every member of the Cabinet was also a member of the Broederbond's Executive Council. It was impossible for any member of the National Party to become Prime Minister without having first been a member of the Broederbond.

The Broederbond had also provided several State Presidents and through its efforts had helped Afrikaners to take control of their own destiny by removing from important positions those arrogant Whites whose first loyalty was to Britain rather than South Africa. By doing so the Broederbond had reversed the trend of Afrikaners being mostly the under-class farmers while the British were the superior class dominating the professions.

The Broederbond had been instrumental in promoting and maintaining the Apartheid policy of separate development so as to retain the purity of the Afrikaner nation. With some seven hundred and fifty cells throughout the country, the Broederbond was the most influential power in Africa. Its influence was probably unequalled by any other similar organisation in the world. A carefully selected membership of more than 11,000 Broeders controlled the destiny of twenty-five million South Africans. The Broederbond was the Government and the

Government was the Broederbond.

The Broederbond's achievements were the result of its efforts being largely unopposed because it was impossible to oppose the activities of those who were unheard, unseen, and unknown. The Broederbond could discredit, demoralize, and ultimately destroy its enemies without its victims even beginning to suspect the source of their damnation. In the 1930's Prime Minister James Hertzog was destroyed after attacking the Broederbond and trying to fuse Afrikaans-speakers and English-speakers into one Afrikanerdom. Prime Minister Jan Smuts had suffered a similar fate in the late 1940's.

Broeders were calculatingly well placed in every important organisation throughout the nation. They were to be found in city and town councils and in the postal service; they were on school boards, within unions, working in state-controlled broadcasting networks and for independent newspapers; they were promoting industry and commerce and managing banks and building societies; they were also prominent within the ranks of the armed forces, the police, and the Dutch Reformed Church. The Broederbond was the heartbeat of the Afrikaner nation and would remain so for as long as God willed it.

After then establishing that the Candidate was prepared to be resolute in his devotion, love, and work for the Afrikaner nation, the Chairman welcomed him into the organisation with the assurance that he would henceforth be recognised and accepted as a fellow Broeder worthy of trust and support.

The Chairman had then introduced Goldman, commended him for his vitally important service to the nation, and pronounced that Goldman, as the first ever non-Afrikaner to attend a Broederbond meeting, was to be given an honorary membership. There followed a brief ceremony during which Goldman was obliged to solemnly vow that he would never divulge anything he had learnt that evening, or might learn at any time in the future.

• • • • •

The events of that memorable evening had taught Goldman the value of secrecy in acquiring power and control over the destinies of men. It had also helped to make him realize that minority rule by Whites through suppression of Blacks would sooner or later have to come to an end.

His many trips to Israel had of course made him aware of the many aspirations for the future that were shared by Israelis and Afrikaners. But he was equally certain that what Jews could get away with in Palestine, the Afrikaners could not hope to continue getting away with in South Africa.

Afrikaners, unlike Jews, had not been the victims of a truly horrendous holocaust; their past suffering was not of a sufficient scale to have accumulated either the amount or kind of international sympathy that would condone continued human rights violations; they did not have a dedicated worldwide network of lobbyists who could diffuse, suppress or influence negative public opinion; and last but not least, unlike Israel, they lacked the benefit of having at their disposal the support of U.S vetoes at the United Nations Assembly. Consequently Goldman's unequivocal conclusion had been that Afrikanerdom was doomed.

By the beginning of 1987 Goldman had begun to lay the groundwork in Israel that would see him take advantage of the Israeli Law of Return which entitled him as a Jew to 'return to his ancestral homeland.' This law — a basic tenet of Zionist ideology — enabled Jews from anywhere and of any nationality who like their ancestors had never been to or had any connection with Israel to "return" to live in a land from which indigenous Palestinians had been terrorized and forcibly expelled by Zionist forces. As a result there are now some seven million Palestinian refugees with no such "right of return" and as stateless individuals they are also being illegally deprived of many of the basic human rights that Westerners take for granted. In July 1988, Goldman and his family "returned" to Israel and became Israeli citizens. They had simply moved from one stolen land with its own particular brand of Apartheid to another form of Apartheid whose insidious nature was far more dangerous because of its masquerade as the only real Middle Eastern democracy and staunch ally of the West: A West which incidentally it assiduously screwed at every given opportunity.

The Regents Canal flowing from Little Venice

Little Venice leading to Grand Union Canal and Paddington Basin

10
Monday, 15 December 2008
Formosa Street, Little Venice, London

As had been arranged, David Reisner travelled the one stop on the Underground from Paddington Station to Warwick Avenue Station where Banner was waiting to meet him at the top of the exit escalator. Seeing Banner's friendly face helped to lift Reisner's otherwise sagging spirits. Since taking refuge in London Reisner had become — not by choice but out of necessity — a virtual recluse whom even fellow journalists politely avoided. It was therefore heartening for him to know that Banner was made of sterner stuff and would at the very least offer some moral support.

They walked the short distance to Formosa Street's family-run Lebanese delicatessen which Banner and Nadine liked to visit whenever they were in London. After ordering their food and drinks, Reisner wasted no time in passing Banner a folded copy of the secret map which Michal Zeldin had given him. "I made a copy for you."

"Thanks." Banner unfolded the map and peered at it intently for several minutes without comment. The map showed the location of two hidden tunnels running westwards from the long tunnel beyond the men's side of the Western Wall towards the Dome of the Rock on Temple Mount. Banner knew that the long tunnel was not a recently rediscovered ancient thoroughfare but had been intentionally dug over a period of twenty years at the instigation of the Israeli Ministry of Religious Affairs following the 1967 Six Day War. The digging had involved going under Palestinian residential neighborhoods with the intention of exposing a strip of the 2,000-year-old Western Wall along its entire length. The massive construction was part of Temple Mount's retaining wall built by King Herod — the Roman client king of Judea who reigned from 37-4 BCE — which included two building stones estimated to weigh around 400 and 570 tons. Banner was thoughtful as he slowly refolded the map and slipped it into the inside pocket of his jacket. "What do you think?" Reisner asked.

"There's always been suspicions about Israel's tunneling activities, but this proves it beyond any doubt."

"They're hell-bent on taking over the Moriah."

"Any response or reaction to your article?"

"Nothing."

"They're staying below the radar. My Masonic contact in Beirut made some enquiries."

"Anything?"

"Zilch. There's about nineteen regular Masonic lodges in Lebanon and no one's heard of the Hiramic Brotherhood. Question is, what's your next step?"

"No option but to reveal everything I know . . . Even my belief that Mossad killed Zeldin." Having then raised the question of which would be the most suitable news outlet for his story, Reisner wondered if he should approach the BBC. This caused Banner to almost choke as he sipped his drink.

"No bloody way." He said emphatically and went on to explain that the BBC was today no better than its corporate-run counterparts throughout the world including Britain and America where BBC America's spurious journalism bombarded its audience with the same American-style news mediocrity and mind-numbing commercialism that kept listeners and viewers uninformed about the vital national and international issues that affected their lives, their well-being, and their security.

"Let me give you an example of the Beeb's so-called journalistic impartiality," Banner continued, "rather than calling Gaza and the West Bank 'Occupied Territories', the BBC calls them 'disputed territories.' Instead of acknowledging that Jewish settlements in the Occupied Territories are illegal according to international law, the BBC will say that Israel disputes the fact that they are illegal. The BBC will refer to Palestinian self-defense as insurgency, militancy, and terrorism but never as resistance against ongoing Israeli incursions which are never called 'acts of aggression.' The BBC even ignores international law and UN Resolutions." Banner said referring to UN Resolution 194.

Towards the end of the 1948 Arab-Israeli War, the UN General Assembly on 11 December 1948 adopted Resolution 194 that defined principles for reaching a final settlement and returning Palestinian refugees to their homes. It called for an establishment of a UN Conciliation Commission to continue the commendable efforts of UN Mediator Count Folke Bernadotte to facilitate peace between Israel and Arab states. The decision to have Count Bernadot assassinated by the militant Zionist terrorist group Lehi, was taken by Zionist leaders including Yitzhak Shamir who later became Prime Minister of Israel. Resolution 194 was adopted by a majority of thirty-five countries from among the fifty-eight members of the United Nations at that time. All six Arab countries then represented at the UN — Egypt, Iraq, Lebanon, Saudi Arabia, Syria, and Yemen who were all party to the conflict — however, voted against it. Israel had not yet been admitted to the UN.

"The BBC's claim of honesty, integrity, and freedom from commercial and political influence is nothing more than a pathetic sham." Banner said.

"That's a bit harsh."

"Not at all. The Director-General, the Executive Board Chairman, the BBC Trust Chairman, and all senior management are government-appointed with the sole responsibility of dishing out meaningless soundbites that don't rock the boat and serve the interests of the elite."

"Even on such an important issue?"

"Irrespective of the issue, war or peace, corporate or state corruption, violation of human rights or social injustice, or simply coverage of national and international conflicts like the Middle East, the government and the establishment can rely on the BBC to be suitably economical with the truth."

"But surely they couldn't bury a story like this."

"They may not bury it, but because of their bias for Israelis and antipathy for Palestinians, they will not accord it the significance it deserves. Believe me the Beeb walks hand in hand with its European and North American counterparts. Israeli interests are of paramount importance while those of the Palestinian people are regarded with indifference. And that's why finding a just solution to that conflict will always be impossible — the mainstream media lacks the independence and courage to report the facts without Israeli bias."

"I suppose you're right. It's just that I've always considered the BBC to be different from the others."

"Let me tell you how different the Beeb is," Banner said before reminding Reisner of the Doctor David Kelly "suicide'" more than ten years earlier. Doctor Kelly was a distinguished government scientist and as a former UN weapons inspector in Iraq was an expert on biological weapons of the kind cited by the Blair government as justification for going to war against the Iraqis who incidentally did not have any. At that time in 2003, a BBC Today program report claimed that the government — as part of its justification for going to war — had embellished or "sexed up" the intelligence it had presented to the public. The report had caused a furor with the Blair government which unleashed its spin doctoring attack dog Alastair Campbell to savage the BBC.

The BBC management — hardly renowned for its staunch defense of just causes — caved in and Kelly, who was subsequently outed as the BBC's source, was reprimanded by his superiors and felt betrayed. He had been publicly humiliated and a reputation built up over a lifetime had been irreparably sullied. According to Kelly's family, they had never before seen him so low as in the days leading up to his taking a walk and having his slumped body discovered in a wood the following day. Kelly's death was followed by an inquest whose suicide verdict failed to satisfy observers. It was, however, a public inquiry by Lord Hutton which provided a rare glimpse into the secretive worlds of Whitehall's civil service, the British intelligence services, the dark side of politics, and the dereliction of journalistic responsibilities by the BBC. Hutton's absolution for the government lacked credibility and his conclusion that Kelly's death was suicide is still to this day being questioned.

Criticism of the BBC by Hutton led to then chairman Gavyn Davies, correspondent Andrew Gilligan, and director general Greg Dyke becoming sacrificial lambs with the latter recently insisting that history had proven the broadcaster to have been right with it now being "very difficult to find anyone who believes they did not 'sex up' that document . . . History tells us Blair was destroyed by Iraq. Blair will be only remembered for that, just as Sir Anthony Eden will be remembered for Suez."

Banner supported the point he was making by referring Reisner to a June 2002 article written by Robin C. Miller (a progressive freelance writer) in which he listed 'The Media's Middle East Rules of Engagement' to which the BBC always adhered rigidly for coverage of the Israeli-Palestinian conflict. The media's role was to maintain a consensus supporting Israel. Americans were to be kept in the dark so that a poll by the University of Maryland's Program on International Policy Attitudes revealed that only one quarter of Americans knew that the majority of countries were more sympathetic to the Palestinian position than to that of Israel; and only one in three were aware that more Palestinians than Israelis had died in the the conflict.

1. See the Middle East though israeli eyes.

2. Treat American and israeli government statements as hard news.

3. Ignore the historical context.

4. Avoid the fundamental legal and moral issues posed by the israeli occupation.

5. Suppress or minimize news unfavorable to the israelis.

6. Muddy the waters when necessary.

7. Credit all israeli claims, even if wholly unfounded.

8. Doubt all Palestinian assertions, no matter how self-evident.

9. Condemn only Palestinian violence.

10. Disgrace the international consensus supporting Palestinian rights.

11. Fabricate information to start wars.

12. The golden rule that hovers above all rules: Equate anti-Zionism with anti-Semitism.

"Believe me," Banner said, "independent journalism is a thing of the past and now consolidation's the name of the game. Ninety percent of what people listen to, read, and watch is controlled by just six media giants with an annual revenue of $276 billion . . . CBS, Disney, General Electric, News Corp, Time Warner, and Viacom . . . And that's a fact and sad state of affairs for the media whose function is to monitor — not assist — the centers of power that influence the cultural, the economic, political and religious institutions of our society."

They discussed the points that that Reisner would reveal in his articles and after they had finished their lunch Banner offered to show Reisner Little Venice by walking back with him along the canal and passing by the Paddington Central development, under Bishop's Bridge, past the Paddington Station entrance and the Bays Building by Paddington Basin and onto South Wharf Road which led to Norfolk Place.

11
Tuesday, 16 December 2008
La Regence Restaurant, King David Hotel, West Jerusalem.

Following his Sunday afternoon arrival in Tel Aviv and his limo journey to Jerusalem's King David Hotel, Steve Appelman, napped for a couple of hours, lingered under a relaxing shower, dined sumptuously, and then returned to his suite to phone Livia, his long-suffering wife back in Washington. He spent Monday morning being briefed by his Mossad controller with whom he lunched before having a meeting with some members of the Israeli security cabinet at the Knesset in the afternoon.

After a meeting at the AIPAC Jerusalem office on Tuesday morning, Appelman was scheduled to have lunch with Abe Goldman who always regaled him with anecdotes of his days in Africa which included ingenious acts of subterfuge to circumvent trade embargoes. Cuisine at La Regence — reputed to be amongst the best in Jerusalem — started to improve in 1934 when the management decided to upgrade the culinary standards of the hotel which had become the central meeting point of Jerusalem society, the British administration, visiting VIPs, and international travelers.

By the end of the 1930's, with the threat of war in Europe becoming more imminent, the King David had become an important stopover on the travel routes of what was then still the British Empire. Kings, princes, and varying grades of nobility from Europe, the Middle East, India, and China all invariably stayed at the hotel. Every year the royal and the wealthy from Egypt and the affluent from the Palestinian coast arrived for the summer where they stayed for up to six months to escape Cairo's heat and the coast's humidity. The men conducted their business in Cairo during the week and returned by train for the weekends. Following the paving of a new road across the northern Sinai in the late 1930's, it had become fashionable to make the ten-hour journey by car.

As former lawyers, Appelman and Goldman, were both versed in the well-practiced art of deft footwork along the thin line that separates the licit from the illicit. As such, they both shared the unspoken knowledge that as covert power brokers they could influence the course of events in the lives of millions. They began by agreeing that though Barack Obama's pronouncements of a new and improved approach to American diplomacy — including a Middle East peace settlement — had beguiled the ever-hopeful international community, Obama would in reality soon come round to realizing — if he was not already aware — that it was the Israelis and not the occupant of the White House, who determined U.S. Middle East and related foreign policy. And if such a realization were to somehow escape Obama . . . then he would be destined to become the second troublesome U.S. president to have been removed by Israel.

As men of influence in the Zionist hierarchy, they knew that peace with the Palestinians had never been, was not now, and never would be an option because implementing the Zionist agenda demanded that the controlled oppression of the Palestinian people and the gradual expropriation of their lands — including the ultimate possession of the Temple Mount for the building of the Third Temple — be ruthlessly maintained. A Middle East peace agreement was a concept that successive U.S. presidents peddled for public consumption while in reality knowing full well that pigs would fly to the moon before that could ever happen. It was a stark reality that Israel nonetheless always felt obliged to impress on all rookie U.S. presidents.

"Cast Lead should do it," said Appelman who had been briefed by the security cabinet .

"He'll get the message alright." Goldman said of Obama.

"Reactions?"

"Little if any with the holiday timing, but we still must keep a lid on it."

"Don't worry. Our people will do their bit," Appelman said referring to CAMERA (Committee for Accuracy in Middle East Reporting in America), which is known for its pro-Israel media monitoring and advocacy. While describing itself as a "non-partisan organization" which "takes no position with regard to American or Israeli political issues or with regard to ultimate solutions to the Arab-Israeli conflict," it will nonetheless attack any organization critical of Israel including the Israeli non-governmental organization B'Tselem which documents human rights violations in the occupied territories.

CAMERA is a member of the Israel Campus Roundtable — an umbrella organization which includes the Anti-Defamation League, The David Project Centre for Jewish Leadership, and other pro-Israel Zionist organizations. As a member, CAMERA operates on college campuses to combat what it perceives to be "propagandistic assaults on Israel . . . creating harmful misperceptions of Israel" and is active on some 50 college campuses and operates the student-focused site, CAMERoncampus. Apart from having 55,000 paying members and thousands of active letter writers to harangue and intimidate the media, it also has overseas affiliates such as BBCWatch in Britain, ReVista in Spain, and a Hebrew-language website.

"Glad to hear it."

"How about the Gelt-lovin goy?" Appelman asked referring to former British Prime Minister Tony Blair who on the day of his resignation in June 2007, also announced his acceptance of the position of special envoy to the Middle East Quartet consisting of the UN, the U.S., the European Union, and Russia.

"We pay the band: we call the tune." Goldman said of Blair who was known for being a compulsive seeker of power, prestige, and pounds sterling and had become — unwittingly or otherwise — an Israeli asset.

Blair's cosy connection with Israel had begun in earnest in 1994 when he first met Michael Levy — a calculated rather than fortuitous encounter — at a dinner party hosted by Israeli diplomat Gideon Meir who, like Blair was friendly with Eldred Tabachnik, a senior barrister and Queens Council at 11 King's Bench Walk, the chambers founded by Derry Irvine where Blair had been a junior tenant on its foundation in 1981. Tabachnik was also a former president (1994-2000) of the Board of Deputies of British Jews.

In February 2007 the organization of Independent Jewish Voices was launched by 150 prominent British Jews including Nobel laureate Harold Pinter, historian Eric Hobsbawm, lawyer Sir Geoffrey Bindman, Lady Ellen Dahrendorf, film director Mike Leigh, and actors Stephen Fry and Zoë Wanamaker. The founding of the organization was "born out of a frustration with the widespread misconception that the Jews of this country speak with one voice — and that this voice supports the Israeli government's policies." The Organization's aim was "to represent British Jews . . . in response to a perceived pro-Israeli bias in existing Jewish bodies in the UK," and, according to Hobsbawn, "as a counter-balance to the uncritical support for Israeli policies by established bodies such as the Board of Deputies of British Jews."

Following their initial meeting Blair and Levy became friends, tennis partners, and political cahoots with Levy running the Labour Leader's Office Fund to finance Blair's 1997 general election campaign which received substantial contributions from notables such as Alex Bernstein (Granada Group Chairman 1979-1996) and Robert Gavron (publishing). Now generally referred to as 'Lord Cashpoint' in media and political circles, Levy was the Labour Party's leading fundraiser with over £100m raised between 1994 to 2007. After becoming Prime Minister, Blair ennobled Bernstein and Gavron and made Levy a life peer whom *The Jerusalem Post* described as "undoubtedly the notional leader of British Jewry." In 1998 Blair appointed Levy as his personal envoy to the Middle East. It is perhaps no coincidence that as a consequence of being financed and in effect controlled by Israeli interests, Blair — like President Bush in the U.S. — was manipulated into launching an illegal war against Iraq despite opposition to the conflict by the majority of British people. On the basis of a doctored intelligence report — that envisaged Iraq using weapons of mass destruction that could be deployed within 45 minutes — the semi-illiterate Bush and the smarmy Israeli asset, Blair, duped their nations into accepting the necessity for war against Iraq.

Everyone now knows that the 45-minute claim was a blatant lie because Iraq had nothing even remotely resembling a weapon of mass destruction. So once again Zionist Israel had successfully managed to influence Western nations into attacking one of its "enemy" Middle Eastern Arab neighbors. Other targets for destruction included Iran and Syria.

Levy, who praised Blair for his "solid and committed support of the State of Israel," maintained close ties with Israel's political leaders and kept a home in Herzliya, a city in the central coast of Israel. Daniel Levy, his son, was active in Israeli politics and at one time served as an assistant to former Israeli Prime Minister Ehud Barak and to Knesset member Yossi Beilin. Now based in the U.S., Daniel is a senior research fellow of the Middle East Task Force at the New America Foundation.

In March 2006 it was revealed that Tony Blair's Labour Party had raised £14 million in loans from private individuals of whom some were later nominated for peerages. Levy was later arrested but released on bail pending Scotland Yard's investigation into what came to be known as the "cash for honors" scandal. In July 2007 the Crown Prosecution Service announced that Levy would neither be prosecuted in connection with the affair nor face any other charges.

When Tony Blair and his disgraced Zionist "Lord Cashpoint" controller voluntarily decided to step down in June 2007, Gordon Brown, the Chancellor of the Exchequer for the past decade, assumed the office of prime minister following the approval of Queen Elizabeth

II. Having been for a long time Blair's bitter competitor for residence at 10 Downing Street, Prime Minister Brown was not to be outdone and was himself bankrolled and influenced by Ronald Cohen who as the Labour Party's fourth largest supporter was also ennobled. The Egyptian-born Lord Cohen was in 2002 an inaugural inductee into the Private Equity Hall of Fame, at the British Venture Capital Association and Real Deals' Private Equity Awards. So long as money — Jewish or otherwise — is permitted by the majority to influence and control the governance of a nation, then there can be no democracy.

"Keeping him sweet?" Appelman asked.

"It's in the pipeline . . . we're pushing for him to receive a Dan David Prize next year." Goldman said with a shake of his head at the thought of Blair being given an award that supposedly recognized achievements that have had an outstanding scientific, technological, cultural or social impact on the world. Dan David was the Romanian Zionist who made his fortune from Photo-Me, the automated photography booths. In 2000 he founded the Dan David Foundation with $100 million endowment. The Foundation along with Tel Aviv University annually awarded three prizes of $1 million each.

"Helping to destroy Iraq for us deserves some kind of reward." Appelman said.

"Can your people do something for him?"

"We're planning to nominate him for, and have him receive the National Constitution Centre's Liberty medal . . . it comes with a $100,000 that'll boost his self-esteem."

"He hasn't any . . . he's just a putz." Goldman said, referring to Blair as a dickhead.

"Even a putz can be useful. How are the Brotherhood doing since Reisner's article last week?"

"We're okay so far, but we may have a problem."

"Serious?"

"Not too big a deal but we could do without it."

"Tell me."

"It's that schmuck Zeldin."

"Thought that was taken care of."

"It was. But now seams he somehow got a copy of an IAA for map for the secret tunnel excavations. Shin Bet found the map in his apartment, but they don't know if he gave a copy to Reisner when they met in London. Mossad's on his case."

"You need that like a hole in the head."

"I also got word this morning that Reisner met with Mark Banner yesterday. They're both being watched."

"Banner . . . that's one son of a bitch Arab lover."

"Don't worry, his time will come."

Their conversation was interrupted by the wine waiter who brought them their 2006 vintage bottle of Cabernet Sauvignon Gamla from vineyards in the the stolen Golan Heights. This was followed shortly afterwards with the arrival of their first course of lamb sweetbreads from the charcoal grill. Over dinner they discussed the possible ramifications of "Cast Lead."

12
Wednesday, 17 December 2008
North Pine Grove Avenue, Chicago

His ever-present charm was laced with a hint of cynical glibness that complimented his inability in either comprehending or respecting the space of others. No one in the apartment block where he lived knew what he did and very few had had an actual conversation with him or knew his name. For the very few that had, he was known simply as Mr. Pyotr Gregov, but his clients referred to him in hushed tones as "The Sweeper." His "sweeping" required an absolute lack of conscience with no capacity whatsoever for remorse. He was not by any means an intellectual, but what he lacked in the IQ department he more than made up for with a cold, calculating cunning that induced "thinking outside the box" to determine the best possible course of action for successful completion of an assignment. To fully exploit the use of such characteristics required versatility that enabled him observe and learn quickly, to immediately adapt to new surroundings, and to employ that charm and glibness to manipulate others into becoming his useful tools.

His necessity for always being in peak condition in readiness to go to work at short notice had to be coupled with a pathological tendency to justify his deadly deeds by regarding them as those of an "avenging angel." He was a restless and untrustworthy character whose life was chaotic and as such he had a "nothing to lose" mentality that thrived on risk-taking with treacherous conditions and dangerous scenarios. He was without any dependency on alcohol, tobacco, or women. Whenever the physical necessity arose for the latter it was always paid for with a cold and polite aloofness that forbade familiarity or unwelcome questions. His existence was one of solitude and meditation dedicated to harmonizing a muscular body with a sick mind.

His clients never met him nor even had a clue what he looked like. He preferred it that way and so did his clients. Only four people — who were themselves of a somewhat shadowy nature — knew who Pyotr Gregov actually was, what he did, and how to contact him. Usually he had a preference for operating on home ground in the U.S., but on this occasion — the fifty percent deposit of U.S. $75,000 in used hundred-dollar bills in a large manilla envelope — had persuaded him otherwise.

Gregov's preferred "sweeping" implements varied according to the task and ranged from a Finnish Sako TRG-42 sniper rifle, a Beretta 92 FS compact handgun, to a silent but equally efficient switchblade for work at close range.

For this particular assignment Gregov had been contacted late Monday evening after he had returned from watching — along with more than 20,000 others — the Chicago Blackhawks ice hockey team beat the Ottawa Senators at the United Centre on West Madison Street. A meeting had been arranged for the following day in a Lake shore Drive cafe where no time had been wasted on formalities. A $150,000 fee was agreed with fifty percent paid up front and the balance on completion. The target to be "swept" away was in London where Gregov would be met at Heathrow Airport by his contact, a katsa known by the alias of Conrad Brown, and be driven — not to a London hotel where he would have to register and be seen on CCTV — but to a North London suburb to stay with a reliable and impeccably discreet old Jewish couple.

During the drive Gregov and Brown would work out a means of communication with code words for use during their telephone conversations. Gregov was to use cash at all times so as not to leave a traceable trail of credit or debit card transactions. On completion of his task he would immediately take a cab to Heathrow airport, while in the meantime Brown would pick up his suitcase and meet him there.

Though no mention had been made as to who his clients were, Gregov was in no doubt as to their identity. All Gregov's requirements in London were to be catered for by Mr. Brown who would provide a "safe" mobile phone for contact purposes, coordinate surveillance of the target so that Gregov would at all times be kept informed of the target's movements and location, and supply Gregov with the necessary implement. Gregov had been impressed by the efficiency and speed with which the operation had been set up and could foresee no problems. The prospect of "sweeping" abroad was quite exhilarating for someone who over the years had become an adrenaline junkie.

A recent Justice Department report suggested that many of those who have committed or attempted to carry out assassinations share certain behaviours. This National Institute of Justice-funded study, conducted by the U.S. Secret Service and the Federal Bureau of Prisons, was compiled "to aid law enforcement agencies in identifying and assessing those who could pose a threat to public figures before that individual comes within lethal range of a target."

The report, "Protective Intelligence and Threat Assessment Investigations," was based on a study of everyone who has attacked or posed a real threat to public officials or figures in the United States over the past fifty years. The report concluded that assassinations and attacks on public figures are not necessarily prompted by mental illness, but are the products of an understandable and often discernible processes of thinking. It also found that most people who attack others perceive the attack as the means to an end or a way to solve a problem, and an individual's motives and selection of a target are directly connected.

The report, which was designed to learn about pre-attack behaviours of persons who target prominent public officials and figures, found that few assassinations in the United States — even those targeting major political figures — have had purely political motives. The study's examination of more than 80 individuals, who either attacked or got within near-lethal range of a public figure target, identified eight major motives which were: to achieve notoriety or fame; to bring attention to a personal or public problem; to avenge a perceived wrong; to retaliate for a perceived injury; to end personal pain, to be removed from society, to be killed; to save the country or the world, to fix a world problem; to develop a special relationship with the target; to make money; and to bring about political change. Pyotr Gregov was not interested in fame or notoriety; he had no personal or public axe to grind; no perceived grievance to avenge; no personal slight that required retaliation; no personal pain that cried out for termination; and no desire to save his country or change the world. In fact his one and only motivation was to get well paid for doing what he enjoyed best.

13
Thursday, 18 December 2008
Jerusalem Technology Park, Malha, southwest Jerusalem

First as part of the Ottoman Empire, and then until the 1948 Arab-Israeli War, Malha was known as al-Maliha and along with other Palestinian villages such as Deir Yassin — the massacre where Palestinians including women and children were either shot or killed by hand grenades being lobbed into their homes — was terrorized by the Irgun Zevai Leumi and Lohamei Herut Israel Zionist paramilitary murdering groups. News of the Deir Yassin Massacre caused fear and panic amongst the Palestinians who fled their homes which were then occupied by Jewish refugees.

Malha was today a modern development that featured a residential neighbourhood, the Jerusalem Malha Railway Station, the Jerusalem Mall, the Teddy Stadium for football, the Jerusalem Tennis Centre, the Biblical Zoo, the Sculpture Garden, and the Jerusalem Technology Park. It was in fact the kind of Judaized development that Palestinians could neither afford nor ever aspire to being a part of. Apart from a predominance of high-tech companies such as IBM R&D Labs in Israel, the Technology Park was also host to a variety of other businesses like Answers.com and media organisations including the BBC Middle East Bureau and Thomson Reuters Israel. It was in the large boardroom of a high-tech company that the Hiramic Brotherhood of the Third Temple meetings were held every four weeks.

Apart from being a member and a Master of Jerusalem's only English-speaking Masonic Lodge which usually convened on the third Monday of each month, Abe Goldman had also been the main driving force behind the Hiramic Brotherhood, a specific agenda shadowy cell that operated under the aegis of Freemasonry but without the knowledge of regular members. The cell consisted of a select number of Masons with zealot tendencies who were totally dedicated to the building of a Third Temple on Temple Mount where the Dome of the Rock, the oldest existing Islamic building in the world, had stood since the year 692. The covert nature of Freemasonry has throughout its history provided a fertile environment for the birth of other secretive cells which with their diverse agendas have managed to secretly exist and operate within the

Masonic framework:

> *Richard Metzger: You have studied the Illuminati for years. Have you come to any conclusion about their aims?*
> *Robert Anton Wilson: Usually when people ask me that question, I give them some kind of a put-on, but I can't think of a good and original put-on that I haven't done several times before. So I'll tell you the truth, for once. After investigating the Illuminati and their critics for the last 30 years, I think the Illuminati was a short lived society of free thinkers and democratic reformers that formed a secret society within Freemasonry, using Freemasonry as a cover so they could plot to overthrow all the kings in Europe and the Pope. I'm very happy that they succeeded in overthrowing all the kings, I just wish that they had completed the job and gotten rid of the Royal family in England too, but they did pretty well on the continent. I'm sorry they haven't finished off the Pope yet, either, but I think they're still working on the project and I wish them luck.*
> **From an interview by Richard Metzger, author and host of the TV show *Disinformation* with Robert Anton Wilson.**

It was for example a Mason and former Confederate Army general, Nathan Bedford Forrest, who with five fellow officers in 1866, founded the Klu Klux Klan (known as the Invisible Empire of the South) in Pulaski, Tennessee. Albert Pike, one of the Klan's main office holders, was simultaneously a Masonic Sovereign Grand Commander of the Scottish Rite's Southern Jurisdiction. Pike, who is the only Confederate military officer to have been honored with an outdoor statue in Washington D.C., was subsequently pardoned for treason due mainly to his Masonic connection with President Andrew Johnson.

Following their defeat in the Civil War, the Southerners tried to regain the governance of their States and ensure a constant supply of cheap labour by enacting laws known as the "Black Codes" which had their roots in the slave codes that had been previously in operation. The assumption behind American chattel slavery was that slaves were property, and, as such, they had few, if any, legal rights. The slave codes were regarded as deterrents against runaways, slave labour unrest, and uprisings. Though the means for enforcing the codes varied, harsh corporal punishment was widely used to maintain strict order. The North's reaction to enactment of the codes was to impose military rule on the South.

Forest, who had been accused during the Civil War of the massacre of coloured Union troops after they had surrendered at the Battle of Fort Pillow in April 1864, had initially formed the Klan as a resistance movement against the oppression being endured by the defeated Southern States. His intention was for the Klan to be a temporary guerrilla organisation that would operate for only as long as it was necessary to oppose Northern carpetbaggers, varmint Southern renegades, and the newly-liberated but mostly illiterate Negro slaves. Though there may have been some initial justification for such an organisation to protect vulnerable Southerners against the freebooters operating in the name of the government, the Klan soon degenerated into hordes of hooded marauders whose anonymity gave licence to numerous murders and outrages.

As a consequence of the rampant violence, Forrest ordered the Klan to be disbanded in 1869 and it almost ceased to exist. In 1915, however, the Klan was reborn when the film *The Rebirth of a Nation* romantically portrayed Klansmen as heroes responsible for preserving America's character and moral fibre. The main architect of this rebirth was another Freemason, W. J. Simmons, and by the mid-1920s the Klan had effective control from the courthouse to the statehouse of some Southern states. Virtually all of the Klan's top officials were also Masons.

A more recent example of chicanery by a rogue Masonic cell was that of Propaganda Due or P2 Masonic Lodge in Italy which operated illegally as a pseudo-Masonic, "black," or "covert" cell in contravention of Italian constitutional laws banning secret lodges, and membership of government officials in such organizations. During the years that the lodge was headed by Licio Gelli, P2 was implicated in numerous Italian crimes and mysteries, including the nationwide bribe scandal Tagentopoli (Bribesville), the collapse of the Vatican-affiliated Banco Abrosiano, and the murder of journalist Mino Pecorelli who was investigating the head of the Vatican Bank and its connections with organized crime.

P2 members were known as "Black Friars" and it was possibly as a warning that the body of fellow member Roberto Calvi, known as God's Banker, had been found in June 1982 hanging beneath Blackfriar's

Bridge in London's financial district. Though initially thought to be a suicide, the death was subsequently judged to have been a homicide.

Calvi had been head of the Banco Ambrosiano when the existence of P2 was discovered during investigations into the collapse of P2 member and Mafia-connected Michele "The Shark" Sindona's financial empire. The day before the discovery of Calvi's body, his secretary also "committed suicide" by falling from the fourth floor window of the bank's headquarters. A mysterious note was discovered that conveniently made Calvi the scapegoat for bringing the bank into disrepute. Like Calvi and his secretary, Sindona was also silenced in March 1986 when he was fatally poisoned in prison while serving a life sentence for the murder of lawyer Giorgio Ambrosoli who had been investigating Sindona's banking malpractice.

Both Calvi and Sindona had dealings with Paul Marcinkus, an American archbishop of the Roman Catholic Church who from 1971 to 1989 was the president of the Istituto per le Opere di Religione, also known as the Vatican Bank. In April 1973 Marcinkus was questioned in his Vatican office by a U.S. federal prosecutor and the head of the Organised Crime and Racketeering Section of the United States Department of Justice regarding his involvement in the delivery in July 1971 of a $14.5 million batch of counterfeit U.S. bonds to the Vatican. The delivery was part of a total of $950 million as requested in a letter on Vatican notepaper. The questioning was part of an investigation into the activities of an international gangster who subsequently served twelve years in prison. Marcinkus said he "considered the charges against him serious but not based enough on fact that he would violate the Vatican Bank's confidentiality to defend himself." U.S. federal prosecutors decided against pursuing the case against him.

In July 1982 newspapers and magazines throughout Europe reported that Marcinkus, a director of Ambrosiano Overseas, was implicated in financial scandals including the collapse of the Banco Ambrosiano in which P2 was involved. Though Marcinkus survived the scandal, he was two years later named in investigative journalist David Yallop's book *In God's Name* as a possible accomplice in the alleged murder of the scrupulous Pope John Paul I who might have taken a closer look at the Vatican Bank's questionable dealings. Other possibilities for the Pope's murder included his belief that the Church's position on contraception was immoral and outdated and that a rethink of the encyclical Humanae Vitae was required so as to allow use of the contraceptive pill. The Pope's opinions on the subject were reinforced by his comments referring to malnutrition in the Third World when he said that "God does not always provide." Prioritizing concern for the living rather than for those not even yet conceived had never been a concept whose humanity was recognized or welcomed amongst the Roman Catholic Church hierarchy.

Yallop alleged that other possible suspects for the Pope's murder were also associated with Marcinkus' business dealings which involved members of the Mafia on behalf of the Vatican Bank. Yallop had concluded that Marcinkus would probably face criminal exposure were he to be removed from his position at the bank. Marcinkus was never charged with any crime and in 1990 returned to the Archdiocese of Chicago before his retirement in Arizona and eventual death in February 2006 from undisclosed causes.

Following on to Yallop's thesis, other investigative writers suggested that another suspect in the Pope's murder was the secretive organization of Opus Dei (initially known as The Prelature of the Holy Cross and Opus Dei) whose pervasive influence was opposed by some within the Vatican. Allegations included the belief that several individuals within the church who had opposed Opus Dei and had supposedly died from heart attacks, may have instead been poisoned: a fate that may also have befallen the late Pope.

Founded in Spain in 1928 by the Catholic priest St. Josemaria Escriva, Opus Dei (Latin for 'Work of God') eventually received final approval from Pope Pius XII in 1950. In 1982 a decision by Pope John Paul II made it into a personal prelature with the jurisdiction of its own bishop covering members wherever they were, instead of them being subject to the authority of geographical dioceses. Approximately 70 percent of Opus Dei's estimated 95,000 members live in private homes and lead traditional Catholic family lives while pursuing a wide range of secular careers including local and national government. The remainder are celibate, of whom the majority live in Opus Dei centers. The organization provides training in Catholic spirituality as applied to daily life which includes personal charity and social work. Members are also involved with the running of universities, university residences, schools, publishing houses, and technical and agricultural training centers. Opus Dei has so far failed to explain why while performing such good works in the name of God, there is a necessity for so much secrecy within its organization.

Often described as the most controversial force within the Roman Catholic Church, Opus Dei has been criticised for its secretiveness, its recruiting methods, its elitism and misogyny, the strictness of rules governing its members, the practice of mortification of the flesh by celibate members, the right-wing tendencies of its members, and the participation by some of those members in authoritarian and extreme right-wing governments such as that of the Francoist Government of Spain until the late 1970s.

During the search of Licio Gelli's villa in March 1981 police discovered list of 962 P2 members including industrialists, members of parliament, military leaders, the heads of all three Italian intelligence services, and prominent journalists. Also discovered were documents for a "Plan for Democratic Rebirth" which called for the rewriting of the Italian Constitution, suppression of trade unions, and consolidation of the media. Gelli was a strong advocate of using money to buy control of the media: a goal which was subsequently achieved by another Mafia-connected P2 member, Silvio Berlusconi, who eventually became Italian Prime Minister.

Sometimes referred to as a "state within a state" or a "shadow government," P2 was also active in Uruguay, Brazil, and especially Argentina where during the height of the "Dirty War" P2 member Raul Alberto Lastiri was interim president from July to October 1973. Others included Emilio Massera who was part of the military junta led by Jorge Rafael Videla from 1976 to 1978; Jose Lopez Rega, minister of Social Welfare in Peron's government and founder of the Argentine Anticommunist Alliance (Triple A); and General Guillermo Saurez Mason who was convicted for Dirty War crimes.

Gelli, who during the 1930s volunteered for the "Black Shirt" expeditionary force sent by Mussolini to Spain in support of Francisco Franco's rebellion, subsequently became a liaison officer between the Italian government and the Third Reich whose contacts included Hermann Göring. He also participated in the Italian Social Republic with Giorgio Almirante, founder of the neo-fascist Italian Social Movement. Gelli's vision of P2's political program was confirmed in July 1982 when two documents were discovered at Fiumicino airport in the false bottom of a suitcase belonging to Gelli's daughter. Entitled 'Memorandum on the Italian Situation' and "Plan of Democratic Rebirth," The documents asserted that Italy's main enemies were the trade unions and the Italian Communist Party which had to be isolated and denied cooperation.

Gelli's goal was to form a new political and economic elite which would lead Italy towards a right-wing, authoritarian form of democracy with a strong anti-communist agenda. A programme of widespread corruption was thus proposed: "political parties, newspapers and trade unions can be the objects of possible solicitations which could take the form of economic-financial maneuvers. The availability of sums not exceeding 30 to 40 billion lire would seem sufficient to allow carefully chosen men, acting in good faith, to conquer key positions necessary for overall control."

Gelli absconded to Switzerland where in September 1982 he was arrested in Geneva while trying to withdraw tens of millions of dollars. Despite being detained in the secure Champ-Dollon Prison near Geneva, he managed by means of a little bribery and corruption to escape and then flee to South America. In 1984 Chilean authorities admitted that Gelli was in the country and he eventually returned to Switzerland in 1987 to surrender to an investigative judge. Gelli was wanted in connection with the 1982 collapse of the Banco Ambrosiano and for subversive association in connection with the 1980 Bologna railway station bombing which had killed 85 people.

Switzerland in due course agreed to extradite Gelli to Italy, but only on financial charges stemming from the collapse of Banco Ambrosiano. His extradition and transfer to Italy in February 1988 required elaborate security measures including decoy cars, road blocks, 100 sharpshooters, a train, and two armoured cars. Legal maneuvering and extradition stipulations, however, ensured that Gelli avoided serious time in prison. Gelli in fact remains unrepentant and his admiration for the notoriously corrupt, underage hooker-hiring Berlusconi is no doubt a reflection of his own charlatan character. In 2003, Gelli boasted to *La Repubblica* newspaper that Berlusconi's program for the reform of the judicial system had been an integral part of his own original project. He also approved of Berlusconi's reorganization of TV networks and suggested that the P2 "democratic rebirth plan" was being implemented by Silvio Berlusconi:

Every morning I speak to my conscience and the dialogue calms me down. I look at the country, read the newspaper, and think: All is becoming a reality little by little, piece by piece. To be truthful, I should have had the copyright to it. Justice, TV, public order. I wrote about this thirty years ago

. . . Berlusconi is an extraordinary man, a man of action. This is what Italy needs: not a man of words, but a man of action.

• • • • •

For the occasion of the Hiramic Brotherhood meetings, the boardroom's vertical slat blinds were shut tight and the lighting subdued. The two framed prints — one with a view of Jerusalem from the Mount of olives and another titled When We Remembered Zion with a depiction of the Star of David — that usually adorned the walls on either side of the long boardroom table, had been replaced by an envisioned image of the Second Temple and a map of the "Promised Land." The map outlined Israel's hoped for territory stretching from the eastern bank of the River Nile in Egypt to the western bank of the River Euphrates. Twenty-six chairs were placed around the long table at the centre of which a golden Menorah was stood between the Masonic symbol of square and compasses and a Hebrew Bible that was opened at the Vision of the Future Temple as described in the Book of Ezekiel which predated the Second Temple.

The Menorah, a seven-branched candelabrum, was said to have been used in the ancient desert Tabernacle and subsequently in the First Temple in Jerusalem. It was both the ancient symbol of Judaism and the emblem of the modern state of Israel. According to the Hebrew Bible the Tabernacle was the portable "residence" for the divine presence that accompanied the Israelites during their mythical Exodus from Egypt, their wanderings in the wilderness, and their conquest of the Promised Land. The Tabernacle was allegedly built in accordance with the specific details that God Himself revealed to Moses on Mount Sinai.

Being one of the cofounders of the Hiramic Brotherhood of the Third Temple and the principal author of the Articles of its Constitution, Abe Goldman held the title of "Master Hiram Abiff" and as such presided over the meetings. So as soon as it had been established that all the members had arrived, Goldman called the meeting to order. The members — who were clad in black suits, white shirts, and their black velvet kippot Jewish hats — then stood behind their chairs and picked up the laminated A5 size cards that were on the table in front of each chair. A designated member lit the Menorah's candles and dimmed the electric lighting even further. The members, in unison with Goldman and with their right hands on their hearts, then read out aloud from the reaffirmation cards as follows:

We of the Brotherhood of the Third Temple hereby reaffirm our commitment to the building of that Temple in accordance with the vision described in the Book of Ezekiel. We fervently vow before God and each other to maintain that commitment and advance its objective whenever possible and in every aspect of our lives, whether at home, at work, or at social events. We shall never forget that according to Israel's great sages, Israel's people are obliged by a specific commandment to rebuild the Holy Temple and to adhere to the dimensions, characteristics and attributes of the Second Temple. Despite there being differences between the First and Second Temples, and vast differences between both of these and Ezekiel's vision, it is the details of the Second Temple that are binding upon Israel for all time. Though many aspects of Ezekiel's envisioned Temple are beyond comprehension because we lack the necessary spiritual and intellectual capacity, we will nonetheless persevere with Judaism's desire to have such a Temple built on Temple Mount as a replacement for the First and Second Temples which were destroyed by the ancient Babylonians in 586 BCE and the Romans in the year 70.

According to Ezekiel's prophecy, the structure of the Third Temple will require immense topographical changes in Jerusalem's environs with the Temple differing dramatically in size from its predecessors. Ezekiel's measurements suggest that the new Temple will be so large as to occupy the entire area of Jerusalem with both the Temple Mount and the Mount of Olives being accordingly enlarged to facilitate its presence. We must not forget that Ezekiel's teachings were part of a larger and broader tradition that he received from his predecessors. Despite the dilemma of comprehending Ezekiel's measurements, we will take them to mean that the areas surrounding the Temple are to be regarded as inviolable and sacred areas that combined together constitute a divine entity at the core of which is the Temple.

On that basis, we the people of Israel, irrespective of any cost or consequence, can never allow the division of our Holy City. Its establishment as the undivided capital of Eretz Israel will consolidate our claim over all of the Holy Land and legitimize the extension of Eretz Israel's boundaries as laid out in the Torah's books of Genesis, Exodus, and the Prophets.

As a fellow Masons we are already aware of the importance of utmost confidentiality with regards to the membership, the vows, the aims, and procedures of any Masonic Lodge, and as such we reaffirm our acceptance that an even greater degree of confidentiality will be required from us as a members of the Hiramic Brotherhood of the Third Temple and solemnly swear under pain of death to never divulge anything that may be discussed, learnt, or determined this evening or at any time in the past or in the future. This our vow, spoken out loud, has a binding force in traditional Jewish Law.

The Brothers then sat down for commencement of the meeting.

"Shalom to all you Brothers. As we are all aware," Goldman began, "our ultimate goal is the building of the Third Temple on Temple Mount . . . but for that to happen we must first Judaize the Negev and all areas inhabited by Palestinians including villages adjoining Jerusalem as well as those in the fertile Jordan Valley which would be essential for any Palestinian state. Areas around the Temple Mount must also be surrounded and isolated to such an extent that the Mount will be swallowed up and forever become an inseparable part of a fully Judaized East Jerusalem. So we shall start with a report from Brother Daniel."

"Shalom to all my Brothers. It is generally agreed within government circles,' Brother Daniel began, 'that Ehud Olmert's legal problems with corruption will force him to step down as Prime Minister and his successor as leader of the Kadima Party will not be able to form a government. This will leave the way open for the return of Benjamin Netanyahu as Prime Minister . . . Probably sometime early next year."

"Having Likud in power would certainly suit our purpose," Goldman said.

"Exactly," Brother Daniel concurred before continuing, "we do

291

know that Netanyahu has delegated his planning policy chief to come up with a plan to solve the question of settlement in and around the Negev which would involve the expulsion of an estimated forty thousand Palestinian Bedouin from their current dwellings — this would be our largest single forced displacement of Arabs since the 1950s. The Plan's main objective is to Judaize the Israeli Negev by offering a positive solution to the region's problem of the forty-five unrecognized Bedouin villages in the region with a population totaling seventy thousand."

"How's that going to be achieved?" Goldman asked.

"As the villages are already classified as unrecognized, they are forbidden by the government from connecting to the electricity grid or the water and sewage systems. Construction regulations will be harshly enforced and thousands of Bedouin homes and animal enclosures which we regard as illegal temporary structures will be demolished. There will be no paved roads and signposts from main roads to the villages will be removed and the villages will no longer be shown on maps because officially they and their inhabitants do not exist."

"And how'll this removal of Arabs be justified?" Goldman asked.

"The government has already been arguing that because these Arabs live in small villages scattered over a large area, it cannot provide them with the basic services that would otherwise be available if the Arabs were to be concentrated into a few townships.

"The township idea certainly worked in South Africa and it is working here in those townships already established," Goldman said.

"Relocation also solves the problem of those seventy thousand Bedouin who have repeatedly refused to sign over their property rights to the State and have continued living in their unrecognized and therefore illegal villages. We have developers waiting to commence building towns for Jews only because we maintain that the Negev's Bedouin inhabitants are robbing the Jewish people of their Israeli land."

"What kind of timescale are we talking here?" Goldman asked.

"Five years. But to speed up forced relocations we have plans for ethnic cleansing by designating zones for national parks, restricted military sectors, and firing ranges which will require the villagers to evacuate for their own safety. The building of new Jewish settlements in the area will of course be continued."

"Anything else?" Goldman asked.

"A concerted effort to implement our plans will be to continue harassing the Palestinians, to continue the eradication of their culture as a people, and to continue forcing them to move to West Bank cities under Palestinian Authority control. The designated Area C in the West Bank — which was temporarily entrusted to Israel under the Oslo Accords — will within a few years have a Palestinian population of no more than 100,000 whom Jewish settlers will outnumber by three to one. Slowly but surely we are reclaiming the land promised to us by God — and by God, we will reclaim it and nobody will stop us."

That was exactly the sentiment of Prime Minister David Ben-Gurion who believed that it was the Negev that would test Israel as a nation so that in 1969 the Ben-Gurion University of the Negev was established with the objective of promoting development of the desert which comprises sixty percent of Israel. This Israeli claim over Palestinian Bedouin land is as usual racist and dishonest and ignores the fact that the first recorded nomadic settlement in Sinai dates back to between 4,000 and 7,000 years — long before the 1313 BCE date that has become traditional in Rabbinic Judaism for the Exodus from Egypt.

In their dishonest and illegal obsession with displacing the Arabs, Israelis have overlooked the fact that scarcity of both water and permanent pastoral land had required the Palestinian Bedouin to be constantly on the move with nomadic herding, periodic agriculture and occasional fishing. They also earned some income by transporting goods and people across the desert. Consequently the Bedouin had been unable to establish more than a few permanent settlements though evidence remains of traditional baika buildings that were seasonal dwellings during the rainy season when some farming was possible. Cemeteries known as "nawamis" dating to the late fourth millennium BCE were also in existence along with some roofless open-air mosques (some still in use) dating back to the early Islamic period. Israelis were adamant that these nomads — who have always minded their own business without oppressing other ethnic groups or waging wars — are not entitled to even a few of the basic human rights that Israelis violently demand for themselves.

"Thank you for that, Brother Daniel. Now Brother Yosef has a progress report for us on the work of the Institute," Goldman said.

"Shalom to all my Brothers. I know everyone here knows that the Institute is a non-profit educational and religious organization located in the Old City's Jewish quarter. Like us it is dedicated to every aspect of building a Holy Temple of God on Mount Moriah in accordance with the positive Biblical commandment which the Torah teaches us was given by God to the Jewish people at Mount Sinai, the day following Yom Kippur. The commandment is counted as one of the 613 mitzvot, the commandments that Israel is perpetually obligated to fulfill.

"The Institute's short-term goal is to rekindle the flame of the Holy Temple in the hearts of mankind through education. Its long-term goal is to do all in its power to bring about the building of the Holy Temple during our time. Its efforts include raising public awareness about the Holy Temple and the central role it occupies in the spiritual life of mankind by conducting activities that combine research, seminars, publications, and conferences, as well as the production of educational materials. It repeatedly emphasizes the importance that the building of the Holy Temple is for all mankind, and not just for Jews. It is important that it continues to emphasize that its goal is for all of mankind and not just for the Jewish people.

"The Institute's major focus is its efforts towards the beginning of the actual rebuilding of the Holy Temple and to this end it has already begun to restore and construct the sacred vessels for the service of the Holy Temple. These vessels, which God commanded Israel to create, can be seen today at the Institute's exhibition in the Old City's Jewish Quarter. They are made according to the exact specifications of the Bible, and have been constructed from the original source materials, such as gold, copper, silver and wood. They are authentic, accurate vessels, not merely replicas or models. All of these items will soon be fit and ready for use in the service of the Holy Temple. Among the many items featured in the exhibition are musical instruments played by the Levitical choir, the golden crown of the High Priest, and gold and silver vessels used in the incense and sacrificial services.

"After many years of effort and toil, the Institute has virtually completed the three most important and central vessels of the Divine service: the seven-branched candelabra, or Menorah, made of pure gold; the golden Incense Altar, and the golden Table of the Showbread. The Institute is also in the process of completing the sacred uniform of the Kohen Gadol, the High Priest with the project being the culmination of years of study and research. The High Priest's Breastplate and Ephod are also near to being completed. The Institute functions on donations and I believe it is deserving of our support, budget permitting of course."

"Brother Avraham?" Goldman asked the Brother responsible for finance.

"Right now we would have no problem with 100,000 shekels."

"It'll have to be anonymous," Goldman said.

"No problem. We can start the ball rolling from the Swiss account." Avraham said referring to the Brotherhood's external numbered bank account in Zurich's Bahnhofstrasse. Apart from being one of the world's most exclusive and expensive shopping avenues, Bahnhofstrasse was also host to numerous commercial and private banks whose underground vaults were crammed full of gold and silver. Furthermore Bahnhofstrasse epitomized not only the national preoccupation with the worship of Mammon, but also the ability to do so with a relatively clear conscience because of the general perception that Switzerland was a clean, efficient, and law abiding country abounding in chocolate, quaint cuckoo clocks, humanitarian neutrality, and numerous obliging banks with unconditional commitment to client confidentiality. It was a perception which in the minds of most people — including the Swiss themselves — mitigated for the unconscionable benefits that the country derived from being a haven for the ill-gotten gains of despots, desperadoes, drug dealers, and more than a few genuine anti-Semite Nazis. Swiss neutrality and banking confidentiality comes at a high cost to the rest of humanity.

Switzerland had served as a repository for Jewish capital smuggled out of Germany and other countries being threatened by the Nazis. Apart from hoarding vast quantities of gold and other valuables plundered from Jews and others all over Europe, it also throughout the war laundered hundreds of millions of dollars in stolen assets including gold pillaged from central banks in German-occupied Europe. When the war ended Switzerland staunchly resisted Allied demands for restitution and following the 1946 Washington Agreement the Allies settled for a measly twelve percent of the stolen gold. Holocaust survivors and the heirs of those who had perished faced an unyielding bureaucracy with only a handful being able to reclaim their assets. To add insult to injury, Swiss authorities appropriated dormant accounts to satisfy claims of Swiss nationals whose property had been seized in East Central Europe by Communist regimes.

With the end of the war approaching, and while other neutral countries were refusing to directly purchase gold from Germany, Switzerland continued profiting from such trade with the gold coming mostly from the reserves of the central banks in occupied countries and gold taken from individuals including gold dental fillings from corpses. Swiss banks conducted lucrative transactions with the German

Reichsbank and individual Nazis with even the royalties from Hitler's book *Mein Kampf* being deposited in a Swiss bank account. Documents recovered in former East German archives suggest that in 1944 Heinrich Himmler — the SS Chief and German Interior Minister who following his capture committed suicide by biting on a cyanide pill hidden in his mouth — sent a special train to Switzerland loaded with gold, jewelry, and art objects worth hundreds of millions of dollars for deposit in Swiss bank vaults. Switzerland's hypocritical claim of humane neutrality and continued refusal to acknowledge its complicity in the theft of European and Jewish assets by Nazi Germany remains a stigma on a neutral nation that as part of the protection for its ill-gotten deposits maintains the largest per capita armed citizen militia in Europe. So while it may appear questionable on moral grounds for the Hiramic Brotherhood to have availed itself of Swiss banking services, Zionism has never been fussy when it comes to collaboration for the achievement of its goals even to the extent — as Lenny Brenner's *51 Documents* clearly established — of not only being prepared to collaborate with the Nazis, but also of being prepared to sacrifice Jewish lives. This is an irrefutable fact that Jewish people should realistically acknowledge and honestly accept.

Over the best part of the next hour the Brothers discussed their agenda with each brother reporting on the progress of the particular task to which he had been assigned. This included the subtle lobbying of municipal officials and government ministers; maintaining 'watch' lists of Jewish individuals and organizations that opposed occupation, Judaization, and the gradual annexation of Temple Mount and Silwan; and the undermining of the reputation of such individuals and organizations. At 8:45 p.m. Goldman finally called the meeting to a close.

14
Friday, 19 December 2008
The Eruv, Golders Green, London

As David Reisner was walking through the Eruv back to Golders Green Underground Station he was both disappointed and alarmed by the cold reception he had just received from his cousin, Aaron Lewis, and the rest of the family. On a previous visit shortly after his arrival in London he had been greeted with a warmth and affection that had to some extent rekindled his faith in humanity. On his way there today he had stopped off at the Kosher bakery in Golders Green Road and picked up some pastries for them to enjoy on the Sabbath — a gesture which had clearly not been appreciated. The stark contrast between his last and today's visit had left Reisner utterly dumbfounded.

Not being an observant Jew, Reisner had never believed in the controversial concept of the eruv which circumvents the Sabbath prohibition the basis of which is cited in the Torah. Apparently the Israelites went out on Sabbath to collect manna despite being forbidden by Moses and being told that on Friday they would receive two day's portions. As a result they were reprimanded by Moses who told them "bide every man in his place, let no man go out of his place on the seventh day.' One interpretation suggests this to mean 'do not go out to collect manna on the seventh day,'" but others have been widened to include the prohibition on walking long distances during the Sabbath.

The eruv is a designated area within which observant Jews can carry or push objects on the Sabbath — lasting from sunset on Friday to sunset on Saturday — without violating a Jewish law that prohibits the carrying of anything outside the home. Though the area must be "completely enclosed," it does not require the building of special walls around it and its boundaries can be marked by existing physical features such as walls, hedges, railings and roads,

The open spaces between the existing features are filled in by erecting poles that are connected by wire or nylon fishing line. The poles and lines are regarded as forming doorways in the boundary with the poles representing the sides of the door and the lines being the lintel along the top. Flimsier parts of the boundary are inspected weekly to ensure that the boundary is intact without damage to any of the poles or connecting lines. The concept appears to imaginatively stretch the interpretation of a religious law so as to circumvent its inconvenience.

Eruvs (or eruvim) mix the boundaries between the areas within the home and the areas outside it so that within eruvs Orthodox Jews can follow the same rules on the Sabbath that they would in their homes. Jewish law stipulates that Jews must not carry any item, no matter how small or for whatever purpose in a Reshus HaRabim — any public domain outside their homes — on the Sabbath, even if they are allowed to carry them within their home. Pushing objects is also forbidden so that those requiring the use of prams or wheelchairs are rendered housebound and cannot even fulfill their religious duties on the Sabbath by going to the synagogue.

Eruvs do not permit Orthodox Jews to carry things that cannot be moved at all on the Sabbath — such as mobile phones, pens, and wallets; nor can they carry things for use after the Sabbath, or perform tasks that break the spirit of the Sabbath such as gardening, shopping, swimming, riding a bicycle, or playing games in the park.

The eruv — regarded as being within the home domain — therefore permits Jews, to both carry and push objects within its boundaries. They can carry reading glasses, house keys (but not car or office keys), a handkerchief, books, food or drink for Sabbath use, a prayer shawl, essential medicines, and extra clothing. An eruv therefore makes it easier for Jews to normalize their lives during the Sabbath without contravening the spirit of its holiness.

There were now over 200 eruvs worldwide whose establishment is always preceded by many years of campaigning and controversy with objections coming from both non-Jews and Jews. Reform and secular Jews' disapproval of eruvs stems mainly from their not seeing a requirement for them. Support for them comes from Orthodox and Conservative Jews, but some Ultra-Orthodox Jews are very rigorous about eruv rules and often for legal reasons refuse to recognize their validity.

Some of the objections to eruvs are that they are a ploy for avoiding the strict rules of the Sabbath; they claim public areas as a private areas; they are visually intrusive; they take over a public space for a religious purpose; they breach human rights by giving a religious Jewish role to the walls and fences of non-Jews; they breach the human rights of non-Jews because they are forced to pass through symbolic Jewish structures when entering or exiting eruvs; they are religiously divisive and may therefore promote anti-Semitism; they create symbolic ghettos, reminiscent of past persecutions; that they encourage separateness and discourage assimilation; Jews will be encouraged to concentrate within eruvs; and they are an archaic idea.

Supporters on the other hand claim that they are a creative use of Jewish law to improve the Sabbath; they are purely symbolic and do not make areas any less public; the poles and lines are barely visible; public spaces are only changed for Orthodox Jews but remain unchanged for non-believers; the symbolic roles that the boundaries have for Jews does not exist for non-Jews and as such does not affect their rights; they are no more religiously divisive than synagogues or Jewish schools; they do not create symbolic ghettos; the questions of separateness and assimilation are of no consequence; the suggestion that Jews will concentrate in eruvs is anti-Semitic; and that their existence follows ancient laws and traditions that are part of Jewish continuity and a vital part of the survival of the Jewish people.

Reisner, however, was too preoccupied with this latest development to worry about the pros and cons of eruvs. His cousin, Aaron, had apparently on Wednesday received a visit from the local synagogue's rabbi whom Reisner now figured was probably a Mossad *sayan* acting on the orders of his *katsa*. The rabbi had informed Aaron that as a respected member of the local Jewish community he had a responsibility to maintain certain standards of loyalty which included not consorting with the enemies of the community and Eretz Israel. Reisner figured that this was just the beginning of the strategy used against Jewish critics of Israel that Michal Zeldin had experienced: Proactive exclusion from the Jewish community, character assassination with smear campaigns, physical assaults including being spat on and slapped, malicious damage of property including offensive graffiti on walls and cars, and verbal abuse with accusations of being a self-hating Jew.

Accusing someone of being a self-hating Jew has been an often used rhetorical device — now appropriated by Zionist supporters of Israel — that prevents a considered exchange of views by forcing those accused to defend themselves against the insult and thereby avoid any further reasonable discussion. The concept gained popularity following publication in 1930 of *Der Jüdische Selbsthass* ("Jewish Self-hatred") by Theodor Lessing, the German Jewish philosopher. The book endeavored to explain the prevalence of Jewish intellectuals inciting anti-Semitism with their extremely hateful view toward Judaism.

Jewish self-hate has been characterised as being a neurotic reaction to the effect of anti-Semitism by Jews accepting, expressing, and even exaggerating the basic suppositions of anti-Semites. The expression consequently became a form of censure during and even after the Cold War-era (1947-1991) debates about Zionism. Similar accusations of discomfort with one's Jewishness were, however, already being made by groups of Jews against each other even before Zionism movement came into existence.

Some academics have suggested that the expression "self-hating Jew" is often used as a designation of unworthiness for those Jews who have different lifestyles, interests, and political viewpoints from those of their accusers. A distinction therefore has to be made between "Jewish anti-Semitism" and "Jewish self-hatred" so that it recognized that Jews who embrace anti-Semitism that is dangerous and damning to all Jews, are not necessarily "self-hating." Self-hatred can also be regarded as distaste or hatred for the group to which one belongs. The expression also has a long history in debates over the role of Israel in Jewish identity, where it is used against Jewish critics of Israeli government policy.

In the 2006 essay *"Progressive" Jewish Thought and the New Anti-Semitism* authored by Alvin H. Rosenfeld and released by the American Jewish Committee, it is claimed that a "number of Jews, through their speaking and writing, are feeding a rise in virulent anti-Semitism by questioning whether Israel should even exist." The American cultural and literary historian, Sander Gilman, believes that "One of the most recent forms of Jewish self-hatred is the virulent opposition to the existence of the State of Israel." He uses the expression not against those who oppose Israeli policies, but against Jews who are opposed to Israel's existence.

Jewish self-hatred as a concept has been described by Antony Lerman — a British writer specializing in the study of anti-Semitism, the Israeli-Palestinian conflict, multiculturalism, and the place of religion in society — as "an entirely bogus concept. . . that serves no other purpose than to marginalize and demonize political opponents," and is used increasingly as a personal attack in discussions about the "new anti-Semitism." Lerman also raises the question of whether extreme vilification of Israel amounts to anti-Semitism and recognizes that sometimes anti-Semitism can be disguised as anti-Zionism.

It must also be recognised that having historically attained the position of always being the presumptive victims, Jews can no longer —

thanks to Israeli crimes against humanity — continue to monopolize the position of always being the victim. Whether it is a Jewish settler who is killed by rocket fire or a Palestinian stone-throwing child who is shot by the IDF . . . the fact remains that both are victims of violence. Therefore if such acts of violence are to always be challenged and condemned in the interest of justice, then the right to freedom of speech without fear of condemnation — such as being accused of anti-Semitism — must always prevail. A victim cannot be judged as being *more* or *less* of a victim because of his or her ethnicity, color, religion, or social position.

For David Reisner — like for numerous other ethically progressive Jews in diaspora and Israel — the question arises as to whether to remain silent over Israeli crimes, or to openly condemn them and consequently be accused of anti-Semitic activities. The mere thought of being thus stigmatized was for any Jew, Reisner included, quite unbearable.

Ultimately everyone including Jews has to decide whether to remain silent and become Israeli collaborators in crimes against humanity, or despite any risk loudly condemn such crimes and be proudly counted with those who did what they could to end the violent repression of the Palestinian people. Reisner's mood as he walked back to the underground station was one of deep melancholy as he contemplated his cousin Aaron's cowardice in having chosen the former course of inaction.

15
Tuesday, 23 December 2008
Little Venice, London

Mark Banner decided to skip last-minute Christmas shopping with Nadine and his parents and instead remained at home to continue working on the final draft of his book. George Herbert Walker Bush (Bush Sr.), the 41st President of the U.S. (1989-1993) was a seasoned politician who served as a congressman (1967-1971), as U.S. Ambassador to the UN (1971-1973), as Chairman of the Republican National Committee (1973- 1974), as Chief of Liaison Office to the People's Republic of China (1974-1975), as Director of the CIA (1976-1977), and as the 43rd Vice President of the U.S. (1989-1993).

Bush Sr. took office at a time of rapid change in the world which witnessed the fall of the Berlin Wall and the collapse of the Soviet Union during the early period of his presidency. He ordered military operations in Panama against Manuel Noriega government and in the Persian Gulf following Saddam Hussain's invasion of oil-rich Kuwait. After having achieved a record-high approval rating of 89%, his handling of the economic recession and broken promise of "no new taxes" subsequently caused a sharp decline in his approval rating.

Banner also noted that more than a few political observers still believed that Bush Sr. lost the 1992 general election because of the Israeli lobby which punished him for his standoff with Israeli Prime Minister Yitzhak Shamir when he tried to stop Israel from building more settlements in the Occupied Territories by opposing a proposed $10 billion loan guarantee to Israel.

Having initially taken on AIPAC over the building of settlements and holding up the $10 billion loan guarantee which Israel required desperately to build housing for its influx of Russian émigrés, Bush Sr. nonetheless caved in over the issue after being given an assurance that the loans would not fund settlements. Banner wondered how long it would take before U.S. presidents would come to realize that assurances from liars, thieves, and murderers are worthless.

Ironically, the first ever U.S. veto to protect Israel was cast in 1972 by Bush Sr. in his capacity as U.S. ambassador to the UN. It was also Bush Sr. who as president temporarily suspended the use of the veto to shield Israel eighteen years later. The last such veto was cast on 31 May 1990 killing a resolution approved by all fourteen other council members to send a UN mission to study Israeli abuses of Palestinians in the occupied territories. Then President Bill Clinton followed up with three more.

Between 1972 and 1997 the U.S. used its veto thirty-two times to shield Israel from critical draft resolutions. This constituted nearly half of the total of 69 U.S. vetoes cast since the founding of the UN. The Soviet Union had cast 115 vetoes during the same period. During the early days of the UN, the Soviet Union commissar and later minister for foreign affairs, Vyacheslav Molotov, vetoed resolutions so many times that he was known as "Mr. Veto." The Soviet Union was In fact responsible for nearly half of all vetoes ever cast — seventy-nine in the first 10 years. Molotov regularly rejected bids for new membership because of the U.S.'s refusal to admit the Soviet republics. Since the dissolution of the Soviet Union, however, Russia has since used its veto power sparingly.

Nonetheless the belief still persists that Bush Sr.'s loss to Bill Clinton in the 1992 election was due to his being thrashed in precincts with substantial Jewish populations in the states of New York, New Jersey, Ohio, and Florida. Despite the Jewish lobby's subsequent denial of having any such power, Bush has since on more than one public occasion condemned AIPAC's influence and power in Washington. Those who dispute such a claim point out that even though the Jewish vote for Bush had dropped from over 30% in 1988 to less than half that in 1992, it made no difference to the end result because Clinton had in any case won the presidency by an overwhelming electoral majority of 370 to 168.

Bush Sr.'s perceived problems with American Jews — not helped by Secretary of State James Baker's remark, "Bleep the Jews; they didn't vote for us anyway" — had less to do with his own position and far more to do with Prime Minister Yitzhak Shamir's uncompromising Zionist stance on settlements and negotiations with the Palestinians which would have made Shamir's relationship with any American president, even under the best of circumstances, extremely precarious. Shamir was after all the Zionist Ingun Zvai Leumi terrorist who said "Israel's days without Jerusalem, Judea and Samaria and the Gaza strip are gone and will not return." In view of such statements, how can any U.S. president with some common sense — even one regarded as being a merely a pragmatic but not very charismatic or imaginative caretaker — seriously believe he can broker an Israeli-Palestinian peace plan based on a two-state solution? So irrespective of the Jewish vote's role in his defeat, Bush Sr.'s public image was of no help in his bid for reelection to a second term.

For Mark Banner it was therefore no surprise that the more flamboyant and charming Bill Clinton who despite Gennifer Flowers — a cabaret singer who came forward during the campaign alleging that she had had a twelve-year relationship with Clinton — easily won the presidential election. Clinton's wife, Hillary, was possibly responsible for saving her husband by going on television to demonstrate her support by making the now famous reference to the country song "Stand by Your Man." During the interview Mrs. Clinton said: "I'm not sitting here, some little woman standing by her man. I'm sitting here because I love him and I respect him." When asked if he had a 12-year affair with Ms. Flowers, Clinton replied that the "allegations are false," but admitted to having "caused pain" in the marriage.

On assuming office in January 1993, President Clinton immediately indicated — by the nature of his high level administrative appointments — that he would maintain the unwavering U.S. diplomatic, economic, military, and political support that Israel had enjoyed since 1967. Clinton's appointments included for the position of senior Middle East advisor on the National Security Council, Martin Indyk, a former head of the pro-Israel think tank the Washington Institute for Near East Policy (WINEP) who later served as two-term ambassador to Israel and assistant secretary of state for Near East affairs. Indyk had also previously served as an advisor to former Israeli Likud Prime Minister Yitzhak Shamir. Although Indyk was an Australian citizen, he was sworn in as a U.S. citizen in an act of peremptory executive privilege at Clinton's express wishes. The position of special Middle East coordinator went to Dennis Ross who served temporarily as interim director of WINEP after Indyk.

When in December 1992 Israel expelled 400 Palestinians for allegedly being Hamas supporters, President-elect Clinton — despite international outrage and condemnation — avoided criticizing Israel and instead connived with Israel to formulate a face-saving exercise for then Prime Minister Yitzhak Rabin. This involved an announcement by the State Department that just 100 of the deportees would in time be allowed to return home; that half of the rest would be allowed to return in September; and the remainder allowed to return in 1994.

In March 1993, Rabin announced the "emergency measures" including the closure of the border between Israel and the Occupied Territories which have in varying degrees of severity remained to this day with a view to oppressing the Palestinian people in the West Bank and Gaza and severely damaging their economies. Having failed to condemn the "emergency measures," Clinton then presided over the signing of the Declaration of Principles on Interim Self-Government Arrangements (The Oslo I Accord) which he achieved by inveigling of the Palestinian leadership with false promises of U.S. evenhanded neutrality. The charming but slimy Clinton — the man who can look you in the eyes and tell sincerely and with hand on heart that he is not screwing around — then proceeded to act as Israel's procurer in the ensuing and seemingly endless negotiations.

Negotiations concerning the agreement, an extension of the Madrid Conference of 1991, were conducted secretly in Oslo, Norway — under the auspices of the Fafo institute (a Norwegian research foundation)— and were completed on 20 August 1993. The Accords were subsequently signed officially at a public ceremony in Washington, D.C., on 13 September 1993 in the presence of PLO chairman Yasser Arafat, the then Israeli Prime Minister Yitzhak Rabin, and U.S. President Clinton. The documents themselves were signed for the PLO by Mahmoud Abbas, Foreign Minister Shimon Peres for Israel, and Secretary of State Warren Christopher for the U.S., and Foreign Minister Andrei Kozyrev for Russia.

The Accord provided for the creation of a Palestinian interim self-government, the Palestinian National Authority (PNA). The PNA was to have responsibility for the administration of the territory under its control. The Accords also called for the withdrawal of the IDF from parts of the Gaza Strip and the West Bank — an aspect that Israel cheated on as subsequently admitted to by Benjamin Netanyahu. It had been anticipated that the arrangement would last for a five-year interim period during which beginning no later than May 1996 a permanent agreement would be negotiated. Issues such as Jerusalem, Palestinian refugees, Israeli settlements, security, and borders were left to future negotiations. In 1995, the Oslo I Accord was followed by Oslo II with neither promising Palestinian statehood.

By August 1993, the delegations had reached an agreement, which was signed in secrecy by Peres while visiting Oslo. The Palestinians and Israelis, however, had not yet agreed on the wording for the Letters of Mutual Recognition, which constituted an agreement in which the PLO would acknowledge the state of Israel and pledge to reject violence, and Israel would recognise the (unelected) PLO as the official Palestinian authority, allowing Yasser Arafat to return to the West Bank. An agreement was eventually reached and signed by Yasser Arafat and Yitzhak Rabin in time for the official signing in Washington which occurred 13 September 1993, at a Washington ceremony hosted by U.S. President Clinton.

Clinton's function as procurer for Israel — instead of for himself — was sidetracked temporarily when Paula Corbin Jones, a former Arkansas state employee sued Clinton for sexual harassment. Clinton brought the case to a close by entering into an out-of-court settlement to pay Jones and her attorneys a total of $850,000 before the lawsuit was dismissed pre-trial on the grounds that Jones failed to demonstrate damages. Jones appeal of that decision prompted Clinton on 13 November 1998 — without any apology — to settle with Jones for entire amount of her claim for $850,000 in exchange for her agreement to drop the appeal. In April 1999, Clinton was found in civil contempt of court for misleading testimony in the Jones case. He was ordered to pay $1,202 to the court and an additional $90,000 to Jones's lawyers for expenses incurred. The Judge then referred Clinton's conduct to the Arkansas Bar for disciplinary action, and on January 19, 2001, the day before Clinton left the office of president, he entered into an agreement with the Arkansas Bar under which he was stripped of his license to practice law in Arkansas for a period of five years. His fine was paid from a fund raised for his legal expenses.

Though not particularly damaging, the Paula Jones case nonetheless precipitated the more serious Monica Lewinsky scandal. News of the scandal first broke on January 17, 1998, on the *Drudge Report* which revealed that *Newsweek* editors were sitting on a story by investigative reporter Michael Isikoff exposing the affair. The story broke in the mainstream press on 21 January in *The Washington Post* and was spun around for several days. Despite immediate denials from Clinton, the clamor for answers was not silenced and on 26 January, Clinton, standing with his wife, addressed a White House press conference, and issued a forceful denial, which contained what would later become one of the best-known soundbites of his presidency:

Now, I have to go back to work on my State of the Union speech. And I worked on it until pretty late last night. But I want to say one thing to the American people. I want you to listen to me. I'm going to say this again: I did not have sexual relations with that woman, Miss Lewinsky. I never told anybody to lie, not a single time; never. These allegations are false. And I need to go back to work for the American people. Thank you!

Clinton was impeached by the House of Representatives on two charges, one of perjury and one of obstruction of justice, on 19 December 1998. Two other impeachment articles, a second perjury charge and a charge of abuse of power, failed in the House. He was acquitted by the Senate on 12 February 1999.

Clinton's cowardly and persistent adherence to the U.S. policy of partisanship towards Israel — coupled with former Israeli Defense Minister and untried war criminal Ariel Sharon's arrogant visit to the Haram al-Sharif (Temple Mount) — served to ignite the tinder box of Palestinian frustration accumulated over years of broken commitments and meaningless negotiations. They had endured continual land confiscation, demolition of property, oppression, poverty, and severe unemployment. Due to the blockades, the majority of them could no longer access education, employment, medical care, or the holy sites in East Jerusalem.

On 28 September 2000, surrounded by hundreds of Israeli riot police, Ariel Sharon and a handful of Likud politicians marched up to the Haram al-Sharif, the site of the golden Dome of the Rock that is the third holiest shrine in Islam. This deliberately staged and provocative visit to a Muslim shrine at the heart of the Israeli-Palestinian conflict resulted in dozens of people being injured during the ensuing rioting on the West Bank and in Jerusalem. Sharon descended 45 minutes later, leaving a trail of fury. Young Palestinians assaulted the Israeli forces with chairs, rubbish bins, stones, and any other available missile. Israeli riot police retaliated with tear gas, rubber bullets, and shooting one protester in the face.

The symbolism of the visit to Haram al-Sharif by Sharon — reviled for his role in the September 1982 Sabra and Shatila massacre of Palestinian refugees in Lebanon — and its timing was deliberate, unmistakable and led to the Second Intifada (Al-Aqsa Intifada). "This is a dangerous process conducted by Sharon against Islamic sacred places," Yasser Arafat told Palestinian television. Sharon's second less obvious motive was to steal the limelight from the former prime minister, Benjamin Netanyahu, who had on the same day returned from the U.S. and was a potential for the Likud party leadership after Israel's attorney general had decided against prosecuting him for corruption.

Sharon's stunt — staged in a place where history, religion and national aspirations converged — enraged the Palestinians who responded with chants of "murderer" and "we will redeem the Haram with blood and fire." The Palestinian protesters then followed Sharon down the Temple Mount but narrowly avoided clashing with Orthodox Jews who shouted "go back to Mecca." Although the Haram is part of Arab East Jerusalem and had been illegally occupied by Israel since 1967, Jews nonetheless revere the "Sacred Esplanade" (Temple Mount) as the site of a Temple destroyed in 70 AD.

The 35-acre site has been the single biggest obstacle to peace which was not helped by Sharon's assertion that it was an inalienable part of the Jewish state. "The Temple Mount is in our hands and will remain in our hands. It is the holiest site in Judaism and it is the right of every Jew to visit the Temple Mount." Palestinians and Israeli liberals denounced Sharon's visit as a dangerous provocation. "The timing and the decision to visit the Haram was taken to flare up the area and to burn up the place," said a blood-splattered Ahmed Tibi, an Israeli Arab member of the Knesset, who suffered a broken wrist in the scuffles at the shrine. "He wants to see more blood and more killing. He wants to kill the peace." Sharon, however, was unrepentant with the downright ridiculous falsehood he had been on a mission of reconciliation. "What provocation is there when Jews come to visit the place with a message of peace? I am sorry about the injured, but it is the right of Jews in Israel to visit the Temple Mount."

Israel's response to the ensuing Intifada was immediate, disproportionate, and brutal. Within 90 days over 350 Palestinians were killed and more than 10,000 sustained injuries of which many were severe. Israel has laid siege to the Occupied Territories and apart from employing starvation and assassination tactics, it also deployed its military might including helicopter gunships against the mostly unarmed civilian population. The final death toll when the Intifada ended in 2005 was an estimated 3,000 Palestinians, 1,000 Israelis, and 64 foreigners.

While the rest of the world denounced Israel's draconian reprisals, the Clinton Administration — in the name of the American people — maintained its unwavering support for Israel; support that was continued by Clinton's successor, George W. Bush. At the start of the violence, France and Germany had both initiated an undeclared embargo on Israel of military equipment and materials. The French and German embargoes were a stark contrast to the U.S. response which was to increase arms deliveries to Israel.

On 14 November 2000, Clinton asked Congress to grant $450 million in extra aid to Israel in addition to the astronomical amount it received annually. In fiscal year of 1997 for example, Israel received $3 billion from the foreign aid budget; $525 million from other U.S. budgets; and $2 billion in federal loan guarantees. Under the new request, the U.S. would give Israel $250 million to defray the cost of the Lebanon withdrawal, and $200 million to develop new weapons such as the Arrow anti-missile shield. The request also included a suggestion that Israel's military aid next year include an extra $350 million. Uncharacteristically, the usually AIPAC-controlled U.S. Congress declined to approve the request.

Under the 17 October 2000 Sharm el-Sheikh agreement (in Egypt) Clinton provided support for Israel's desire to return to the status quo ante (the way things were before) and revive the Oslo process while also heavily pressuring Arafat to 'stop the violence.' Furthermore, Clinton oversaw a secret agreement at Sharm el-Sheikh between Palestinian Preventive Security head Jibril Rajoub and Israel's General Security Services head Avi Dichter for resumption of their cooperation in 'counter-terrorist' activities. These included the re-arrest of Hamas and Islamic Jihad activists, disarming the Tanzim militias (a counter to Palestinian Islamism), joint operations to prevent the creation of "terror cells," and other shared activities so that by the end of December, a special Israeli military unit had assassinated eight senior Fatah leaders. Implementation of the deal was to be overseen by CIA chief George Tenet and the CIA's representative in Tel Aviv. It is also worth noting that an important aspect of the Oslo Accords involved the CIA training of Palestinian policemen to become Israeli surrogate informers and enforcers of "order" in the Occupied Territories.

With U.S. administrations being in cahoots with and brown-nosing Israel, the Oslo accords were in reality nothing but a sham that resulted in the inevitable Palestinian uprising against the new and more oppressive form of occupation imposed by the so-called "peace process." Though the purpose of the Oslo Accords was to provide limited autonomy for the Palestinians, their areas of actual control were segregated into separate enclaves that were surrounded by Israeli-controlled borders; that were punctuated with settlements and settlement roads that violated the territories' integrity; that have witnessed the mushrooming of continued land expropriations, bypass road building, and a rise in the number of new settlements as Palestinian homes are demolished. All these abominable Israeli actions were carried out without any admonition by U.S. administrations who instead increased U.S. economic and military support.

Because Clinton — as he approached the end of his presidential tenure — feared that history may not credit him with some genuine achievement, he convened a summit in July 2000 at Camp David in the hopes of concluding a final Israeli-Palestinian peace agreement. By trying to achieve such an agreement with the usual U.S. predilection for Israel, the U.S. presented the Israeli agenda to the Palestinians as a fait accompli. When, for the first time, the Palestinians did not accede to the U.S.-fronted Israeli proposals, the Clinton Administration unjustly blamed Arafat for the failure of the summit. Shortly thereafter, Clinton appeared on Israeli television in a strong but shameful display of support for the Jewish State, repeating his guarantees of military aid, an upgrading of the strategic relationship, and consideration of moving the U.S. embassy to Jerusalem. Mark Banner concluded his summary of the Clinton Presidency by noting that the man who liked a good screw, had once again screwed both the American and the Palestinian people.

16
Saturday, 27 December 2008
Little Venice, London

Like most people after Christmas and Boxing Day, Mark Banner was trying to recover from having over-indulged so after a light breakfast of toast, coffee, and scanning through the morning papers, he decided on a leisurely walk along the Regent's Canal which branched off from Little Venice and flowed eastwards past Regent's Park. When he reached the towering aviary which as part of London Zoo overlooked the canal, he turned around and walked back home where his parents and Nadine were watching the breaking news on TV.

At about midday Israeli forces without warning had begun a devastating bombing campaign on the Gaza Strip with the stated intention of ending rocket attacks into Israel by armed groups affiliated with Hamas and other Palestinian factions. Though initially surprised by the Israeli tactic of launching its attack on the Jewish Sabbath, Banner quickly realised that the attack was deliberately timed — timing had always been an important factor in all acts of Israeli aggression — to take advantage of the fact that Western nations were still preoccupied with the Christmas Holiday season.

> *Israel should have exploited the repression of the demonstrations in China, when world attention focused on that country, to carry out mass expulsions among the Arabs of the territories.*
> **Benyamin Netanyahu speaking to students at Bar Ilan University, from the Israeli journal *Hotam*, November 24, 1989.**

Banner was equally certain that the military offensive was also a clear message to the incoming U.S. president that it was the Israelis and not the Americans who decided when, where, and how Israel would conduct its Middle East policies. Shortly afterwards Banner received a phone call from an astonished Reisner and they discussed the ramifications of the Israeli assault for about fifteen minutes.

With the arrival of nightfall further reports stated that Israeli missiles had destroyed security compounds and militant bases with Palestinian officials claiming a casualty count of 225 people killed and about 700 wounded. Israel had in the meantime claimed it was responding to an escalation in rocket attacks from Gaza and would continue bombing for "as long as necessary." Israeli Prime Minister Ehud Olmert — who throughout his premiership had been accused of corruption — said the operation "may take some time" and proffered one of the standard Israeli high-principled but totally insincere pledges that a humanitarian crisis would be avoided. Flanked by Israeli Defense Minister Ehud Barak and Foreign Minister Tzipi Livni, Olmert said in a televised statement: "It's not going to last a few days."

Back in August Banner had entered the Gaza Strip from Egypt through the Rafah crossing because to have done so through Israel would have resulted in his getting an Israeli stamp in his passport which would have subsequently prevented him from entering most Arab countries including Lebanon. Rafah had a history dating back thousands of years with it being first mentioned in an inscription of the Egyptian Pharaoh Seti I (1303 BCE). The purpose of Banner's visit had been to report on the Strip's need for humanitarian aid — mainly food and medical supplies — which was a constant necessity due to Israel's land, sea, and air blockade which in 2001 saw Gaza's only airport being bombed and bulldozed by so-called Israeli Defense Forces.

Banner's three-day stay had been during a period of relative calm due to a ceasefire agreement between Israel and the Hamas movement which had subsequently ended on 19 December. Ending of the ceasefire without its renewal had been announced by Ezzedin al-Qassam, the armed wing of Hamas, which blamed the "Zionist enemy" for violating the conditions of the ceasefire by maintaining its blockade of the Gaza Strip. When the political-military movement in control of the Gaza Strip resumed launching rockets at Israeli targets, Israel retaliated on 20 December 2008 with missiles strikes close to the Jabaliya refugee camp. According to Agence France-Presse the rocket fire from the Strip had then been stepped up with around 200 being fired between 19 and 27 December resulting in the death of an Israeli civilian at Netivot.

Banner feared that this offensive was not going to be simply a retaliatory measure by Israel, but a crushing reminder to the Palestinian people that they were still — and would forever continue to be — brutally oppressed; that the West was either morally insolvent, indifferent, or incapable of taking positive action to end such brutal oppression; that any form of Palestinian dissent or resistance to that brutal oppression would be met by an overwhelming and disproportionate Israeli military response; and that such military response would be portrayed — and unquestionably accepted by the West's Holocaust-industry-muzzled-media — as being of a defensive nature in the ongoing "War on Terror." Banner was also certain that Israel would trot out the usual excuses (blatant lies) for the ensuing Palestinian casualties by claiming that the Palestinians had killed their own refugees; that the Palestinians had disinterred bodies from cemeteries and planted them in bombed-out buildings; that the ultimate blame lay with the Palestinians themselves because they backed a terrorist faction; and that armed Palestinians deliberately used innocent refugees as shields during combat.

●　●　●　●　●

As it eventually transpired, the first phase of the operation — lasting from 27 December 2008 to 3 January 2009 — consisted of ongoing air and naval bombardment of Hamas-controlled security posts, smuggling tunnels, Palestinian Authority ministries, jails, and presidential compounds. According to the Israel Defense Forces more than 100 tons of explosives were dropped in the first nine hours of the offensive on a list of targets that had been earmarked over the previous six months — a statement that would suggest Israel had already long planned to launch an offensive which would provide an opportunity for the testing of new state of the art weaponry and serve as a training exercise for the IDF.

The Israeli offensive codenamed Operation Cast Lead had begun with an almost four-minute "shock and awe" campaign by 64 of Israel's fleet of approximately 300 U.S.-supplied F-16 warplanes. Regarded as the IDF's "bomber workhorse," the F-16s were armed with various air-to-ground missiles, rockets, and bombs. Being a multifunctional tactical aircraft, the F-16 could be outfitted with navigation and targeting equipment to also provide support for infantry and artillery units. The combination of such features with the plane's light, compact construction; its ability to travel at supersonic speeds; and its enhanced maneuverability made it ideal for any operation requiring close coordination and rapid response to intelligence data between ground and air combat units intending to strike Palestinian targets.

The F-16s heavily bombed structures across Gaza including more than 50 allegedly Hamas-related security targets and smuggling tunnels along Rafah's border. The F-16s' "general purpose" munitions consisted of M-82 and M-84 high-explosive unguided "dumb bombs," which can be upgraded with precision guidance systems (U.S.-made Paveway II and JDAM kits, respectively). The smaller M-82 carries a 500-lb. warhead, whereas the M-84 carries a 2,000-lb. warhead. The latter is capable of forming craters as big as 50 feet wide and 36 feet deep and can — depending on the height from which it is delivered — penetrate up to 15 inches of metal or 11 feet of concrete with a lethal fragmentation radius of 400 yards. The obliging U.S. had over the years supplied Israel with not less than 1,500 M-82s and 13,500 M-84s along with 4,000 Paveway II and 10,000 JDAM precision guidance upgrade kits. Israel had itself produced a laser-guided variant of the M-83 "dumb bomb" called the PB500A1 which were used to destroy tunnels on the Rafah border. With its sophisticated design, the PB500A1 is a hard-target penetration 1,000-lb. bomb with a blast impact equal to a bomb twice its size and can blast through 6.5 feet of reinforced concrete.

In addition to its warplanes, Israel also deployed U.S.-made AH-64 Apache attack helicopters and AH-1F Cobra helicopter gunships. Apart from their standard equipment with a 1,200-round M230 30 mm cannon, the Apaches were loaded with AGM-114 Hellfire guided missiles and probably Hydra 70 rockets which can be upgraded to carry white phosphorous munitions. Apart from multiple rocket launchers, the Cobras were also equipped with TOW 2 missile systems with each helicopter carrying eight that were guided heavy antitank, anti-bunker, and anti-fortification missiles. The Israeli air force subsequently released disinformation that claimed standing orders during the operation were to use only laser-guided weapons so as to minimise collateral damage and that over 1,000 Hellfire and Orlev missiles were fired by Israeli helicopters during the offensive.

The Israeli navy was used predominantly in a support role with its extensive intelligence capability being fully exploited while its fleet of Super Dvora-class fast patrol boats directed cannon and machine gun fire along the coast. Naval artillery was also involved in the coordinated shelling of inland targets.

The next stage of the operation had then begun at around 8:00pm local time on 3 January when, having struck all possible preselected targets from the air, Israeli ground forces crossed into Gaza with a view to establishing control over Palestinian rocket-firing areas and more precisely targeting Hamas-affiliated facilities. This included occupation of open areas, encirclement of towns and refugee camps, but avoidance of deep penetrations into densely populated areas. In both this and the following stages of the operation Israel relied heavily on UAVs (drones) to provide vital surveillance and remote strike capability. Though primarily providing support to IDF units, UAVs were also frequently used to carry out strikes.

Having helped pioneer the controversial global development and use of unmanned aerial vehicles (UAVs) — more commonly referred to as drones — Israel, as part of its intelligence and remote operating strategy, had fully utilized such vehicles for their ability to provide an agile and mobile aerial advantage that was even beyond the capability of helicopters. For basic intelligence gathering — known as ISTAR: intelligence, surveillance, target acquisition, and reconnaissance — Israel relied on three types of unarmed UAVs: the Hermes 450, the Heron, and the Searcher 2. Though slightly differing in their specifications, they were all designated as medium-altitude/long-endurance (MALE) UAVs with capability of missions of 20–40 hours at heights of 9,500–35,000 feet.

MALE UAVs provided excellent surveillance with day or night imaging (infrared and visible light), a combination of state of the art intelligence systems for the detection of communications between people and electronic communications between machines, GPS navigation or radar systems for precise targeting, sophisticated communications capability for the transfer of images and data in real time wherever needed, and inaudible operation to avoid detection.

For ISTAR and attack purposes, Israel deployed the MQ-1 Predator UAV system which consisted four MALE UAVs, a ground control station, and a satellite communication suite operated by a total of 55 people. Apart from the ISTAR equipment, the UAVs were also loaded with two AGM-114 Hellfire guided missiles. With their infrared and digitally enhanced zoom cameras, the UAVs were able to identify the heat signatures of human bodies from a height of 10,000 feet.

During the offensive Israel also deployed a modified Hermes 450s equipped with 2 Hellfire missiles and 2 domestically made missiles; and the recently developed and largest Eitan UAV which carried more than a ton of weapons. The Eitan, which had been developed for a strike on Iran and tested in war games over the Aegean in July 2008, made its combat debut in the offensive by firing Spike missiles. Human Rights Watch, Amnesty International, and other rights organizations subsequently noted that despite the precise imaging and targeting capabilities of Israeli UAVs, missiles fired from drones appear to have been responsible for a high number of Palestinian civilian deaths. Human rights organizations also confirmed that in a significant number of cases, drones had fired an unidentified missile that dispersed tiny, sharp-edged cubes of purpose-made shrapnel similar to a flechette — a pointed steel projectile with a vaned tail to provide stable flight.

Israel's ground force offensive was supported by one of the world's most technologically advanced artillery corps which connected with the IDF's sophisticated radar and navigation networks so as to maximize accuracy. The corps' most used equipment was the Soltam M-71 towed howitzer, the M109 self- propelled howitzer, the Sholef 155 mm self-propelled howitzer, and the M270 MLRS multiple rocket launcher.

Israel had a standard munitions stockpile of 100,000s of artillery shells supplied courtesy of U.S. taxpayers. Most of the shells were M433 40 mm high-explosive, dual-purpose (HEDP) cartridges and M889A1 81 mm high explosive cartridges. The U.S. had also supplied M107 155 mm high explosive artillery rounds, M141 83 mm bunker defeat munitions, and M930 120 mm illuminating cartridges. The HEDP, M889A1, and M107 provide armour-piercing capability against vehicles and buildings, but were all designed or modified to also serve as anti-personnel fragmentation devices. The M107 sprays about 2,000 pieces of shrapnel; the M141 breaches walls; and the M930 provides phosphorous-free battlefield illumination. In addition to buying general purpose munitions from the U.S., Israel has also jointly developed and produced with U.S. manufacturers its own artillery ammunition, including the M971 120 mm dual-purpose improved conventional munition (DPICM) used during OCL. Intended as an anti-armor and antipersonnel weapon, this artillery shell is essentially a cluster bomb that separates into 24 sub-munitions, each containing more than 1,200 fragments that explode above the target to create a wide and dense area of coverage within a 350-foot radius.

It is estimated that the IDF fired 7,000 of the above mentioned artillery shells as well as numerous antipersonnel fragmentation weapons which apparently did not include the M483A1 DPICM artillery-delivered cluster munition for which Israel received international condemnation during the 2006 Lebanon war. Nonetheless, unexploded ordnance (UXO) was an issue following the operation with two children being killed near Jabaliya refugee camp and the International Committee of the Red Cross issuing an alert as to their existence.

Ground assaults into the Gaza Strip were led by tanks and armored vehicles which attacked identified targets of structures and personnel, and offered troops protection with a standard infantry division operating some 300 tanks and 100s of APCs (armored personnel carriers). Merkava II, III, and IV main battle tanks were also deployed with their 105 mm or 120 mm laser-guided antitank missiles, multiple 7.62 mm or 12.7 mm heavy machine guns, 60 mm mortars, and smoke grenades. The main tank guns were capable of firing high-explosive antitank (HEAT) rounds and sabot rounds that disperse armour-piercing flechettes; upgraded models have superior firing control systems that facilitate a lock on moving targets while on the move with real-time encrypted intelligence data from the IDF drones.

The tanks are routinely armed with grenades, missiles, and heavy machine guns, and guided TOW and Spike missiles. Ground forces following the tanks carried antitank rocket-propelled grenades (RPGs) which can target vehicles or buildings. All battle tanks were heavily armored and resistant to anything less powerful than an antitank guided missile of which Palestinian factions possessed few if any. Human Rights Watch and Amnesty International stated that Israel's precision-guided tank shells were so accurate that they were capable of being fired into windows from a distance of a mile (1.5 km). Numerous reports of tank shells being fired directly into Palestinian homes would therefore suggest that Israeli soldiers routinely targeted homes and buildings whenever signs of movement were detected by tank vision systems. Such a blanket open fire policy was regarded as being illegal under international law.

Israeli Infantry troops were transported in armored personnel carriers equipped with remotely operated machine guns, RPGs, smoke grenades, mortars, rockets, and antitank missiles. APC modifications included the addition of armour, weapons, and in some cases mine ploughs or rollers to clear improvised explosive devices (IEDs). Further modifications included bulldozer blades for demolition, radar assistance for artillery, and communications equipment for command and control in the field.

To further assist its troops, the IDF also deployed some 100 armored CAT D9 bulldozers which in conjunction with the U.S. had been specifically modified to meet IDF requirements which included building barriers and fortifications, demolition; creating routes for other fighting vehicles and infantry, clearing land mines, IEDs, booby traps, and other explosives. The bulldozers were modified with armour and bulletproof windows for protection against IEDs, RPGs, and heavy machine gun and sniper fire. They were equipped with crew-operated machine guns, smoke projectors, and grenade launchers.

The IDF also had at its disposal the use Viper miniature robots, electronic jamming devices, special weapons systems and a variety weapons whose use was controversial and in some cases even illegal. White phosphorous for example was used by infantry, artillery, and helicopters and was exploded both in the air and on impact. It is usually used for signalling, screening, obscuring enemy vision, to block targeting equipment, and incendiary purposes to eliminate enemy resources such as vehicles, fuel depots, and ammunition storage areas.

White phosphorous causes immediate, deep, excruciating chemical burns similar to those caused by napalm and results in delayed healing of wounds. Spraying white phosphorous fires with water — as any chemistry student will know — will only increase the intensity of its chemical reaction. Though white phosphorous munitions are considered legal under international law when used for their intended purposes, their use in areas with dense civilian populations may legally constitute a war crime. Use of such munitions was initially denied by Israel — despite live footage and still photographs showing clearly that white phosphorous was used as early as 5 January — but in the face of irrefutable evidence eventually admitted to their use after the operation had ended.

In view of the glaring disparity between the military resources available to the blockaded and ill-equipped Palestinian factions and the extremely well U.S.-financed and equipped Israelis during Operation Cast Lead, any attempt at comparison between their respective weaponry and resources would be ludicrous.

During what proved to be the last week of the offensive from January12 while the Israeli government debated the wisdom of opening a third stage that would deal Hamas a "knockout blow" Israel concentrated on previously damaged Palestinian rocket-launching sites and mop up operations. The Israeli government was ultimately persuaded against launching a third stage by military and intelligence assessments indicating that such an attempt would require weeks of fighting deep in the Strip's urban areas and refugee camps resulting in heavy casualties on both sides. Such an outcome would undoubtedly have eroded existing strong domestic support for the war, and result in increased international condemnation. So on 17 January — after 22 days of conflict — the Israeli security cabinet adopted a resolution for a unilateral ceasefire with the last of the Israeli soldiers withdrawing from the Gaza Strip on 21 January 2009 — just one day after the inauguration of the new U.S. President, Barack Obama.

A subsequent United Nations report revealed that the Israeli offensive had killed 1,330 (including 431 children and 112 women) and wounded 5,380 Palestinians with only 14 dead Israelis (10 soldiers, of whom four were killed by "friendly fire" and four civilians). According to the Palestinian Authority's central statistics bureau, more than 4,000 Palestinian homes were completely demolished and over 17,000 others were damaged with estimated losses totaling more than two billion dollars.

It could be argued that the casualty totals of Operation Cast Lead were relatively light when compared to the 17,500 — virtually all civilians with the majority being women and children — killed in Israel's 1982 invasion of Lebanon; the conservative estimate of 1,750 Palestinian civilians killed in the Sabra-Chatila massacre; the 106 killed and 116 injured Lebanese civilian refugees —more than half of them children— during the April 1996 Israeli shelling of a United Nations compound near Qana in Southern Lebanon; the 1,000 civilians killed during the Israeli invasion and bombardment in 2006; and at the same time the massacre of the Marwahin where refugees were ordered from their homes before being slaughtered by an Israeli helicopter crew. Needless to say no Israelis have been indicted for any of these crimes because as Israeli Prime Minister Ariel Sharon said in 2001: "Israel may have the right to put others on trial, but certainly no one has the right to put the Jewish people and the state of Israel on trial." Interesting Jewish logic which presumably assumes that having appointed themselves as "God's chosen people," they can only be judged for their crimes against humanity by God Himself in the afterlife.

The Palestinian people were not the only casualties of Operation Cast Lead and the following excerpt from a report by the organisation Reporters Without Borders serves to cast further doubt on Israel's claim to be the only democracy in the Middle East:

News was also a casualty of the conflict. Six journalists were killed between 27 December 2008 and 17 January 2009, two while working, and at least three buildings housing media were hit. Foreign journalists were banned from entering the Gaza Strip throughout the conflict and they were forced to 'cover' at a distance a war which attracted world-wide attention. The blockade prompted protests and indignation from the entire profession.

Israeli journalists have been banned, because of their nationality, from entering the territories for more than two years and the Gaza Strip is regularly closed to foreign journalists by the Israeli authorities. But this ban, from 27 December onwards, while the military offensive had just started, had serious consequences for the work of Palestinian journalists who were the only ones able to cover the conflict. "I wouldn't wish on anyone to live through what we lived through. Every evening, I asked myself how come I was still alive," Shohdi el-Kashef, head of the broadcast news agency Ramattan, in Gaza, told Reporters Without Borders.

Reporters Without Borders went to Israel, the Gaza Strip and the West Bank at the end of January to assess the extent of press freedom violations committed during the conflict.

As Israeli aviation launched its offensive on 27 December 2008, the military authorities closed the Gaza Strip to foreign journalists.

During the second war in Lebanon, in July-August 2006, journalists had been 'embedded' with Israeli troops so as to follow military operations, as reported by Nahum Barnea, of the daily Yedioth Aharonoth. And soldiers used their mobile phones to describe the war live to their families, but also to journalists, sometimes with film as well.

In Gaza, in December 2008, the Israeli military command, drawing lessons from the free media coverage that exposed its shortcomings to the whole world, adopted a completely different approach. They closed the Gaza Strip making it impossible for any foreign journalist to reach the field of battle.

● ● ● ● ●

By the end of that 27 December day, David Reisner had finished his article "telling all" about the illegal tunneling under Temple Mount towards the Dome of the Rock. He had been invited by Banner and Nadine for Sunday lunch the following day which would give him an opportunity to get Mark Banner's opinion on the article before sending it to the *Guardian* newspaper. Right now, however, he needed some fresh air to clear his head and decided that a leisurely retracing of his steps along the canal walk that Banner had shown him was just what he needed. He checked the weather and discovered it was very cold but dry. Easterly winds had ushered in some very cold low-level air from the continent that would result in sharp frosts during the night and early morning.

Though Reisner suspected that Mossad was no doubt monitoring his movements, he had never imagined that his nuisance value warranted their assigning a team of twelve agents to his case. So when he came out of the Frontline Club at around 7:30 p.m., two of them were sitting shivering in a parked car in Norfolk Place. As Reisner reached the junction with Praed Street, one of the agents got out of the car and followed him as he crossed Praed Street and headed northwards towards South Wharf Road and the Paddington Basin. The Mossad agent made a quick call on his mobile which precipitated a flurry of activity amongst the rest of the team members including the rushing by car of a female and two male agents to Little Venice. It had become obvious to them that Reisner was going to walk along the canal.

It was a quiet, cold, overcast evening and with it still being the Christmas holiday weekend, there was hardly anyone to be seen as Reisner turned right from South Wharf Road onto the Paddington Basin. As he reached the Bays Building before the northern entrance to Paddington Station, he was surprised to see three people walking towards him and as they got closer he could make out it was a women between two men and all three appeared to be cheerfully involved in a lively discussion. As their paths crossed just past the Bays building, the man nearest to Reisner suddenly wheeled around and slammed his right hand into Reisner's back. The hand was holding a syringe filled with succinylcholine, a fast-acting muscle relaxant that induces short term paralysis and which has occasionally been used as a paralysing agent for executions by lethal injection. All three agents then grabbed hold of Reisner whose feeble attempt at struggling failed due to loss of his muscle function. There was absolutely nothing he could do to defend himself.

17
Sunday, 28 December 2008
Grand Union Canal Paddington Arm, London

The elderly man with the tartan-coated Scottish terrier on a retractable lead was smartly dressed in a brown herringbone city coat and Dirleton tweed cap which covered most of his greying hair. His customary early morning stroll along the Paddington Arm of the Grand Union Canal which passed through Little Venice always required patience because his dog, Alastair, had a mind of his own with a sniffing curiosity that knew no bounds. They had strolled from Warwick Crescent along Little Venice, under Bishop's Bridge Road, and past the northern entrance to Paddington Station when the man happened to notice something that was much larger than the bits of waste that might be occasionally seen floating in the canal. He walked to the canal bank's edge for a closer look from which point he could clearly discern the shape of what looked like the back of a man's body being gently lapped by the partly frozen water.

The man quickly overcame his initial sense of alarm and after establishing there was no one around to help, he used his mobile phone to dial the 999 emergency number and ask for the police. After giving his details and location to the operator, he was told to wait there until help arrived. The man reckoned on not having to wait too long because about half a mile away was Paddington Green High Security Police Station which happened to be the most important in the United Kingdom. Terrorist suspects were always taken to Paddington Green to be detained and interrogated in the underground cells whose walls, as a precaution, were lined with brown paper. The paper-lining ensured that if any trace of explosives was found on the bodies of suspects, then it could be proven not to have been picked up from the cells. Within ten minutes of the elderly man's call, police units had arrived at the scene to cordon off the area as divers proceeded to retrieve the body.

● ● ● ● ●

Not too far away in Maida Avenue after having a light breakfast with Nadine and his parents, Mark Banner decided to spend the morning going over his chapter on the George W. Bush Jr. presidency. As David Reisner was joining them later for lunch, Banner figured he could make use of the peace and quiet in his father's study for a good three or four hours.

The chapter began by noting that unlike his father, the first President Bush — who regarded himself as an impartial arbiter in the precarious and often violent environment of Middle East politics — Bush Jr. viewed his presidential role as being a righteous crusade against terror. Bush Jr., once again unlike his father, was part of an evangelical Christian community that was a staunchly pro-Israeli component of his conservative Republican constituency.

While Bush Sr. had been tough on Israel — especially with regards to the Israeli settlements in the Occupied Territories that Ariel Sharon had helped develop — Bush Jr. made very clear to then Israeli Prime Minister Ariel Sharon that he would not be following in his father's footsteps, and that he would "use force to protect Israel." This powerful predisposition to support Israel was revealed to Sharon in the Oval Office in March 2001 six months before the 11 September attacks that served to strengthen U.S.-Israeli bonds.

Bush Jr.'s unconditional commitment to Israel represented a generational and philosophical gap between him and his father, one that intensified the mounting friction between their respective foreign policy advisers. Bush Sr.'s advisers expressed deep concern over Bush Jr.'s support for Israel in its campaign against Hezbollah, despite a weekend attack that caused many Lebanese civilians fatalities and triggered international condemnation.

Bush Jr. had hardly settled into the Oval Office when on the morning of 11 September 2001, nineteen hijackers took control of four commercial passenger jets flying out of U.S. east coast airports. Two of the aircraft were deliberately flown into the Twin Towers of the World Trade Centre in New York; a third crashed into the Pentagon (headquarters of the U.S. Department of Defense) in Arlington County, Virginia; and the fourth plane crashed in Pennsylvania without reaching its intended target because the hijackers may have been overpowered by the passengers and crew.

The twin hundred and ten-floor World Trade Center towers — widely regarded as being symbolic of America's power and influence — collapsed as a result and the Pentagon sustained substantial damage. Numerous other buildings at the World Trade Centre site in lower

Manhattan were also destroyed or severely damaged with attack time fatalities totaling 2,977 including the nineteen hijackers.

Suspicion without positive proof immediately fell on the radical Sunni Islamist group al-Qaeda because of its past terrorist activities and opposition to the U.S. starting in 1993 with the first World Trade Centre car bombing with five fatalities and scores of injuries; the shooting down of two American Black Hawk helicopters in Somali in October 1993; the 1996 call by al-Qaeda leader Osama bin Laden for his followers to 'launch a guerrilla war against American forces and expel the infidels from the Arabian Peninsula'; the killing of nineteen Americans in a bombing at a military housing complex in Saudi Arabia in 1996; the bombing of U.S. embassies in Dar Es Salaam and Nairobi in 1998 with the loss of 223 which prompted the Federal Bureau of Investigation (FBI) to place bin Laden on their Ten Most Wanted list with a reward offer of $25million for his capture; and the suicide attack on USS Cole in 2000 killing seventeen servicemen and wounding thirty-nine.

On the evening of 11 September, with al-Qaeda being widely suspected of having conducted the attacks, Bush Jr. — whom Banner refrained from calling a moron so as not to offend morons — described that day's events as "evil, despicable acts of terror" and said that the U.S. was "at war with a new and different kind of enemy." In the following month of October, western coalition forces in conjunction with the anti-Taliban Afghan Northern Alliance launched attacks on Afghanistan.

Though bin Laden had initially denied any involvement in the 11 September 2001 attacks, in 2004 he claimed responsibility citing as his motive the U.S. support for Israel, the presence of U.S. troops in Saudi Arabia, and the sanctions against Iraq. Bin Laden's delay in taking responsibility may have been due to the fact that al-Qaeda was not actually responsible — there are some credible conspiracy theories including an Israeli false flag operation — and it was only subsequently that he decided to exploit the situation by claiming responsibility so as to enhance al-Qaeda's standing and reputation.

Irrespective of who was responsible for the 11 September attacks, the fact remained that terrorism had struck a blow against freedom because many countries reacted by strengthening their anti-terrorism legislation and expanded law enforcement powers to a draconian extent that encroached on civil liberties in the name of national security. Unfortunately the concept of national security has since been cited not only to justify state intrusion into the lives of private citizens, but also to eliminate the need for transparency by governments — a definite victory for terrorism over democracy.

Following the 11 September attacks on New York, Bush Jr. launched the War on Terror by having a U.S. military and a limited international coalition invade Afghanistan on 7 October 2001 where Osama Bin Laden — the alleged brainchild of the New York attacks — was in hiding. In his January 2002 State of the Union address, Bush Jr. referred to an axis of evil including Iraq, Iran, and North Korea. The well-intentioned but somewhat wacko President appeared to be sadly oblivious to the existence of that other axis of evil consisting of the U.S., Israel, and Saudi Arabia.

As part of his war on terror, Bush Jr. issued an executive order authorizing the President's Surveillance Program which included allowing the NSA to monitor communications between suspected terrorists outside the U.S and parties within the U.S. without obtaining a warrant as required by the Foreign Intelligence Surveillance Act (FISA). Other provisions of the surveillance program have remained highly classified and when the Department of Justice Office of Legal Counsel questioned the program's original legal opinion that FISA did not apply in a time of war, the program was subsequently re-authorized by Bush Jr. on the basis that the warrant requirements of FISA were implicitly superseded by the subsequent passage of the Authorization for Use of Military Force Against Terrorists.

The program proved to be controversial with critics of the administration and organisations such as the American Bar Association who argued that it was illegal. A U.S. district court judge ruled in August 2006, that the NSA electronic surveillance program was unconstitutional, but on 6 July 2007, that ruling was annulled by the U.S. Court of Appeals for the Sixth Circuit on the grounds that the plaintiffs lacked standing (failed to demonstrate to the court sufficient connection to and harm from the law).

In a fit of arrogant superpower petulance, Bush Jr. wasted no time in implementing counter-productive Neocon policies starting with the 13 December 2001 withdrawal of the U.S. from the 1972 Anti-Ballistic Missile Treaty because he concluded it hindered the U.S.'s ability to develop ways to protect the American people from future terrorist or rogue state missile attacks. Instead he supported a National Missile Defense project being designed to detect intercontinental ballistic missiles and destroy them in flight. Critics doubted the efficacy of the project which at the cost of $53 billion was the Pentagon's largest funding for any single item.

Bush Jr. also cranked up diplomatic tensions with the People's Republic of China and North Korea with the latter in 2003 admitting to being in the process of building nuclear weapon which it threatened to use if provoked by the U.S. There was also grave U.S concerns — vigorously encouraged by Israel — that Iran may also be developing nuclear weapons despite Iran's insistence that its nuclear energy program was for peaceful use. Strained relations between the U.S. and North Korea, and doubts over Iran's nuclear intentions have remained to this day.

Bush Jr.'s first visit to Europe in June 2001 was met with criticism from European leaders over the U.S. rejection of the Kyoto Protocol which was intended to reduce the carbon dioxide emissions that were contributing to global warming. Despite criticism by many governments, he asserted that the Protocol was "unfair and ineffective" because it would exempt 80 percent of the world and "cause serious harm to the U.S. economy."

In a 22 January 2002 press conference, the Bush Administration's Secretary of Defense Donald H. Rumsfeld gave three reasons for the decision to establish the Guantanamo Bay detention camp (Gitmo) which were: to detain extraordinarily dangerous prisoners, to interrogate prisoners in an optimal setting, and to prosecute prisoners for war crimes. This controversial U.S. military prison was located within the Guantanamo Bay Naval Base in Cuba where the Global War on Terror's captives — mostly from Afghanistan with smaller numbers from Iraq, the Horn of Africa and Southeast Asia — were transported and detained incommunicado.

After Bush Jr.'s political appointees at the U.S. Office of Legal Counsel at the Department of Justice advised his administration that the Guantanamo Bay detention camp could be considered outside U.S. legal jurisdiction, the administration asserted that detainees were not entitled to any of the protections of the Geneva Conventions. Since then U.S. Supreme Court decisions starting in 2004 have determined otherwise with the ruling that the courts have jurisdiction. On 29 June 2006 the court ruled in *Hamdan v. Rumsfeld,* that detainees were entitled to the minimal protections listed under Common Article 3 of the Geneva Conventions. The ruling was followed on 7 July 2006 with the issue of an internal Department of Defense memo stating that prisoners would, in the future, be entitled to protection under Common Article 3.

Current and former prisoners have reported abuse and torture which the Bush Jr. Administration — led by Vice President Dick Cheney (an unindicted war criminal you would not want walking behind you in a dark alley) — strenuously denied. In an Amnesty International 2005 report, the facility was called the "Gulag of our times." The UN in 2006 was unsuccessful in its bid to have the camp closed with one judge observing that "America's idea of what is torture . . . does not appear to coincide with that of most civilized nations."

On 1 July 2002 the International Criminal Court (ICC) came into being as the first ever permanent, treaty based, international criminal court established to promote the rule of law and ensure that the gravest international crimes do not go unpunished. Later in August of that year, the American Service-members Protection Act (ASPA) was passed by the U.S. Congress "to protect United States military personnel and other elected and appointed officials of the United States government against criminal prosecution by an international criminal court to which the United States is not a party."

One of Bill Clinton's legacies for the Bush Jr. Administration was his 1998 signing into law of the Iraq Liberation Act with the U.S. government officially calling for regime change in Iraq. Subsequently the Republican Party's 2000 campaign platform called for "full implementation" of the act and the removal of Iraqi president Saddam Hussein by focusing on the rebuilding a coalition, the imposition of tougher sanctions, the reinstating of inspections, and support for the Iraqi National Congress (an umbrella opposition group led by Ahmed Chalabi).

The controversial and somewhat shady Chalabi, with the assistance of lobbying powerhouse BKSH & Associates — known for representing anti-democratic dictators and regimes in Nigeria, Philippines, Somalia, and Zaire — provided most of the information on which U.S. Intelligence based its condemnation of the Iraqi president Saddam Hussein including reports of weapons of mass destruction and alleged ties to al-Qaeda. Most, if not all, of Chalabi's information turned out to be false with Chalabi being a concocter who may possibly have been — and probably was — assisted, encouraged, and financially rewarded by Mossad.

In his 2007 book, *The Blair Years,* Alastair Campbell, former British Prime Minister Tony Blair's communications director and vicious attack dog, revealed that in conversations with Bush Jr. in late 2002, then Israeli Prime Minister Ariel Sharon threatened to nuke Baghdad if Saddam Hussein launched missiles against Israel as had occurred during the 1991 Gulf War. Considering that Iraq's hardly state of the art Soviet SCUD missiles could never have been a serious threat to Israel, the threat to use nuclear weapons was the response expected from responsible and sane political leaders. The psychotic unindicted war criminal Sharon no doubt intended his threat to pressure Bush Jr. to attack Iraq.

In their book, *The Israeli Lobby,* John Mearsheimer and Stephen M. Walt contend that one of the main driving forces behind Bush Jr.'s invasion of Iraq in 2003 was the Israeli lobby. As evidence for this contention the authors cite the central role played in propagandizing for the war by Neoconservative figures such as Richard Perle (chair of the Defense Advisory Committee), Paul Wolfowitz (deputy Secretary of Defense), Douglas Feith (undersecretary of Defense for planning who also happened to be a militant West Bank settler), other officials such as Irv Lewis "Scooter" Libby (convicted of perjury), David Wurmser and John Hannah — who all at one time or another were high-ranking members of Israeli lobbies.

Mearsheimer and Walt noted that for decades, and especially since the Six-Day War in 1967, the focus of U.S. Middle Eastern policy had been its relationship with Israel. Unwavering support for the Israelis coupled with U.S. Attempts to foist 'democracy' on the region had inflamed Arab and Islamic perceptions and compromised the security of both the U.S. and of much of the rest of the world. U.S. willingness to set aside its own security and that of many of its allies in order to advance the interests of another state, was an unequalled situation in American political history. Though it could be argued that the bond between the two nations was based on shared strategic interests or compelling moral imperatives, such an argument does not account for the extraordinary level of material and diplomatic support that the U.S. provides.

Furthermore, the main thrust of U.S. policy in the region is derived almost entirely from domestic politics driven by the activities of the Israel lobby. Though other special-interest groups have managed to occasionally skew U.S. foreign policy, none has managed to divert it as far from what the U.S. national interests required while simultaneously convincing the American people that U.S. interests and those of the other country — in this instance, Israel — were inherently synonymous.

According to Mearsheimer and Walt, Since the October 1973 War, the U.S. has provided Israel with a level of support dwarfing that given to any other state. Israel had been the largest annual recipient of direct economic and military assistance since 1976, and was the largest recipient in total since World War Two, to the tune of well over $140 billion (in 2004 dollars). Israel receives about $3 billion in direct assistance each year, roughly one-fifth of the foreign aid budget, and worth about $500 a year for every Israeli. This largesse is especially striking since Israel is now a wealthy industrial state with a per capita income roughly equal to that of South Korea or Spain.

Other recipients of U.S. aid receive their money in quarterly instalments, but Israel gets its entire appropriation at the beginning of each fiscal year and can thus earn interest on it. Most recipients of aid given for military purposes are required to spend all of it in the U.S., but Israel is allowed to use roughly 25 per cent of its allocation to subsidise its own defence industry. Israel is also the only aid recipient that does not have to account for how that aid is spent, thereby making it virtually impossible to prevent the money from being used for purposes opposed by the U.S. such as the building of illegal settlements on the West Bank. Moreover, the U.S. has provided Israel with nearly $3 billion to develop weapons systems, and given it access to such state of the art weaponry as Blackhawk helicopters and F-16 jets. Finally, the US gives Israel access to intelligence denied to its NATO allies and while insisting on non-proliferation of nuclear weapons in the Middle East, it hypocritically ignores Israel's possession of nuclear weapons.

The U.S. gives Israel consistent diplomatic support with more than thirty U.S. vetoes since 1982 of Security Council resolutions critical of Israel — more than the total number of vetoes cast by all the other Security Council members. The U.S. blocks Arab state efforts to put Israel's nuclear arsenal on the International Atomic Energy's agenda; it comes to the rescue in wartime and takes Israel's side when negotiating peace; the Nixon administration protected it from the threat of Soviet intervention and resupplied it during the War; it was deeply involved in the negotiations that ended that war, as well as in the lengthy step-by-step process that followed; and it played a key role in the negotiations that preceded and followed the 1993 Oslo Accords. In each case there was occasional friction between U.S. and Israeli officials, but the U.S. consistently supported the Israeli position. One American participant at Camp David in 2000 later said that "far too often, we functioned . . . as Israel's lawyer." Finally, the Bush Jr. administration's ambition to

330

transform the Middle East was at least partly aimed at improving Israel's strategic situation.

Such extraordinary U.S. generosity might be understandable if Israel were a vital strategic asset or if there were compelling moral grounds for unconditional U.S. backing. But neither possibility provides convincing justification. It could be argued that Israel was an asset during the Cold War; that by serving as America's proxy after 1967, it helped contain Soviet expansion in the region; that it inflicted humiliating defeats on Soviet clients like Egypt and Syria; that it occasionally helped protect U.S. allies such as King Hussein of Jordan; that its military prowess forced Moscow to spend more on backing its own client states; and that it provided useful intelligence about Soviet capabilities.

Backing Israel — as President Truman had suspected prior to its 1948 establishment as a state — has been not only a heavy financial burden for the U.S., but it has also complicated U.S. relations with the Arab world. The U.S. decision to give Israel $2.2 billion in emergency military aid during the 1973 October War triggered an OPEC oil embargo that inflicted considerable damage on Western economies. Furthermore Israel's armed forces were not in a position to protect U.S. interests in the region because the U.S, could not for instance rely on Israel when the Iranian Revolution in 1979 raised concerns about the security of oil supplies, and had to create its own Rapid Deployment Force instead.

The extent to which Israel was becoming a strategic liability became apparent during the first Gulf War when the U.S. avoided using Israeli bases so as not to rupture the anti-Iraq coalition. Instead resources (e.g. Patriot missile batteries) had to be diverted to prevent Tel Aviv doing anything that might harm the alliance against Saddam Hussein. The problem reoccurred in 2003 when despite Israel's eagerness for the US to attack Iraq, Bush Jr. could not request its assistance without triggering Arab opposition. So Israel once again remained on the sidelines while others did the dirty work and paid the price.

During the 1990s, and even more so following the 9 September attacks, U.S. support has been justified by the false assertion that both states were threatened by terrorism originating from the Arab and Muslim world, and by "rogue states" that backed these groups seeking weapons of mass destruction. This is was interpreted as meaning not only that the U.S. should give Israel a carte blanche in dealing with the Palestinians — while not pressing for it to make concessions until all Palestinian "terrorists" were imprisoned or dead — but that the U.S.

should also aggressively pursue countries like Iran and Syria. Israel was thus portrayed as a crucial ally in the war on terror, because its enemies were America's enemies. In reality, Israel is a liability in the war on terror and the broader effort to deal with rogue states.

Mearsheimer and Walt's book makes it clear that "terrorism" is not a single adversary, but a tactic employed by a wide array of political groups. The terrorist organizations that threaten Israel do not threaten the United States, except when it intervenes against them as was the case in Lebanon in 1982. Furthermore, Palestinian "terrorism" is not indiscriminate violence directed against Israel or the West; it is more precisely a desperate response to Israel's prolonged brutal campaign to colonize the West Bank and Gaza Strip.

To therefore suggest that Israel and the U.S. are allied by a shared terrorist threat is a cockeyed explanation that disregards the fact that the U.S. problem with terrorism is mostly due to its being so closely allied with Israel, not the other way around. U.S. support for Israel is not the only source of anti-American sentiment and terrorism, but it is a vital one that makes winning the war on terror much more difficult. There is no question that many al-Qaida leaders, including Osama bin Laden, were motivated by Israel's presence in Jerusalem and the plight of the Palestinian people. Unconditional support for Israel makes it easier for extremists to rally popular support and to attract recruits of whom many are motivated by a sense of injustice.

As for the so-called Middle Eastern rogue states, they are not in any way a serious threat to U.S. interests, except in that they are a threat to Israel. Even if those states were to acquire nuclear weapons — an obviously undesirable situation — neither the U.S. nor Israel could be blackmailed, because the blackmailer could not carry out the threat without suffering overwhelming retaliation. The danger of a nuclear handover to terrorists is equally remote, because a rogue state could not be sure the transfer would go undetected or that it would not be blamed and punished afterwards. The close relationship with Israel actually makes it harder for the U.S. to deal with those states. Israel's nuclear arsenal is the main reason why some of its neighbors desire nuclear weapons, and threatening them with regime change merely increases that desire.

Finally, another reason to question Israel's strategic value is its blatant failure to behave like a loyal ally. Israeli officials repeatedly ignore U.S. requests and renege on pledges such as to stop building settlements and to stop the "targeted assassinations" of Palestinian leaders. In order to serve its own interests Israel has provided sensitive military technology to potential U.S. rivals like China, in what the State Department inspector-general called "a systematic and growing pattern of unauthorized transfers." According to the General Accounting Office, Israel also "conducts the most aggressive espionage operations against the US of any ally." In addition to the case of Jonathan Pollard, who gave Israel large quantities of classified material in the early 1980s — which it reportedly passed on to the Soviet Union in return for more exit visas for Soviet Jews — a new controversy erupted in 2004 when it was revealed that a key Pentagon official called Larry Franklin had passed classified information to an Israeli diplomat. Israel is hardly the only country that spies on the US, but its willingness to spy on its principal patron casts further doubt on its strategic value as a so-called ally.

As was to be expected, Mearsheimer and Walt's well-documented and reasoned book was met not by an equally well-documented and reasoned rebuttal, but by the ever so familiar and tiresome ploy of denouncing the authors as "anti-Semites"; and this from a bunch of warmongering bigots with racist tendencies towards Arabs. There was not only the suggestion that the book lacked sufficient evidence, but there was also a choreographed chorus by prominent politicos who pushed the bounds of credibility by denying the existence of either Neoconservatives or an Israeli lobby. The audacity of such denials represents the lowest form of chicanery given that it is no secret that AIPAC vigorously pushed for the invasion of Iraq in the U.S. Congress. Having successfully inveigled the U.S. into invading Iraq, APAIC could then concentrate on coercing the U.S. into also destroying Syria and Iran.

Bush Jr., who In November 2001 had asked then Secretary of Defense Donald Rumsfeld — the same Rumsfeld who in 1983 met with Saddam Hussein in Baghdad and arranged U.S. military assistance for Iraq's war against Iran — to begin developing a war plan for Iraq, began in early 2002 to publicly press for regime change on the grounds that the Iraqi government had ties to terrorist groups, was developing weapons of mass destruction, and did not cooperate sufficiently with UN weapons inspectors. Having by January 2003, convinced himself that diplomacy was not working, Bush Jr. began notifying allies such as Saudi Arabia that war was inevitable and imminent.

Despite there being no agreement within the UN Security Council authorising the use of force, the war was nonetheless launched after Bush Jr., in a speech on March 17, effectively declared war on Iraq with the objective of ensuring U.S. national security with "no more poison factories, no more executions of dissidents, no more torture chambers and rape rooms." It can only be assumed that Bush Jr.s righteous revulsion over the use of torture was not applicable to the U.S. Guantanamo Bay detention camp. It has been suggested that Bush Jr. once read a book, if he did, then it was not ***The Arrogance of Power*** by **William J. Fulbright from which the following is a quote about pre-emptive war:**

A pre-emptive war in "defense" of freedom would surely destroy freedom, because one simply cannot engage in barbarous action without becoming a barbarian, because one cannot defend human values by calculated and unprovoked violence without doing mortal damage to the values one is trying to defend.

In preparation for the invasion, one hundred thousand U.S. troops were assembled in Kuwait by 18 February and on 19 March 2003 the illegal invasion of Iraq — Operation Iraqi Freedom — was launched because of Iraq's alleged possession of weapons of mass destruction (WMDs). The invasion involved twenty-one days of major combat operations by a combined force — with troops from the U.S. (148,000), the UK (45,000), Australia (2,000), and Poland (194) — that deposed the Ba'athist government of Saddam Hussain. The invasion stage of the war was primarily conventionally-fought and ended with the capture by U.S. forces of the Iraqi capital, Baghad. While the combined invading force consisted mostly of American troops, support was also received from Kurdish irregulars in Iraqi Kurdistan with thirty-six other countries becoming involved in the aftermath of a seemingly endless war.

Saddam Hussein was deposed when Baghdad was captured on 10 April 2003 and went into hiding in a narrow underground passage on a remote farm near his home town of Tikrit. He was subsequently located and arrested after being betrayed by a relative who had been one of his closest bodyguards. The ensuing trial was regarded by many as being a show trial in a kangaroo court with Amnesty International stating that the trial was "unfair." Saddam was in due course found guilty of crimes against humanity, and hanged on Saturday 30 December 2006. Human Rights Watch noted that Saddam's execution followed "a flawed trial and marks a significant step away from the rule of law in Iraq." Those who denied Saddam Hussein due process — irrespective of how vile and despotic he was — are no better than he was.

The occupation of Iraq ultimately proved extremely onerous with many Iraqis and foreigners attacking U.S. forces stationed in the country. Eventually, the U.S. death toll in the post-war occupation surpassed that of the actual war itself. Iraqi violence and fatalities are still occurring on a daily basis and will go on occurring for an indefinite time. As the invasion was deliberately launched on the false premise that Iraq possessed weapons of mass destruction, it has to be asked whether Bush Jr. and Tony Blair were any less guilty of crimes against humanity than that despot Saddam Hussein. These two war criminals who claim to having received divine guidance, are also guilty of sending young American and British military personnel to Iraq to be unnecessarily killed, seriously maimed, or mentally scarred for life.

As part of his war on terror, Bush Jr. authorised the CIA to use waterboarding as one of several enhanced interrogation techniques (torture) which between 2002 and 2003 the CIA considered to be legal based on a secret Justice Department legal opinion arguing that terror detainees were not protected by the Geneva Convention's ban on torture. Based on and under the authority of the Bybee Memo from the Attorney General — subsequently withdrawn — the CIA had water-boarded certain key terrorist suspects. Though not permitted by U.S. Army Field Manuals which assert "that harsh interrogation tactics elicit unreliable information," the Bush administration nonetheless believed that such enhanced interrogations "provided critical information" that would save American lives. Some critics including author and former CIA officer Robert Baer, who stated that such information was suspect because "you can get anyone to confess to anything if the torture's bad enough." Baer's books *See No Evil* and *Sleeping with the Devil* were the basis for the 2005 Academy Award-winning motion picture *Syriana* with George Clooney in the role of Bob Barnes, a character loosely based on Baer.

Bush Jr. and Blair are also guilty of undermining the concept of democracy because the majority of the people in the U.S. and the UK — not to mention in over sixty countries worldwide — were fervent in their opposition to war. On January 16, 2003, protests were held worldwide in opposition to the war including in Argentina, Belgium, Egypt, Japan, Pakistan, Turkey, the Netherlands, and the U.S. where Americans attended a rally in Washington, D.C. on the National Mall.

Two days later anti-war demonstrations took place in villages, towns, and cities around the world, including Auckland, Bonn, Cairo, Christchurch, Cologne, Dublin, Dunedin, Florence, Gothenburg, Istanbul, London, Montreal, Moscow, Oslo, Ottawa, Paris, Rotterdam, Tokyo, Toronto, and in the U.S. NION (Not in our Name) and ANSWER (Act Now to Stop War and End Racism) jointly organised protests in Washington, D.C. and San Francisco with other protests taking place all over the United States. Even before the invasion it became clear to many observers that this was a hurried, botched-up operation with insufficient planning having been made for the stability of post-war Iraq. Consequently both Bush Jr. and Blair were throughout the course of the Iraq war the target of severe criticism.

On 1 May 2003, a smiling, swaggering Bush Jr. — in an olive flight suit, ejection harness between his legs, and helmet tucked under his arm — emerged from a fixed-wing Lockheed S-3 Viking aircraft after an arrested landing on the aircraft carrier USS Abraham Lincoln. Then standing directly under a "Mission Accomplished" banner, he arrogantly declared that "In the battle of Iraq, the United States and our allies have prevailed." Yeah right!

Having "accomplished" his mission in Iraq (for Israel), Bush Jr. refocussed his spasmodic attention span on resuming the Israeli-Palestinian peace process by declaring his desire for a Palestinian state to be created before 2005. He outlined a road map for peace in cooperation with the European Union, Russia, and the UN which outlined compromises that had to be made by both sides before the goal of Palestinian statehood could become a reality. One of his proposals was the insistence on new Palestinian leadership which saw the appointment of the first ever Palestinian Prime Minister on April 29, 2003. Bush Jr. had denounced the Palestinian Liberation Organization's leader Yasser Arafat for continued support of violence and militant groups. Following continued violence, however, and the resignation of the new Palestinian Prime Minister Mahmoud Abbas, the road map for peace stalled within months and by the end of 2003 neither side had done what had been outlined in the plan.

Also in 2003 — as a result of the Second Intifada which started in September 2000 and ended in 2005 — Israel's economy experienced a sharp downturn which the U.S. alleviated with $9 billion in conditional loan guarantees made available through 2011 with an annual negotiation at the U.S.-Israel Joint Economic Development Group. Though All recent

U.S. administrations had to some degree shown disapproval of Israel's settlement activity which undermined the emergence of a contiguous Palestinian state, Bush Jr. — no doubt prompted by his Israeli lackey advisors — stressed the need to take into account changed "realities on the ground, including already existing major Israeli population centers" as it was "unrealistic to expect that the outcome of final status negotiations will be full and complete return to the armistice lines of 1949." He subsequently emphasized that it was a subject for negotiations between the parties which was his way of copping out because continued Jewish settlement building in the Occupied Territories was Israel's way of making a de facto claim — possession is ninety percent of the law — on Palestinian land. So while realizing and admitting that continued Jewish settlement building in the Occupied Territories was a major and possibly even permanent obstacle to a two-state solution, the U.S. nonetheless continued to tolerate and support illegal Israeli settlement policies.

In April 2004 Bush announced his endorsement of Israeli Prime Minister Ariel Sharon's plan to disengage from the Gaza Strip but retain the illegal Jewish settlements in the West Bank. He also confirmed his agreement with Sharon's policy of denying the right of return to Palestinians who had previously lived in Palestine, while simultaneously offering the "right of return" to Jews who had never previously set foot in the Holy Land. This major departure from previous U.S. foreign policy in the region resulted in condemnation from Arafat, European governments, and Arab leaders with Egyptian President Hosni Mubarak commenting that Bush Jr.'s policies had led to an "unprecedented hatred" by Arabs for America.

During Bush Jr.'s presidency, several American politicians sought to either investigate him for allegedly impeachable offenses, or to bring actual impeachment charges on the floor of the of the U.S. House of Representatives Judiciary Committee. The most significant attempt occurred on 10 June 2008, when two Congressmen introduced thirty-five articles of impeachment against him to the U.S. House of Representatives. Of the thirty-five articles, most were related to the 2003 invasion of Iraq with another fifteen directly concerning alleged misconduct by Bush Jr. in seeking authority for the war, and in the conduct of that military action. The House voted 251 to 166 to refer the impeachment resolution to the Judiciary Committee on 11 June where no further action was taken. Bush Jr's presidency ended on January 20,

2009 and with the completion of his second term in office, impeachment efforts were left unresolved.

Bush Jr. had begun his presidency with approval ratings of around fifty percent. Following the 11 September attacks those ratings shot up to ninety percent where they remained for about four months before dropping to around fifty percent for the rest of his first term. During most of his second term the ratings fell as low as nineteen percent. In a 2006 Siena College survey which asked experts — seven hundred and forty-four professors responded — this question: "George W. Bush has just finished five years as President. If today was the last day of his presidency, how would you rate him?" The responses were Great: two percent; Near Great: five percent; Average: eleven percent; Below Average: twenty-four percent; Failure: fifty-eight percent. To the question "In your judgment, do you think he has a realistic chance of improving his rating?" Sixty-seven percent responded no; twenty-three percent responded yes; and ten percent chose no opinion or not applicable.

The question of how Bush Jr. had managed to get any kind of following at all may be answered by the fact that in the U.S. there are numerous households where the size of the TV screen exceeds by far the size of the bookshelf. Otherwise how else could TV channels like Rupert Murdoch's so-called Fox News Channel manage to get viewers? Furthermore, Surely the citizens of a superpower deserve much more than the biased, low-IQ political comments of a Rush Limbaugh — who in fairness — may be marginally more intelligent than Bush Jr..

● ● ● ● ●

It had been arranged that Reisner would come around at one o'clock for a leisurely drink and chat before they all lunched at two, but when by one-thirty he had not arrived, Banner tried calling his mobile only to get the voicemail. When Reisner had not arrived by two o'clock and was still not answering his phone, banner tried the club but no one had seen him that morning. Banner and family waited another half hour before starting to have lunch which being a roast could not be kept waiting any longer. What should have been an enjoyable afternoon was somewhat marred by Banner's obvious preoccupation and concern for his friend. Later that day as the family watched the early evening news, they learnt that an unidentified body had been found in the canal. An alarmed Banner immediately phoned Paddington Green Police station and informed them that the unidentified body could be that of David Reisner and was told that they would call him back to arrange for him to view the body.

18
Monday, 29 December 2008
Oxford Street, London

Mark Banner had a busy schedule for the day ahead of him starting with a formal identification of Reisner's body at the St. Pancras mortuary followed by a visit to Paddington Police Station where he was due to help the police with their enquiries by providing a full statement regarding what he knew of Reisner. The postmortem had yet to be completed but bruising and a needle mark in the lumber region of the back suggested that death was neither accidental nor from natural causes. *The murdering bastards got to him,* Banner thought to himself as he resolved that he would continue with what Reisner had planned on doing.

Later at the police station, Banner enquired from the officers if they had found a map amongst Reisner's personal effects, but was informed that apart from some books, magazines, and his laptop with his newspaper articles, there was no map in his room which did not appear to have been broken into. Banner concluded that Reisner must have had the map on him and his killers had taken it. Banner conveyed everything he knew to the officers but did not hold out much hope of their catching the culprits who had probably already left the country with their false identities and passports.

• • • • •

Nadine had offered to go with Banner to the mortuary and the police station but as they had already planned to visit the Wallace Collection, he insisted on her going ahead without him and arranged to meet her at the main entrance to the Selfridges department store at one o'clock after which they would go for lunch at steakhouse in nearby Maddox Street. On her two previous visits to London with Banner Nadine had wanted to visit the Collection but a tight schedule had prevented them from doing so.

As a national museum, the Wallace Collection at Hertford House in Manchester Square displayed the amazing works of art collected in the eighteenth and nineteenth centuries by the first four Marquesses of Hertford and Sir Richard Wallace, the son of the fourth Marquess. The

Collection was bequeathed to the British nation by Sir Richard's widow, Lady Wallace, in 1897. Hertford House, the main London townhouse of its former owners, provides a sumptuous setting for the nearly 5,500 objects of which the quality and breadth of eighteenth-century French paintings, Sèvres porcelain, and French furniture is best known.

After spending almost three hours going through the six curatorial departments of Pictures and Miniatures, Ceramics and Glass, Sculpture and Works of Art, Arms and Armour, Sèvres porcelain and Gold Boxes and Furniture, Nadine left Hertford House and walked southwards along the east side of Duke Street to the corner of Oxford Street where she joined a large crowd of shoppers waiting for the traffic lights to change before crossing over. As it was winter, there was nothing unusual about the man standing behind Nadine and whose features were barely discernible because of the Trapper Hat he was wearing.

The traffic lights changed and the crowd surged forward to cross over and as Nadine stepped on the curb on the other side, the man close behind her with his gloved right hand by his side, flicked open a nine-inch switchblade stiletto, expertly stabbed her, and left the knife sticking in her lower back. As she fell forward there was no immediate reaction from the people around her who were more intent on rushing to their destinations. It was not until one woman screamed on seeing the knife in Nadine's back that some other people stopped to help. By that time the man had casually veered away to his left and threaded his way through the slow moving traffic to the other side of Oxford Street where he hailed a cab and climbed in.

"Heathrow Airport, terminal three," Pyotr Gregov said as he removed his Trapper Hat, sat back, took out the mobile, and called Conrad Brown, "The package has been dispatched."

"Okay, I'm on my way . . . see you there."

●　●　●　●　●

When Mark Banner arrived in a cab and got out by Selfridges main entrance there was a lot of commotion and a crowd milling around the Duke Street corner. The priority of meeting with Nadine overcame his natural journalistic curiosity and he remained by the main entrance to the store as the sound of deafening sirens preceded the arrival of a police car followed minutes later by an ambulance. Two more police cars soon arrived and started moving the crowd back, cordoning off the area, and closing Duke Street to traffic.

As Banner stood there patiently waiting for Nadine, he heard a passer-by mention that a woman had been stabbed. He was suddenly overcome by a chilling sense of foreboding. *Oh no,* he thought as he panicked and started running towards the scene of the incident. He explained to a policeman who tried to keep him back that the woman might be his girlfriend and was escorted towards the prostate body on the stretcher. The woman's face was obscured by the two kneeling paramedics but seeing the woman's face was not necessary for Banner who instantly recognized Nadine's distinctive camel-hair trench coat and sage calf boots. The sudden and overwhelming torment deep within the pit of his stomach built up and like the molten-lava of an erupting volcano surged upwards but when he opened his mouth to vent his anguish, there was no sound. He fell to his knees and sobbed quietly like a child.

The ensuing ambulance rush to hospital and the events that immediately followed were but a haze of bewilderment and concern as an agitated and now angry Banner paced the A&E reception floor awaiting news of Nadine's condition. Banner's shocked parents arrived at 2:45 p.m. to console their grief-stricken son but to no avail. Finally at 3:50 p.m. they were informed that Nadine was in a coma on life support in intensive care as a result of having her spinal cord severed by the extremely sharp blade.

The doctor was sympathetic and explained that the spinal cord was about eighteen inches long extending from the base of the brain, surrounded by the vertebral bodies, down the middle of the back, to about the waist. Nerves situated within the spinal cord were upper motor neurons and their function was to carry messages to and from the brain to the spinal nerves along the spinal tract. Spinal nerves that branched out from the spinal cord to the other parts of the body were the lower motor neurons. Spinal nerves entered and exited at each vertebral level and communicated with specific areas of the body. In Nadine's case the severe damage of the spinal nerves would most certainly result in paralysis.

Having to contend with two calamities — first the murder of a journalist friend and now the vicious and unwarranted attack on someone he loved dearly — within a period of little more than twenty-four hours, was emotionally overwhelming and Banner was near to collapse. He was, however, determined to remain at the hospital all night and after his own parents left, he phoned Nadine's who promised to catch the first available flight to London. It was going to be a long, sleepless, and heartbreaking night for a man who had spent a good part of his life reporting on violence and human despair.

19
Tuesday, 30 December 2008
Little Venice, London

Having spent most of the previous night dozing in a chair by Nadine's bedside, Banner looked a sorry mess in the morning and had been persuaded by the nurses to at least go home for a shower, a change of clothing and some breakfast. After a hurried breakfast of two cups of strong black coffee, Banner grabbed his laptop and rushed back to the hospital to learn that there was no change in Nadine's condition. The sight of her lying there on life support was heartbreaking and though he was physically and mentally drained he was spurred on by the realization that they had punished him by hurting the one person who meant more to him than anything and anyone else in the world. He opened his laptop, paused for a moment, and then started to pound the keypad furiously:

Mark Banner

Tuesday, 30 December 2008
London

Israel's Ruthless Quest fir Temple Mount

Back in 1976 Bob Greene — a pioneering investigative journalist who uncovered corruption in Arizona after a journalist was murdered there and during thirty-seven years as a reporter and editor at *Newsday* twice helped win the Pulitzer Prize for Public Service — said that conducting a journalistic investigation was like climbing a mountain studded with bear traps. When you finally reach the top, you find the glory all too short-lived. En route you pass lawsuits, embarrassed publishers, and boycotts by advertisers. You lose your friends and get threatened with prison. Sometimes you die.

Last Saturday evening, David Reisner, an Israeli investigative journalist, died. Or to be more precise — he was murdered by the Mossad. This is a tribute to Reisner who belonged to that small sector of the Israeli media, led by the *Haaretz* newspaper, that reported on Israeli-Palestinian conflict with the kind of courage and integrity that is rare in Europe and certainly nonexistent in North America. For having that courage and integrity Reisner was made to pay with his life by his own government — a Zionist government whose abhorrent Apartheid policies against the Palestinian people are fascist, racist, totally lacking in moral principles, and in direct violation of every international law relating to humans rights.

The seed for the Israeli-Palestinian conflict was planted in the late 1800s when a group of Jews in Europe known as Zionists decided to colonise Palestine. Zionists represented an extremist Jewish minority whose goal was to create a Jewish homeland for which various locations were considered including Africa and the Americas, before Palestine was finally chosen. Initially, there were no problems with this immigration, but as more and more Zionists immigrated to Palestine — where the vast majority of the population had been Arabic since the seventh century CE (over 1200 years) — for the specific purpose of taking over the land for a Jewish state, the indigenous Palestinian population became increasingly alarmed and Inevitably fighting broke out. The fact of Hitler's rise to power combined with Zionist determination to prevent the placement of Jewish refugees in western countries, resulted in further Jewish immigration to Palestine.

As Palestinians became increasingly aware of Zionist intentions to dispossess them of their land for an entirely Jewish state, they opposed further Jewish immigration and the Jewish National Fund's buying of land which was held in trust for the Jewish people and could never be either sold or leased back to the Palestinians — a situation which exists to this day. Consequently Palestinian opposition was not of an anti-Semitic nature, but simply due to an understandable fear of the dispossession of their people. Because of this opposition, Zionist intentions could never have been realized without the military backing of the still colonial British Mandate. In other words, Zionism was based on the flawed colonialist perception that the rights of indigenous inhabitants were immaterial.

Western nations, under considerable Zionist pressure and use of the Holocaust as a means of blackmail, were then quite happy to regard Jewish immigration to Palestine as being more preferable to having Jewish refugees resettled in the West. With this in mind, and under the auspices of the UN, they recommended giving away fifty-five percent of Palestine for a Jewish (Zionist) state. They did so without consulting with — and at the expense of — the indigenous Palestinian people. This was done despite the fact that Jews represented only thirty percent of the population while owning only seven percent of the land.

The resulting 1947-1949 Arab-Israeli war was in the West portrayed as a 'David and Goliath' battle between Israel and five Arab armies. What was not reported was the fact that throughout the war Zionist forces outnumbered all Arab and Palestinian fighters by a ratio of three to two with all battles being fought on Arab land because the Arabs never actually invaded Israel. It should also be noted that Arab armies entered the conflict only after the Zionists committed some sixteen massacres including the infamous one at Deir Yassin where over one hundred men, women, and children were slaughtered. Menachem Begin, a then Jewish terrorist leader and future Israeli Prime Minister, described this atrocity as "splendid . . . As in Deir Yassin, so everywhere we will attack and smite the enemy. God, God, Thou has chosen us for conquest." Was it in God's name that Zionist forces committed a total of thirty-three massacres?

By the war's end, Israel had taken (stolen) seventy-eight percent of Palestine; caused 750,000 Palestinians to become refugees; obliterated over five hundred towns and villages; drew up new maps in which every feature was given a new Hebrew name; and began erasing every vestige of Palestinian culture. It was an achievement that even Hitler's Nazis would have been most proud of. Having in the past been regarded as nothing more than serfs in the lands of Diaspora, these newly-liberated Jews in Palestine — a great many of them from homicidal Russia — were transformed by the intoxicating effects of freedom into despicable despots who treated Palestinians with cruel hostility; attacked them and their property; deprived them of their natural and legal rights; insulted and abused them without justifiable cause; and then — as "God's chosen people" — arrogantly boasted about it amongst themselves.

Total commitment to that same Zionist philosophy has been ruthlessly maintained to the present time with accelerated efforts to grab more Palestinian land by means of illegal expropriation, cultural genocide, ethnic cleansing, and the use of archaeology and biblical history. It was precisely for his opposition to such policies, and particularly the misuse of archaeology, that the late Michal Zeldin, an archaeologist with the Israel Antiquities Authority, was unceremoniously killed by a Mossad car bomb. Zeldin, having accidentally discovered a map showing the location of two illegal tunnels under the Temple Mount, passed the information on to David Reisner whose enquiries uncovered the existence of a secret Masonic cell calling themselves the Hiramic Brotherhood of the Third Temple.

Investigating this Judaic preoccupation with the building of a Third Holy Temple is what got David Reisner killed, and — because he shared that information with me — got this correspondent's innocent partner brutally stabbed, no doubt as an intended warning. This warning from murderous Zionist thugs, however, will be totally ignored with this announcement that Israel is illegally tunneling under Temple Mount and that such knowledge including the attached map is what got an archaeologist and a journalist killed, and an innocent acquaintance of another journalist seriously stabbed.

Since its accursed inception Israel has continuously busied itself with the creation of misery and misfortune not only to its immediate neighbours and allies, but also to the rest of the world. Though paragraph six of article forty-nine of the Fourth Geneva Convention explicitly stipulates that "the occupying power shall not deport or transfer parts of its own civilian population into the territory it occupies," Israel does so while pursuing many other policies that violate international law. Discriminatory measures against Palestinians including racial profiling; imprisonment without charges or proper judicial procedures; destruction of the public and private properties; disruption and prevention of medical care; refusals to permit Palestinians to join their families in the Occupied Territories; systematic isolation of Palestinians in their own lands; and the continued blockade of the Gaza Strip are all policies that inflict incalculable human suffering on a people who barely survive in what is an open prison maintained by an evil Apartheid regime which was apparently chosen by God.

Israel's criminality with impunity is only possible because whenever other nations reach a consensus for condemnation at the UN, the U.S. — an evil empire if there ever was one — will veto the resolution. Even more galling is the fact that thanks to special-interest Israeli lobbying groups, Israel's criminality is subsidized by U.S. taxpayers to the tune of more than $8 million per day. Can the God-loving American people justify the morality of such unconditional support for an Apartheid state, or do they not have any say in the Matter?

The central fact of the conflict is that Zionists sought sovereignty in Palestine. From this, all else follows: the Arab response and all that came after . . . Israel is the illegitimate child of ethnic nationalism.
Michael Neumann, *The Case Against Israel*, AK Press, 2005.

20
Wednesday, 11 February 2009
The Corniche, Beirut, Lebanon

Since writing his tribute to David Reisner on 30 December 2008, Banner had not had the heart to do any more writing, and despite his recent resolve to commence work again, he was still having difficulty getting started. The loss of Nadine, who after two weeks following the attack had been taken off life support and died, was too much for him to bear. Nonetheless he had to make an effort, if only for her sake and in her honor.

He started by reading the document on the screen of his laptop several times before wondering if Israel had launched Operation Cast Lead on December 27 not only to take advantage of the holiday season and the power vacuum in the U.S. White House, but also to benefit from the forthcoming London Declaration on Combating Anti-Semitism — organized by Israel with the assistance of its bought and paid for parliamentarians — which would serve to frighten would-be critics into silence. Banner felt that as some kind of response was required, it was time to put the boot on the other foot. As more than a few American conservative blogs — who had in taken exception to his critical commentaries of U.S. foreign policy and unconditional support for Israel — had in the past reprinted his dispatches on their blogs and then proceeded with their own paragraph-by-paragraph dissection and debunking of the facts and his opinions, he would now do likewise with this Declaration which sought to prevent anyone — even those with no anti-Semitic sentiment whatsoever — from demanding human rights for the Palestinian people.

The London Declaration on Combating Anti-Semitism

Preamble

We, Representatives of our respective Parliaments from across the world, convening in London for the founding Conference and Summit of the Inter-parliamentary Coalition for Combating Anti-Semitism, draw the democratic world's attention to the resurgence of anti-Semitism as a potent force in politics, international affairs and society.

We note the dramatic increase in recorded anti-Semitic hate crimes and attacks targeting Jewish persons and property, and Jewish religious, educational and communal institutions.

We are alarmed at the resurrection of the old language of prejudice and its modern manifestations in rhetoric and political action — against Jews, Jewish belief and practice and the State of Israel.

We are alarmed by Government-backed anti-Semitism in general, and state-backed genocidal anti-Semitism, in particular.

We, as Parliamentarians, affirm our commitment to a comprehensive programme of action to meet this challenge.

We call upon national governments, parliaments, international institutions, political and civic leaders, NGOs, and civil society to affirm democratic and human values, build societies based on respect and citizenship and combat any manifestations of anti-Semitism and discrimination.

MB: Could these same hypocritical Zionist lapdog national governments, parliaments, international institutions, political and civil leaders, NGOs, and civil society — while they are at it — also affirm and enforce democratic and human values that enable the Palestinian people to build their own society based on respect and citizenship within Occupied Territories that have been their homeland for hundreds of years.

We today in London resolve that;
Challenging Anti-Semitism

1. Parliamentarians shall expose, challenge, and isolate political actors who engage in hate against Jews and target the State of Israel as a Jewish collectivity;

MB: Sorry, but Israel has been a collective since its inception as verified by the following statements from The Declaration of the Establishment

349

of the State of Israel on 14 May 1948 whose high-sounding professed aims the Israelis have also violated:

> *We appeal to the Jewish people throughout the Diaspora to rally round the Jews of Eretz Israel in the tasks of immigration and up-building and to stand by them in the great struggle for the realization of the age-old dream — the redemption of Israel . . . The State of Israel will be open for Jewish immigration and for the Ingathering of the Exiles; it will foster the development of the country for the benefit of all its inhabitants; it will be based on freedom, justice and peace as envisaged by the prophets of Israel; it will ensure complete equality of social and political rights to all its inhabitants irrespective of religion, race or sex; it will guarantee freedom of religion, conscience, language, education and culture; it will safeguard the Holy Places of all religions; and it will be faithful to the principles of the Charter of the United Nations.*

MB: Evidently the Declaration's guarantee of human rights precludes Arab people in general and Palestinians in particular so that the Declaration is a useless document laced with unmitigated hypocrisy and blatant Zionist lies.

> **2. *Parliamentarians*** *should speak out against anti-Semitism and discrimination directed against any minority, and guard against equivocation, hesitation and justification in the face of expressions of hatred;*

MB: Why should discrimination against Jewish people (anti-Semitism) be distinguished from discrimination against other minorities including Palestinians? Once again there is that inference of "separateness" and "superiority." So it is okay to oppose anti-Semitism, but if anyone opposes the violation of Palestinian human rights, then that is anti-Semitic.

> **3. *Governments*** *must challenge any foreign leader, politician or public figure who denies, denigrates or trivializes the Holocaust and must encourage civil society to be vigilant to this phenomenon and to openly condemn it;*

MB: Quite Right! But when Zionists use the memory of the Holocaust to stifle legitimate criticism of Israeli violations of human rights, then they are themselves trivializing the Holocaust.

> ***4. Parliamentarians*** *should campaign for their Government to uphold international commitments on combating anti-Semitism — including the OSCE [Organization for Security and Co-operation in Europe] Berlin Declaration and its eight main principles;*

MB: Governments should uphold international commitments to combat racism against any and all ethnic groups and not just racism against Jews. To combat racism is to enforce human rights; and the enforcement of human rights cannot be achieved by selectivity, but by impartiality towards all human beings including the Palestinian people who — despite the on record opinions of Israeli leaders and others of their ilk — are not beasts, but human beings.

> ***5. The UN*** *should reaffirm its call for every member state to commit itself to the principles laid out in the Holocaust Remembrance initiative including specific and targeted policies to eradicate Holocaust denial and trivialization;*

MB: No reasonable person with intelligence would deny or trivialise the Holocaust and only diehard racists — of which Israel has more than its fair share — would do so as a result of their hate fuelled by ignorance.

> ***6. Governments and the UN*** *should resolve that never again will the institutions of the international community and the dialogue of nation states be abused to try to establish any legitimacy for anti-Semitism, including the singling out of Israel for discriminatory treatment in the international arena, and we will never witness — or be party to — another gathering like the United Nations World Conference against Racism, Racial Discrimination, Xenophobia and other related Intolerances in Durban in 2001;*

351

MB: Despite their undoubted intelligence, the majority of blinkered-racist-view Israelis refuse to accept that they are not being 'singled out' because of anti-Semitic sentiments, but because of their inhuman criminality towards the Palestinian people. You do not have to be an Einstein to figure that out.

> *7. **The OSCE** should encourage its member states to fulfill their commitments under the 2004 Berlin Declaration and to fully utilize programs to combat anti-Semitism including the Law Enforcement program LEOP;*

MB: The OSCE should certainly use the LEOP (Law Enforcement Officer Program) while simultaneously demanding that Israel, as a member of the United Nations General Assembly, must in turn stop relying on U.S. vetoes to avoid accountability for its violations, and instead honestly comply with the Universal Declaration of Human Rights.

> *8. **The European Union,** inter-state institutions, multilateral fora and religious communities must make a concerted effort to combat anti-Semitism and lead their members to adopt proven and best practice methods of countering anti-Semitism;*

MB: But shouldn't they be making concerted efforts to combat racism irrespective of who the victims are?

> *9. **Leaders of all religious faiths** should be called upon to use all the means possible to combat anti-Semitism and all types of discriminatory hostilities among believers and society at large;*

MB: Great idea. But when are Jewish religious leaders going to start practicing what they preach by preventing discriminatory hostilities towards Palestinians?

> *10. **The EU Council of Ministers** should convene a session on combating anti-Semitism relying on the outcomes of the London Conference on Combating Anti-Semitism and using the London Declaration as a basis.*

MB: Another great idea. So why not also convene a session for combating anti-Palestinian Israeli atrocities and use the London Declaration as a basis?

Prohibitions

*11. **Governments** should fully reaffirm and actively uphold the Genocide Convention, recognizing that where there is incitement to genocide signatories automatically have an obligation to act. This may include sanctions against countries involved in or threatening to commit genocide, referral of the matter to the UN Security Council, or initiation of an interstate complaint at the International Court of Justice;*

MB: Fine words coming from an illegitimate nation that regards the UN Security Council and the International Court of justice with nothing but contempt and is itself actively involved in the cultural genocide of the Palestinian people.

*12. **Parliamentarians** should legislate effective Hate Crime legislation recognizing 'hate aggravated crimes' and, where consistent with local legal standards, 'incitement to hatred' offenses and empower law enforcement agencies to convict;*

MB: Does this smack of hypocrisy and double standards or will Israel do likewise so as to ensure Israeli law enforcement agencies apprehend and convict all those armed Jewish settlers in the occupied territories who incite and commit hatred offenses against unarmed Palestinian civilians?

*13. **Governments** that are signatories to the Hate Speech Protocol of the Council of Europe 'Convention on Cybercrime' (and the 'Additional Protocol to the Convention on cybercrime, concerning the criminalization of acts of a racist and xenophobic nature committed through computer systems') should enact domestic enabling legislation;*

353

MB: What? Do they mean domestic enabling legislation that does not specifically single out Apartheid Israel for special consideration and dispensation?

Identifying the threat

*14. **Parliamentarians** should return to their legislature, Parliament or Assembly and establish inquiry scrutiny panels that are tasked with determining the existing nature and state of anti-Semitism in their countries and developing recommendations for government and civil society action;*

MB: Before doing that the parliamentarians concerned should first declare any connections with, or benefits received from either Israel or Jewish lobby groups.

*15. **Parliamentarians** should engage with their governments in order to measure the effectiveness of existing policies and mechanisms in place and to recommend proven and best practice methods of countering anti-Semitism;*

MB: Do elected parliamentarians not have an obligation to ensure protection against racism for all constituents without favoring any one group? Or would that be undemocratic?

*16. **Governments** should ensure they have publicly accessible incident reporting systems, and that statistics collected on anti-Semitism should be the subject of regular review and action by government and state prosecutors and that an adequate legislative framework is in place to tackle hate crime;*

MB: Once again should incident reporting and monitoring systems not be applicable for everyone without special consideration for any one group? The belief by any individual that he or she was chosen by God does not entitle them to special consideration in a secular and democratic society.

*17. **Governments** must expand the use of the EUMC [European Monitoring Centre on Racism and Xenophobia] 'Working Definition of anti-Semitism' to inform policy of national and international organizations and as a basis for training material for use by Criminal Justice Agencies;*

MB: Why expand the "the working definition of anti-Semitism" when the definition of racial discrimination is already covered by the United Nations Convention on the Elimination of all Forms of Racial Discrimination: "The term 'racial discrimination' shall mean any distinction, exclusion, restriction, or preference based on race, color, descent, or national or ethnic origin that has the purpose or effect of nullifying or impairing the recognition, enjoyment or exercise, on an equal footing, of human rights and fundamental freedoms in the political, economic, social, cultural or any other field of public life."

If Israelis were to abide by and respect the preceding definition which happens to also cover Palestinian people, then not only would they have taken one giant leap towards Middle East peace, but they would also eliminate the criticism of their country which they deceitfully brand as anti-Semitism. Deceit, however, will prevail as their modus operandi perpetuates and promotes the perception that anti-Semitism is on the rise so as to create a smokescreen behind which they can continue to lie, cheat, bribe, violate human rights, and illegally occupy or steal Palestinian lands. And if anyone dares to suggest that what they are doing is wrong, then all hell will break loose with shrill accusations of anti-Semitism and Holocaust denial. You just have to admit they have no shortage of criminal chutzpah!

*18. **Police services** should record allegations of hate crimes and incidents —including anti-Semitism — as routine part of reporting crimes;*

MB: Are they not doing that already?

*19. **The OSCE** should work with member states to seek consistent data collection systems for anti-Semitism and hate crime.*

MB: *What about racism and hate crimes — especially by Israel — against other ethnic groups?*

Education, awareness and training

*20. **Governments** should train Police, prosecutors and judges comprehensively. The training is essential if perpetrators of anti-Semitic hate crime are to be successfully apprehended, prosecuted, convicted and sentenced. The OSCE's Law Enforcement Program LEOP is a model initiative consisting of an international cadre of expert police officers training police in several countries;*

MB: Yet another demand for special consideration for anti-Semitic crimes without mention of the obligations that government representatives have to all constituents.

*21. **Governments** should develop teaching materials on the subjects of the Holocaust, racism, anti-Semitism and discrimination which are incorporated into the national school curriculum. All teaching materials ought to be based on values of comprehensiveness, inclusiveness, acceptance and respect and should be designed to assist students to recognize and counter anti-Semitism and all forms of hate speech;*

MB: Should students not also be taught the UN Universal Declaration of Human Rights; that 'universal' means for everyone including Palestinians; and that Israel contemptuously violates all of its articles?

*22. **The Council of Europe** should act efficiently for the full implementation of its 'Declaration and Program for Education for Democratic Citizenship based on the Rights and Responsibilities of the Citizens', adopted on 7 May 1999 in Budapest;*

MB: The Rights and Responsibilities of citizens include the right to criticize and condemn all violations of human rights — including those committed by Israel — without fear of being vilified, threatened, and slandered as an anti-Semites.

*23. **Governments** should include a comprehensive training program across the Criminal Justice System using program such as the LEOP program;*

MB: Governments have a responsibility not only to do that, but also to ensure that it is clearly understood by all law enforcement officers that enforcement is applicable to all ethnic groups and not just Jews.

*24. **Education Authorities** should ensure that freedom of speech is upheld within the law and to protect students and staff from illegal antisemitic discourse and a hostile environment in whatever form it takes including calls for boycotts.*

MB: In the U.S. — that champion of free speech — hostile environments exist in all major colleges where active monitoring of professors and students by Jewish pressure groups ensures that any debate on the rights of Palestinians is stifled and punished even to the extent of having professors dismissed. Freedom of speech? What a bunch of hypocrites.

Community Support

25. The Criminal Justice System should publicly notify local communities when anti-Semitic hate crimes are prosecuted by the courts to build community confidence in reporting and pursuing convictions through the Criminal Justice system;

MB: Should that not automatically apply to all hate crimes irrespective of who the victims are?

*26. **Parliamentarians** should engage with civil society institutions and leading NGOs to create partnerships that bring about change locally, domestically and globally, and support efforts that encourage Holocaust education, inter-religious dialogue and cultural exchange.*

MB: Once again the constant reminder and implication that only Jews are victims of hate and suffering is being imposed without reference to all the other people in the world for whom daily hate and suffering is all that they have known.

Media and the Internet

27. Governments *should acknowledge the challenge and opportunity of the growing new forms of communication;*
MB: Yes, they certainly should. But they should also ensure that unfettered use of these new forms of communication is in no way restricted by Israeli sponsored declarations such as this one in London.

28. Media Regulatory Bodies *should utilise the EUMC 'Working Definition of anti-Semitism' to inform media standards;*

MB: Anti-Semitism! Anti-Semitism! Anti-Semitism! What about working definitions and media standards for the rest of the people in the world?

29. Governments *should take appropriate and necessary action to prevent the broadcast of anti-Semitic program on satellite television channels, and to apply pressure on the host broadcast nation to take action to prevent the transmission of anti-Semitic program;*

MB: By anti-Semitic programs they presumably mean any programs that in any way question or criticize Israeli policies towards the Palestinian people. The concept of a free press is an illusion that all responsible people should ensure becomes a reality despite undue influence and control by the Jewish lobby.

30. The OSCE *should seek ways to coordinate the response of member states to combat the use of the internet to promote incitement to hatred;*

MB: What? Something is wrong here because there is no mention of incitement to hatred against Jews in particular?

*31. **Law enforcement authorities** should use domestic 'hate crime', 'incitement to hatred' and other legislation as well as other means to mitigate and, where permissible, to prosecute 'Hate on the Internet' where racist and anti-Semitic content is hosted, published and written;*

MB: That's more like it. Back onto the theme of anti-Semitism.

*32. **An international task force** of Internet specialists comprised of parliamentarians and experts should be established to create common metrics to measure anti-Semitism and other manifestations of hate online and to develop policy recommendations and practical instruments for Governments and international frameworks to tackle these problems.*

MB: How very generous of them — as well as anti-Semitism they have grudgingly included 'other manifestations of hate online'.

Inter-parliamentary Coalition for Combating Anti-Semitism

*33. **Participants** will endeavor to maintain contact with fellow delegates through the working group framework, communicating successes or requesting further support where required;*

MB: No doubt they will be able to do that while enjoying free junkets to Israel.

*34. **Delegates** should reconvene for the next ICCA Conference in Canada in 2010, become an active member of the Inter-parliamentary Coalition and promote and prioritize the London Declaration on Combating Anti-Semitism.*

MB: More Israeli-sponsored free junkets?

Lancaster House, 17 February 2009

After he had finished commenting on the Declaration's thirty-four articles, Mark Banner decided that he would start keeping a diary of notable world events. It would serve not only as a check on Barack Obama's influence and achievements for the good of humanity during his first term in office, but also to track any changes in U.S. Middle East policies should Obama win re-election and no longer have to worry about AIPAC lobbying pressure.

2009 DIARY OF NOTABLE WORLD EVENTS

18 February '09: According to a Global Research report last month by Mahdi Darius Nazemoraya — an award-winning author and geopolitical analyst — in November 2008, barely a month before Tel Aviv started its massacre in the Gaza Strip, the Israeli military held drills for a two-front war against Lebanon and Syria called Shiluv Zro'ot III (Crossing Arms III). The military exercise included a massive simulated invasion of both Syria and Lebanon. (For full report *See Israel's Next War: Today the Gaza Strip, Tomorrow Lebanon?* Global Research, 17 January 2009).

20 February '09: Several weeks ago the national Boycott Israeli Goods (BIG) campaign, led by a coalition of pro-Palestine and anti-war groups, carried out nationwide protests to boycott the sale of Israeli goods on UK high-streets with a view to impacting on Valentine's Day sales of flowers, many of which are imported from Israel.

5 March '09: A *Lancet* medical journal report of a new study shows Palestinians in the West Bank and Gaza suffer from an 'ailing landscape' of health services with 10% of Palestinian children now suffering from stunted growth. The healthcare system in the Palestinian territories is described as "fragmented and incoherent." An Israeli government spokesperson said *The Lancet* had failed to seek its view and that the report was one-sided, adding that many Palestinians had accessed medical care in the country. No mention was made of either why *The Lancet* should seek the view of a government that never cooperates with such reports, or the number of Palestinians that had actually been allowed to access medical care in the country. As a medical journal that has been published since 1823, *The Lancet* has the kind of repute and integrity that the Israeli government has always lacked and will never have.

21 March '09: As a follow-up to their indefensible conduct in Operation Cast Lead — when hundreds of civilians were killed including many of them women and children — the Israeli Defense Force is now mired in more controversy following the latest revelations about the conduct of its soldiers by the Israeli newspaper *Haaretz.* The newspaper revealed that t-shirt designs for IDF soldiers make light of shooting pregnant Palestinian women and children and include images of dead babies and destroyed mosques. One of the t-shirts — printed for a platoon of Israeli snipers — depicts an armed Palestinian pregnant women caught in the crosshairs of a rifle with the caption in English: "1 shot 2 kills."

Another t-shirt shows an Israeli soldier blowing up a mosque with the caption "Only God forgives." Yet another bears the caption above the figure of a ninja "Won't chill until I confirm a kill." Even more shocking is one showing a Palestinian grieving mother — also in the crosshairs of a rifle — weeping next to her dead baby's grave with the caption "Better use Durex" implying that it would have been better if the child had never been born.

Michael Maniken, an ex-soldier and campaigner with Breaking The Silence, said that the revelations suggest a pattern of immoral conduct in the army and that "The army keeps on saying we're talking about a few rotten apples but it seems the army doesn't understand there's a norm in this kind of action . . . We're hearing about this time and time again and the army seems disconnected from reality." An IDF spokesman said the t-shirts were printed on the private initiative of the soldiers and their designs "are not in accordance with IDF values and are simply tasteless. This type of humor is unacceptable and should be condemned." While acknowledging that they "should" be condemned, the spokesman did not actually condemn them. Is this the world's most moral army, or just a bunch of utterly contemptible racists?

29 March'09: Today, Palestinian Land Day, is an annual day of commemoration for Palestinians of the events of that date in 1976 when in response to the Israeli government's announcement of a plan to expropriate thousands of dunams of land for security and settlement purposes, a general strike and protest marches were organized in Arab towns from the Galilee to the Negev. During the ensuing confrontations with the Israeli army and police, six Palestinians were killed, some one hundred were wounded, and hundreds of others arrested.

Now every year in commemoration Palestinians walk the streets of every major Palestinian town denouncing the Israeli occupation; the confiscation of Palestinian land; the building of illegal Israeli colonies; the Israeli demolition of Palestinian homes; and demanding freedom, the liberation of all occupied Palestine, and the establishment of an independent Palestinian state.

15 April '09: The Palestinian people are mainly farmers who depend on agriculture with citrus products and olive production being an essential part of their livelihood. Olive trees, with many as old as five thousand years, are scattered all over Palestine and year after year keep yielding olives in abundance. Almost half of the agricultural land of occupied Palestine is planted with some ten million olive trees with the vast majority being in the West Bank.

Yet this symbol of peace is now the main target for destruction by Israeli religious extremist armed settlers who having forcefully occupied Palestinian land, vent their venom during every harvest by attacking Palestinian farmers, preventing them from cultivating their land and harvesting their own crops. Even the Israeli Defense Force is in on the act by preventing Palestinian farmers from accessing their field by means of claiming them as military areas. Then having denied the Palestinian farmers access to their fields, Israeli settlers under the protection of the army steal the olive crops. They then cut down the trees with chain saws, spray chemicals on them, set the whole field ablaze, and uproot the trees with bulldozers. The venomous hate of these God chosen settlers knows no bounds.

17 May '09: Unindicted war criminal and former British Prime Minister Tony Blair received the $1 million Dan David prize at a Tel Aviv university ceremony. Blair's office stated that 90 percent of the money from the prize — which is named after Dan David, the Jewish-born Romanian international businessman who made his millions by setting up Photo-Me booths in shopping malls around the world — would be donated to the Tony Blair faith foundation that promotes religious understanding by bringing together young people of different faiths. As this inter-faith rapprochement amongst the young does not obviously include Palestinian children, there are those who assume that Tony Blair was, is, and always will be a smarmy, two-faced, money-grabbing hypocrite who can be bought for a few lousy shekels. The real tragedy of all this is that the majority of people stand by and allow the Tony Blairs of this world to get away with it.

17 August '09: Sweden's *Aftonbladet* tabloid newspaper has sparked a fierce debate in Sweden and abroad after alleging that Israeli troops harvested organs from Palestinians that died in their custody. The article has created a rift between the Swedish and Israeli governments with

Israeli officials denouncing the report — surprise, surprise — as "anti-Semitic" but without commenting on the specific allegations. The article was written by a Swedish freelance photojournalist and was entitled *"Våra söner plundras på sina organ"* ("Our sons are being plundered for their organs"). It alleged that in the late 1980s and early 1990s, many young men from the west Bank and Gaza Strip had been seized by Israeli forces and their bodies returned to their families with organs missing.

The Israeli government — hardly renowned for Kosher denials — along with several of its U.S. lapdog congresspersons condemned the article as baseless and incendiary, while noting the history of anti-Semitism and its blood libels against the Jews, they asked the Swedish government to denounce it. The Swedish government refused, citing freedom of the press and the country's constitution. Swedish ambassador to Israel Elisabet Borsiin Bonnier condemned the article as "shocking and appalling," stating that freedom of the press carries responsibility. The Swedish government, however, distanced itself from her remarks while The Swedish Newspaper publishers Association and Reporters Without Borders supported Sweden's refusal to condemn it. This is yet another example of the Israeli government screaming "anti-Semitism" instead of dealing with the allegations and disproving them — which invariably in Israel's case means the allegations are true.

15 September '09: A 575-page report by The United Nations fact-finding mission on the Gaza conflict during Israel's Operation Cast Lead was released today ahead of its presentation to the UN's Human Rights Council in Geneva on 29 September. The mission found evidence that both Israeli forces and Palestinian militants committed serious war crimes and breaches of humanitarian law, which may amount to crimes against humanity: "We came to the conclusion, on the basis of the facts we found, that there was strong evidence to establish that numerous serious violations of international law, both humanitarian law and human rights law, were committed by Israel during the military operations in Gaza," head of the mission, Justice Richard Goldstone, said at a press briefing. "The mission concluded that actions amounting to war crimes and possibly, in some respects, crimes against humanity, were committed by the Israel Defense Force."

He continued that "There's no question that the firing of rockets and mortars [by armed groups from Gaza] was deliberate and calculated to cause loss of life and injury to civilians and damage to civilian structures. The mission found that these actions also amount to serious war crimes and also possibly crimes against humanity. The mission finds that the conduct of the Israeli armed forces constitute grave breaches of the Fourth Geneva Convention in respect of willful killings and willfully causing great suffering to protected persons and as such give rise to individual criminal responsibility," the report's executive summary said. "It also finds that the direct targeting and arbitrary killing of Palestinian civilians is a violation of the right to life."

The report went on to criticise the "deliberate and systematic policy on the part of the Israeli armed forces to target industrial sites and water installations," and the use of Palestinian civilians as human shields. On the objectives and strategy of Israel's military operation, the mission concluded that military planners deliberately followed a doctrine which involved "the application of disproportionate force and the causing of great damage and destruction to civilian property and infrastructure, and suffering to civilian populations."

With regards to the firing of mortars from Gaza, the mission concluded that they were indiscriminate and deliberate attacks against a civilian population and "would constitute war crimes and may amount to crimes against humanity." It added that their apparent intention of spreading terror among the Israeli civilian population was a violation of international law.

There was a recommendation that the Security Council should require Israel to take steps to launch appropriate independent investigations into the alleged crimes committed, in conformity with international standards, and report back on these investigations within six months. It further called on the Security Council to appoint a committee of experts to monitor the proceedings taken by the Israeli Government. If these did not take place, or were not independent and in conformity with international standards, the report called for the Security Council to refer the situation in Gaza to the Prosecutor of the International Criminal Court (ICC). It also called on the Security Council to require the committee of experts to perform a similar role with regard to the relevant Palestinian authorities.

At today's briefing, Justice Goldstone said the mission had investigated 36 incidents that took place during the Israeli operation in Gaza, which he said did not relate to decisions taken in the heat of battle, but to deliberate policies that were adopted and decisions that were taken. As an example, he described one such incident: a mortar attack on a mosque in Gaza during a religious service, which killed 15 members of the congregation and injured many others. Justice Goldstone said that even if allegations that the mosque was used as sanctuary by military groups and that weapons were stored there were true, there was still "no justification under international humanitarian law to mortar the mosque during a service" because it could have been attacked during the night, when it was not being used by civilians.

Justice Goldstone added that the report reflected the unanimous view of the mission's four members of Christine Chinkin, Professor of International Law at the London School of Economics and Political Science at the University of London; Hina Jilani, Advocate of the Supreme Court of Pakistan and former Special Representative of the Secretary-General on Human Rights Defenders; and retired Colonel Desmond Travers, member of the Board of Directors of the Institute for International Criminal Investigations (IICI).

27 October '09: An Amnesty International report describes the grim reality of many Palestinians struggling — and more often than not falling — to obtain enough water for drinking, washing, and agriculture while Israelis, including those in illegal Jewish settlements in the West Bank, have all they need for lush, irrigated farmland, swimming pools, and gardens. Israel is denying Gaza and the West Bank access to adequate water through a 'total' and "discriminatory" control that enables its own people to consume four times as much water as do the Palestinians. The report claims that the 450,000 Jewish settlers who have taken up residence in the West Bank and East Jerusalem since the 1967 Six-Day War consume as much or more water than 2.3 million Palestinians. It also points out that the overall Palestinian per capita consumption of seventy liters per day compares with the World Health Organization recommended level of one hundred liters and Israeli consumption of three hundred.

4 November '09: Jewish settlers have taken over another house in East Jerusalem after an Israeli court granted an order supporting their claim of ownership. Twenty-nine members of the al-Kurd family who had been living there were forcibly removed by the Jewish settlers who had hired their own security guards. Palestinians claimed that the frequency of such removals was part of a systematic policy by Israel to force them out of East Jerusalem. UN chief Ban Ki-moon called on Israel "to cease such provocative actions." Sure, that will happen when kosher pigs fly.

The report adds that between 180,000 and 200,000 Palestinians living in rural communities — especially the Israeli controlled "Area C" which comprises sixty-percent of the West Bank — have no access to running water. Furthermore the Israeli Defense Force (the most humane army in the world) "often" prevents Palestinians from accessing rainwater by for example destroying water-harvesting cisterns or even confiscating water tankers. Those who are capable of such barbarous conduct have no right to regard themselves as human beings — let alone God's chosen people.

3 December '09: An Israeli rights group, Hamoked, said a record number of some 4,570 Palestinians have been stripped of their right to live in East Jerusalem. Following Israel's illegal annexation of East Jerusalem in 1967, Palestinians living there were offered Israeli citizenship — proof that Israel had already resolved never to give back Palestinian territories it had occupied — which many refused on the grounds of not wanting to recognize Israeli sovereignty and were instead granted residency. Israel stated that most of those stripped of their rights were living abroad but according to Hamoked some of those Palestinians — if they live abroad for seven years or residency or citizenship elsewhere — may now be stateless or even unaware that they have lost their citizenship. The fact that this can happen to Palestinians while Jews who have never been to Palestine have a "right of return," is racist, supremacist, and a blatant contravention of the Universal Declaration of Human Rights.

8 December '09: European ministers have called for Jerusalem to serve as the capitol of both Israel and a future Palestinian state as part of a negotiated peace. These gutless European foreign ministers had, however, dropped an earlier reference explicitly stating that East Jerusalem should be the capitol of a Palestinian state. The EU foreign ministers' statement said "if there is to be a genuine peace, a way must be found through negotiations to resolve the status of Jerusalem as the capitol of two states." Israel's response was "nothing new" which was a polite but unmistakable way of saying "screw you" and "dream on."

2010 DIARY OF NOTABLE WORLD EVENTS

6 January '10: U.S. Middle East peace envoy George Mitchell — who successfully brokered peace in Northern Ireland — dared to suggest that the U.S. "could withhold support on loan guarantees to Israel" as means of pressuring the Israelis to seriously engage in peace negotiations. His remarks have caused an uproar among Zionist extremists who remain intransigent over settlement expansion and the economic blockade of Gaza. The Israeli *Maariv* newspaper referred to Mitchell's suggestion as a "bombshell," while Israeli Finance Minister Yuval Steinitz barked, "We don't need to use these guarantees. We are doing just fine." Senior members of Benjamin Netanyahu's Likud Party made it clear in a statement that they would not be "threatened" by the U.S., knowing full well that AIPACS's Capitol Hill paid for lackeys would not allow it.

Right on cue, a group of U.S. legislators, — Senators Joe Lieberman, John Barrasso, John Thune, and John McCain — appeared at a Jerusalem press conference to criticize Mitchell's candid suggestion. Lieberman confirmed the fact that AIPAC controlled Congress and the White House by saying that an administration official had already disavowed Mitchell's statement, and that in his opinion "any attempt to pressure Israel, to force Israel to the negotiating table by denying Israel support, will not pass the Congress of the United States. In fact, the Congress will stop any attempt to do that. I don't think we will come to that point." Not to be outdone, McCain was equally categorical in saying that this type of pressure would not be helpful "and I don't agree with it." He added that he was certain that the administration would in the future clarify that this was not its policy.

Mitchell's right-wing critics appear to have forgotten that threatening to freeze loan guarantees was hardly a new ploy with the last such threat being made under President George W. Bush in 2003 when Israel's expansion of their "security fence" cut deep into Palestinian territory.

19 January '10: Senior Hamas Commander Mahmoud al-Mabbouh was today killed in his Dubai hotel room. He had been followed by at least eleven Mossad agents who were carrying fake or fraudulently obtained passports from various Western nations, of which seven assumed the names of Israeli dual citizens. Reports indicated that al-Mabhouh was tracked by his killers from Damascus to Dubai. He was traveling without bodyguards, and was en route to Bangkok.

25 January '10: Israeli Prime Minister Benjamin Netanyahu took part in a tree-planting ceremonies in the West Bank while declaring that that Israel would never leave these areas which with their Jewish settlement blocks would always remain a part of Israel. The rabid, racist, and ranting Netanyahu said "Our message is clear: We are planting here, we will stay here, we will build here. This will be an inseparable part of Israel for eternity."

18 February '10: The International Committee of the Red Cross (ICRC) has said that Israeli restrictions make normal life "close to impossible" for West Bank Palestinians with many unable to reach a hospital or visit relatives and with up to fifty percent of them living in extreme poverty. Furthermore, attacks and harassment by Jewish settlers prevented many Palestinian farmers from cultivating their land while some ten thousand Palestinian olive trees have been either cut down or burnt in the past three years. Beatrice Megevand-Roggo, the ICRC head of operations in the Middle East said that the "ICRC has repeatedly called for action to be taken to allow Palestinians to live their lives in dignity . . . we reiterate our call on Israel to do more to protect Palestinians in the West Bank against settler violence."

24 March '10: Following the assassination in Dubai in January of Palestinian Hamas leader Mahmoud Mabhouh by Israel's Mossad (probably assisted by the rogue and corrupt Palestinian Mohammad Dahlan) the aftershock finally reached the British Parliament yesterday with the revelation that some of the Mossad hit-squad were traveling on cloned British passports. The large hit-squad of men and women had travelled to and from Dubai using cloned passports originally issued to citizens of Australia, France, Germany, Holland, Ireland and the United Kingdom.

All twelve of the forged passports that were British, were copies of UK originals issued to British citizens who had settled in Israel and who, under the *Law of the Return* had also taken Israeli citizenship. The Israeli government's only comment to date had been that "there is no evidence that Israel was responsible."

In his ministerial statement to a hushed House of Commons, David Milliband the Labour government's Foreign Secretary announced that following an investigation by Scotland Yard's Serious and Organised Crime Agency (SOCA), a decision had been taken to require a senior member of the diplomatic staff of the Israeli Embassy in London to quit Britain immediately. Though the diplomat was not named in the statement, it has been assumed that he or she would be Mossad's "head of station" in London.

David Miliband is the Jewish but not Zionist son of Marion Kozak, a Polish-born Holocaust survivor who immigrated to the United Kingdom in the 1950s. In 1961 she had married Ralph Miliband, a sociologist and prominent Marxist thinker, with whom she had two sons who were now both prominent in British politics.

Kozak, who has been a long-standing human rights campaigner and an early activist with the Campaign for Nuclear Disarmament (CND), was also a long-standing supporter of left-wing and pro-Palestinian organisations and is a signatory of the founding statements of both Jews for Justice for Palestinians (founded in 2002) and a supporter of Independent Jewish Voices (launched in 2007).

In his statement Miliband informed the Commons that the SOCA investigation had been able to establish that the authentic UK documents had only ever left the hands of their owners when they were taken into the temporary possession of Israeli officials either in London or in transit at Ben Gurion Airport in Israel. He added that:

> *We have concluded, that there are compelling reasons to believe that Israel was responsible for the misuse of the British passports. Such misuse is intolerable. It represents a profound disregard for the sovereignty of the United Kingdom. The fact that this was done by a country which is a friend, with significant diplomatic, cultural, business and personal ties to the UK, only adds insult to injury. No country or government could stand by in such a situation. I have asked that a member of the Embassy of Israel be withdrawn, and this is taking place.*

So what is new? Zionists have been consistently pissing on their allies even before the state of Israel had been established in 1948.

370

12 May '10: In their recently released very important book *The Politics of Genocide,* authors Edward Herman and David Peterson (an independent journalist and researcher based in Chicago), document the double standards by which the U.S. government, the mass media, and the intellectual establishment label, or refuse to label, particular events such as "genocide." In other words whether an action is labeled "genocide" or not depends on the simple question of who committed the act in question?

If for example the U.S. and/or its allies are responsible for the acts in question, then it is a certainty that those acts will not be labeled "genocide." If on the other hand the perpetrators are regarded as ostensible enemies of the U.S. alliance — even if their acts may may have resulted in massively less deaths than those created by the U.S. or its allies — then there is every likelihood that the acts will be considered "genocide."

As an example of this double standard, the authors cite the U.S. wars and intervening sanctions regime against Iraq that resulted in the killing of approximately 1,800,000 Iraqis. But despite the fact that those killings were known to be the probable consequence of the U.S'.s conduct — including the targeting in the first Gulf War of soft civilian targets such as water treatment, sanitation, and electric plants; roads and railways; and hospitals and clinics; and subsequent sanctions that prevented the repair of infrastructure essential to the survival of the Iraqi people — very few have dared to label the U.S. actions as "genocide."

By contrast there was no hesitation in applying the "genocide" label to the killing of 4,000 in Kosovo, 33,000 Bosnia, 300,000 in Darfur, and 800,000 in Rwanda. The authors also noted that the only country in the world where more civilians were murdered than by U.S. and allied forces in Iraq, was in the Democratic Republic of the Congo (DRC) where an estimated 5.4 million civilians have been killed during that country's ongoing hostilities. This estimate of DRC deaths, however, was to said to be closer to 7 million in a February 2010 report by Nicholas Kristoff in *The New York Times.* However, as with Iraq, the DRC is also hardly ever stigmatized with the "genocide" label because the U.S. and its allies — in their rapacious quest for the rare minerals in the DRC — are responsible for the bulk of those killings. But due to the fact that the Western Alliance controls the political discourse, those killings will never be given the "genocide" label.

Edward Herman is an American economist and media analyst who

371

also co-authored the *Manufacturing Consent: The Political Economy of the Mass Media (*1988) with Professor Noam Chomsky (MIT). The book, according to the publishers, showed "that, contrary to the usual image of the news media as cantankerous, obstinate, and ubiquitous in their search for truth and defense of justice, in their actual practice they defend the economic, social, and political agendas of the privileged groups that dominate domestic society, the state, and the global order . . ."

6 July '10: Twice a year, American evangelicals show up at a winery in the West Bank Jewish settlement of Har Bracha in the hills of ancient Samaria to take part in the biblical prophecy of picking grapes and pruning vines. They do so in the belief that Christian assistance for Jewish winemakers in the occupied West Bank foretells Christ's second coming. These evangelicals are recruited by a Tennessee-based charity called HaYovel that invites volunteers "to labour side by side with the people of Israel" and "to share with them a passion for the soon coming jubilee in Yeshua, messiah."

HaYovel is one of many groups in the United States using tax-exempt donations to help Jews establish permanent residence in the Israeli-occupied territories which would effectively prevent the creation of a Palestinian state as part of a two-state solution. So while the U.S. government seeks to end a four-decade Jewish settlement enterprise and foster a Palestinian state in the West Bank, the American Treasury helps sustain the settlements through tax breaks on donations to support them.

13 September '10: Today the National Constitution Center's Liberty Medal and $100,000 prize was awarded by Former President Bill Clinton to unindicted war criminal and former British Prime Minister Tony Blair. The National Constitution Center is an independent, non-profit organization that promotes understanding of the US constitution and its relevance. Recipients of the Liberty Medal receive $100,000 (£65,000) which in Blair's case was to be donated to his charitable foundations. Officials acknowledged that Blair, who had just been forced to cancel promotional events for a new autobiography amid protests by critics of his role in the U.S.-led Iraq war, was a contentious choice. The Center's Jewish president, David Eisner, said that "there is always an element of controversy when you pick people at the forefront of change. They are usually very controversial figures. We understand . . . how differently

Tony Blair appears to be viewed by many people in the UK as compared with many people in the US." That is probably because the British people have not forgotten how he deliberately involved Britain in a war on the strength of a barefaced lie that Saddam Hussein could unleash weapons of mass destruction within forty-five minutes.

24 September '10: Member nations at the annual conference of the International Atomic Energy Agency (IAEA) narrowly rejected an Arab-backed resolution calling on Israel to join a global treaty limiting nuclear arms. The resolution — backed by 46 nations but rejected by 51 with 23 abstentions — had expressed "concern about the Israeli nuclear capabilities" and called on Israel to join the nuclear Non-Proliferation Treaty (NPT) which would require it to open any of its nuclear activity to IAEA inspectors.

Before the vote, the ever arrogant Israelis warned the gathering in Vienna against approving the non-binding resolution and was backed by its lapdog the U.S. which also urged a vote against by suggesting that a vote for would undermine a conference on a nuclear-free Middle East in 2012. Israel's envoy to the IAEA, Ehud Azoulay, said prior to the vote that "Adopting this resolution will be a fatal blow to any hope for future co-operative efforts towards better regional security in the Middle East." When translated from the Hebrew that means better security for Israel which alone must remain as the only Middle Eastern nation with nuclear weapons.

The IAEA's U.S. envoy and Israeli puppet, Glyn Davies, said "The vote sent a 'positive signal' to the Israeli-Palestinian peace process . . . What's important is that we've stopped some action from occurring that would have made it very difficult to move forward with both the peace process and toward a Middle East free of weapons of mass destruction when that peace is achieved." Coming up with such a supposition must have required a great deal of coaching and much disjointed thinking. The NPT came into effect in 1970 and has yet to be signed by Israel, India and Pakistan. A similar resolution, expressing concern at "Israel's nuclear activities," passed at the IAEA last year.

3 October '10: An Israeli military court has convicted two Israeli soldiers for using a Palestinian child as a human shield in 2009 during Operation Cast Lead in Gaza. It is reportedly the first such conviction in Israel — where the use of civilians as human shields is banned. They were found guilty of reckless endangerment and conduct unbecoming for forcing the nine-year-old boy to check suspected booby-traps. The southern command military court found the two soldiers guilty of "exceeding their authority to the point of endangering life" and conduct unbecoming in the incident in Gaza City's suburb of Tel al-Hawa on 15 January 2009.

A summary of the verdict by the three-judge panel said that — when rounding up residents of Tel al-Hawa — the soldiers came across bags in a home and ordered the Palestinian boy to search for suspected booby-traps. "The boy, who feared for his fate and was under the stress of the situation, wet his pants." The court also noted that "unlike the soldiers, the child was, naturally, bereft of any form of protection." The bags that the boy had checked did not have any hidden explosives and the child was later returned to his family unharmed. Sentencing is to be decided at a later date (if at all).

4 October '10: In what has come to be known as the "price tag" policy under which Palestinians are attacked in retaliation for any Israeli government measure that appears to threaten Jewish settlements, hardline Jewish settlers set fire to a mosque in the West Bank. An Israeli military spokesman said it was taking the incident very seriously with every effort being made to catch the perpetrators. Needless to say, previous Israeli "thorough" investigations of such "price tag" attacks have failed to result in any convictions.

11 October '10: An Israeli parliamentary committee has been debating the issue of the involvement of children in violent protests after two young Palestinian boys were run over and injured by an Israeli right-wing activist. David Be'eri claimed he hit the boys in the East Jerusalem district of Silwan because they were throwing stones at him. Silwan sees frequent protests by local Palestinians against Jewish families and organizations who have arbitrarily moved into the area after Palestinian property is bulldozed to make room for them.

Video footage and photographs of the incident appear to show Mr Be'eri's car swerving to the wrong side of the road, accelerating towards the boys and hurling one of them into the air. Be'eri is the chairman of the right-wing Elad organization which promotes Jewish settlement in Arab East Jerusalem.

After being questioned by police, Be'eri was released on bail which came as no surprise because two weeks ago, an Israeli security guard was released after killing a young Palestinian man. Be'eri's supporters in the Israeli parliament, the Knesset, claimed the incident highlighted the Palestinian tactic of using children to terrorize local communities.

23 October '10: United Nations human rights rapporteur Richard Falk said continued settlement construction will probably make Israel's occupation of Palestinian land irreversible. Consequently the peace process aimed at creating an independent and sovereign Palestinian state was an illusion. He added that the UN, the U.S. and Israel had failed to uphold Palestinian rights.

With nearly half a million Jews living in more than 100 settlements built since Israel's 1967 occupation of the West Bank and East Jerusalem, Jewish settlement construction had become so extensive it amounted to de-facto annexation of Palestinian land.

In his report for the UN General Assembly, Mr Falk stated that this undercut assumptions behind UN Security Council resolutions which said Israel's occupation of Palestinian territory in 1967 was temporary and reversible. Such assumptions which had always been the basis for the peace process aimed at achieving an independent Palestinian state alongside Israel, were in reality just an illusion. Israel's official response — in keeping with its usual position that anything unfavorable said or written about Israel was irrespective of justification automatically deemed to be biased and anti-Semitic — was that Mr. Falk's report on the Palestinian territories was biased and served a political agenda.

2 November '10: According to a report by two Israeli rights groups B'Tselem and Hamoked, Israel's internal security service subjected Palestinians to abuse and torture while in custody. The report — based on interviews with 121 Palestinians held in the Petah Tikva detention centre in 2009 — said Israeli agents bound detainees to chairs during lengthy interrogations that included insults, threats, and beatings.

In a written response to the report's authors, Israel's Justice Ministry denied many of the charges by claiming it respects the law and interrogations were conducted according to law in order to prevent illegal activity that would harm state security. The world is only too familiar with Israel's lies and respect for the law.

Also published on the B'Tselem website are detainees' claims that they were held in isolation, kept in "appalling" unhygienic conditions, and subjected to physical abuse and sleep deprivation. Many also reported that the interrogators used family members as a means of pressure. The report cited the case of a 63-year-old widow who was brought to the facility apparently so that her incarcerated relatives could witness her anguish in detention. She was released without charge two days later.

The rights groups said the procedures constituted "cruel, inhuman and degrading treatment, at times amounting to torture" and that Palestinians have filed 645 complaints with the Justice Ministry about interrogation techniques since 2001, but none has led to criminal investigations. The ministry responded that military police had opened 427 investigations of alleged violence against Palestinian detainees between 2000 and 2007 but gave no information on any results of these investigations — probably because there were very few if any of those responsible were either investigated, charged, or convicted. It should be remembered that the people committing these crimes against humanity insist that they were chosen by God Himself.

10 November '10: Having to share a small, cramped house with 12 other family members in northern Gaza is difficult enough, but for 24-year-old Basam in his wheelchair — with his younger brother Mustapha sitting on the floor, crutches by his side — life is even more arduous. The brothers, with heavily bandaged feet, were shot by Israeli soldiers while working close to the border. According to Basam Israeli soldiers usually fired a warning shot, but on the occasion when they were shot a month earlier there had been no such warning.

The two brothers had been collecting rubble and gravel — a task which scores of young men can be found doing daily — from the abandoned industrial areas in northern Gaza, close to the Erez crossing into Israel. Loading rubble onto donkey carts is hard, dirty work but the rubble can be recycled to make bricks. Due to the Israeli blockade there is a shortage of construction materials so that on a good day the brothers can make between $10 and $15 (£6-£9) each. Despite their injuries, the brothers vowed to return to collecting rubble and gravel because with there being no other jobs available, they had no other option.

The work, however, is perilous with the United Nations saying that eleven Palestinians civilians, including four children, had been killed by Israeli fire in the past six months in the restricted areas around Gaza's borders. At least seventy civilians had also been injured in the same period, including at least forty-nine who were working collecting rubble and scrap metal. There are claims that the figures are even higher. According Basam al-Masri, head of orthopaedics at the Kamal Edwan hospital in Beit Lahiya in northern Gaza, at his hospital alone in the last six months they have had over sixty patients who were shot while collecting rubble and gravel near the border with nearly all of them — everyone one of them a civilian young man or teenager — having been shot in their legs or feet. One had died from a chest wound while five others had required leg amputations.

The UN said that so far in 2010 fifty-five Palestinians including twenty-two civilians had been killed by Israeli military action in Gaza with a more than 200 others being injured during the same period. In response to being asked why Israeli soldiers felt compelled to shoot Palestinians working near the border, an Israeli military source said it was standard procedure because they could not take chances whenever Israeli lives were at risk. The source added that the "buffer zon"e was only enforced to 300m (326 yards) but the UN and Palestinians dispute this.

Farmer Khalil Zanin who grows oranges said that because of the buffer zone, his family has lost about 60,000 square metres [14.8 acres] of arable farmland near the fence which the Israelis have bulldozed. The UN estimated that more than thirty percent of arable land in Gaza has been lost to the "buffer zone" with a devastating impact on Gaza's farming community and the Gaza Strip's economy. Though Israel had withdrawn its forces from Gaza in 2005, it continued to control its borders as well as Gaza's airspace and access to the sea. When passing through Erez, the main Israeli border crossing into Gaza, it is quite common to hear the sound of gunfire from the Israeli watch towers whose alleged purpose is to protect Israeli communities living just over the border from Gaza.

22 November '10: Almost two years after the event, two Israeli soldiers — "members of the most moral army in the world"' — were convicted of using a Palestinian child as a human shield during the 2009 offensive in Gaza, but were inappropriately punished with only suspended sentences and demotion. They had forced the nine-year-old boy — who in fear of his life had wet his pants — to open suspected booby-trapped bags at gunpoint. As this is the first such conviction in Israel, where the use of civilians as human shields is banned, the lenient punishment will hardly discourage any further ill-treatment of Palestinian children by members of this irreproachable army of brutal occupation.

1 December '10: A new report by the New York-based Human Rights Watch group (HRW) says two of five laws applied in the Indonesian province of Aceh violate peoples' rights and are implemented abusively. Based on the Shariah legal code, they discriminate against women with the laws against "seclusion" and dress codes not being applied against rich or well-connected people, The report, "Policing Morality: Abuses in the Application of Sharia in Aceh, Indonesia," notes that the rights group takes no position on Shariah law as a whole which its supporters say is a system that provides a comprehensive guide to behavior.

The "seclusion" law which makes association by unmarried individuals of the opposite sex a criminal offense in some circumstances, along with laws on dress requirements, discriminatory. The two laws deny people's right to make their own decisions about who they meet and what they wear. The laws, and their selective enforcement, are an invitation to abuse with the word "seclusion" being used to bar people from simply meeting and talking in a quiet place. Abuses include aggressive interrogations and attempts to force people to marry against their will. There has also been at least one case of a woman being raped by the Shariah police officers while in detention.

Shariah police officers had admitted that they sometimes force women and girls to submit to virginity exams as part of the investigation. The laws also allow for members of the public to identify, report and punish alleged misbehaviour which has also led to further violence and abuses which usually go unpunished. Other Islamic laws applied in Aceh relate to charitable giving, gambling, Islamic ritual and proper Muslim behaviour. They were applied as part of the central government's attempts to appease the Islamic lobby in Aceh, where separatists have for years criticised unfairness in the distribution of wealth from Aceh's considerable oil and gas resources. Surveys in the province have regularly highlighted local residents' unhappiness with the laws. Neither the central nor the local government have responded to the HRW report.

10 December '10: A group of 26 ex-EU leaders has urged the European Union to impose sanctions on Israel for continuing to build settlements on occupied Palestinian territory. In their letter they said Israel "like any other state" should be made to feel "the consequences" and pay a price for breaking international law. The signatories include the former EU foreign affairs chief, Javier Solana.

Britain's pro-Israeli Catherine Ashton, Mr. Solana's successor, said in a written response that the bloc's approach would remain unchanged. This was followed by a response from an Israeli foreign ministry official who said the proposal represented "a giant leap of bad faith" — no doubt as opposed to Israel's Apartheid state of "good faith" and respect for human rights. Then in keeping with its AIPAC-designated supporting role, the U.S. announced it was abandoning efforts to persuade Israel to renew a partial settlement construction freeze so that direct peace talks with the Palestinian Authority could resume after being suspended by the Palestinians in September because a 10-month freeze on settlement in the West Bank, excluding East Jerusalem, had expired.

Yigal Palmor, an Israeli Foreign Ministry spokesman said "It is difficult to see how the call for sanctions and Israel's isolation will promote peace, but clearly this will diminish the EU's capability to play a constructive role in promoting peace."

The letter sent to European governments and EU institutions, asked EU foreign ministers to reiterate that they "will not recognize any changes to the June 1967 boundaries and clarify that a Palestinian state should be in sovereign control over territory equivalent to 100% of the territory occupied in 1967, including its capital in East Jerusalem." It also asked ministers to set the Israeli government an ultimatum that, if it has not fallen into line by April 2011, the EU will seek an end to the U.S.-brokered peace process in favor of a UN solution with the EU linking its informal freeze on an upgrade in diplomatic relations with Israel to a settlement construction moratorium; banning imports of products made in settlements; and forcing Israel to pay for the majority of the aid required by the Palestinians. It also urged the bloc to send a high-level delegation to East Jerusalem to support Palestinian claims to sovereignty and reclassify EU support for Palestine as "nation building" instead of "institution building."

The letter added that "Israel's continuation of settlement activity . . . posed an existential threat to the prospects of establishing a sovereign, contiguous and viable Palestinian state," and that "time is fast running out."

According to B'Tselem's 2008 official statistics, Israeli settlements on Palestinian land so far — and increasing — comprised 485,000 settlers in the West Bank and East Jerusalem, alongside 2.5 million

Palestinians; 12 settlements in East Jerusalem and 121 others in the West Bank, covering 40% of the territory; and another 100 settlement "outposts" not authorized by the Israeli government in the West Bank.

Baroness Catherine Ashton said: "The EU position on settlements is clear: they are illegal under international law and an obstacle to peace. Recent settlement related developments, including in East Jerusalem, contradict the efforts by the international community for successful negotiations."

Israeli Foreign Ministry spokesman Yigal Palmor replied that he had not seen a copy of the former European leaders' letter, but believed their focus on the settlements issue seemed "strange and harmful." It must have seemed "strange and harmful" to him because God's chosen people never do anything "strange' or 'harmful."

2011 DIARY OF NOTABLE
WORLD EVENTS

14 January '11: The Tunisian revolution which began in December 2010 with a campaign of civil resistance has today resulted in the ousting of longtime President Zine El Abidine Ben Ali who officially resigned after fleeing to Saudi Arabia. The revolution was precipitated by poor living conditions, food inflation, high unemployment, a lack of free speech, and political restrictions. The revolution's success could encourage similar protests and uprisings throughout the Arab world.

19 February '11: In keeping with its now traditional subservience to Israel — and following pressure from Israel and a Congress influenced by a strong pro-Israel lobby — on February 19 the U.S. vetoed an Arab resolution at the UN Security Council condemning Israeli settlements in the Palestinian territories as an obstacle to peace. Though this may have appeared to be a defeat for the Palestinians, the extent of the support they received was an overwhelming and gratifying "victory." Co-sponsored by some 130 countries the resolution had also been voted for by all fourteen other members of the Security Council. Such an endorsement of the Palestinian position on Israeli settlements — that they are illegal, and an obstacle to peace — served to isolate the U.S. and Israel. While asserting that it was opposed new Israeli settlements, the Obama administration made gutless, feeble excuses that taking the issue to the UN would only complicate attempts by both Palestinians and Israelis to reach an agreement.

20 February '11: Arab nations — having formally submitted a resolution to the UN Security Council condemning Israeli settlement building in the occupied West Bank and East Jerusalem — were not particularly surprised that despite having made a settlement freeze the focus of its attempts to resurrect direct Israeli-Palestinian negotiations, The Obama administration cast its first UN veto by rejecting the resolution which all other fourteen members of the Security Council had backed.

U.S. Secretary of State Hilary Clinton had recently echoed Israeli wishes by stating "We continue to believe strongly that New York is not the place to resolve the long-standing conflict and outstanding issues between the Israelis and the Palestinians." During the past twenty years, the framework for peace talks has shifted from the UN to a U.S.-led bilateral process and the Israelis want to keep it that way because they know they have far greater control of the U.S. government than they do over the UN.

Having vetoed the resolution, U.S. Ambassador to the UN Susan Rice then explained that even though the U.S. had vetoed the resolution, such opposition should not be misunderstood to mean that the U.S. supports illegal Israeli settlement activity:

> *The US still rejects in the strongest terms the legitimacy of continued Israeli settlement activity. For more than four decades, Israeli settlement activity in territories occupied in 1967 has undermined Israel's security and corroded hopes for peace and stability in the region . . . Continued settlement activity violates Israel's international commitments, devastates trust between the parties, and threatens the prospects for peace . . . While we agree with our fellow Council members — and indeed, with the wider world — about the folly and illegitimacy of continued Israeli settlement activity, we think it unwise for this Council to attempt to resolve the core issues that divide Israelis and Palestinians. We therefore regrettably have opposed this draft resolution.*

The contradiction between what the U.S. believes and what it actually does was not, however, explained by Ambassador Rice because that would have required the admission that U.S. Middle East policy is not based on principles of international law and justice, but is instead dictated by AIPAC — who has most U.S. politicians in its pockets — on behalf of Israel. While Prime Minister Benjamin Netanyahu's office issued the statement that "Israel deeply appreciates the decision by President Obama to veto the Security Council Resolution," many Israelis disagreed including Gideon Levy, columnist for the Israeli newspaper *Ha'aretz* :

> *This weekend, a new member enrolled in Likud — and not just in the ruling party, but in its most hawkish wing . . . The first veto cast by the United States during Obama's term, a*

veto he promised in vain not to use as his predecessors did, was a veto against the chance and promise of change, a veto against hope. This is a veto that is not friendly to Israel; it supports the settlers and the Israeli right, and them alone.

2 March '11: Last month in the UK, *The Promise*, a British television serial in four episodes written and directed by Peter Kosminsky premiered on Channel 4. It is about a young woman who travels to present-day Israel/ Palestine and is determined to find out about her soldier grandfather's involvement in the final years of Palestine under the British Mandate. Apart from a few exceptions, reviews were full of praise with Rachel Cooke in the *New Statesman* and *The Observer saying* it was " . . . the best thing you are likely to see on TV this year, if not this decade." As was to be expected, however, a press attaché at the Israeli embassy in London condemned the drama to *The Jewish Chronicle* as the worst example of anti-Israel propaganda he had ever seen on television, adding that it "created a new category of hostility towards Israel." The Zionist Federation and Board of Deputies of British Jews also lodged letters of complaint no doubt because of scenes showing the atrocities carried out by Jews against the Palestinian population. *The Promise* is a must-see for anyone interested in understanding what was done and is still being done to the Palestinians while majority of the high-principled people in the world stand on the sidelines watching and doing absolutely nothing.

7 March '11: An imam has retracted statements about evolution and the right of Muslim women not to cover their hair after death threats were made against him. Dr Usama Hasan, a science lecturer, has voluntarily suspended his role in taking Friday prayers at Leyton Mosque in east London. He said he had gone too far in the way he defended the theory of evolution and acknowledged that many British Muslims believed in creationism, adding that he intended only to begin a debate.

Dr Hasan — a senior lecturer at Westminster University trained in physics and engineering — used an opinion piece on the *The Guardian* newspaper's website in 2008 to suggest Darwin's theory of evolution was not incompatible with the teaching of Islam. He asserted that there were numerous Muslim biologists who had no doubt about the essential correctness of evolutionary theory and added that "many believers in God have no problem with an obvious solution: that God created man via evolution."

Dr Hasan also stated that "snazzy websites, videos and books produced by fundamentalist Muslim 'creationists' were obscuring clear scientific thinking . . . One problem is that many Muslims retain the simple picture that God created Adam from clay, much as a potter makes a statue, and then breathed into the lifeless statue and lo! it became a living human. This is a children's madrasa-level understanding and Muslims really have to move on as adults and intellectuals."

In a separate article he claimed the requirement for women to cover their hair in public was cultural in origin, and that British Muslims should have the choice. His remarks have led to fatwas denouncing him from Muslim scholars in several countries. He was more recently subjected to death threats when he delivered a lecture in January and that a leaflet campaign had been mounted against him. Dr Hasan, who is vice chairman of Leyton Mosque — which houses one of the country's largest Shariah courts — has agreed he went too far in suggesting that the Adam of the creation story would have had human parents. This is yet another example of how religion violates the rights of people who happen to have different opinions.

28 March '11: Willaim Kristol, the Jewish neo-conservative founder and editor of The Weekly Standard ("the neo-con bible"), and regular commentator on the Murdoch-owned Fox (so-called) News Channel, stated in an editorial that U.S. military interventions in Muslim countries (including the Gulf War, the Kosovo War, the Afghanistan War, and the Iraq War) should not be classified as "invasions," but rather as "liberations." This proponent of U.S. military "liberations" had previously in 2010 — during the disclosure of U.S. diplomatic cables by Wikileaks — bitterly criticized the organization and advocated using "our various assets to harass, snatch or neutralize Julian Assange and his collaborators, wherever they are." Kristol, with his warped neoconservative venom, is also associated with more than half a dozen prominent conservative (Zionist) think tanks including the Emergency Committee for Israel (ECI).

2 May '11: Osama bin Laden, the founder of Al-Qaeda the jihadist organization allegedly responsible for the September 11 attacks, was today shot and killed by U.S. Navy SEALs and CIA operatives in a covert operation ordered by President Barack Obama. On the Federal Bureau of Investigation's (FBI) list of "most wanted" with a $25 million bounty on his head, bin Laden was a major target of the War on Terror. Though much welcomed, his death has left Western Neocon warmongers with the dilemma of having to find some other individual or organization capable of taking on the lead role of being a prime target for the War on Terror which at any cost must continue endlessly for the benefit of the Military Industrial Congressional Complex (MICC).

8 May '11: Renowned UK cosmologist Professor Stephen Hawking has withdrawn from a high-profile Israeli conference, in support of an academic boycott of the country. Previous speakers at the Israeli Presidential Conference include former UK Prime Minister Tony Blair, former U.S. President George W. Bush, and former U.S. Secretary of State and Nobel Peace laureate Doctor Henry Kissinger — with all three of them being unindicted war criminals.

Israel reacted with its usual Zionist vitriol with Presidential Conference Chairman, Israel Maimon, saying that "the academic boycott against Israel is in our view outrageous and improper, certainly for someone for whom the spirit of liberty lies at the basis of his human and academic mission. Israel is a democracy in which all individuals are free to express their opinions, whatever they may be. The imposition of a boycott is incompatible with open, democratic dialogue." The only conclusion to be drawn from that statement is that Israel is a democracy in which all individuals are free to express their opinions so long as they are not Palestinians or have opinions that are critical of Israel.

Not to be outdone, Alan Dershowitz in New York, attacked Hawking for his boycott in protest at Israel's treatment of Palestinians by calling him an "ignoramus" and just another anti-Semite "lemming" being pressured by the BDS (Boycott-Divestment-Sanctions) movement which was gaining ground around the world. And Dershowitz is the guy who has been hailed as "the nation's most peripatetic civil liberties lawyer" and "one of its most distinguished defenders of individual rights." As Palestinians are regarded by Zionists to be inhuman, they unfortunately do not qualify for Dershowitz's "most distinguished defense of individual human rights." Dershowitz should stop judging others by his own nasty Zionist disposition.

21 May '11: In an on camera Oval Office appearance Israeli Prime Minister Netanyahu undercut U.S. President Barack Obama with a seven-and-a-half minute lecture after Obama had called for 1967 borders with "mutually agreed land swaps." This had always been an agreed-upon solution to any peace deal, but Netanyahu tore into Obama with the confident knowledge that he could get away with it because of the staunch and absolute bipartisan support that Israel commands in the U.S. Netanyahu vowed that Israel would never return to its 1967 borders and laid down a set of non-negotiable conditions for peace talks with a warning that Obama should not chase what he described as a Middle East peace "based on illusions." Continuing with his confrontational manner, Netanyahu stressed that "While Israel is prepared to make generous compromises for peace, it cannot go back to the 1967 lines — because these lines are indefensible." Netanyahu also played the usual Zionist card by lecturing Obama on the historic struggles of the Jewish people — once again overlooking the ongoing struggles of hundreds of millions of people all over the world.

1 June '11: The Committee to Protect Journalists has reported that more than 251 journalists in 13 countries were killed "with impunity" in the past decade with the unpunished murders leading to self-censorship and press silence. Singled out as the worst environments for journalists were Iraq, Somalia, the Philippines and Sri Lanka with the 2010 situation for journalists worsening in Mexico but improving in Russia. Executive Director Joel Simon said "The targeted killing of journalists serves as a silencing message to others, ensuring that sensitive issues are not subjected to public scrutiny . . . many journalists who were murdered had been threatened beforehand but were left unprotected. Governments can either address anti-press violence or see murders continue and self-censorship spread." The really sad thing about this is the fact that the mainstream media fails to report on and highlight this extreme form of censorship.

8 July '11: Yesterday, after a delay of more than a year, the Canadian Parliamentary Coalition to Combat Antisemitism (CPCCA) released the report of its inquiry. Born out of the February 2009 London Declaration on Combating Antisemitism, the report raises question about such organizations who dedicate themselves to combating only anti-Semitism and not racism against all peoples. The CPCCA will also be hosting an international conference in the Canadian Parliament Buildings with doors closed to the public and the media. It will be financed by U.S. $451,280 of public funds, provided by Jason Kenney, the Minister of

Citizenship, Immigration and Multiculturalism. Guests will include the Inter-Parliamentary Committee to Combat anti-Semitism (ICCA) and payed-for supporters of Israel who are Parliamentarians in various countries.

Canadians for Justice and Peace in the Middle East (CJPME) questioned grave misrepresentations in the report with critics pointing out that Prime Minister Stephen Harper's government is so pro-Israel that It will vote at the UN against recognition of a Palestinian state on only half the land that Canadian diplomats promised Palestine 60 years ago; that it will support illegal settlers and the extreme right in blocking recognition that would redress a travesty of justice; that it would do so despite Canada having spent tens of millions of dollars on "state-building" measures for Palestinians; that it will do all this despite the fact that more Canadians are in favor of the Palestinian bid for UN membership, than voted Conservative in the last election.

Stephen Harper — a contemptible brown-noser of the Jewish lobby — has described criticism of Israel as a new form of anti-Semitism and it was obvious that his motive was to stifle criticism of Israeli policies and disrupt pro-Palestinian solidarity organizations and events in Canada, including Israeli Apartheid Week (IAW) lectures and rallies. Most of the CPCCA's findings have been rejected as having recklessly undermined the combating of real occurrences of anti-Semitism by stifling freedom of speech and the right to peacefully protest.

Between November 2009 and January 2010, the CPCCA held ten separate hearings during which time representatives of various non-governmental organizations, religious institutions, police departments and Canadian and Israeli universities presented papers meant to assess the level of anti-Semitism in Canada. Though groups critical of Israel were denied the opportunity to address the committee, major Zionist organisations like B'nai Brith Canada, Friends of the Simon Wiesenthal Centre for Holocaust Studies, and the Canadian Jewish Congress were embraced with open arms.

During the entire consultation process, the CPCCA repeatedly focused on Canadian university campuses which were falsely described as hotbeds of anti-Semitism with the accusation being made repeatedly and included in the final report. This was despite the fact that Dr. Fred Lowy, President Emeritus of Concordia University in Montreal, stated in his address to the CPCCA that, "by and large, Canadian campuses are safe and are not hotbeds of anti-Semitism of any kind."

In its final report, the CPCCA made some two dozen recommendations on how best to fight anti-Semitism in Canada. Though the report stated that "criticism of Israel is not anti-Semitic, and saying so is wrong," it also found that "singling Israel out for selective condemnation and opprobrium . . . is discriminatory and hateful" with many of its recommendations dealing with combating this "new anti-Semitism." Having had to face the reality that there is very little of the "old anti-Semitism" about, they have had to invent a "new anti-Semitism" with which to intimidate and bludgeon into silence anyone who dares criticize Israeli crimes.

Amongst the CPCCA's threat-to-free-speech recommendations was that Canadian university administrators should condemn "discourse, events and speakers which are untrue, harmful, or not in the interest of academic discourse, including Israeli Apartheid week." In a further display of prejudice in favor of Israel, it was also recommended that even the use of the word "Apartheid" in relation to Israel constituted anti-Semitism with the "denial of the Jewish people their right to self-determination . . . by claiming that the existence of a State of Israel is a racist endeavor." The sheer hypocrisy of this finding beggars belief while overlooking the Palestinian right to also have self-determination.

Such recommendations are a blatant violation of freedom of speech intended to stifle a healthy exchange of ideas on university campuses and vilify the IAW. This is despite the fact that individuals of distinguished international repute such as Ali Abunimah (a Palestinian American journalist), Judith Butler (American post-structuralist philosopher), Noam Chomsky (American activist, cognitive scientist, linguist, logician, philosopher, and political critic), and Ronnie Kasrils (South African politician) were brought together to openly discuss Israeli-Palestinian issues by the IAW.

Contrary to the CPCCA's suggestion that the IAW is a "uniformly well-organized, aggressive campaign designed to make the Jewish state and its supporters pariahs," the IAW simply exposes Israeli Apartheid policies such as the separate legal systems for Israelis and Palestinians in the occupied West Bank; highlights Israel's use of discriminatory land ownership laws; and supports the ever-growing non-violent campaign of Boycott, Divestment and Sanctions (BDS) which aims to pressure Israel into respecting international laws.

Yet another obtuse CPCCA recommendation was that the Canadian Committee of Foreign Affairs should undertake a study on the United Nations Human Rights Council with particular regard to "its over-emphasis of alleged human rights abuses by Israel, while ignoring flagrant human rights abuses of other member states." By confusing anti-Semitism with criticism of Israel and casting questionable aspersions on UN bodies, the CPCCA was inhibiting public discussion of Israeli violations and contributing to the ongoing erosion of what was once Canada's impeccable international standing.

Independent Jewish Voices (IJV) Canada was also critical by stating, "The CPCCA's goal is to criminalize criticism of Israel and Zionism, not to hold impartial hearings. Therefore we oppose the CPCCA as an ideologically biased organization with an agenda that will harm free speech and human rights activity in Canada. We oppose the CPCCA's Orwellian distortion of anti-Semitism. It is a danger to both Canadian liberties and to the genuine and necessary fight against anti-Semitism."

This is not a view shared by Prime Minister Stephen Harper who at the 2010 Ottawa Conference sang from the same Zionist hymn sheet with "when Israel, the only country in the world whose very existence is under attack, is consistently and conspicuously singled out for condemnation, I believe we are morally obligated to take a stand. Demonization, double standards, de-legitimization, the three D's, it is the responsibility of us all to stand up to them." This ingratiating politician — of the same sellout mould as Britain's Tony Blair — added that "harnessing disparate anti-American, anti-Semitic and anti-Western ideologies, it targets the Jewish people by targeting the Jewish homeland, Israel, as the source of injustice and conflict in the world and uses, perversely, the language of human rights to do so. We must be relentless in exposing this anti-Semitism for what it is." So Harper is not only of the opinion that the language of human rights is not applicable to the Palestinian people, but he also feels free to use double standards to demonize and de-legitimize Palestinian rights while in the same breath accusing others of doing so to Israel. If this smarmy individual represents the majority view of Canadians, then the majority of Canadians should take a good look in the mirror while trying to define what it is to be Canadian.

One of CPCCA's more important recommendations was that the Canadian government should promote the working definition of anti-Semitism as used by The European Union Monitoring Centre on Racism and Xenophobia (EUMC). This definition categorizes "applying double standards by requiring of [Israel] a behavior not expected or demanded of any other democratic nation" as anti-Semitic. The recommendation, however, did not cite any examples of other democratic nations that enforce brutal Apartheid policies and commit crimes against humanity to the extent that Israel does with impunity.

11 July '11: The Israeli parliament has passed a controversial law that will punish any Israeli individual or organization that boycotts West Bank settlements. Rights groups complain that the legislation stifles freedom of speech and compromises Israeli democracy. After failed attempts to delay the debate, the law was voted through by 47-36. It follows several Israeli calls to boycott individuals or organizations linked to Jewish settlements on occupied Palestinian land.

The Association for Civil Rights in Israel (ACRI) described the law as "deeply anti-democratic" and a violation of Israelis' freedom of speech. ACRI executive director, Hagai el-Ad said that "there is no question that promoting boycotts is a legitimate, democratic, non-violent form of protest that is being used by Israelis on a wide variety of issues from environmental issues to opposing the prices of certain products . . . No reasoning has been suggested to explain why the boycott of settlement goods should be uniquely cherished as opposed to the right of the Israeli citizen to protest."

Among the recent initiatives that angered settlers and their influential political cohorts was a pledge by Israeli academics and artists to boycott the West Bank settlement of Ariel. Under the new law those sponsoring a "geographically based boycott"' — which includes any part of the Jewish state or its settlements — could be sued for damages in a civil court by the party injured in the boycott call. The petitioner is not required to prove that "economic, cultural or academic damage" was caused, only that it could reasonably be expected from the move. Lawmaker Zeev Elvin, the author of the legislation, said that "the State of Israel has for years been dealing with boycotts from Arab nations, but now we are talking about a homegrown boycott . . . It is time to put an end to this travesty. If the State of Israel does not protect itself, we will have no moral right to ask our allies for protection from such boycotts."

30 July '11: Kuala Lumpur witnessed an Occupy Dataran protest that was directed against economic inequality, corporate greed, corruption, and influence over government such as that by the financial services sector. There was also discontent over lobbyists and the jobless rate.

11 August '11: In a television interview Retired U.S. Army General Wesley Clark (Supreme Allied Commander Europe of NATO from 1997-2000) reiterated what he had previously revealed in his 2003 book *Winning Modern Wars:*

> *As I went back through the Pentagon in November 2001, one of the senior military staff officers had time for a chat. Yes, we were still on track for going against Iraq, he said. But there was more. This was being discussed as part of a five-year campaign plan, he said, and there were a total of seven countries, beginning with Iraq, then Syria, Lebanon, Libya, Iran, Somalia and Sudan.*

Clark's revelation was further confirmation of reports an extended Middle East and Central Asian war has been on the Pentagon's drawing board since the mid-1990s as part of US-NATO alliance plans to wage a military campaign against Syria under the guise of a UN sponsored "humanitarian mandate" U.S.-NATO coordinated military planning includes conflict escalation and destabilization of sovereign states through "regime change" with war preparations to attack Syria and Iran having been in an advanced state of readiness for several years. The Syria Accountability and Lebanese Sovereignty Restoration Act passed by the U.S. Congress in 2003 categorizes Syria as a "rogue state" that supports terrorism.

President Bush Jr. confirmed in his Memoirs that he had ordered the Pentagon to plan an attack on Iran's nuclear facilities and [had] considered a covert attack on Syria. Going to war against Syria is viewed by the Pentagon as part of the broader war which would also include Iran as part of a broader military agenda closely related to strategic oil reserves and pipeline routes.

The July 2006 bombing of Lebanon and the extension of that war into Syria had been coordinated by U.S. and Israeli military planners, but was abandoned following the defeat of Israeli ground forces by Hizbollah. This war on Lebanon also intended to establish Israeli control over the North Eastern Mediterranean coastline including offshore oil and gas reserves in Lebanese and Palestinian territorial waters. Despite Israel's setback in the July 2006 War, plans to invade Lebanon and Syria have since remained on the Pentagon's drawing board.

Any US-NATO sponsored war on Iran would first have to start in

Damascus with a destabilisation campaign including covert intelligence operations in support of rebel forces so as to achieve "regime change" that would also contribute to the ongoing destabilization of Lebanon. It would be billed as a "humanitarian war" under the smokescreen of the "Responsibility to Protect" (R2P) UN initiative established in 2005 consisting of a set of principles based on the claim that sovereignty is not a right, but a responsibility. R2P focuses on preventing and halting the four crimes of genocide, war crimes, crimes against humanity, and ethnic cleansing. The irony and hypocrisy of all this is that Israel — which is guilty of all four of the aforementioned crimes — would be either directly or indirectly involved in the military and intelligence operations. Israel's insidious influence on the U.S. — and through the U.S. and its allies, also on the UN — will eventually lead the West into a broader Middle East-Central Asian war, engulfing an entire region from North Africa and the Mediterranean to Afghanistan and Pakistan.

Also today final approval was given for the construction of 1,600 settler homes in occupied East Jerusalem by the Israeli interior ministry. A spokesman for the interior ministry, told Agence France-Presse (AFP) that minister Eli Yishai had given approval for the 1,600 homes in Ramat Shlomo and will approve 2,000 more in Givat Hamatos and 700 in Pisgat Zeev. The initial go-ahead for the 1,600 homes in Ramat Shlomo had previously been announced in March 2010 during U.S. Vice-President Joe Biden's visit to Israel when he had called for the resumption of Palestinian-Israeli peace talks. The announcement was yet another deliberately-timed Israeli slap in the face for the U.S which caused a diplomatic row between the two countries. Israel's reiteration of its unshakable intent to continue with settlement expansion come what may, was on this occasion timed to preempt the Palestinian Authority's attempt to have a Palestinian state recognized at the United Nations: a move that was strongly opposed by the Israelis who were confident they could rely on a UN Security Council veto from their ever- subservient U.S. ally.

16 August '11: Four days after Israel's approval for the construction of more homes for Jewish settlers in East Jerusalem, a further approval for 300 homes for Ariel which apart from being deep inside the occupied West Bank, is also the largest of the Jewish settlements. So while Palestinians have their homes demolished, new homes are built for Jewish settlers on Palestinian land. The U.S. responded with its usual meaningless and ineffectual announcement that the move was "deeply troubling" and "counter-productive" to the resumption of peace talks. The move also prompted the Palestinian leadership to reassert its intention to pursue UN recognition of a sovereign Palestinian state while also noting that Israeli plans to expand settlements was "new evidence that Israel is not serious about negotiating a two-state solution."

30 August '11: The Israeli army has announced that it is training Jewish settlers in the West Bank in anticipation of protests by Palestinians when they make a bid for separate statehood at the United Nations in September. Israel has not only always permitted settlers to carry weapons which human rights groups claim are used for attacks on Palestinians, but has also been extremely lax with its investigation of such settler criminality. In view of the fact that many of these armed settlers are ultra-orthodox, it can only be assumed that their refusal to serve in the Israeli army has nothing to do with conscientious objection. They are obviously prepared to use violence and if necessary even kill in order to retain that which they have stolen.

2 September '11: The UN-appointed expert panel led by South African judge Richard Goldstone — which in September 2009 accused Israel of using disproportionate force, deliberately targeting civilians, destroying civilian infrastructure, and using people as human shields — has unsurprisingly had a change of mind with the report's author, saying that new accounts indicated Israel had not deliberately targeted civilians. He said that if he had known what he knew now, "the Goldstone Report would have been a different document." Mr. Goldstone did not explain what it was that he failed to learn back in 2009, which he had now suddenly discovered. This is not the first time where criticism of Israel by a Jew had subsequently been withdrawn following Israeli lobbying and pressure.

In an opinion piece in *The Washington Post*, Mr. Goldstone wrote that his conclusions about Israel appeared to have been wrong. He said the Israeli investigations, which were recognized by a UN committee, indicated that "Civilians were not intentionally targeted as a matter of policy." He explained, "we know a lot more today about what happened in the Gaza war . . . If I had known then what I know now, the Goldstone Report would have been a different document." Mr Goldstone also noted

393

that "Hamas had 'done nothing' to examine its rocket attacks, which were 'purposefully and indiscriminately aimed at civilian targets."

In view of Israel's track record for always denying any wrongdoing — along with the tendency to rewrite history so as to sanitize its image — it is highly unlikely that the Israeli investigations were unbiased. Israeli Prime Minster Benjamin Netanyahu wasted no time in claiming that "everything we said has been proven to be true . . . Israel does not purposely target civilians and its investigative institutions are competent, while Hamas intentionally fires at innocent civilians and does not investigate anything . . . The fact that Goldstone has backtracked means the report should be buried once and for all."

During the transition from apartheid to multi-racial democracy in the early 1990s, Goldstone had led the influential Goldstone Commission investigations into political violence in South Africa between 1991 and 1994. His work had enabled multi-party negotiations to remain on course despite repeated outbreaks of violence, and his willingness to criticise all sides led to him being dubbed "perhaps the most trusted man, certainly the most trusted member of the white establishment" in South Africa. He was credited with playing a vital role in the transition and became a renowned public figure in South Africa while attracting widespread international interest and respect.

Goldstone's work investigating violence led directly to his being nominated to serve as the first chief prosecutor of the United Nations International Criminal Tribunal for the former Yugoslavia and for Rwanda from August 1994 to September 1996. He prosecuted a number of key war crimes suspects including the Bosnian Serb political and military leaders, Radovan Karadžić and Ratko Mladić. On his return to South Africa he took up a seat on the newly-established Constitutional Court of South Africa to which he had been nominated by President Nelson Mandela. Goldstone's current retraction of his previous findings regrettably marks the denouement of his international credibility and reputation for impartiality. He should be ashamed of himself for succumbing to Israeli pressure.

9 September '11: As George Bernard Shaw, the Irish dramatist and socialist (1856-1950) once observed: "If history repeats itself, and the unexpected always happens, how incapable must Man be of learning from experience." So with the approach of the tenth anniversary of 9/11, and as was previously the case when people in the West were conditioned to believe that regime change in Iraq was essential, the West is yet again about to be brainwashed into accepting another war. Unindicted war criminal and former British Prime Minister (and Israeli asset) Tony Blair rather than admit to the Blair/Bush collaborative deception in launching an illegal war on Iraq which is still ongoing, has instead blamed Iranian intervention for prolonging the conflicts in Iraq and Afghanistan. He added that regime change in Tehran would make him "significantly more optimistic" about the region's prospects and that Syrian President Bashar al Assad's position was untenable. It would appear that the moneygrabbing, contemptible and brown-nosing Blair's thirst for more blood is unquenchable. It is no wonder that the Palestinians have always suspected that this war mongering criminal was biased towards Israel.

10 September '11: Not wishing to lose momentum, Tony Blair stated that the killing of Osama bin Laden was "immensely important" in the battle against terrorism but that al-Qaeda remained a threat because "large numbers of people'"still shared its ideology. Blair maintained that "risk is still there, but we have gone after them [al-Qaeda]. We have degraded their capacity and capability. We have either captured or killed many of their leading people." Blair added "I think the narrative and ideology of the movement is still there. So killing him [bin Laden] was actually immensely important, because it dealt a huge psychological blow to their movement but it doesn't alter the fact there are still large numbers of people out there who buy the narrative of this terrorist movement, even if they do not share or agree with its methods." The two-faced hypocrisy of this low life knows no bounds especially as Israeli and U.S. and Saudi Arabian intelligence services are supporting al-Qaeda's mischief-making in Syria with a view to achieving "regime change."

21 September '11: President Obama at the U.N. received an appropriately lukewarm response without applause for his arrogant and meaningless lecture which featured the usual load of presidential crap about "peace." This was in stark contrast to the U.S. President's first ever appearance at the U.N. where with time the realization had now dawned that the once apparent champion of multilateralism and hope for the future was no match for those who actually controlled a U.S. foreign policy that relied heavily on aggressive militarism. Obama's main objective was to lend support to a backstage campaign of threats and intimidation designed to force the Palestinian Authority to abandon its application for a UN Security Council vote on recognition of Palestine as a sovereign member state. "Peace will not come through statements and resolutions at the UN," Obama said, thereby raising the question as to why — if that is the case — do nations bother having a UN General Assembly? By also saying that "ultimately, it is the Israelis and Palestinians — and not us — who must reach agreement on the issues that divide them," Obama merely persisted with the West's refusal to learn from history and acknowledge that Zionist Israel does not want a peace that may either require the return of some land to its original and rightful owners; or that might prevent the stealing of even more Palestinian land.

Following his fatuous sermon, Obama immediately rushed to huddle and appear with Israel's Benjamin Netanyahu who by praising Obama's remarks merely confirmed that they were both working to strong-arm Palestine Authority head Mahmoud Abbas into dropping the bid for statehood. One such ploy was to try and persuade the Palestinian delegation to simply make a symbolic application for recognition, while agreeing to postpone any vote until after the resumption of US-brokered negotiations with Israel.

Decades of such talks have always failed because Zionist Israel has remained relentless in expanding Israeli settlements that over the past two decades have served to more than double the number of settlers in Jerusalem and the occupied West Bank. The West Bank is now a territory fragmented by Israeli settlements, security roads, checkpoints, and an apartheid security wall separating it from Israel.

Obama's speech failed to repeat his previous request — which provoked an outcry from Netanyahu, the Israeli right, the U.S. Jewish lobby, and the Republican Party — of a return to the 1967 borders and a halt to the illegal expansion of settlements. Instead, in a gutless u-turn, Obama acknowledged that such conditions were to be dictated by Israel: "Israelis must know that any agreement provides assurances for their security. Palestinians deserve to know the territorial basis of their state."

In an effort to further placate right-wing and Israeli lobby criticism, Obama proceeded to dismiss the historical grievances of the Palestinian people and to unconditionally identify with Israel: "America's commitment to Israel's security is unshakable, and our friendship with Israel is deep and enduring." Obama also obligingly described Israel as being "surrounded by neighbors that have waged repeated wars against it," whose "citizens have been killed by rockets fired at their houses and suicide bombs on their buses." Obama then wound up with both the reminder that Israel was a "small country" in a world "where leaders of much larger nations threaten to wipe it off of the map," and the inevitable invocation of the Holocaust.

Needless to say, this erstwhile champion of peace and justice for all chose to overlook the fact that some 4 million Palestinians live under the oppression and constant violence of Israeli occupation, and that another 5 million driven from their homeland who remain as stateless refugees. There was also no mention of the wars that Israel continually wages against it neighbors such as that against Lebanon in 2006 which left 1,200 civilians dead and much of the country's infrastructure in ruins: and the 2008 Operation Cast Lead in Gaza which ended with nearly 1,500 Palestinians dead, as opposed to just 13 Israelis.

23 September '11: After submitting a bid to the UN for recognition of a Palestinian state, Palestinian leader Mahmoud Abbas called on the Security Council to immediately approve full Palestinian membership of the UN. He pointed out that the Palestinians had entered negotiations with Israel with sincere intentions, but failure had been due to the continued building of Jewish settlements.

It also emerged today that while U.S. President barack Obama was publicly feigning pressure on Israel to make concessions to the Palestinians over the settlements issue, he was secretly selling the Israelis deep-penetrating bombs ("bunker busters") which they had long sought but had hitherto been unable to obtain from previous U.S. administrations. Such sales served to further strengthen the military relationship with Israel which could now use its "bunker busters" in any future strikes against Iranian nuclear sites.

27 September '11: To further emphasize its arrogant disregard for the internationally held opinion that continued settlement expansion was both illegal and a stumbling block to peace negotiations, Israel gave approval for the construction of 1,100 new homes in the Jewish settlement of Gilo on the outskirts of Jerusalem. That meant that in the past two years construction of 3,000 new homes in Gilo had been approved by the Jerusalem planning committee one of whom claimed it was "a nice gift for Rosh Hashanah [Jewish New Year] ."

Three UN special rapporteurs responded by calling for an immediate end to the demolition of Palestinian-owned homes and other structures in the West Bank, including East Jerusalem. A statement by the rapporteurs on housing, water, sanitation and food rights asserted that there had been a dramatic increase in the number of demolitions this year, and that "the impact and discriminatory nature of these demolitions and evictions is completely unacceptable. These actions by the Israeli authorities violate human rights and humanitarian law and must end immediately." Despite all these violations, the majority of Jews around the world with their Judaic moral sense of right remain amorally silent.

Dismay was also expressed by Western nations with the European Union (EU) calling for a "reversal" of the plan. The indecisive Obama administration, having previously on February 19, 2011 vetoed an Arab resolution at the UN Security Council condemning Israeli settlements in the Palestinian territories as an obstacle to peace, now flip-flopped with U.S. Secretary of State Hillary Clinton stating that the move was "counter-productive" to peace talks. Hilary Clinton had flip-flopped at least once before in 2000, when on realizing that she could not win the New York Senate seat without the Jewish vote, she quickly changed her mind about a previous statement in which she had sympathized with the plight of the Palestinian people.

4 October '11: In response to the Palestinian application for UN membership as a fully fledged state, the Israeli controlled U.S. Congress has frozen $200m U.S. aid to the Palestinian Authority. U.S. Defense Secretary Leon Panetta and a state department spokeswoman condemned the move as counterproductive. It would appear that the Congress of the superpower nation that spends hundreds of billions of dollars fighting wars to give democracy and the right to self-determination to others; is the same nation which excludes the Palestinian people from that same inalienable right for fear of upsetting the Jewish lobby.

5 October '11: A senior official of the Palestinian Authority has urged the Quartet for Middle East peace to reconsider Mr Blair's appointment after declaring that his "bias" towards Israel had shorn him of credibility. The official added that "Our general evaluation of his efforts is that he has become of no use at all, and that he has developed a large bias in favor of the Israeli side and he has lost a lot of his credibility. We hope the Quartet will reconsider the appointment of this person." The demand for Blair's dismissal reflected Palestinian disillusionment and utter contempt for the former unindicted war criminal prime minister.

18 October '11: In the latest TV debate for Republican presidential hopefuls, Texas Governor Rick Perry, who like his predecessor George W. Bush is also intellectually challenged, suggested that the U.S. should consider "defunding" the United Nations because of its recent acceptance of a Palestinian application for membership. Was this guy chasing the Jewish vote or what?

On another note, following Gilat Shalit's release in exchange for Palestinian prisoners — he was captured and held by Hamas militants since 25 June 2006 — Emergency Committee for Israel (ECI) board member Rachel Abrams (and frequent contributor to William Kristol's The Weekly Standard) had this to say on her blog:

> *GILAD!!!!!!!!!!*
> *He's free and he's home in the bosom of his family and his country. Celebrate, Israel, with all the joyous gratitude that fills your hearts, as we all do along with you. Then round up his captors, the slaughtering, death-worshiping, innocent-butchering, child-sacrificing savages who dip their hands in blood and use women —those who aren't strapping bombs to their own devils' spawn and sending them out to meet their seventy-two virgins by taking the lives of the school-bus-riding, heart-drawing, Transformer-doodling, homework-losing children of Others —and their offspring — those who haven't already been pimped out by their mothers to the murder god — as shields, hiding behind their burkas and cradles like the unmanned animals they are, and throw them not into your prisons, where they can bide until they're traded by the thousands for another child of Israel, but into the sea, to float there, food for sharks, stargazers, and whatever other oceanic carnivores God has put there for the purpose.*

It is perhaps no surprise that such a venomous diatribe would come from a board member of ECI, an organisation that in the same vein opposes the election of politicians who refuse to sign a pledge — circulated by AIPAC — for the defense of Israel. It must be extremely sad for any human being — especially one allegedly chosen by god — to be so consumed with hate for other humans. Apparently god's spawn — at least in this instance — is no better than that of the devil.

20 October '11: Libya's Colonel Muammar Gaddafi was captured alive and then murdered by his barbaric captors who denied him any vestige of justice such as the show trial accorded to that "most evil of dictators" Saddam Hussein of Iraq. Subsequent video images show Gaddafi being abused and possibly sodomised with some sharp implement by a vengeful and frenzied God-worshipping crowd shouting Allāhu Akbar (God is Great). Indeed He is.

21 October '11: U.S. President Barack Obama announced that before the end of December remaining U.S. troops would be withdrawn from Iraq: a country which Israel had long regarded as an enemy to be destroyed. With the help of an Israeli controlled U.S. Congress, Israel had achieved its goal by using the U.S. in a proxy war that destroyed a once strong Iraqi infrastructure, killed an estimated million and a half Iraqis, cost the lives of 4,400 Americans, and more recently squandered nearly $1 trillion during a time of economic crisis. Are the American people really happy about being thus used to expend their resources helping Israel instead of looking after America?

In 1952 segregation on inter-state railways in the U.S. was declared unconstitutional by a Supreme Court judgment which was followed in 1954 by a similar ruling concerning inter-state buses. In the Deep South, However, states continued with their own policy of transport segregation which allowed for whites to sit at the front while blacks sitting nearest to the front had to give up their seats to any whites that were standing. African American people who disobeyed such transport segregation policies were arrested and fined. On December 1, 1955, Rosa Parks (1903-2005), a middle-aged African American tailor's assistant from Montgomery, Alabama, who was tired after a hard day's work, refused to give up her seat to a white man. Following her arrest, Martin Luther King, a pastor at the local Baptist Church, helped to organize protests against bus segregation. It was decided that black people in Montgomery would refuse to use the buses until passengers were completely integrated. King was arrested and his house was fire-bombed while others involved in the Montgomery Bus Boycott were also subjected to harassment and intimidation, but the protest continued. For thirteen months the 17,000 black people in Montgomery walked to work or obtained lifts from the small car-owning black population of the city. Eventually, the loss of revenue and a decision by the Supreme Court forced the Montgomery Bus Company to accept integration.

Today, almost 56 years later, New York City officials have disclosed that a bus service running through an Orthodox Jewish area could be shut down for asking women to sit at the back. While the B110 bus service is operated by a private company under a franchising agreement with the city, it is nonetheless open to the public. A New York Times report stated that a woman passenger on the B110 had said men and women also sat apart on similar bus services catering for the city's Hasidic Jewish community. The city's Department of Transportation director has asked the company that operates the route to respond to the claims. It would seem that religious extremists with their false and outdated religious doctrines and traditions — be they Jewish, Islamic, Christian, or some other denomination — are still flouting equal rights legislation by treating women as an inferior gender of the species.

25 October '11: While appearing as a guest on the Tonight Show with Jay Leno, President Barack Obama said that the death of Libya's Colonel Muammar Gaddafi "sends a strong message to dictators" that "people want to be free." Judging by the Obama administration's Israeli-dictated Middle East policy it would seem that Barack "Uncle Tom" Obama — a major hypocrite and miserable excuse for an international statesman — is apparently not aware that Palestinians are also "a people who want to be free."

Also on this day A New York Times/CBS poll augured badly for President Obama and Congress with its findings that distrust of government is at its highest level ever with 89 percent of Americans saying they distrust government to do the right thing. The poll also revealed that 74 percent think the country is on the wrong track, 43 percent feel that wealth should be distributed more evenly, and 84 percent disapprove of Congress. When asked specifically about the 'Occupy Wall Street' movement, 43 percent of Americans agreed with its views while 27 percent disagreed and 30 percent were unsure.

31 October '11: The UN cultural organization (UNESCO) has voted in favor of membership for the Palestinians: of the 173 countries voting, 107 were in favor, 14 opposed, and 52 abstained. Those opposed included the U.S., Israel, and Canada where — despite the controlling influence of its own Jewish lobby — it still claims to be impartial, independent, and in no way a U.S. lapdog. UNESCO — like other UN agencies who do not require full UN membership — has separate membership procedures and can make its own decisions regarding which countries become members. Being thus deprived of its usual veto power, the U.S., at the instigation of the pro-Israel Jewish lobby, immediately announced that its funding of UNESCO — about 22 percent of the agency's total budget — would be withheld starting with the the $60 million payment due in November. The move was dictated by a longstanding 1990s congressional ban on the funding of any agency recognizing Palestine as a state before Israel and Palestine reach a peace agreement. By acting in accordance with Israel's bidding, the U.S. could be stripped of its vote if delinquent in paying its dues for two years, become further isolated, and have its influence diminished in global affairs. No prize for guessing which lobby group initiated that particular congressional ban.

1 November '11: Being somewhat alarmed and piqued that so many nations dared to support the Palestinian cause, Israel announced that not only would it speed up Jewish settlement construction in the West Bank and East Jerusalem, but that it would also temporarily freeze the transfer of funds to the Palestinian Authority. It said that Prime Minister Benjamin Netanyahu had called for the accelerated construction of about 2,000 housing units with the construction being within "areas that in any future arrangement will remain in Israel's hands." An Israeli foreign ministry spokesman said that the measures were intended to increase pressure on the Palestinians following the "tragedy" of the UNESCO vote.

3 November '13: Despite the U.S. government's reiteration of its commitment to online free speech since Obama took office in January 2009 — and Secretary of State Hillary Clinton's affirmation of U.S. support for freedom of expression and opinion — the leak of classified

U.S. diplomatic cables has initiated many U.S. free speech violations at the federal government's bidding. WikiLeaks announced on 24 October that it was suspending its activities due to lack of funding, as a result of economic censorship in the form refusals by Visa and MasterCard to process donations to WikiLeaks.

Reporters Without Borders noted that the White House had issued a directive on 3 December 2010 forbidding unauthorised federal employees from accessing classified documents available on WikiLeaks. The Library of Congress and State Department responded a few hours later by blocking access to WikiLeaks from their computers. As well as WikiLeaks the US Air Force blocked access to the websites of the five newspapers that had worked closely with WikiLeaks — *The New York Times, The Guardian, Le Monde, Der Spiegel, and El Pais* — and around 20 other media and blogs that had been publishing the Cables. And this is the country that lectures the rest of the world about "freedom."

7 November '11: After speaking publicly for a G20 press conference last Thursday, French President Nicolas Sarkozy and President Obama reportedly had a heated exchange in which Sarkozy declared he could not "stand' Israeli Prime Minister Benjamin Netanyahu and called him "a liar" The report was posted by French website *Arrêt Sur Image* which reported that the conversation turned to Netanyahu after President Obama berated Sarkozy for not having warned him that France would vote in favor of Palestinian membership in UNESCO. The report claimed that both presidents were unaware that their microphones were still on while discussing the Israeli prime minister. Obama's reported response was: "You're fed up with him, but I have to deal with him every day!" The website stated that reporters had been asked to sign papers promising not to leak the "private" conversation.

15 November '11: Israeli police have detained six Palestinian "West Bank Freedom Riders" who boarded a Jerusalem-bound bus used by Jewish settlers. The activists claimed that their inspiration was drawn from the 1960s U.S. civil rights demonstrators who had campaigned against segregated buses. Palestinians from the West Bank are not permitted to cross into Jerusalem without Israeli permission — a restriction which Israel justifies for security reasons. The six protesters had travelled from a West Bank bus stop on an Israeli bus to an Israeli checkpoint at the edge of Jerusalem where they were eventually arrested for refusing to leave the bus. The protesters claimed that by only serving Jewish settlements and not Palestinian areas in the West Bank, Israeli bus companies and the entire Israeli system were discriminating against them.

23 November '11: A five-panel Kuala Lumpur War Crimes Tribunal in Malaysia has found former U.S. President George W. Bush and former British Prime Minister Tony Blair guilty of war crimes for their roles in the Iraq war. The Tribunal concluded that Bush and Blair committed genocide and crimes against humanity by leading the invasion of Iraq in 2003. The invasion — carried out under the pretext of finding former Iraqi dictator Saddam Hussein's alleged stockpile of weapons of mass destruction — was in blatant violation of international law.

The tribunal judges ruled that the decision to wage war against Iraq by the two former heads of government was a flagrant abuse of law and an act of aggression that led to bombings and other forms of violence resulting in large-scale massacres of the Iraqi people. The judges also stated that the U.S., under Bush's leadership, had fabricated documents to suggest that Iraq possessed weapons of mass destruction despite the U.S. and British leaders' knowledge to the contrary. According to the California-based investigative organization Project Censored, over one million Iraqis were killed during the invasion. The judges also stated that the court findings should be made available to signatories to the Rome Statute, which established the International Criminal Court (ICC), and that Bush and Blair should be registered as war criminals and tried by the ICC. The likelihood of that ever happening is, however, extremely remote considering that the ICC — like other entities such as the U.N., NATO, and the IMF World Bank — is under the corrupt and self-serving influence of the U.S.

23 November '11: A bench of Justices Dalip Singh and Sajjan Singh Kothari in High Court of Rajasthan – the largest state in India by area — has stated that the marriages based on right to choose (love marriages) are examples of "lust and greed." Such a repugnant conclusion was one of several made by the Bench on October 21 during their ruling on a Habeas Corpus petition filed by a 34- year-old man. The man was forced to file the petition after his 18-year-old wife was forcibly taken back by her parents when they learnt of the marriage. The High Court's conclusions were as quoted as follows: "The pious purpose of the Arya

Samaj mission has been lost by local units in the State and they are becoming a tool for pacification of 'greed and lust' for girl and boy, and once it is over the marriage lands in courts resulting in irreversible breakdowns."

Furthermore "it takes them one hour to solemnize a marriage between an 18-year-old girl and a 40-year-old gentleman, which leaves scars forever in the life of parents who bring up their children with great passion and aspirations. Such marriages in lust and greed by young blood cannot be said to be correct." Such conclusions by the renowned judges merely reinforces the legal violation of human rights by a society still trapped within the confines of religious bigotry and an outdated and abhorrent caste system.

30 November '11: A pro-Israel lobbying group modeled on AIPAC — which lobbies for pro-Israel policies in the U.S. — was launched yesterday in South Africa. The Cape Town-based South African Israel Public Affairs Committee, or SAIPAC, said it aims to establish relationships (bribe) with members of Parliament, and other community leaders, as well as strengthening the South Africa-Israel relationship. According to David Hersch — who cofounded SAIPAC with Kenny Penkin — there was "a gap and a desperate need for a lobby in Parliament and to get the truth out to those who support us."

Hersch, who sat on the Cape committee of the South African Jewish Board of Deputies and served as national vice-chairman and Cape chairman of the South African Zionist Federation, claimed he was in touch with AIPAC, attended its conference in Washington some years ago and lobbied with the group in the U.S. Congress. "There's no doubt that this is an uphill battle, but we will do it," Hersch said alluding to the pro-Palestinian stance of the country's ruling African National Congress. Though he stressed that SAIPAC would be "completely independent" and not affiliated "in any way" to the Board of Deputies or any other Jewish body, Hersch, nonetheless did not rule out dialogue with key Jewish groups.

SAIPAC, however, would "always be in sync and close association with the Israeli Embassy," he added while emphasizing that the group was not in the employ of the embassy but was simply pro-Israel, regardless of who is running the government. The group would also draw on the experience of its antipodean counterpart the Australian Israel & Jewish Affairs council (AIJAC). Apart from Cape Town, satellite SAIPAC branches were also being planned for Johannesburg and Durban. Funds would be raised partly by hosting expert speakers and analysts from Israel and elsewhere as a means of "keeping our community and others informed and empowered with knowledge and information." Knowledge and information that would no doubt be skewed towards Israel while ignoring to mention its violations of international laws.

In view of the fact that Penkin had noted that the community needed "a vibrancy" in that regard and to "stand up and be counted, be proud Jews," would it be impertinent and anti-Semitic to ask whether South Africa's "proud Jews" are equally proud of what Israeli Jews are doing to the Palestinian people?

2 December '11: A report in Saudi Arabia — whom Amnesty International has accused of reacting to the Arab Spring by launching a wave of repression — has warned with inexplicable religious absurdity that if Saudi women were granted the right to drive, it would result in the end of virginity in the country. Though there is no formal ban on women actually driving, they do nonetheless face arrest if they get behind the wheel. The report was prepared for Saudi Arabia's legislative assembly, the Shura Council, by a well-known conservative academic. The report's aim was to counter both King Abdullah's recent cautious attempts at reform, and campaigns by Saudi women. The report provided graphic warnings that allowing women drive would increase prostitution, pornography, divorce, and homosexuality. It, however, failed to explain how allowing women to drive would increase homosexuality.

6 December '11: Israel has expelled a senior Hamas MP from Jerusalem on the grounds that he was living in the city illegally. Ahmed Attoun, whose Israeli-issued residency permit was revoked in 2006, was forcibly transferred to the Palestinian-controlled West Bank. He had been released after previously spending 70 days in an Israeli prison for living without a permit in Jerusalem which has been controlled by Israel since the 1967 Middle East war. Mr. Attiun was one of three Hamas members who had been staging a sit-in inside the offices of the International Committee of the Red Cross (ICRC) in East Jerusalem since July 2010 in order to avoid being expelled. The other two men — former Palestinian Minister for Jerusalem Affairs Khaled Abu Arafah and MP Mohammed Totah — are still holed up inside the ICRC compound. Though Jerusalem's status remains disputed and Israel's occupation of East Jerusalem is regarded as illegal under international law, Israel is nonetheless determined that Jerusalem becomes its undivided capital despite Palestinian hopes of establishing their capital in East Jerusalem. "This is one of the hardest moments of my life," Mr. Attoun told journalists as he crossed the Qalandia checkpoint leading to Ramallah. "We are the original residents of this country and the occupation is the one that should leave the country, not us," he added.

The the ICRC urged the Israeli authorities to rescind the expulsion order because East Jerusalem was occupied territory under international humanitarian law and Palestinians were protected by Article 4 of the Fourth Geneva Convention from being forcibly transferred. The Palestinian Authority President, Mahmoud Abbas, has cited Mr Attoun's case as an example of Israel's 'ethnic cleansing' of Jerusalem. Hamas won a majority in the 2006 Palestinian Legislative Council elections and governs Gaza. It is designated as a terrorist group by Israel.

9 December '11: If there is any doubt in the minds of the American people that all current and aspiring U.S. politicians are fully aware of an inescapable obligation to brownnose the Israeli lobby, then they should consider Newt Gingrich's latest neo-fascist diatribe. Gingrich, an opportunistic political buffoon with questionable integrity and a hope to become the Republican Party's presidential candidate, strongly implied that under his presidency, the American position would be that of Netanyahu's. "I believe that the Jewish people have the right to have a state, and I believe that the commitments that were made at a time. Remember there was no Palestine as a state. It was part of the Ottoman Empire. And I think that we've had an invented Palestinian people, who are in fact Arabs, and were historically part of the Arab community. And they had a chance to go many places. And for a variety of political reasons we have sustained this war against Israel now since the 1940's, and it's tragic." Gingrich overlooked the fact that Jews have lived everywhere and can also go to many places. He is also not aware that most historians mark the start of Palestinian Arab nationalist sentiment as 1834 when residents of the region revolted against Ottoman rule. To suggest that Palestinians are "an invented people" is a deliberate and outrageous attempt to undermine Palestinian national identity and to conveniently overlook the fact that "Israelis" never even existed before 1948. While it is undeniable that Palestinian nationalism is a 20th-century phenomenon, Israeli nationalism is an even later 'invention,'

The implication from Gingrich is that there should have been a mass Palestinian exodus even from their now illegally and brutally occupied territories.

In Israel this month a board member of the Jewish National Fund's US fundraising arm resigned in protest after a 20-year legal process came to a head with an order for the eviction of a Palestinian family from a JNF-owned home. The home had been acquired via the Absentee Property Law. Several days before the order was carried out, JNF announced it would be delayed.

2012 DIARY OF NOTABLE WORLD EVENTS

10 January '12: A new report by Peace Now's Settlement Watch project reveals that 2011 was a record year in West Bank Jewish settlement construction. Such construction was a dangerous trend whose only outcome would be the torpedoing of a two-state solution with the Israeli government intending to legalize illegal outposts so as to transform them into full-fledged settlements. Building in sensitive locations such as E-1, Efrat, and Givat Hamatos, would also serve to deny contiguity for a future Palestinian state. Peace Now's objectives and positions are as follows:

- *Two states for two nations — Israel and Palestine*
- *A Palestinian state alongside the State of Israel, based on the borders of June 1967 with land swaps agreed upon by both sides*
- *Jerusalem — In an official document from 1982 Peace Now advocated for an undivided Jerusalem as Israel's capital. It has since shifted its position to two capitals for two states — a solution based on demographic breakdowns with a special agreement for the Old City.*
- *Peace with Syria — A peace agreement based on secure and recognised borders, and the regulation of relations between the two countries is the primary strategic issue for the people of Israel and Syria.*
- *Beginning negotiations with Syria is a gateway to negotiations with Lebanon and will help create a new international mood in the region.*
- *Peace Now views the settlements as a threat to the existence of Israel as a democratic and Jewish state.*
- *Peace Now views the settlements as a main obstacle to any future peace agreement.*
- *Peace Now views the settlements as an element that harms the State of Israel on many fronts: security, economically, morally culturally. They also harm Israel's standing in the international community.*

4 April '12: The prosecutor of the International Criminal Court (ICC) has rejected a request by the Palestinian Authority to recognize the court's jurisdiction. The decision blocks a move to have the war crimes tribunal based at The Hague investigate the 2008-2009 Gaza war. The prosecutor said it was up to "relevant bodies" at the UN or ICC member countries to determine whether Palestine qualified as a "state." Only then could it sign the court's founding treaty, the Rome Statute. An Israeli foreign ministry spokesman welcomed Friday's decision, while noting that Israel did not recognize the ICC's jurisdiction.

In January 2009, the Palestinian Authority's justice minister had lodged a declaration with the ICC unilaterally recognizing its jurisdiction for "acts committed on the territory of Palestine since 1 July 2002." Luis Moreno-Ocampo, the ICC's chief prosecutor, had said at the time that a decision on whether the Palestinian Authority was legally entitled to do so, could not be made immediately.

The Office of the Prosecutor announced On Tuesday, that it could not act on the Palestinian declaration because Article 12 of the Rome Statute established that only a "state" could confer jurisdiction on the court and deposit an instrument of accession with the UN secretary general. It added that "in instances where it is controversial or unclear whether an applicant constitutes a 'state,' it is the practice of the secretary general to follow or seek the General Assembly's directives on the matter . . . this is reflected in General Assembly resolutions, which provide indications of whether an applicant is a 'state'. Though Palestine has been recognized as a state in bilateral relations by more than 130 governments and certain international organizations, including UN bodies, the current status granted by the General Assembly to the Palestine Liberation Organization (PLO) is that of 'observer,' and not 'non-member state.' "

Amnesty International said the decision by the ICC prosecutor meant Palestinian and Israeli victims of crimes allegedly committed during the Gaza war were unlikely to be get justice. Marek Marczynski, head of Amnesty's International Justice campaign, said that "This dangerous decision opens the ICC to accusations of political bias and is inconsistent with the independence of the ICC. It also breaches the Rome Statute which clearly states that such matters should be considered by the institution's judges."

In September, the Palestinians submitted an application for admission to the UN as a member state, but the Security Council has yet to make a recommendation. Israel's lapdog, the U.S., has promised to veto any vote on the matter.

28 April '12: Yuval Diskin, the former head of Shin Bet — Israel's domestic intelligence agency — has accused the country's leadership of "misleading" the public on the merits of a possible military strike on Iran. He said an attack might speed up any attempt by Iran to obtain a nuclear bomb. Diskin, who stepped down last year after six years as chief of Shin Bet, added that he had "no faith in the current leadership . . . I don't believe in a leadership that makes decisions based on messianic feelings . . . They are misleading the public on the Iran issue. They tell the public that if Israel acts, Iran won't have a nuclear bomb. This is misleading. Actually, many experts say that an Israeli attack would accelerate the Iranian nuclear race."

Diskin's comments followed remarks by other leading Israeli figures contradicting the prime minister and defense chief's views on the subject. Israeli Prime Minister Benjamin Netanyahu and Defense Minister Ehud Barak have repeatedly said Iran must be prevented from building nuclear weapons and have not ruled out military action to disrupt its nuclear program. Diskin's harsh criticism is yet another sign of deep disquiet within the Israeli military and intelligence community over Prime Minister Netanyahu's threats to attack Iran.

The former Shin Bet chief's comments came days after Chief of Staff Lt. Gen. Benny Gantz, Israel's military chief, said he did not think Iran had yet decided to build nuclear weapons and believed international sanctions against Iran were bearing fruit in dissuading it from taking such a decision. Earlier in March, the former head of Israel's foreign intelligence service, Mossad, publicly opposed military action against Iran. Meir Dagan said an Israeli attack would have "devastating" consequences for the Jewish state and would not prevent Iran from obtaining nuclear weapons.

Such views are at odds with those of the prime minister and defence chief. Prior to Dagan's remarks on US television, Mr Netanyahu had inferred he would not countenance a long delay before taking direct action against Iran's nuclear programme if all other options failed . . . "We can peacefully convince them to tear down their nuclear program . . . the result has to be that the threat of a nuclear weapon in Iran's hands is removed." The cause of world peace would be better served not by removing "Iran's nuclear program," but by removing from power warmongering fascist maniacs like Benjamin Netanyahu.

14 June '12: According to the charities Save the Children and Medical Aid for Palestinians, Gaza's only fresh source of water is too dangerous to drink due to contamination by fertilizers and human waste. The new report claims that the number of children being treated for diarrhoea has doubled in five years, and that Israel's five-year blockade of the territory is preventing the import of crucial sanitation equipment resulting in a "completely broken" sewage system.

The report, *Gaza's Children: Falling Behind,* blames high levels of nitrates and other contaminants in the main water supply. As well as the blockade, war damage and chronic underinvestment is also blamed. Desperate families are resorting to private water sources without realizing that such water has 10 times the contamination of safe level water. While Israel insists that the blockade of Gaza has been eased considerably in recent months, the report insists that, "as a matter of urgent priority for the health and well-being of Gaza's children, Israel must lift the blockade in its entirety to enable the free movement of people and goods in and out of Gaza."

28 August '12: The South African social rights activist and 1984 Nobel Peace Prize winner for his opposition to Apartheid, Archbishop Desmond Tutu (retired), has pulled out of an event because he refuses to share a platform with Tony Blair. The veteran peace campaigner stated that Mr. Blair's support for the Iraq war was "morally indefensible" and it would be "inappropriate" for him to appear alongside Blair in Thursday's one-day leadership summit in Johannesburg.

30 August '12: According to Associated Press, a new resolution passed by the California State Assembly attempts to limit criticism of Israeli policy on college campuses by equating it with anti-Semitic hate speech. Drafted by Republican Linda Halderman and passed without public discussion, the resolution was voted on — with the usual under the radar Israeli lobby tactic — when most students were between semesters and away from their campuses. Supporters of Israel's Zionist regime had also employed the sleight of hand maneuver by combining any criticism of the Israeli state's policies or of the U.S. government's support for them with racist attacks on Jews. The law urged "California colleges and universities to squelch nascent anti-Semitism" and encouraged university leaders to combat a wide array of anti-Jewish and anti-Israel actions.

The Assembly's resolution drew criticism from free speech advocates with Carlos Villarreal, director of the San Francisco chapter of the National Lawyers Guild, calling the resolution irresponsible and dangerous because it combines legitimate condemnations of acts of intimidation and hate with specific objections to tactics used to support the Palestinian people. He said "In doing so, it can be seen as having no other purpose than to demonize all those who criticize the nation-state of Israel or support the rights of the Palestinian people." This bill attempts to codify into law an obligation to "squelch" activism and speech objecting to Israeli government actions. Fortunately, growing criticism of the bill has led the University of California to refuse to support it.

2 September '12: Archbishop Desmond Tutu followed up his refusal to share a platform with Tony Blair by calling for Tony Blair and George W. Bush Jr. to be taken to the International Criminal Court in The Hague over the Iraq war. Writing in the UK's *Observer* newspaper, he accused the former leaders of lying about weapons of mass destruction to justify a military campaign that had made the world more unstable "than any other conflict in history."

6 November '12: U.S. Presidential Elections result in President Barack Obama being re-elected with fifty-one percent of the popular vote.

29 November '12: The Emek Shaveh, website — an organization opposed to the politicization of archaeology — challenged Israeli plans to build a military college on the Mount of Olives by suggesting that "If the Churches get involved and oppose the plan it could have a great impact. If the churches mention the holiness of the mountain, it might affect the plan. The most effective work, for you as outsiders, will be to influence the churches to object to the plan. I think that the Israeli authorities will be affected by pressure from churches and foreign governments." The Mount of Olives is one of the most disputed pieces of land in Jerusalem with deep religious significance.

20 December '12: The UN in another futile attempt to appear to be doing its job, stepped up pressure on Israel over its settlement building on occupied Palestinian land in the West Bank and East Jerusalem. The secretary general and all Security Council members except the U.S. demanded an immediate halt to new construction. Despite its usual protection of Israel at the UN, the U.S. state department accused Israel of "a pattern of provocative action," and that settlement activity put the goal of peace "further at risk." If that is the case, then why give Israel unconditional support.

Israeli Prime Minister Benjamin Netanyahu gave both the UN and the U.S. his kosher one-fingered salute by announcing that his government would press ahead with settlement expansion — an announcement substantiated by Jerusalem's planning committee which granted approval for 2,610 homes in a new settlement in East Jerusalem called Givat Hamatos. Meanwhile, tenders were also announced for several settlements in the West Bank for a total of 1,000 new homes.

2013 DIARY OF NOTABLE WORLD EVENTS

29 January '13: *Global Research* reports that in August 2010, the Yesha Council together with Israel Sheli (My Israel), organized a workshop — with a video pertaining to the art of manipulating online content on Wikipedia entries — in Jerusalem to teach people how to edit Wikipedia articles in a pro-Israeli way. The Yesha Council which is the Hebrew acronym for Yehuda Shomron, Aza, lit. ("Judea Samaria and Gaza Council") is an umbrella organization of municipal councils of Jewish settlements in the West Bank (and formerly in the Gaza Strip), known by the Hebrew acronym Yesha. My Israel (Israel Sheli) is an Israel right wing extra-parliamentary Zionist movement, which deals with PR across the internet and especially social networks. The training program's stated objective is to "teach people how to edit Wikipedia: the number one source of information . . . We want to be there . . . We want to influence what is written, how it is written, ensure that it is balanced and Zionist in nature . . . [To ensure that] our side of the story is getting coverage." Enough said, what chance have the stupid goyim against such determined and organized Zionist censorship.

6 March '13: A UN report has stated that the ill-treatment of Palestinian children in Israeli jails is "widespread, systematic and institutionalized." The study by the Children's fund UNICEF, described some of the practices used in dealing with children as "cruel, inhuman or degrading." According to the report, an estimated 700 Palestinian children aged 12 to 17 are arrested every year by Israeli security forces in the West Bank with ill-treatment typically beginning with arrests carried out in the middle of the night and continuing through to prosecution and sentencing.

The report also said that unacceptable practices included "blindfolding children and tying their hands with plastic ties, physical and verbal abuse during transfer to an interrogation site, including the use of painful restraints." It said during interrogation, some detained children had been "threatened with death, physical violence, solitary confinement and sexual assault, against themselves or a family member."

Treatment inconsistent with child rights continues during court appearances, including shackling of children, denial of bail and imposition of custodial sentences and transfer of children outside occupied Palestinian territory to serve their sentences inside Israel.

The report noted that a number of "positive changes" recently made by Israel in its handling of Palestinian minors included new hand-tying procedures to prevent pain and injury, informing parents of a child's detention, and informing children of the right to a lawyer. How very magnanimous of God's chosen people.

12 April '13: Former President Jimmy Carter accepted an award from the Yeshiva University law school's journal, despite protests from pro-Israel supporters. In a New York ceremony the Cardozo Journal of Conflict Resolution bestowed its International Advocate for Peace prize on Carter for his political activism. Carter's nomination had come under the customary and now tiresome but inevitable attack by pro-Israel groups, who accused the former president of being biased towards Israel. They cited his comparison of Israel's West Bank policies to that of Apartheid and his meetings with leaders of the 'terrorist' group Hamas. They did, however, conveniently — in keeping with their usual less-than-honest Zionist missives — omit to mention that some of Carter's meetings with Hamas leaders involved relaying messages from the family of Gilad Shalit, an Israeli soldier held captive by the group from 2006 to 2011. Prior to the ceremony Alan Dershowitz, a Harvard law professor and notorious fanatical pro-Zionist Israel supporter, challenged Carter to a debate with the lunatic and false accusation that "Carter has prevented peace, encouraged terrorism and done more than anyone else to isolate and demonize the Middle East's only democracy, Israel." Presumably Dershowitz was referring to that Middle Eastern democracy of Israel which as a matter of policy illegally occupies Palestinian lands; carries out wholesale evictions of Palestinians families by bulldozing their homes and possessions; creates Palestinian ethnic cleansing zones to make way for Jewish settlements and in so doing routinely violates international laws and human rights. And this mentally deranged fanatic is a professor of law?

16 April '13: The recently released *The Gatekeepers,* a film by Dror Moreh, uses newsreel material to support interviews with six former chiefs of Shin Bet which since the six-day war of 1967 has become more influential by controlling the West Bank and Gaza Strip. They speak frankly with eloquence of their successes and failures during forty-five years fighting "terrorism" with "no strategy, only tactics" that included forgetting "about morality." The honesty of one of them offers encouragement with his admission that the conduct of Israel in the West Bank was comparable to that of the Nazis towards the non-Jewish civilian population of occupied western Europe during the second world war.

18 April '13: In keeping with its policy of strictly controlling movement in and out of Gaza so as to make it difficult for Palestinians to make the short trip (33.5 kilometers) from there to the West Bank, Israel has refused permission for Palestinian runners from the Gaza Strip to take part in a marathon in the West Bank city of Bethlehem. The race due to start on 21 April will be the first marathon to be held in the occupied Palestinian territory.

The twenty-two Gazan runners including a former Olympian and one woman —planning to participate in the shorter race — have been deemed by the Israeli military as not meeting the criteria required to leave Gaza. Israel, which also controls entry to the West Bank via the border with Jordan, stated through an Israeli military source that "the entrance of the Gaza Strip residents to Israeli territory, and their passage to the West Bank, is possible only in exceptional humanitarian cases, mainly urgent medical cases."

The athletes, the race organizers and the Palestinian Olympic Committee have asked the Israeli authorities to reconsider their position but have not received a reply. They are of the view that the marathon has nothing to do with politics and should be regarded by the Israelis purely as a sporting event in the West Bank that every Palestinian, not just athletes, should have the right to attend. But then as Israelis regard Palestinians as being beasts, they are not obliged to grant them any rights.

5 May '13: Retired U.S. Army Colonel Lawrence Wilkerson, who once served as Secretary of State Colin Powell's Chief of Staff, has made the not so astounding assertion that the chemical weapons used in Syria may have been an Israeli "false flag" operation aimed at implicating Bashar Assad's regime. Israel has a historical propensity for "false flag" operations which it uses for covert attacks on foreign or domestic soil with a view to placing the blame on its enemies.

Wilkerson — a former Army helicopter pilot who flew numerous combat missions in Vietnam — served as Colin Powell's chief of staff between 2002 and 2005 and was responsible for reviewing the intelligence information used by Powell in his by now infamous February 2003 United Nations Security Council appearance on Saddam Hussein's weapons of mass destruction. Following his retirement, Wilkerson described Powell's presentation as "a hoax" and became an outspoken critic of the Bush Administration's handling of the Iraq war. He now serves as a professor at Virginia's William and Mary College and is a guest commentator on several U.S. television networks.

11 May '13: Today witnessed the start of an antipodean stampede with over 100 Jewish lobby stooges — Australian federal and state members of parliament — rushing for an en masse signing of the London Declaration on Combating Anti-Semitism. The Israeli newspaper *Haaretz* reported that even more of the nation's 226 federal parliamentarians in Canberra were expected to add their signatures as had all 105 federal Liberal MPs and senators. According to a spokesperson from the Inter-parliamentary Coalition for Combating Anti-Semitism, about 300 other lawmakers from some 60 countries have So far signed with 50 of them being Canadian, 18 British, six Israeli, and for some inexplicable reason: only two are American.

Furthermore, last month Australia's Julia Gillard became the fourth prime minister to sign following Britain's Gordon Brown and David Cameron, and Canada's ingratiating Stephen Harper, who in 2010 signed the Ottawa Protocol, reaffirming the London Declaration. So the Jewish lobby's global campaign for legislation to criminalize criticism of Israel continues unabated. Such efforts are a threat to free speech and must be challenged so as to maintain the concept of democratic governance by the people for ALL the people — and not just the Jewish people. The enactment of laws that give immunity from criticism to habitual lawbreakers is preposterous and intolerable. Disregard for the rights of Palestinians by Australian politicians should come as no surprise because they have already had a lot of practice disregarding Aboriginal rights in Australia.

29 May '13: Germany has agreed to help care for Jewish survivors of the Nazi Holocaust by paying an extra 800 million euros (£685 million/ U.S.$1,064 million) which is thought will benefit about 56,000 people worldwide with a third of them being in Israel. The object is to help elderly Holocaust survivors to live their final years in dignity. Germany also agreed to widen the scope of those eligible to include people who lived in open ghettos.

The Jewish Claims Conference, which represents Jews caught up in the Holocaust and their descendants, welcomed the announcement: "We are seeing Germany's continued commitment to fulfil its historic obligation to Nazi victims," said Stuart Eizenstat, the Claims Conference's special negotiator, in a statement on the organization's website. Mr Eizenstat, who is a former US ambassador to the European Union, added that the move was "all the more impressive since it comes at a time of budget austerity in Germany." He added that the main beneficiaries would be people whose "early life was filled with indescribable tragedy and trauma."

According to the Claims Conference, the open ghettos referred to were those without walls where residents "lived in constant fear of deportation by the Nazis." The former West German government acknowledged the murder of six million Jews by the Nazi regime and began, in 1952, to pay compensation to Israel. Last year, the German finance ministry said it would make one-off payments worth 2,556 euros (£2188/U.S.$3,400) each to Jewish victims of the Holocaust who had still not received any compensation. It is only right that people who suffer atrocities and loss of their property should receive compensation. The question now is when will the Israelis compensate the Palestinian people whom they are continuing to abuse, dispossess, and murder?

1 June '13: The United Nations has stated that more than 1,000 people were killed in Iraq during the month of May which makes it the highest monthly death toll for years and the deadliest month since the wide sectarian violence of 2006-7. The vast majority of the casualties were civilians with the capitol Baghdad being the worst hit area of the country that now appears to be returning to civil war. Did the God that advised George W. Bush and Tony Blair to go to war in Iraq in 2003 not tell them that death and destruction on this scale would still be occurring a decade later?

7 June '13: Downing Street announced that Prime Minister David Cameron will attend the Bilderberg meeting in Hertfordshire in his capacity as head of the host nation. Bilderberg —an annual behind-closed-doors meeting of the world's political and financial elite— is pitched as a forum for "informal, off-the-record discussions about megatrends and the major issues facing the world." Of the 140 guests attending only 14 are women.

Bilderberg — founded in 1954 when it took its name from the Dutch hotel where the first meeting took held — has no detailed agenda, no proposed resolutions, no voting, and no release of policy statements. The Bilderberg Group contends that the private nature of the conferences allows people to 'listen, reflect and gather insights' without being bound by 'pre-agreed positions.' Critics, however, assert that with so many important and well-intentioned people from Europe and the US attending, the Bilderberg should be fully transparent and accountable to the people for whose benefit it purports to be working.

9 June '13: In an interview broadcast today a senior member of Prime Minister Benjamin Netanyahu's Likud Party said that the Israeli government will not accept a Palestinian state with the borders favored by the Palestinians and the international community — a statement that reconfirms the Zionist state's deceit in speaking of peace while thinking only of removing Palestinians from their land and replacing them with Jewish settlers. Typically, the not-so-independent mainstream media — especially in the U.S. — studiously avoided commenting on, or pointing out the glaring contradiction between what Israel says and what Israel actually does.

10 June '13: UN expert Special Rapporteur Richard Falk has called for an international inquiry into Israel's treatment of Palestinian prisoners, alleging that torture and other abuses were occurring "on a massive scale" including the "collective punishment" of 1.75 million Palestinians resulting from Israel's blockade of Gaza which had to end. He added that "With 70% of the population dependent on international aid for survival and 90% of the water unfit for human consumption, drastic and urgent changes are urgently required if Palestinians in Gaza are to have their most basic rights protected." Mr. Falk, a Princeton University law professor, said the situation was of great concern and called for an international investigation.

In his annual report, which he presented at a meeting of the UN Human Rights Council in Geneva, Mr. Falk said that "the treatment of thousands of Palestinians detained or imprisoned by Israel continues to be extremely worrisome," and accused Israel of subjecting Palestinian prisoners to serious violations. This, according to his report included detention without charges, "torture and other forms of ill, inhumane and humiliating treatment," and solitary confinement, including that of children. There are currently about 4,500 Palestinians in Israeli jails with a UN estimate that more than 700,000 Palestinians have gone through detention in Israeli jails since Israel launched the 1967 war.

Israel, which with its criminal expertise in denying any wrongdoing — and has in the past accused Mr. Falk of being biased against the Jewish state — on this occasion left it to its U.S. stooges to comment on the report with disapproval from Susan Rice, the outgoing US ambassador to the UN and U.S. National Security adviser-designate; and the US ambassador to the United Nations Human Rights Council, Eileen Chamberlain Donahoe, branding Richard Falk as "unfit to serve in his role as a UN Special Rapporteur."

Donahoe's biography on the U.S. mission website assumes the role of moral superiority with the following piece of high-toned hypocrisy: "On the front lines of the Obama administration's strategy of multilateral engagement to promote democracy and respect for universal human rights, Ambassador Donahoe and the US delegation work to ensure that the courageous voices of human rights defenders from around the globe are heard" — so long, of course, as they are waving an Israeli flag while singing Hava Nagila (let us rejoice) over the persecution of the Palestinian people.

In 2008, Mr Falk drew widespread criticism for comparing Israeli actions in Gaza to those of the Nazis and in fairness to him it should be asked whether such an assertion is that far off the mark. *The Times of Israel,* reported that Abraham Foxman, the national director of the Anti-Defamation League, said his organization agrees with Donahoe that Falk is unfit to serve in his role. "If he does not leave voluntarily, the Human Rights Council should remove him. Mr Falk's attempt to paint himself as the victim of an Israeli government-sponsored defamation campaign, carried out by UN Watch, has echoes of classical anti-Semitic conspiracy theories." So here we go again with the anti-Semitic gambit.

Several weeks earlier some average IQ Americans may have just wondered whose national interests these American government representatives were actually serving when the American Jewish Committee (AJC) with its hypocritical stated vision of embracing "democratic values, respect for human rights and peaceful conflict-resolution" enthusiastically welcomed the appointment of Susan Rice as

President Obama's National Security Adviser as follows:

> *With regard to the Middle East, Ambassador Rice has strenuously opposed Iran's nuclear ambitions and human rights transgressions . . . She has sought to mobilize international action in the face of the ever mounting death toll in Syria, and stood up for Israel whenever needed, which in the UN, regrettably, is all too often, whether in the Security Council, General Assembly or other UN organs . . . Again and again, she has tried to block Palestinian efforts in the world body to do an end-run around direct negotiations with Israel . . . For all these reasons, AJC was very proud to present Ambassador Rice with our Distinguished Public Service Award . . .*

Palestinians authorities have criticized Israel after official statistics revealed a rise in new house building in West Bank settlements. A report by Israeli settlement watchdog, Peace Now, stated that settlement building had reached a seven-year high and that many new units were located in the settlements of Modin Illit and Beitar Illit.

Construction had begun on 865 settler homes in the first quarter of this year compared to 313 in the same period of 2012. In keeping with standard Israeli strategy, the data was released just as U.S. Secretary of State John Kerry tries to revive Israel-Palestinian peace talks.

An adviser to the Palestine Liberation Organisation's negotiating team stated that "Once again the Israeli government has ratified that they have a plan for settlement and colonization and not a plan for peace, and that they are destroying any prospect for a two-state solution."

Figures released last month by the Central Bureau of Statistics detail construction across Israel with construction of new settler homes in the occupied West Bank representing the highest year-on-year increase. Though Palestinians insist they will only resume direct talks if Israel stops construction of Jewish settlements, deep in their hearts they know — as Israel and the U.S. also know — that is never going to happen.

11 June '13: In a statement on the House floor today, Kansas Republican Congressman Mike Pompeo said that there had been a relative silence from Islamic community leaders in the wake of the Boston bombings and that such silence was "deafening" and "dangerous." He further suggested that by not condemning acts of terrorism against the U.S. — not true because the Islamic community has been extremely vocal over the years regarding the actions of the extremists — they were therefore complicit in those and any future attacks.

Even assuming Congressman Pompeo's facts were correct, which they were not, then on the basis of his reasoning — backed by his having majored in Mechanical Engineering at the U.S. Military Academy and having graduated from the Harvard Law School — the majority of Americans and Jews worldwide by virtue of their silence over Israeli violations of international law and Palestinian human rights, are also complicit with, and as guilty as, Israel.

13 June '13: The Holocaust industry's relentless onslaught continued today with Israeli Prime Minister Benjamin Netanyahu opening a Holocaust exhibition at the Auschwitz Nazi death camp site in southern Poland. Overseen by Israel's Yad Vashem Holocaust institute, the display in Block 27 was intended to place the former camp in the broader context of Nazi Germany's systematic attempt to destroy Europe's Jewish population.

Earlier in Warsaw, the as usual raving, belligerent, and fascist Netanyahu accused Iran — regarded by Israel as one of its more powerful enemies — of planning a new Holocaust. Really? Unlike Israel, Iran has not in recent history invaded and occupied any neighboring country, oppressed its people, stolen their land and water, and blockaded them in "open prisons" that restrict movement and limit opportunities for social development and commercial trade.

It was Iraq that invaded Iran on 22 September 1980 as a result of years of border disputes and Iraqi fears that the 1979 Iranian Revolution would inspire insurgency among Iraq's long-suppressed Shia majority. There was also Iraq's desire to replace Iran as the dominant Persian Gulf state — a desire covertly welcomed and encouraged by Israel and the U.S. with President Reagan's Special Envoy — the warmongering neocon Donald Rumsfeld — meeting with Saddam Hussein in Baghdad to discuss U.S. military aid. This was the same Reagan administration that was subsequently mired in the Iran-Contra affair of secret arms sales to Iran.

16 June '13: Zionist Israeli Prime Minister Benjamin Netanyahu with his strutting racist arrogance has warned that international pressure on Iran must not be loosened in the wake of the election of reformist-backed Hassan Rouhani as president. Netanyahu said Iran's nuclear program must be stopped "by any means" and there should be no "wishful thinking" about Mr Rouhani's victory. He added that "The international community should not fall into wishful thinking and be tempted to ease pressure on Iran to stop its nuclear program . . . Iran will be judged on its actions. If it insists on continuing to develop its nuclear program the answer needs to be clear — stopping its nuclear program by any means."

This was despite one of Rouhani's main election pledges to try to ease international sanctions imposed on Iran over its nuclear programme, and his promise for greater engagement with Western powers. So once again Israel warns the international community, with threats, that Israel alone must remain as the only nuclear power in the Middle East.

19 June '13: The release of a new Israeli documentary film, *The Lab*, provides an incisive and alarming commentary on the true character, the objectives, and the worldwide destructive role of Israel as a Jewish state. In his film, director Yotam Feldman interviews key figures in Israel's "security" trade — who appear to have no qualms about answering questions with arrogant pride at their destructive achievements — and exposes the Israeli military industry and and the manner in which it operates. He reveals the evolving role within Israel of a "security" industry whose exports have reached an unprecedented $7 billion a year. Twenty per cent of Israeli exports are now military or military related with some 150,000 Israeli families being dependent on an industry that has made Israel the the world's fourth largest military exporter. During the past decade every Israeli military aggression has led to an instant and steep increase in worldwide Israeli military related exports including doctrines, experience, intelligence, knowledge and strategies.

Even more alarming is the film's clear evidence that the West Bank and Gaza's Palestinian civilians are being used as guinea pigs for the development of Israeli tactics, weaponry, and philosophy of aggression — the "Fighting Torah" (Torat Lechima) — as Israelis call it. There appears to be no reservations about the manner in which the cold, calculated destruction of the Palestinian people has been adapted by the Israelis to serve their immensely lucrative industry.

The Lab leaves no doubt that what Israel is doing is fundamentally and irrefutably a premeditated war crime committed with a total lack of compassion that leaves no room for "two-state solution." It becomes abundantly clear that the Israelis conducting this experiment in the destruction of a people have no intention of ever negotiating with their "guinea pigs." Anyone who thinks otherwise is due for a reality check that will first require acceptance of the fact that the dream of a Jewish state has instead become a huge nightmare military enterprise as a direct result of the Zionist supremacist ideology.

Feldman's film provides an insight into an efficient Israeli industry with worldwide weapons fairs where foreign diplomats, high-ranking military officers, and defense officials shop for Israeli military hardware. By thus becoming interlocked with the political and military elite of numerous other countries, the Israeli military-industrial complex has acquired for the Jewish state much needed influence and support. One of the films interviewees points out that those who on the one hand criticize Israeli policies, have no problem in then flocking to Israeli armaments fairs to learn about Israeli "tricks." It becomes apparent that nations who to some extent become dependent on military supplies from Israel, will soften their position with regards to Israeli violations of human right and international law.

21 June '13: Being in the service of god does not preclude religious leaders from dabbling in a bit of sexual abuse and good old fashioned corruption — and that includes rabbis. Anti-fraud detectives stated that for months they have been carrying out an undercover investigation into financial dealings Yona Metzger, one of Israel's two chief rabbis whom they have placed under house arrest on suspicion of corruption. Rabbi Metzger, the spiritual leader of Ashkenazi Jews, and three associates, are suspected of receiving bribes, of theft, and of money laundering. Metzger had been previously questioned on suspicion of fraud in 2005, but was not prosecuted. As well as providing spiritual leadership, the Chief Rabbinate is responsible for legal and administrative aspects of religious Jewish life in Israel. Chief rabbis are appointed from both the Ashkenazi and the Sephardi communities. Metzger's ten-year term as a state-appointed chief rabbi is due to end in July and his arrest may have been delayed until now so as to avoid miring the position of chief rabbi. It seems that God does not always choose wisely.

29 June '13: During his visit to South Africa, U.S. President Barack Obama dropped in on Soweto — once at the very heart of the black struggle against white minority rule — and was greeted not by adoring multitudes, but by an angry group of demonstrators protesting against

U.S. foreign policy. The South African people's indifference no doubt stemmed from their realization that Obama's charming, magical black oratory was laced with meaningless white-man political glibness rather than fruitful substance and that he had turned out to be no better — if not even worse — than some of his white sell-out-to-AIPAC predecessors.

16 July '13:   Israel has condemned new European Union guidelines banning EU funding of projects in territories occupied by Israel since the 1967 Middle East war. As of 2014, such agreements between the EU and Israel will exclude East Jerusalem, the West Bank, Gaza Strip and the Golan Heights. Under the guidelines Israeli projects applying for EU funding will be required to sign a clause to state that it will not apply to the occupied territories.

Israeli minister Silvan Shalom said the measure was a "big mistake" which cast doubt on the EU's impartiality in the Israel-Palestinian conflict. The truth is that Israel's objection has nothing to do with concern over the EU's lack of impartiality, but with the EU's long overdue attempt at impartiality in dealing with Israeli-Palestinian issues by moving from ineffective statements, declarations and denunciations to making more effective policy decisions. Israel, like any spoilt brat, will always throw a temper tantrum and malign others whenever it does not get its way.

Also today, new historical research has revealed a worrying Canadian government policy toward Aboriginals following World War II in which Canadian Aboriginal children and adults were used as unwitting subjects in nutritional experiments by the Canadian government. During the 1940s and 50s Aboriginal children were deliberately starved by government researchers in the name of science.

For many years milk rations were halved at residential schools across the country and Essential vitamins were kept from people who needed them. Dental services were also withheld because gum health was a measuring tool for scientists and dental care would have distorted research results. This revelation is yet another example of attitudes towards aboriginal people of the First Nations.

23 July '13: In Germany a poster campaign has been launched to track down the last surviving Nazi war criminals and to bring them to justice. Some 2,000 posters showing the entrance to the Nazi Auschwitz death camp and asking people to come forward with information have been displayed in Berlin, Hamburg and Cologne. The U.S.-based Simon Wiesenthal Centre offers rewards for useful information and estimates that there about sixty people alive in Germany who are fit to stand trial with some of them being suspected of having been guards at Nazi death camps or members of death squads responsible for mass killings.

Efraim Zuroff, a leading international Nazi hunter and the centre's Jerusalem branch director said that "unfortunately, very few people who committed the crimes had to pay for them . . . The passage of time in no way diminishes the crimes." As part of its "Operation Last Chance II" the centre has set up a hotline for tip-offs and is offering rewards of up to 25,000 euros (£21,500; $33,080) for information which helps to prosecute war criminals in Germany. Perhaps Efraim Zuroff would like to clarify whether all war criminals — including Israelis guilty of crimes in the Occupied Territories — should be prosecuted, or are God's chosen people exempt from such prosecutions. Did the god whom Moses met on Mount Sinai decree that His "chosen people" had his divine permission to to commit crimes with impunity?

25 July '13: Following revelations of data collection of U.S. phone calls by the National Security Agency (NSA), the U.S. House of Representatives narrowly rejected an attempt to restrict the NSA's ability to collect electronic information. Despite always insisting on their constitutional right to bear arms, it would appear that Americans do not give a damn when it comes to their right to privacy. By abandoning such rights, the American people — rather than helping to defeat terrorism — have allowed their fixation with "the war on terror" to force them to surrender the very liberties which "the right to bear arms" is presumably supposed to help defend.

Roger Waters — co-founder of the progressive rock band Pink Floyd — a critic of Israeli policies and supporter of BDS, released the following letter:

'To My Colleagues in Rock and Roll

In the wake of the tragic shooting to death of un-armed teenager Travon Martin and the acquittal of his killer Zimmerman, yesterday, Stevie Wonder spoke at a gig declaring that he will not perform in the State of Florida until that State repeals it's 'Stand Your Ground' Law. In effect he has declared a boycott on grounds of conscience. I applaud his position, and stand with him, it has brought back to me a statement I made in a letter I wrote last February 14th, to which I have referred but have never published.

The time has come, so here it is.

This letter has been simmering on the back burner of my conscience and consciousness for some time.

It is seven years since I joined BDS (Boycott Divestment and Sanctions) a non- violent movement to oppose Israel's occupation of the West Bank, and, violations of international law and Palestinian human rights. The aim of BDS is to bring international attention to these Israeli policies, and hopefully, to help bring them to an end. All the people of the region deserve better than this.

To cut to the chase, Israel has been found guilty, independently, by international human rights organizations, UN officials, and the International Court of Justice, of serious breaches of international law. These include, and I will name only two:

1. The Crime of Apartheid:

The systematic oppression of one ethnic group by another. On 9 March 2012, for instance, the UN Committee on the Elimination of Racial Discrimination called on Israel to end its racist policies and laws that contravene the prohibition against racial segregation and apartheid.

2. The Crime of Ethnic Cleansing:

The forcible removable of indigenous peoples from their rightful land in order to settle an occupying population. For example, in East Jerusalem non-Jewish families are routinely physically evicted from their homes to make way for Jewish occupants.

There are others.

Given the inability or unwillingness of our governments, or the United Nations Security Council to put pressure on

Israel to cease these violations, and make reparations to the victims, it falls to civil society and conscientious citizens of the world, to dust off our consciences, shoulder our responsibilities, and act. I write to you now, my brothers and sisters in the family of Rock and Roll, to ask you to join with me, and thousands of other artists around the world, to declare a cultural boycott on Israel, to shed light on these problems and also to support all our brothers and sisters in Palestine and Israel who are struggling to end all forms of Israeli oppression and who wish to live in peace, justice, equality and freedom.

I am writing to you all now because of two recent events.

Stevie Wonder.

Word came to me, the first week of last December that Stevie Wonder had been booked to headline at a gala dinner for the Friends of The Israeli Defense Force in LA on 6th December 2012. An event to raise money for the Israeli armed forces, as if the $4,3,000,000,000 that we the US tax payers give them each year were not enough? This came right after The Israeli defence Force had concluded yet another war on Gaza, (Operation Pillar of Defence), according to human rights watch, committing war crimes against the besieged 1.6 million Palestinians there.

Anyway, I wrote to Stevie to try to persuade him to cancel. My letter ran along these lines, "Would you have felt OK performing at the Policeman's Ball in Johannesburg the night after the Sharpeville massacre in 1960 or in Birmingham Alabama, to raise money for the Law Enforcement officers, who clubbed, tear gassed and water cannoned those children trying to integrate in 1963?"

Archbishop Desmond Tutu also wrote an impassioned plea to Stevie, and 3,000 others appended their names to a change .org petition. Stevie, to his great credit, cancelled!

2. Earlier that week I delivered a speech at The United Nations. If you are interested you can find this speech on YouTube.

The interesting thing about these two stories is that there was NOT ONE mention of either story in the mainstream media in the United States.

The clear inference would be that the media in the USA is not interested in the predicament of the Palestinian people, or for that matter the predicament of the Israeli people. We can only hope they may become interested as they eventually did in the politics of apartheid South Africa.

Back in the days of Apartheid South Africa at first it was a trickle of artists that refused to play there, a trickle, that exercised a cultural boycott, then it became a stream, then a river then a torrent and then a flood, (Remember Steve van Zant, Bruce and all the others? 'We will not Play in Sun City?') Why? Because, like the UN and the International Courts of Justice they understood that Apartheid is wrong.

The sports community joined the battle, no one would go and play cricket or rugby in South Africa, and eventually the political community joined in as well. We all as a global, musical, sporting and political community raised our voices as one and the apartheid regime in South Africa fell.

Maybe we are at the tipping point now with Israel and Palestine. These are good people both and they deserve a just solution to their predicament. Each and every one of them deserves freedom, justice and equal rights. Just recently the ANC, the ruling party of South Africa, has endorsed BDS. We are nearly there. Please join me and all our brothers and sisters in global civil society in proclaiming our rejection of Apartheid in Israel and occupied Palestine, by pledging not to perform or exhibit in Israel or accept any award or funding from any institution linked to the government of Israel, until such time as Israel complies with international law and universal principles of human rights.

Roger Waters '

26 July '13: In retaliation for the EU's banning of funding for projects in the territories occupied by Israel, Defense Minister Moshe Ya'alon ordered defense officials to halt cooperation on the ground with EU representatives including the refusal of permits to humanitarian aid staff. The directive includes any assistance to EU infrastructure projects in Area C, which is under full Israeli civilian and military control. Ya'alon also intends to make it more difficult for EU officials to pass through the Erez Crossing to either the Gaza Strip or back to Israel. It is high time for all EU states to abandon the inimical position of gutless subservience and instead fight back in the face of bullying by Israel and the U.S. When is the rest of the world going to make it difficult for Israel to violate human rights and international laws?

29 July '13: The steadfast and blind U.S. bias towards Israel continues unabated with the announcement that Martin Indyk has been appointed as Washington's special Middle East envoy for the resumption of peace talks between Israel and the Palestinian Authority. Indyk served as U.S. ambassador to Israel and Assistant Secretary of State for Near East Affairs during the Clinton Administration. He is was the brains behind the U.S. policy of *dual containment* which sought to "contain" Iraq and Iran which were both viewed as being — with much prodding and prompting from Israel — the two main strategic U.S. adversaries at the time.

Born in London, England to a Jewish family, Indyk is an Australian-trained academic who in 1982, following his position as Australian deputy director of current intelligence in the Middle East, started setting up a research department for AIPAC. Because of his affiliation with AIPAC, however, Indyk felt his research wasn't being taken seriously enough and so he helped found the Washington Institute for Near East Policy (WINEP) in 1985 to convey an image that was accommodating to Israel but with the appearance of doing credible research on the Middle East that was realistic and unbiased.

The two other candidates for the position — also well established Israeli partisans with the necessary Star of David credentials — were Dennis Ross, co-founder with Indyk of the AIPAC backed WINEP, and Daniel Kurtzer, another former ambassador to Israel prior to becoming Commissioner of Israel's Baseball League. In 2008, Indyk endorsed then-Senator Barack Obama's successful candidacy for the presidency. Kurtzer, James Steinberg, and Dennis Ross were among the principal authors of Barack "Uncle Tom" Obama's 2008 brown-nosing address to the AIPAC conference.

U.S. Secretary of State John Kerry who is responsible for

conducting the negotiations, with subservience to Israel, suggested when announcing Indyk's appointment that success would depend on the willingness of both sides to make "reasonable compromises." Is this man an unwitting, well-intentioned fool or just a calculating shyster politician? Does he really believe that Benjamin Netanyahu and his Zionist pro-settler government would consider reasonable compromises on the questions of pre-1967 borders; on East Jerusalem as the Palestinian capitol in a two-state solution; on an end to Jewish settlement building in the occupied territories that serves to steal Palestinian land and render as impossible the concept of a two-state solution; or on the right of return for Palestinian refugees?

So once again the periodic pantomime billed as "the peace process" will be played out at great cost to the Palestinians and with U.S.-backed benefits for the Israelis. The Illegal and brutal Israeli occupation with all its hardships and humiliations will continue; settlement expansion will be increased and accelerated; the portrayal of Palestinians as terrorists and the genocide of their culture will be maintained; the prospects of a genuine and unified leadership for the Palestinian people will remain elusive; and any attempt to make Israel accountable for its violations at the UN will be vetoed by the Israeli-shackled and amoral government of the U.S.

1 August '13: The UN mission in Baghdad has released casualty figures showing that 1,057 Iraqis were killed in July, making it the most violent month in years. So far this year at least 4,137 civilians have been killed and 9,865 injured with Baghdad seeing the most bloodshed. Sectarian strife has fueled a wave of violence across Iraq in the past six months with Sunni Islamist militant groups targeting Shia districts. In July there was a series of bombings in streets, cafes and mosques. Militants also broke into two prisons and set inmates free.

There were 928 civilians' fatalities in July including 204 civilian police, and 2,109 injured civilians including 338 civilian police. A further 129 members of the Iraqi security forces were killed and 217 injured. Many of the provinces affected were dominated by members of the country's Sunni minority who resent the Shia-led government that took power after Saddam Hussein was toppled in 2003. Those pious Christians Bush and Blair still insist they did the Iraqi people a favour by launching an illegal war for regime change and so-called liberation.

8 August '13: After recently setting up a commission to investigate the Vatican bank's decades of corruption and report back to him personally, the Pope has has finally announced measures to strengthen supervision of its financial transactions. The decree issued by Pope Francis is the latest attempt to eliminate abuses that include money-laundering, the occasional financing of terrorism, and the proliferation of weapons of mass destruction.

The bank — officially known as the Institute for Religious Works — which handles funds for the Catholic Church and the payroll for some 5,000 Vatican employees, last month froze the account of a senior cleric, Monsignor Nunzio Scarano who was suspected of involvement in money-laundering. He and two others were arrested by Italian police in June on suspicion of trying to move 20m euros ($26m; £17m) illegally.

The Pope's first priority is to sort out the financial mess at the bank by setting up a financial security committee to coordinate the anti-corruption effort. Church spokesman Federico Lombardi said the decree would help the Vatican resist "increasingly insidious" forms of international financial crime. This has come at a time when the French-based financial watchdog, Moneyval, after carrying out a review of the Vatican bank's operations, concluded that the bank had not always exercised due diligence.

12 August '13: Saudi Prince Khaled Bin Farhan Al-Saud has defected from his country saying that he and his family left because of suppression of free speech, monarchical corruption, and the arrest of anyone who dares to dissent: "There is no independent judiciary, as both police and the prosecutor's office are accountable to the Interior Ministry. This ministry's officials investigate 'crimes' (they call them crimes), related to freedom of speech. So they fabricate evidence, don't allow people to have attorneys," the prince told RT Arabic. "Even if a court rules to release such a 'criminal' the Ministry of Interior keeps him in prison, even though there is a court order to release him. There have even been killings! Killings! And as for the external opposition, Saudi intelligence forces find these people abroad! There is no safety inside or outside the country."

Political parties are banned with anyone wishing to campaign for civil rights having to obtain permission from the monarchy. The Saudi Civil and Political Rights Association (ACPRA) — which failed to obtain permission — has reported that more than 30,000 of its members have been imprisoned. According to Human Rights Watch, "Saudi Arabia has stepped up arrests and trials of peaceful dissidents, and responded with force to demonstrations by citizens." Anti-government sentiment has increased with the "Saudi Million" group of mostly young activists being independently formed of other political groups and demanding the release of political prisoners.

19 August '13: At last under the Freedom of Information Act the CIA has released documents which confirm its long-suspected key role in the 1953 coup which ousted Iran's democratically elected Prime Minister, Mohammad Mossadeq. So much for the U.S.'s respect for democracy which is always sidelined when oil is at stake. The documents came from the CIA's internal history of Iran from the mid-1970s and were published on the independent National Security Archive on the coup's 60th anniversary which had been carried out under CIA direction as an act of U.S. foreign policy.

Prime Minister Mossadeq's overthrow came after it had become apparent by the end of 1952 that his Iranian government was incapable of reaching an oil agreement with interested Western countries. It was felt that Mossadeq's desire for personal power was responsible for reckless policies based on emotion; for weakening to a dangerous degree the roles of the Shah and the Iranian Army; and for close cooperation with the Tudeh (Communist) Party of Iran. It was therefore believed that Iran was in real danger of falling behind the Iron Curtain thereby providing the Soviets with a victory in the Cold War that would be a major setback for the West in the Middle East.

Release of the documents were the CIA's first admission — having previously issued "blanket denials" — to having been involved in the coup in concert with MI6, the British intelligence agency. CIA preparations for the coup included the placing of anti-Mossadeq stories in both the Iranian and US media together with the U.S. and UK intelligence agencies bolstering pro-Shah forces and helping organize anti-Mossadeq protests which persuaded the Army to join the pro-Shah movement leading to Tehran and certain provincial areas being controlled by pro-Shah groups and Army units. The ensuing coup strengthened the position of Shah Mohammad Reza Pahlavi who having fled Iran following a power struggle with Mossadeq, returned to rule with an iron fist and become a close U.S. ally and puppet.

We'll know our disinformation program is complete when everything the American public believes is false.
William Casey, CIA Director (from first staff meeting in 1981)

20 August '13: Angela Merkel, in the first such visit by a German chancellor, today visited the former Nazi concentration camp of Dachau which was the first camp built by the Nazis in March 1933. The visit — which was part of Mrs. Merkel's election campaign — was described as a "tasteless and outrageous combination" by political opponents, but as "historic" and a "signal of respect for the former detainees" by Max Mannheimer, the 93-year-old president of the Dachau camp committee, who had long lobbied for Mrs. Merkel to go to the camp near Munich in southern Germany. Some 30,000 people died in Dachau before it was liberated by US soldiers on 29 April 1945.

It would also be "historic" and a "signal of respect" if Mrs. Merkel were to visit the persecuted Palestinians of the occupied territories and the graves of their deceased and murdered. After all, it was the Palestinians whom the West offered up as sacrificial lambs to compensate for the guilt felt over the atrocities committed by Nazi Germany. Surely such selfless Palestinian sacrifice to alleviate the sense of Western guilt should be afforded some token recognition? Perhaps a truly self-governed state of their own on neither blockaded or occupied territory? Or would such an act in today's intimidated environment with its constant reminders of the Holocaust constitute anti-Semitism?

21 August '13: Private First Class Bradley Manning, 25, who was convicted in July of 20 charges including espionage, showed no emotion as Judge Colonel Denise Lind sentenced him to a dishonorable discharge from the US Army, forfeiture of some of his pay, and to 35 years in prison. While stationed in Iraq in 2010, Manning had passed hundreds of thousands of battlefield reports and diplomatic cables to Wikileaks, the pro-transparency group headed by Julian Assange.

Manning's "show trial" which precluded any semblance of due process was preceded by his being mentally and physically tortured while in solitary confinement for almost a year, of his being imprisoned for three years prior to his trial, and of having his right to presumption of innocence — until proven otherwise — being undermined by prejudicial public pronouncements by President Obama, numerous legislators and

435

the mainstream media.

Manning's disclosures of U.S. war crimes against Iraqi and Afghan civilians had aroused worldwide disapproval which the Obama administration countered by trotting out "another" imaginary terror threat to coincide with Manning's pre-judged conviction and to justify the allegation that his exposure of gross U.S. war crimes "served the enemy" rather than the American people.

Manning had previously apologized for hurting the U.S. and for "the unexpected results" of his actions which he claimed at pre-trial hearing were carried out in the hope of starting a public debate regarding U.S. foreign policy and the military. The many people around the world who had applauded Manning's actions now feel he should have been honored rather than imprisoned. Though governments pay lip service to the idea of support for whistleblowers, they do not take kindly to being the victims whistle-blowing.

27 August '13: Dan Goldberg has today reported in the Israeli newspaper *Haaretz* that "Jewish community leaders in Australia have virtually abandoned support for the governing Labor Party, with most privately hoping the conservative Liberal Party wins the federal election next weekend. The near consensus in favor of replacing Kevin Rudd with Tony Abbott as the next Australian Prime Minister comes as the Liberal Party reportedly plans to upgrade relations with Jerusalem, facilitate easier visa applications for Israelis, ban more terror groups, and stop financial support to any Australian organization that supports the boycott Israel campaign."

This has come about some four months after Julie Bishop — then Deputy Leader of the Liberal Party-National Party Coalition Opposition and now Foreign Minister of Australia— told the pro-Zionist Murdoch-owned newspaper *The Australian* the "the coalition will institute a policy across government that ensures no grants of taxpayers' funds are provided to individuals or organizations which actively support the BDS campaign. It is inappropriate for Associate Professor Lynch to use his role as director of the taxpayer-funded CPACS [Centre for Peace and Conflict Studies, University of Sydney] . . . in support of the anti-Semitic BDS campaign."

Anti-racist Jewish Australian academic Professor Jake Lynch's reaction at the time was that "the number two in the incoming government has vowed to use the coercive power of the state to stifle dissent on a contested policy issue . . . According to Julie Bishop, shadow foreign minister and deputy Liberal leader, I and other supporters of an academic boycott of Israel will be penalized under the Coalition, by having our access to public research funds summarily cut off . . . The charge of anti-semitism [against BDS supporters] fails its only salient test. The target of BDS is not Jews or Judaism, but militarism and lawlessness. A systematic study by an international expert panel found that discriminatory laws and practices, confining non-Jews to second-class status, do indeed put Israel in breach of the Apartheid Convention. That obliges governments to "co-operate to end the violation; not to recognize the illegal situation arising from it; and not to render aid or assistance to the State committing it." So it seems that Israeli blackmail, bribery, and coercion of Western politicians is just as relentless and flourishing Down under where Rupert Murdoch's News Corp Australia — the nation's number one media company — helps Zionism to call the political shots.

28 August '13: Earlier this month the U.S. Department of Education's Office for Civil Rights (OCR), struck a blow for freedom of speech by throwing out claims that three University of California campuses — Berkeley, Irvine and Santa Cruz — violated Title IV of the Civil Rights Act by fostering anti-Semitic climates that allowed protests against Israeli policies to take place. As part of the ongoing "lawfare" campaign to silence pro-Palestinian speech, some Jewish UC students claimed that the political speech expressed in these demonstrations created a "hostile" atmosphere and amounted to illegal harassment and intimidation.

The OCR, however, concluded that encountering views contrary to one's own, hardly constitutes harassment and appropriately stated: "In the university environment, exposure to such robust and discordant expressions, even when personally offensive and hurtful, is a circumstance a reasonable student in higher education may experience." That something so obvious and fundamental would be contested through a series of formal complaints suggests that there is nothing "reasonable" about Jewish students and their supporters cynically endeavoring to silence political opponents.

30 August '13: The experience of being lied to by Tony Blair over Iraq's alleged possession of WMD's has not been entirely lost on the majority British politicians who today must be commended for resisting hysterical Israeli-U.S. calls for the military action against Syria. The 285-272 rejection of possible British military action against Syrian President Bashar al-Assad's government to deter the use of chemical weapons, does not only serve notice that Britain will not always support Israeli-U.S. agendas, but also suggests that Prime Minister David Cameron's apparent loss of control over foreign and defense policies will diminish his international standing.

In files disclosed to the Washington Post by Edward Snowden — currently in Russia after being granted a year's asylum — it is revealed that U.S. intelligence agencies have multi-billion dollar "black budget" with the CIA alone receiving $14.7 billion (£9.5 billion) out of $52.6 billion total for 16 intelligence agencies of which two are actively hacking into foreign computer networks. Though the U.S. has not made public its total intelligence budget breakdown, the newspaper published detailed charts without posting all the documents because of U.S concerns over "sensitive details" that may jeopardize methods and sources.

The CIA, whose budget has grown more than 50% since 2004, allocated almost $5 billion to human intelligence operations, with some $67 million of that total being used to fund false identities of its overseas spies. The files also revealed that the budget of the National Security Agency (NSA), America's electronic spying organisation, was apparently $10.8 billion for 2013, making it second only to the CIA. The two agencies had also launched "offensive cyber operations" to hack into or sabotage enemy computer networks with "priority" counterintelligence targets being China, Russia, Iran, Cuba and Israel. It would seem that finally the "U.S. Empire"' — a victim of incessant espionage by Israel — is striking back with token retaliation against the ungrateful recipient of its unconditional backing and financial largesse.

31 August '13: Further evidence of Jewish lobby interference within the mainstream media has come to light this week with news that Raffi Berg, the editor of the BBC News website's Middle East section, has been sending his staff emails advising them to write more favorably about Israel. Berg had been promoted to his current position earlier in August, having already worked as a journalist on the Middle East desk. He replaced Tarik Kafala, who has moved over to head the BBC's Arabic Service.

In emails to his BBC colleagues he not only asked them to word their stories in a way which does not blame or "put undue emphasis" on Israel for starting the prolonged attacks, but he also encouraged them to promote the Israeli government line that the "offensive" was "aimed at ending rocket fire from Gaza."

In a second email, sent during the same period, this pathetic excuse for an impartial journalist informed BBC reporters: "Please remember, Israel doesn't maintain a blockade around Gaza. Egypt controls the southern border." Berg unashamedly omitted to mention that the UN viewed Israel as the occupying power in Gaza and has called on Israel to end its siege of the Strip. Israel's refusal to do so is a violation of UN Security Council Resolution 1860. Unfortunately the BBC is riddled with vermin such as this man who hide he truth from the British listeners and viewers who are responsible for financing the BBC.

1 September '13: A controversial Vietnamese law that has come into effect, known as Decree 72, has been criticized by human rights groups, internet companies, and even the U.S. government which is hardly a paragon when it comes to respecting the privacy and rights of its own citizens. The decree states blogs and social websites should be used only for personal information and not for the sharing of news articles. It also bans Vietnamese online users from discussing current affairs and requires foreign internet companies to keep their local servers inside Vietnam.

So far this year dozens of activists and bloggers have have been convicted for activities against the state which has one-party communist rule with authorities maintaining a tight grip on the media. The new law is specific that social networking sites such as Twitter and Facebook should only be used "to provide and exchange personal information" and prohibits the online publication of material that "opposes" the Vietnamese government or "harms national security."

The U.S. embassy in Hanoi had previously said it was "deeply concerned by the decree's provisions" and that "fundamental freedoms apply online just as they do offline." Right. Tell that to the hundreds of millions around the world on whom the U.S. is electronically spying. Reporters Without Borders, the Paris-based group that campaigns for press freedom worldwide, has said the decree will leave Vietnamese people "permanently deprived of the independent and outspoken information that normally circulates in blogs and forums." Meanwhile the Asia Internet Coalition, an industry group representing companies such as Google and Facebook, said the move would "stifle innovation and discourage businesses from operating in Vietnam."

6 September '13: Israel's stooge Tony Blair has said the aftermath of the invasion of Iraq has made the UK "hesitant" to intervene in Syria. The former prime minister told BBC Radio 4 that he was disappointed the UK would not be taking part in military action especially as it was not that members of parliament had not trusted the government's assessment of the threat posed by Syria, as chemical weapon use had been proved. And this comes from the two-faced liar who had "proof" of Iraqi weapons of mass destruction. Blair added that he "disagreed" with Labour leader Ed Miliband, who helped defeat the government in a Commons vote last week. A Labour source rejected Mr Blair's analysis, saying the lessons the Labour leader had learned from Iraq was the importance of avoiding an "ill-judged and reckless rush to war."

Because Western powers suspect Iran of trying to develop nuclear weapons, they had frozen the assets of various Iranian businesses thought to be linked to that program. Today, however, the EU's top court, the European Court of Justice (ECJ), ruled that the EU should unfreeze the assets of seven Iranian banks and other businesses hit by sanctions. The court said there was insufficient evidence that the businesses concerned were involved in nuclear proliferation. While the ruling may appear to be a blow to Western efforts to exert pressure on Iran over its nuclear program, it is unlikely to counter the West's Israeli-driven vilification of Iran in preparation for an attack against that country. Israel's constant exploitation of anti-Semitism and the Holocaust to blackmail Western powers into launching wars against its Middle East neighbors has to stop, and only the people can force their governments to do that.

11 September '13: According to a top-secret document provided to *The Guardian* by whistleblower Edward Snowden, the U.S. National Security Agency (NSA) routinely shares raw intelligence data with Israel without first sifting it to remove information about U.S. citizens. Information about the intelligence-sharing agreement spelled out in a memorandum of understanding between the NSA and its Israeli counterpart that shows the US government handed over intercepted communications likely to contain phone calls and emails of American citizens. The agreement places no legally binding limits on the use of the data by the Israelis.

This disclosure contradicts Obama administration assurances that there are rigorous safeguards to protect the privacy of U.S. citizens caught in the dragnet. The intelligence community refers to the process as "minimization," but the memorandum makes clear that the information shared with the Israelis would be in its pre-minimized state. According to an undated memorandum which specifies the rules for the intelligence sharing, the deal was agreed to in principle in March 2009. The five-page memorandum, regarded as an agreement between the U.S. and Israeli intelligence agencies "pertaining to the protection of U.S. persons," repeatedly emphasizes the constitutional rights of Americans to privacy and the need for Israeli intelligence staff to respect these rights.

The spirit of the agreement is, however, undermined by the fact that Israel is allowed to receive "raw Sigint" (signal intelligence). The memorandum states that "Raw Sigint includes, but is not limited to, unevaluated and unminimized transcripts, gists, facsimiles, telex, voice and Digital Network Intelligence with metadata and content."

The agreement states that the intelligence being shared would not be filtered in advance by NSA analysts to remove US communications. Also that the "NSA routinely sends the ISNU [Israeli Sigint National Unit] minimszed and unminimised raw collection." Though the memorandum specifies that the material provided had to be handled in accordance with U.S. law — with the Israelis agreeing not to deliberately target Americans identified in the data — there are no legal obligations to back up the rules. The document states that "this agreement is not intended to create any legally enforceable rights and shall not be construed to be either an international agreement or a legally binding instrument according to international law."

An NSA spokesperson in a statement to the Guardian did not deny that personal data about Americans was included in raw intelligence data shared with the Israelis, but insisted that the shared intelligence complied with all rules governing privacy. "Any U.S. person information that is acquired as a result of NSA's surveillance activities is handled under procedures that are designed to protect privacy rights," the spokesperson added. The NSA, however, declined to answer specific questions about the agreement, including whether permission had been sought from the Foreign Intelligence Surveillance court for handing over such material.

The memorandum of understanding allows Israel to retain "any files containing the identities of US persons" for up to a year, and requests only that the Israelis should consult the NSA's special liaison adviser when such data is found. Significantly a much stricter rule was set for US government communications found in the raw intelligence whereby the Israelis were required to "destroy upon recognition" any communication "that is either to or from an official of the US government." Such communications included those of "officials of the executive branch including the White House, cabinet departments, and independent agencies, the US House of Representatives and Senate members and staff, and the US federal court system including, but not limited to, the supreme court."

Whether any communications involving members of U.S. Congress or the federal courts have been included in the raw data provided by the NSA, is not clear, nor is it clear how or why the NSA would be in possession of such communications. The possibility of such possession, however, was confirmed in 2009 when the *New York Times* reported on "the agency's attempt to wiretap a member of Congress, without court approval, on an overseas trip."

The law stipulates that The NSA can target only non-U.S. persons without an individual warrant, but it can collect the content and metadata of Americans' emails and calls without a warrant when such communication is with a foreign target. U.S. persons are defined in surveillance legislation as U.S. citizens, permanent residents and anyone located on US soil at the time of the interception, unless it has been positively established that they are not a citizen or permanent resident. Furthermore, with much of the world's internet traffic passing through U.S. networks, large numbers of purely domestic communications also get scooped up incidentally by the agency's surveillance programs. The document mentions only one check carried out by the NSA on the raw intelligence, stating the agency will "regularly review a sample of files transferred to ISNU to validate the absence of US persons' identities." It also requests that the Israelis limit access only to personnel with a "strict need to know." It should be noted that Israel — a country that does not respect human rights or international law — is hardly likely to respect an informal arrangement that is not "a legally binding instrument according to international law."

Israeli intelligence is allowed "to disseminate foreign intelligence information concerning U.S. persons derived from raw Sigint by NSA" on condition that it does so "in a manner that does not identify the U.S. person." The agreement also permits Israel to release U.S. person identities to "outside parties, including all INSU customers" with the NSA's written permission. Although Israel is one of America's closest allies, it is not one of the inner core of countries involved in surveillance sharing — collectively known as Five Eyes — consisting of the U.S., Australia, Britain, Canada and New Zealand.

16 September '13: Sixteen Israeli Knesset right-wing ministers and members have called on Prime Minister Benjamin Netanyahu to inform John Kerry, who was in Jerusalem on Sunday, that they wanted the "wretched" Oslo Accords scrapped and that Israel will not give up land to the Palestinians. This has occurred at a time when Israeli and Palestinian negotiators had announced that they will resume agricultural cooperation after a 13-year hiatus and amid reports that more economic gestures from Israel to the Palestinians would follow in the weeks ahead. The letter which provides further proof that Palestinian peace talks with Israel are a waste of time, categorically stated that "twenty years have elapsed since the implementation of the wretched Oslo Accords. We call on the Prime Minister to present to the US Secretary of State our unequivocal position that Israel will not return to the Oslo plan, and will not hand over any more regions of the homeland into Palestinian hands."

18 September '13: According to U.S. Census data the number of Americans in poverty rose slightly last year to 46.5 million despite a stock market recovery. Though the U.S. has been out of recession since 2009, this is the sixth consecutive year that the rate has failed to improve so that the national poverty rate — the poverty threshold last year was income below \$23,492 (£14,700) for a family of four — remains unchanged at 15%.

Analysts blamed the lingering poverty on changing employment patterns and tightening of the social safety net. Of the jobs added since the recession, many have been in the lower-paying services industry such as retail and catering.

- Rate among blacks highest at 27.2%; 25.6% for Hispanics; 11.7% for US-Asians; 9.7% for whites
- Mississippi residents had the highest poverty rate, at 22%
- It was followed by Louisiana, New Mexico and Arkansas
- The state of New Hampshire had the lowest share, at 8.1%

Though the Standard & Poor's 500 index gained 16% on a total return basis last year, the Census Bureau report shows median household income remained statistically the same, at \$51,017. The bureau also estimated about 16.1 million children and 3.9 million people aged 65 years and older were living in poverty last year.

Instead of spending billions of dollars supporting an Apartheid Israeli state and financing illegal overseas military intrigues that only serve the industrial-military complex, shyster U.S. politicians could start considering the novel idea of serving and looking after their own.

20 September '13: Israeli arrogance and contempt for everyone but themselves continues unabated as diplomats from the UN and several European countries were prevented by Israeli soldiers from delivering aid to Bedouins in the West Bank. The diplomats said that as soon as they arrived, about a dozen Israeli army jeeps converged on them and ordered them not to unload their truck. The diplomats reacted angrily with one French diplomat complaining she had been dragged out of the truck and forced to the ground with no regard for her diplomatic immunity. "This is how international law is being respected here."

The aid was destined for the Bedouins in Khirbet al-Makhul where their homes had been demolished after Israel's High Court ruled that they had been built without the correct permits. This is yet another example of how Israeli courts with their fascist and warped sense of justice are used to oppress Arabs and drive them from their homes.

A European official described the Israeli actions as "shocking and outrageous," while a spokesman for the British Consulate General in Jerusalem said it was "concerned at reports that the Israeli military authorities have prevented the affected community from receiving humanitarian assistance . . . We have repeatedly made clear to the Israeli authorities our concerns over such demolitions, which we view as causing unnecessary suffering to ordinary Palestinians; as harmful to the peace process; and as contrary to international humanitarian law." A UN Humanitarian Co-ordinator said the Israeli authorities should "live up to their obligations as occupying power to protect those communities under their responsibility."

A forked tongue Israeli spokesman said it was reviewing whether the diplomats had abused their privileges as opposed to why thuggish Israeli soldiers waylaid diplomats endeavoring to deliver humanitarian aid. As for houses being built without the correct permits, it should be noted that the Bedouin villagers — who have refused to leave — have been living and grazing their sheep on that land for generations long before Zionists conned and coerced the UN into allowing them to steal a "Zionist homeland" in Palestine.

According to *Global Research* Israeli officials are said to be increasingly nervous that international efforts to destroy Syria's chemical weapons might serve as the start of demands on Israel to eliminate its own, undeclared weapons of mass destruction. Israel has so far maintained a posture termed "ambiguity" on the question of whether it possesses either nuclear or chemical weapons. It is, however, known that Israel has concealed from international scrutiny its large arsenal of nuclear weapons and there are also strong suspicions that it has secretly developed a chemical weapons program.

Such concerns have intensified following this month's disclosure of a confidential CIA report suggesting that Israel had created a significant stockpile of chemical weapons by the early 1980s. Israel has refused both to sign the 1968 Non-Proliferation Treaty, covering the regulation of nuclear arms, and to ratify the 1993 Chemical Weapons Convention, which obligates states to submit to international oversight and destroy chemical agents in their possession.

Over the past few days there have been a series of moves by other states in the Middle East to bring international attention to Israel's WMD. Those efforts followed Damascus' ratification of the Chemical Weapons Convention last week and the announcement at the weekend of a timetable agreed by Russia and the U.S. to disarm Syria of its chemical stockpiles by the middle of next year.

Israel remains one of only six states refusing to implement the convention, along with Egypt, Myanmar, Angola, North Korea and South Sudan. That has prompted concerns that Israel could rapidly become a pariah state on the issue. The *Haaretz* daily newspaper reported this week that the prospect of mounting international pressure on Israel to come clean on its WMD was "keeping quite a few top Israeli defense officials awake at night."

This week Arab states submitted a resolution to the UN's nuclear watchdog body, the International Atomic Energy Agency, calling on Israel to place its nuclear facilities under the IAEA's inspection regime as part of efforts to create a nuclear arms-free zone in the region. The Nuclear Non-Proliferation Treaty, which Israel has refused to sign, was drawn up in 1968, the year after Israel is widely believed to have produced its first warhead.

23 September '13: In a series of four articles in *AlterNet,* Elly Bulkin (a writer and editor) and Donna Nevel (a community psychologist and educator), state that "as American Jews who work with groups to challenge Islamophobia and anti-Arab racism, we are particularly committed to engaging with the Jewish community about the ways that Israel and the war on terror intersect with Islamophobia . . . In the United States, the separation of the world into 'good Muslims' and 'bad Muslims' is integral to U.S. domestic and foreign policy, which encompasses the 'special' relationship between the U.S. and Israel and the 'war on terror.' Within the mainstream Jewish community, the litmus test that determines which Muslims (or Arabs or others) are 'good' or 'bad' relates most often to Israel."

In another of their articles, Bulkin and Nevel discuss the 2005 film *Obsession: Radical Islam's War Against the West* and note that "the people bankrolling illegal Israeli expansionism in the occupied West Bank are the same people fomenting anti-Muslim sentiment in the U.S." They note that within a minute into the film you "begin to see how inextricably it ties Islamophobia to hardline Israeli policies. Despite its initial disclaimer, the film demonizes all Muslims, and through explicit statements and rapid-fire images, makes clear the filmmaker's view that there is a direct connection between Nazis and both Palestinians and Muslims." And this is despite the irrefutable fact that it was the Zionists who actively sought to collaborate with the Nazis.

Obsession had brief but extensive exposure during the 2008 presidential election campaign when the Clarion fund — founded in 2006 by Canadian-Israeli film producer and rabbi, Raphael Shore — distributed 28 million DVDs as a newspaper insert in swing states. In 2008 Clarion's *The Third Jihad: Radical Islam's Vision for America* — about an alleged Islamic enemy that "the government is too afraid to name" — acquired its own share of notoriety when it was reported that the New York City Police Department had showed the film to some 1,500 police officers. In 2011 Clarion scored a hat trick with its third big film, *Iranium* which hyped Israeli and neo-conservative scaremongering about the dangers of Iran's nuclear program and the need for preemptive military action against the Iranians.

In Bulkin and Nevel's article on the Anti-Defamation League (ADL) — which bills itself, and is typically seen by many in the mainstream Jewish community and beyond, as the "nation's premier civil rights/human relations agency" — the authors show that the ADL's conduct over the years is in fact at odds with this one-dimensional view of the group as a long-time champion of civil liberties. The ADL's mission statement for example, describes itself as a group that "fights all forms of bigotry, defends democratic ideals and protects civil rights for all." Its record going back decades, however, contradicts such a perception and includes a shift "from civil rights monitoring to espionage and intelligence gathering." Consequently there is mistrust of the ADL among those deep rooted concerns about civil and human rights.

During the 1970s, the ADL, which had concerned itself with tracking neo-Nazis and other U.S. right-wing groups, began to also monitor critics of Israeli policies. Since then the ADL and its chapters have issued numerous publications to expose alleged "Arab propaganda" on university campuses and to silence and intimidate Arab Americans and others who did not share their perspective on Israel. By branding any criticism of Israel as "anti-Semitism," ADL publications such as the 1983 *Pro-Arab Propaganda in America: Vehicles and Voices, a Handbook,* effectively developed a "blacklist" of faculty, staff, and campus groups. The Middle East Studies Association singled out "the New England Regional Office of the ADL for circulating a document on college campuses listing factually inaccurate and unsubstantiated assertions that defamed specific students, teachers, and researchers as pro Arab propagandists."

Front-page investigative reports in the *San Francisco Examiner* during the winter and spring of 1993 revealed that the ADL had been carrying out surveillance of almost 10,000 people and 950 organizations. The newspaper reported that the ADL particularly targeted Arab Americans and Arab American organizations and also spied on such groups as the ACLU, ACT UP, Artists Against Apartheid, Americans for Peace Now, Asian Law Caucus, Greenpeace, NAACP, New Jewish Agenda, and the United Farm Workers, as well as three current or past members of Congress. The FBI had also found that the ADL had been sending surveillance information on U.S. anti-apartheid groups to South Africa which at that time was still an ally of Israel.

The *San Francisco Examiner* exposé revealed that the ADL's domestic spying involved a San Francisco police officer and a full-time salaried undercover investigator, who had been working for the ADL for 32 years. While running "a public/private spying ring," the ADL received aid from local police and federal agencies. Also revealed was that 'FBI documents released through the Freedom of Information Act show that special agents in charge of FBI field offices throughout the nation were explicitly ordered by Bureau headquarters in Washington,

D.C. during the 1980s to cooperate with the ADL.

Six years after the filing of a class action suit coordinated by the American-Arab Anti-Discrimination Committee (ADC), the ADL was fined in 1999 and under the permanent injunction issued by Federal Judge Richard Paez . . . [was] permanently enjoined from engaging in any further illegal spying against Arab-American and other civil rights groups. Nabeel Abraham had written in *Anti-Arab Racism and Violence in the United States,* that "the overall effect of the ADL's practices is to reinforce the image of Arabs as terrorists and security threats, thereby creating a climate of fear, suspicion, and hostility toward Arab-Americans and others who espouse critical views of Israel, possibly leading to death threats and bodily harm."

The ADL's anti-Arab, staunchly pro-Israel mindset, which was behind decades of illegal spying, enabled it to easily incorporate an anti-Muslim worldview that has become increasingly pervasive after 9/11. This has been a period of growing popularity for the "clash of civilizations theory" which characterizes the causes of conflict in the post-Cold War world as fundamental "cultural" differences between Islamic and Western civilizations, rather than history, politics, imperialism, neo-colonialism, struggles over natural resources, or other factors. Further, the Islamophobic belief that all Muslims were responsible for the 9/11 attacks and that all Muslims, as well as Arabs and South Asians, should be targeted provides a dominant U.S. narrative that brands all members of these groups as terrorists, potential terrorists, or terrorist-sympathizers. Like others within and outside the Jewish community, the ADL views the U.S. focus on the domestic and global "war on terror" as integral to ensuring Israeli security and maintaining the United States' special relationship with Israel.

26 September '13: A new campaign requesting that women be given the right to drive in Saudi Arabia has attracted more than 12,000 signatures in support. Scheduled for 26 October, the campaign has asked Saudi women to take to the roads in defiance of the informal ban on women drivers. As confirmation of how online social network use is becoming widespread even in Saudi Arabia. This campaign — the brainchild of the activist, Eman al-Nafjan — was started on Twitter with a simple message stating that Saudi women would express their feelings about driving on 26 October and that there is no justification for the Saudi government to prohibit adult women citizens who are capable of driving cars from doing so. Ms Nafjan hopes that women will come out en-masse to drive on the day of the campaign which is intended as a grassroots movement open to all Saudis so that men can also show their support. Some influential Saudis have given their public support while several videos of women driving have been posted on the campaign's website.

The Saudi response to this "outrageous" request by women for parity with men verges on insanity and definitely belongs in a Ripley's Believe it or Not arcade. A conservative Saudi cleric in this ultra-conservative kingdom invited a wave of online mockery when he warned women against driving because it would affect their ovaries and bring "clinical disorders" upon their children: "Physiological science has found that driving automatically affects the ovaries and pushes up the pelvis," Sheikh Saleh bin Saad al-Lohaidan warned women in remarks to local news website Sabq.org. "This is why we find that children born to most women who continuously drive suffer from clinical disorders of varying degrees."

In a further informed response to the use of online social networks, Sheikh Abdul Latif Abdul Aziz al-Sheikh said that anyone using social media sites — and especially Twitter — has lost this world and his afterlife, and that Twitter was the platform for those who did not have any platform. His comments reflect Saudi Arabia's concern that Saudis are using Twitter to discuss other sensitive issues including politics. Saudi Arabia is believed to have experienced the world's fastest increase in the use of Twitter and the sheikh's comments echoed those of the imam of the Grand Mosque in Mecca who in April used his sermon — watched by millions on TV — to warn that Twitter was a threat to national unity. Earlier, Saudi Arabia's grand mufti, the kingdom's most senior Muslim cleric, had dismissed Twitter users as fools.

Also today declassified documents revealed that during the height of protests against the Vietnam War, the U.S. National Security Agency (NSA) spied on civil rights leader Martin Luther King, boxer Muhammad Ali, two senators, and journalists from the *New York Times* and the *Washington Post*. The operation, dubbed "Minaret" was subsequently described by some NSA officials as "disreputable if not outright illegal." Though originally exposed in the 1970s, the names of those on the phone-tapping "watch list" had remained secret until now.

Publication of the secret papers became possible after a government panel ruled in favour of researchers at George Washington University.

The university's National Security Archive — a research institute that seeks to check government secrecy — described the names on the NSA's watch-list as eye-popping. Other victims of the NSA's eavesdropping included civil rights leader Whitney Young, *New York Times* journalist Tom Wicker, and *Washington Post* columnist Art Buchwald.

The rising tide of the anti-war campaign in 1967 had led President Lyndon Johnson to ask U.S. intelligence agencies to establish whether some protests were being encouraged by foreign governments. Watch lists of anti-war critics were drawn up and their phone calls were tapped. The operation continued following Richard Nixon election as U.S. President in 1969. US Attorney General Elliot Richardson, however, shut down the NSA's operation in 1973 as the Nixon administration became embroiled in the Watergate scandal.

This latest declassification of secret documents has come at a time when the NSA is embroiled in further controversy over its surveillance operations as a result of the exposure —by U.S. intelligence leaker Edward Snowden — of far-reaching electronic surveillance of phone records and internet traffic.

2 October '13: The majority of people worldwide who have welcomed Iran's efforts for rapprochement with the West in general, and the U.S. in particular, are apparently all wrong. Who said so? Who else but the Israelis who are always right while everyone else is always wrong. Furthermore, whoever happens to disagree with them, does so because he or she is an anti-Semitic Holocaust denier. Instead of taking the opportunity to seek harmonious relations and avoid conflict — Presidents Obama and Rouhani recently spoke on the phone together in what was the first top-level conversation between the two countries for more than 30 years — Israel instructs us that we should instead tighten sanctions against the Iranian people and then bomb the hell out of them.

As part of an Israeli offensive to counter any such rapprochement, Israeli Prime Minister Benjamin Netanyahu in his usual hawkish insanity mode along with his not so demure hawk-eyed wife — both exuding dovish love and humanity — flew to the U.S. to warn against working with the Iranian government. In a harangue to the UN General Assembly, Netanyahu referred to President Hassan Rouhani and his more hard-line predecessor Mahmoud Ahmadinejad by saying "Ahmadinejad was a wolf in wolf's clothing. Rouhani is a wolf in sheep's clothing." In response to President Rouhani's strong denial that Iran was seeking to manufacture nuclear weapons, Netanyahu said "I wish I could believe Rouhani. But I don't." So once again the silent and peaceful worldwide majority will have to continue abiding by what Israel — through the obsequious mainstream media — tells it what to listen to, what to read, what to watch, what to believe, and what to do — Which is to keep waging wars that distract from the fact that it is Israeli violations of international law and human rights in the occupied territories — not to mention assassinations, espionage, false flag operations, and provocative subversion throughout the region — that are the main causes of the problems in the Middle East. Can there be any doubt that Benjamin Netanyahu belongs in a straitjacket.

3 October '13: The UN has released figures that show that in September almost 1,000 people were killed and more than 2,000 wounded in violence in Iraq. Baghdad was the worst affected province with 887 civilians and 92 members of the Iraqi Security Forces dying nationwide. The death toll was lower than July's 1,057 death toll, but still one of the highest in years with a death toll 5,740 so far this year. The UN's envoy urged Iraqis to strengthen their efforts to promote national dialogue and reconciliation, and urged that political, religious and civil leaders as well as the security services must work together to end the bloodshed and ensure that all Iraqi citizens feel equally protected.

A statement posted online by the Islamic State in Iraq and the Levant (ISIS), an umbrella group to which al-Qaeda in Iraq (AQI) belongs, said the bombings were revenge for a "campaign of torture, displacement, detainment and liquidation" of the Sunni minority by the Shia-led government.

Apart from the Shia-Sunni conflict, Iraq has also seen a spill-over of violence from the conflict in Syria, where jihadist rebels linked to the Islamic State of Iraq, a Sunni militant umbrella group that includes al-Qaeda, have risen to prominence. During the past two months, Iraqi security forces have reportedly arrested hundreds of alleged al-Qaeda members in and around Baghdad as part of a government campaign called "Revenge for the Martyrs." The operations, however, which have taken place mostly in Sunni districts, have angered the Sunni community and failed to halt the violence. It would appear that the execution of Osama bin Laden and the disposal of his body at sea has by the U.S. failed to curb the terrorist activities of Al-Qaeda.

4 October '13: The Supreme Court in Jerusalem has rejected a request by twenty-one people to be registered as Israeli nationals rather than Jews or Arabs. This is because Israel's population register — in a nation that is hyped and sold to the world as the Middle East's only democracy — does not permit the concept of Israeli nationality. Most of the Petitioners — described in the population registry as Jewish — claimed that this was undemocratic and exposed minorities to discrimination. The court's explanation in its 26-page ruling, was that it did not have the authority to determine ethnicity in statehood.

The ruling was described as a "defeat for Israeliness." In an editorial by the *Haaretz* newspaper which added that "the state and its legislators must relate to all its citizens as Israeli citizens and eliminate the nationality line item in the Population Registry." The court had said that any recognition of Israeli nationality would have "weighty implications" on the state of Israel and endangered Israel's founding principle of being a Jewish state for the Jewish people. Is that a democracy?

Anita Shapira, a professor emeritus of Jewish history at Tel Aviv University, revealed her fear that if nationalism developed into an Israeli one, the Jewish essence would be lost and added that "the attempt to claim that there is a Jewish nationality in the state of Israel that is separate from the Jewish religion is something very revolutionary." According to figures obtained from the Israel Democracy Institute think tank, about fifty percent of Israel's Jewish population define themselves first and foremost as Jewish, while forty-one percent define themselves as Israeli. Jewish religious holidays are also national holidays in Israel.

The main petitioner — a linguistics professor at the Technion-Israel Institute of Technology in Haifa — was ninety year-old Uzzi Ornan who by running a small group campaigning for the recognition of Israeli nationality felt that "with an Israeli identity, we can be secure in our democracy, secure in equality between all citizens." Professor Ornan should know by now that equality for all citizens including Arabs, is a concept that is a complete anathema to the majority of Israel's chosen people.

7 October '13: Despite vigils that had been held for the past month at a hospital in Jerusalem where he was being treated, the influential leader of Israel's Sephardic Jewish community, Rabbi Ovadia Yosef, has passed away at the age of ninety-three. As well as being a leading Torah scholar and arbiter of Halakha (Jewish law), he was also the spiritual leader of the Shas party, which he founded in 1984 to boost representation for Jews of Middle Eastern and North African origin. Until that time, Israel's government and religious institutions had been dominated by Ashkenazi Jews — those of European descent.

Though currently in opposition, Shas party has been a kingmaker in several coalition governments. After Rabbi Yosef's death was announced, Shas leader Arye Deri sobbed uncontrollably and asked "How will we remain alone? Who will lead us?" he added, referring to the rabbi as "our father."

Israel's Prime Minister Benjamin Netanyahu expressed "deep sorrow" at the news of Rabbi Yosef's death, describing him as "among the greatest rabbis of our generation . . . Rabbi Ovadia was a giant in Torah and Jewish law and a teacher for tens of thousands . . . the Jewish People have lost one of the wisest men of this generation."

This wisest of men was an Iraqi-born cleric who was also known for his controversial comments about Arabs, secular Jews, liberals, women and gays. He once likened the Palestinian people to snakes, and in 2010 called for Palestinian Authority President Mahmoud Abbas to "vanish from our world." Why do people continue tolerating the hate-spewing pronouncements of religious leaders and let them influence the course of humanity?

According to the Nigerian-based *Ventures* financial magazine, there are now more billionaires in Africa than previously thought. The fifty-five billionaires on record include three women — the mother of Kenya's president, a daughter of Angola's president, and a Nigerian oil tycoon and fashion designer. The richest amongst them is Nigeria's Aliko Dangote, with a fortune of $20.2 billion (£12.5 billion). Earlier this year the World Bank said the number of people living in extreme poverty in Africa had risen in the past three decades from 205 million to 414 million. Such statistics will no doubt reignite the debate about inequality between the very rich and the very poor people in Africa.

Inequality in African wealth distribution was just one of the more calamitous legacies of colonial rule in Africa whereby colonial corporate interests prepared for the independence of African nations by buying and corrupting the African politicians who were about to take over the governance of their own countries. Before South Africa's 1994 independence from White minority rule, mining and other conglomerates started splashing out with the cash that saw potential Black South African leaders buying and moving into exclusive Whites-only residential areas. Thus began the divide between those who would become rich and those who would remain poor.

Venture magazine estimated that the combined fortunes of the fifty-five billionaires was $143.88 billion (£89.55 billion), an average of a $2.6 billion (£1.62 billion) per person. Twenty were Nigerian, nine were South African and eight were Egyptian. The richest woman was Nigeria's Folorunsho Alakija, who made her $7.3 billion (£4.79 billion) fortune mainly in the country's oil industry. The other two women were Isabel Dos Santos, an Angolan investor and the eldest daughter of Angolan President Jose Eduardo dos Santos; and Ngina Kenyatta, the mother of Kenya's President Uhuru Kenyatta. This is the same Uhuru Kenyatta whose trial is due to commence next month at the International Criminal Court (ICC) as an indirect co-perpetrator of crimes against humanity including murder, deportation or forcible transfer, rape, persecution, and other inhumane acts. Kenyan preparations for this trial have resulted in the bribing of witnesses and of parliamentary vote last month to back a call for Kenya to pull out of the ICC.

In African politics, nepotism goes hand in hand with corruption that sees the majority of African people — despite their having gained so-called independence — remain in poverty and squalor while their political leaders' plundered wealth is safely ensconced in tax havens like Switzerland where the issue of humanity's well-being is swiftly sidestepped in the rush to worship at the alter of Mammon.

10 October '13: Pakistani schoolgirl and campaigner Malala Yousafzai, who was shot in the head by the Taliban, has won the EU's Sakharov human rights prize. The sixteen-year-old activist was shot a year ago for campaigning for better rights for girls. The 50,000 euro ($65,000) prize is considered Europe's top human rights award. Malala rose to prominence in 2009 after writing a blog anonymously for the BBC Urdu service about her life under Taliban rule and the lack of education for girls. She lived in Pakistan's mountainous Swat Valley and her name became internationally known after the Pakistan army pushed the Taliban out of the area in 2009. The Taliban's Islamist doctrine puts harsh restrictions on women's rights and one of the militants shot her as she was riding in a bus with school friends.

The head of the conservative European People's Party (EPP), Joseph Daul, said "Today, we decided to let the world know that our hope for a better future stands in young people like Malala Yousafzai." Malala had received a standing ovation in July this year for an address to the United Nations General Assembly, in which she vowed she would never be silenced. Members of the European Parliament said Malala — who now lives in Birmingham, England — was incredibly brave to continue promoting the rights of children. She joins a distinguished list of winners of the Sakharov Prize which includes South Africa's Nelson Mandela and Aung San Suu Kyi in Burma (Myanmar). The award will be officially presented at a ceremony in Strasbourg in November.

Another Nominee for the Sakharov prize for freedom of thought was Edward Snowden, the fugitive American former CIA and NSA intelligence employee. Snowden was nominated by Green politicians in the European Parliament for leaking details of U.S. surveillance. His nomination was prompted by the recognition that his disclosure of U.S. surveillance activities was an enormous service to human rights and European citizens. Snowden, who has sought asylum in Russia, said in a statement read out in parliament that he was grateful to Europe's politicians for "taking up the challenge of mass surveillance . . . the surveillance of whole populations, rather than individuals, threatens to be the greatest human rights challenge of our time."

The prize is awarded annually in memory if Andrei Sakharov, a Soviet nuclear physicist, dissident, and human rights activist. Sakharov was arrested on January 1980, following his public protests against the Soviet intervention in Afghanistan in 1979 — a failed intervention which the U.S. is destined to repeat — and was sent to the off-limits to foreigners city of Gorky (now Nizhny Novgorod) for internal exile. In December 1985, the European Parliament established the Sakharov Prize for Freedom of thought, to be given annually for outstanding contributions to human rights. On 19 December 1986, Mikhail Gorbachev who had initiated the perestroika and glasnost policies, called Sakharov to tell him that he and his wife could return to Moscow.

14 October '13: Following Israeli Prime Minister Benjamin Netanyahu's deranged rant at the opening of the Knesset's winter session that it would be a historic mistake to ease pressure on Iran, Israel continued with its arrogant persistence in telling the world what to do. Israeli Minister for Strategic Affairs, Yuval Steinitz, has also warned against easing sanctions on Iran in return for its consent to suspend uranium enrichment. This comes on the eve of talks on Iran's nuclear program in

Geneva which are scheduled to resume today and are the the first under the recently elected administration of Hassan Rouhani.

15 October '13: *The Washington Post* reports that the secretive National Security Agency (NSA) is not limiting itself to the bulk collection of Americans' phone metadata, but is also collecting and holding hundreds of millions of e-mail and instant messaging contacts. This latest information from documents leaked by Edward Snowden reveal that the NSA is doing so without any oversight or approval from the Foreign Intelligence Surveillance Court. Such foreign intelligence collection is carried out under executive authority which precludes Congressional intelligence committees from having full knowledge about the program.

Data from Americans' e-mail address books are being swept up in the dragnet, but the federal surveillance court does not need to approve the collection because the access points are all over the world, instead of U.S.-based. Data from instant messaging "buddy lists" is also being swept up. The number of e-mail address books and instant messaging contacts being harvested is staggering. The *Post's* Barton Gellman and Ashkan Soltani report that "according to an internal NSA PowerPoint presentation, during a single day last year, the NSA's Special Source Operations branch collected 444,743 e-mail address books from Yahoo, 105,068 from Hotmail, 82,857 from Facebook, 33,697 from Gmail and 22,881 from unspecified other providers." Such figures which are described as typical daily document intake, correspond to a rate of more than 250 million a year. The NSA is able to do so because of arrangements with foreign telecommunications companies and allied intelligence agencies.

This dragnet can reveal much about Americans because address books can include telephone numbers, street addresses, family and business information, and the first few lines of the content of e-mails in inboxes. Such data would enable the NSA to draw detailed maps of an individual's life as revealed by personal, professional, political and religious connections. The information gathered, however, could be misleading by creating false "associations" with people with whom an account holder has had no contact for many years.

The program is defended by NSA officials who claim the agency is "focused on discovering and developing intelligence about valid foreign intelligence targets like terrorists, human traffickers and drug smugglers. We are not interested in personal information about ordinary

Americans." The American Civil Liberties Union's response was that "this revelation further confirms that the NSA has relied on the pretense of 'foreign intelligence gathering' to sweep up an extraordinary amount of information about everyday Americans . . . The NSA's indiscriminate collection of information about innocent people can't be justified on security grounds, and it presents a serious threat to civil liberties." And this is the nation that conducts wars globally in the name of liberty for all.

16 October '13: An academic study by university researchers in the US, Canada, and Iraq suggests that about half a million people died in Iraq — including avoidable fatalities linked to infrastructure collapse, but excluding an additional estimate of 56,000 deaths that were not counted because of the emigration of households from Iraq — as a result of war-related causes between the US-led invasion in 2003 and mid-2011. The researchers based their estimate on random surveys of two thousand households. The figure exceeds the 112,000 violent civilian deaths reported by Iraq Body Count, the British-based organization which bases its tally on media reports, hospital and mortuary records, and information from official and non-governmental sources.

According the UN, the past year has seen a surge in sectarian violence in Iraq with almost five thousand civilians killed in attacks between January and September, an increase on the three thousand that died in 2012. The study by researchers — from the University of Washington, Johns Hopkins University, Simon Fraser University and Mustansiriya University — covers the period from March 2003 until June 2011, six months before the US withdrawal.

The study concludes that more than 60% of the estimated 461,000 excess deaths were directly attributable to violence, with the rest associated with the collapse of infrastructure and other indirect causes. These include the failures of health, sanitation, transportation, communication and other systems. The most common causes of non-violent deaths linked to the war were heart attacks or cardiovascular conditions, followed by infant or childhood deaths other than injuries, chronic illnesses and cancer.

Amy Hagopian, Associate Professor of Global Health at the University of Washington and lead author of the paper, said "In a war situation, people can't leave their homes to get medical care. When they do leave their homes to get medical care, they arrive at institutions overwhelmed with violent injuries . . . The water is compromised. Stress is elevated. The power is out. The distribution networks for medical supplies are compromized." The researchers, however, did warn that their estimates were associated with "substantial uncertainties." Nonetheless the fact remains that those who perpetrated this illegal war —Israeli puppets Bush Jr., Blair et al — have not been held accountable and continue to enjoy the inevitable trappings that result from having been in positions of political power.

17 October '13: Despite all the human, monetary, and other resources expended on wars perpetrated with the excuse of liberating the people of the world, almost thirty million are —according to the latest Global Slavery Index 2013 ranking 162 countries — still living as slaves with India accounting for almost half of them at fourteen million with other estimated numbers being as follows:

1.	*India*	*— 13,956,010*
2.	*China*	*— 2,949,243*
3.	*Pakistan*	*— 2,127,132*
4.	*Nigeria*	*— 701,032*
5.	*Ethiopia*	*— 651,110*
6.	*Russia*	*— 516,217*
7.	*Thailand*	*— 472,811*
8.	*DR Congo*	*— 462,327*
9.	*Burma*	*— 384,037*
10.	*Bangladesh*	*— 343,192*

It comes as no surprise that India with its multiple deities and Brahmin-enforced caste system, shamelessly leads the way with the highest number of slaves while claiming to be the world's largest democracy. The report said India's ranking was mostly due to the exploitation of Indian citizens within the country itself. Mauritania — with about four percent of its population being enslaved — had the highest proportional figure followed by Haiti, Pakistan, India, Nepal, Moldova, Benin, Ivory Coast, The Gambia, and Gabon.

The index was compiled by Australian-based rights organisation Walk Free Foundation by using a definition of modern slavery that includes debt bondage, forced marriage and human trafficking. The authors of the report hoped that it would assist governments in tackling what they called a hidden crime.

20 October '13: *The Lancet,* one of the world's leading medical journals, has published a report supporting the theory that Yasser Arafat was poisoned with polonium-210. Arafat, then president of the Palestinian Authority, died in a French military hospital in November 2004 after falling ill at his headquarters in Ramallah. The report was produced by scientists from the Institute for Radiation Physics in Lausanne and the University Centre of Legal Medicine, Lausanne-Geneva. The Swiss examination of Arafat's medical records and some of his belongings — including toothbrush, clothes and kaffiyeh provided by his widow Suha Arafat — showed traces of polonium.

The study addressed neither the question of whether Arafat had been assassinated, nor how he might have come into contact with polonium. The presence of the radioactive isotope, however, pointed irrefutably to Arafat having been murdered. Given the difficulty of obtaining the isotope by anyone other than the nuclear powers and by asking who benefits, the murder could only have been planned — if not carried out — by either Israel or the United States. Israeli Prime Minister Benjamin Netanyahu's office dismissed the report with the comment that he had "nothing new to say" on the death of Arafat.

21 October '13: Amnesty International has accused Saudi Arabia — which has a unitary Islamic absolute monarchy government — of having failed to act on recommendations by a UN body to improve human rights and that promises made by the Gulf Kingdom to the UN Human Rights Council in 2009 were nothing but hot air. The Saudi authorities have instead "ratcheted up" repression with continued crackdowns on activists through "arbitrary arrests and detention, unfair trials, torture and other ill-treatment." Amnesty said the kingdom had failed to implement any of the main recommendations from its last Universal Periodic Review by the Human Rights Council which is due to review Saudi Arabia in Geneva next week.

Amnesty's report documents what it describes as a new wave of repression against civil society that has taken place since 2011 with human rights activists and supporters of political reform in the country facing repressive measures that include arbitrary arrest, detention without charge or trial, unfair trials and travel bans. Such violations of human rights, however, is to be expected because Saudi Arabia is almost unique in giving the ulema — the body of Islamic religious leaders and jurists — a direct role in government with the only other example being Iran.

459

Apart from having direct influence over major government decisions, the ulema also plays a major role in the judicial and education systems and monopolizes authority over religious and social morals.

23 October '13: In Yemen — where traditional Muslim tribal customs in some parts of the country prohibit contact between men and women before marriage — a man was arrested for burning his fifteen-year-old daughter to death after he caught her speaking to her fiancé on the phone. The UN Human Rights council had already raised concerns over so-called "honor killings" in the country where perpetrators escaped being charged with murder and were usually only given a light prison sentence of six months to a year. Many Yemeni women are accorded a low family and community status that sees them subjected to various forms of violence, deprivation of education, early and forced marriages, sexual abuse, and restrictions over freedom of movement, forced pregnancy, and female genital mutilation. So yet another victory can be chalked up for God and religion.

29 October '13: In an *Information Clearing House* book review, Rania Khalek —an independent journalist living in Washington, DC— had the following to say:

> *In his new book,* Goliath: Life and Loathing in Greater Israel, *award-winning journalist Max Blumenthal goes deep inside Israeli society, offering a rare and unfiltered lens into the hideous implications of Israel's commitment to Jewish supremacy.*
>
> *With his fearless brand of uncompromising honesty, Blumenthal exposes Israel as a racist colonizer that more closely resembles the American Jim Crow South and Apartheid South Africa than a modern-day democracy. In one gripping scene after another, Blumenthal shows Israel to be a nation infused with nationalistic fervor, where mainstream political leaders routinely incite hatred against non-Jews and use the Holocaust to justify violence and discrimination against Palestinians and African migrants, a far cry from the picturesque 'Jewish and democratic state' revered in the establishment press.*

Meanwhile, daily life for Palestinians between the river and the sea has deteriorated to levels of epic misery, as Israel continues its illegal campaign of dispossession and ethnic cleansing inside and outside the green line, all in the name of maintaining its demographic imperative as a majority Jewish state. Even those who disagree with Blumenthal's analyses will come away shocked at just how far mainstream Israeli culture has descended into fascism, the inevitable outgrowth of a national identity based on ethnic purity.

Rania Khalek: *Challenging the pro-Israel narrative, as your book does, isn't the most lucrative career move for an American journalist. With that in mind, why did you write this book?*

Max Blumenthal: *I was following a really successful book called Republican Gomorrah that got me on MSNBC, Air America [and] NPR, and I had a big liberal Democrat-oriented audience who were eager for my analysis of the radical right. I could've leveraged that into another book deal about Republican racism, made loads of money and sold tons of books. But this isn't why I'm in journalism. I don't look at journalism as a career. I look at it both as a profession and a craft and also as a means for exposing injustice. I've been watching the increasing violence and racism of Israeli society for most of my adult life, especially in their treatment of Palestinians. Having been born in 1977, I came of age during the First Intifada and then watched during the Second Intifada as Israel destroyed the Jenin Refugee camp. And then the Second Lebanon invasion happened. Israel basically carpet-bombed southern Lebanon, turning one-quarter of the country into refugees. Then there was Operation Cast Lead, the three-week assault on the besieged Gaza Strip that left 1,400 dead. It was so hard to watch, and it occurred after Barack Obama had been elected, someone I was deeply skeptical of. During the slaughter, I went to midtown New York and filmed a few hundred Jewish-Americans celebrating the attack. They were dancing a hora line outside the Israeli consulate and offering very clearly genocidal statements about the need to* *eradicate the cancer in Gaza. I put this online as a video, and it went viral. Before long, I was contacted by all kinds of people from across the Middle East who are directly affected by the Israel-Palestine crisis, inviting me to come there to see the situation on the ground. I agreed, and I put a lot of my book advance into the first extended reporting trip there in May 2009. That's what led to me getting the deal to write* Goliath *and to spending the last four to five years of my life writing about this situation. It definitely changed my life in a lot of ways that I never expected, and I don't think I'll ever be able to see things the same way again.*

Rania Khalek: Goliath *came out October 1. What has the reception been like so far, compared with that for* Republican Gomorrah?

Max Blumenthal: *Pro-Israel partisans in the U.S. typically get hysterical about books like this because the real Israel is really impossible for them to grapple with. It shatters the dream castle Israel that goes to the heart of their identity as tribalistic, secular American Jews. I really believe that they are determined to ignore this book for as long as they can. It may take me going on national TV with one of those foam giant fingers and twerking on Abe Foxman for them to pay attention.*

1 November '13: Marilyn Kleinberg Neimark reports in *MuzzleWatch* that what Canada's relatively small population of Jews lack in numbers — some 370,000 with about half living in Toronto and a quarter in Montreal — they more than compensate for with the ferocity of their organized community's defense of what they regard as Israel's interests. They have for example tried — so far unsuccessfully — to keep Queers Against Israeli Apartheid out of the city's annual Gay Pride parade since the group was founded in 2008.

In the latest attempt to muzzle critics of Israel, as reported in the Electronic Intifada (24/10/13), "The Toronto Transit Commission (TTC) has rejected a group's bus advertisement showing Israel's appropriation of Palestinian land over time, claiming the advertisement could incite anti-Jewish discrimination and violence," — the implication being that the problem is not due to Israel's despicable land-grabbing conduct, but to the reporting and criticism of that conduct.

Even in Canada's second city, Montreal, censorship of Israel's critics has ramped up so two panels scheduled for the November 3rd Le Mood — an annual festival aimed at engaging Jewish youth in Montreal — were peremptorily cancelled because the festival's major funder, Federation CJA (Combined Jewish Appeal), objected to the panel hosts. Le Mood festival director, Mike Savatovsky, is reported to have told one of the hosts "You have a specific instance when you did go against a program that our funders support; we're not willing to create a platform for people whose mission goes against the beliefs of our funders." And these are the people who support Israel with the claim that it is the only democracy — a concept that includes the right to free opinions and speech — in the Middle East.

3 November '13: Back in April the BBC — no doubt pressured by BBC Watch which ensures the silencing of any coverage critical of Israel — cancelled the showing of Lian Ziv's documentary *Jerusalem: An Archaeological Mystery Story* which questioned the scale and veracity of the Jewish exile from Jerusalem in 70CE. When questioned about the cancellation by Palestine Solidarity Campaign (PSC), the BBC replied "We originally acquired Jerusalem: An Archeological Mystery Story to supplement BBC Four's season exploring the history of archeology. However, we have decided that it doesn't fit editorially and are no longer planning to show it as part of the season."

The BBC's claim was subsequently disputed by Lian Ziv on his blog which felt the reason for his film being dropped was "a mixture of incompetence, political naiveté [and] conscious or subconscious political pressure." Ziv had also explained how BBC executives had wanted to make substantial cuts to the film, including removing one scene about the Palestinians which, he wrote, was deemed "too emotive" by an internal BBC review. Consequently six organizations, including the PSC, Middle East Monitor, Friends of Al Aqsa, and Jews for Justice for Palestinians wrote an open letter in June to the BBC's director general, Tony Hall, in which they questioned the broadcaster's reasons for discarding the documentary. The letter concluded "we write to ask if a reason can be provided for removing *Jerusalem* from the BBC's schedule that can disprove the reasons given by Mr. Ziv."

While no reason countering Ziv's claims was ever provided, the

PSC was, however, informed that the film would be shown in November with an accompanying discussion program to give "context and balance." So today BBC Four broadcast a sanitized version repackaged as *Searching for Exile: Truth or Myth* followed by a debate chaired by Ed Stourton and featuring Lian Ziv and three historians but without any Palestinian or Muslim representatives. The film made it clear that Jewish communities continued to exist for long after 70CE and raised the point of whether the story of the exile was now being used to justify the "return" of the Jews to Palestine.

4 November '13: The UN warns that Gaza's population of 1.6 million Palestinians are without clean drinking water with the only source they can access — the underground water aquifer — being over-utilized and now highly polluted with sea water and sewage intrusions. The UN added that unless a solution is found to provide Gaza with safe and affordable water, Gaza's aquifer will become unusable by 2016, and irreversibly damaged by 2020. Currently only five percent of the water extracted by Gazans from the Coastal aquifer is safe to drink. Most Gazan families are forced to buy drinking water from private Israeli companies at a high cost that in some cases accounts for as much as a third of a family's income.

The portion of the Coastal aquifer running beneath Gaza represents only a small percentage of the total freshwater resources available to Israelis and Palestinians. Israel, with its usual predatory selfishness, continues to exploit ninety percent of the available freshwater — particularly the underground Mountain aquifer in the occupied West Bank — for exclusive Israeli use while Palestinians have access to less than ten percent. Israel does so in violation of international water laws, which call for these resources to be shared "equitably and reasonably" between Palestinians and Israelis. As God's chosen people, Israelis do not give a damn for international laws.

There is apparently a solution which can start with the implementation of Palestinian water rights. If Palestinians have access to their rightful share of the available water resources, and if Israel lifts its blockade over the Gaza Strip, which restricts water imports as well as the entry of materials and goods needed to upgrade and repair its deteriorating water infrastructure, many of Gaza's water problems would be solved. Unfortunately, however, any solution that requires unselfish Israeli cooperation, will in reality mean that there is no available solution.

Is it possible that the hardline supporter and probable agent of Israel, Rahm Emanuel —Obama's former chief of staff and now mayor of Chicago — had anything to do with Rasmea Odeh's arrest and detention? The International Jewish anti-Zionist Network had the following protest on its website:

ACTION ALERT: Support Rasmea Odeh

Monday, November 04, 2013

The International Jewish Anti-Zionist Network (IJAN) protests in the strongest possible manner the arrest and detention of civil rights worker Rasmea Yousef Odeh, on October 22, 2013, from her home in Chicago.

Ms. Odeh, a Palestinian lawyer, arrived in the United States 20 years ago after suffering brutal arrest by the Israeli military for her work for Palestinian freedom and rights. Rasmea's arrest led to years of unspeakable, inhumane, and illegal torture by Israeli prison authorities. Since her arrival, she has worked for the civil and human rights of Palestinians and Arabs. Since 2004, she has worked with the Arab American Action Network (AAAN) as the Associate Director. She also managed the Arab Women's Committee of the AAAN and fought to defend women's and immigrants' rights. She recently won the Outstanding Community Leader's Award from the Chicago Cultural Alliance.

Ms. Odeh was charged with an immigration violation, but we believe that this is an excuse to remove an effective human rights worker from the American society and instill fear in others who dare to work for human rights and equal rights for Palestinians. As with the Grand Jury subpoenas of the 23 Palestinian human rights and anti-war activists in Minneapolis and Chicago in 2010, the inhumanely long prison sentence of the Holy Land 5, and the infiltration and targeting of Muslim groups by FBI informants, the arrest of Ms. Odeh is meant to send a message to those who work for and believe in human rights for all people: the U.S. will not tolerate criticisms of its pro-Israeli policies and support.

465

This reflects a long history of collaboration between the United States and Israeli government, military and police in repressing popular movements for justice and liberty and organizations that work on their behalf. Beyond the Palestine liberation movement, this includes the Black Liberation Movement, the South African anti-apartheid struggle, the United Farm Workers, the Center for Constitutional Rights and countless others. Most recently, the US National Security Administration was exposed for spying on its general population and sharing the information it gathers with the State of Israel. The lead contracting agencies the NSA partners with in its spying are run by former personnel of the intelligence branch of the Israeli military.

IJAN calls on the US Attorney Barbara McQuade to drop the charges against and immediately release Rasmea Yousef Odeh, and the cessation of policies to instill fear in human rights activists and workers.

6 November '13: One year has now passed since Barack "Uncle tom" Obama was reelected for a second term as U.S. President and as expected — even with having been relieved of concern over upsetting AIPAC by pursuing an independent and just U.S. Middle East policy — he has clung to a cowardly White House bias towards Israel. To celebrate the anniversary of its first year in its second term the Obama administration has conducted itself as follows:

Has responded to the latest exposures of the massive NSA spying operations by insisting that all programs will be retained, while in the meantime intensifying its campaign against NSA whistleblower Edward Snowden. Leaks from Snowden during the past few weeks include the exposure of an intelligence apparatus aimed at collecting all significant electronic communications worldwide, the monitoring of dozens of heads of state using US embassies as NSA outposts, and the secret theft of communications from Internet giants Yahoo and Google. Such activities — which are both illegal and unconstitutional — have provoked international outrage and caused a diplomatic crisis for the United States.

Referring to one program, which collects phone records, the *New York Times* wrote that "...but for now, President Obama and his top advisers have concluded that there is no workable alternative to the bulk collection of huge quantities of 'metadata,' including records of all telephone calls made inside the United States." The telephone records program constitutes only a small part of an all-encompassing intelligence apparatus. A *New York Times* article — "No Morsel Too Minuscule for All-Consuming NSA" — based on thousands of documents provided by Snowden to the *Times* and *The Guardian,* documents an electronic omnivore of staggering capabilities, eavesdropping and hacking its way around the world to strip governments and other targets of their secrets, all the while enforcing the utmost secrecy about its own operations.

The NSA seems to be listening everywhere in the world . . . Gathering every stray electron that might add, however minutely, to the United States government's knowledge of the world . . . It sucks the contents from fiber-optics cables, sits on telephone switches and Internet hubs, digitally burglarizes laptops and plants bugs on smartphones around the globe . . .

Among the activities documented by the newspaper are the collection of text messages from all over the world, the daily monitoring of the movements and communications of Iranian leader Ayatollah Khamenei and Venezuela government officials, and many other operations.

According to the *Times* "the agency, using a combination of jawboning, stealth and legal force has turned the nation's Internet and telecommunications companies into collection partners, installing filters in their faculties, serving them with court orders, building back doors into their software and acquiring keys to break their encryption."

The fact that in the mainstream media and the political establishment are treating such operations — conducted in flagrant violation of international law and the Fourth Amendment prohibition of unreasonable searches and seizures — as a non-issue is extremely alarming. Furthermore, the latest revelations directly contradict previous Obama administration denials that the NSA does not monitor the phone conversations and emails of US citizens. In order to diffuse the crisis, the administration has proposed a few minor modifications such as decreasing the amount of time that the NSA can keep telephone records in its own storage facilities from five to three years. There is also a suggestion to develop methods for the NSA to access the data on the servers of telephone companies directly, so that it would not have to store the information itself. Such modifications — storing records for three instead of five years — still do not address the fact that the acquisition of such records in the first place contravened international law and the Fourth Amendment of the U.S. Constitution.

Despite the willingness of Iran's new and less belligerent President, Hassan Rouhani, to make reasonable nuclear program concessions to U.S. demands, war-mongering Israeli pressure groups in Washington continue to demand a military offensive against Iran. If their demands are successful — which is not inconceivable because the majority of politicians on Capitol Hill have accepted either favors or money from Israel — then those bought and paid for members of the U.S. Senate and House of Representatives will add to the treasonable offenses already committed not only against the U.S., but also against the rest of the world.

A recent series of in-depth investigations by human rights groups, United Nations agencies, and some news organisations have highlighted the stark reality of U.S. drone warfare. So instead of adding to the condemnation of such warfare, the mainstream media has sided with the U.S. government by either ignoring or downplaying the exposures. Detailed examination of these reports reveals not just that most of these attacks — which the human rights reports document — are not only illegal, but also illegitimate and immoral.

This raises the question of whether President Obama's targeted killing program, implemented through the use of drone strikes, complies with both international human rights law and international humanitarian law. International human rights law is applicable "outside of a defined conflict zone" and demands significantly more stringent rules for the use of lethal force than does humanitarian law. If the U.S. is only involved in an armed conflict in Afghanistan, international human rights law would be the regime that regulates the use of lethal force in Pakistan and Yemen. Therefore, as noted by Amnesty International, the use of lethal force outside of Afghanistan is legal when it can be demonstrated that:

> *[It was] only used when strictly unavoidable to protect life, no less harmful means such as capture or non-lethal incapacitation was possible, and the use of force was proportionate in the prevailing circumstances.*

Amnesty International's conclusion was that it was highly likely that drone strikes in Pakistan had failed to "satisfy the law enforcement standards that govern intentional use of lethal force outside armed conflict," and therefore:

> *[T]heir deliberate killings by drones ... very likely violate the prohibition of arbitrary deprivation of life and may constitute extrajudicial executions.*

If the Bush Jr. and Obama administrations' argument that the U.S. is involved in an armed conflict with al-Qaida and associated forces wherever they are engaged — international humanitarian law is the *lex specialis* (overriding law) in Pakistan and Yemen. Yet, even with less rigorous limitations on the use of lethal force under international humanitarian law, there is mounting evidence that the Obama administration's use of drones constitute violations of international law in the form of war crimes.

Furthermore, Obama has used tactics that inherently violate the laws of war which include the use of so-called "signature strikes" and "double taps." According to Amnesty International:

> *Under international humanitarian law, US drone operators must at all times abide by the principle of distinction; namely distinguish between civilians and combatants . . . All feasible precautions must be taken in determining whether a person is a civilian . . . In case of doubt, the person must be presumed to be protected against direct attack.*

Signature strikes target individuals for death based not on the confirmed identity or activities of the targets, but rather their "behavioral characteristics" which may resemble those typical of militants. This constitutes a clear violation of the principle of distinction. Amnesty also questioned President Obama's assertion that drone strikes are only launched when there is "near certainty" that civilians will not be killed in the strike — which may be a reference to President Obama's disputed method of counting "all military-age males" in the vicinity of an alleged target as militants.

Amnesty argues that the president's precautionary measures "are only relevant if the US applies the status of 'civilian' to unidentified individuals, rather than presuming they are combatants whom they deem directly targetable. Otherwise, these killings could constitute war crimes or extrajudicial executions."

The "double tap" involves launching an initial drone strike, which is followed by a second strike that targets rescuers and first responders. The rationale behind the use of double taps is that those who converge on the scene of the initial strike must be militants themselves. Thus, the use of double taps relies on two assumptions. The first is that the victims of the initial strike were militants — an assumption that on numerous occasions is not corroborated by the facts. And the second assumption that first responders must also be militants also fails because of the first assumption's failure. Even if the victims of the initial strike had been legitimate targets, to subsequently assume those who converge on the scene are also legitimate military targets, clearly fails to satisfy the principle of distinction.

So yet again, the U.S. is faced with a dilemma. It can either immunize President Obama and members of his administration from accountability — as it did President Bush Jr. and his administration — or it can subject its leaders to the same standards it demands of others. By choosing the former option, the U.S. has fully exposed the double-standards and hypocrisy of the administration's counter-terrorism policy.

Since the 11 September 2001 attacks, the U.S. has been waging what was initially called a global "war on terror" which under various guises has included the invasion and occupation of Afghanistan and Iraq; the setting up of a massive apparatus for spying on people globally; and the increased use of global drone warfare (the firing of missiles from unmanned aircraft, or drones). Since then there have been hundreds of drone strikes in Afghanistan, Pakistan, Somalia, Yemen, and probably other countries with thousands having been killed.

In response to criticism, the U.S. government has steadfastly claimed that drone strikes are necessary, legal, and just. President Obama — who has radically escalated U.S. drone warfare — said the U.S. only targets terrorists who pose a continuing and imminent threat to the American people. He added that "before any strike is taken, there must be near-certainty that no civilians will be killed or injured." Because of such criteria, Obama's administration claims that very, very few non-"'terrorist" civilians have been killed and according to Obama himself: "Our actions are effective . . . Simply put, these strikes have saved lives." Lies! Lies! And more damned Lies! But then they apparently also had political professional scumbag liars even in ancient times.

When one with honeyed words but evil mind, persuades the mob, great woes befall the state.
Orestes, a late tragedy by the ancient Greek playright Euripides (c. 480 BCE - c. 406 BCE)

10 November '13: Following the exhumation of Yasser Arafat's body last year, a Swiss report said tests on the body showed "unexpected high activity" of polonium which "moderately" supported the poisoning theory. Bearing in mind that Arafat's uncompromising stance was an obstacle to the Israeli agenda, it may safely be assumed that Israel — a state with access to polonium — was instrumental in his murder.

14 November '13: After years of denial — which included accusing anyone who mentioned organ harvesting in Israel of committing a "blood libel" against Israel and Jews — following controversial allegations in a Swedish newspaper (17 August 2009) that Israel had a shoot-to-kill policy that enabled it to secretly harvest body parts from Palestinians in the occupied territories, this shameless, lying excuse for a democracy of God's chosen people has finally admitted to its crimes and agreed to return organs of dead Palestinians harvested by its forensic pathologists during autopsies. How can anyone ever believe these people?

15 November '13: Following on from the U.S. and Israel losing their UNESCO voting rights for non-payment of contributions, Israel's ambassador to UNESCO, Nimrod Barkan said his country supported the U.S. for "objecting to the politicization of UNESCO, or any international organization, with the accession of a non-existing country like Palestine." Palestine-denial and violent ethnic-cleansing are sinister Israeli ploys to wipe the Palestinian people off the face of their own ancestral land in order to lay a spurious Jewish claim to the whole of historic Palestine.

17 November '13: Thousands of people in the UK and U.S. united in a mass protest to reject the mainstream media by targeting the headquarters of media giants like Fox News, the BBC and NBS, denouncing their narrow coverage of world affairs. The March Against Mainstream Media (MAMM) organized the international protest via social media and challenged the established media to cover it.

In a statement posted on the MAMM website, the organisation

said big media outlets had two options: "report on the fact that thousands of people are currently protesting outside of their buildings because they are keeping important news from the public's eyes" or ignore them. Americans turned out brandishing banners, condemning established news channels with banners such as *Boycott the media!* and *America deserves the truth*. Americans may "want the truth" but AIPAC and news organizations owned by people like Rupert Murdoch are not going to let them have it.

24 November '13: Despite raving lunatic threats from Benjamin Netanyahu against a deal with Iran at the Geneva talks, Iran agreed to curb some of its nuclear activities in return for about $7billion (£4.3billion) in sanctions relief which U.S. Secretary of State John Kerry described as an agreement that would make the region safer for all its allies including Israel. Loony warmongering Israeli Prime Minister Benjamin Netanyahu, however, informed his cabinet it was a "historic mistake" and that Israel reserved the right to defend itself. Israel always "defends itself" by persecuting the Palestinian people and attacking its neighbors —something that Iran has not done in recent history.

He continued, "Today the world became a much more dangerous place because the most dangerous regime in the world made a significant step in obtaining the most dangerous weapons in the world." He later added at a news conference that Israel would not be bound by the agreement. And why should it when it is not even bound by international law. The most dangerous regime in the whole world is not Iran but Israel which has nuclear weapons and raving lunatic leaders.

28 November '13: A document provided by NSA whistleblower Edward Snowden, reveals that the NSA has been gathering records of online sexual activity and evidence of visits to pornographic websites as part of a proposed plan to harm the reputations of those whom the agency believes are radicalizing others through incendiary speeches. The document identifies six targets, all Muslims, as "exemplars" of how "personal vulnerabilities" can be learned through electronic surveillance, and then exploited to undermine a target's credibility, reputation and authority. Among the vulnerabilities listed by the NSA that can be effectively exploited are "viewing sexually explicit material online" and "using sexually explicit persuasive language when communicating with inexperienced young girls."

The Director of the National Security Agency — described as DIRNSA — is listed as the originator of the document. Beyond the NSA itself, the listed recipients include officials with the Departments of Justice and Commerce and the Drug Enforcement Administration. U.S. agencies have in the past used similar tactics against civil rights leaders, labor movement activists and others.

Under J. Edgar Hoover, the FBI harassed activists and compiled secret files on political leaders such as Martin Luther King, Jr. whose wiretapped sexual exploits used to provide President Johnson with hours of listening pleasure. The extent of the FBI's surveillance of political figures is still being revealed to this day, as the bureau releases the long dossiers it compiled on certain people in response to Freedom of Information Act requests following their deaths. The information collected by the FBI often centered on sex with homosexuality being an obsession of Hoover who was himself a homosexual. Information about extramarital affairs was reportedly used to blackmail politicians into fulfilling the FBI's requirements.

30 November '13: Bedouin Arabs living in Israel have been protesting in the Negev Desert, in towns, and in cities over Israeli government plans to resettle them. Thousands took part in a 'day of rage' in the Negev, Haifa, Jerusalem, the West Bank, and Gaza. The Bedouin rightly claim that the plan will force them out of their ancestral land, while Israel says it aims to provide better services, infrastructure, and settle long-standing land disputes which means stealing even more Palestinian land. An open letter backing the campaign against the legislation, and signed by celebrities including Peter Gabriel and Julie Christie, was published in a British newspaper on Friday.

Now that the first year of his second term has passed and it has become apparent that Barack "Uncle Tom" Obama is not going to do the right thing for the Palestinian people by exploiting the fact of his not having to worry about reelection — what is to become of them? To begin with, their desperate plight will continue to deteriorate because not only will the leaders of the Western world ignore them, but their own leaders will betray them while jockeying amongst themselves for positions that are self-serving rather than for the benefit of their forsaken people.

One of the many less than reputable Palestinian leaders who has regained a position of prominence despite past omissions is Mohammad Dahlan whom Israel, the U.S. and some Arab countries regard as someone who could be relied on to serve their combined agendas

473

rather than the Palestinian cause. It was following the signing of the Oslo Accords that Dahlan first gained notoriety when he commanded some 20,000 Palestinian security personnel who were accountable to Mossad and the CIA while obligingly arresting and torturing members of of Hamas throughout the 1990s. The scale of Dahlan's corruption was most impressive with an estimated 40 percent of taxes raised from Palestinians being diverted to his personal bank accounts. In 2005, an Israeli think tank conservatively estimated his personal wealth at around $120 million.

Dhalan is the kind of man Israeli and other intelligence services love to deal with because he can be bought and he has in fact been accused by both Fatah and Hamas of being an agent for Egyptian, Israeli, Jordanian and U.S. intelligence services. Dahlan has been involved in many conspiracies and assassinations including — on behalf of Israel — that of Yasser Arafat. Ultimately it is up to the Palestinian people themselves to ensure that the Israeli-U.S. alliance does not impose upon them a corrupt leader like Dahlan who will instead of representing Palestinian aspirations, will serve the interests of his paymasters.

ISRAEL AND SAUDI ARABIA
The Middle East's Major Violators of the Universal Declaration of Human Rights

Israel and Saudi Arabia who as a members of the United Nations General Assembly are obligated to abide by and enforce the Universal Declaration of Human Rights, are in fact both culpable of horrendous human rights violations. Saudi Arabia violates the rights of its own citizens and is therefore not racist but simply repressive. Israel on the other hand with its brutal Apartheid-style persecution of the Palestinian people, is definitely racist. Though one nation is Judaic and the other Islamic, they nonetheless — in a somewhat bizarre fashion — rely on each other for survival because the West led by the U.S would not allow Israel to directly interfere with any of the Persian Gulf's oil-rich Arab states of Bahrain, Kuwait, Oman, Qatar, Saudi Arabia, and the United Arab Emirates.

Saudi Arabia arms its forces to the teeth — thanks mainly to a ravenous and obliging U.S. and EU armaments industry — ostensibly for protection against Israel, but in reality it is for maintaining the House of Saudi royal family's control over the nation's wealth and its people. In order to maintain control over their own country, Saudi rulers cannot have an "Arab Spring" with Arab democracies all around them because that might lead to the Saudi people also becoming desirous of political reform as happened in other Gulf states with a series of petitions and calls for meaningful change having rattled more than a few authoritarian Gulf monarchies where the boundaries of permissible opposition were severely tested. This led to repression as regimes sought to tighten political control and delegitimize all forms of dissent. The result was that western policy makers and institutions were left with the the difficult quandary of trying to balance engagement with strategic Gulf partners without appearing to betray the universal principles of human rights.

Saudi Arabia is already causing chaos and bloodshed in Middle Eastern and North African countries by providing millions-of-dollars-worth of armaments to al-Qaeda and other Takfiri networks — Muslims accusing other Muslims of apostasy — that are destabilizing and destroying once proud civilizations in Iraq, Lebanon, Libya, and Syria by fomenting sectarian unrest. Therefore by serving its own purpose, Saudi Arabia is also fulfilling Israel's desire for political instability and chaos within the predominantly Muslim countries that surround it. Furthermore, Israel's existence as a state serves to have Gulf state Arab populations focussing on Israel as the enemy rather than their own autocratic monarchies — not legally bound or restricted by a constitution — that rule their own countries.

The real motive behind Saudi Arabia's interference in Syria is its desire to neutralize Iran's regional influence. So all the talk about supporting democracy in Syria is just a political pantomime with the actual objective being the installation in Damascus of a regime subservient to Saudi Arabia — which in turn means subservient and subject to the geopolitical control of the U.S., Israel, and tag-along allies who constitute the imperialist hostile thrust against Iran. Britain, France, and the U.S. have in the meantime continued to diligently claim that they are supporting "a pro-democracy uprising" in Syria which of course is to be expected from noble honest-to-goodness proponents of freedom and human rights. That claim, however, is nothing but a Western criminal conspiracy that also happens to satisfy the feudal-style Gulf state dictators who are cherished for their oil.

Though Saudi Arabia and Israel enjoy the commonality of sowing discord in the Middle East and violating human rights, it is Israel who is culpable of violating all the Declaration's 30 Articles and it is therefore hoped that all those who back Israel — with justification and a clear conscience — are proud of their support and contributions to an Apartheid state which lies, cheats, steals, and murders without compunction or regard for human rights or international law. Furthermore, to add insult to injury, this ungrateful state not only spies on and ruthlessly exploits the goodwill of its closest allies, but is also by nature apparently parasitic. In his book *Jews Must Live*, Samuel Roth is bitter in his denunciation of Jews as a race of predatory businessmen, shyster lawyers, money-grubbing doctors, soulless land-grabbers and uncultured show-business hustlers.

> *Jewish history has been tragic to the Jews and no less tragic to the neighboring nations who have suffered them. Our major vice of old as of today is parasitism. We are a people of vultures living on the labour and good fortune of the rest of the world.*
> **Samuel Roth, *Jews Must Live: An Account of the Persecution of the World by Israel on All the Frontiers of***

Civilization. **New York, The Golden Hind Press, 1934.**

The fact is that the Jews were known only as destroyers in ancient history, not creators. They have developed no science, have produced no art, have built no great cities, and alone have no talent for the finer things of civilized life. The Jews claim to be the torchbearers of civilization, but through their parasitic habits have deteriorated or destroyed every nation in which they have existed in large numbers.

Charles A. Weisman, *Who is Esau-Edom?* Weisman Publications, 1996.

The Universal Declaration of Human Rights

PREAMBLE

Whereas recognition of the inherent dignity and of the equal and inalienable rights of all members of the human family is the foundation of freedom, justice and peace in the world,

Whereas disregard and contempt for human rights have resulted in barbarous acts which have outraged the conscience of mankind, and the advent of a world in which human beings shall enjoy freedom of speech and belief and freedom from fear and want has been proclaimed as the highest aspiration of the common people,

Whereas it is essential, if man is not to be compelled to have recourse, as a last resort, to rebellion against tyranny and oppression, that human rights should be protected by the rule of law,

Whereas it is essential to promote the development of friendly relations between nations,

Whereas the peoples of the United Nations have in the Charter reaffirmed their faith in fundamental human rights, in the dignity and worth of the human person and in the equal rights of men and women and have determined to promote social progress and better standards of life in larger freedom,

Whereas Member States have pledged themselves to achieve, in co-operation with the United Nations, the promotion of universal respect for and observance of human rights and fundamental freedoms,

Whereas a common understanding of these rights and freedoms is of the greatest importance for the full realization of this pledge,

Now, Therefore THE GENERAL ASSEMBLY proclaims THIS UNIVERSAL DECLARATION OF HUMAN RIGHTS as a common standard of achievement for all peoples and all nations, to the end that every individual and every organ of society, keeping this Declaration constantly in mind, shall strive by teaching and education to promote respect for these rights and freedoms and by progressive measures, national and international, to secure their universal and effective recognition and observance, both among the peoples of Member States themselves and among the peoples of territories under their jurisdiction

Article 1. *All human beings are born free and equal in dignity and rights. They are endowed with reason and conscience and should act towards one another in a spirit of brotherhood.*

Article 2. *Everyone is entitled to all the rights and freedoms set forth in this Declaration, without distinction of any kind, such as race, colour, sex, language, religion, political or other opinion, national or social origin, property, birth or other status. Furthermore, no distinction shall be made on the basis of the political, jurisdictional or international status of the country or territory to which a person belongs, whether it be independent, trust, non-self-   governing or under any other limitation of sovereignty.*

Article 3. *Everyone has the right to life, liberty and security of person.*

Article 4. *No one shall be held in slavery or servitude; slavery and the slave trade shall be prohibited in all their forms.*

Article 5. *No one shall be subjected to torture or to cruel, inhuman or degrading treatment or punishment.*

Article 6. *Everyone has the right to recognition everywhere as a person before the law.*

Article 7. *All are equal before the law and are entitled without any discrimination to equal protection of the law. All* are entitled to equal protection against any discrimination in violation of this Declaration and against any incitement to such discrimination.

Article 8. *Everyone has the right to an effective remedy by the competent national tribunals for acts violating the fundamental rights granted him by the constitution or by law.*

Article 9. *No one shall be subjected to arbitrary arrest, detention or exile.*

Article 10. *Everyone is entitled in full equality to a fair and public hearing by an independent and impartial tribunal, in the determination of his rights and obligations and of any criminal charge against him.*

Article 11. *(1) Everyone charged with a penal offence has the right to be presumed innocent until proved according to law in a public trial at which he has had all the guarantees necessary for his defence. (2) No one shall be held guilty of any penal offence on account of any act or omission which did not constitute a penal offence, under national or international law, at the time when it was committed. Nor shall a heavier penalty be imposed than the one that was applicable at the time the penal offence was committed.*

Article 12. *No one shall be subjected to arbitrary interference with his privacy, family, home or correspondence, nor to attacks upon his honour and reputation. Everyone has the right to the protection of the law against such interference or attacks.*

Article 13. *(1) Everyone has the right to freedom of movement and residence within the borders of each state (2) Everyone has the right to leave any country, including his own, and to return to his country.*

Article 14. *(1) Everyone has the right to seek and to enjoy in other countries asylum from persecution. (2) This right may not be invoked in the case of prosecutions genuinely arising from non-political crimes or from acts contrary to* *the purposes and principles of the United Nations.*

Article 15. *(1) Everyone has the right to a nationality. (2) No one shall be arbitrarily deprived of his nationality nor denied the right to change his nationality.*

Article 16. *(1) Men and women of full age, without any limitation due to race, nationality or religion, have the right to marry and to found a family. They are entitled to equal rights as to marriage, during marriage and at its dissolution. (2) Marriage shall be entered into only with the free and full consent of the intending spouses. (3) The family is the natural and fundamental group unit of society and is entitled to protection by society and the State.*

Article 17. *(1) Everyone has the right to own property alone as well as in association with others. (2) No one shall be arbitrarily deprived of his property.*

Article 18. *Everyone has the right to freedom of thought, conscience and religion; this right includes freedom to change his religion or belief, and freedom, either alone or in community with others and in public or private, to manifest his religion or belief in teaching, practice, worship and observance.*

Article 19. *Everyone has the right to freedom of opinion and expression; this right includes freedom to hold opinions without interference and to seek, receive and impart information and ideas through any media and regardless of frontiers.*

Article 20. *(1) Everyone has the right to freedom of peaceful assembly and association. (2) No one may be compelled to belong to an association.*

Article 21. *(1) Everyone has the right to take part in the government of his country, directly or through freely chosen representatives. (2) Everyone has the right to equal access to public service in his country. (3) The will of the people shall be the basis of the authority of government; this will shall be expressed in periodic and genuine elections which* *shall be by universal and equal suffrage and shall be held by secret vote or equivalent voting procedures.*

__Article 22.__ Everyone, as a member of society, has the right to social security and is entitled to realisation, through national effort and international co-operation and in accordance with the organisation and resources of each State, of the economic, social and cultural rights indispensable for his dignity and the free development of his personality.

__Article 23.__ (1) Everyone has the right to work, to free choice of employment, to just and favourable conditions of work and to protection against unemployment. (2) Everyone, without any discrimination, has the right to equal pay for equal work. (3) Everyone who works has the right to just and favourable remuneration ensuring for himself and his family an existence worthy of human dignity, and supplemented, if necessary, by other means of social protection. (4) Everyone has the right to form and to join trade unions for the protection of his interests.

__Article 24.__ Everyone has the right to rest and leisure, including reasonable limitation of working hours and periodic holidays with pay.

__Article 25.__ (1) Everyone has the right to a standard of living adequate for the health and well-being of himself and of his family, including food, clothing, housing and medical care and necessary social services, and the right to security in the event of unemployment, sickness, disability, widowhood, old age or other lack of livelihood in circumstances beyond his control. (2) Motherhood and childhood are entitled to special care and assistance. All children, whether born in or out of wedlock, shall enjoy the same social protection.

__Article 26.__ (1) Everyone has the right to education. Education shall be free, at least in the elementary and fundamental stages. Elementary education shall be compulsory. Technical and professional education shall be made generally available and higher education shall be equally accessible to all on the basis of merit. (2)

Education shall be directed to the full development of the human personality and to the strengthening of respect for human rights and fundamental freedoms. It shall promote understanding, tolerance and friendship among all nations, racial or religious groups, and shall further the activities of the United Nations for the maintenance of peace. (3) Parents have a prior right to choose the kind of education that shall be given to their children.

Article 27. *(1) Everyone has the right freely to participate in the cultural life of the community, to enjoy the arts and to share in scientific advancement and its benefits. (2) Everyone has the right to the protection of the moral and material interests resulting from any scientific, literary or artistic production of which he is the author.*

Article 28. *Everyone is entitled to a social and international order in which the rights and freedoms set forth in this Declaration can be fully realised.*

Article 29. *(1) Everyone has duties to the community in which alone the free and full development of his personality is possible. (2) In the exercise of his rights and freedoms, everyone shall be subject only to such limitations as are determined by law solely for the purpose of securing due recognition and respect for the rights and freedoms of others and of meeting the just requirements of morality, public order and the general welfare in a democratic society. (3) These rights and freedoms may in no case be exercised contrary to the purposes and principles of the United Nations.*

Article 30. *Nothing in this Declaration may be interpreted as implying for any state, group or person to engage in any activity or to perform any act aimed at the destruction of any of the rights and freedoms set forth herein.*

ONCE UPON A PALESTINE
by *Mhara Costello*

Once upon a distant time, there was a land called Palestine
Is it yours or is it mine, this land they once called Palestine
And who am I to stand and stare, in disbelief at land stripped bare
Banished people, stolen homes, broken dreams, crumbling stones
Of ancient graves and ghostly moans, silenced by Israeli drones

Who is this God that would erase, a people from their own birthplace
What kind of God would curse and smite, to please the cruel Israelite
*Thugs! Thieves! Parasites! How **dare** they speak of wrong and right*
Whilst dragging children thru' the night, from their beds, pale with fright
Bound and shackled, in a cell, just a kid, alone in hell

No mother, father, man of law, allowed to enter thru' that door
Till false confession fear has wrought, a boy alone must face the court
His crime? With stones he bravely fought, at those he knows his enemy
Till flows the river to the sea, young freedom fighter he will be
To set his land and people free

Who was it made the desert bloom, filled the air with sweet perfume
Jasmine, peaches, sage, and thyme, 'Once upon a Palestine'
Who was it made the desert bleed, raped and pillaged, sowed their seed
Of death, destruction, theft and greed, with every twisted word and deed
The Bedouin who stands alone, midst debris of his bulldozed home
Stares out upon once cherished earth, whose forbears, long before his birth
Toiled this land for all their worth

Oh ancient well of water sweet, that once did quench God's thirsty sheep
Now doomed to choke in desert heat, with nought to drink but dry concrete
Courtesy of Israeli jeep
Manned by robots, following orders, "erase those Palestinian borders"!
Hide all trace of Arab culture, replace it with the Zionist vulture

Sly alibi's and dirty lies, of traitor Brits, whose stitched up lips
Couldn't wait, to seal the fate, of Arab Nation extermination
Condemned to brutal occupation; Well done! Balfour Declaration

For every drop of blood been spilt, every settlement ever built
Every teardrop ever shed, every bullet thru' the head
Every precious child laid dead and every Zionist lie been said

*"The old will die, the young forget"- **Ben Gurion,** do not hold your*
breath!
Your words of bile, we won't forget; this battle is not over yet!
We'll see you burn in hell, you bet!

The wise man teaches, so I'm told, revenge is a dish best served cold
*For every **Freedom Fighter** bold, enshrine their name in letters gold*
Let their stories brave be told, till time stands still and hell turns cold!

The fishermen who dare not fish, what kind of unjust law is this!
Lets mighty Israel take the piss, whilst sinking in its own abyss
Of cruel rule and iron fist; dares mock at International Law
Is this what brave souls gave life for?

Enough's enough! We'll have no more! of got at, shot at! Bashed up
boats
Impounded! Hounded! Freedom floats, to plumb the depths of deep
despair
*In a world that's neither sane nor fair-**United Nations**, are you **there??***
*Shame on you! To stand and stare; **Ban Ki Loon,** how do you dare!*
Gutless wimps of Zionist pimps! Tyrant's answer to a prayer

Pollute the water! Cut the power!
Close the checkpoints! Wait for hours
No matter if you're old or sick, held fast in vile Israeli grip
Watch the clock hand slowly tick, see the blood begin to drip
Newborns die, mothers cry, fathers sigh, world asks why
So do I

Cries of children; Run! Run! Staring down Israeli gun
Hey! It's just a bit of fun! Watching school kids bleed and run

***Remember Tom,** noble, strong*
In act so brave, his life he gave
"Spare the child, but mark your grave"
Heaven smiled, Tom's choice was made

485

One life lost, another saved
Laid to rest, 21 of age
Angels sang and Gaza prayed
A light went out — true Martyr made

Zionists fiddle, whilst Israel burns
Same old same old, no lessons learned

March to the sound of the war drum you beat
Trample the truth as it clings to your feet
In the slime and the grime of your 'Jews Only' street
Shalom! Dogs and Irish, no Arab you'll meet
On Streetwise Apartheid, Gods 'Chosen Elite'

Shine up your trophies, just so you can brag
*As you count every corpse on **Obama's** false flag*
Caught, bought and paid for, in each body bag
Three billion dollars! Guess who's been had!

So innocent children can burn to a crisp
Xmas in Gaza snows white phosphorus!
***'The Most Moral Army'** that doesn't exist*
*Who's kidding who? But **if** you insist!*
*There in the glass is your real **Terrorist!***

Cowards and bullies, two of a kind
Sound in the body, but sick in the mind
*Spawn of the **Stern Gang** and vile **Haganah***
*Irgun's Ms. **Livni,** her Ma and Papa*

Who would you believe it? But hush now! Don't tell!
*Blew up us Brits in **King David's Hotel!***
We know who our friends are, didn't we do well!
Birds of a feather, we'll meet them in hell!

But hey! What's your problem? We're all best mates now
Changing our laws to protect 'Sacred Cows'
The woman who boasted, with no sense of shame
***Operation Cast Lead,** she'd do all again*
Proud of her role in this orgy of pain

*It's all so confusing, speak **up! Hague! Explain!***
Shielding war criminals, since when was our game
There's blood on your hands and it's staining our name
The wrong side of history is where lies your fame
Next to your Masters of Zionist shame!

The pride and the glory and God save the Queen
Won't save us now from an act so obscene
'Great British Empire'? Shamed old has been!
Farewell Magna Carta; Impossible dream

You lie down with dogs and you get up with fleas
Dance with the Devil and crawl on your knees
At the skirts of Ms. Livni, to plead "pretty please"
Daughter of Zion, slaughters with ease
It's only an Arab, shoot with the breeze

Streets hung with netting, no prizes for guessing
Stench is quite telling, you know what you're getting
*When **Settler Scum's** yelling, with IDF'S blessing*
Hatred is spreading, no forgive, no forgetting
Shit sticks where it hits, defiles sacred dwellings

Grapes of wrath, spoils of war
Sixty-five years, how many more
Ask yourselves, what was it for
Karma's knocking upon your door
You stole another people's land
What part of that, don't you understand

Arabs made homeless, clutching a key
Forced from their homes, fled into the sea
Proud noble race to sad refugee
*Shame of the **Nakba! Catastrophe!!!***

Show me the Fuhrer to lay all the blame
Where were the cries of "not in my name"
As you watched from the sidelines, 'Gurion's Game'
Immune to the suffering of grief loss and pain

Dave to Goliath, roles now reversed
Victim to bully, chapter and verse
Goebbels to Gaza, shades of Mein Kampf
Checkpoints and cameras, ID cards to stamp

Hard to believe, in the land of one's birth
1.7 million denied freedom, self worth
*Whilst **'W*nkers in Whitehall'***
Free roam this earth

Friends in high places, puppets on strings
*These are a few of my **not** favourite things*
Dope smoking soldiers, not human kind
***'The Most Moral Army'** stoned out of its mind!*

***God's chosen people??** God must be blind!!*
*But God's seen the light and the sights blown **his** mind!*
*Hey! God's new commandment! **"Occupy-Stop"** !*
God's smelt the coffee and thrown in his lot!
*With those pesky Arabs; deserve all they got**?***

*God begs to differ; **why** would they **not?***
Fight for the right to a life without strife
Free from the Jackboot of Zionist might

Pilgrims and poets, music and song
Writers, the fighters, record right and wrong
Power of the people, united we're strong!
Come join the dance! It's where you belong!

*Words are **our** weapon, who needs a gun*
*Armed with the truth, Justice will come**!***
Garden shed rockets and rocks in kids pockets!
No Army! No Navy! No train with the gravy!
Just a will and a way, no if's buts or maybe!

No brute F16's or killing machines
Just a girl's silent screams, crushed with her dreams

Casually slaughtered, one brave precious daughter
*When **'Catakillerd'** its quarry*
*God blessed **Rachel Corrie***

Fate will take her pound of flesh, plucked within the gory mess
Of crimes against humanity, etched into eternity
*Pray tell, 'Isra-hel', where will **you** be*
In the Hague, for all to see
Down on your knees, begging Merci
Outcasts of society
Que Sera, what must be, will be

Time and Tide for no man waits
When stood before those pearly gates
Locked and barred, be in no doubt
The tide brings in what the world casts out

Written in the sands of time, sins of man
Yours and mine; but let the punishment fit the crime
Of persecution by design; what's mine's my own
What's yours is mine; speaks the bully, none so blind

Once upon a distant time, I was yours and you were mine
Rise again! Sweet Palestine!
History's page turns one last time
Desert breeze draws a line
Apocalypse now!!! Free Palestine!!!

© **Copyright Mhara Costello**

- **Mhara Costello** is a pro-Palestinian activist , writer, poet, living in the United Kingdom.

- **Tomas "Tom" Hurndall** (1981-2004) was a British photography student, a volunteer for the International Solidarity Movement (ISM), and an activist against the Israeli occupation of the Palestinian territories. On 11 April 2003, he was shot in the head in the Gaza Strip by an IDF sniper, Taysir Hayb. Hurndall was left in a coma and died nine months later. Thanks to the persistent efforts of Tom's family Hayb was convicted of manslaughter and obstruction of justice by an Israeli military court in April 2005 and sentenced to eight years in prison. On 10 April 2006, a British inquest jury returned a verdict of unlawful killing meaning "illegally killed," or, in the opinion of the Hurndall family's QC, "murdered."

Tom's mother Jocelyn Hurndall wrote a biography of him called *Defy the Stars: The Life and Tragic Death of Tom Hurndall*, published in April 2007 and reprinted in May 2008 with the alternative title *My Son Tom: The Life and Tragic Death of Tom Hurndall*. Tom's sister, Sophie, works for Medical Aid for Palestinians whose stated aim is to meet the humanitarian needs of the Palestinian people. It was founded in 1984 by Major Derek Cooper and his wife, Pamela Cooper in the wake of the 1982 Sabra and Shatila massacre in Lebanon. Dr Swee Chai Ang FRCS is also a founding Trustee.

• **Rachel Aliene Corrie** (1979-2003) was an American peace activist and ISM member who was crushed to death by an IDF armored bulldozer in the Gaza Strip while engaged with other ISM activists in efforts to non-violently prevent the Israeli army's demolition of Palestinian homes. She was killed while standing in the path of a bulldozer wearing a bright orange fluorescent jacket and a megaphone. The exact nature of her death and the culpability of the bulldozer operator are still disputed, with eyewitnesses saying that the Israeli soldier operating the bulldozer deliberately ran over Corrie, and the Israeli government saying that it was an accident since the bulldozer operator could not see her.

In 2005 Corrie's parents filed a civil lawsuit that charged Israel with not conducting a full and credible investigation into the case and with responsibility for her death, contending that she had either been intentionally killed or that the soldiers had acted with reckless neglect. They sued for a symbolic one U.S. dollar in damages to make the point that their case was about justice for their daughter and the Palestinian cause she had been defending.

Finally in August 2012, an Israeli court rejected their suit and upheld the results of Israel's 2003 military investigation by exonerating the Israeli government and ruling that Corrie was to blame for her own death. The ruling, the Israeli justice system, and the investigation it exonerated were subsequently severely criticized. Former President Jimmy Carter called "unacceptable" the court's ruling that declared the State of Israel as being not responsible for the death of American activist Rachel Corrie. "The killing of an American peace activist is unacceptable. The court's decision confirms a climate of impunity, which facilitates Israeli human rights violations against Palestinian civilians in the Occupied Territory," Carter said in a statement from the Atlanta-based Carter Center.

Rachel Corrie's life has been memorialized in several tributes, including the play *My Name is Rachel Corrie* and the cantata *The Skies are Weeping* which also memorialized Tom Hurndall. Corrie's collected writings were published in 2008 under the title *Let Me Stand Alone,* which opened "a window on the maturation of a young woman seeking to make the world a better place." The Rachel Corrie Foundation for Peace and Justice has been established to continue her work.

EPILOGUE

Cowardice asks the question — is it safe?
Expediency asks the question — is it politic?
Vanity asks the question — is it popular?
But conscience asks the question — is it right?
And there comes a time when one must take a
position that is neither safe, nor politic, nor
popular; but one must take it because it is Right.
Dr. Martin Luther King Jr.

It is high time — because time is certainly running out — for the silent majority of "the people" to take conscionable positions and make their voices heard despite the inevitable possibility of being universally vilified by the reverent, the righteous, and the raving; of being unjustly branded as anti-Semites by God's chosen spewers of hate; of being falsely accused of blasphemy by fanatical religious bigots; and perhaps even of being subject to the malevolent machinations of those maladjusted and probably mad merchants of mendacity, mischief, and murder — the Mossad. Though all of the aforementioned God-fearing, upstanding and open-minded inhabitants of this planet have the inalienable right to disagree with what "the people" believe and say, they also have the moral obligation to acknowledge and fiercely defend "the people's" right to believe and say it. Because in the event of their failing do so, then all the sacred religious doctrines and fine ethical standards that they so overtly and vociferously profess to live by are nothing but a huge heap of hypocritical horse shit wherein they wallow while attempting to compensate for the inadequacy of their existence as human beings by posing as God's guardians of what are in reality their own warped perceptions of morality. Furthermore, "the people" should make it very clear to them that they must refrain from justifying their heinous crimes against humanity by either quoting from religious scriptures concocted by the ancients, or by invoking fictional covenants with non-existent gods.

Morality and religion are but words to those who crouch
behind barrels in the street to cut the icy blasts, or fish in the

492

gutters for the means to sustain life.

Horace Greeley (1811-1872), American newspaper editor, founder of the Liberal Republican Party, reformer, politician, and an outspoken opponent of slavery. Greeley founded and edited *The New York Tribune* which was the most influential newspaper in the U.S. from the 1840s to the 1870s and as such established Greeley's reputation as "the greatest editor of his day".

People who call themselves supporters of Israel are actually supporters of its moral degeneration and ultimate destruction.

Noam Chomsky (born 1928) American linguist, cognitive scientist, logician, and political commentator and activist.

The majority of "the people" who are critical of Israeli policies are not anti-Semitic: they are simply of an opinion that was once expressed by former U.S. Senator William J. Fulbright:

Israel, I am convinced, can and should survive as a peaceful, prosperous society — but within the essential borders of 1967 . . . That much we owe them, but no more. We do not owe them our support of their continued occupation of Arab lands . . . The Palestinians have as much right to a homeland as the Jewish people.

No honest, self-respecting Jew could either deny Palestinians that right or try to justify the human rights violations and atrocities that Israel has been, and still is, perpetrating against the Palestinian people.

We cannot achieve world peace without first achieving peace within ourselves . . . Inner peace. In an atmosphere of hatred, anger, competition, violence, no lasting peace can be achieved. These negative and destructive forces must be overcome by compassion, love and altruism.
The 14th Dalai Lama. (born in Tibet 1935)

For Real News and Information on a World in Crisis or to Become Involved with Peaceful Activism, Visit Websites for the Following Organisations:

ADDAMEER (Arabic for conscience): A Jerusalem based Palestinian non-governmental, civil institution offering support for Palestinian prisoners and torture victims through monitoring, legal procedures and solidarity campaigns. Needless to say, fascist Israeli security forces have responded in the only way they know how by breaking into and trashing Addameer's office; and by harassing, arresting, barbarically interrogating, and unjustly imprisoning its volunteers.

Al-Monitor: *Al-Monitor* is a new media website providing original reporting and analysis by prominent journalists and experts from the Middle East and offering in-depth analysis through its Iran, Iraq, Israel, Lebanon, Palestine, and Turkey 'Pulses.'

Alternative Information Centre (AIC): "The Alternative Information Centre (AIC) is a joint Palestinian-Israeli organization promoting justice, equality and peace for Palestinians and Israelis . . . The AIC believes that peace can be just and lasting only when based on ending Israel's colonial occupation, securing the right of the Palestinian people to self-determination and the right of refugees to return. Only such a just peace, based on international law, can guarantee individual and collective rights of both Palestinians and Israelis . . . The AIC promotes a joint Palestinian-Israeli struggle and strongly opposes 'normalization,' those actions that 'normalise' Israel's occupation policies while presenting the Israeli-Arab conflict as one of conflicting narratives, lack of understanding or something to be overcome through personal relationships and getting to know the 'other.'"

Alternet: a project of the non-profit Independent Media Institute, is a progressive/liberal activist news service.

Amnesty International: Working to protect people wherever justice, fairness, freedom and truth are denied.

Atheist Alliance International: A nonprofit global federation of atheist groups and individuals committed to educating the public about atheism, secularism, and related issues.

Avaaz: The globe's largest and most powerful online activist network with over thirty-five million members in 194 countries using 15 languages.

BDS: (BDS) is a truly global movement of Boycott, Divestment and Sanctions against Apartheid Israel until it complies with international law and Palestinian rights; ends its occupation and colonization of Arab land; provides full equality for Arab-Palestinian citizens of Israel, and respects the right of return of Palestinian refugees.

Breaking the Silence: An organization of veteran combatants who have served in the Israeli military since the start of the Second Intifada and have taken it upon themselves to expose the Israeli public to the reality of everyday life in the Occupied Territories. We endeavor to stimulate public debate about the price paid for a reality in which young soldiers face a civilian population on a daily basis, and are engaged in the control of that population's everyday life.

B'Tselem: An Israeli Information Centre for Human Rights in the Occupied Territories. It was established in February 1989 by a group of prominent academics, attorneys, journalists, and Knesset members. It endeavors to document and educate the Israeli public and policymakers about human rights violations in the Occupied Territories, combat the phenomenon of denial prevalent among the Israeli public, and help create a human rights culture in Israel.

Coalition to Oppose the Arms Trade: COAT is a national network of individuals and organizations in Canada that began in late 1988 to organize opposition to ARMX '89, which was the country's largest weapons bazaar. COAT has continued to expose and oppose Canada's role in the international arms trade, particularly where there is trade to governments which are engaged in war or which violate human rights.

Code Pink: Women for Peace is an American grassroots peace and social justice movement whose positions include Palestinian statehood.

CJPME: Canadians for Justice and Peace in the Middle East whose mission is to enable Canadians of all backgrounds to promote justice, development and peace in the Middle East and in Canada.

Committee to Protect Journalists (CPJ): Independent nonprofit organization promoting press freedom and defending the rights of journalists.

Common Dreams: a non-profit independent news centre created in 1997 as a new media model that publishes a diverse mix of breaking news, insightful views, videos and press releases covering issues that resonate with progressives in every corner of the globe. The compilation is on one easy-to-access online location, and is presented in a clean, uncomplicated format, uninterrupted by pop-ups, advertising or gimmicks.

Countercurrents: Alternative web journal culling news and analysis on the fight against economic globalization and other issues.

Counterpunch: A U.S. monthly magazine that is not afraid to tackle controversial issues including criticism of Israeli government actions.

Dissident Voice: "Is an internet newsletter dedicated to challenging the distortions and lies of the corporate press and the privileged classes it serves. The goal of Dissident Voice is to provide hard hitting, thought provoking and even entertaining news and commentaries on politics and culture that can serve as ammunition in struggles for peace and social justice."

Emek Shaveh: An organization of archaeologists and community activists with an excellent website focusing on the role of archaeology in Israeli society and in the Israeli-Palestinian conflict.

Foreign Policy Journal: Is an online publication dedicated to providing critical analysis of U.S. foreign policy outside of the standard framework offered by political officials and the mainstream corporate media. FPJ offers original news, analysis, and opinion commentary from perspectives all too lacking in the public debate on key foreign policy issues. The goal of FPJ is to provide a valuable alternative source for news and insight into world affairs, to encourage citizen journalism, and to promote broader discussion of important global issues.

Global Research: A Centre for Research on Globalization with a website offering news articles, commentary, background research and analysis on a broad range of issues, focussing on social, economic, strategic and environmental processes.

Global Witness: Investigates and campaigns to prevent natural resource related conflict and corruption, and associated environmental and human rights abuses. From undercover investigations, to high level lobby meetings, Global witness aims to engage on every level where it might make a difference and bring about change.

HaMoked: "Centre for the Defense of the Individual is an Israeli human rights organization whose main objective is to assist Palestinians of the Occupied Territories whose rights are violated due to Israel's policies . . . The site contains information relating to these human rights violations. It gives the texts of Israeli laws and regulations, including those of the Military Government; international conventions; petitions to the Israeli High Court of Justice; claims for compensation for damages; decisions by Israeli and other courts; and other official documents and reports."

Human Rights Watch: Dedicated to protecting the Human rights of people around the world. Stands with victims and activists to prevent discrimination, to uphold political freedom, to protect people from inhumane conduct in wartime, and to bring offenders to justice. Investigates and exposes human rights violations and holds abusers accountable. Challenges governments and those who hold power to end abusive practices and respect international human rights law. Enlists the public and the international community to support the cause of human rights for all.

If Americans Knew: A nonprofit organization with an excellent website focussing on U.S. financial and military support for Israel and critical analysis of American media coverage of the Israeli-Palestinian conflict.

IJAN: International Jewish anti-Zionist Network uncompromisingly committed to struggles for human emancipation, of which the liberation of the Palestinian people and land is an indispensable part.

Information Clearing House: offers 'news you won't find on CNN or Fox news.'

Independent Jewish Voices: A network of Jews committed to certain principles, especially with the Israeli-Palestinian conflict in mind: putting human rights first, rejecting all forms of racism, and giving equal priority to Palestinians and Israelis in their quest for a peaceful and secure future. They believe that those principles, rather than group loyalty, should determine the parameters of legitimate debate.

Jews not Zionists: Holds the unadulterated Torah position that any form of Zionism is a heresy and that the existence of the so-called 'State of Israel' is illegitimate.

J Street: Is the political home for pro-Israel, pro-peace Americans fighting for the future of Israel as the democratic homeland of the Jewish people. It believes that Israel's Jewish and democratic character depend on a two-state solution, resulting in a Palestinian state living alongside Israel in peace and security.

Medecins Sans Frontieres; Doctors Without Borders helps people worldwide where the need is greatest, delivering emergency medical aid to people affected by conflict, epidemics, disasters or exclusion from health care.

Mondoweiss: A news website blog that is part of the CenterCentre for Economic Research and Social Change co-edited by journalists Philip Weiss and Adam Horowitz. According to the editors, Mondoweiss is "a news website devoted to covering American foreign policy in the Middle East, chiefly from a progressive Jewish perspective'. They state that they 'maintain the blog because of 9/11, Iraq, Gaza, the Nakba, the struggling people of Israel and Palestine, and our Jewish background."

MuzzleWatch: A project founded in 1996 by Jewish Voice for Peace which is a national grassroots organization dedicated to promoting U.S. foreign policy in the Middle East based on peace, democracy, human rights and respect for international law. With over 90,000 supporters and members, JVP's board of Jewish American and Israeli advisors includes Pulitzer and Tony award winner Tony Kushner, actor Ed Asner, poet Adrienne Rich as well as other respected rabbis, artists, scholars and activists.

MuzzleWatch is dedicated to creating an open atmosphere for

debate about US-Israeli foreign policy by:
- shining a light on incidents that involve pressure, intimidation, and outright censorship of critics of US-Israeli policy
- showing that there is a real environment of intimidation that keeps people from speaking honestly and openly.
- making groups that use silencing tactics accountable

Mystic Politics: Claims its mission is to instigate debate on politics, religion, and science towards a more informed society. Its goal is to increase the authority of alternative media and citizen journalism, to change the geopolitical narrative and the way in which you see the world.

openDemocracy: A website for debate about international politics and culture, offering news and opinion articles from established academics, journalists, and policymakers covering current issues in world affairs.

Palestinian Counseling Centre: 'The Palestinian Counseling Centre (PCC) was established in Jerusalem by a group of psychologists, sociologists, and educational experts in 1983. The Centre was established to work on developing and improving mental health concepts and services in Palestine. Since the establishment of the PCC in 1983, the Centre's vision has remained the same, and that is, to have a healthy Palestinian society that is productive in an independent Palestinian state with Jerusalem as its capital. This vision focuses on building the balance between the individual and her/his surrounding environment. In order to reach this vision, counseling as a concept had to be introduced, understood, and accepted in Palestinian society. Since its establishment in 1983, it was very important for the Centre to maintain a clear ideological approach that ran parallel to our work undertaken with the individual and community from a mental health perspective.' This website has many informative articles regarding the psychological effects of brutal Israeli policies on the Palestinian people.

Peace Now: A non-governmental organization in Israel seeking to promote a two-state solution to the Israeli-Palestinian conflict

PEN International: An organization whose first affirmation is that 'literature knows no frontiers and must remain common currency among people in spite of political or international upheavals'.

rabble.ca: A progressive, left-wing Canadian online magazine with the tag line 'news for the rest of us' whose stated intention is to publish original news stories, in-depth features, provocative interviews, commentaries and more from some of the few progressive voices in mainstream media.

Redress Information and Analysis: Exposes injustice, disinformation and bigotry.

Reporters Without Borders: A nonprofit organization defending the freedom to be informed and to inform others throughout the world.

The Electronic Intifada: Is a not-for-profit, independent online publication which covers the Israeli-Palestinian conflict from a Palestinian viewpoint 'aimed at combating the pro-Israeli, pro-American spin' which its editors believe exists in mainstream media reporting.

The International Solidarity Movement (ISM): "Is a Palestinian-led movement committed to resisting the long-entrenched and systematic oppression and dispossession of the Palestinian population, using non-violent, direct-action methods and principles. Founded in August 2001, ISM aims to support and strengthen the Palestinian popular resistance by being immediately alongside Palestinians in olive groves, on school runs, at demonstrations, within villages being attacked, by houses being demolished or where Palestinians are subject to consistent harassment or attacks from soldiers and settlers as well as numerous other situations."

The Real News: A member-supported, global online video news network using internet broadcasting and describing itself as "focused on providing independent and uncompromising journalism," on "the critical issues of our times." It relies exclusively on donations by supporters, and does not accept funding from advertising, government, or corporations.

The Truth Seeker: Provides crucial articles, documents and perspectives that have either been suppressed by the authorities, or altogether ignored by the mainstream media.

The Washington Report on Middle East Affairs: Is published by the American Educational Trust (AET) which is a non-profit foundation incorporated in Washington, DC in 1982 by retired U.S. foreign service officers to provide the American public with balanced and accurate information concerning U.S. relations with Middle Eastern states. AET perceives a dearth in knowledge about the Middle East, Arabs, and Muslims, in the U.S., and pursues an educational mission of "Interpreting the Middle East for North Americans; Interpreting North America for the Middle East."

Transparency International: An organisation that strives for "a world in which government, politics, business, civil society and the daily lives of people are free of corruption"

Zochrot: "Zochrot and other Israeli NGOs have been fairly successful over the past few years in raising the Nakba to the awareness of the broad Jewish public. The destruction of hundreds of villages and resulting hundreds of thousands of Palestinian refugees in the 1948 War have become part and parcel of current Israeli discourse; nevertheless, its mere presence in Jewish Israeli discourse still does not mean broad acknowledgement of and accountability for the Nakba. This gap is largely due to the continued adherence of Jewish Israeli society to colonial concepts and practices."

Needless to say Zochrot has been subjected to Zionist vitriol with some of the nastiest coming from extreme right-wing groups like Im Tirtu and NGO Monitor which are both closely connected to the Israeli government. Recently, in response to an NGO Monitor report attacking it, Jewish Voice for Peace, a U.S. group, wrote: "NGO Monitor has a long history, broadly documented, of attacking any organization that it believes is effectively criticizing Israeli policies. The organizations NGO Monitor has attacked include Human Rights Watch, Amnesty International, B'Tselem, Breaking the Silence, Al Haq, and the New Israel Fund, to name just a few. We are honored to be among them."

www.ingramcontent.com/pod-product-compliance
Lightning Source LLC
Chambersburg PA
CBHW070826260626
47170CB00007B/2275